Raves for [image]

"Cherryh has given us an alien psychology story, and she has done a grand job. It is a mark of Cherryh's success that here it is the human who seems alien."
—*Analog* (Lester Del Rey)

"This book and the rest of the Chanur series . . . comprise one of the best science fiction tales ever. Don't miss it."
—*Minneapolis Star and Tribune*

"Furiously paced action—intricate, interesting, precarious alien politics."
—*Publishers Weekly*

"Cherryh's performance as a writer is . . . on a level of quality which few writers will ever attain . . . an uncommonly deft storyteller . . . a major talent . . . a *tour de force* . . . quintessential SF."
—*The Magazine of Fantasy and Science Fiction*

"WONDERFUL . . . energy and suspense . . . great aliens . . . a terrific adventure story . . . spectacular battles and escapes . . . scenes that I could easily imagine being done by today's special effects wizards to terrific effect."
—*Locus*

And for the Science Fiction of C. J. Cherryh:

"Cherryh provides a riveting plot that emphasizes intense human/alien interactions instead of physical violence. Perhaps undervalued because she writes in traditional forms that don't appeal to the literati, while too difficult for some fans of space opera, Cherryh remains one of the most talented writers in the field."
—*Publishers Weekly*

"One of SF's most powerful imaginations."
—*Booklist*

"A seriously probing, thoughtful, intelligent piece of work, with more insight in half a dozen pages than most authors manage in half a hundred."
—*Kirkus Reviews*

"Cherryh is a born storyteller."
—*The Magazine of Fantasy and Science Fiction*

CHANUR'S ENDGAME

CHANUR'S HOMECOMING

CHANUR'S LEGACY

C. J. Cherryh

DAW BOOKS, INC.

DONALD A. WOLLHEIM, FOUNDER

375 Hudson Street, New York, NY 10014

ELIZABETH R. WOLLHEIM
SHEILA E. GILBERT
PUBLISHERS

http://www.dawbooks.com

CHANUR'S
ENDGAME

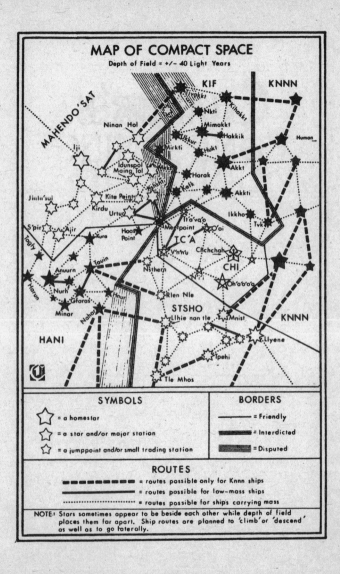

MAP OF COMPACT SPACE
Depth of Field = +/– 40 Light Years

KIF
KNNN

MAHENDO'SAT

Tyokki
Nkti
Kihokki
Mimakkt
Hakkik
Human
Ninan Hol
Ukkur
Huk't
Iji
Hirkti
Akkt
Idunspol
Maing Tol
Harak
Akkti
Kkshsht
Kefk
Jinlu'sui
Kita Point
Ikkho
Tvk
Kirdu
Urtur
It'a'va'o
Meetpoint
O'oi
S'pir
Ajir
Hoas
Point
IC'A
Chchchah
CHI
Jaoly
Kura
V'n'n'u
Tauin
Anuurn
V'i'i
Oh'a'b'o'o
Harun
Nsthern
Nurh
Gfaras
Rlen Nle
STSHO
Minar
Nohor
Llhie nan tle
Mnist
HANI
T.Llyene
Ipehi
KNNN
Tle Mhos

SYMBOLS

☆ = a homestar

☆ = a star and/or major station

☆ = a jumppoint and/or small trading station

BORDERS

─── = Friendly

▓▓▓ = Interdicted

░░░ = Disputed

ROUTES

▄ ▄ ▄ ▄ = routes possible only for Knnn ships

──── = routes possible for low-mass ships

──── = routes possible for ships carrying mass

NOTE: Stars sometimes appear to be beside each other while depth of field places them far apart. Ship routes are planned to 'climb' or 'descend' as well as to go laterally.

CHANUR'S
HOMECOMING

In our last episode . . .*

Two years previous, the aggressive kif, natives of Akkht, had a *hakkikt,* a leader so fearsome he united more than the usual number of kif behind him in a pirate band. This *hakkikt,* Akkukkak, had seized a ship of a hitherto unknown species, humanity; and acquired ambitions beyond the usual kifish banditry against other species. With a species to prey on which was without the protections of the Compact, he might grow powerful enough to gather the whole kifish species under his influence, sweeping down on the Compact in a wave of conquest unprecedented in history.

But his human prey escaped him. While the *hakkikt* was docked at Meetpoint star station, the last surviving prisoner ran to shelter aboard *The Pride of Chanur,* a hani merchant ship captained by one Pyanfar Chanur, who in no wise solicited this refugee.

Still Pyanfar and her crew as a matter of policy refused to surrender the human to Akkukkak's demand. This was a two-fold calamity for the kif: first the loss of the human and all the information he held about his species; and then this defiance from a mere hani merchant—who continued to elude the great *hakkikt* in a multi-star chase. Akkukkak was suddenly fighting not only for his prey but for his life, for a kif who loses face rapidly loses followers, and becomes the target of other kif with ambitions. Akkukkak was compelled to seek vengeance on a scale sufficient to cover this humiliation; and this humiliation involved an ambition large enough to shake worlds.

He took the unprecedented step of moving on the hani homeworld, seeking first the humiliation and removal of

*as told in *The Pride of Chanur, Chanur's Venture,* and *The Kif Strike Back.*

Pyanfar Chanur and all her clan, in what may have been a kifish misapprehension of the importance of any single hani; he was thinking as a kif, and interpreted Pyanfar's moves as aggressive ambition. He also demanded the return of his property. In all these demands he seriously misjudged the hani, for no action he could have taken would have rallied the hani against him more than this intrusion on hani home territory and the demand to surrender a living being who had taken shelter within a hani clan. Hani resisted in a battle at Gaohn station, and they received mahen help in the persons of two hunter captains, known to Pyanfar (mahendo'sat names are not easy for outsiders) as Goldtooth and Jik. This firefight would have been serious enough; but the hostilities disturbed yet another species of the Compact, the methane-breathing knnn, aliens of direst reputation and the highest technology in known space. The knnn, intervening, took Akkukkak away to a fate unguessed. And that settled that. The human Tully went home to his people. Pyanfar Chanur looked forward to a new era of trade and prosperity in which not only Clan Chanur, but all hani-kind would profit from human contact.

She reckoned, unfortunately, without the stsho, whose station at Meetpoint was the hub of all trading routes of the Compact. Total xenophobes, the stsho withdrew Chanur's trading permit. More, Akkukkak had indeed caused a profound disturbance in hani affairs by the manner of his demise. Chanur was forced to defend itself against challenge by hani enemies who took advantage of popular fears of the knnn, and though Lord Kohan Chanur held on, Chanur lost valuable allies whose support in council Pyanfar and other women of the clan very greatly missed.

To add to the difficulties, no one kept their promises. The humans did not return and the mahendo'sat withdrew into isolation.

Two impoverished years later, Pyanfar Chanur was doing all she could to keep *The Pride* running—and she was not the only Chanur captain in deep trouble.

Then by some unforeseen miracle her papers cleared and she was invited back to Meetpoint to recover her trading license.

She pulled into Meetpoint with the last cargo she could afford to buy, and fell right into the welcoming arms of

Goldtooth the mahendo'sat, who handed her a courier packet with the human Tully as a secret passenger and told her to run for her life: the kif were hunting him.

Now among Pyanfar's other troubles, she had defied hani custom. Hani males were traditionally a protected class within hani society, the few who made successful challenge becoming clan lords, ceremonial heads of clans, who in fact had no meaningful authority at all, the real legal and financial power resting with the clanswomen who conducted exterior business. The rest of the males lived and died in rural exile, excluded from all society but their own; and to this pool of males a defeated clan lord must retire, to a short and wretched life among younger, ambitious males practicing their combat skills. Pyanfar's husband Khym Mahn was defeated by their son Kara, and deposed; but he postponed his exile to help her in her fight against the kif, and became one of the few hani males ever to leave the planetary surface—by interstellar agreement, they were in fact barred from doing so, since they had a reputation for berserker rages dangerous to life and property.

But Pyanfar, faced with the prospect of sending Khym downworld again to die, defied treaty and custom and took him aboard *The Pride;* more, she secured working papers for him by bribing a mahendo'sat official, and listed him as crew. Having traveled and worked with alien males, Pyanfar had begun to see in her own husband traits no hani has ever looked for in a male of her species; she conceived the idea in her heart of hearts that the berserker rages might be due more to upbringing than biology, and yet— and yet she *was* hani; and to doubt something out of all folk wisdom, something built into all language and custom and tradition, is very difficult, the more so that Khym himself doubted her theories; he was, after all, a product of his culture too, and all the complex of beliefs which encouraged him to be a man also fostered his aggressive impulses and his doubts about his faculties. It was not, in sum, a comfortable situation for *The Pride*'s crew either, who still could not figure out whether they ought to treat Khym as a man or try to ignore that handicap and treat him as one of themselves—in which case modesty and custom and language were in the way: female humor and traditional curses involve sons and males; pausing to dress in shipboard emer-

gencies is not practical; ship facilities are not designed to
accommodate a man's larger stature; and male thinking is
traditionally given to be hasty and imprecise, not the sort
of thing anyone wants to rely on in any use of hazardous
machinery.

But Khym once-lord of Mahn acquired the unprecedented (for a hani) designation of crewman aboard *The
Pride of Chanur.*

The worst happened forthwith: Khym was involved in a
riot that heavily damaged Meetpoint station. Pyanfar escaped a second loss of her license only by charging the
entire bill to the mahendo'sat, who had given her a credit
slip for quite different purposes—to aid her with the transport of the human, Tully.

Unfortunately this riot happened under the disapproving
witness of one Rhif Ehrran, an agent of the hani government.

Now Rhif Ehrran had come to Meetpoint on quite different business. So many of the spacing clans of the hani had
taken heavy damage at Gaohn that the groundling clans
had seized control of the *han,* the hani senate. Meanwhile
the xenophobic stsho, wealthiest species of the Compact,
had bribed certain hani politicians, wanting to subvert hani
politics from the inside for fear of two other species: first,
humans, who had trespassed stsho borders and might do so
again; second, the kif, because two of Akkukkak's erstwhile
lieutenants, one Akkhtimakt and one Sikkukkut, had risen
to declare themselves *hakkikktun.* These two kif were currently battling it out between themselves, but they had already polarized kifish society into a frighteningly few
predatory bands. From a fragmented piratical species, kif
had suddenly achieved unity to a degree Akkukkak himself
never effected.

The burning issue, among kif as elsewhere, was humanity;
and the persistent rumors held that humanity was coming to
the Compact right through methane-breather space, to unite
with the mahendo'sat, which meant trouble for the kif. The
rumors happened to be true. And the stsho, who, incapable
of fighting, had long relied on mahen guards for protection,
suddenly suspected they could no longer trust mahendo'sat.
Hence the sudden coziness with the groundling hani clans
and the flood of stsho money to certain hani pockets.

The *han* had heard rumors too; and heard rumors, moreover, of one hani actively cooperating with the kif—the hani pirate Dur Tahar of *Tahar's Moon Rising.* That was the ship Rhif Ehrran had gone out there to hunt. But Ehrran was also there on secret business: negotiating with the stsho on behalf of certain of her own political patrons. Certainly Ehrran was interested when Pyanfar Chanur involved herself in a major riot aboard Meetpoint, entangled with both mahen secret agents and a high-ranking kif. So when Pyanfar paid a huge bribe to the stsho stationmaster, Stle stles stlen, and made a hasty departure from Meetpoint with the human Tully aboard, Rhif Ehrran followed, smelling political blood and seeing in this move of Pyanfar's a threat to all she stood for.

Akkhtimakt headed Pyanfar off by occupying Kita Point, strategic gateway to mahen and hani space, forcing all traffic to detour into the Disputed Zones along the kifish/mahen border. With *The Pride* damaged enroute, Pyanfar had no choice but to go to Kshshti Station in the Zones, seeking repairs and help. Her intended destination was Maing Tol, the mahen regional capital; her aim, to deliver Tully and his message from humanity into the hands of Goldtooth's superiors. But on her arrival at Kshshti, she ran into Rhif Ehrran, the kif Sikkukkut, and the hani trader *Ayhar's Prosperity,* which had lost its cargo at Meetpoint thanks to her: its captain Banny Ayhar was not pleased.

Rhif Ehrran demanded Tully's surrender to her; and her attempt to take custody of Tully resulted in a dock fight which put Tully and Pyanfar's young niece Hilfy Chanur into the hands of their enemy Sikkukkut. Sikkukkut left, leaving Pyanfar the message that she could recover the hostages at Mkks, a station right on the kifish border. It was too obviously a trap.

In the midst of all this, Goldtooth's partner Jik (whose true mahen name is Keia Nomesteturjai) showed up at Kshshti with his powerful hunter-ship *Aja Jin;* and sent the hani captain Banny Ayhar on to Maing Tol with the message Pyanfar had brought this far. He supported Pyanfar in her decision to go to Mkks: he went along and somehow argued Rhif Ehrran into joining them.

At Mkks, Sikkukkut returned Hilfy and Tully in a negotiated settlement. He also gave Pyanfar a gift of kifish esteem—a slave named Skkukuk.

And all they had agreed to do in return was to cross into kifish territory and help Sikkukkut take Kefk station, the main kifish link to Meetpoint, in an act of outright piracy.

Jik agreed, to Pyanfar's consternation. Moreover, Rhif Ehrran did, after listening to Jik's persuasion.

They made the jump and they succeeded. Their ships occupied Kefk kifish-fashion, by superior bluff and with very little damage.

Goldtooth showed up then, furious with his partner Jik, for Goldtooth had been lying silent just off Kefk monitoring the situation. He had been off a time fighting Akkhtimakt, trying to open the way for a human fleet now enroute to Compact space, and now Jik had made a deal which would effectively bring Sikkukkut into alliance with the mahendo'sat against Akkhtimakt, emphatically not the situation Goldtooth was working toward. Humans were headed into Compact space in great number, and Goldtooth's whole plan for human-mahen alliance now was jeopardized by the taking of Kefk and its delivery to Sikkukkut, who consequently would bring the kif into unity under one *hakkikt* much faster than Goldtooth's plans called for.

Pyanfar meanwhile received a second gift of esteem from Sikkukkut, the person of her old enemy Dur Tahar the pirate, who had been a respectable hani merchant captain before she opposed Pyanfar at Gaohn and accidentally ended up in alliance with the kif, her reputation ruined. Now a prisoner of Sikkukkut, captured along with Akkhtimakht's partisans on the station, Tahar had reached the nadir of her fortunes and begged Pyanfar to intercede with the kif for the lives of her cousins still in Sikkukkut's hands.

Rhif Ehrran at once stepped in to demand custody of Tahar. Pyanfar refused, having nothing but disgust for Ehrran's secret police methods and police state mentality. Tahar would go home to hani justice, but aboard *The Pride of Chanur*. It was a direct slap at Ehrran and a threat to her prestige; and a countermove against her patrons' ambitions. It served notice that Chanur, instead of bowing to political force, was going to exercise the ancient authority of a clan to take its own prisoners and administer its own justice before turning the offender over to the *han*. This effectively meant that Rhif Ehrran's superiors and political allies could not touch Tahar without dealing with Chanur as a head-of-cause in open council, and without bringing the whole foreign policy issue into debate in the *han* with Chanur as the chief spokeswoman for the opposition, precisely the situation Chanur's enemies did not want.

Then, while Pyanfar went to negotiate with Sikkukkut, Goldtooth secretly met with Ehrran. And some unknown agency started a riot on the docks, which set Akkhtimakt's hitherto cowed partisans on the station to attacking Sikkukkut's forces. Pyanfar and the Tahar crew, whose freedom she had just negotiated from Sikkukkut, were caught in the middle of the firefight, as Goldtooth and Rhif Ehrran both took advantage of the confusion to break dock and run for Meetpoint—together.

The slave Skkukuk saved Pyanfar's life in the riot, to her profound distress at the debt.

But Jik, also attempting Pyanfar's rescue from the firefight, fell into the hands of Sikkukkut, who had some new and hard questions to ask of Jik regarding Goldtooth, mahen ambitions, and the whereabouts and course of human ships.

Chapter 1

The Pride's small galley table was awash in data printout, paperfaxes ringed and splotched with brown gfi-stains, arrowed, circled, crossed out, and noted in red and green ink till they were beyond cryptic. The red pen made another notation and another snaking arrow; and the bronze-pelted hani fist that held it flexed claws out and in again in profoundest frustration. Pyanfar Chanur sat in this sanctuary gnawing her mustaches and drinking cup after cup of lukewarm gfi amid her scribbles on the nav and log records.

Pyanfar was not her usual meticulous self—rough blue spacer-breeches instead of the bright red silk she favored, and not a single one of the bracelets and other gold jewelry she usually wore, just the handful of spacer rings up the sweep of her tuft-tipped ears. Her best pair of red silk breeches had gone for rags, perished of the same calamity which had stiffened her joints, left several knots on her maned skull, and made small puncture wounds all over her red-brown hide. Her niece's deft fingers had tweezed out the metal splinters down in sickbay, with the help of the magnetic scanner, and patched the worst cuts with plasm and sticking-plaster. Haral, her second in command, had suffered the same, and limped about her duties on the bridge, running printouts and sitting watch in her turn, while the rest of the crew was in scarcely better shape, hides patched, manes and beards singed, with bandages here and there about their persons. That had been a memorable fight on the docks, indeed a memorable fracas; but Pyanfar could have recalled it with more pleasure if it had come to better success.

Scritch-scratch. Another note went down on the well-worn starchart. She studied it and restudied it, gnawed her mustaches and refigured, though all but the finest decimal exactitudes of current star-distances were in her memory. There were surely answers in that map; and she racked her wits to find them, to discover what the opposition planned and what her allies (treacherous though they be) might be figuring to do, and to juggle all the variables at once. The answer was *there,* patently there, in the possibilities of that starmap and in the self-interests of eight separate and polylogical species.

Knowing all the options, all those self-interests, and all the capabilities of the ships involved, a hani merchant might conceivably manage to think of something clever. She needed something clever. Desperately.

She sat at Kefk, inside kifish space where no hani of right mind would ever consent to be, allied to kif no hani in her right mind would ever trust; she sat in the same space station with nervous methane-breathers (tc'a and chi) who had lately been raided (reprimanded? attacked? congratulated?) by an intruding knnn ship, which had carried off a tc'a vessel. Gods knew what was in the tc'as multipartite minds; the chi *had* no minds that any oxy breather had ever proved; and as for the knnn, no one had any least idea what they were up to. Wherever those black hair-snarls on thin black legs intruded their influence (and the power of their strange ships), things bent. Fast. But the knnn had withdrawn and Kefk occupied itself with its own affairs, like repair of its fire-ravaged docks and placating its new master, the *hakkikt* Sikkukkut, whose ships now numbered thirty-two (the count was rising). It occupied itself with the hani pirate Dur Tahar, lately at liberty by the *hakkikt*'s grace; with the mahen hunter-ship *Aja Jin,* lately outside the *hakkikt*'s good graces, and still at dock, sitting beside *The Pride* and not daring to send a compromising query across the dockside communication lines. Kefk had a great deal to worry about, not least of which was the missing hunter-ship *Mahijiru* and its captain, one Ana Ismehananmin, aka Goldtooth, and the hani ship that had run with him.

Along with major structural damage, a breached sector, fire, disruption of the lifesupport systems, the remnants of a revolution and other nagging difficulties.

Another flurry of figures and pen-corrections. There was, number one, the mahendo'sat territory to reckon with: a wide sprawl of stars into which at least one message had

gone and might have gotten through, knnn and the gods
willing. Banny Ayhar would have done her best to get it
through, as much as any merchant captain could do: she
might have lived to get it to Maing Tol, if the knnn had
not stopped her or if the kif had not been laying for her.
The mahendo'sat, tall black-furred primates with enough
double-turning motives involved to baffle a tc'a's multipartite brain (but antagonism toward their neighbors the kif
was always high among them), *might* have made a move if
that message had gotten through. Down the line via Kshshti
and out to Mkks might be a good course of action for the
mahendo'sat to take, if they hoped to forestall any kifish
breakout along that border; but Meetpoint station or Kita
Point, critical to all trade routes, was most likely the object
of any major push from the mahendo'sat. That effort would
have to come via Kshshti if Kita was still blocked; while
Kefk, in kifish territory, was not a likely route for them.
Not impossible, given the current state of borders in the
Compact, just less than likely.

Also reckoning mahendo'sat moves, it was very likely
there were one or more mahen hunter-ships escorting the
human ships; and *they* were coming in toward Meetpoint
from Tt'a'va'o and tc'a/chi space.

With human ships and human captains; still another set
of motives and self-interests, on gods-knew-what orders
from their own authorities. (Or lack of them—who knew
what human minds were like?)

Further complication: kifish forces under the rival *hakkikt* Akkhtimakt had likely moved in to take the mahen/
tc'a station at Kshshti. That might stand off any mahen
flanking move to Meetpoint, if Akkhtimakt's forces still
controlled Kita as well. Akkhtimakt might have Kita, Urtur,
Kshshti, or all three, and advance from any or all of those
points against Meetpoint and/or Kefk itself, if the report
Goldtooth had brought was true and the stsho had been
fools enough to invite Akkhtimakt in as hired help.

There was, lure to Akkhtimakt, his greatest enemy Sikkukkut, sitting here at Kefk gathering to his control every
ship that came into port. And revenge was always high on
any list of kifish motives. *Pukkukkta,* they called it. Advance retaliation was better than revenge after the fact.

Having an enemy *know* his calamity before he died was best of all.

Yet another move of the pen, another arrow, lurid green: one could not exclude interference from the methane-breathers, whose motives no oxy breather could guess.

And, certainly not to be forgotten, there were the stsho who owned Meetpoint, congenitally noncombatant, but hiring alien, aggressive help right and left and forming reckless associations.

While the *han*—gods, the hani senate was up to its nose in politics as usual, and Rhif Ehrran was on her way to Meetpoint with evidence enough to outlaw Chanur once and for all.

The Pride of Chanur sat at a kifish dock six to seven jumps from homestar, no matter which way she figured it. Six or seven jumps was a long way, a very long way, measured in stress on ship and on body; and gods knew what would follow on her heels, if she did what she would gladly do now and broke dock at Kefk and ran for their lives, withdrawing herself like a good law-abiding hani from all the affairs of kif and mahendo'sat and multifarious aliens.

But the trouble would surely follow her home; she knew beyond a doubt that it would. She had involved herself in the affairs of kifish *hakkiktun* and she had acquired their notice. She had made herself a name in kifish eyes. She had gotten *sfik,* face. And that meant that kif would never let her alone so long as she lived.

Her uneasy partner Sikkukkut an'nikktukktin would never forget her; certainly (gods forbid he should replace Sikkukkut in power) her personal enemy Akkhtimakt would not.

Pyanfar scribbled, flicked her ears, and the rings of forty years of voyages chimed in her hearing. A pearl swung from her right ear, a Llyene pearl from the oceans of the stsho homeworld; she still wore that gift, regardless of the perfidy of the giver, who was Goldtooth, friend, traitor, flatterer, and tenfold liar.

Curse him to his own deepest hell.

Goldtooth was bound for Meetpoint with Rhif Ehrran, beyond a doubt he was, the conniving bastard. He was dealing with the stsho and anyone else who offered his species an advantage, and he was betting opposite to the alliance

his own partner Jik had made—to which maneuver Sikkukkut took strongest and understandable exception.

Another scribble.

A quick movement caught her eye, a black blot speeding
across the floor, sinuous, small, fast.

She leapt to her feet. "Haral!" she yelled, while paper
cascaded off the table and the black thing paused for one
beady-eyed stare before it skittered on, faster than her
limping dive to stop it.

Haral appeared, hobbling in by the short bridge-galley
corridor, and did a fast skip and wince as it dived between
her feet and vanished.

Pyanfar snatched up a handful of jumbled papers. "Fry
that thing!"

"Sorry, captain. We're setting traps—"

"Traps be bothered, they're *breeding,* I swear they are!
Get Skkukuk on it, they're his by-the-gods dinner. Let *him*
find 'em. Gods-be mess. Vermin!" The hair stood up on
her shoulders and she stared at her first officer in bleakest
despair. No one in the crew was up to more orders, more
duty, or more trouble.

"The things might get into something vital," Pyanfar said.
Common sense, covering absolute revulsion. "Gods, get
'em *out!*"

"Aye," Haral said, in a voice as thin and hoarse as hers.
And Haral limped away, to get their own private kif to
ferret his dinner out of the *The Pride*'s nooks and crannies
before something else went wrong. That took a guard, to
watch Skkukuk; and gods curse the luck that had set the
things free on the ship in the first place. She had heard the
story, inspected the burned patch on *The Pride*'s outer airlock seal. And she blessed Tirun Araun's quick hand that
had gotten that door shut—vermin and all.

Gods *knew* how those black slinking pests had gotten up
from lowerdeck.

Climbed the liftshaft? The airducts?

The thought of myriad little slinking black bodies loping
along the airshafts and into lifesupport lifted the hairs at
her nape.

What were the gods-be things *eating?*

She scooped up a last couple of papers with a wince and

a grimace and sat down again. Rested both elbows on the table and rested her aching head in her hands.

She saw within her mind a dark kifish hall; sodium-light; and a table surrounded by insect-legged chairs—her partner Jik sitting there with one of Sikkukkut's minions holding a gun to his head, and that bastard Sikkukkut starting to ask closer and closer questions.

She had not had a way to help him. She had been lucky to get her own crew out of there alive; and to keep herself and her ship as free as it was, under kifish guns at a kifish dock.

Send another appeal to Sikkukkut to ask for Jik's release? Sikkukkut's patience with her was already frayed. Perhaps it was personal cowardice not to send another message. Perhaps it was prudence and saving what could be saved, not to push Sikkukkut into some demonstration of his power—at Jik's expense. Kifish heads adorned the stanchions of Sikkukkut's ship-ramp. That image haunted her rest and her sleep. A moment's off-guard imagining set Jik's head there beside the others.

She opened her eyes abruptly when that vision hit, focusing instead on the maps and charts and printout, where the answer had to lie, where she was convinced it was, if she could cudgel her aching skull and battered brain just a little farther through the maze.

Jik had left them another legacy: a coded microfiche which even Soje Kesurinan, in command of *Aja Jin,* might not know existed. And *The Pride*'s computers had been running on that, trying to break that code, ever since they had gotten back to the ship and had a chance to feed it in.

"Again," said Sikkukkut an'nikktukktin, *hakkikt* and *mekt-hakkikt,* lately provincial boss and currently rival for ultimate authority among his kind; while Jik, Keia Nomesteturjai, kif-hunter, captain, and what other rank among mahendo'sat this kifish pirate would earnestly like to know—focused his eyes with difficulty and managed a twisted grin. That tended to confuse hell out of the kif, who knew facial expressions were a second and well-developed language especially among mahendo'sat, and who had never quite learned to interpret all their nuances.

"Again," said Sikkukkut, "Keia, my old friend. *Where are the human ships? Doing what? Intending what?*"

"I've told you," Jik said. He said it in mahensi, being perverse. Sikkukkut understood that language, though many of his listening subordinates, standing about their table in this dim, sodium-lit hall, were not as educated. Sikkukkut, on the other hand, had a good many talents.

Interrogation was one of those. Sikkukkut had performed that office in the service of Akkukkak, of unlamented memory. All these questions, each pacing and each shift of mood Sikkukkut displayed, were calculated. It was, at the moment, the soft touch. *Have a smoke, my old friend. Sit and talk with me.* But now the frown was back, a slight drawing down of Sikkukkut's long black snout. Hooded and inscrutable he sat, on his insect-legged chair, in the baleful light of the sodium-lamps, while Jik smoked and stared at him eye to eye. There were numerous guards about the shadowed edges of the hall, always the sycophants and the guards. In a little time the order would come to take him back to lowerdecks; and they would try the harder course again. Constant shifting of strategy, the hard approach and the soft, Sikkukkut usually the latter. Usually.

Jik kept himself mentally distant from all these changes, observed the shifts and absorbed the punishment with a professional detachment which was Sikkukkut's (surely, Jik reckoned) intention to crack. And he looked Sikkukkut in his red-rimmed eyes with the sure feeling that the kif was analyzing his every twitch and blink, looking for a telling reaction.

"Come now, Keia. You know my disposition, how patient I am, of my kind. I know that you had ample time to consult with your partner before the shooting started. We've been over these questions. They grow wearisome. Can we not resolve them?"

"My partner," Jik said, silken-slurred: Sikkukkut afforded him liquor, and he pinched out a dead smokestick and took a sip from the small round footed cup, and drew a long, long breath. Pleasures were few enough. He took what he could get. "I tell you, *hakkikt,* I wish *I* knew what my partner's up to. God, you think I'd have been out on that dock if I'd known what he was about to do?" He fumbled after his next smoke and his fingers were numb.

Doubtless the drink was drugged. But there were enough of them to put the drug into him another way, so he took his medicine dosed in very fine liquor and quietly gathered his internal forces. He was deep-conditioned, immune to ordinary efforts in that regard: he knew how to self-hypnotize, and he had already focused on a series of mantras and mandalas into which he had coded what he knew, down paths of dialectic and image no kif could walk without error. He smiled blandly, in secret and bleak amusement that Sikkukkut's methods had incidentally eased the aches and the pains of previous sessions. His thoughts swayed and wove, moved in and out of focus. The docks and fire. His crew. *Aja Jin.* Friends and allied ships were just down the dock and as good as lightyears away. "Let me tell you, *mekt-hakkikt,* I know Ana's style. Think like a mahendo'sat who knows kif, *hakkikt.* If he'd asked you for leave to operate on his own you'd never have given it."

"Therefore he wrecks Kefk's docks."

Jik shrugged and drew in a puff, blinked and stared at the kif beneath heavy lids. "Well, but independence is Ana's way. I've known him for years. He's damn stubborn. He thinks he sees a way and he takes it. Agreements to this side and that—sure, he's working the mahen side. And maybe the human side too. Most of all he's gathering assets—" (Careful, Keia, the brain's fogged; stay to the narrow, the back-doubling path and lead us all round again.) Jik drew in smoke and let it out again in a shaky exhalation. "He'll negotiate with you. Eventually. But think like a mahendo'sat. He has to get something in hand to negotiate with, something to offer you, *hakkikt,* to demonstrate his worth."

"Like Meetpoint? You weigh upon my credulity, Keia." Silk, silk and soothing-soft. "Try again."

"Not Meetpoint. But some matter of substance he can come to you with. I think he means to come back to talk. But he will bring something."

Sikkukkut's snout twitched in a dry sniffing, kifish laughter, which came for many reasons, not all of which were civilized. "Like a million human ships and a great number of guns?"

"Now, that is possible, *hakkikt.*" Jik blinked and narrowed his focus still tighter on what he had resolved to say, never on what he was hiding. Find the threads of the story and stay to them, walk the narrow path, while the drug and the alcohol and the stimulants in the smoke flowed through his veins. "That is remotely possible; but the advantage would be too onesided for the humans. What good to mahendo'sat, to exchange one powerful neighbor for another of unknown potential?"

"Unknown, is it?"

"You speak excellent mahensi. Far better than I speak your language. Mechanical translators arc hardly a substitute for living and fluent brains. The best human translator we know can ask for a cup of water and say he wants trade. Now, what does that tell us about human motives, human government, human minds, a? Friend, they say. You say friend, I say friend. Do we mean the same thing? What do humans mean with that word? Assuredly Ana doesn't know; and I much doubt he means to upend the Compact as long as he doesn't know." Jik held up a blunt-clawed forefinger, to maintain attention to a point. "Goldtooth, our esteemed Ana, takes orders. He also interprets them freely. This is the danger in him. The Personage who sent us both knows this. Therefore he sent me to restrain Ana from his excesses. I have failed in this. But I know Ana's limits. I am saying this to you, and you speak such excellent mahensi; but I don't know whether you know the meaning of this word *limits* in the way we do. It implies the edge of Ana's personal assumptions. Ana still obeys the Personage at Maing Tol. As I do. And I tell you that negotiation with you is in the Personage's interest and human ships running freely through Compact space is not in those interests. Therefore I make alliance with you, as I would have made it simultaneously with Akkhtimakt if he were not the fool he is."

This pleased Sikkukkut, perhaps. The dark eyes flickered. Sikkukkut picked up his cup and the thin tongue exited the v-form gap of his outer teeth and lapped delicately at the petroleum-smelling contents. "I have known mahen fools," Sikkukkut said.

"Don't number Ana among them."

"Or yourself?"

"I hope not to be."

"I have a notion what you might have been doing out on

that dockside, Keia, my friend. Ana Ismehanan-min wanted confusion behind which to depart. And *someone* fired the shot that touched off the riot."

"Rhif Ehrran."

"The hani? Come now, Keia. Hani gave no orders to the mahendo'sat."

"It's not certain that they take them either, your pardon, *hakkikt*. Myself, I look for a fool to do a fool's work; and Ehrran is the greatest fool I know."

"Ehrran isn't sitting here at this moment."

Jik drew in a long breath of smoke and let it go again. "It did give her the diversion she needed. And indeed, she isn't sitting here at this moment. At cost to me, to Chanur—in fact, *hakkikt,* expensive as it may be to her in the long run, in the short, it served her very well. And what my partner is thinking of in her regard I wish I could tell you. I wish I knew. I think he has use for that hani he took with him, use he couldn't get out of Chanur—Chanur being no fool."

"Perhaps he has made use of all the hani. Perhaps he has secured his retreat from among us, and that is all he hoped to do—might that not be, Keia? I only wonder what you are doing here."

"Perhaps he only followed her because he saw no way to stop her."

"His ship has armaments," Sikkukkut said dryly. "He was close behind her before her ship reached velocity."

"I mean within his intentions he had no way to stop her."

"And those intentions are?"

Jik spread his hands. "I keep my agreements, *hakkikt.* And if he has abrogated our partnership—" It was his best argument, his most desperate. His brain fuzzed and the drug meandered through his veins with the force of a tidal bore. "If he has cast me off, *hakkikt,* I still keep my agreements with you. That's my job to do; and if I fare better than he does, then that will prove to my Personage which agreement is the better to keep."

"Mahen mentality."

"I tell you: it's very like *sfik.* Give me status and I'll outweigh him with the Personage at Maing Tol. It's that simple. It's not unknown that the mahendo'sat conclude conflicting treaties. And if my course looks wiser than

Ana's, mine will be honored and his will be set aside. If both of us look like fools, our Personage will lean on other agencies—nor can either of us know if our Personage is not concluding a *third* treaty with the stsho. If all fail him, he will fall and another Personage's agents will be to deal with. The mahendo'sat is easy to predict and reasonable to deal with. It will always go for its greatest advantage.''

"Kk-kk-t. And will this Personage of yours stir forth in action or wait for events?"

"Outcome from the subordinates is always the deciding factor.''

"Where has Ismehanan-min gone? Where is this human fleet? What agreements has he made with the methane-breathers? What of your own?''

They returned to old questions, the same questions, bringing the interview in its usual circle. "Again, *mekt-hakkik,* I don't know. They may aim at Meetpoint. It's not impossible the humans might come here. And I don't know of any agreement with the knnn. I asked the tc'a to come here to assure that there was no panic on methane-side—"

"Why did the knnn take your tc'a?"

"I don't know. Who knows the knnn? Who can make an agreement with them—"

"Except the tc'a. Except the tc'a, Keia. Tell me what dealings *you* have had with them.''

"God help me, none." He held up a protesting hand. "I never deal with knnn." And carefully, with his sense in rags from drugs and drink: "That's Ana's department.''

"You wish to alarm me.''

"*Hakkikt,* I am alarmed. I don't know whether Ana is in control of it, or whether the knnn are doing something independent."

"In control of it."

It did sound stupid. Jik blinked slowly and took another drag at the smoke. "I mean maybe he's in consultation with them." The *hakkikt* feared the methane-breathers. Their irrationality, their technology, their vapors and tempers or whatever it was that sent them into frenzies, made the methane-folk a force no one sane wanted to stir up. "Or they approached him." That was enough to send the wind up Sikkukkut's back. "I don't know, *hakkikt.* I swear. God witness. I don't know. I did send a message to Maing Tol. So did Goldtooth. What was in his packet I don't know."

"What was in yours?"

Jik shrugged. "My deal with you. My urging they accept this treaty. I tell you, *hakkikt,* I'd urge you—all respect, *hakkikt,* you let me go back to my ship. I have a personal interest in seeing this agreement of ours flourish. It'll make me a very powerful man at home."

Give the kif something he understood, an ambition within kifish comprehension.

"You're attempting to use psychology on me," Sikkukkut said.

"Of course I am. It also happens to be true."

"What happened to *friendship?* You know I know words like this. I am not stupid, Keia; I can study up on a concept without having the—internal circuitry to process it. Friendship means that you work in concert with Ismehanan-min. Loyalty means that you might become a martyr—I learned that word of *ker* Pyanfar. An appalling concept. But there it was in the mahen dictionary. I was curious. Martyr. Martyrdom. The whole of mahen history teems with martyrs. You place value on them. Like the hani. Have you wish to become one, Keia?"

Jik lifted his brows. "Martyr is another word for fool."

"I found no such cross-reference. Tell me: Keia: I want to know this: where do the knnn fit into Ismehanan-min's arrangements? What arrangements has he made with the stsho?"

"He would betray them."

"And your opinion of them?"

"They would betray us."

"They have. Stle stles stlen is a deadly creature. For a grass-eating stsho. Is he dealing with this person?"

"I don't know. No. Yes." God help him, the drug was fuzzing up his mind again. For a panicked instant he lost all the threads and got them back again, remembering his story. "But not at depth. Ana doesn't trust the stsho. It's mutual. Of course. The humans will come to Meetpoint— eventually. I think they'll come there. And Stle stles stlen will Phase when *gtst* sees it. No sts-stsho can withstand that kind of blow to *gtst* reputation. Ana will take advantage of the confusion and seize the station. If he can."

"And Akkhtimakt will allow this."

"Ana will have to anticipate him there. Perhaps—perhaps, *hakkikt,* Ana moved so quickly because he knows something of Akkhtimakt's intentions. That there was no more time—in Ana's estimation."

"And why would he go with the hani?"

"Look for advantage." That questioning made him nervous. It was a new tack; he tried to think his way through it and in desperation went back to old answers. "I think—think he hopes to use Rhif Ehrran to get into Meetpoint itself *without* having stsho techs Phase and bring the systems down. Now you doubt this. I well know. But stsho react badly to surprises; from kif, they expect threats. Even from hani. But mahen threats unbalance them. They're *unaccustomed.* Ehrran has a treaty with them. That's all I can guess about it. She's a key. That's all. A fool and a key."

"To do what?"

"*Hakkikt,* I'm not privy to his plans."

Upon that, they were back to old matters. He sat and smoked while Sikkukkut thought that reply over once more, hunched faceless within the hooded robe, on his insect chair, the silver emblem of his princedom among kif shining on his breast stained with sodium-glow. Now and again from the shadows about them came the rustling of other robes, the restless stirring of subordinates who waited on their prince's pleasure.

In a moment Sikkukkut would negligently lift his hand and those waiting about the room would close in, to bear their prisoner back downship and belowdecks to a different sort of questioning, now that he was sufficiently muddled and drugged. Jik did not let himself doubt that. He did not let himself hope that his argument might sway the *hakkikt;* least of all did he hope that his hani allies on *The Pride of Chanur* and his own crew back on *Aja Jin* would effect a rescue. That was the core of his defense here among the kif, the hard center to his resistance that let him sit here so placidly taking his smokestick down to a stub and watching heavy-lidded while Sikkukkut an'nikktukktin meditated what next to do to him; it was the center of all secrets he held, that he counted himself already dead, from which position it was possible to be quite patient with all manner of misery, since, dead, he was enjoying a degree of sensation and occasional pleasant interlude no one dead had a right to. Even when the pain was extreme, it was better than not feeling anything at all. Ever.

Besides, he was mahendo'sat, and curiosity was second nature to him: he was still picking up information, skilled as Sikkukkut was. He had learned, for instance, that *Aja Jin, The Pride of Chanur,* and *Tahar's Moon Rising* were all at dock and all seemed free: that was very pleasant news. That Pyanfar Chanur was at hand to lend her experience to his own second in command was very good news; that Pyanfar still had credit enough with Sikkukkut to keep Dur Tahar's throat uncut was excellent news as well, and if there was still enough hani left under Tahar's red-brown hide, the pirate would adhere to her old enemy like burr to fur: hani paid their debts, if nothing else; and Tahar owed Chanur enough to stick to hell and back.

All of this he had learned in these sessions, as he knew that the human Tully was indeed safe aboard *The Pride of Chanur,* so Sikkukkut evidently valued Pyanfar more than he wanted the human to question and for other purposes, which was a mighty great deal of value for any kif to put on a non-kif. This was a double-edged benefit, of course: knowing kifish mindset, value-as-ally could turn with amazing swiftness to high-status-target. Friend in a kif's doubletoothed mouth had no overtones of loyalty or self-sacrifice at all, was in fact nearly the opposite. Ally-of-convenience, rather. Potential rival, rather. Or poor fool.

The hani knew these things; and he knew well that his second in command knew. So they would both keep one finger to the wind; and he hoped that heads would stay cool if, as seemed possible and even likely, portions of himself turned up as decoration on Sikkukkut's ship-ramp. He loathed stupidity, himself; he had sinned in that regard or he would not be here. But he truly abhorred the thought that he might singlehandedly serve as trigger to the undoing of the Compact. That was the one thing even a dead man could fear, the legacy he might leave the living for generations to come. That thought was the crack in his defense: Sikkukkut, being kif, taking no thought to posterity, was not capable of reaching that chink without a strong hint.

It was very easy for species to misunderstand each other, particularly when it came to abstracts.

It was possible, for instance, that he and Pyanfar had persistently misinterpreted Sikkukkut's lack of metaphysics as a lack of emotional abstracts and irrational desires. He had come to know the kif with unwanted intimacy, and now suspected Sikkukkut of a kifish sentimentality, a preference for intimate targets for his most personal satisfaction, while Akkhtimakt was less personal in his mayhem, and more catholic in his attacks.

Akkhtimakt operates with the fist, Sikkukkut was wont to say, *and I with the knife.*

It was kifish poesy; it was also a profound statement of styles which might, if a mahendo'sat were well-educated in kifish mentality, say more than its surface content, and delve into those deep things language barriered away from translation between species.

He smoked the butt down to the last possible remnant, and carefully pinched it out instead of stubbing it, spacer's affectation. Fire never hurt if one's moves were definite and one's mind was set firmly on the extinguishing and not on the fire. Spacer's affectation, because when the fingers could bear it comfortably, it was safe to put away. He dropped the butt into the side of the pouch reserved for that and laid the pouch on the table. They never let him keep it. The pouch, with the liquor and Sikkukkut's good humor, was delivered only in this room. So he let it lie, and met Sikkukkut's eyes with lazy amusement.

Perhaps he perplexed the *hakkikt* with his attitude, a coolness between defiance and alliance and certainly not the behavior of a kif; perhaps that was what kept his head off the spikes outside. Sikkukkut gazed at him a moment in what seemed interest, then lifted his hand as he had done before, and signaled his removal.

"There it goes," someone cried down the hall, and footsteps went thundering past Chur Anify's door, disturbing her convalescence. "*Kk-kk-kt,* something else called out, and that brought Chur's eyes open and set a little quicker pulse into her heart, so that needles jumped on the machine to which she was bound by a large skein of tubes, indicating an increase in pulse rate; in response to that, a flood of nutrients and appropriate chemicals came back into her bloodstream, automatically supplied.

Living bound to a machine-extension which thought it knew best what a body ought to feel was bad enough; lying there while riot went on in the corridor was another thing, and Chur edged her way off the bed, carefully (the spring extensions on the skein of tubings made it possible for her to reach the bathroom and saved her some indignities). In this case she gripped the various tubes in one fist to keep the extension from jerking painfully at the needles and padded over to the bureau where she had her gun, hearing the kifish clicking going on out there. Her head spun and her heart raced and the gods-cursed machine flooded her veins with sedative when it sensed her elevated pulse, but she made it to the door and pushed the button with the knuckle of her gun-hand.

The door shot open. She slumped lazy-like against the wall and stared at a kif who turned up directly opposite her and her pistol; then her eyes went strange-focused and her mind went here and there again, so that she had difficulty recalling where she was or why there should be a kif in *The Pride*'s corridor looking as horrified as a kif could look (not extremely) and why the peripheries of her vision informed her there were her cousins and a human standing there in shock and in company with this kif. It was a great deal to ask of a drugged hani brain, but the kif had its hands up and she was not crazed enough to go firing off a gun in a ship's corridor without knowing why.

And while her brain was sorting through that crazy sequence, something small and black ran right over her foot on its way into her room. "Hyaa!" she yelled in revulsion, and the kif dived for the wall beside her as she swung to keep a bead not on the thing but on the kif. A hurtling mass of her friends overtook her from behind—not to help her, to her vast bewilderment: they grabbed her and the gun, while the kif flinched and pasted himself tight to the wall, making himself the smallest possible target.

"Chur," her sister Geran was pleading with her, and she supposed that it was Geran prying the gun loose from her fingers: she was dizzy and her vision fuzzed. She heard her cousin Tirun's voice, and human jabber, which was her friend Tully; and she dazedly let herself be dragged one step and another into the room, someone else taking the skein of tubes. A bell was going off: the infernal machine was telling off on her, that she was stressed.

"Gods rot it," she cried, remembering. "There's something in here." And then she remembered that she had seen little black things before, on the bridge, and could not remember whether they were hallucinations or not, or whether her sister took her seriously. It was embarrassing to see hallucinations. And the cursed machine kept pouring sedative into her, so that they were going to leave her alone in here and drugged, with whatever-it-was: she did not want that either.

"Look under the bed," Geran said, while Geran was putting her back into it, and she could not remember where the gun had gotten to, which was against ship's rules, which was against all the regulations, to lose track of a firearm; and there was a kif trying to crawl under her bed. A sweat broke out on her, cold on her ears and nose and fingertips. "Where's my gun?" she asked hazily, trying to sit up again; and "There it is!" someone shouted from the floor.

"My gods," Chur murmured, and her sister put her flat on her back again. She blinked, blinked again in the crazed notion that there was a kif on his hands and knees at her bedside and people were trying to get her hallucination out from under her bed.

"Sorry," Geran said fervently. "Stay down. We've got it."

"You're crazy," Chur said. "You're stark crazy, all of you." Because none of it made sense.

But something let out a squeal under her bed, and something bumped against the secure-held braces, and there was an ammonia smell to the room which was no illusion, but a kif's real presence.

"He got," said Tully's voice, and he loomed up by her bedside. "Chur, you all right?"

"Sure," Chur said. She remembered at least where she was now, tied to a machine in *na* Khym's cabin because she was, since the kif had shot her on a dock at Kshshti, too sick to be down in crew quarters; and Goldtooth had given them this fine medical equipment when he had met them here at Kefk, which was before the docks blew up in a firefight and she had been holding the bridge single-handed when the little black things started coming and going like a nasty slinking nightmare. There *was* a kif aboard, his name was Skkukuk, he was a slave and a gift from the *hakkikt* and he stood there with his black snout atwitch and his Dinner clutched in both bony hands as he stared at her. She curled her lip and laid her ears back, head scantly lifted. "Out!"

The kif hissed and clicked and retreated in profound offense, teeth bared, and Chur bared hers, coming up on her free elbow.

"Easy," Geran said, pushing her back; and Tirun chased the kif on out, Haral's sister Tirun, big enough to make a kif think twice about any argument, and owing that slight limp to a kifish gun some years back: Chur felt herself safe if Geran was by her and Tirun was between her and the kif. She looked up at Tully's gold-bearded face and blinked placidly.

"Gods-be kif," Geran said. "Readout jumping like crazy—Tully, here, get this gun out of here."

"No," Chur said. "Drawer. Put it back in the drawer, Tully."

"Out of here," Geran said.

"Gods rot," Chur yelled, *"drawer!"* Living around Tully, a body got to thinking in pidgin and half-sentences. And the voice came out cracked. Tully hesitated, looking at Geran.

An even larger figure showed up in the doorway, filling it. Khym Mahn, male and tall and wide: "What's the trouble?"

"No trouble," Geran said. "Come on, close that door, everyone out before another of the gods-be things gets in. *Who's watching the godsforsaken kif?*"

"Put the gun in the drawer," Chur said firmly. "Tully."

"You leave it there," Geran said, getting up, as Khym vanished. She stood looking down a moment, while Tully did as he was told. Then the two of them stood there, her sister, her human friend; if there was ever truly such a thing as friendship between species. And the gods-be kif down the hall— Was *that* thing a friend, and did they have it running loose on the ship now? Had the captain authorized that?

"O gods," Chur murmured, too tired and too sick for

thoughts like loose kif, and for uncharitable thoughts toward Tully, who had done his unarmed best to save all their hides more than once. But it was in her heart now that she would not see home again, and that this was her last voyage, and she wanted to go home·more than anything, back to Anuurn and Chanur and to have this little selfish time with things she knew and loved, familiar things, uncomplicated by aliens and strangeness—wanted to be young again, and to have more time, and to remember what it was to have her life all in front of her and not behind.

Wanted, gods help her, to see even her home up in the hills, which was purest stupidity: she and Geran had walked out of there and come down to Chanur when they were kids as young as Hilfy, because a young fool of a new lord had gotten himself in power up there over their sept of clan Chanur, and she and her sister had pulled up roots and left for Chanur's main-sept estate with no more than the clothes on their backs.

And their pride. They had come with that intact. The two of them.

"Never looked back," she said, thinking Geran at least might understand. "Gods be, odd things were what we were looking for when we came down the hills, wasn't that it?"

Geran made a desperate motion at Tully that meant get out, quietly, and Tully went, not without a pat at Chur's blanketed leg.

Chur lay there and blinked, embarrassed at herself. She looked like something dead. She knew that. She and Geran had once looked a great deal alike, red-blond of mane and beard and with a sleekness and slimness that was the hill-woman legacy in their sept; not like their cousins Haral and Tirun Araun or their cousin Pyanfar either, who had downland Chanur's height and strength, but never their highlands beauty, their agility, their fleetness of foot. Now Geran's shoulders slumped in exhaustion, her coat was dull, her eyes unutterably weary; and Chur had seen mirrors. Her bones hurt when she lay on them. The sheets were changed daily: Geran saw to that, because she shed and shed, till the skin appeared in patches, all dull pink and horrid through her fur. That was her worst personal suffering, not the pain, not the dread of dying: it was her vanity the machine robbed her of, and her dignity; and watching Geran watch her deteriorate was worst of all.

"Sorry," Chur said. "Gods-be machine keeps pouring sedative into me. I don't always make sense."

Rotten way to die, she thought to herself, drugged out of my mind. Scaring Geran. What kind of way is that?

"Unhook me from this thing."

"You said you'd leave it be," Geran said. "For me. You told the captain you'd leave it be. Do we need to worry about you?"

"Asked, didn't I?" The voice came hoarse. The episode had exhausted her. Or it was the sedative. "We letting that gods-be kif loose now?"

"Khym's got an eye on him."

"Uhhn." There was a time that would have sounded crazy. Men did not deal with outsiders, did not take responsibility, did not have any weight of decision on their shoulders, on their berserk-prone brains. But nothing in the world was the same as it had been when she was a girl. "We left home to find strange things," Chur said, bewildered that she ended up trusting a man's good sense and an alien human's good will, a hillwoman like her. "Found 'em, didn't we?" But she saw that pained drawing about Geran's mustaches, the quivering flick of Geran's ears, well-ringed with voyages. She saw how drained Geran was, how her maundering grieved Geran, had a sure instinct that if Geran had one load on her shoulders, she had just put another there, almost unbearable for her sister. "Hey," she said, "I was pretty steady on my feet. Machine helps. Think I'll make it. Hear?"

Geran took that in and the slump left her shoulders and the grief left her eyes so earnestly and so trustingly it hurt.

Gods, Chur thought, now I've done it, I've promised her, haven't I?

Stupid to promise. Now I have to. I'll lose. It'll hurt, gods rot it. I'll die somewhere in jump, O gods, that's an awful way, to go out there, *in the dark between the stars, all naked.*

"Not easy," Chur murmured, heading down to sleep. "Easier to go out, Gery. But I'll get back up there, b'gods. Don't you let the captain assign me out. Hear?"

"Chair's waiting."

"You want to fill me in, treat me like I was crew?" It was
hard to stay interested in life, with the sedatives drawing a
curtain between herself and the universe. She remembered
her promise and fought to keep it. "What f'godssakes is
going on out there?"

"Same as before. We're sitting at dock waiting for that
gods-rotted kif to make up his mind to go left or right, and
so far nothing's worse."

"Or better."

"Or better. Except they're still talking. And the *hakkikt*'s
still real polite."

"Jik hasn't cracked."

"Hasn't cracked. Gods help him."

"How long are we going to sit here?"

"Wish we all knew. Captain's figuring like mad, Haral's
laying in six, seven courses into comp. We may get home
yet."

"Doublecross the kif? They'd hunt us." Her voice grew
thick. "Meetpoint's the only way out of here. That's where
we've got to go."

Geran said nothing. The threads grew vague, but they
always came to the same point. Goldtooth had left them
and his partner in the lurch and run for Meetpoint, and
Tully's folk were headed into the Compact in numbers, all
of which meant that a very tired hani who wanted the universe to be what it had been in her youth was doomed to
see things turned upside down, doomed to see Chanur allied with kif, with a species that ate little black things and
behaved badly on docksides, and did other things an honest
hani preferred not to think about.

Gods-rotted luck, she thought; and thought again about
the hills of home, and the sins of her youth, one of which
she had left with its father; but it was only a gods-be boy,
and not a marriage anyhow, and she had never written back
to the man, who was no happier at getting a son than she
was at birthing one (a daughter would have done him some
good in his landless station), but his sisters would treat the
boy all right. Rest of the family never had known much
about it, except Geran knew, of course; and it was before
she had joined *The Pride*. The kid would have come of age
and gone off to Hermitage years ago; and probably died,
the way surplus males died. Waste. Ugly waste.

Wish I'd known my son.

Maybe I could find him. If his father's still alive. If he's like na Khym, if— Maybe, maybe if I could've talked to him he'd have sense like na Khym.

Never asked that man—never much talked to him. Never occurred to me to talk to him. Isn't that funny? Now I'd wonder what he was thinking. I'd think he was thinking. I'd find me a man and make love to him and gods, I'd ask him what he was thinking and he'd—

—I'd probably confuse him all to a mahen hell, I would; aren't many men like Khym Mahn, gods-rotted nice fellow, wished I'd known him 'fore the captain got him. If he was ever for anybody but her. If a clan lord like him could've ever looked at an exile like me. I'd like to've loved a man like him. I'd have got me a daughter off him, I would've.

But what's the captain got of him? Gods-rotted son like Kara Mahn and a gods-forsaken whelp of a daughter like Tahy, no help there, gods fry 'em both, no sense, no ears to listen, no respect—doublecrossing gods-be cheats.

Want to find me a man. Not a pretty one. A smart one. Man I can sit and talk with.

If I ever get home.

She pursed her lips and spat.

"You all right?"

"Sure, I'm sleeping, get out of here. I'm trying to get my rest. What in the gods' name *are* those black things?"

"Don't ask. We don't."

The lift opened belowdecks, and Hilfy Chanur, coming back onshift, stepped back hastily as the doors whisked back and gave her Skkukuk all unexpected, Skkukuk clutching a squealing cageful of nasty black shapes, which apparition sent her ears flat; but Tirun and Tully were escorting the kif, which got Hilfy's ears back up again and laid the fur back down between her shoulderblades. She stepped aside in distaste to let the kif out and stood there staring as the door waited to her hold on the call button.

"We think we got 'em," Tirun said.

"They got," Tully said, amplifying his broken pidgin with a gesture topside. "Eat fil-ter. Lousy mess."

"Good gods, *what* filter?"

"Airfilter in number one," Tirun said. "Sent particles all

over the system: we're going to have to do a washdown on the number two and the main."

"Make electric," Tully said.

"We made it real uncomfortable in that airshaft," Tirun said.

"Kkkkt," Skkukuk said, "these are Akkhtish life. They are *adaptive*. Very tough."

The creatures started fighting at the sound of his voice. He whacked the cage with his open hand and the Dinner subsided into squeals.

"Gods," Hilfy said with a shudder of disgust.

"Two of them are about to litter," Tirun said. "Watch these gods-forsaken things. They're born fighting."

"Tough," Skkukuk said conversationally, and hit the Dinner's cage again, when the squeals sharpened. There was quiet, except for a hiss. "Kkkt. Excuse me." He clutched the cage to him and headed off down the hall with the Dinner in his arms, happy as ever a kif could be.

Hilfy's lip lifted; an involuntary shiver went through her as Tirun turned and went to keep an eye on the kif. Tully stayed, and set a hand on her shoulder, squeezed hard. *Tully* knew. He had been with her in the hands of the kif, this same Sikkukkut who was their present ally; who sent them this slavish atrocity Skkukuk to haunt the corridors and leave his ammonia-stink everywhere in the air, a smell which brought back memories—

A second time Tully squeezed her shoulder with his clawless fingers. Hilfy turned and looked at him, looking up a bit; but he was not so tall, her Tully, that she could not look him in the eyes this close. Those eyes were blue and usually puzzled, but in this moment there was worry there. Two voyages and what they had been through together had taught her to read the nuances of his expressions.

"He's not bad kif," Tully said.

That was so incredible an opinion from him she blinked and could not believe she had heard it.

"He's kif," Tully said. "Same I be human. Same you hani. He be little kif, try do what captain want."

She would not have heard it from anyone else. She had her mouth open when Tully said it. But this was a man who had been twice in their hands; and seen his friends die; and killed one of them himself to save him from Sik-

kukkut: more, he had been there with her in that kifish
prison, and if Tully was saying such an outrageous thing it
might have any number of meanings, but emptyheaded and
over-generous it was not. She stared at him trying to figure
out if he had missed his words in hani: the translator they
had rigged up to their com sputtered helpless static at his
belt, constant undertone when he spoke his thickly accented hani or pidgin. Maybe he was trying to communicate
some crazy human philosophy that failed to come through.

"Little kif," Tully said again. She had lived among kif
long enough to know what he meant by that, that kif were
nothing without status, and that kif of low status were everyone's victims.

"If he was a big kif," she said, "he'd kill us fast."

"No," Tully said. "Captain be Pyanfar. He want be big,
she got be big."

"Loyalty, huh?"

"Like me," Tully said. "He one."

"You mean he's alone."

"He want be hani."

She spat. It was too much. "You might be." And not
many hani in space and certainly none on homeworld
would be that generous, only a maudlin and lonely young
woman a long way from her own kind. "Not a kif. Ever."

"True," Tully admitted, twisting back on his own argument in that maddening way he had of getting behind a
body and leaving them facing the wrong way. He held up
a finger. "He kif, he same time got no friend with kif, he
be little kif. They kill him, yes. He want not be kill. He lot
time wrong, think we do big good to him. You watch, Hilfy: crew be good with him, he be happy, he got face up,
he be brave with us, he talk. But we don't tell truth to him,
huh? What good truth? Say him, 'kif, you enemy,' he got
no friend, got no ship, got no *hakkikt*. He don't be hani,
he die."

"I can't be sorry for him. He wouldn't understand it.
He's kif, gods rot him. And I'd as soon kill him on sight."

"You don't kill same like you be kif." He patted her arm
and looked earnestly at her, from the far side of a language
barrier the translator never crossed. "He makes a mistake,"
the translator said as he changed into his own language for
words he did not have. "He's lost. He thinks we like him

more now. We ask him go die for help us, he go. True, he will go. And we hate him. He doesn't know this. He's kif. He can't understand why we hate him."

"Well, let's not confuse him," Hilfy snarled, and turned and stopped the lift door which had started to close on auto when she let go the button. It recoiled, held for another wait. She looked back at Tully, who looked back, aggrieved and silent. She knew his shorthand speech better than anyone else aboard: ship's com officer, linguist, translator, she had helped set up his translation system and help break through to him when they first met him. And what he was saying now made more sense than she wanted it to—that a kif, cold-blooded tormentor and killer that it was, was also a helpless innocent in their hands. If a kif saw another kif in his way, he killed; his changes of loyalty were frequent but sincere and self-serving. And if the captain's subordinates treated him better, it was because the captain had accorded him more status: it was all a kif could think, it was all a kif knew how to imagine. Pyanfar let Skkukuk loose more often, Pyanfar cared to feed him, the crew was civil to him: his place in the universe was therefore improving. Gods help them, the kif became conversational with them. Two and more centuries of contact and the kif had never let slip any casual detail about their homeworld, which no one visited but kif; and here Skkukuk, bragging on his nasty little vermin as Akkhtish and adaptive, hinted at more of kifish life and kifish values than kif had said about themselves in all of history.

And what would a man know about anything? was her gut reaction, staring into Tully's eyes. She did not think of Skkukuk as male, gods knew; hardly thought of Jik or Goldtooth as anything but female and rational, despite the male pronouns which were ordinary in pidgin and otherwise in hani: but Tully was definitely male to her, and stood there saying crazy things about an enemy, talking to *her* about self-restraint, which was a female kind of thought, or Pyanfar was right and males had a lot of hidden female about them: it was an embarrassing estimation. But the sense that it made also reached somewhere inside and found a sore spot, that Tully had found some kind of peace with the thing that had happened to them among the kif, where a sane, technically educated woman failed.

Because he's older, Hilfy thought. She had always thought of him as near her own age: and suddenly she thought that he must be, of his kind, old as Khym, whose years had burned the tempers out of him and given him self-control and lost him his lordship over Mahn. Suddenly she suspected that she had always been wrong about Tully, that he was wiser than a young man could possibly be, and cooler-headed: and there was something still he had not been able to tell her. There was something still bottled up in him, she could almost read it, but it was too alien an expectation; or too simple. She could not guess it. The lift door hit her in the shoulder again and gave up, and she reached out and gently touched Tully's face with the pads of her fingers.

"If you were hani," she said, "we'd—" But she did not say that. It sounded too foolish; and hurt too much, without an answer that resulted in anything but both of them being fools. Laughable fools.

"Friend," he said in a small voice, and touched her face. While the lift door hit her again, on shorter and shorter reminder. "Friend, Hilfy." With a peculiar stress in his voice, and a break, as it would do when he was grieved. There were things he did not commit to the translator. More and more he tried to speak hani. And to be hani. And he grew sadder and more wistful when he would look at her and say a thing like that, making fools of them both.

Gods, Hilfy Chanur, she thought, *what can you do? When did you go crazy? When did he? When we were alone and we were all we had, with kif all about? I want him.*

If he's older than me, why doesn't he have an answer for this?

Then an alarm went off. For a moment she thought she had tripped it by holding the door, and Pyanfar was going to skin her.

"Priority, priority. We've got a courier at the lock," Haral's voice said then from com, from every speaker in the hall. *"All secure below. Hilfy, Tirun, arm and stand by: looks like you're the welcoming committee, captain's compliments, and she's staying topside. Protocols. You get that?"*

"I got it," Hilfy said.

Lock up the kif, that meant. Fast.

"Tully," she said, and motioned to the lift. Panic had

started a slow, hysteric beat in her heart; habit kept her face calm as she stepped aside and held the door with her arm for Tully.

I could help, that look of his said; I could be down here, I want to be here. I want to help you—

It was not the kif's feelings he had so laboriously described: *you make him part of the crew, you let him believe it, you don't know how cruel you are to let him believe you.*

He'd go out and die for you, Hilfy Chanur. Because he believes you.

No. It was not true of the kif. It was what he felt in himself.

"Up," she said. "Bridge. Haral needs you. I got enough down here."

And, gods, why put it that way? She saw the pain she caused.

He went into the lift, and turned and pushed the Close, so that the door jarred her obstructing arm and she drew it back in confusion. She opened her mouth to say something like *you can't help in this,* which was no better than she had already said; but the door closed between their faces, and left her speechless and harried in recalling that it was an emergency Haral had just sent her on—kif, and trouble, and gods knew what.

The whole situation could be unraveling. Jik might have talked, might have spilled something; it might be the beginning of the attack they had feared; it might be anything, and gods help her, she had just fouled it up with Tully and there was no time, no time, never time to straighten it out betweeen them.

Gods, gods, gods, I hurt him. I never wanted to hurt him, we can all die here and I can't get past that gods-be translator.

Why is it all so complicated?

Chapter 2

It was not a situation Pyanfar enjoyed, sitting on the bridge and watching on the vid as a pair of armed kif headed toward her airlock. They wore no suits, only the hooded black robes universal with their kind. That meant the kif put some reliance on the jury-patches and the repressurization of this zone of the dock, more than she herself would have liked to put on it—kifish repair crews had been thumping and welding away out there, motes on vid, getting a patch on those areas the decompression had weakened.

So finally the *hakkikt* seemed to have settled accounts with the rebels inside his camp to the extent that now he could send a message to the friends of the mahen and hani traitors who had made such a large hole in his newly-acquired space station, who had disturbed the tc'a into riot on their side of the station, and incidentally sent over five hundred unsuspecting kif out into space on the wind of that decompression.

Sikkukkut had a very legitimate grievance; even a hani had to admit as much. Though the kif that had gone on that unscheduled spacewalk were many of them Sikkukkut's enemies, a good many had been partisans of his, and while no kif had ever been observed to grieve over the demise of any other kif, and while the incident might even have contributed to stopping the rebellion, still it had embarrassed him—and embarrassing a kifish leader was a very serious matter. It was not an accustomed feeling, to have a sense of wrong on her side when she was dealing with the kif; and to know, the while those black-robed figures cycled through the lock, that *The Pride* was not in a position, nose to a wrecked dock and outnumbered ten to one in ships and multiple thousands to one in personnel, to negotiate anything at all, not regarding what this mass of

ships chose to do, not regarding their own position within
the kifish power structure, not even regarding their safety
or their lives.

So bluff was still the game, status and protocols, which
was why she was sitting up here gnawing her mustaches
and having her crew meet with an armed delegation that
neither they nor she had power to negotiate with. She tried
to use kifish manners, which kif understood, and she hoped
to the gods the kif did understand the gesture she was making, which meant that Pyanfar Chanur had just abandoned
her inclination to meet the *hakkikt*'s messengers on hani
protocols, with hani courtesies: now she withdrew to a re-
moteness which to a kif (she hoped) signaled not fear (a
frightened kif would show up to placate the offended party,
and thrust himself right into the presence of his potential
enemy to try to patch it up) but rather signaled that the
captain of this hani freighter turned hunter-ship considered
herself risen in the *hakkikt*'s favor, to the extent that she
intended henceforth to receive her messages through subordinates. She sensed that self-promotion was the way things
worked with kif: she sensed it by experience, and kifish manners, and Skkukuk's inside-out advice: their own much-
bewildered kifish crewman alternately shrank and flourished
in every breeze of her tempers, crushed by a moment's
reprimand, bright-eyed and energetic on her next moment's
better humor; and jealous and paranoid in his constant suspicions the crew would undermine him—as he tried to undermine them, of course, but less zealously of late, as if he
had finally gotten it through his narrow kifish skull that
that was not the way things worked on a hani ship; or that
the crew was too firmly in the captain's favor to dislodge;
or perhaps the crew's own increasing courtesy with him had
sent his mind racing on a new stratagem down some path
thoroughly mistaken and thoroughly kif: it was enough to
give a sane hani a headache. But Skkukuk had shown her
a vital thing: that a kif took all the ground he could get at
every hour of every day, and if he made a mistake and got
a reprimand, he did not, as a hani would do, cherish a
grudge for that reprimand: where a hani would burn with
shame and throw sanity and self-preservation to the winds,
and where a hani who chastised another hani knew that

she was asking for bloodfeud to the second and third generation, involving both clans and affiliate clans to the eighth degree, a kif just accepted a slap in the face with the same unflappable sense of self-preservation that would make him go for his own leader's throat the moment that leader looked vulnerable, at the very moment a reasonable hani might stand by her leader most loyally. Pyanfar had puzzled this out. In a total wrench of logic she could even understand that kif being dead as they were to any altruistic impulse, had to move to completely different tides, and the most urgent of those tides seemed to be the drive to inch their way up in status at every breath if they could get away with it.

It was a good question whether Sikkukkut understood hani half that well, despite his fluency; and upon that thought a logical gulf opened before her, whether a kif could ever truly understand the pride of the lowliest hani hill woman, who would spend the last drop of blood she had settling accounts both of debt and bloodfeud with anyone at all, headwoman or beggar; the kif had not the internal reflexes to feel what a hani felt; and how, good gods, could a hani know the compulsion that drove a kif, lacking whatever-it-was which was as natural to kif as breathing.

Gods help us, if I had enough credit with him to get Jik loose—if anyone did—if I could crack that gods-be code of Jik's, over there in comp, if I knew what Jik was holding out against Sikkukkut, what kind of craziness he passed me at Mkks—is it his will and testament? Something for his Personage? Some gods-cursed plan of attack?

Goldtooth's plan of action?

What do the kif want *down there, why come in person, why not use the com?*

While the kif arrived in their fire-scarred airlock and prepared to deal with her niece and her cousin, both of whom had gotten scars before this at kifish hands.

Don't foul it, Hilfy, don't give way— Gods, I should have called her up and sent—

—Geran? With Chur shot and Geran in the mood she's in?

—not Haral, I need her.

Not a place for the menfolk down there either. Hilfy's all

*right, she's stable, she'll carry it off all right—she knows
the kif, knows them well as anyone—knows how to hold
herself—*

*O gods, why'd I ever let her and Chur go off the ship at
Kshshti? It was my fault, my fault and she'll never be the
same—*

*—isn't the same, no one's ever the same; I'm not, the ship
isn't, Chur isn't, none of us are, and I brought us here, every
gods-be step along the way—*

Haral cycled the lock and two unescorted kif walked into
The Pride's lowerdeck; while Geran powered the airlock
camera about, tracking them, and Khym and Tully hovered
over separate monitors. Haral kept cycling her own checks,
keeping an eye to the whole godsforsaken dockside, screen
after screen at Haral's station shifting images so that they
were never blinder than they had to be.

No way they were going to be caught in distraction, even
if, gods forbid, the kif tossed a grenade through the lock.

"Record," Pyanfar said. "Aye," Geran said; and flicked a
switch, beginning to log the whole business into *The Pride*'s
records. Then:

"Those are rifles," Geran muttered.

The kif carried heavy weapons, besides the sidearms. The
dim light and poor camera pickup had obscured those black
weapons against the black, unornamented robes. But the
rifles were slung at the shoulder, not carried in the hand.
That much was encouraging. "Polite," Pyanfar said through
her teeth, while below, from the spy-eye:

"Hunter Pyanfar," one kif said as he met *The Pride*'s
welcoming committee.

"Tirun Araun." Tirun identified herself—scarred old
spacer with gray dusting her nose and streaking her red-
gold mane. She had a way of holding herself that seemed
both diffident about the gun she held (surely civilized beings ought not to hold guns on each other) and very likely
to use it in the next twitch (there was not the least com-
punction or doubt in her eyes). *"I trust you've come from
the* hakkikt,*"* Tirun said. *"Praise to him"*—without the least
flicker, kifish courtesy.

"Praise to him," the kif said. *"A message to your captain."* It took a cylinder from its belt, with never an objection to the leveled guns or Hilfy's flattened ears. *"The*

hakkikt *says: the docks are secure. The matter is urgent. I say: we will stand here and wait for the Chanur captain.*"

Tirun reached out and took the cylinder. And delayed one lazy moment in a gesture that could not have been wasted, especially on a kif. *"Be courteous, Hilfy."*

With fine timing, with a little flattening of the ears that might be respect and might be something else again, ambiguous even to hani eyes—Tirun delivered her signal to Hilfy and turned with authority and walked off, at a pace both deliberate and fast enough.

While Hilfy stood there with the gun in her fist and two kif to watch.

Steady, kid. For the gods' sakes, Tirun's done it right, don't wobble.

No one said a thing on the bridge. It remained very, very quiet until the lift worked, back down the corridor from the center of the bridge. Then Pyanfar got out of her chair and went to wait for Tirun, who came down the corridor at a much faster clip than she had used below. While at the boards, Haral and Geran kept to business, monitoring everything round about the ship and inside it and everything coming from station.

"Captain," Tirun said by way of courtesy, and handed over the cylinder.

The cap stuck when she pulled at it. For one awful moment Pyanfar thought of explosives; or deadly gas. "Wait here," she said, left Tirun standing on the bridge, and stepped outside into the corridor, pushing the door switch to close it between them.

She hooked a claw into the seal then and gnawed her lip and pulled the cap. Nothing blew. Nothing came out. It was a message, a bit of gray paper.

The door shot open again in the same instant, which was Tirun; and Tirun stood there aggrieved in the tail of her eye while she fished the paper out and read it.

Hunter Pyanfar: you have made requests. I will give you my reponse aboard my ship at 1500, expecting that you will come with ranking personnel of allied ships.

"Captain?" Tirun said.

She passed the letter over and cast a second look up at the chrono in the bridge display: 1436.

"It's a trap," Tirun said.

On the bridge even Haral had taken one quick look around.

"Invitation from the kif," Pyanfar said. "Ranking personnel of allied ships. On his deck. Fast."

"My gods," Khym exclaimed.

"Unfortunately," Pyanfar said, and thought of Hilfy down there in the corridor with two kif alone. "Unfortunately we haven't got a real choice. Get Tahar and get Kesurinan. I'm not taking any of you—"

Mouths opened.

"It's a trap," Khym said, his deep voice quivering with outrage. "Py, Tirun's right, listen to her."

"Not taking any of you," she said carefully, "except our friend the kif. Get to it, Geran, get our friends out there."

"That dock," Geran said.

"We got worse risks than a leaky dock, cousin; one of 'em's being late and one of them's missing a signal with that kif. I'm going down there, I want Tahar and Kesurinan just the way the kif asked, and about the time I clear the lock down there I want *The Pride* powered up and held that way till I get back again. Make the point with 'em we still got teeth, hear? And that my crew's on full alert."

"Aye," Haral muttered, far from happy.

Neither was Pyanfar happy. She went and pulled one of their APs out of the locker by the bridge exit and headed back down the corridor, with the heavy sidearm and its belt in hand.

Not to the lowerdeck straightway.

First came a stop in her own quarters, for a fast exchange: for a bit of glitter, because appearances counted, a psychological weapon as essential as the gun at her side.

Sikkukkut meant to move now. In some regard.

She clenched her jaw and started cataloging things, fast, things that wanted doing. In case she had just said goodbye to her crew and her husband.

Gods, Khym had just stood there and took an answer for an answer. Her heart did a little painful thump of pride when she realized belatedly what that had cost him: he was not the gentle ignorant she had married, not the feckless man who had walked out on the docks at Meetpoint and run straight into a kifish trap. If she died today at kifish hands he would not act the male; would not rush out there like a lunatic to take the kif on hand to hand—he had grown a lot on this voyage, had Khym, when he was no longer a boy and no longer young at all. He had finally found out what lay outside his limits and what the universe was like—had found friends, b'gods, female friends and one who was even male, friends which she suddenly realized in grief that Khym had never had in all his adult life, excepting her and his other wives, and them but scarcely: clanlord, shielded from all contact with the world by his wives and his sisters and his daughters, he had finally come out into the real world to find out what it was, and he was not just *her* Khym anymore; or even Khym lord Mahn; he was something more than that, suddenly, long after he should have gone to die in Hermitage, outworn and useless—he grew up and became what he always could have been; discovered the universe full of honest folk and scoundrels of all genders, and learned how to win respect, how to ignore the barbs and become ship-youngest and work his way out of a second youth, with utterly different rules. That was more change than most women had the fortitude to take in their lives; but by the gods he had made it complete back there; he would do his fighting from that bridge and that board, under Haral's command if something went wrong, part of the crew that drove a ship of mass enough and internal power enough to turn Kefk and Sikkukkut and all his ambitions into one briefly incandescent star.

The docks were the shambles she had expected, gray metal still supercooled under her bare feet, with a good many of the lights out—blown when the pressure went and when this dock had opened to space. Gantries loomed up down the righthand side of the docks, subtly tilting in the positive curvature of the deck, which was the torus-shaped station's outermost edge, to anyone who saw it as a wheel, from the outside. Here that rim was *down,* and floored in bare metal—Kefk had mining, metal-rich in the debris that floated around its double stars; therefore Kefk was gray and dull, except for the dirty orange of the sodium-lights kif preferred—because it never occurred to the colorblind kif to paint anything for decorative purposes, only for protective ones: they literally had to use instruments to determine what color a thing was, and gods knew whether their

homeworld Akkht had ever offered them dyes other than
black—though it was rumored that they had learned their
color-taste from the pastel, opalescent stsho, who dispar-
aged the riot of color which hani and mahendo'sat loved
about themselves; having discovered a range of distinctions
beyond their senses, having the pale example of the stsho
before them, and flinching before the stsho's concept of
value (such affluent consumers they set the standard for
the whole Compact's economy) and further daunted by the
stsho's disparagement of species who put strong color with
color, the kif were all very insecure in their own dignity
before the stsho and before others: above all no kif wanted
to be laughed at. True black was one distinction they could
make, true black and true white: so they naturally chose
the dark that matched their habitat and their desire to
move unseen, and became aesthetes of only one color, the
blackest black. They valued silver more than gold because
to their eyes it shone more; and they valued texture above
other things in aesthetics, because they were more tactilely
than visually stimulated in their pleasure centers: in fact
they must be virtually blind to sight-beauty, and loved to
touch interesting surfaces—that was what she had heard
from an old stsho once upon a time, when the stsho had
gotten quite giddy on a tiny cupful of Anuurn tea (it had
a substance in it which reacted interestingly with stsho metabolism, which did nothing at all to a hani: such were the
oddities of vice and pleasure between species). The kif in
earliest days, this stsho said, had been victims of mahen
practical jokes, who sold them clashing colors; and the kif
did not forget this humiliation.

Kif were vastly changed, that was the truth, even from a
few years ago: then they had been scattered and petty pirates, dockside thieves a hani could bluff into retreat, kif
whose style was to whine and accuse and frequently to
launch lawsuits in stsho courts which might make a freighter
pay out of court settlement just to get the matter clear.
That was the style of kifish banditry before Akkukkak.

Now she walked onto this dock in the company of a
prince's escort, and had her own bodyguard—Skukkuk
walking along with her, armed with the gun he had taken
from a kif in the fighting, looking like every other kif in
his black robe and his hood and the plainness of his gear:

if she looked about and if Skkukuk and one of her escort had changed places, she would not be able to tell them apart at any casual glance. That was another effect of kifish dress: of black hoods that deeply shaded the face and left only the gray-black snout in the light; it made targets hard to pick.

And from *Aja Jin*'s berth—nothing of that ship was visible nor any of the others, only the tangle of lines and gantries that held those lines aloft to the several ports that valved through to t'   'p—from behind that tangle came another pair, mahen,   of them male. The other was Soje Kesurinan, Jik's second in command. Kesurinan was a tall black mahe, scarred and missing half an ear, but handsome in the way she carried herself—dour as Jik was cheerful, but she lifted her chin as she saw Pyanfar, and her diminutive mahen ears, whole and half, flicked in salutation.

"Kesurinan," Pyanfar said quietly, as Kesurinan walked up to her. And: "Kkkkt," from her kifish escort. "Tahar is on her way. An escort is going to pick her up; we can go on down."

"Got," Kesurinan said, which was agreement, economical and expressionless in a woman who had to be worried. Very worried. But they had to play everything to the kif who watched them, and give away nothing. Pyanfar nodded to the escort, and they started walking then, along the dock, the belt of the AP gun heavy about her hips, a pocket pistol thumping against her leg on the other side. Kif went armed to the teeth and so did she and so did Kesurinan, and, kifish taste and kifish eyesight notwithstanding, she had used that trip to her room to put on a pair of dress trousers, silk and not the coarse crewwoman's blues she had taken to wearing aboard; silk trousers, her best belt, the cord-ends of which were semiprecious stones and *ui,* polyp skeletons from Anuurn seas, and worth more than rubies off Anuurn: hani were not divers, as a rule, but they were traders, and knowing the substance, had suspected the stsho would prize this pale rarity—quite correctly, as it developed. In this splendor and with a couple of gold bracelets and a silver one, not mentioning the array of earrings, she headed for a meeting with the self-appointed prince of pirates, in all the arrogance a hani captain owned.

She had gotten out the door in good order, had gone

down the lift, joined Hilfy in the short lock corridor and informed the kif that she was expecting her own escort, while Haral used the intercom and the central board's unlock-commands to release Skkukuk from his prison and to direct him to the lift by the farside corridor, where Tirun brought his gun to him—all managed so that it saved Skku-kuk's dignity. The ammonia-smelling rascal had come stroll-ing up on them from the direction she had come, armed and suitably arrogant with his fellow kif: after all, his captain had an appointment with the *hakkikt* and he had just been chosen over all the other crew as her escort: he was posi-tively cheerful.

Hilfy, on the other hand—

Hilfy's ears had gone flat when she saw what was toward, and there had been starkest horror in her eyes, which the kif might well have attributed to seeing herself shunted aside for a kifish escort—correct; but for the wrong reasons.

But the kid, in fact, had kept her mouth clamped shut and taken it all in grim silence. Gods knew Hilfy would probably say something considerable when she got topside, which was probably where she had gone the moment that lock shut, topside so fast the deck would smoke.

A strobe light began to flash behind them, pulses hitting the gantries and the girders; she knew what it was, knew when Kesurinan turned, and when the kif turned in one move— "Kkkt," one said, "kkkt—"

And looked back at her again as the others did, head lifted in threat, tongue darting in nervousness: his rifle slid to his hands.

Pyanfar only stood there. Grinned at him, which was not humor in a hani as it was in a mahendo'sat or a human; but which at this moment approached it. *The Pride of Cha-nur* had just powered up and the sensors on the gantry-fed power lines had just shut off the flow and triggered an alarm, the same alarm that would have sounded when Goldtooth's *Mahijiru* and *Ehrran's Vigilance* had powered up to leave dock—if the station had not been too occupied for anyone to react to it. "We're not leaving," she said to the kif quite cheerfully. "It's honorific. So you know who you're dealing with— Praise to the *hakkikt.*"

Kif might be blind to a great many things: not to sarcasm and not to arrogance and not to a gesture made to the whole of Kefk station and the whole of the *hakkikt's* power. They would not rally to their *hakkikt* in the sense that hani would rally round a leader; she bet her life on that; he was just The *Hakkikt* and there might arise another without warning. Kif would not defend him against someone of status enough to make that kind of gesture to him: such a status only made them uneasy, in the absence of orders which might have told them how the *hakkikt* would play the matter. They could anger the *hakkikt* by creating him a problem, too. She faced a pair of very uneasy kif. And grinned in something very like primate humor as she turned and walked down the dock as she had already done, with the kif at her back, with Kesurinan at her side and Skukkuk guarding her flank, armed and deadly. That was perhaps another very worried kif: his own *hakt'-mekt,* his great captain, had just defied the highest power in local space.

She had just served notice to that Power what the stakes were, by the gods; and what her life was worth to her crew.

That was power of a sort no kif wielded, of a sort no kif could easily foresee.

Martyrdom was a concept that had gotten a shiver even out of Sikkukkut.

"Word from *Harukk,*" Hilfy said, coldly and calmly as she could, though her hand trembled as it hovered over the com console: "Quote: *We demand cause for this violation of regulations.*"

"Reply," said Haral Araun, her low voice quite calm, "we have obeyed instructions from our captain."

The hair rose on Hilfy Chanur's spine. She was more fluent in main-kifish than most hani, than most communications officers far senior to her, in fact. And what Haral was telling the kif was precisely the correct response, a very kifish thing to say, whether or not the old spacer knew it: Hilfy would have bet her scant possessions that Haral had calculated it, not by book-learning, but by decades of dockside give and take with the kif. She punched in and rendered it in main-kifish to the *hakkikt's* communications officer, who let a considerable stark silence ride after it.

Click.

"*Harukk*-com just went offline," Hilfy said, still calmly, though her heart was slamming away at her ribs. Beside

her, Tully and Geran and Khym sat keeping an eye on
scan, on the limited view they had with their nose into
station and the scan output from station. Tirun Araun ran
Haral's copilot functions from her post over by the aft bulkhead, the master-alternate, acting as switcher and sequencer,
Haral's usual job; and Tirun had armaments live back there
too. In case.

"Haa," Khym muttered suddenly.

"We just lost station output," Geran said.

Sikkukkut's officials had just blinded them, at least inso-
far as station could. Doubtless someone was on the com to
Sikkukkut personally, to tell him that there was a hani ship
live, armed, and with its powerful nose stuck right into
Kefk's gut.

Not mentioning what those engines back there could do
if they cycled the jump vanes sitting at dock. Some of their
particles would stay in realspace, mightily agitated; others,
in their random way, would enter hyperspace, and stream
for the depths of the local gravity wells, the greatest of
which was Kefk's main star. Everything would part company in a rather irretrievable fashion, either turning into a
bright spot or a failed attempt at a black hole, stripping its
own substance down, since it had no directional potential
except the station and the star's own motion through the
continuum. Probably not enough to prevent implosion. Hilfy
activated a keyboard in her idle moment, fed in *The Pride*'s
mass and her best guess at total station mass, adding in the
number of ships tied into the station, a moment of black
self-amusement, filling her mind with numbers and school-
book calculations.

It was significant that the kif had not immediately demanded that they shut down the internal power: the kif
knew they had no power to enforce that until they had
Pyanfar in their hands.

And Hilfy did not want to think about that at the moment. She simply ran the numbers on their own possible
dissolution, and whether they would actually form the hyperspace bubble, and whether with all those ships and that
station and all that mass, they might actually have a hyper-
spatial effect on the largest star when they plowed into it.

She sent it into Nav, since the bubble variables resided
there in standard equations; and of a sudden her comp

monitor blinked, beeped, and came up with output too soon to have responded to that complex query: TRLING/PR1, it read, PSWD.

Password?

Nav query?

Those were the two thoughts that hit her brain while her eyes were in motion back to the top of that screen where the program name was listed: they found that PRIORITY ONE code and the Linguistics Path Designator as the implication suddenly hit like a wash of cold water.

YN she typed, which was the shortest city name on Anuurn and the standard password for their lightly coded systems: fast keys to hit.

Syntax achieved, the screen said. *Display/Print?/Tape?/All?*

She hit *D* and *P*; the screen blinked text up, full of gaps and mangled syntax: it was running a code-cracker set in the assumption it was mahensi, but it was not mahen standard, it was some godsforsaken related language, though the computer was making some sense of it on cognates. Jik's message. The coded packet he had dropped in their laps back at Mkks.

Dialect. Which?

She punched more buttons, desperately, asking for the decoded original. It came up, vaguely recognizable as mahen phonemes. "Gods be," she muttered. "Haral, Haral, the comp just spat out Jik's message but it's still hashed up, it's got a string of words together but it's still sorting—we got a breakthrough here."

The screen blinked with a red strip across the top, which was Tirun using her keyboard to snatch information across to her board and probably to Haral's.

"Keep on it," Haral said. "Tirun, monitor com."

"Aye," Tirun said, and "Aye," Hilfy muttered, punching keys, with the hair bristling on her neck and her ears flicking in half-crazed vexation with the computer, which had thrown her a half-solved problem in her own field here on the very edge of oblivion.

Kif could call our bluff any second now.

Haral could push that button.

We could go streaming for that sun and the gods rot it what language is he using that comp hasn't got? O gods be!

*when's that alarm going to come? We're going to die, gods
rot it, and it's giving me something to chase, and gods rot
it, Haral, let me finish this gods-be silly problem before you
push the godsforsaken button, it's a rotten thing to die with
a question in your head, if this thing's got the whole why
and wherefore of it, all Jik's conniving, all his secrets—hold
off the button, Haral, tell me when we go, I don't want to
die till I get this—*

The computer beeped and sorted and ticked away,
launched on a new hunt with a little hani shove in a certain
direction for its research. It blinked away to itself and Hilfy
clasped her hands in front of her mouth and stared at the
screen in mindless timestretch.

*Probably a letter to his wife. Gods know. Has he got a
wife? Kids?*

*We're going to die here and this stupid machine can't go
any faster and what can we do anyway? Pyanfar's already
out there with the kif.*

And we can't get to her. Whatever happens.

Harukk occupied a berth well around the rim, beyond
the weakened section, but not beyond the damage: wreckage lay about them, walls and decks were fire blackened
and pocked with shells and laser-hits.

And the approach to the *hakkikt*'s ship was more ghastly
than before, hedged with a veritable forest of poles and
stanchions on which he had put the heads of enemies and
rebels against his power.

Pyanfar had seen the display before; so had Kesurinan.
Hope he changes them off, was the wisp of thought that
leapt into Pyanfar's distressed mind. *M'gods, putrefaction.
The things life-support has to put up with on this station—
filters must be a gods-be mess.*

—in a distracted, callous mode because she had gotten
used to such horrors, and only her heart flinched in a forlorn, pained recollection that there were places where such
things did not happen, where naive, precious folk went
about their lives never having seen a sapient head parted
from its body and hung up like a traffic warning.

*This kif is going to expand beyond Kefk. Going—gods
know how far. Gods help the civilized worlds.*

A sneeze hit her. She stifled it, turned it into a snarl and wiped her nose. She was allergic to kif—had taken another pill when she changed clothes, but the air was thick hereabouts. Her eyes watered. Lives rode on her dignity and she was going to sneeze, the very thought that she was going to sneeze made her nose itch and the watering grow worse. But she squared her shoulders and put the itching out of her mind, eyes fixed on the ramp, on the access which lay open for them.

"It's coming, it's coming," Hilfy murmured, as the screen came up with more and more whole words, as it broke the code on a few key ones and spread the pattern wider: a makeshift job of encoding, a kind of thing one ship's computer could do and another one could unravel, if it had a decoding faculty; and *The Pride*'s did. *The Pride*'s fancy-educated communications officer had taken her papa's parting-gift in the form of the same system she had studied on by com-net back on Anuurn; it cost; and it worked, by the gods, it sorted its vast expensive dictionaries for patterns, spread its tentacles and grabbed every bit of memory it could get out of the partitionings, and sorted and cross-checked and ran phonemic sorts, linked up with the decoder-program in the fancy new comp-segment the mahendo'sat had installed in *The Pride* back at Kshshti—gods knew what all it did. While no one who wanted to keep a document in code was going to be fool enough to drop proper names through it or use telltales like *t'* or *-to,* or *-ma* extensions, it had the advantage of that mahen code program it sorted in as a cross-check. The result was coming out in abbreviated form, truncated, dosed with antique words and code phrases no machine could break, but it was developing sense.

Prime writes haste* not * runner/courier accident* eye/see.

Events bring necessity clarify actions take* prime/ audacity. . . .

She added a hani brain's opinion what the choice ought to be in two instances. The computer flicked through another change.

Number one writes hastily {?} Do not hold this courier or risk disclosure. Events compel me to clarify actions which Number One has taken—

"Haral," she said, and felt a shiver all over as she added another suggestion to comp.

*. . . since {ghost?} is not holding to agreements support
will go {to?} opposition all efforts supporting candidacy—*

"We got some stuff here," Tirun muttered. "Jik's talking
doublecross of somebody."

"Who's *Ghost?*" Hilfy said. "Goldtooth?"

"Akkhtimakt?" Tirun wondered in her turn.

"Ehrran?" Geran wondered, which possibility of double-
dealing sent a chill down Hilfy's back.

"Maybe some human," Haral said, and the hair bristled
all the way down.

O gods, Pyanfar needs to know this.

And may never know it.

*If they lay a hand on her; if we blow this place; gods
know what we're taking out—if we have to. If they make us
do that.*

*Good gods, we're talking about conspiracy all the way to
Maing Tol or wherever—Candidacy, who in creation has a
candidacy anyone out here worries about—*

—except the hakkikt.

The corridors of *Harukk* would haunt her dreams—
ammonia-smelling and dim, with none of *The Pride*'s
smooth pale paneling: conduits were in plain view, and bore
bands of knots on their surfaces that, Pyanfar suddenly realized in a random flash, must be the kifish version of color-
coding. The codings added alien shadows to the machinery,
shadows cast in the ubiquitous and horrid orange of sodium-
light and the occasional yellow-green of a coldglow. Tall
robed shadows stalked ahead of them and others walked
behind, as a door opened and let her and Kesurinan and
Skkukuk into the *hakkikt*'s meeting-room.

Sikkukkut waited for them, in a room ringed with black
kifish shadows. Two incense-globes on tall poles gave off
curls of sickly spicy smoke that curled visibly in front of
the sodium-lights mounted to the side of the room, while
another light from overhead fell wanly on Sikkukkut's floor-
hugging table, himself and his chair, the legs of which
arched up about him like the legs of a crouching insect.
Sikkukkut sat where the body of the insect would be, robed
in black edged with silver that took the orange light, with
the light falling on his long, virtually hairless snout and the
glitter of his black eyes as he lifted his head.

"Hunter Pyanfar," he said. "Kkkt. Sit. And is it Kesurinan of *Aja Jin?*"

"Same, *hakkikt,*" Kesurinan said. And did not say: *where is my captain?* which was doubtless the burning question in her mind.

Pyanfar settled easily into another of the insect chairs and tucked her feet up kif-style as one of the *skkukun* brought her a cup, one of the ball-shaped, studded cups the kif favored, and another poured parini into it. Kesurinan had hesitated to sit: "You too," Sikkukkut said, and as Kesurinan took another of the chairs, next Pyanfar, he looked in Skkukuk's direction. "Kkkkt. Sokktoktki nakt, skku-Chanuru."

A moment's hesitation. It was courtesy; it was invitation to a kifish slave to sit at table with the *hakkikt* and his captain. "Huh," Pyanfar said, sensing Skkukuk's crisis; and her flesh shrank at the sudden purposeful grace with which Skkukuk came around that table and assumed the chair beside her—he *slithered,* on two feet: was, she suddenly recognized those moves, not skulking, not slinking—but moving with that fluidity very dangerous kif could use; very powerful kif; kif whose moves she instinctively kept an eye to when she saw them dockside and met them in bars. This was a fighter, among a species who were born fighting. And all hers, for the moment.

She sipped her parini. Sikkukkut sipped whatever he was drinking while a *skku* served the others in turn.

"Tahar," Sikkukkut said, "is on her way in. And your ship is *live,* hunter Pyanfar. Have you noticed this?"

"I've noticed," she said, and kept all her moves easy.

Sikkukkut's long tongue exited the v-form gap of his teeth and extended into the cup, withdrew again. "So have I. Your crew claims they're following orders. Is this so?"

"Yes."

"Kkkt." Silence a moment. "While you are on the dock."

"I hope," Pyanfar said ever so softly, "that nothing's been launched toward my ship—bearing in mind there might be agencies still on the station that would like to damage the *hakkikt*'s ally. I hope the *hakkikt* will protect us against a thing like that."

Deathly stillness. At last the *hakkikt* lapped at his cup

again and blinked with, for a kif, bland good humor. "You have been foolish, hunter Pyanfar. There's far too much opportunity for error. And you have delivered far too much power into the hands of subordinates. We will talk about this."

Another weighty silence, in which perhaps she was expected to reply. She simply sat still, having achieved a position in which she could sit and stare thoughtfully at the *hakkikt*.

Eggsucking bastard, she thought. *Where's Jik, you earless assassin?*

She tried not to think of what kind of demonstration Sikkukkut was capable.

"We will have a discussion on the matter," Sikkukkut said; and there was the subtle, soft whisper of arrival in the outer corridor. "Is that Tahar? Yes. Alone except for my escort. I wonder at this new tactic."

Tahar hesitated in the doorway, then ventured close—a quiet step, a quiet settling into place when the *hakkikt* gestured her to sit at the table: a rippled-maned, bronze-pelted southern hani with a black scar across her mouth that gave her a grim and raffish look.

"So all the ships in your hand," Sikkukkut said, looking at Pyanfar, "are in mine."

"*I* am in your hand," Pyanfar said, with as steady a voice as ever she faced down a dockside official bent on penalties. *But never suggest I don't control those ships, no, not to a kif. Status, Pyanfar Chanur. Status is all there is with him.* "It's a complex situation, *hakkikt*. Hani minds are not, after all, kifish. But that's my value to you."

"Godsawful gibberish," Haral said from her station. The printout was ten pages long, and full of code words that only Jik and his Personage might know. Hilfy Chanur stared at the same set of papers and flipped this way and that, trying to get some idea what they applied to.

—*Ghost is proceeding on the course suggested in her previous report.*

Pieces and bits of information depending on other information.

—*reports from inconvenience/Inconvenience? are negative.*

"I think Inconvenience is another codename," Hilfy said.

"We knew," said Tirun, from the end of the consoles, "that that son was in connivance up to his nose."

"Who are we?" Haral wondered. "Could we be that *Ghost?*"

"*Inconvenience,*" Hilfy suggested. "If—"

"Priority," Geran exclaimed, atop a sound from Tully. "Priority, engine live, coming over station rim vicinity berth 23—"

Harukk's neighborhood. Kif ship.

"I am glad to know your value to me," said Sikkukkut carefully. "It's always helpful to have those things explained." His fingers moved delicately over the projections on the cup he held, restless, sensual movement. "I have held such a discussion with my friend Keia. He has tried to explain. I'm not sure with what success."

"He's very valuable," Pyanfar said, her heart thudding the harder against her ribs. *Careful, careful, don't tie the crew and all we've got to him.* "He's a force we'd miss. Against Meetpoint."

"You assume Meetpoint."

"*Hakkikt,* I've expected the order hourly."

"Is *that* why your ship's engines are live?"

She grinned, honest hani grin, a gentle pursing of the mouth. "I'm quite ready to go."

"Kkkt. *Skku* of mine."

"Congruent interests."

"And do your subordinates share your enthusiasm?"

"They'll follow."

"They've followed you here. Meetpoint might be far more dangerous."

"They're well aware of that."

"What is their motive, do you suppose?"

"Self-interest. Survival."

"They think then that your guidance will advance them."

"Evidently they think that. They're here."

"You see outside my ship the results of miscalculation."

"I noticed, *hakkikt.*"

"You still consider Keia Nomesteturjai a *friend,* hunter Pyanfar."

"*Hakkikt,* when you use that word it makes me nervous. I'm not certain we understand each other."

"When you say *subordinate* I suffer similar apprehensions. What *is* that ship of yours doing?"

"Following my orders."

"Which are?"

"Are we to *later?* I'm willing to discuss it if we are." In the *hakkikt*'s stony silence she sipped at the cup. "On the other hand, we were talking about Meetpoint. That *is* where we're going."

"Do be very careful, hunter Pyanfar."

She lowered her ears and pricked them up again. But a kif might not read that hani apology; and galling as retreat was: "I retract the question then."

"Nankt." The kif waved a hand; a door opened and someone moved; it was a name he had called. It sounded like one. The hand flourished and took up the cup again from the table. "Well that you learn caution, hunter Pyanfar."

"It's holding stationary," Geran said, and Hilfy watched the development on her own number two monitor, where the limited sweep of their scan picked up a ship which had risen to station zenith, hanging where it had a free shot at everything.

"That's *Ikkhoitr*," Haral said. "One of the *hakkikt*'s oldest pets."

"If they're not talking," said Tirun, "and they're not moving, that means they're at the limit of their orders."

"Move and countermove," Haral said.

Hilfy flexed her claws out and in again with an effort at control. Her stomach hurt. She felt a shiver coming on at the thought of that button near Haral's hand. *You going to tell us before you push it? Or just surprise us all, cousin?*

With a mental effort she shifted her eyes back to the translation problem and got herself busy, leaving the ship over their heads to Haral's discretion.

From Khym and Tully, not a word; silence; Chur had not cut in her monitor: Geran had gone back to Chur's room briefly when it all started, and pushed a button on the machinery, ordering sedative, putting her sister out cold before it got to the noise of locks opening and the ship powering up. Or other things Chur might want to listen in on; and learn too much of situations that she could do nothing about. Geran quietly put her sister out, turned her back and walked back to the bridge to do her job, which she sat doing, businesslike and without a shake or a wobble in her voice or a trace of worry on her face.

Gods-be coward, Hilfy Chanur, do your own job and quit thinking about it.

It was Jik they brought into the hall—Jik, a dark, dazed figure between two kif who held him by either arm: who had to go on holding him on his feet after they brought him to the table. Jik lifted his head as if that took all his strength. Pyanfar's stomach turned over; her ears twitched against her determination not to let them flatten, and then she let them down anyway: any hani smelling that much drug-laden sweat and pain would wrinkle up the nose and lay the ears down, even if it was not a friend held there in such condition before her eyes.

"Keia," said Sikkukkut. "Your friends have come to see you."

"Damn dumb," Jik said thickly; and Kesurinan climbed slowly to her feet, stood there with her hands at her sides, a holstered pistol brushing one of them. Kesurinan had the cold good sense to go no farther than that. Tahar tensed in her seat, but she made no further move either, and Pyanfar nodded in Jik's direction.

"You don't look too good."

"Lot drug," Jik said, head wobbling. "You damn fool. Go ship. Private, huh?"

"It is the drug," said Sikkukkut. "I forgive his discourtesies. Do you want to cede him your place in our council, Kesurinan? Or not, as you please."

Do you repudiate your captain? Do you want his post?

Perhaps Kesurinan had no idea what was being asked. She moved and took Jik's arm from the kif who held it, flung her arm about him and gently eased him down onto the chair.

"Kkkt. Mahen behaviors." Sikkukkut lapped at his drink while Jik leaned on one of the upraised insect-legs of the chair his first officer had yielded him and stared through a pair of them at Pyanfar.

"H'lo," he said. "Damn mess."

"Godsrotted mess for sure. What've you been telling the *hakkikt,* huh? You going to go with us to Meetpoint?"

"I dunno," he said. He shut his eyes as if he had gone away a moment and opened them again. They shone dark and desperate in the orange light, spilling water onto his black skin and black fur. His nostrils widened and sucked in air. "Go ship, Pyanfar."

"You see," said Sikkukkut, "we *are* moving at some deliberate speed. Kesurinan, Tahar, I tell you what I have told my other captains: follow your orders. You came here, which is very well. Now you will go to another room; and you will stay there. Until I release you. Tell them they will do this, hunter Pyanfar; and dismiss this *skku* of your own ship."

"Do it," Pyanfar said. It was protocols. Or a demonstration of power. There was no choice, not even with all of them armed. She looked at Tahar as the scar-nosed pirate got up and stared back at her with that expressionless calm that had carried her through two years of close dealing with kif. Skkukuk got to his feet on the same order.

And:

"You go," Jik murmured on his own, speaking to Kesurinan.

"A," Kesurinan agreed.

"Kkkt," Sikkukkut said, not missing that little distinction, it seemed, of control in that exchange. He waved his hand: kif cleared a way and one of the ranking *skkukun* motioned to Tahar and to Kesurinan and Skkukuk. There was, Pyanfar noted with some relief, no question about the weapons they wore, and Skkukuk had not signaled any warning. If he had not changed sides altogether when he sat down at that table.

"Would you," Sikkukkut said, when the others had gone, "like something to drink, Keia?"

"No," Jik said thickly.

"He still has his wits," Sikkukkut said, turning his head slightly to Pyanfar. "And he still has all else he was born with, by my strict order. In consideration of an old friendship, kkkt, Keia? But you don't then order *Aja Jin,* hunter Pyanfar. Nor order this one. He makes that quite clear, doesn't he?"

"He'll do what I ask him. As an ally."

"If he does what you ask, as an ally, do you then do what he asks?"

"I have in past. I think he owes me one."

"Merchants. But Keia professes not to be a merchant at all. I don't think he will trade. Will you, Keia?"

Silence. Long silence.

"Stubborn. He is very stubborn." Another lap at the cup. "Tell me, *Chanur-skku*, what am I to think about that ship of yours?"

"That we're ready to go to Meetpoint, *hakkikt*."

Sikkukkut's long jaw lifted. It was not a friendly gesture, that shift of the head that stared more nearly nose-on: that was threat, the eyes glittering cold black with the sulfurous highlights of the lighting. "Ismehanan-min went to Meetpoint, *skku* of mine: now, I am not patient of this. By now there is a ship of mine over the station axis with its guns aimed at your ship. And we are at impasse."

"*Hakkikt,* when I go back to my ship I'll power down. My crew has its orders until then."

"That's a very stupid bluff, hunter Pyanfar."

"I'm not bluffing. We can all die here. You're not dealing with a kif, *hakkikt*. I'm hani. Remember?"

There was a stir all about the hall. Clicks and subsequent red gleams of weapons ready-lights. And Jik pushed his hands against the insect-leg and lifted his head slightly.

"Your ship isn't moving on mine," Pyanfar said, "since you don't want your station damaged. And mine won't move. Leaving dock isn't what I ordered them to do. I told them if I die here, or if they're attacked from your side, to cycle the jump vanes."

Chapter 3

There was stark silence in the hall.

"Cycle the vanes," Sikkukkut repeated, and rested his hands on the legs of the insect-chair. "That would be a curiously futile gesture for them."

"What should I care," Pyanfar said, "if I were dead? But never doubt that my crew is prepared to do that."

"Martyr," Jik said in his hoarse voice, and hauled himself by his arms on the chair to face Sikkukkut: he rested there leaning on the upraised arch of the chair legs, head on forearms and a grin on his face. "She *hani*. She tell crew blow us all to hell, they do it. You deal with damn fine hani crew. Same be lot brave for you. You got use right."

More profound silence. Then Sikkukkut lifted his cup and lapped at it delicately. "*Bravery*. This is another of those words which sounds kifish until one looks more deeply at the mindset. I distrust it. I distrust it profoundly."

"Just consider it," said Pyanfar, "a longrange survival plan. But *don't* consider it." She waved her hand. "What I'm truly interested in, what I'm sure we're all interested in, is what we do about Meetpoint, *hakkikt*. You want Jik's cooperation; I can get it for you."

"I remind you that you failed miserably with Goldtooth. We *assume* that you failed there. In certain moments I wonder."

"In certain moments *I* wonder, *hakkikt;* and I still don't know what he's up to. I'm more concerned what the humans are up to; and I can tell you plainly—" she held up a forefinger, claw extended—"Tully doesn't know. I've questioned him closely on it, and I know when that son is lying and when he isn't. He was a courier who didn't know his own message; Goldtooth used him and dumped him, which is a little habit of Goldtooth's that I want to talk to him about. Goldtooth doublecrossed Tully, doublecrossed Jik. Doublecrossed me. And to confuse it all he gave me help, in the form of medical supplies we needed. *I* don't know how to read his signals. I'm being perfectly frank with you. I can tell you that Ehrran and I aren't friendly; and she's dealing with the stsho, which I trust even less. That's where I stand. I want Jik back. Under *my* command, *hakkikt.*"

"Damn," Jik said. "Hani—".

"He's honest," Pyanfar said. "If you do that favor to him, at my request, he'll be caught in a moral tangle his government won't like at all. But we don't need to tell them that, do we? And we don't need to leave Goldtooth alone to represent the mahendo'sat. *Jik* supports your side. And if you lose him, *hakkikt,* you'll have no chance in a mahen hell of getting the mahendo'sat to make any treaty. Give him to me. I can handle him."

"Prove it now. Get the truth from him. Have him say where the humans are going, what Ismehanan-min said to him before he left, and what agreements he knows of with the methane-folk."

Pyanfar let go her breath slowly. Her laboring heart found a new level of panic.

Fool. Now you get what you bargained for. Don't you, Pyanfar?

But what else is there to do? How do we win anything without this kif?

She looked toward Jik as he shifted his hold on the chair to face her direction. A fine dew of perspiration had broken out around his eyes, running down into his black fur; his eyes glittered in the orange light and the darkness, and there were lines about them she was not accustomed to see there. "Jik," she said. "You heard him. You know what he wants."

"I know," Jik said, with no intimation he was going to say a thing.

"Listen." She reached out and took hold of his arm where it rested on the chair; she smelled the sweat and there was the stink of drugs in it; drugs and raw terror. "Jik. I need you. Hear? Hear me?"

Jik's face twisted, showed teeth, settled again in exhaustion. His eyes shut and he got them open again. "Get hell

out. Hear?" And he meant more than get out of *Harukk:*
she read that plainly.

"If the *hakkikt* fails," she said, "what does that leave us
with? Jik. Jik—" *There's a reason I can't tell you.* She tried
to send that with her eyes, with the sudden force of her
hand; and with her thumb-claw, dug in so hard he winced.

"Damn!" he cried, jerking back; she held on.

"Listen to me. If the *hakkikt* fails, where are we? That
bastard Akkhtimakt—" She tensed the thumb-claw again.
J-i-k. In the blink-code. "Do you hear me? Do you hear?"

He no longer pulled back. His hand twitched. "I hear,"
he said in a hoarse, distracted voice. "But—"

"You'll take my orders. Hear?" And: h-u-m-a-n-t-r-e-a-
c-h-e-r-y she spelled into his flesh. The sweat ran in rivulets
past his eyes, in the thin areas of his facial hair. "Jik. Tell
him everything."

A long moment he hesitated. She felt the tremor of muscles in his arm. The fear-smell grew stronger. The look on
his face was a thing to haunt the sleep: he poured all his
questions into it, and there was nothing she knew how to
send back—let one kif note that hidden move of her thumb
on the underside of his hand and they were both in it. But:
T-r-u-s-t, she signaled him. *D-o.*

He broke away from her eyes. He leaned himself on the
other side of the chair, facing Sikkukkut. "Ana say—
humans come Meetpoint. Truth. They go fight Akkhtimakt.
Gather hani, make fight 'gainst kif. Then got—" His voice
broke. "Got—hani, stsho, human, mahendo'sat, all fight
kif."

"And it's your task," Sikkukkut said quietly, "to see that
I reach Meetpoint to engage my rival Akkhtimakt—all
while being attacked by all the others. Is *that* what your
partner told you to do?"

Prolonged silence.

"Answer," Sikkukkut said.

"He not tell me what he do. He say—say I got go Meetpoint, wait orders."

"To turn on me at the opportune moment. Kkkkt. And
now what will you do?"

"I think he damn fool, *hakkikt.*" Again Jik's voice
cracked. "I think I first time got better idea, help you take
out Akkhtimakt."

"And then to turn on me."

"Not. Not. I think Ana got wrong. I damn scared, *hak-kikt,* he got number one bad mistake. I don't think he do what he do, damn, I come on dock, try get Pyanfar out lousy mess, I don't know my damn partner going to blow the damn dock, I don't know he going outsystem, I don't know he got deal with Ehrran and the damn stsho— What happen? I get shoot at, I get caught, I get lousy drug and beat up, you think I be damn fool, *hakkikt,* come outside if I know what he do? Hell, no. Maybe Ana same time got smart idea, but he don't know I be out there, I don't know he be going to leave the dock—lousy mess. Ehrran be the one break dock, she be the one kill you people; I don't think he know what she do."

"They met. They talked. We know this."

Jik's head dropped, his shoulders slumped. He looked up again, leaning on his arms. "I think they talk stsho deal. I think Ana not know, not know what she do— He just got move fast. He plan go, yes. Not then. No so fast. He think got time. Ehrran make him move. Maybe he think I be dead, I don't know; maybe he think we all be on that dock, maybe he think *The Pride* crew be gone, maybe think ever'thing be gone to hell—I don't know, *hakkikt.* I don't know."

"You contradict yourself."

"Not lie. Don't know. I don't know."

"And the methane-folk? What dealings with them?"

Jik's head dropped again onto his arms. For a moment he was utterly still, and a kif moved closer at his side. Pyanfar sat quietly, forcing a calm over her nerves from the outside in, till it got to the depth of her mind.

We're talking about the whole gods-be Compact going up in smoke.

We can take him, at any time, we can take this kif bastard, if we're willing to die—and we're both dead now, Jik and I. It doesn't matter. Doesn't matter that he's in pain, it's nothing, nothing in the balance, nothing that really matters. I'm sorry, Jik; I can't care, can't afford to care, can't stink of fear, I daren't. Not if we've got a chance. And I'll take it wide and high, Jik, if I have to. You're a professional, you know what I'm doing, you know I can't do anything else, drug-drunk as you are. We can settle it later.

"Answer him, Jik." *And gods, come up with a good one.*
I need you, Jik.
I can't play this throw alone.

He moved. He lifted his head again. "Tc'a," he said
thickly.

"What about the tc'a?" Sikkukkut asked.

"I talk with. Lot scare'." His hands slipped. He caught
himself and lifted his head with an effort. "Knnn lot disturb. Humans come through knnn space. Maybe shoot at
knnn ship."

"Kkkkt."

"Damn fool. Tc'a want keep knnn quiet. They want mahendo'sat make all quiet, quick. Tc'a lot mad with Ana.
Talk me—talk me—want make knnn be quiet. I say tc'a—
tc'a, you got help Sikkukkut. Fine fellow, Sikkukkut. So
tc'a come with us to Kefk. But knnn—"

"The knnn took it."

"Took. Don't know why. Maybe want ask why come with
us. Maybe want ask what we do. Knnn lot crazy. No know
knnn mind. I tell Ana—he be crazy want talk to knnn.
Make quiet, I tell Ana, you got make quiet. Knnn be disturb, I don't know, don't know, don't know—"

Both hands went. He hit the arch of the chairlegs and
hung there.

Pyanfar carefully took up her cup and sipped at it. *Don't
think, don't react, he's not in pain now. Be cold and careful
and don't care. There's no guarantee what the bastard's
going to do with either of us now he has what he wants.*
"That, I think, was the truth. It jibes with other things he's
said. Mahendo'sat have their own ways. And it's very likely
that Goldtooth is pursuing some contrary course, giving his
Personage a second option. Unfortunately that course seems
to involve helping Ehrran ruin me—friendship is worth
something, *hakkikt,* but species-interest in Goldtooth's case
is a great deal more potent. He'll be sorry to see me ruined
and my influence broken—I was useful to him once; we
even had a personal debt. But sorry is as far as it goes.
Ehrran seems to him to have what he wants right now:
influence in the *han.* Jik is pursuing a totally different
course for the Personage they both serve—so Goldtooth
wouldn't work directly against Jik, in the interest of giving
the Personage that double choice; but he'll by the gods cut

Jik's throat when he thinks it's come to crisis. And it will be crisis at Meetpoint, when we all go in there. That's how Goldtooth will deal with the methane-folk: kill Jik and remove the one person who can deal with the tc'a—because Jik does work with them." She took a second sip. "You told me back at Meetpoint, that one day I'd want revenge on my enemies. *Pukkukkta.* I had to look that word up. I know now what you offered me. You said at the same time that if I didn't want it then, I'd want it later. That was before I knew my enemy was a bastard of a hani who was out to get me from the start. I'll give you a hani word. *Haura.* Bloodfeud. Ehrran's got that now, with me, with Chanur, with Geran and Chur Anify; and Haral and Tirun Araun have a grudge or two themselves. And I'll get Rhif Ehrran if I have to go through Goldtooth and the stsho and the mahendo'sat and the humans to do it. *Pukkukkta's* a cold emotion; *haura's* a hot one; but that doesn't mean it can't last years. Am I making clear sense? However long it takes, I'll get her."

"You make sense, hunter Pyanfar."

"Tahar also has a bloodfeud with Ehrran. And Tahar interests are linked to mine. I'm her only hope of recovering her reputation. And her power."

"That also makes sense."

"I also have a certain matter to settle with Goldtooth. A personal matter. And Jik is the best leverage on that. That's why I want him."

"No kif would be as forward."

"No kif can offer you what I do."

There was a soft clicking about her, a stirring; and the guns were still live.

"What do you offer?"

"An alliance with non-kif."

"Kkkt." Sikkukkut placed his hands on the chair, lifting his jaw. "Where is it?"

"Lying in that chair; and sitting in this one. And neither's inconsequential. Neither's without ties that go far beyond one ship and a small authority. Give me Jik and give me *Aja Jin,* and I'll use him to settle with Goldtooth *and* Rhif Ehrran. A weapon in my hand is a weapon in yours."

"Is it?"

"Since we have common interests. A hani is very easy

to understand. Look for clan interest. And Rhif Ehrran is out to destroy my clan, with Goldtooth's help. I told you I'd go through all the others to get her. And that's exactly what I'll do."

Sikkukkut leaned his long chin on his fist, the silver-bordered sleeve fallen back from a thin and muscular arm, the light gleaming on his eyes. "I well tell you, hunter Pyanfar, you will have the chance to make good what you say." The forefinger lifted. "You will have everything you ask."

O gods, the thought hit her then. *Too easy. Too fast. Too complete.*

"You will take *Aja Jin* and *Moon Rising* and you will take Meetpoint."

"Hakkikt—"

"You claim a great deal for yourself. Can you deliver more than words? Or perhaps—will you defect to my enemies?"

"To Ehrran?" Her ears went flat. It took no acting at all. "No."

"You encourage me." A second finger lifted beside the first. "So I will give you Keia. On condition."

"That being, *hakkikt?"*

"He will go aboard *The Pride.* In your charge."

"He's the best pilot—"

"I know his skill. I know Kesurinan's, which is considerable. But she has less recklessness. I tell you how I will arrange things and you will accept them for your own good, hunter Pyanfar. Keia would betray your interests, left free to follow those he serves. Instead I give him to you, and you will use him wherever it profits you, but most of all where it profits me. I insist on this point. Do you understand me?"

Her ears twitched again, and it was not acting either. "You're very clear. And you may be absolutely right. I agree."

"I *may* be right. How generous of you. Is that the word—generous?"

"I'm taking your orders. Those who know me would be shocked to hear that. I'm a bastard, *hakkikt,* and a gray nosed old bastard at that, and I'm not in the habit of taking orders, but I'm taking yours." *You don't back me up, son. You don't treat me like one of your rag-eared lot.* "You impress me and your opinions make absolute sense to me. You give me Jik here, I'll keep Kesurinan in line. And him. I know what you're saying, and yes, you're right. You want me to take Meetpoint, I can't do that. Even with Jik for a wedge. But if you're coming in behind me and want the stsho all dithered—" *Which is what you plan, isn't it, you son?* "—I can by the gods keep them busy."

Sikkukkut sipped at his drink. "You'll have to be more than that, *skku* of mine. I have a ship to spare. Do you know what a single hunter-ship can do to an inhabited world?"

O my gods.

"No warning would travel faster than that ship. It would strike and go. And hani would be removed from the question. The power I give you would be removed, *skku* of mine. Always remember I can take it away. I can remove Anuurn from consideration as an inhabited world. Do you understand me?"

"Entirely." *Bastard. Thanks for the warning.* Haura, *bastard. You know how long Akkht itself would survive a move like that? Let's talk about life in the Compact. Let's talk about wiping out species.* "When do I go?"

"I have a packet for you. You'll have it. With the person of my friend Keia. Treat him gently." Sikkukkut's nose twitched. "And under no circumstances set him free. I have uses for him myself: he's a loan, not a gift." Another lap at the cup. And a wave of Sikkukkut's hand, at which several kif near him stirred forth from the shadows, passing in front of one of the lights and casting long shadow over the table.

The shadow enveloped her, enveloped Jik as they laid hands on him and gathered him up with soft clickings and chatter among themselves. Jik lolled limp, in a way that said he was not shamming: his arm swung down, his head fell back when they lifted him, and there was no muscle tone in the arm they grasped—kifish fingers bit deep when they swung him up to carry him.

"Your leave," Pyanfar murmured, set her drink down, and stood up. She bowed, as carefully and formally as ever before the leadership in the *han*. She kept her ears up and her face calm as she glanced aside to their handling of Jik, and looked again to Sikkukkut for instruction.

He waved his hand again. A second time she bowed, and walked out the door, into the dim corridor outside, into the presence of lesser kif who gave way to someone of her evident status, who edged out of her path, lowered their faces and made themselves shadows against the walls and the conduits.

Her knees were going to be weak. The ammonia smell dizzied her: she had not sneezed, thank the gods, she had snuffled once or twice and covered it; but of a sudden her stomach felt queasy and her heart which had exhausted itself in terror, labored away in slow, painful beats.

The nightmare was not going away. They were bringing Jik, she had to pick up her three companions, mahe, hani, and kif, on her way out; and she had to get down that dock and observe whatever the kif sent her in the way of instructions.

Had to.

"I got him," she said curtly to Kesurinan when the kif brought her companions to her in the exit corridor. "He's staying in my custody."

And it hurt, somewhere dimly and at the bottom of her soul where she had put all her sensibilities—the quick lift of Kesurinan's ears, the dismay, the instant smothering of all reaction, because Kesurinan was not a fool, and knew where they were and who was listening, and then that they would have to do everything the kif insisted on to get her captain out of *Harukk*. Kesurinan thought she was talking to an ally.

Sikkukkut was absolutely right: the mahendo'sat would be an ally right down to the point their own species-interest took over. And then Jik would save his own kind.

So, she discovered, would she.

They made slow progress down the unstable docks—a gang of kifish *skkukun* carrying a stretcher with Jik strapped tightly to it; Jik's first officer walking along by him, anger and concern in every line of her back: and with a gun on her hip. Pyanfar walked to the side and a little behind, with Dur Tahar on her right and Skkukuk at her left, Tahar inscrutable as Tahar had become in her life among kif, while Skkukuk gave few signals either—except in squared shoulders, except in less nervousness than he had ever shown; except in every subtle move that said here was a kif whose status was no longer that of an outright slave, a kif whose captain had just dealt with the *hakkikt* and won. He carried a weapon beneath his outer robes and gods knew what ambitions in his narrow skull. If ever a kif was pleased, this one positively basked in his change of fortunes, inhaled the chance in the air, savored the sight of the *hakkikt*'s slaughtered enemies, his dreadful signposts— and the sight of his captain rising in that service.

Cold in all the warm places and fever-warm in all the cold ones, gods, a hundred eighty degrees skewed. Alien. *The kif are that thing in doubles and triples.*

Stay cold, Pyanfar Chanur. Save it. Jik's a piece of meat. Tahar an ally-of-fortune, Kesurinan's potential trouble, and this gods-be son of a kif is a convenience.

Kesurinan's not going to make trouble, not yet. She'll let us take Jik aboard.

Gods, don't let Jik come to out here.

Slowly, slowly they walked up the dock past the section seal, into that area where there were no pedestrians. Where there was no traffic at all but themselves.

And there was *The Pride*'s berth ahead, still flashing with those warning lights. She took her pocket com out, within range of the pickup now: "This is the captain. I'm coming in."

"Aye," Haral's voice came back to her, thin with static: that formality she had used was warning, and Haral took it: *I've got company, Haral; don't get easy with me.*

Another eternity, walking that fragile dock: and gods help them, Tahar and Kesurinan had farther still to go. "Skkukkuk," Pyanfar said, and the kif beside her was all attention. "Tell the *skkukun-hakkiktu* I want Tahar escorted to her ship by the quickest and safest route. Through the central corridors if they can."

"Hakt'," Skkukuk said, acknowledging the order; and walked up with the litter-bearers and gave that instruction with all the kifish modulations of a superior's relayed instructions and his own high status with that superior. Then he fell back a step or two and lifted his face in satisfaction.

She said not a word to Tahar, and Tahar offered not a word to her; that was the way of things.

Toward _The Pride_'s open accessway, then. "Wait here," Pyanfar said to Tahar and Kesurinan, and with a special coldness in Kesurinan's direction, when they reached that gateway: her flesh crawled in that earnest look of Kesurinan's scar-crossed face. "Aye, captain," Kesurinan said, all unknowing.

And betrayed her own captain into foreign hands.

"Chanur-hakto," the foremost kif said, when they had deposited Jik on his litter in _The Pride_'s airlock. That kif took a packet from within his robes and offered it.

Skkukuk intercepted it in one smooth move. And waved his hand, dismissing the other kif out the airlock.

"Seal us up," Pyanfar said to the air and the crew watching on monitor.

The lock shot closed, hissed and thumped into electronic seal.

"Power down," Pyanfar said.

"Aye," Haral's voice came to her. All business, even yet. Pyanfar took the packet Skkukkuk offered her officiously, with the stretcher lying on its supports at her feet. Now the shivers wanted to come, but she kept her ears up and looked her own kif in his watery, red-rimmed eyes.

"Good job," she said to Skkukuk.

"Kkkkt," the kif said. "You need me, hakt'. Who else of your crew has manners?"

Her gorge rose. She swallowed and tucked the small packet into her pocket, squatted down by Jik's stretcher and patted his face gently. It was cold and there was no reaction.

"This is an ally?" Skkukuk asked.

"This is a complicated situation," she said, trying to tell a kif the truth; and then a second thought ruffled the hair down her back. _Gods, this is a killer I'm talking to. With hairtrigger reflexes._ "Yes. An ally." She moved her hand down to Jik's neck and felt the pulse there. "Haral. Get Khym down here. We got Jik to move. He's still out."

"On his way, captain. You all right?"

"Fine. I'm fine. We got out in good shape. Open that

door." She patted Jik's face again. "Hey. Friend. Come out of it. You hear me? You're all right."

Friend.

He was under. Deep. She heard the lift work: Khym had either been on his way or he had run that topside corridor. And *The Pride* was proceeding with powerdown, a series of subtle noises that her ear knew in every nuance. "Skkukuk. You'll help Khym. You'll do what he says."

"Kkkt. This is your mate."

She stood up and looked flat-eared at Skkukuk, with the ammonia-stink in her nostrils and the antiallergents drying her mouth. Something about the asking crawled along her nerves. This alien, this unutterable alien, was feeling out who was to consider among the crew, who he could displace, who he could get around and who not.

That's one job you can't work your way into, you slithering earless bastard. You keep your mouth off my husband's name. You better figure that, fast.

A thousand thousands of years of hani instinct ran up her spine. And Skkukuk read that look and took on one of his own.

Caution.

Footsteps in the lowerdecks corridor. Rapid ones, more than one set.

Don't run, Khym. Dignity, Khym. In front of the kif, gods rot it, Khym.

She was still standing squared off with Skkukuk when Khym showed up in the doorway with Tully close behind.

"You're all right," Khym said.

"I'm just fine. Take Jik to sickbay. Get Tirun onto it. Skkukkuk—"

The kif was still waiting. Armed. Their ex-prisoner, possessing a gun that could blow a hole in armor plate. And expecting in his aggressive little kifish soul that he had just won his freedom.

"You're offduty," she told Skkukuk. "You'll keep that gun in your quarters. You've got a lowerdecks clearance. You understand me."

"Kkkt. Absolutely."

"Move."

Everyone moved. Skkukuk got himself out of her sight,

correctly reading her temper. Khym and Tully got to either
end of the stretcher, got it lifted with its not inconsiderable
dead weight of tall mahendo'sat, and maneuvered it out
the hatch.

"Tirun's on her way to sickbay, captain." That from her
niece. While the powerdown proceeded.

"Understood," Pyanfar said calmly. And stood there a
moment staring at the wall. With a kif's orders in her
pocket. She fished them out and broke open the brittle seal
to look at the written portion.

"Departure at 2315," was the center of that detail. It was,
at the moment, all she was interested in. The kif gave them
time enough to get organized. Barely. With precise course
instructions, aborting one that they had laid in.

"Hilfy."

"Aye," the subdued voice reached her.

"Message to Kesurinan and Tahar: stand by departure;
they'll have a bit over six hours. So will we."

A pause. *"Aye."*

Silence after. *The Pride* was at rest again. The crew on
the bridge could see her, where she stood. The camera was
live. She looked up at it. "Things could be worse," she said
glumly. "I can think of one way right off. But we got Jik
in our custody, we got Tahar and *Aja Jin* with us, and we've
got the *hakkikt's* orders: it's Meetpoint. His way."

A longer pause.

"Aye," Haral said simply, as if she had given a routine
order.

The largest space station in the Compact.

And a forewarned one.

"Clear the boards, stand offduty; I got Jik to see to."

"Aye, captain."

She walked out of the airlock. And only then it occurred
to her, like the ghost of an old habit that no longer meant
anything, that she had just packed her husband and another
crewman off to tend another man, knowing beyond the last
twitch of instinct, if it was ever instinct, that Jik was safe
with them, safe as that kif was safe to send down the corridor in the other direction, because even the kif was a rational mind and sane and sensible, while the universe quaked
and tottered on all sides of them.

She walked down the corridor and into the open door of sickbay, their little closet of a facility. Tirun had beaten her there. Khym and Tully were taking Jif off the stretcher and laying him on the table.

"He'll have some bruises," Pyanfar said. "You'd better run a scan on him. He may have more than that." She went to the med cabinet, keyed the lock with a button-sequence, and sorted through a tray of bottles—hani-specific; hani drugs did strange things with some mahendo'sat. No telling what the kif had given him even if she ran a query into Library, and it was better to stick to the simple things. She pulled out an old-fashioned bottle of ammonia salts and brought that over to hold under Jik's nose.

Not a twitch.

"Gods-be." She capped the stinking bottle and slapped Jik's chill face. "Wake up. Hear me?"

"What did they give him?" Tirun asked, lifting Jik's eyelid, peering close. "He smells like a dopeden."

"He's a hunter-captain, gods rot it, his own precious government's got him mind-blocked, gods know how far down he's gone." She turned around, shoved her way past Khym and got to the intercom. "Bridge! Get *Harukk* on, tell 'em I want to know what they dosed Jik with, fast."

"*Aye,*" Haral's voice came back.

Tirun was counting pulsebeats. And frowning.

"Gods, he doesn't know where he is." Pyanfar crossed the deck again, shoving roughly past both the men, to grab at Jik's shoulders. "*Jik, gods fry you, it's Pyanfar, Pyanfar Chanur, you hear me? Emergency, Jik, wake up!*"

Jik's mouth opened. His chest moved in a larger breath.

"*Come on, Jik—for the gods sake, wake up!*" She yelled it into his ear. She shook at him. "*Jik! Help!*"

Tension began to come back to his musculature. His face acquired familiar lines. "Come on," she said. "It's me, it's Pyanfar."

Help, she said. And the great fool came back to her. He hauled himself out of whatever mental pit his own people had prepared for him, the way he had run out onto that dock to fight for her and her crew, when an absolute species-loyalty had dictated he save himself. *Help.* More strangers handled him, dumped him from stretcher to table, gods, not unlike what the kif must have done to him, and he went away from them, deeper and deeper, only knowing at some far level that he was being touched.

Knowing now that there was a hani cursing him deaf in one ear and asking something of him, but nothing more than that.

O gods. Gods, Jik.

His eyes slitted open. He was still far away.

"Hey," she said. "You're all right. You're on *The Pride.* I got you out. Kesurinan's gone back to *Aja Jin,* you hear me, Jik, you're not with the kif anymore. You're on my ship."

He blinked. His mouth worked, the movement of a dry tongue. He heard her, she thought, at some level. He was exploring consciousness and trying to decide if he wanted it.

"It's me," she said again. "Jik," She patted his arm and stooped with a sick feeling at the gut when he flinched from her touch. "Friend."

"Where?" he said, at least it sounded like that.

"On *The Pride.* You're safe. You understand me?"

"Understand," he said. His lids drifted down over the pupils. He was gone again, but not so deeply gone. She hesitated a moment, then turned in a blind rage at two fool men who had not sense enough to clear out of sickbay's narrow space and give them room to work.

She found herself staring eye to eye with Tully—with Tully who had been twice where Jik had been, and whose face was stsho-white and his eyes white round the edges. She had been about to shout. The look on Tully's face strangled the sound in her throat.

"Out," she said, and choked on the word. "Clear out of here, you're not doing anything useful."

Khym flattened his ears, thrust out an arm and herded Tully away; Tully went without seeming to notice it was Khym who had touched him. The human was a shaken man.

So was she, shaken. The hair was standing up all down her back.

"*Captain,*" Haral's voice came, "*it's sothosi. Library's sending to labcomp right now.*"

"We're on it."

Tirun was on it, a quick move for the comp unit; a glance at the screen and a dive for the medicine cabinet. She broke open a packet, grabbed an ampule and an astringent pad, and made herself a clean spot on Jik's arm.

The stimulant went in. In another moment Jik made another gasp after air, and another, a healthier darkness returning to his nose and lips. "There we go," Tirun said, monitoring his heartbeat. "There we go."

Pyanfar found herself a chair and sat down, before her knees went. She bent over and raked her hands through her mane, conscious of the uncomfortable weight of the AP at her hip and the prodding of the gun in her opposite pocket. She stank. She wanted a bath.

She wanted not to have done what she had done. Not to have made the mistakes she had made. Not to be Pyanfar Chanur at all, who was responsible for too much and too many mistakes. And who had now to think the unthinkable.

"You all right?" Tirun asked.

She looked up at her cousin, her old friend. At a crewwoman who had been with her from her youth. "Tirun." She lapsed into a provincial hani language and kept her voice down. "He'll stay here. I want this room safed, I want him left under restraint—"

She tried to keep the cold distance she had had on *Harukk*. It was hard when she looked into an old friend's eyes and saw that natural reaction, that dropping of Tirun's ears.

"Tirun," she said, though she had meant to justify nothing; she found herself pleading, found a shiver going through her limbs. "We got a problem. I'll talk about it later. Do it. Can you? Stay with him till he wakes up and make sure he's breathing all right. And for godssakes leave those restraints on him. Can you do that?"

"Yes," Tirun said. No doubt. No question, from an honest hani who handed her captain every scruple she had and expected her captain was going to explain it all. Eventually.

"Tell him I'm going to come back down. Tell him it's because we've got a few hours, I want him to rest and I can't think of any other way to make sure he does." She still spoke in chaura, a language no mahendo'sat was going to understand; and that was statement enough how much truth she was handing out. Tirun stared at her and asked no questions. Not even with a flick of her ears. Lock up a friend who had saved their lives and come back in this condition from doing it. Lie to him.

If she could knock him cold again without risking his life she would do that too.

She got up and walked out, raked a hand through her mane and felt the stinging pain of exhaustion between her shoulders, the burn of cold decking on her feet. Kif-stink was still in her nostrils.

She flung the kifish packet onto the counter by her own station on the bridge.

No one had left post; or if Geran had left to check on Chur she had come back again in a hurry. Solemn faces stared at her: Hilfy, Geran, Khym, and Tully; Haral kept operations going.

"Leave it, Haral," Pyanfar said.

Haral swung her chair about, same as the others.

"You know the way we came in here," Pyanfar said, "and took Kefk. We got orders to do it again. At Meetpoint."

Ears sank. Tully sat there, the human question, hearing what he could pick up on his own and what garbled version whispered to him over the translator plug he kept in one ear.

"You've heard bits and pieces of it," she said, and sat down on the armrest of her own cushion, facing all of them. "We've got to follow orders the way they're given. Or we've got to blow ourselves to particles here at dock. And that takes out only one kif faction. It leaves the other one the undisputed winner. And by the gods, I'd rather they chewed on each other a while and gave the Compact a chance. That's one consideration. But there's another one. Sikkukkut's threatened Anuurn."

"How—threatened?" Haral asked.

"Just that. One ship—if he thinks we're getting out of line. He's not talking about an attack at Gaohn. Nothing like it. He means an attack directly on the world. That's the kind of kif we're dealing with. One large *C*-charged rock, hitting Anuurn, before Anuurn can see it coming, gods know. It was a threat. I hope it was a remote threat. We're dealing with a kif who knows too gods-be much about hani and too gods-be little: he was a fool to tell me that and maybe he doesn't imagine what we'd do to stop him—before or after the event. But I don't think he's the only kif who'd think of it. I hope they chew each other to bloody rags. We arrange that if we can—but we've got to do what we're told right now or we find ourselves looking the wrong way at one of Sikkukkut's guns, and we don't get the chance to warn anybody, or work our way around this, or save a gods-be thing."

"Captain," Haral said, "we got a kif up there at zenith. He's got position on us."

"I know about it. We're not going to take 'em on. We just get out of here. We've got six hours, we're dropping into a Situation at Meetpoint, and the Compact may not survive it in any form we understand it. *That's* what we've got. That's what we're up against. I don't know what we're going to find at Meetpoint. Tully—are you following this? Do you understand me?"

"I understand," he said in a faint voice. "I crew, captain."

"Are you? Will you be, at Meetpoint?"

"You want me sit with Hilfy at com, speak human if humans be there." His voice grew steadier. "Yes. I do."

With all he could and could not understand. She gazed on him in a paralysis of will, as if putting off deciding anything at all could stop time and give them choices they did not have.

Jik, they had locked up below. A kif and a human were loose among them. The human sat in their most critical councils.

But Tully had given them the warning she had passed to Jik, a warning blurted out in one overcharged moment that Tully had stood between her and Hilfy and she had questioned his motives.

Don't trust humans, Pyanfar.

On one sentence, one frightened, treasonous sentence in mangled hani, they bet everything.

Gods, risk my world on him? Billions of lives? My whole people? My gods, what right have I got?

"I'll think on it," she said. "I haven't got any answers." She picked up the packet and flung it down again. "We've got our instructions. We've got Tahar with us. We've got Jik's ship. And we've got orders to keep Jik with us and keep that ship of his under tight watch."

"There's something else," Hilfy said. And took up a

piece of paper and got up and brought it to her. It trembled in Hilfy's hand. "Comp broke the code. Maybe he meant us to break it. I don't know."

She hesitated in the dim doorway of sickbay, with that paper in her pocket; Jik was awake, Tirun had said.

He was. She saw the slitted glitter of Jik's eyes, saw them open full as she walked in, quiet as she was. She went and laid her hand on his shoulder, above the restraint webbing. Tirun had put a pillow under his head and a blanket over his lower body.

His eyes tracked on her quite clearly now, gazed up at her sane and lucid. "Come let me go, a? Damn stubborn, you crew."

But she did not hear the edge of annoyance that might have been there. It was all too quiet for Jik, too wary, too washed of strength. It was—gods knew what it was.

Apprehension, comprehension—that he might not be among friends?

That for some reason she might be truly siding with the kif—or that she was operating under some other driving motive, in which they were no longer allies?

He had for one moment, in that kifish place, drugged and on the fading edge of his resources, answered questions he had held out against for days, answered because she got through his defenses with a warning his mind had been in no shape to deal with, and because she had signaled him that he had to do this.

Now he was clear-headed. Now he knew where he was, and perhaps he recalled, too late, what he had done. That was what came through that faint voice, that failing attempt at good humor.

"Hey," she said, and tightened her hand. "You got nowhere to go, do you?"

"Aja Jin."

"Told you about that. Kif'll shoot your head off. We're clear. Got it all patched up with Sikkukkut. You passed out on me. Missed the good part. I need to talk to you."

"I got talk to my ship."

"That can wait. You'll fall on your nose if you try to get up. Don't want you trying it, hear? Tirun fill you in?"

"Not say."

"Your ship's fine; the dock's patched; I got you clear and got everything fixed up with Sikkukkut: he's a gods-be bastard, but he does listen. He's still suspicious, but he's put you aboard *The Pride,* says you've got to ride out the next move aboard my ship and let Kesurinan handle *Aja Jin.* That was all I could get. We've got to live with that."

"I got damn itch on nose, Pyanfar."

She reached and rubbed the bridge of it. "Got it?"

"Let me go. I walk fine."

"Haven't got time. We're moving. Going to Meetpoint. You're going to have to ride it out where you are. I'm sorry about that, but we haven't got another cabin we can reach till we undock. And then things are going to go pretty fast."

He was quiet a heartbeat or two. Then: "Pyanfar—"

"I got a question for you. I want to know what we're headed into. What did Goldtooth tell you before he left us, huh?"

A silent panic crept into his eyes. He lifted his head and let it fall back against the pillow, still staring at her. "Not funny."

"*I* need to know, friend. For your sake, for that ship of yours, gods know, for mine. What are we headed for? What's he doing?"

"We talk on bridge."

Bluff called. She stared at him and he at her and there was a knot at her gut. "You know how it is," she said.

"A," he said. "Sure."

"I got this thing to ask you. I want to know the truth. You understand me."

He ran his tongue over his lips. "What this deal with humans?"

"Tully told me—told me flatly not to trust them. You know Tully; he's not too clear. But what he said, the way he said it—I think they're going to doublecross your partner. I think they're not the fools Goldtooth thinks they are. And they're not taking his orders."

"Maybe you do better talk to Tully."

"I have. We've got a problem. Sikkukkut wants Meetpoint. He wants us three to go in first, *The Pride, Aja Jin,* and *Moon Rising*. You see how much he trusts us. He wants us to go in there and shake things up and crack Meetpoint so he can walk right in easy."

"Akkhtimakt maybe be there."

"So's everyone else. Aren't they? I got one more question. What about the methane-folk? What's the real truth?"

"Lot—lot mad." Another pass of Jik's tongue across his lips. "I try talk to tc'a. They want keep like before. Knnn—different question. Goldtooth said—said got maybe trouble."

"Who's *Ghost?*"

Jik blinked. His eyes locked on hers, pupils dilated.

"When you were in trouble," Pyanfar said, "I hauled out that little packet you gave me at Mkks and started it through comp. We got a number one good linguistics rig. The best. *Mahen* make, a? Why'd you ever give me that packet, huh?—to carry on for you. In case something happened here at Kefk? So I could get through to Kshshti or Meetpoint? Gods-be careless job of encoding if we could break it—but then, then it might have had to go to a mahen ship way out from your Personage, mightn't it? Someone like Goldtooth, maybe? And the real code's in the language—*isn't it?*"

"Maybe same—want you to have."

"You knew gods-be well we'd have to go to mahen authority to read it! You by the gods knew we'd have to run to your side when it got hot—we'd be held to being your courier again, that's what you knew, that's what you set us up for, rot your conniving, doublecrossing hide!"

He lay there and blinked at her.

"*Was* it because you thought something might happen to you, Jik? Or did you already plan to do what Goldtooth did for you here at Kefk? Blow the docks and run and leave me to get anywhere I gods-blessed could, with your confounded message? *Was it you who gave Goldtooth the orders to break dock?*"

"Hani, you got damn nasty mind."

"I'm dead serious, Jik."

"You crazy." He gave a wrench at the restraints. "Damn, Pyanfar? I walk fine."

"Answer me."

"What you think, I run out on you, leave you talk to kif? *I on that damn dock myself!*"

"You weren't in the zone that blew! That's by the gods close timing, Jik!"

"I not do!"

"Didn't you? I think you knew with Chur sick I wasn't free to run for it. That it'd kill her and I wouldn't move if I had a chance in your coldest hell. *Goldtooth* gave us that med unit—fine, so I could run. *You* gave me that gods-be packet back at Mkks before we knew we'd find him here— you gave it *in case* something happened to you, a packet we'd *have* to take to mahen authorities. And what does it talk about? People reneging on agreements, that's what; it talks about contingencies, talks about supporting some candidacy—*whose?* Sikkukkut's? What agreements?"

"Sikkukkut. Same. You know agreement."

"You're lying, Jik. By the gods, you show up at Kshshti and help me out of one mess, then you help me all the way here, deeper and deeper you helped me, you and your godsforsaken partner, you and your gods-be deals—"

"I come out on that dock save you damn neck!"

"Where were you planning to ditch us? *Where,* huh? Here? Or later, at Meetpoint? Where was it I was supposed to find this gods-be packet was the only currency I had, where was I supposed to go? Kshshti? Back through kif territory, get my ship and my crew shot up one more time, end up on mahen charity because there's no gods-be help else when you've got through using me and mine for every gods-be gods-rotted piece of mahen politics you've got going? Or maybe I get to Meetpoint and find you'll drop me to politic with the stsho to save them from the kif— some mahen squeeze play, throw one kif at them from Kefk, another from Kita and Kshshti, catch them between your ships and the humans and haul the whole gods-be Compact into your lap, with me and the *han* left the way you left us the last time, out in the cold with our ships shot up, our station in ruins, and nothing this time to do but come crawling to your gods-be charity! Is that the way your favors go? Am I what you think you're buying with this little packet that tells your authorities how to deal with me?"

"I not do!" Jik fell back from a convulsive shout, breathing hard, and they stared at each other for a moment.

"Then who's this Ghost? What's the rest of it?"

Silence. Jik only stared and breathed.

"It's another doublecross. Isn't it? *They've threatened my world, you hear me?*"

He blinked. That was all.

"Gods rot you—" She snatched the paper from her pocket and waved it in his face. "What's this thing mean? What's this gods-be message worth if the humans double-cross you?" And when his mouth only clamped the tighter: "Jik—"

"My nose itch, Pyanfar." Quietly. With full self-possession. And when she lost the breath to shout with: "Damn miserable, Pyanfar, damn ridic'lous situation, you and me. You come get me. Now what we do? What you think do?"

She took the paper and folded it, absorbed in that meticulous task.

"You got too good heart deal with kif," Jik said.

"What's our choice? What gods-be choice have we got? Your whole plan's blown up, we've got the Compact coming apart around our ears—"

"Same you, me, a?" He made a grimace, blinked sweat and strained to see her. "What we do, a? How far we want go, you, me?"

"I don't know." She shoved the message into her pocket and leaned into his view, close, ears flat and a shaking in her knees. "How far *do* I go, huh, Jik? How far'd you go? This mess you put in motion is threatening to take my *world* out. We talk about friendship now? We talk about what you'd do in mahendo'sat interests? About two mahen bastards who'd doublecross every friend they got, all for the Personage?"

"You want try drug next?"

"Don't push me."

"What *we* got, huh? Damn Anuurn hani sit and wait, good friend? You longtime got mind like rock, Pyanfar, whole damn *han* got own interest, let mahendo'sat fight kif pirate, let mahe do, hani too damn busy make politic—"

"Why blame us? You created the *han,* take the poor hani bastards, teach 'em spaceflight, shove 'em into your own gods-rotted politics with the stsho, and to a mahen hell with the clans—"

"What you want? Sit on world, be sit there when politic

in the Compact roll over you heads like wave in the sea? Be sit there when kif eat our heart and come find hani? Maybe all time you like sit on world, Pyanfar, maybe you get old, want go sit in damn dirt and wait for kif?"

"So what d'we get? The kif or you?"

"You got choice."

"Gods blast you!"

"If we want you damn world, Pyanfar, we one time got, first time we land on Anuurn you got nothing but point' sticks. You forget? You ask us leave, we go."

"Sure, you went. You never turned loose of us. Manipulate our trade, shape our government, let us here and let us there and *don't* let us get beyond ourselves—"

"Fine. You make fine deal. Maybe you like kif lot better. Wish you luck, Pyanfar. Or you got trust me—"

"*Trust* you!"

"Damn, you come, I crazy drunk, *talk kif,* you say; I do, I *do,* Pyanfar, I got so much trust in you, I *do.* All diff'rent, you say; got human louse things up, got bad trouble—'*Talk, Jik: tell the kif what he want, I get you out—*' God! what kind fool I be with trust?"

"I should let you loose on my ship? Let you loose with my crew? Jik, I got you out of there. I did that for you. If you trusted me you'd tell me what's in this paper, but you won't do that. You can't do that, and I know why, like you know why I don't dare let you go. I've got to survive. I have to stay alive in this gods-rotted mess you handed me. I've got to hold a position where I can still do something. You understand me? I'm *going* to do something."

"I tell you paper." Jik's voice came faintly, almost inaudible. "You know mahendo'sat—know I got power to make agreement for my Personage. I make now—with you. With hani."

"Same as you make with Sikkukkut, huh? Same as you make with Akkhtimakt and set them at each other's throats."

"Same I keep. Same I give him Kefk, same I fight with. You same know mahendo'sat. I keep agreement. I don't say Personage keep. But—" Jik blinked again and licked his lips, eyes lively as if he had already won his point. "—if you get this kif, we got deal with you fair, a?"

"Tell me the paper."

"Let go first."

"Oh, no, friend. You listen to me. You listen good. We're going out of here, going to come kiting blind into whatever you set up over at Meetpoint, and Kesurinan's going in there on my directions. It's your ship. Your crew. I'd think you'd be a little concerned."

"Damn kif heart, you got kif heart, Pyanfar."

"I got a hani one, same as you're working for your own." She laid her hand on his shoulder, even knowing it was unwelcome. "Listen, you bastard, you and I had rather deal with each other. I take your agreement. I'll *sleep* with your gods-be Personage if it gets us out of this, but the first thing I got to do is get us into Meetpoint in one piece. And I want those code names and I want every gods-rotted thing you've been holding out on me. Right up front, I want to know what's in that message, and what kind of a deal you and Goldtooth have already made."

He shut his eyes, blinked at the sweat. "Paper say—most this you got to know already: the stsho betray us; the human maybe ally; hani—hani not reliable; I make deal with Sikkukkut to make him *hakkikt,* I got also deal with tc'a—Pyanfar, you say this wrong ear, you blow Compact to hell."

"That's real fine. What of it we've got left. Keep talking."

"Tc'a long time take knnn orders: why they change now. I don't know. Got some crazy input from chi, damn lunatic chi got notion want go out from Chchchcho, want expand—"

"You mean the *chi* are pushing the knnn? Good gods, those—"

"Not sure. Maybe tc'a idea. Methane-breather be lot crazy. But knnn—we not be sure, think maybe knnn got eye on chi. Also human got lot planetaries, got lot thing knnn want, maybe; also got humanity, number one problem. Long time problem. Stir up kif. Stir up methane-folk. Big trouble. You not know."

"The Akkukkak business?"

"Before Akkukkak." Jik explored a cut on his lip with his tongue and drew a deep breath. "Old *hakkikktun* be small stuff; lot little *hakkikktun* be lousy neighbor, lot trouble, steal you cargo, do little pirate stuff, easy we keep lanes clear—few hunter-ship take care these bastard number one good. Then we get fellow name Afkkek, nasty lot trouble.

He go down, we get 'nother, name Gotukkun. He got own authority, take what belong Afkkek too. After Gotukkun be Sakkfikktin. Kasotuk. Nifekekkin. Each more big."

"Each adding his own followers to what he'd taken."

"You got. Long time kif be fight at Akkht, lot internal stuff. Long time we know kif got more big and more big *hakkikt.* So we try—try push *hakkiktun* make difficulty with methane-folk. Sometime work good. Now—we got mistake. Big mistake. We been get human signal, longtime."

"You *asked* them in? Gods blast—!"

"Not ask. We try take quiet look, see what be this kind. Lose ship. Lose two ship, we think be knnn, maybe kif take those ship. Maybe knnn same time got curiosity 'bout humanity. I think, me, I think Akkukkak set up trap, bring human, take. But we not know this: he be dead; maybe no one know."

"Of course you didn't share this information with anyone."

"Who we tell? Stsho? *Han?* You got Tully. We don't know what else you got. We don't know what he tell you— I tell you, Pyanfar, you come mahen station, bring human— you trust us damn too much. 'Cept we be friend, a? We don't tell you all thing we know. But we fight with you keep kif off Anuurn. Lot thing then we don't know. We got find out. You know when Tully 'scape kif? Lot time kif operate at Meetpoint, make trade with stsho. They got Akkukkak, got couple kif be rival—lot trouble with kif. Ana try—not know what that ship got; he know one kif ship chase 'nother, Akkukkak come there 'cause he got no safe route else. Then he not be real happy find my partner Ana come in port. He 'fraid stay, got other kif; 'fraid go, 'fraid Ana get on his tail, he got tail in vise number one good. So he sit at dock. He so damn busy watch Ana he forget watch other kif. One kif inside ship make snatch Tully; Tully run like hell down dock—you got rest. Now Ana lot worry, not know what this be, not know if this be species we know about, or be something lot different. He try find Tully. Kif try find. Tully go *you* ship and start damn lot trouble. Now you got stsho go crazy, all scare' 'bout knnn, scare' 'bout humans come, damn mad 'bout you damage station— Mahendo'sat work hard, bribe lot stsho, make so hani come back to Meetpoint. We *need* hani. Need bal-

ance with kif, damn sure stsho no good, tc'a and knnn lot
disturb. We get hani back to Meetpoint, go try make careful
new contact with humanity, try find out what they be, how
big, what they minds be like—find out what knnn want."

"And the kif took offense at it."

"Kif damn busy big fight on Akkht. We know we got
worry 'nother *hakkikt* grow up; so we got make opposition,
hit here, hit there, try make lot little *hakkiktun*. Then we
got Sikkukkut. My mistake. Sikkukkut."

"Who already had his hands into Akkhtimakt's organization. He got that ring, Jik, that ring Tully has on his hand.
He got it from a human prisoner in Akkhtimakt's hands—
Sikkukkut was already poised with his spies and his organization before we ever got to Kshshti, before you dealt with
him at Mkks. This wasn't a little provincial boss we were
dealing with, this was a kif already on his way to being
what he is. Sikkukkut knows humans. He was Akkukkak's
interrogator, he killed all of Tully's crew except the one
Tully killed himself, when it got that bad, Jik, and you
know better than I do what it could get to. This is the gods-
be kifish *expert* on humanity we're dealing with, and if kif
have anything like a security organization, I'm guessing
some of Akkukkak's old staff that got swept up into Akkhtimakt's organization—never were Akkhtimakt's. They
were Sikkukkut's partisans all along. Am I wrong?"

Jik stared at her. "You got damn good ears."

"I'm an old trader and I know how to add. You knew
this. You knew some of it; and you went right ahead and
you promoted this kif of yours at every step. The wrong
gods-be kif. I didn't see it. You didn't see it till Kefk. Jik,
I could take this dock out. I could stop this one. And that
still leaves Akkhtimakt—"

"Same damn bastard. I be right, Pyanfar, still be right
'bout that one. Akkhtimakt got no bottom. Swallow everything. Sikkukkut—want *use* everything. Ana—Ana got this
idea he use human for break the kif. But if *they* got
motive—"

"Tully's got no reason to lie. They're *big,* Jik. You're not
dealing with one human government. There's their homeworld, but there's two other powers. Tully's from their
homeworld. It's fighting the other two and it wants to beat
them—you tell me how. They've shot at the knnn. The

knnn are putting up with it for reasons the gods and the
knnn only know; we've got one human planet out there at
odds with every other human in space, and there's gods
know how many worlds the other side of their homestar
from us. Their homeworld is cut off, isolate, having bloodfeud with its own outposts—what in the gods' name can
you imagine we're dealing with? What's this lot after, when
they've got a dozen worlds in the other direction and all
of them are shooting at each other?"

"Tully say this?"

"By bits and pieces. Yes. That's what he's told me. We've
just got the tail of the creature. When it turns around—"

"God."

"If you and your earless Personage had told the same
truth twice in a day we might not be in this mess. You
understand me?"

"If we not got damn hani traitor, if we not got the *han*
screw up—we both got damn fools, Pyanfar, both kind. We
got be fools too? Let me go. You got one of you crew sick.
You want damn good pilot, you want me sit boards, you
got. You want chain me to damn chair, you got. Pyanfar.
I don't want lie down here in dark!"

She stood there on yea and nay, reached as far as the
release and took her hand back. "Agreement?"

"You got."

She pulled the first release; and the second.

And stood there remembering the power there was in a
mahen arm. And the wit there was in this mahendo'sat,
and all his twists and turns: make a simple move against
her he would not—until it was profitable.

Fool, a small voice said, while Jik slowly lifted his hands
to his face and wiped the sweat, while he groped for the
edge of the table and gave every indication of weakness
and disorientation. He looked apt to pitch onto his face.
She made a grab for him and steadied him as he got his
feet over the edge and sat there blinking and grimacing as
if his head hurt considerably. He put a hand up to his brow,
wiped his eyes and looked at her.

As well admit Skkukuk to the bridge during jump. Much
rather admit Skkukuk—who *was* on their side.

Of all the things I've done, she thought to herself, staring
into Jik's alien eyes, *this is the one I'll deserve to die for. I*

know I'm making a mistake. I'm wrong. I'm going to foul up and the kif'll launch that ship, that ship no one can stop and no one can catch, and there won't be hani left except those of us who happen to be in space, that the kif will hunt down one by one. All because there's this chance that we need him, and Tully, and that gods-be kif who thinks I'm his ticket to kifish glory; because I'm an old fool of a hani who's been out in the dark too long and I can't shake if off and think clear of it any longer.

"Pyanfar," he said gently, "you be damn bastard."

"Got you out, didn't I?"

"You got."

"You know you're not sitting a post on this ship."

"What you want?" He held out his hands together. "Chain to chair? Do! I want be on bridge. Want talk to my ship. Want hear my ship."

"Hear them, I'll give you."

Fool, Pyanfar. This isn't Anuurn. He isn't hani. Parole means nothing to him weighed against his orders.

And how do I treat him like this and trust him again, ever?

"Agreement, Jik. You put this one in my hands. You stay on the bridge, but you keep your mouth shut and you keep your hands off controls."

He turned his hands, showed blunt mahen claws which nature had never made retractable, or fine enough for the smaller controls on hani boards; and they were broken and bloody, the fingertips swollen and coated with plasm from Tirun's caretaking: it was sure the kif had done no good for them.

She felt a cold shiver inside, a sympathetic twitch of her own claws in their retractile sheaths. But she set her face all the same. "Is that all the answer I get? Or do you give me those codewords and give us some honest help?"

He looked at her straight from under his dark brow, a hard glitter in his eyes. "I do, Pyanfar. Now you got believe what I say, a?"

Chapter 4

I am writing this in haste at Mkks. Do not hold or compromise this courier. Present crisis compels me to clarify the actions which I have taken in support of Ismehanan-min, since his lines of operation have crossed mine. I trust his report has reached you, but have placed a duplicate in the care of the Personage at Kshshti should the courier have failed. Since Stle stles stlen is not holding to treaty agreements both Ismehanan-min and I are taking measures to support other candidates and to prevent replacement of mahen personnel with hani. Here at Mkks we have retrieved all hostages and have suffered no damage at present. We are requested by Sikkukkut to add support to his candidacy by moving on Kefk. I am not apprised of Ismehanan-min's whereabouts and do not speculate. I advance on Meetpoint by that route. All reports from tc'a sources indicate that Stle stles stlen is proceeding as in the previous report, and reports from our contact inside stsho space are not encouraging. . . .

Tc'a contacts report knnn agitation in urgent terms. . . .

I have given Ehrran a false packet. Evidently this is a stsho agent and I dispense only disinformation into this outlet. Her willingness to participate I am certain is only a means to gather information on our activities which I am sure she has gained through stsho contacts of her own and which she has twice attempted to relay through furtive contact with stsho agents, some of which have eluded the net. Our movements are reported through an efficient system of couriers and I maintain a close watch over Ehrran's transmissions.

Thus far Chanur remains reliable. Support for this agent must be managed with extreme discretion on all levels. I would send her on to Maing Tol but I see no means to do this over Sikkukkut's objections and considering Ehrran's present state of mind. Therefore Chanur remains with us, under utmost priority of protection. Particularly alarming is Sikkukkut's courting of Chanur. Leverage will have to be arranged to counter this. . . .

Pyanfar looked away from the translation on screen, and Jik, sitting in a ring of Chanur at the bridge com station, gave a pained shrug as she flattened her ears. "What kind of leverage?"

"Money," Jik said faintly. "Debt. Like maybe—a, Pyanfar, I not arrange these thing. This *gover'ment* stuff. They also help. Who repair you ship, a? Who bribe Stle stles stlen get you license back?" He looked around him, at face after face, looked again as Khym leaned a huge hand on the back of the cushion, and gazed up at Khym's glowering countenance before he thought otherwise and turned back to Pyanfar. "No good this read message," Jik said. "Damn, you read mail you going find stuff don't got all the truth. Truth, truth I can't say in letter— What you want, I write to Personage say I want help friend, I say I want them do good to you? No. I do quiet. I push make Personage you friend, I push keep you out trouble, I down on knee ask Personage treat Chanur right—" He reached and made a backhanded gesture toward the screen. "This, this be *evidence* in law. You know what I mean say. You don't write down some thing. No want enemies get, not kif enemy, not hani enemy, not mahe, not stsho. God, Pyanfar, you know what I try say."

She stared at him bleakly, saw the tremor in his hand and the pain etched around his eyes and his mouth, saw— maybe she *wanted* to see past the damning words on the screen.

"I know," she said, and saw the tremor grow worse in his arm before he let it down. Proud Jik, vain Jik, pressed to give accounts he would not have given, not for any threat, except for hope of help from the friends he had doublecrossed, with his ship held hostage and more than his freedom and his reputation at stake. What she saw hurt. And rang clearer than any protestations. "I know, gods rot it, we both got a mess. Haral, what's status on our allies out there?"

"*Aja Jin* and *Moon Rising* both report on schedule. I reported ourselves the same, all well aboard."

"So we've told Kesurinan you're fine," Pyanfar muttered to Jik. "So what was the hope—send me off sideways about the time you made the jump with Sikkukkut to Meetpoint?"

"We not want lose you," Jik said.

"I ought to be flattered," she said in her throat, and looked up at the others. Tully was on the bridge with them. Everyone but Skkukuk. Tully as usual lost all of it. He looked confused. So did the crew, confused and on the edge of anger. "We got a value to the mahendo'sat," she said. "They like their friends to survive. Gods know what else they want. It's fair, I guess. We have certain mahendo'sat we favor more than others. No great wrong in that, as far as it goes. You're off shift. Whole crew. Get a good meal in your stomachs: we got gods know what coming up. We got more than Meetpoint laid into Nav. If we have to."

She looked toward Jik. Jik leaned back in his chair, folded his hands across his stomach with something more like his usual ease. His eyes were tired. But the gesture at least looked like Jik, bedraggled as he was and lacking his usual finery.

"You too," she said. And for a moment the lids half-lowered on his eyes, the faintest of warnings.

Don't give me orders, that was to say. *I've had enough.*

Well, it was Jik, and he was only trying to recover a bit of his dignity. She let her ears dip: *all right.*

Then he unfolded his arms, pried his stiffening frame out of the chair, and gave himself up to Tirun Araun, who indicated the galleyward corridor.

Fool, she told herself again. It was not just Jik she was trusting. It was a mahe the mahendo'sat put ultimate confidence in, one of a few who were turned loose in the field to make decisions across lightyears too many for the central government to be consulted on every twitch and adjustment of policy—places where agents had no time to consult, and a hunter-captain like Jik had to make up his own law and make treaties and direct local ships with the authority of the whole mahen government behind him.

Personage was more than an individual back in Maing Tol and another at Iji. It was the whole concept on which the mahendo'sat concluded anything: when a mahe was right he was right as law, and when he made a mistake he fell from power. His superiors would disown him. And if

he made too great a mistake the superior who appointed
him might fall: so there might be more than one agent in
the field making contradictory arrangements.

The most viable would be acknowledged, the agents who
stood too visibly for the nonviable policies would fall from
power, and the mahen government went smoothly on.

Doublecross was the standard order of business. Betrayal
of each other, of everyone but the superior. That he protected his own agents was Jik's saving honesty, and Goldtooth's, who had run and left Jik because he had to. It took
this many years in space for an old hani to understand how
it worked and to understand *that* it worked.

And there was still the question whether Jik might turn
back on an agreement he had made, and repudiate it himself.

He had made a hard one, gods knew, with Sikkukkut.

And a contradictory one with her.

She frowned, and walked on the way others had gone,
into the galley, where Tirun had gotten Jik seated at table
and where Haral and Hilfy and Khym and Tully were all
delving into the cabinets and the freezer hunting quick-fix
edibles. There was the bitter odor of dry gfi in the air: Tirun
was filling a pot. There was the rattle of plastic: disposables.
Pyanfar leaned on the table with both hands and looked
Jik in the eyes.

"Got a question for you. Say you got two agreements,
you, yourself. And the people you made them with—get at
odds. How do you resolve that?"

Jik frowned. His eyes still wept. His sweat smelled of
ammonia and drug even yet. "You, Sikkukkut?"

"Me and Sikkukkut."

"I keep best agreement."

"The one that serves the mahendo'sat best."

"A." He blinked and gazed at her like a tired child.
"Always."

"Just wondered," she said. "In case."

Something else occurred to her, when she turned to the
cabinet and took a packet of dried meat out of the storage.

Jik had just, for whatever reason, told the truth. Against
his own Personage and all those interests. Which made him,
in mahen terms, a dishonest man.

Gods, what's gotten into us on this ship? We got nobody

aboard who hasn't gone to the wrong side of her own species' business—Tully, Skkukuk, all us of Chanur and Mahn: now Jik's sliding too.

Treason's catching, that's what it is.

She got a cup, wrinkled her nose as Khym dosed his gfi with tofi. She poured her own from the fastbrewer, looked back at their unlikely crew crowded into the galley. At Jik sitting disconsolate and hurting and trying his best to choke down a sandwich and a cup of reconstituted milk; no one in Chanur put off any temper on him, not Hilfy and not Khym either.

So. Crew was going to give him a chance. For their own reasons, which might include latitude for the captain's judgment; but maybe because of past debts.

It was hard, being hani, not to think like one. There were times they had been as glad to see Jik as he had surely been to see her come after him on *Harukk.* Even if on his side it was all policy and politics. He had saved their skins many a time.

Even if it was always to bet them again.

Chur slitted open her eyes, wrinkled her nose, and blinked sleepily at her sister. Her heart sped a bit. She had dreamed of black things in the corridors, had dreamed of something loose on the ship. Noise in the corridors. It felt as if some time had passed.

And Geran had noted that little increase in pulse rate. Geran had this disconcerting habit of taking glances at the monitors while she talked, and whenever she reacted to anything. Geran's be-ringed ears flicked at what she saw now; and it was a further annoyance that the screen was hard to see from flat on one's back.

"We got Jik out," Geran said.

Chur blinked again. So much that came and went was illusion and it was the good things she most distrusted, the things she really wanted to believe. "He all right?"

"Knocks and bruises and the like. Told Tirun he'd run into a wall trying to leave. Likely story. You know you never get the same thing twice out of him. How are you feeling?"

"Like I ran into the same wall. What'd you do to that gods-be machine? You put me out?"

"Got pretty noisy around here. I thought you might need the sleep."

"In a mahen hell you did!" Chur lifted her head and shoved her free elbow under her. "You want my heart-beat up?"

"Lie down. You want mine up?"

"What happened out there?" She sank back, her head swimming, and tried to focus. "Gods, I still got that stuff in me. Cut it out, Geran. F'gods sakes, I'm tired enough, hard enough to go against the wind—"

"Hey." Geran took her by the shoulder.

"I'm awake, I'm awake."

"You want to try to eat something?"

"Gods, not more of that stuff."

Foil rustled. A sickly aroma hit the air, which was otherwise sterile and medicated. Food, any food was a trial. Chur nerved herself and cooperated as Geran lifted her head on her arm and squirted something thin and salty into her mouth. She licked her mouth and took a second one, not because she wanted it. It was enough.

"Not so bad," she said. It was so. She had missed salt. It did something more pleasant in her mouth than the last thing Geran had brought her. She cautiously estimated its course to her stomach and felt it hit bottom and lie there gratefully inert. She looked up at Geran, who had a desperately hopeful look on her face. "You worried about something, Gery?"

The ears flicked. "We're doing all right."

Lie.

"Where's those gods-be black things?"

"Got 'em all penned up again." Change of subject. Geran looked instantly relieved. And the traitor machine beeped with an increased heartbeat. Geran looked back at it and the facade fell in one agonized glance.

"We under attack?" Chur asked.

"We're prepping for jump," Geran said.

Scared. Gods, Gery, you'd send a monitor off the scale—

"Huhn," Chur said. "What're you thinking? That I won't make it?"

"Sure, you'll make it."

"How far're we going?"

Geran's ears went flat and lifted again. There was a draw-ing round her nose, like pain. "Home, one of these days."

"Multiple jump?"

"Don't think so."

"Maybe, huh?"

"Gods rot it, Chur—"

I haven't got the strength. I can't last it out. Look at her. Gods, look at her. "Listen. You mind your business up for'ard, f'godssakes, what d'you want, me make it fine and you marry this ship up with a rock? You pull it together. Me, I'm fine back here. Back here feeding me—" The mon-itor started going off again. She let it. "When'd *you* eat, huh? Take care of yourself. I got to worry whether you're doing your job up there?"

"No," Geran said. She gave a furtive glance at the moni-tor and composed herself sober as an old lord. "I just want to make sure you get anything into your stomach you can."

"Don't trust this machine, do you? I make you a deal. You cut that gods-be sedative out of the works and I'll try to eat. Hear me?"

"Stays the way they set it."

The monitor beeped again.

"Gods fry that rotted thing!" Chur cried, and the beep became a steady pulse. Geran reached and hit the interrupt; and it prevented the flood of sedative.

"Quiet," Geran said.

She subsided. Her temples ached. The room came and went. But in the center of it Geran stayed in unnatural focus, like hunter-vision, hazed around the edges.

I can think my way home, she thought, which was rankest insanity, the maundering of a weakened brain. *Just got to hold onto the ship and get there with it.*

That was crazy. But for a moment she seemed to pass outside the walls, know activity in the ship, feel the rotation of Kefk station, the whirling of the sun, a hyperextension like the timestretch of jump, where time and space rede-fined themselves. An old spacer could take that route home. She could not have explained it to a groundling, never to anyone who had not flown free in that great dark—she stopped being afraid. It was very dangerous. She could see the currents between the stars, knew the dim-

plings and the holes, the shallows and the chasms planets
and stars made. She smiled, having mindstretched that far,
and still being on her ship.

I can think the way home. Bring us all home.

"Chur?"

"I'll be with you," she said. "No worry. Wish they could
move this gods-rotted rig onto the bridge." She shut her
eyes a moment, shut that inward eye that beckoned to all
infinity, then looked at Geran quite soberly. "When?"

"Bring *him,* captain?" It was not Tirun Araun's way to
question orders; but there was reason enough, and Pyanfar
let her ears down and up again in a kind of shrug that got
a diffident flattening from Tirun's ears and put a little stam-
mer in Tirun's mouth. "That is to say—"

"Skkukuk's not the one I'm worried about," Pyanfar said
quietly. They were outside the lift, in upper main, and the
ship hummed and thumped with tests and closures, auto-
rigging for a run. And if there was a place Tirun ought to
be it was at her boards down on lowerdeck, in their cargo
bridge; and *The Pride* ought to have a cargo to carry, and
a trader's honest business. But those days were past for
them. There was only something dreadful ahead; and she
went from one to another of the crew and spoke with them,
quietly, of things that had to be done, and never of the
situation they were in. With Tirun it was just a matter of
giving her orders, and of telling her, obliquely, in that way
they had talked for forty years and more, that she knew
that she asked a great deal; and Tirun's worried look settled
and became quiet again, still as deep water. "How many
rings you got, cousin?"

"Oh, I don't know." Tirun flicked her ears and set the
ones she wore to swinging. " 'Bout many as proves I've got
good sense, captain."

"We get out of this one, cousin, I'll buy you a dozen
more."

"Huh," Tirun said. "Well, I got enough. We get out of
this one, captain, you and I'll both be surprised, and that
son Sikkukkut no more than most."

"All of our allies will," Pyanfar said. "Skkukuk's safe.
He's *on* this ship, isn't he? Kif don't understand that kind
of suicide. You know Jik had to explain to Sikkukkut we'd

really blow the ship? Couldn't figure why you'd do that. You can tell a kif about it all you like. He'll think it's a lie. A bluff. Skkukuk's no different, I think. Tell the son I'm going to give him a job to do: he'll handle kif-com. I'm putting him under Hilfy's orders."

"My gods, cap'n."

"Tully's sitting com too, this jump. No choice, is there? You've got to handle armaments—this time for real, I'm very much afraid; and back up Haral, and keep an eye on scan: I'm putting Jik in Chur's seat, but his board stays locked, whatever condition his hands are in; and sure as rain falls down I'm not giving him com. While we're at Kefk we've got one excuse; at Meetpoint we may have to contrive another. But I don't want to put him between his ethics and our survival. Gods know, maybe it'll take something off his shoulders, in some bizarre turn of the mahen mind. He *wants* to help us; he *wants* to carry out his own orders; he probably *wants* to save Goldtooth's neck in spite of what the bastard did to him, he *wants* a whole lot of things that are mutually exclusive. Or that may turn that way in a hurry. And gods know I don't want him in reach of your board and the guns."

"He won't like Skkukuk there."

"He'll know why, though. I figure he'll know inside and out why that is."

"Him knowing the kif and all, yes."

"Him knowing the kif and knowing what his own side wants from him, gods save him—gods save us from mahen-do'sat and all their connivances. And watch Goldtooth, cousin, for the gods' own sakes, if we do spot him, keep us a line of fire there. I don't like the rules in this game either, but we didn't make them up. They're his, they're that bastard Sikkukkut's, and gods know who else has a finger in it. Watch them all."

"Aye," Tirun said in a hoarse, faint voice. "Them and Ehrran."

"Everyone else for that matter. I don't know a friend we've got."

"Tahar," Tirun said.

"Tahar," she recalled.

A pirate and an outlaw.

* * *

And: "I've got *Skkukuk?*" Hilfy said. Her jaw had dropped, her ears were flat.

Pyanfar nodded. They stood where she had caught up with Hilfy, in the galley. And Tully sat sipping a cup of gfi, his blue eyes following their moves and his human, immobile ears taking in the whole of it. His com-translator would whisper it to him.

"Luck of the draw. He's sitting down by Tirun on the jumpseat, but he'll be working off your board. Just keep your finger by the cutoff. If we have to. And get your wits about you when we come out of the drop. I have to ask you this: how good are you on kifish nuance?"

"I'm good."

"Objective assessment: good enough to pick up the subtleties in a kif's transmissions?"

Hilfy paused, and gathered her cup off the counter. She glanced Tully's way and back again. There was clearest sanity in her golden eyes. "I know what you're saying. No. But Skkukuk can do it. What I've got to do is watch what *he's* saying. And be fast on the cutoff."

"You tell me this: is a kif going to damage a ship he's on?"

Hilfy thought about that one too. Her ears dropped and lifted again. "No," she said. "Not when you put it that way. But there is a point he'd turn on us."

"He'd be alone. Crew wouldn't go along with him the way it might on a kifish ship. Kifish crew'd turn on their captain and mutiny. Hani won't. I think maybe Skkukuk's got a glimmering of that. It'll make him behave."

Again a dip of Hilfy's ears. One ring swung there. But the eyes were not that young any longer. "I tell you what that son's thinking. He's thinking the crew's conserving its own position and it's rallied around you out of fear of him. That's what he's thinking. He's thinking if we got into trouble we'd do a real stupid thing, standing by you just for fear of him. He thinks if we prove tough enough other hani will join us on Sikkukkut's side. It's all very simple to him. One thing I've found the kif astonishingly free of is species-prejudice."

"I think you're right."

That seemed to soothe some raw spot in Hilfy. The ears

came up again, pricked in an expression that made her look young again. And they flagged when she looked at Tully.

So you're not a fool, Pyanfar thought. *Thank the gods great and lesser.* And did not miss that distracted look that passed between those two. No species-prejudice there either. Too little species prejudice. *O Hilfy, you're a long way from home and gods-be if I care if you're two outright fools in that regard. I ought to be shocked. I can't even find it anymore. Gods save you both, I hope you've done what I don't even want to think about. I hope you've had a little bit of what I've had forty years of.*

And what kind of thinking's that?

Khym was sleeping when she came into their quarters. She dropped the trousers on the floor, quietly, pocket-gun and all; and came and got into the bowl-shaped bed, down in the middle of it where he was, a huge warm lump all hard with muscle and tucked up like a child. She put her arms around his back, buried her head against his shoulder. He turned over and nuzzled her shoulder.

Sleep, she wished him, with a bit of regret. Among pleasures in life a warm bed and a nap in her husband's arms was not the least. She had not the heart to wake him, not when he was this far gone.

"Py," he murmured, in that breathy rumble of his voice at whisper. And bestirred himself, perhaps for his own sake, perhaps just in that way a man would who knew he was wanted: matter of kindness, for a tired wife who came to him for refuge. What they did had nothing to do with time of year. That would have shocked the old gray whiskers back home. Wives and husbands were a seasonal matter: men were always in and wives got around to it when they were home, by ones and twos and, in spring, a confounded houseful of women with hairtrigger tempers and demands on a single, harried man; then the house lord got round to driving out all the young men who had overstayed their childhood, before some scandal happened: young women went to roving, older sisters heaved out any near-adult brother the lord happened not to take exception to. It was housecleaning, annual as the spring rains.

A spacer missed the seasons. She just came home when

she got the chance, and tried to make it coincide with
spring, a little visit to her brother Kohan, who was glassy-
eyed and distracted with affairs in Chanur at such a time,
she paid a little courtesy to his wives and any sister or
cousin who lived in the house or just happened to be
home—

—then it was up in decent leisure to Mahn in the hills,
where Khym and his groundling wives held court. His other
wives had never much gotten in her way: they were out-
fought and knew it, and hated her cordially in that way of
rivals who knew she would be gone within a week or two,
back to her ship and her gadding about again: if one had
to have a rival one could not shove out, best at least she
be the sort who was seldom home.

Now where were those wives? Hating her still, because
she had him to herself at last and he was not decently dead,
in his defeat? They would pity him and hate her, and call
it all indecent, as if he himself had not had a choice in the
world about being snagged up onto a Chanur ship and carried away to a prolonged and unnatural preservation. It
ruined his reputation. It touched on their honor. Likely
they imagined just such lascivious and libertine unseasonal
things as she had led him into, or worse, that he was the
prize of all the crew.

She thought about that. "What do you think," she said
into his ear, "do you think you'd object to one of the crew
now and again? How do you feel about that?"

"I don't know," he said. "I mean—they're—" He was
quiet a long time. "They're friends."

"I don't mean you should." She brushed his mane straight,
dragged a clawtip along beside his ear. "I never meant that.
I was asking if you ever wanted to."

"They're your friends."

She felt his heart beating faster. Like panic. And cursed
herself for bringing it up at all. "They never asked. Gods,
what a mess. Don't even think about it. I'm sorry I said it.
I just felt sorry for them."

"So do I. I'd do it. Tell them that if you want to. Like
friends. I think they'd be sensible about it. I think I could
be."

Ask *sensible* of a man. Trust him. *Gods, that's what's
changed, isn't it? He's steady as a rock. He wouldn't play*

*games about it. They wouldn't, with him. They respect him.
They'd treat him like a sister—in crew matters. Not one of
them is petty and not one is the sort that has to prove a
point in bed or after. You know that about women you work
with for forty years; and they'd know he was a loan. I'd
take that risk for them.*

*But what's good for him, that matters; that, they'd never
question. Gods know I wouldn't.*

"I think you could trust them," she said. "It's all of them
if it's one, you understand that. I'm just telling you it's all
right with me. Won't make me happy or unhappy. I just
thought—well, if it ever does happen, you don't have to
slip around about it."

"I never—!"

"I know that. I'm just telling you how I feel. If it's ever
one, it's all. Remember it. Gods, back home I'd drop in on
you for a hand of days and shove your other wives out;
been the longest five days yet, hasn't it? I'm feeling guilty
about hanging onto you so long. It's getting obsessive. I
thought maybe, if things settle down again—" Thoughts
crowded in that made it all remote and hopeless and stupid
even to talk about it; but it was peace that she had come
here for: she shoved Meetpoint aside and pretended. "Well,
I thought I ought to give you a little breathing room. I
shove you into my room, I don't give you much choice, do
I? I want you to know you've got a berth on this ship. On
your own. As much as you want to be. Or where you want
to be. You want not to share my bed a while, that's fine.
I'd miss you. But I don't want you ever to think that's what
you're aboard for."

"I'm aboard because I'm a total fool." A frown was on
his face, rumpling up his brow. "The rest came later. Py,
don't talk like this."

"Gods, you don't understand."

"I don't own this ship. It's Kohan's. I can't come here,
bed his kin—"

Male thinking, hindend-foremost and illusionary. Downworld thinking. It infuriated her in him, when so much else
was extraordinary. "This ship is *mine,* gods rot it, Kohan's
got nothing to do with it. And if you want to bed down
with Skkukuk, he's mine, too. I'll also shred your ears."

That struck him funny. And wrinkled his nose in disgust.

"I didn't consult with Kohan," she said. "I don't consult. You know gods-be well how the System works, how it always worked, your sweat and your blood and you never *owned* a gods-be thing. Now you really do. Something you can't lose. You can do as you gods-blessed please, and you *do* it, husband. Forty years I've been out here. You've been here two and already your thinking's skewed. You at least listen to my craziness. All those years in Mahn, you used to ask me what the stars were like. Now you know what I come from, why I didn't get along with the rest of the women . . . why I never could make our daughter understand me. Tahy thinks I'm crazy. Some kind of pervert, probably. Kara knows I am. I just can't get excited about what they think down there. I don't have those kind of nerves anymore. Their little laws don't seem important to me. That's dangerous, I think. I don't know how to get back to where I was. None of us do. Haral's got a bastard daughter off in Faha; Tirun's got a son somewhere still alive, left him in Gorun. Gods know they usually take precautions. But they've never married; they never will; they just take their liberties down in Hermitage with whatever takes their fancy, and I don't ask. You know why they do that? I was lucky. My sister Rhean—one spring that we coincided down in Chanur I asked her how her husband was, you know, not a loaded question. But she got this look like she was dying by inches: 'Pyanfar,' she said, 'the man doesn't know where Meetpoint is. He doesn't know *what* it is. That's how my husband is.' And I never asked her. That's lord Fora she was talking about."

"He's not stupid, I knew him in Hermitage."

"No, he's not stupid. Rhean just can't talk to him. Her world isn't where he lives. His isn't where she lives. Nowadays she comes home as little as she can. If she could go to Hermitage and do her planettime there, I think she would far rather. A man you pick up in the hills, he'll pretend you're all his dreams, won't he?"

"You ever do it?"

She hesitated. Which was as good as yes. She shrugged. "Not after we were married."

"A Morhun found me like that; and left me a week later. Me, a kid out in the bush, hoping for an ally. Playing games with a boy like that—that's cruel."

"I was honest about it. I said I was down on leave. When I was. When I was younger than that I was honestly looking."

"No boy of that age'd know you meant gone in the morning. No boy would know that that ship's worth more to you than he ever could be. No boy would know he couldn't follow you where you'd go, that the territory you want isn't—isn't something he could take for you. And he'd want to lay the whole world in your lap, Py, any man would want to, and he'd try to talk to you and maybe learn by morning he couldn't give you anything you cared about. That's a hard thing, Py. It was hard for me."

"You were lord of Mahn!"

"I was lord of the place you used to go hunting, the house you lived in when you wanted a rest. I was a recreation. I never could give you anything. And I wanted to give you everything."

"O gods, Khym. I said I was lucky."

"But I could never give you anything. And I wanted to. When I went up to Gaohn to fight for you, gods, it was the first time I ever felt I was worth anything. When you wanted me to go with you—well, I followed you off like some boy out of Hermitage, didn't I? Go off and fight our way up in the world like two teenaged kids? Didn't know then the size of the farm you had picked out for me to take. Gods, what an ambition you've got! Give you a spacestation or two, shall I?"

"Gods, I wish you could." For a moment Meetpoint was back in bed with them. The room felt cold. His arms tightened. He gave her what he had, and she still did not know whether it was out of duty or out of his own need; but at least it was a free gift, not something she demanded by being there. That was what she hoped they had won, after all these years, and this far removed from all the rules.

"You never were a recreation," she said. "You were my sanctuary. The place I could go, the ear that would listen."

"Gods help me, my other wives always knew who I was waiting for. Who I was always waiting for. They took it out on Tahy and Kara. I tried to stop that. Py, I spent thirty-odd years buying my other wives off our kids' backs and it didn't work."

It was like a light going on, illuminating shadow-spots.

Corners of the old house at Mahn she had never seen. The reason of so many things, so evident, and so elusive. "You never told me, rot it."

"The times you were home—were too good. And you couldn't stay. I knew that. I did what I could."

Gods, I poisoned the whole house. All the other marriages. Ruined my kids—hurt Chanur in the long run, when my daughter turned on Khym and took our staunchest ally out. My doing. All of it mine.

He sighed, a motion of his huge frame against her. "I didn't mean to say that. Gods blast, Py, I just fouled it up, is all."

That was his life. That was why he walked on eggshells round those women, lost the kids. O gods. Lost Mahn alone, finally. And came back to Chanur like a beggar when I finally came home. Alienated his sisters. Everything. His sisters—for an outsider. They couldn't forgive that. And the wives' clans too. All for one wife. That's crazy.

But, gods, what I've done—for a husband. I think I love this great fool. Isn't that something? Love him like he was clan and kin. Like he was some part of me. It's gotten all too close. He needs someone else for balance. Some sense of perspective. So do I. And I'm not interested. Handsomest man on Anuurn could walk in stark naked, I'd rather Khym. Always would. And he'd rather me. I never saw that part of it. I never saw that that was always what was wrong with us, and look what it did. We did so much damage, never meaning to; I did so much to him. Gods, I wish I could turn him over to the others.

They wouldn't know how to treat him but they'd try. Even Tirun.

He wants so much to be one of them. That's what he really wants. And they'd forget that. They'd forget because I can't tell them any way I could make them understand what goes on in him.

Haral would. Haral might make a dent in Tirun, the old reprobate: gods, Khym, if you knew what good behavior Tirun's been on—not laid a hand on you, has she? Because you're mine. She'd go off and get drunk with you and take you home nice as milk, she would, because she's onship and you're offlimits and gods know she likes you, thinks you're

*something special. I don't know. She might be the real lady
with you, you're so much the gentleman. Funny what a
crooked line we walk.*

*No, if you knew either side of Tirun, really knew her,
you'd like her.*

*Geran and Chur—gods. I wish you'd known them before
this mess. So pretty. But deep water, both of them. And
dark. You don't ever pick a fight with either. But they've got
a gods-rotted broad sense of humor . . . never told you those
stories. Not planetside. They don't go down so much. Not
comfortable around groundlings. That's the awful thing:
sometimes you want the land under your feet and the sun
on your back, and then you've got to deal with the people
that live there.*

*And Hilfy—you see what's going on, her and Tully? My
poor, conservative, ex-groundling man—not a flicker. We're
too well-bred. We don't see. We don't know what to do
about it, so we don't see; and we wish them by the gods
well, because you and I, Khym, we're on the downside of
our years and we've got enough to do just to do for ourselves, in the mess we're in.*

*You couldn't sleep with Hilfy; never her. She's the odd
one out. Species she can get across. But the generations she
can't bridge. Can't figure me out; gods, she can't figure herself out. You'd confuse everything. And you're uncle to her,
you always will be, even if you haven't a corpuscle in
comon. You're her substitute for Kohan. She loves her father
so much. That's why she fusses over you like a little grandmother.*

*Bring her out here, never give her a stopover at home,
and her in the growing years— She takes what she can. It
was all so pat for us. And we wasted so much time. Good
for her, I think. Good for Hilfy.*

Thank the gods you're here.

2342 and *The Pride* was stretching muscles, electronic
impulses sending tests down to systems aft and bringing
internal support up full, while lights on the bridge flickered
and instruments blipped, routine departure-prep.

Given a kifish ship still stationary over station axis, bow-
down so that its guns were constantly in line with every

ship on the rotating station, but most notably the ones whose systems were now live, the ones full of non-kif who thought non-kifish and unpredictable thoughts.

But they kept com flowing naturally between *The Pride* and station central, which was partly *Harukk* personnel. And com operations went on likewise between *The Pride* and *Aja Jin* and *Tahar's Moon Rising,* nothing compromising in any fashion, just the necessary coordination of three ships which planned to put out close together. There was still the coder they might have used. There were languages the kif might not understand.

There was also that ship over their heads, and mindful of that and of the firepower here gathered, they refrained from all such options.

"Hilfy," Pyanfar said, "take message on your three: first thing at Meetpoint, auto that escape course out to both our partners."

"Aye," Hilfy said. "Understood."

Hilfy and Haral and Tully were all settled in, Khym was settling. Haral was still running Geran's station from the co-pilot's board, but that was all perfunctory: there was not one gods-be thing scan could tell them at this point. If the kif decided to fire, they fired. That was all. And lost part of their station doing it.

"Geran come," Tully said, doing—gods witness, the service Hilfy had drilled him on at that board: he had a pick to use where his poor clawless fingers had not a chance, he stuck it into the right holes in the right sequence, and he was at least adequate to keep an ear to internal operations. Even trusting him with that was taking a chance: Tirun was downside with Skkukuk and Jik was loose, but Pyanfar got a firm grip on her nerves and figured that (gods save them from such insanity) Tirun and Skkukuk between them could handle Jik if he had something inventive in mind.

While Tully, in a good moment and with the gods' own luck on his side, might handle an emergency call down there: *The Pride*'s autorecognition was set on the word *Priority,* which no one let past their teeth during ops if it was not precisely that: *Priority* got flashed to Hilfy's board and Haral's simultaneously, and Tully would have to make an unlikely sequence of mistakes to take the lower corridors off wide open monitor.

Geran arrived, she saw that in the conveniently reflective monitor, a shadow arriving from the main topside corridor, larger and larger until the bridge lights picked out Geran's red-brown coloring and the glint of the gold in her ear-rims. "H'lo," Geran said. After putting Chur to bed, and walking out of that room. With all the chance of finality. *H'lo*, to Hilfy, when Geran normally said nothing at all when she walked on-shift. *I'm all right*, that meant. *Don't doubt I'm on.*

"We're routine right now," Hilfy said quietly. Which was the right tack to take with Geran. No fuss. No emotional load. Pyanfar kept an ear to it all and keyed an acknowledgment to dockside's advisement they were about to withdraw power.

"Tirun," Tully said.

"I've got it," Khym said, second-com, picking that up; and: "Right. I'll tell him. *Na* Jik, you'll come topside now; Tirun's on her way."

"Geran," Pyanfar said on bridge-com, "Jik's in your charge. Best I can do." There was the matter of Jik's hands, which would heal of injuries in the several day subjective transit before systemfall; but recuperation and jump was not a matter she wanted to open up with Geran at the moment. "I don't much want him on your elbow, but I haven't got a place else to put him."

"I'll watch him."

Enough said, then. If Geran buckled there was still Tirun on Jik's other side. And that left Tully down at that end of the boards with Skkukuk. She might have put Khym in that seat. But Khym was getting used to the com board; he was actually worth something with it in a pinch. Putting Khym at Tirun's confusing second-switcher post handed him a system that had a completely different set of access commands. Tully could learn a sequence from scratch; Khym, jump-muzzy and in emergency, might touch a control he thought he knew. Disastrously.

"Yes, *Harukk*-com," Hilfy said. "That data is current. Captain, they're inquiring again on departure time and routing."

"It stands as instructed."

Uncoupling began, a series of crashes as *The Pride* disengaged itself from dock under Haral's signal to the other side of that station wall, and Haral's touch at the controls of her board. There was the low drone of Khym's voice, making routine advisements to the dockers and station com, and Hilfy's voice talking quietly to *Aja Jin* and *Moon Rising*.

"Captain," Tully said, "Tirun come."

"Got that," Pyanfar murmured.

If Tirun was on her way, that was the last and they were going to make schedule easily. So much the better with nervous kif all about. Pyanfar flicked her ears and settled her nerves, while *The Pride*'s operating systems made noise enough to mask the lift and rob them of other cues to movement in the ship. There were the telltales on the board—if she chose to key the matrix over to access-monitor. Her nose twitched at the mere thought of Skku-kuk in proximity. She dared not take the allergy pills. She needed her reflexes. She rubbed her itching nose fiercely with the back of her hand, curled her lip, and looked up at the convenient reflection in a dead monitor as the gleam of the lift's internal light reflected a motley assortment of silhouettes in the distance down the corridor at her back.

Her eyes flicked to the chrono.

2304.

"*Moon Rising* reports all ready," Hilfy said.

"Got that," Haral said.

Tahar was showing off. Flouting the schedule on the short side. Which took work.

Tahar clan was Tahar clan, even when it owed Chanur its mortgaged hide.

The lift door had closed back there. The shadows in the reflective glass had come closer. Pyanfar slowly rotated her chair to face the last-comers. Courtesy. Tirun walked beside Jik, Jik beside Skkukuk's dark-robed shape. They had washed Jik's clothes for him, had not even dared have clean ones couriered over from *Aja Jin,* for fear of rousing kifish suspicions. And someone of the crew must have lent him the bracelet on his arm. The kif had robbed him of the gaudy lot of chain he usually wore.

"This person," Skkukuk said the moment he got through the door, "this *person* refuses your order, *hakt'*."

"He means the gun," Tirun said.

"We don't carry firearms up here," Pyanfar said patiently. With spectacular patience, she thought. "Nor do we change captains under fire." With an internal shudder and a thought toward Jik: *I hope.* "Tirun will give you instructions. If you're that good, *prove it.*"

So much for kifish psych.

But the son moved. Jik was still looking at her.

"How my ship?" he asked, very quiet, very civilized. She would not have been that restrained, under similar circumstances.

"Hilfy, give his station that comflow on receiving only."

"Aye," Hilfy said. "It's in."

"That's scan two," Pyanfar said, meaning seat assignment; and he gave a short, more than decent nod of his dark head and went to belt in, wincing a bit as he sat down. He spoke quietly to Geran; and Pyanfar found her claws clenched in the upholstery: she released her grip, carefully; and turned her seat around again.

2313.

"We're on count," Haral said. "*Aja Jin* reports ready. We're on."

"Standby."

"We going to show the *hakkikt* punctuality?"

She considered the potential for provocation. Considered the kif. And considered another possibility as she put their engines live. There was another set of switches by her hand, safety-locked by a whole string of precautions which they had a program now to bypass. Input three little codes and that set of key-slots would light. And *The Pride* would have a last chance to take out a space station full of kif, a handful of innocent methane-breathers; a doublecrossing allied ship that held one of two plans for a mahen hegemony over the Compact; a kif who was very close to having a kifish hegemony, and who with cold intent, threatened the whole hani species. Half the whole problem in the Compact was sitting right here at this station, with the solution within reach of her hand; and for one ship to take out half the problems in the immediate universe was not a bad trade, as trades went.

It also assured by default the immediate success of their rivals, whose intentions were also mahen and kifish hegemonies, maybe a human one, a methane-breather action, and the immediate collapse of the stsho and then the *han* into the control of one or the other hegemonies. Which meant years of bloody fighting. Not taking into account

humanity, which was already at odds within its own compact, and whose ships they knew were armed.

Take out one set of contenders here or make Jik's throw
for him and play power against power.

She was not even panicked in contemplating that sequence
of bypasses. She felt only a numb detachment: she could give
it, and only Haral would know; Haral would look her way
with a slight flattening of the ears and never pass the warning
to the crew. Just a look that said: *I know. Here we go.*

Perhaps Haral was thinking the same thing about now,
that it was one last chance, while their nose was still into
the station's gut and they were an indisputable part of station mass. Haral went on flicking switches, the shut-down
of certain systems no longer necessary, along with the check
of systems-synchronization and docking jets.

2314.

"We break on the mark," Pyanfar said in the same tone
in which they threw those checkout sequences back and
forth. "Advise them down the line. Advise station."

"Aye," Haral said. "Hilfy."

"I got it," Hilfy said.

The minute ticked down.

2314.46.

"On mark," Pyanfar said. "Grapple."

Clang. The station withdrew its grip.

Thump. They withdrew their own as the chrono hit 2315;
and Pyanfar hit the docking jets. Precisely. And hard. *G*
shifted, momentum carrying them in a skew the jets cor-
rected, and more so, as *The Pride* left the boom and the
hazard of collision with the kifish ship down-wheel from
them.

Another *G* shift, no provision for groundling stomachs,
as she sent *The Pride* axis-rolling on a continual shove of
the docking jets.

"Show those bastards," Haral muttered beside her. As
The Pride finished her roll with never a wasted motion,
precisely-angled the jets and underwent outbound impulse.

"*Aja Jin*'s cleared on mark," Geran said. "Precisely."

Pyanfar flicked her ears, rings jingling, and her heart
picked up.

Show these bastards indeed. That was a fancy new engine

rig *The Pride* carried, the ratio of those broad jump vanes to her unladed mass was way up since Kshshti; and any kif who saw *The Pride* and *Aja Jin* move out in close tandem, would remark the peculiar similarity between their outlines, give or take the cargo holds which were firmly part of *The Pride* and which were stripped off the hunter-ship's lean gut and spine.

"Tahar's away."

Routine out to startup. The mains cut in on mark; *Aja Jin* was on the same instant, and Tahar, playing the same insolent game.

It was quiet on the bridge. No chatter, none of the talking back and forth between stations that was normal, all of them kin and all of them knowing their jobs well enough to get them done through all the back-and-forth. They were not all kin on this trip. And none of them were in the mood. Only she looked over at Haral, the way she had looked a thousand times in *The Pride*'s voyages; it was reflex.

Haral caught it and looked back, a little dip of one ear and a lift of her jaw, a cheerfulness unlike Haral's dour business-only blank.

Same face she might have turned her way if she had decided to blow the ship. Pyanfar made a wry pursing of her mouth and gave the old scoundrel the high sign they had once, in their wilder days, passed each other in bars.

They had a word for it. Old in-joke. *Meet you at the door.*

She drew a wider breath and flexed her hands, reached across and put the arm-brace up, when they would need it.

She had never been so outright scared in her life.

"Coming up," Haral said finally. But she knew that. The numbers kept ticking off to jump. They took the outbound run with less haste than they could use, on the mark the kif gave them. There was a little leisure, a little chance for crew to stand up and stretch and flex minds as well as bodies; but no one left the bridge. Not even Geran.

She's asleep, Geran had said when Pyanfar offered her the chance to leave scan and take a fast walk back to Chur's cabin while they were inertial and under ordinary rotation. So that was that. Pyanfar gnawed her mustaches and offered no comforts; Geran was not one to want two words on a topic where one had said it, and she was focused down tight; took her little stretch by standing up beside her chair, and kept her eye still to her proper business; answered Jik's rare comments with a word or two.

"Tully," Pyanfar said, "get ready."

"I do," he said. He had his drugs with him, the drugs that a human or a stsho needed in jump. He prepared to go half to sleep in his chair, sedated so heavily he could hardly stay upright.

Interesting to contemplate—a horde of human ships, all of them that automated. Like facing that many machines.

Set to do what? React to buoys and accept course without a pilot's intervention?

Defend themselves? Attack? A horde of relentless machines whose crews had committed themselves to metal decisions and a computer's morality, because their kind had no choice?

Stsho did that, because stsho minds also had trouble in jumpspace; but stsho were nonviolent.

Gods, so gods-be little he says, so little he's got the words for.

"Tully. Are human ships set to fire when they leave jump?"

He did not answer at once.

"Tully. You understand the question?"

"Human fire?"

"Gods save us. Do their machines—fire after jump? Can they?"

"Can," Tully said in a small voice. "Ship be ##."

Translation-sputter.

"Captain," Hilfy said, "he's got to go out now. Got to."

His mind was at risk. "Go to sleep," Pyanfar said, never looking around; his back would be mostly to her anyway, the bulk of the seat in the way.

"Not trust human," Tully said suddenly.

"Go *out*," Hilfy said sharply. "You want me to put that into you? *Do it.*"

While the chronometer got closer and closer to jump.

"Tully," Pyanfar said. "Good night."

"I go," he said.

"He's got it," Tirun said. "He's all right."

"We're on count," Haral said.

"You give me com we come through," Jik said.

"*Aja Jin* has its orders." They had talked through that matter already. Jik made a last try.

And: "You got anything last minute you want to own up to?" she asked. "Jik?"

"I damn fool," he said.

"Count to ten," Haral said, and the numbers on the corner of the number-one monitor started ticking away.

"Take her through," Pyanfar said. They did that, traded off; and she suddenly decided on the stint at exit.

"Got it," Haral said. That section of the board that pertained to jump was live. "Referent on, we got our lock."

Star-fixed and dead-on. It was a single-jump to Meetpoint from dusty Kefk, with its armed guardstations and its grim gray station—

—to the white light and opal subtleties of a stsho-run station.

If that was what was still there.

"Going," Haral said.

Down. . . .

They stopped being at Kefk.

. . . *Gods save us,* Pyanfar thought, which thought went on for a long long timestretch.

She dreamed of ships in conflict in their hundreds, burning like suns.

Of strange gangling beings that had walked the dock once at Gaohn, sinister in their numbers and their resemblance to a creature she had befriended (but too many of them, and too sudden, and with their Tully-like eyes all blue and strange and malevolent). They carried weapons, these strangers; they talked among themselves in their chattering, abrupt speech, and laughed their harsh alien laughter out loud, which echoed up and down the docks.

What do they want? she asked Tully then, in that dream.

Look out for them, he said to her. *And one of them drew a gun and aimed it at them both.*

What does it say? Pyanfar asked when it spoke.

But the gun went off and Tully went sprawling without a sound; in slow motion the tall figure turned the weapon toward her—

Chapter 5

. . . it went off.

The Pride made the drop into realspace and Pyanfar blinked, gasped a breath, and felt an acute pain about the heart which confused her entirely as her eyes cleared on *The Pride*'s boards and blinking lights and her ears received the warning beeps from com: *Wake up, wake up, wake up—*
Meetpoint?

Her eyes found the data on the screen, blurred and focused again with a mortal effort. "We're on," she said around the pounding of her heart, "Haral, we're on."

And from elsewhere, distant and echoing in and out of space: *"Chur, do you hear me? Do you hear?"*

From still another: *"We've got passive signal. Captain! We're not getting buoy here. They've got Meetpoint image blanked!"*

"Gods and thunders. Geran!"

"I'm on it, I'm already on it, captain."

—Hunting their partners, who could make a fatal mistake in a jump this close, looking for the first sign of signal, and themselves rushing in hard toward Meetpoint, into crowded space, where the scan's bounce-back could only tell them things too late and passive reception might not have all the data. They were blind. Meetpoint wanted them that way. It was somebody's trap.

"Priority," Hilfy said. "Buoy warning: *dump immediately.*"

"Belay that," Pyanfar said. With two ships charging up behind them out of hyperspace, she had no wish to have herself slowing down in their path. Collision to fore was an astronomical possibility; behind was a statistical probability.

And the kif who gave them orders meant business.

"Acquisition," Geran said, "your one, Haral."

"Your two," Haral said; and id chased the image to Pyanfar's number-two monitor. *Aja Jin* was in.

"What've we got here? Geran—"

"I'm working on it. We got stuff all over the place on passive, nobody outputting image, lot of noise, *lot* of noise, we got ships here—"

"Mark," Haral said, "less twenty seconds."

"That's it, that's it, brace for dump."

She sent it to auto; *The Pride* lurched half into hyperspace again and fell out with less energy—

—gods, gods, sick as a novice— What in a mahen hell's in this system? Come on, Geran. Get it sorted. O gods— At forty-five percent of Light. With the system rushing up in their faces. Their own signal going out from that traitor buoy at full Light. Themselves about to become a target for someone. She fumbled after the foil containers at her elbow, bit through one and let the salt flood chase down the nausea. There was a meeting of unpleasant tides somewhere behind the pit of her throat and her nose and hands and the folds of her body broke out in sickly sweat. "Geran. *Get me ID.*"

"Working, I'm working."

Dump fouling up the scan; nothing where it ought to be, the comp overloaded with input and trying to make positional sense out of it before it got around to analyzing ship IDs.

"Multiple signal," Hilfy said. "Nothing clear yet. Multispecies."

"Arrival," Jik said. "*Moon Rising* is in."

"On the mark," Haral said. "Second dump, stand by."

Taking it down fast. The pain in her chest refused to leave. The nausea all but overcame her; but she hit the control anyway—

—down again.

—Gangling figures against white light. *Captain,* a voice said, and Chur was there with the light shining about her, in the midst of a long black hallway, and shafts of light spearing past her as she moved in the slightest. She turned her shoulder and looked back into the light—

—"*Chur—*"

—they cycled through again, back in realspace. And the

weakness that ran through her was all-enveloping. She fought it back and groped after another of the packets. Bit into it and drank the noisome stuff down in a half dozen convulsive gulps.

"We got signal on *Moon Rising*," Geran's voice reached her, indistinct; she heard Tully talking, some half-drunken babble.

"Chur," he was saying. "Chur, you answer. Please you answer."

No sound out of Chur, then. It might still be the sedative. The machine would knock her out in stress. They had plenty of it. Pyanfar blinked again, flexed her right arm in the brace, withdrew it and shoved the mechanism aside, out of her way. Her hands shook. She heard the quiet, desperate drone of Tully's alien voice: *"Chur, Chur, you hear?"*

While Geran battled the comp for ID they desperately needed. Mind on business.

"We got recept on Meetpoint," Hilfy said. "Lot of output. Busy in there. I'm trying to link up with our partners, get a fix on those ships—"

"We've got to keep going," she muttered. "Got to. No gods-be choice. Blind. We got our instructions, we got—"

"Kif," Skkukuk said suddenly. "Kifish output!"

"Audio two," Hilfy said.

It was. Some kifish ship was transmitting in code. Unaware of them yet, it might be. Or close enough to have picked them up, inbound from Kefk. "Going to have an intercept down our necks any minute," she muttered, and sweated. "Akkhtimakt. He's on guard here. Or he's running the whole gods-be station—"

"Image, *priority*," Geran said. "My gods."

Passive scan came up with resolution, a haze to this side, to that, all in differing colors indicating different vectors and slow, virtually null-movement, relative. Big hazy ball where Meetpoint ought to be. Haze to zero-ninety-minus sixty. Haze to minus seventy-thirty-sixty. Another ball out to one-ten. The only thing that made sense was the Given in the system, the Meetpoint Mass itself, big and dark and dead from its eons-old formation. And the station itself. The rest—

"Khym," Pyanfar snapped. "Interior com. Tully! Audio one. Listen sharp. We don't know what we've got here. Could be humans, could be anything. Whatever we got, it's a lot of it."

"Got it," Khym said; and: "Got," from Tully.

The comp main panel between Haral and Hilfy was a steady flicker of inter-partition queries and action from this and that side of its complex time-sharing lobes. Like the lunatic tc'a: it had several minds to make up, and they were all busy.

She rubbed her chest where the pain had settled and swiped the back of the same hand across an itch on her nose.

And listened to Khym trying over and over again to raise Chur on the com.

"Chur," he cried suddenly. "Geran—I got her, she's answering! Chur, how are you?"

She was alive back there. Someone switched Chur's answer through. It was scatologically obscene.

Pyanfar drew one painful breath and another.

"Thank the gods," Haral murmured in a low voice. And from Khym: "*Ker* Chur, we have a problem just now—"

"That's stsho," Hilfy said. "I'm picking up something near the station. Stsho. And hani. More than one. You got data coming, Geran, Jik.—I hear that." To someone on com. And Geran:

"Gods rot it, I'm working." Then: "Yeah, just take it easy, hear?"

"I got," Jik said quietly. "They be here they don't—"

"Ten minutes station AOS," Haral said. "Mark."

Pyanfar drew another breath and flexed her hands. "Hilfy, output to Meetpoint traffic control: coming in on standard approach."

"Aye, done, standard approach data in transmission."

"*Aja Jin* make dump," Jik said.

"Stand by our final."

The wavefront of their arrival had not yet gotten to Meetpoint central. The robotic beacon in the jump range knew as much as its AI brain was capable of knowing anything; but the buoy was not communicating data back to them even after it had had time to receive their ID squeal.

It was certain that it was a trap. Stsho had no nerve sufficient to antagonize an armed enemy, blinding them as they came in. It was what they hired guards to do.

"No telling where Sikkukkut is," Pyanfar muttered. "It'd take him maybe another hour to get that lot away from Kefk. But he's fast."

"Kkkkt," Skkukuk said, which sound sent the hair up on her back. Not a comment except that click which meant a thousand things. "You all right back there: Skkukuk, you all right?" she asked the kif. And deliberately pleased the bastard. It was a genuine question; nourishment for him was a problem. *No gods-be little vermin on my bridge,* was her ultimatum; and Skkukuk had come up with his own answer. Straight simple-sugars and water, into a vein.

"Kkkkt," he said again. "Yes, hakt'." Doubtless coming to a whole array of mistaken kifish conclusions about his status, the crew's, Jik's and Tully's; that elongate, predatory brain was set up to process that kind of information constantly, inexorable as a star in its course. Claw and crawl and climb. With a sense of humor only when it was in the ascendancy and demonstrating its power.

Creator Gods, if You made that, You must've had something in mind. But what?

"Imaging," Tirun said; "priority channel four."

"Your two," Haral said; but that change was already there, the hazy ball of Meetpoint separating into a whole globe of points. So did one of the other patches of haze. Another remained indistinct.

"We got a lot of company," Haral said.

It was a swarm for sure. A monstrous swarm sitting around Meetpoint station, like insects around a corpse.

"Migods," she murmured.

Another blur materialized. About ten minutes Light off station nadir. Unresolved yet, and small. It could get a lot wider.

"There's another one," Haral said; on the second Geran and Jik both came in on com.

"Got that," Pyanfar muttered, her mind half there, half on what the comp was bringing up, color-code spotted into the station-mass that said *stsho/hani ID.*

More IDs. There were stsho and hani in the station imaging, there were mahendo'sat and kif outlying. But not a single methane-breather in the output, which could mean that imaging had ignored them; or that no methane-breather was outputting; or that the methane-breathers had gotten the wind up them at some time earlier in events and lit out for their own territories.

"Captain," Geran said.

"I got it, I got it."

"Not a methane-breather anywhere," Haral muttered. "I don't like this."

"Got to be Akkhtimakt out there," Tirun said. "Looks like we got a real standoff here."

"Mahen ships out there," Pyanfar said. "Goldtooth, I'll bet you that, eggs to pearls. And too many ships. Gods, *look* at that."

"Humans," Haral said in a low voice. *Not* on bridge-com; voice-only.

"Yeah."

Tully knows it. Got to know it. He's not deaf. Not blind either.

"Pyanfar," Jik said. "Give com."

"In your own hell I will. Sit still."

Stsho and hani sitting there dead at dock with kif in full view, kifish ships with the advantage of position and startup time and the mass of Meetpoint's dark dwarf to pull them in?

But so had those other blotches on scan, mahen and alien. Standoff for sure.

We got troubles, gods, we got troubles.

"Hilfy: to both our partners; stand by hard dump, at the 2 unit mark; gods-be if we're going into that. Hard dump and brake. We're going to sit."

"You got damn kif come in here behind us, upset ever'thing!" Jik cried. "Give com, dammit, I talk!"

"Sit still while you got ears!"

"*Aja Jin*'s outputting," Hilfy said. "Jik. Translate."

Faster than the mechanical translation.

"They make ID. Say hello to Ana. Say got kif coming behind us."

"Gods rot them." Monitors flicked and shifted. They were being inundated with com input, faster than their operators could handle it. Transcriptions were coming over. Kifish com. Hani ships were standing out from station.

Stsho were in panic. Their wavefront had gotten to the station but not to the outliers they had seen on passive. Three more minutes for Akkhtimakt's kif to notice them. Seven for the unidentifieds that might be mahendo'sat. Eight for the ones farthest out, who might be human. And double that for response time. "We're going to have kif up our backsides."

"You going have damn kif break through system, they don't stop, you hear? Pyanfar! Give com!"

"Shut it up. Haral! Dump us down."

Haral hit the switches. *The Pride* shed *V* in a single lurch to a lower state; space went inside out—

 . . . another lurch. The universe spun once about. . . .
       . . . revised itself.

Instruments cleared. Broke up again with a heartstopping jolt and cleared, some ship too near them and themselves displaced off their nav-fix as the field popped them down the gravity-slope.

The rate was far less. Easy from here. Two more blips reappeared: *Moon Rising* and *Aja Jin* matched them and came *down* again widely spaced from them and a little to the rear.

"Reacquire," Geran said.

"Com output to my board," Pyanfar said; and when the light went on: "All ships: this is Pyanfar Chanur, *The Pride of Chanur*. Take precautions; all station personnel, go to innermost secure areas. Maintain order. All ships drop to low-*V* for your own protection.—We have limited time. This is *The Pride of Chanur* and allied ships urging all ships to maintain position and take no action. The *hakkikt* Sik-kukkut is inbound with a large number of ships. Take precautions—"

"Sheshe sheshei-to!" Jik cried. And Geran:

"Priority, Priority!" Geran cried, as the scan-monitor went red all across the top, with a breakout behind them like plague in the jumprange.

"Gods-be!" Pyanfar cried; and hit the alarm.

Useless. With ships coming up their backsides and under their bellies at *V* that could cross a planetary diameter in seconds. The informational wavefront was on them at *C* and the ships a fraction behind it—

Instruments jumped and went crazy. Her heart slammed

in her chest, and the first firing of panicked neurons said
they were dying—the second, that they had not died and
the encounter was over in nanoseconds.

It passed like a storm. It was inbound to Meetpoint with
a dopplered flare of output, like devils screaming down on
the damned, Meetpoint with minutes left and mortal reflexes hopeless of mounting any response—

"O gods," she said for the third time. It came out with
what felt like the last of her breath.

"Give com," Jik yelled. *"Give—"*

"Stay in your seat!" Tirun snarled back.

"Priority, com," Hilfy snapped. "Tully!"

And hard on that a stream of alien language, Tully's
voice, rapid-paced: ". . . to all ships," the words turned up
on monitor, translator-function. "This is # Tully ###, ask
you # stay #####—"

Total breakup. Whatever he was speaking, it was not in
the com-dictionary.

"Damn," Jik said. "Ana!"

While a mass of kifish output raced ahead of them, *Sikkukkut,* howling down on the station, nadir-bound, past a
stationful of stsho who could not fight; and a cluster of hani
ships who might try. And die doing it.

"Gods curse that bastard," Pyanfar muttered, and something hurt deep in her gut, diminishing that pain about her
heart. "Gods curse him. Haral. To my boards. Hilfy: tell
our partners stand by. Haral: course to Urtur."

"Aye," Hilfy said.

"Do it," Pyanfar said, "Haral."

A code flashed to her screen. *Priority four. Personnel
emergency.* From Tirun's hand.

"Pyanfar!" Jik's voice. She spun the chair, saw Jik unbuckled and rising to his feet as Khym scrambled for his
and Skkukuk moved faster still.

But Jik stopped. Stopped still. So did everything else
when she held up a hand. "Pyanfar, you got give me
com—"

"Aja Jin's outputting code," Hilfy said. "Inputting to
code faculty, Haral."

"Jik," Pyanfar said, "I don't want my crew hurt. Don't
want you hurt. You're about to give me no choice. You
hear me?"

"Damn fool hani, that be *Mahijiru,* Ana be wait signal—
he get your message, he go from here. He got go from
here. I give you message. You send: say *Sheni.* He understand, give you same cooperation. *I tell truth, Pyanfar.*"

"Directive to that ship can't go out from here," she said,
ears flat. All but deaf. Her heart was pounding. "You trying
to fry us good, Jik? Mahen ships are dead-stopped out
there. They're caught, same as hani are. We haven't got a
choice here and Sikkukkut isn't just real pleased with us to
start with. Khym. Skkukuk. I think you better get Jik off
the bridge."

"No! Pyanfar! Damn fool, you need me. Need me here.
You send message!"

"I can't trust you. I'm going to ask you to leave. Quietly.
Right now. Or you sit in that chair."

Jik's hand tightened on the chair back. Not going to
move, she thought; it seemed forever. Khym would never
delay so long. Time spooled itself out the way it did in
jump. She had to think of her own ship; and of the gun in
her pocket. *I'll use it, Jik; I'd use it if you made me, for
godssakes, don't, don't make me, I've got my ship to
protect—*

He moved to put himself in the chair. And she let go the
breath she had forgotten, and spun her chair back again.

The translations were multiplying on the screen. *Aja Jin*
was spilling out everything, a flood of com-sent explanations, coded and headed out toward the mahen ships. Tully
was still sending on their com, never having stopped. It was
a guess what he was sending. Saying everything they could
not, dared not, in a code no one could crack.

Treason against the *hakkikt.* Perhaps against them.

Or against humankind itself.

But what did the *hakkikt* expect, sending them in first,
to paralyze the system—when his own arrival hard upon
their own would send ships running like leaves in the wind?

She switched that to Jik's monitor. Silent comment.

It's getting done, Jik. And it may kill all of us.

Tully's output made no sense at all, misapplications or
coded applications of vocabulary driving the translator to
lunacy. What came out of *Aja Jin* achieved syntax. It made
no sense in some of its parts. But did in others. They were
onto those codewords. If Kesurinan over there had truly

suspected something she might have used some alternate; it was a guess that the mahendo'sat *had* alternates. But Kesurinan did not suspect. That was the best guess: Kesurinan did not suspect that they had those words at least; or that Jik would have given them out against his will, to a ship that had a mahen-given translation program.

While the ship hurtled on at its reduced V and duty stations talked back and forth to each other in muted voices and the blip and click of instruments and boards.

For Jik it was already past. And there was the kif in front of him, and hani who had kept him from his ship at a moment that might prove decisive in all history.

She found not a thing to say either.

Sikkukkut's kif hurtled on toward attack on Akkhtimakt and on Goldtooth and the humans, if that was what that mass was out there. While the stsho and any other noncombatants on that station abided the outcome in helpless terror.

"Priority," Geran said. Scan went red-bordered, a group of outlier ships went from stationary blue to the blinking blue of a low-V ship from which passive-recept had picked up some activity. Like engine-firing.

Akkhtimakt.

Her claws dug into the upholstery. "What AOS are they on?"

"That's our message," Tirun said. "They don't know Sikkukkut's here yet. That AOS is coming up minus three. I've got ID on some of those hani ships at station. Negative on Ehrran. That's *Harun's Industry* and *The Star of Tauran,* stsho ship *Meotnis;* hani vessel *Vrossauru's Outbounder; Pauraun's Lightweaver; Shaurnurn's Hope—*"

Old names. Spacer names. The clans of Araun. Pyanfar heard them and clenched her hands on the arms of the chair.

As the color-shift on Akkhtimakt's kif went over from blue to blinking green. To purple, like the image on Sikkukut's ships. But a double hand of Sikkukkut's ships were shifting down, going brighter blue-green, and two brighter still. Different assignments. Stopping in midsystem. Where they could shift vector and strike at Meetpoint Station. Or at the mahendo'sat.

"Priority," Geran said.

"I got that," she said. "Sikkukkut's got his tail guarded, he does."

"AOS on our message," Tirun said, monotone. "Akkhtimakt's present position."

"Gods." *Vector, gods rot it, Geran. What's Akkhtimakt's vector?* "Geran, can you get me a—"

The projection took shape. "Priority, priority," Geran said. And her answer came up two-vectored, one part of Akkhtimakt's group bound nadir, twenty ships for Urtur and ten for Kshshti. Her heart seized up and beat painfully against the stress.

"Gods and thunders."

"Sikkukkut may just chase 'em," Haral said. "Gods send he chases 'em clear to Urtur, get him by the gods out of here."

"Give me com," Jik said in a low voice. As if he had no hope of it already. "Give me com. I talk to Ana—"

But suddenly Goldtooth's image was blinking too. Imminent motion, as yet undefined in the comp. The doppler shift could tell it what it had, and comp was working on the precise figure.

"Pyanfar."

"*No,* gods rot it. *Gods-be,* that bastard's just AOS on that move of Akkhtimakt's and he's losing no time taking out of here. Whatever *Aja Jin* sent may not reach him before he goes. Running. Where? How far's he going?"

"Not know," Jik aid.

"Outsystem? Turn around and come in?"

"Give com. I tell him, he do! Code. God! Kif not break fast enough! Give com."

"You might not catch him. And he might not listen. And that leaves us with the kif, doesn't it? *All* alone; and us transmitting to his enemies in code. No thanks."

While, beside them and behind, *Aja Jin* kept quiet. Perhaps Kesurinan believed that that order for silence came from Jik, relayed because he was not on the bridge; or Kesurinan still trusted. Perhaps.

"Mahen ships are AOS of our number-two message," Tirun droned placidly, their relativity-timekeeper, while disaster went on shaping up around them. "Going to be a while on Kesurinan's. It may not make it."

The Goldtooth-human aggregate went green. Retreating. Faster and faster.

Jik swore. In mahensi. "All way doublecross. Pyanfar. You, me, Ana. Damn, *damn!*"

"Shut it down."

"Kif—damn, kif do this thing, you don't go in fight, don't go in, Pyanfar."

"That, you got. No way are we going into that."

While the recent past unfolded on the screen, the computer struggling to make sense of it and sending out image that had two shades of the same kifish color on the ID monitor.

"Gods-be fool kif've hardly dumped," Haral muttered at her side. "Carrying sixty-five of light. Gods, *look* at that."

"I'd rather not," she said back. And felt sick at the stomach. Felt a tremor in all her limbs. "Bastard's got enough *V* to hyper out of here, right up Akkhtimakt's tail."

"Dangerous," Haral said. Meaning collisions on the other side, where they would drop down into the well at Urtur not knowing the trim and the precise capacity on the ships ahead of them. It was asking for it.

And the godscursed mahendo'sat were leaving system. *Abandoning* them. There were other conclusions, but none of them were enough to pin hope on. Knowing Goldtooth, whose priorities were all mahendo'sat.

That's one more I owe you, Goldtooth, you bastard.

We got hani ships at station. We got three hundred thousand stsho who can't defend themselves.

She reached after the last of the food packets by her chair and got it down; her mouth tasted of dry fuzz and copper. She was aware of loose fur rubbing between her skin and the chair leather; of hair sticking to the console-rim where it had rubbed from her arm; sweat had soaked her trousers and made the leather of the seat moist wherever she touched it.

Once at Urtur Akkhtimakt might turn about and come back with *V* on his side. Even if it took four months. But beyond Urtur was hani territory; the conflict might keep going.

Four months out and back, again and again and again. Years of maneuvering as the ground-bound saw it. Mere weeks in the time-stretch of ships that made virtually no system-time at all. Years of fighting, with ship-crews caught in virtual stasis, unaged.

How does anything survive in that kind of lunacy? What have we got at the end of it?

Gods fry him, what game is Goldtooth playing now? Him and the humans. All running. What in a mahen hell good are they?

What doublecross are the humans planning?

What did Tully tell them?

"Priority," Hilfy said. "Message from Sikkukkut: quote: Dock and hold the station."

Got our orders, do we? Kiss the hakkikt's feet, do his work, move at his order. Go in there like a bunch of gods-be pirates?

I wish I were dead before this.

"Advise *Aja Jin* and Tahar," she said.

"Aye," Hilfy said. And a moment later: "They acknowledge: final message: *Going on your signal.*"

We're worrying about what Goldtooth's doing. What Akkhtimakt's doing. We forget one important thing: Sikkukkut's no fool. He's had time to think this thing through. He's got something planned. He's thinking ahead of Akkhtimakt. Gods, what's the next move?

"Put us in," she said.

"Aye," said Haral. And began to lay course. They were moving in approximately the right vector. Haral hit the directionals and they started hammering off the *V*, turning, bringing the mains to bear on it. *Those* cut in, a one-*G* push, sudden and solid against the downward *G* they had from the rotation, a steady discomfort.

"Chur all right back there?" she asked. "Khym?"

"Chur's asked," Khym said, "What we're doing. I've tried to explain. I think she's drugged. She says she wants free of the machine. I said no, we had enough trouble."

"We got enough trouble," she muttered, and punched in all-ship. "Chur, we're all right. We got our hands full up here, huh? Just don't worry your sister."

"Aye," Chur's voice came back to her. She had been Geran's partner at that board. Now she lay listening while scan tried to track a Situation multiplied by fives and worse. "Geran, I'm . . . going to sleep . . . gods-be machine."

"*G*-stress," Pyanfar said.

Is it? Gods, cousin, hang on.

"We're headed into station," Geran said. "Hear that, sister of mine?"

"Got it," Chur murmured. It sounded like that. But she was far from the pickup.

The mains cut in, hard acceleration. And cut out again.

"We're on," Haral said. "We're going to be inertial. Take our time getting in there."

Preserve our options. Haral was reading her mind again. And inertial-time was rest-time.

She dropped her hand from the boards and sat there a moment while her muscles went weak and she was not at all certain that she could stand up. The interval between the two groups of kif narrowed further and further, changes perceptible only in the data-tags, but definitive. That would go on for the better part of an hour till someone got in position to do something. Jump and shoot, respectively. Then it remained to see what Sikkukkut would do.

Leave us to hold onto Meetpoint while he chases that bastard down?

Us to hold Meetpoint with Goldtooth loose? Goldtooth's taking his options. He won't jump till he has to, he wants to know what Sikkukkut's doing; and Sikkukkut's going to give him no options, going to follow right on his tail till he jumps. There's some small chance that Sikkukkut might leave if he can get Goldtooth out. He might rip loose everything he can pirate here and go for Akkhtimakt at Urtur. Akkhtimakt's got to go slow on the turnaround there, all that gods-be dust. Got to. Then Sikkukkut could catch him up and hammer him good.

If we knew Goldtooth's mind. Kifish ships are going to run up his backside, make him jump for Tt'av'a'o, they got V on him, he's got no choice either.

And once Goldtooth goes, he and the humans've got a three, four month turnaround to get back here. Gods, think, Pyanfar! What are *the options?*

"Tirun. Take watch. All the rest of you, you're off. Get something to eat. Geran, you're cleared aft; Skkukuk, belowdecks. Take what you can set. Jik. You I want to talk to."

Seats moved, restraints clicked open. Everyone was in

motion, Haral as well. Pyanfar turned her own chair and stopped. Jik still sat in his place, staring at the screens. Tirun was beside him, keeping her station. And Tully, though Hilfy had him by the elbow, lingered with a confused and sorrowful look toward the boards. Toward—gods knew, his own people starting off in retreat with Goldtooth, leaving him behind, perhaps forever, who knew? It was not a time to say anything. Pyanfar stared their way till Hilfy prevailed and they went out the door.

"Haral," she said. "Take the long break. Tirun, board to you, you go off when we get to final. Sorry about it."

"Got it," Tirun said hoarsely. "I'm fine, captain."

That left Jik to deal with. Khym had lingered in the corridor. She saw him standing down near Chur's door, looking back toward the bridge.

In case.

"Haral," she said in deepest and most impenetrable hani: "You want to bring me up a sedative. Something our guest can take. If we have to do that."

"Aye, captain," Haral said.

"I'll be in galley."

She wanted to be clean. She wanted to go back to her cabin and run herself under the shower. The whole bridge smelled like ammonia and hani and human and mahen sweat, an aroma even the fans did not totally disperse. But there was no time for that. It was far from over.

Even on this deck.

"Get me up," Chur said, with a move of an aching arm. "O gods, prop this gods-be bed up. I'm a mess."

"That's all right." Geran sat down on the bedside and checked the implanted tubes with a quick glance, bit a hole in the packet she had brought, and offered it to Chur. "Take this and you get the bed propped up."

"Unnhhn." The very thought hit her stomach and lay there indigestible. "Prop it first."

"You promise."

"Gods rot you, I'll rip your ears."

Geran touched a control and the bed inclined upward. Chur flexed her legs and shifted her weight and grimaced in pain as the arm with the implants shifted down. But

Geran, relentless, got an arm behind Chur's head and held the packet where she could drink.

It hit her stomach the way she had feared. "Enough," she said, "enough." And Geran had the sense to quit and just let her lie there drifting a moment, in that place she had discovered where the pain was not so bad. "Where's the shooting?" she asked finally.

"Hey, we ducked out of it."

Chur lay there a moment adding that up and rolled her head over where she could look at her sister, one long stare. "Where'd we duck to? Huh?"

"Kif are about to chew each other to rags about fifteen minutes off. We're headed to station for R & R. Maybe I'll buy you a drink, huh?"

"We take damage?" She recalled a lurch, like the thrust of the mains from the wrong angle . . . impossible to happen. Recalled a long hard acceleration, till the machine put her out cold. "Geran, what's the straight of it?"

"That is the straight of it. We're in one piece, we're going into station while the kif work it out. That's all."

Too gods-be cheerful, Geran. Whole lot too cheerful.

"Give me the truth," Chur said. "That's a gods-be dumb move. Sit at dock. Who knows what could come in? Huh? What's going on?"

"You want to try something solid?"

"No," she said flatly. And lay there breathing a moment, and turned her face toward Geran's stricken silence. Gods, the pain in Geran's face. "But I have to, don't I?" Her stomach rebelled at the thought. "Bit of soup, maybe. Nothing heavy. Don't push me, huh?"

"Sure," Geran said. Her ears had pricked up at once. Her eyes shone like a grateful child's. "You want the rest of this?"

O gods. Don't let me be sick. "Soup," she said, and clamped her jaws and tried not to think about it. "I rest, huh?"

"You rest," Geran said.

She shut her eyes, turning it all off.

You're still lying, Geran. But she did not have strength to face whatever it was Geran was lying about. She hoped not to discover. Her world limited itself to the pains in her joints and the misery of her arm and her back. The world could be right again if she could keep her stomach quiet and ease the pain a little. She just wanted not to throw up her guts again, and any problem more than that was more than she could carry.

It was impossible not to ask. But in a dim, weary way, with the data that came over the com all muddling in her head and promising nothing good at all, she thanked the gods Geran held back the answers.

"Jik," Pyanfar said.

Jik pushed himself back in his chair and looked at the board in front of him, its screens all dark and dead. And turned his chair then and stared at her across the width of the bridge.

A word was too much. Till she had something to offer him from her side. Time seemed to stretch further and further like the eeriness of jump. And there was no rescue and no way out of the impasse they were in. Him on *The Pride*'s bridge. *Aja Jin* ignorant and silent beside them.

His allies outbound. Unless by some monumentally unexpected turn the kif all went after their enemies and left them alone.

And none of them believed that.

Down the corridor the lift worked, and opened, and let Haral out. Pyanfar got up and went to the door of the bridge and out it, to intercept her in the hall; and Haral slipped her a couple of pills. "Thanks," she said; "you sure about this stuff."

"This'll make it sure," Haral said, and fished a flask out of her capacious pocket. Parini. Pyanfar took it and gestured with a move of her jaw back the way Haral had come. Haral went.

And Pyanfar turned back toward the bridge, where Jik sat quietly in his chair, caring not to turn it when she came up on him. She walked back to the fore of the bridge, and stood there looking back. "I want to talk to you. Private." Only Tirun was left with the boards; and she herself was not up to a hand-to-hand with a taller, heavier mahendo'-sat, even if he was jump-wobbly too. *Fool*, she thought. But some courses had to be steered. Even at risk to the ship.

"Come on," she said again. "Jik."

He got to his feet. She walked away, deliberately taking her eyes off him, though it was sure Tirun was alert to sudden moves.

But he came docilely after her, and followed her through the short corridor to the galley.

Tirun being Tirun, she would both monitor it all on the intercom and pass the word to all aboard that the galley had just gone offlimits.

She turned when she had gotten as far as the counter and the cabinet with the gfi-cups.

"Captain," Tirun said via com. *"Pardon. Goldtooth's group has started shifting out, first one just went. Before AOS on Kesurinan's message. Close, but they're not going to get it. Thought you'd want to know."*

"Huh," she said. "Pass that to the crew."

"Aye." The audio cut out. The com stayed live, its telltale still glowing on the wall-unit.

And Jik stood there, just stood, with a slump in his shoulders and a set like stone to his face. "Sit down," she said, and he did that, on the long bench against the wall, elbows on the table. She got a glass from the cabinet, the flask from her pocket, poured a shot of it and set it in front of him.

"No," he said.

"That's prescriptive. You drink. Hear?"

He took it then, and took a sip and shuddered visibly. Sat there looking nowhere. Thinking of friends, maybe. Of Goldtooth, outbound and not to return for months.

Of his ship, so close and himself helpless to reach them.

"Take another," she said. He did, shuddering after that one too, and that shudder did not stop. Liquor spilled out onto his hand, pooled on the table as he set the glass down. He put the hand to his mouth and sucked at the knuckle where it had spilled. His eyes glared at her.

She sat down, opposite him. If Tirun wanted her, there was the alarm. Her own aches could wait. She was prepared to wait. For whatever it took.

It was a long time before he moved at all, and that was to lift the glass and take it all down in one long stinging draught. He shuddered a third time, set the glass down empty and she filled it.

Got a crate of the stuff in storage. Pour it all down him if we have to.

"Hao'ashtie-na ma visini-ma'arno shishini-to nes mura'-ani hes." Whoever he was talking to, she did not follow it. Something about dark and cold. It was that dialect he spoke with Kesurinan. "Muiri nai, Pyanfar."

"Mishio-ne." *I'm sorry.*

"Hao. Mishi'sa." —*Yes. Sorry.* "Neshighot-me pau taiga?" *What the hell good is it?*

"None. I know that. Species-interest, Jik. I warned you of that. Now you can try to break my neck. It won't get you our access codes. What it will get you is a lot of grief. You don't want it; I don't want it. We're old friends. And you know down that one way's a lot of trouble and no good at all and down the other's a hani whose interests might be a lot the same as yours in the long run."

For a while he said nothing. After a while he picked up the glass again and took a tiny sip. "Merus'an-to he neishima kif, he?"

Something about damned kif, himself, and bargains.

"I want my people safe, Jik."

"You damn fool!" His hand came down on the table, jarring the liquid. "Give me com."

"So you can doublecross me again? No. Not this time. Too many lives here."

While pacifist stsho ran in gibbering terror in the corridors of their station and discovered there were species which could neither be hired nor bribed nor prevented from being predators.

"Humans," she said; "and mahendo'sat. If Tully's right, if Tully's telling the truth, and I think he is—there's one more doublecross in the works. The humans will betray Goldtooth. Hear? And you know and I know Sikkukkut's got to do something here. Your partner's going to push and herd the kif into fighting. He thinks. But in the meanwhile who does the bleeding? They'll herd him right away from mahen space. Right? Where does that leave? Stsho? Tc'a? Goldtooth's defending that. That leaves hani space—*friend.* You don't push me right now. My people have got *me* between them and *that,* and don't push me, Jik!"

"You—" Jik fell silent a moment, coughed and rested there with his mouth against his hand as if he had lost his way and his argument. "Merus'an-to he neishima kif. Shai."

Bargains and the kif again. Then: *I.* Or something like

that. He spoke mahensi. As if he had forgotten that he was not on his own ship. Or as if, exhausted as he was and wrung out, he lacked the strength to translate. He had that glassy look. Jump healed, but it took it out of a body too. And he had gone into it hurt, in body and spirit.

He was still reasonable. Still the professional, getting what he could get. She counted on that.

"I have to go in there to Meetpoint," she said. "I got to get what I can get. I won't doublecross you. Won't do any hurt to the mahendo'sat. I swear that, haur na ahur. But I don't want you against me either. I don't want you trying to get at controls, I don't want you trying to get at my crew. And everything you tell me's going to be a lie. Isn't it? Con the hani again." She fished in her pocket and laid the two pills on the table. "You take those when you want 'em. Nothing but sleeping pills. I got enough troubles. You got enough. You're strung. You know it. I want you to go out of here, mind your manners with my crew, get some sleep. That's all you can do. All I can do for you. Like a friend, Jik. But first I want to ask you: have you held out on me? Conned me? You got anything you think I better know? 'Cause we are going in there. And we're going to get blown to a mahen hell if this is a trap. And Sikkukkut just might not go with us, which would be a real shame."

He shoved the glass up against her hand. "You want talk? Take bit."

She had no business taking anything of the sort, straight out of jump, with a ship to handle in what was going on out there. But it was cheaper than argument. She picked up the glass and took a sip that hit her dehydrated throat and nasal passages like fire, and her stomach like an incandescence. She set the glass down and slid it across the table to touch his hand again. He sipped a bit more and blinked. Sweat moistened trails down his face and glistened on black fur; the dusky rim around his eyes was suffused with blood and they watered when he blinked. And after all that liquor on an empty stomach and straight from injuries and jump, he showed no sign of passing out.

"I want stay on bridge," he said. "Py-an-far. Same you don't trust me, this know. All same ask."

"I can't shut you up. I can't have you distracting my crew. I can't risk it. I'm telling you. I can't risk it. You

want your ship to survive this? You help me, gods rot
you, *cooperate.*"

He lifted his face then, his eyes burning.

"Survival, Jik. Is there anything we'd better know? Because we've got two kif out there fighting over everything
we've got, and gods rot it, I *hate* this, Jik, but we got no
gods-be *choice,* Jik!"

His mouth went to a hard line. He picked up the glass
and drank half the remainder. Shoved it across to her. "I
deal with that damn kif, set up whole damn thing." His
hand shook where it rested on the table. "*Drink,* damn
you, I don't drink without drink *with.*"

She picked it up and drank the rest. It hit bottom with
the rest and stung her eyes to tears.

"We got make friend this damn kif," he said, all hoarse.
"I don't know where Ana go, don't know what he do. We,
we got go make good friend this kif. This be *job,* a? Got
go be polite." A tic contorted his face and turned into a
dreadful expression. "Pyanfar. You, I, old friend. You, I.
How much you pay him, a?"

A chill went up her back and lifted the hair between her
shoulderblades. "I won't give you up to him. Not again."

"No." He reached across and stabbed a blunt-clawed
finger at her arm. "I mean truth. We got to, we *deal* with
this damn kif. You got to, you give him me, you give him
you sister, we got make surround—" His finger moved to
describe a half-circle in the spilled liquor. "Maybe Ana
damn fool. Maybe human lot trouble. We be con-tin-gency.
Con-tin-gency for whole damn Compact. We be inside.
Understand?"

"I don't turn you over to him again."

"You do. Yes. I do job. Same my ship. Same we got
make deal." His mouth jerked. "Got go bed this damn kif
maybe. I do. Long time I work round this bastard." He
shoved the glass at her again. "Fill."

"I'm not drinking with you. I got a—" —*ship to run.* She
swallowed that down before it got out. "Gods rot. You got
to get something real on your stomach." She filled the glass
and got up, jerked a packet of soup out of the cabinet and
tore the foil, poured it into a cup and shoved it under
the brewer. Steam curled up. It smelled of salt and broth,

promised comfort to a stomach after the raw assault of the parini. She took a sip herself and turned around to find him lying head on arms. "Come on," she said. "I'll drink this one with you, turn about. Hear? You take the pills."

He hauled himself off the table and took a sip of the cup. Made a face and offered it back.

One and one. She gave him the next sip. "Just keep going," she said. "I got a sick crewwoman to see about back there." Her stomach roiled. She still tasted the parini and she never wanted to taste it again in her life. But it was to a point of locking a friend into a cubbyhole of a prison and letting a kif loose as crew to walk the corridors where he liked. That was the way of things.

He was right. He was utterly right, and thinking, past all the rest of it.

They might have no choice at all.

"Come on," she said. "While you can walk. Going to put you to bed myself. Pills in the mouth, huh?"

"No." He picked them up and closed his fist on them. "I keep. Maybe need. Now I sleep. Safe, a? With *friend*."

He gathered himself up from the table. Staggered. And gained his balance again.

She motioned toward the number-two corridor. The back way toward the lift, that did not pass through the bridge, past delicate controls.

He cooperated. He went with her quietly, when he had every chance to try something. But that would be stupid, and gain him nothing, in a ship he could not control.

He had also told her nothing, for all his talking.

That in itself said something worrisome.

They went down to the lift; and down to the lower level; and as far as Tully's cabin, far forward. Next to Skkukuk's.

Tully was not there. That meant he was in crew quarters. That did not surprise her.

"Get some sleep," she said.

"A," he said. And parked his wide shoulders against the door frame, leaned there reeking of parini and looking as if he might fall on his face before he reached the bed.

"And don't forget the safety, huh?"

The next door opened. Skkukuk was there, bright-eyed and anxious to serve.

"You don't be fool," Jik said to her. *"Friend."*

And spun aside into the room and shut the door between them.

She locked it. And turned and looked at Skkukuk. "This man is valuable," she said. Kifish logic.

"Dangerous," Skkukuk said.

She walked off and left him there. Took out the pocket-com and used it and not the intercom-stations along the way. "Tirun, we got it all secure down here."

"Kif are pounding each other hard. We got approach contact from Meetpoint. Stsho are being extra polite, we got no trouble if the poor bastards don't Phase on us in mid-dock, I got no confidence I'm talking to the same stsho from minute to minute. Scared. Real scared. I got the feeling kif-com isn't being polite at all. Ships inbound are Ikkhoitr *and* Khafukkin."

"Gods. Wonderful. Sikkukkut's chief axe. You could figure."

"You going on break?"

"I'm coming up there." No way to rest. Not till they had an answer. Even if her knees were wobbling under her. She envied Jik the pills. But not the rest of his situation.

Tirun caught her eye as she walked onto the bridge and looked a further worried question at her. Tirun, who looked deathly tired herself. "No change," Tirun said. "Except bad news. Goldtooth's bunch had two chasers on his tail when he went out. Akkhtimakt's got to jump any minute now. Got to. He's getting his tail shot up. Some of those ships may not make it otherside. They got to clear out of here." Pyanfar looked. Everyone was still running for jump. The last of Goldtooth's company was gone. And a flock of stsho, fortunate in being out of range of all disasters and *not* being tied up dead-*V* at station. Not a sign of a methane-breather. Anywhere.

No hani was moving. They were caught at dock. And there was not a way in a mahen hell to get out vectored for hani space with the angle and the *V* Sikkukkut's two station-aimed ships had on them. *Ikkhoitr* and *Khafukkin* were going to make it in before their own three ships. Kif were going to have control of that dock, and gods help the hani who took exception to it.

"We got one more ship ID: a Faha. *Starwind*."

"Munur." That was a youngish captain. A very small ship. And a distant cousin of Hilfy's on her mother's side. Ehrran?"

"Not a sign."

"With Goldtooth or kited out of here home a long time ago. Want to lay odds which?" Exhaustion and nerves added up on her. She shivered, and a great deal of it was depletion. "Yeah. Stay on it." She indicated the direction of the galley and marshaled a steady voice. "Jik's going to rest a bit. He's plenty mad. And crazy-tired. I hope to the gods he takes those pills and settles down, but I don't think he'll do it. Pass out awhile, maybe. Maybe come to with a clearer head. Right now he's real trouble. He's not thinking real clear. Me, I'm not, either. We put his quarters on opscom when he wakes up. *Maybe* let him up here, I don't know yet. It's *my* judgment I don't trust. I'm going to clean up, pass out a few minutes. How are you holding?"

"I'm all right," Tirun said. It was usual sequence: Haral first on the cleanup; Haral first to snatch a little rest, Haral the one whose wits had to be sharpest and reflexes quickest, their switcher; and Haral generally shorted herself on rest-time to pay her sister for it. " 'Bout time, though." And before she could leave the chair she was leaning on: "Captain, Chur's wanting a bit of something hot. Geran went to the lowerdecks to fix it."

That was the best news since the drop. "Huh," she said. "Huh." With a little relaxation in tensed muscles. She shoved off and walked on down the corridor. She wanted food. Wanted a bath. Wanted, gods knew, to be lightyears away from all of this. But they did not have that choice. They could run for it and get out of Meetpoint system while Sikkukkut was busy. But he would find them; and anyone they were attached to. Their world was held hostage. Not mentioning the immediate threat to three hundred thousand gods-be stsho and a handful of hani ships.

A kif could not forget an insult.

No more than a hani forgot harm to her friends.

It was a quiet gathering down in crew quarters, in the central area where they had a microwave, and a little store of instant food: one of those amenities they had installed

along with the high-V braces and the AP weapons they had
acquired on the black market. A couple of little couches
and a table or two in a lounge, and a common-room for
sleeping, in which they could have installed partitions, but
they had never gotten around to that—never much wanted
it, truth be known. A body learned to sleep with cousins
trekking in and out, and there was never any urgent reason
to change, even in the days when they had had wealth.

Right now, Hilfy thought, it was the best reason of all; a
body wanted company in this crisis. Geran came kiting in
and out again with two cups of soup, gods only hope she
got one into her own stomach on the way topside; Chur
was evidently awake and willing to try it eating, which was
one heart-lightening event among all the bad news. Haral
was sitting on the couch opposite with a bit of jerky in one
hand and her mouth full, while she raked her damp mane
into order with the other. Her eyes had that distracted,
glassy weariness jump left in a body. Tully came out of the
common bath with a towel over his shoulders, wearing a
pair of Khym's trousers, a rust silk pair which he had had
to pin at the waist, but Haral was out of spares and the
other pair was going through the laundry. He staggered
over to the cabinet and got a cup and poured soupmix and
water into it, shoved it in the microwave and sat down to
towel his head and beard dry. Pale, old scars stood out on
white-skinned shoulders; and pinker, recent ones.

"Akkhtimakt's jumped out," came the bulletin from the
bridge. And: *"We got a general slow-down on Sikkukkut's
side, sure enough, 'cept for two of 'em it looks like Sikkukkut's sending out to keep 'em worried, same as he did with
Goldtooth's lot. Looks for good and sure like Sikkukkut's
going to stay with us. Thought you'd like to know."*

"No surprise," Haral muttered. *"Couldn't* be that lucky.
Couldn't be lucky enough to get help out of Goldtooth.
Sikkukkut's going to have this place stripped to the deck-
plates before he gets back."

"Going to do whatever he wants," Hilfy said, "that's
sure."

"Lousy mess."

Tully had lifted his face from the towel and looked at
them, yellow hair tousled, eyes showing lines of strain
about the edges. Sometimes he seemed too tired even to

make the effort of speech. Or to listen for the translator's sputtering whisper giving him its mangled version of things around him. The things hardest to get across were the delicate topics, like: *How's Chur—honestly?* Or: *What do you think Jik will do?* And: *What are we going to do when the kif move into the station?* He seemed to go away at times. At others he seemed desperate to say something of too much difficulty to attempt it.

Things like: *My people are going. I talked to them. Even if the message didn't get there. I was that close.*

I didn't betray you.

I swear I didn't try.

The microwave bleeped Finished; and Tully got up and got his soup, with a package of shredded meat and a packet of mahen fuyas, which he and Haral thought edible and everyone else aboard loathed. He offered one of the grain-meat sticks to Haral: she took it and stirred her soup with it, and he settled down with the other packets in his agile fingers, cup in both hands and elbows on his knees, to drink a sip and sigh in profoundest weariness.

"I figure," Hilfy said, to fill the quiet, and to answer questions Tully did not ask, "Goldtooth rendezvoused here with the human fleet. *That's* why he kited out on us at Kefk. He and Ehrran came in here, *he* got stuck here, in a standoff with Akkhtimakt. Maybe he got Akkhtimakt pried loose from the station. He did that much for the stsho. But Ehrran's on her way to Anuurn. Bet."

"Gods-rotted well has to be," Haral muttered. "But with Goldtooth in it we got to wonder, don't we?"

"Like what happened here?" That bothered her. The whole arrangement of things bothered her. The lack of methane-breathers. And Akkhtimakt and Sikkukkut, if they both wanted to be fools, could go on trading that position till the suns all froze. Every few shipboard days, every few ground-bound months, one side could do a turn-around at Urtur or Tt'av'a'o or Kefk or wherever, and come in and strafe the other who had taken possession of Meetpoint. Or Kefk. Or wherever. If ships got to trading positions like that, time-dilation got to stretching lives wider and wider; no in-system passages. No slow-time. Just run and run and run as long as a ship could take it and a body could take the depletion. A merchant ship did its jumps with a lot of slowtime and dock-time in between; and a tradeoff like that could do as much timestretch in a month of their own perception as a trader did in a decade. Before flesh and bone and steel had gone their limits. "Wonder is he didn't come in on Kefk."

"Kefk's got two guardstations. Kefk's got position on him."

Tully stared at them both. He had lost that, probably. But of a sudden the problem had found itself a cold spot in Hilfy's gut. She took a sip of her cup to warm that cold and licked the soup off her mustaches.

"Sikkukkut's got something in mind. He's sure not going to sit here."

"There *are* fools in the universe," Haral said.

"What if he isn't? What if he's not sitting still here? What if he's got something else in mind?"

But Goldtooth was out on the Tt'av'a'o vector. Methane-breather territory. Logical choice: the stsho feared the humans like plague. Stsho would deal with Ehrran; they would deal with the kif before they dealt with Goldtooth and his human allies. They would go with the known villains.

Stsho had no armaments. No capability for that kind of stress. Stsho would run if they could. Evade it all.

Tc'a and chi and—gods save us—knnn—they're not here, they're always here. Where are they? Knnn aren't afraid of anything. They won't run. Avoid, maybe; run in panic—not the knnn. Ever.

"Methane-breathers," Hilfy said. "Gods rot it, Haral. It's a trap. Sikkukkut's and Goldtooth's both."

Haral's ears flagged and lifted again, and a thinking look got through the exhaustion in Haral's eyes.

"Hilfy." Tully held his cup between his knees and his brow furrowed with worry under its fringe of pale wet hair. "Goldtooth not go Tt'av'a'o."

"You mean you *know* that?"

"I think. He come—turn, go *whhhsss,* like Tt'av'a'o. Not."

"You mean he faked a jump? Stopped out there in deep space? You think he can *do* that?"

Tully might or might not have gotten all of that. "Mahe," he said. "Human do."

"Stop a jump short?"

"Same."

"Good gods."

"Makes sense," Haral said. "If they've got the stuff to do that. If they got it from humans— He waits here to fake a run."

"And Ehrran runs for good and real and leaves hani here to catch it when Sikkukkut came through? Gods-be, she's got a *treaty* with the stsho!"

"Give her credit. What could she do—if Akkhtimakt was here first. Goldtooth *wanted* Akkhtimakt intact. He's shoving the two kif into a fight, by the gods, that's what he's doing!" Haral rubbed her graying nose and it wrinkled up again. "Let them weaken each other before he throws the humans at them and before the mahen forces come in here. That's what he's up to. Let Jik hang; let Jik keep at least one gods-be kif halfway tame if he can while Goldtooth sets it up so he can take out both kif. That's what the mahendo'sat would really like. Throw the humans at 'em. Let the humans get shot up. That's why he left Jik behind at Kefk."

"No mahen workers left here onstation, I'll bet on that."

"Gods-rotted sure. Goldtooth could have had the word out long before this. Routed everything out of here. Cleared it all out when the stsho broke that treaty."

"Eggs to pearls Goldtooth's left a spotter here."

"No contest."

"*It's* still insystem," Hilfy said. "*It's* still in position to get whatever happened here, maybe there's more than one of them, huh? Maybe a couple of spotters, one drifting out slow, going to fire up when it's outside normal pickup, just sneak out of here. And if Goldtooth's out there in the deep and those fool kif that were tailing him jump all the way to Tt'av'a'o—"

Haral's ears lifted. The exhaustion melted from her eyes and replaced itself with a hard, hard look. "Keep going."

"Goldtooth might wait for news. Before his turnaround. If he makes one. He may have put more than one or two spotters on the outside of this system. He's used up all his credit with Sikkukkut himself, he's out there in the dark with the humans, with the tc'a that Jik was working with, he's got some credit with the *han*, maybe some with the knnn. What if he decided there wasn't any choice and he just lets the kif fight it out?"

"Maybe that's the safest thing we could all do."

"But—"

"I'm listening."

"But—you know the mahendo'sat are going to save their own hides. Ehrran's left him. We can't speak for the *han.* We got kif going to go head-on against each other with the humans on their backside. If both of them get busy, if the mahendo'sat hit them in the back—neither Akkhtimakt nor Sikkukkut can stand for that chance. They're in a mess. They can't leave the mahendo'sat armed at their backs. They're *kif,* and Goldtooth's going to attack and they know it. My gods, we got one kif making a threat against Anuurn. What's *Akkhtimakt* going to threaten, huh? Or is he just going to turn around and send a ship apiece at every mahen world and station?"

Haral's ears were all but flat. She was still listening.

"Ask Skkukuk," Tully said suddenly.

"Ask him *what?*" Hilfy asked.

"He kif. Ask what kif do."

"He's not on Sikkukkut's level. If he'd outthought him, we'd have Skkukuk to worry about."

"Kif mind. Lot dark. *I* go ask."

"Man's got a point," Haral said. "But no way we talk to the kif. Better we talk to the captain. Py-an-far, you understand me, Tully?"

"You think I'm right?"

"I been in space forty some years, kid, I never been real close to kif on their terms. You have. And you speak mainkifish. Which I still don't, not real well. But I've had a look at our passenger, 'bout enough to get an idea or two. And between the mahendo'sat and that kif, I'm real anxious. We got that other bomb aboard. And sorry as I am for him, he scares me worse'n Skkukuk."

"Jik," Hilfy murmured. And took another sip that failed to warm her gut.

"He's got a lot on him," Haral said, "and much as we owe him and he owes us—first, he's hurting; second, he's *been* hurt, by the kif *and* by his own partner and by us on top of it all; and thirdly, he's mahendo'sat and seeing his whole species in danger, and *maybe* he's got more information than we've gotten out of him. What's he going to do?"

The cold got worse. For one uneasy moment Hilfy could not even look at Tully. For one uneasy moment he was like Jik, alien and full of strange motives and unpredictabilities. And she was female and he was not, with all the craziness on that score. *No place for him to be sitting. Listening to us. Gods, what if he was only waiting, all this time? He's alien. Isn't he? Same as Jik. And we've been through so gods-be much—and I don't know what's in his mind right now. My friend. My—* She gave a mental shiver, looked at the time. "Gods," she said, "we better get topside. Tirun—"

"Yeah," Haral said. And: "You want me to talk to the captain?"

"She listens to you more than me."

"Hey," Haral said. And fixed her with a lazy, flat-eared stare. Reprimand for that small remark. Hilfy dipped her ears.

"Kif," Tully said.

"No," Haral said. "We let that son sleep. You stay here. Rest. Understand. You go down that hall to talk to that kif, I'll skin you. Hear?"

"I understand," Tully said. His mouth had that set it got in unhappiness. "Not right, Haral. I sit here."

"Argues," Haral said. "Huh."

"He wasn't juniormost on his ship," Hilfy said. "I know that. He's not a kid, Haral."

"Who is, on this ship? Tully. You want to come? Talk to the captain?"

He had a few bites left. He made it one, drank the cup dry, and got to his feet, still trying to swallow what he had.

"How's it going?" Pyanfar asked quietly, leaning showerdamp and exhausted over Tirun's chairback. Khym had come back to his post, far from skilled enough to relieve Tirun, but there, at least for support. Tirun looked back at her with flagging ears and a desperate weariness. Tirun had not had a chance at the showers. That was evident.

"No answers yet," Tirun said. "*Na* Jik's asleep, I think. Stopped stirring around down there after I heard the safety-web go." She tilted an ear generally downships and down below. "We got our routine instructions, I just fed it into auto. All the kif are on schedule, Sikkukkut's pair's in final just now and the stsho're sweating it."

"Huhhhh." Pyanfar had an eye on the scan from her vantage; ships proceeding sedately on course. No one out there had done anything definitive. And she leaned closer to Tirun's ear, her elbow on the chairback. "Get out of here, huh? I'll take it."

"Haral'll be here." The voice came out hoarse. "You want to go catch a bite? I c'n take a little longer, 'm not doing anything but sit."

"Neither am I. Get. I'll hold the boards." She shoved off from the chair back and paused half a heartbeat considering her husband, who had never looked away from the screen in all this time. Covering, while she distracted Tirun, though the board was audio-alarmed, and her own eye had automatically held on that screen the minute Tirun looked her way. Tirun had known where she was looking—experience, decades of it. Bridge rules. But Khym covered. That was bridge rules too. She gave Khym's chairback a pat, approval, with a little unwinding of something at her gut. Closer and closer to reliable. On the standard of the best crew going. An impulse came to her; she unclipped one of her earrings.

"Hey," she said, and leaned next to him where her breath stirred the inner tuftings of his ear. "Huh," he said, as if it were some intimacy.

"Hold still. Don't flinch." She nipped right through the edge of his ear. *"Owwh!"* he grunted, and did flinch, turning half about in indignation and then—perhaps he thought it was some bizarre test of his concentration—jerked his gaze right back to the boards.

She slipped the ring right into the wound and clipped it.

"Uhhhn," he said, and felt of what she had done. Never looked around.

"Good." She patted his shoulder, remembered then that he had once upon a time reacted with temper over that gesture of shoulder-patting. But maybe it felt different somehow. He did not object. And she went off to her own station, sat down and brought in the scan images and the com.

Sikkukkut was still on course. *Ikkhoitr* and its partner were docking ahead of them, and *The Pride* was on a course right down lane-center, neat and precise.

They were going to have some specific docking instructions very soon. *The Pride* and *Aja Jin* and *Moon Rising* were about to put themselves where the kif could get at them.

And where Sikkukkut could make demands of them. Jik, for instance. Jik, for a very large instance. Or even Tully. Or Dur Tahar. All of which items Sikkukkut might want back. She sat and gnawed her mustaches, wishing she dared talk back and forth with Dur Tahar over there, who assuredly knew something about kifish mentality. But absolute com silence seemed the best policy at the moment. Gods knew she wanted no questions out of *Aja Jin,* where Kesurinan still followed her orders. And did not ask, as Kesurinan might well have asked: How is my captain? Is he recovered? Why do I have no instructions from him?

Kesurinan believed she knew the answers to all these things, perhaps. And stayed patient. So far.

But on that dockside Kesurinan was bound to ask questions that needed direct lies. And inventive ones.

Goldtooth, gods curse you, what have you set up here?

Made an agreement *with someone, have you?*

Or have we got something else lurking out there, outsystem, that we're going to find out about when our wavefront gets to them and they get themselves run up to attack speed?

Gods, gods, this is no situation to be in. What's Sikkukkut doing? Is that son really depending on us, *for godssakes? Are* we *the backup he thinks he has?*

Fool, Sikkukkut. Can a kif mind be that tangled, to trust us now?

Or are you no fool at all?

Com beeped. "Py," Khym said, and cut it in from his board.

"I got it." It was station, talking to them in effusive jabber. A stsho told them that they could, if they wished, have any free berth, but suggested numbers twenty-seven, twenty-eight, twenty-nine. Which the lord captain of *Ikkhoitr* had suggested, praise to the *hakkikt.*

"Affirm," she said, and with a flattening of her ears: "Praise to the *hakkikt.*"

"No real choice, do we?" Khym asked.

"Life and not. We got that."

"What are we going to do?" There was the faintest note
of despair there. A man asking his wife for reassurance.
Tell me there's something you can do. Tell me it's not that
bad, not that hopeless. A man lived within the small borders
of his estate—never tell a man a thing: never worry him
with problems he had no capacity to deal with. And no
power. *Old habits, Khym, gods rot it, grow up!*

No. It's crew talking to captain. That's all. Get off him,
Pyanfar.

"Feathered if I know what we're going to do," she muttered. *No mercy, Khym.* "Got an idea?"

"He's going to ask for Jik."

"I'm afraid he is."

"What are we going to do?"

"I'll make something up."

Nothing to do but watch it unfold. Obey instructions,
take the berth.

You got it, husband. There isn't an answer. I haven't got
a miracle to pull off. I don't know what in a mahen hell
we're going to do and most of all I don't know how we're
going to get out of here.

Thank gods Ehrran's headed home to warn the han. *Even*
if she goes for Chanur in the process. Better the clan goes
down than the whole world. Better a whole lot of things
than that.

But, gods, Ehrran's a fool. What's a fool going to tell
them? What's a fool going to persuade those fools to do?

Gods, give her good sense just once and I'll go religious,
I swear I will. I'll reform. I'll—

Haral startled her, settling ghostlike into place beside
her.

"Captain," Haral said. "What we got?"

She turned the chair half-about, saw Tirun out of her
place and Tully and Hilfy settling into theirs, ghostlike silent under the noise of operating systems. "We got our
docking instructions. Give Tirun time to get herself down
to quarters. We can brake a little late. Meetpoint sure as
rain isn't going to file any protest on us for violations." She
swung the chair about again and punched in com. Two
veteran crewwomen in their places and two novices. But it

was a routine docking, whatever else was proceeding. "Geran," she said. "Five minutes."

"I'm on my way," Geran answered back from somewhere.

"Captain," Haral said, "Hilfy's got this idea—"

"Tahar acknowledges recept on docking instructions," Hilfy said. "They're on our lead."

"—Akkhtimakt's just lost any reason he had for restraint," Haral said. "He's losing. *Mahendo'sat* aren't dealing with him. He's gone off toward Urtur; there's two moves he could make. One's us. One's the mahendo'sat. Things could get ugly. Real ugly. That's what we been thinking."

"Huhhhn." Another body hit the cushions, hard. She heard the click of restraints. Geran was in. Heard a wild high chittering coming down the corridor, which was a kif in full career, headed for his station and trying to tell them to wait for him: a shove of *The Pride's* mains would send him smashing back into the lift door with the same force as if he had fallen off a building roof.

"We hear you," she said over general com. "You got time, Skkukuk."

And thought about the web of jump-corridors around Meetpoint and where they led.

Gods know what's already been launched at us. "Mahendo'sat aren't going to sit still for it," she said. "It's not their style."

"If they push back," Haral said, "it's going to shove that bastard right into hani space. We figure there's a push coming here. Cap'n, Tully says human ships can drop out of hype in deep space. Do a turn. Says he thinks the mahendo'sat can do it too."

She shot Haral a look. It was a knnn maneuver, that stop-and-turn. Or tc'a. "Friends turning up in odd places."

"From here, cap'n, it's a real pocket out Kura-way."

It was: hani space was an appendix of reachable space, right on the mahendo'sat underbelly, near the mahen homestar. But the accesses in that direction were few and defensible.

"Yeah," she said, thinking of that geometry, which thought suddenly shaped itself into coherent form, in full light. "Yeah. It might work. If they can do that kind of thing. But that'd mean those human ships aren't freighters in any sense of the word—wouldn't it? What's a ship with holds need with that kind of rig, huh?"

"Sure seems like not. And a strike coming in here rams it right down hani throats. Again."

"It does that, too. If they can do that." Another and worse thought. "If mahendo'sat can pull this—wouldn't be the first time they had some new rig they didn't tell us about. Wouldn't be the first time the kif turned up with it too. Before we did. Praise to the mahendo'sat. More gods-be careful of what their allies learn than what gets to their enemies."

Gods, don't let Ehrran be a fool.

Then, down the boards: "Priority," Geran said. "Priority, we got a shift going on, we got a vector change on some of Sikkukkut's lot. That's *Noikkhru* and *Shuffikkt*—"

It came up on the monitor, part of the image changing color again as kifish ships finished their braking and began to slew off on new headings.

Headings at angles to Sikkukkut's.

Chapter 6

Color-shifts multiplied on the scan.

"Gods," Pyanfar muttered, and put in the general take-hold. Alarm's rang up and down the corridors. In case. "Message to our partners: hold steady, keep course; Khym, advisement to Chur: Take precautions, we got kif moving gods know where. Tirun, feed scan down to Jik's monitor; tell him we're all right, we're still on course, we just got something going here."

Acknowledgments came back.

"Captain," Haral said, "Hilfy's got this idea—"

"Tartar acknowledges," Hilfy said. "They're on our lead. Aye—we got that, *Aja Jin*. Thanks—"

"—Akkhtimakt's got bad troubles," Haral said. "I think we got 'em too."

She waited. Waited till she heard Tirun report all personnel accounted for; Tirun had made it onto the bridge. A last safety snicked into place.

They were secure for running. If they had to.

On the screens the flares continued as the doppler recept sorted it out and got information trued again.

And one and another of Sikkukkut's ships flaring green and going into maneuvers.

Not all on the same vector. They were headed out like thistledown scattering from a pod. Everywhere.

In every direction open to them, mahen space and hani and stsho and tc'a.

"*They go,*" Jik exclaimed over the open com. And something else profane in mahensi. He was monitoring the situation, down there in his sealed cabin. "*Damn, they go, they go—*"

To every star within reach. To strafe every station and every system where there might be a hostile presence.

"Priority, priority," Hilfy said, overriding something Geran was saying: "*Harukk*-com says: *Pride of Chanur,* proceed on course."

"*They go hit ever' damn target in Compact,*" Jik cried. There was the sound of explosion. Or of a mahen fist hitting something. "*Damn! Let me out!*"

"She was right," Haral muttered. "Gods-be right. They're going to do it anyhow and we got kif every which way. Captain, they're going to push Akkhtimakt right down that open corridor, to *Anuurn,* captain, by the gods they are."

"We got problems," Pyanfar muttered.

While a stream of mahen profanity warred with Chur's insistent question on the com.

"Kkkkt." From a forgotten source behind them.

And station was ahead. Meetpoint, with three hundred thousand stsho and a handful of hani citizens. With kif closing in on them with declared intent to dock.

"Transmit," Pyanfar said. "*The Pride of Chanur* to all hani on station: prepare to assist in docking for incoming ships. Join us. This is your greatest hope of immediate safety."

Offer a hani an overlord, a master, a foreign hegemony—

They would spit in Sikkukkut's face. And die for it. That, beyond doubt.

But if they heard the reservation in that message, if they keyed on the nuances of safe-shelter-in-storm and all the baggage that went with it—even if the kif did, it was no more than kif expected, even if it was something no kif dared say: *until we find a better.*

"Repeat?" Hilfy queried.

"Repeat."

"Still braking," Geran said.

And the brightness on the amber lines that was their own position crept closer and closer to their own brake-point for station approach.

"*Harun's Industry* responds," Hilfy said, "quote: We take your offer enthusiastically."

It took awhile, for ships to reduce *V.*

It took awhile for outbound kifish ships to go their way, leaping out into the dark, toward Hoas Point and Urtur

System, toward Kshshti and Kefk and Tt'av'a'o and V'n'n'u and Nsthen. Seven ships, to follow right down Akkhti-makt's tail in a second strike after the first one; and right down the throats of Goldtooth and humans and mahendo'-sat and whoever else might be coming in if they could find them.

It was, Pyanfar reckoned bleakly, both ruthless and effective.

"Kkkkt," was Skkukuk's comment. "Kkkkt."

"Kkkt," said Skkukuk. "He is challenging you all. Kkkkt. But his throat is unprotected. *You* are here. He thinks to daunt you. Surprise him, hakt'."

She spun her chair about to face the kif who sat at the aft of the bridge. And there was not a hair on her unbristled. "What has he in mind for us?"

"You are part of his *sfik*. You increase him. Kkkkt. His move is very good. He has penned you all in with his main force. Any attempt to exit toward your territories of resource are blocked first by his enemy and then by his own ships, whose capacities you do not know. It is a fine move, hakt'. But I have faith in you."

"Faith."

"Inappropriate word? *Sgotkkis*."

"Call it faith." She laid her ears back and stared at her private curse with coldest, clearest threat. "Since you don't have an idea in a mahen hell what I'm likely to do about it. But *I* am still here. And my resources have not diminished."

"Kkkkt, kkkt, skthot skku-nak'haktu."

Your slave, captain.

"Captain," Hilfy said. "Communication from *Harukk*. Quote: You have made a proposal to hani ships. You will gather these captains for my inspection on-station. End message."

Second move. It's going too fast. O gods.

"Acknowledge," she said, cold as routine. While they slogged their way at a sedate pace through a system laced with kif, toward a station which was going to be under kifish occupation. "Sikkukkut's going into dock. Cocky son's going to bring that ship in."

If Goldtooth and the humans have stopped short and the kif pass them by in hyperspace, we could get hit here.

Hilfy and Haral have got it figured. All of us do.

If Akkhtimakt's set up to dive in here again—an attack could be poised at system's edge right now. Or already inbound. Not saying whether the kif are onto that trick of stopping a jump. They could well have it. Maybe and maybe. It's not saying all their ships can do it.

"Transmit," she said. "Honor to the *hakkikt:* beware system edges. I fear more than spotters."

"Done," Hilfy said.

We help the bastard we're with. While we're with him.

We take whatever they want to do. And maintain our options. Ehrran's lost all hers. We got hani on that station and gods know how many fluttering stsho. Keep a cool head, Pyanfar Chanur. It's by the gods all the chance you've got.

"We're getting docking instructions," Hilfy murmured finally. They turned up on screen, where kifish ships were already well toward touch with station.

And from Chur, plaintively over com:

"What in a mahen hell's going on?"

"Easy," Geran said. "It's all all right."

"Got crew falling on their noses tired," Pyanfar muttered. "Haral, keep it steady, standard dock. Tirun, get yourself below, take the rest of your break."

"Aye," Tirun said. Old spacer. *And* falling-down tired. A belt snicked. Tirun went away in silence, to food, sleep, anything she could get.

"Jik's requesting to be out," Khym said. So that voice had vanished off com. Khym had silenced him. A mahen hunter captain, locked in a lowerdecks cabin and probably trying to think how to shortcircuit the latch or take the door apart.

"Jik," she said, cutting in on that blinking light on her com section. "We're all right. F'godsakes, be patient, get some rest, we've got our hands full, you got our scan image. We're moving in on dock and that's all that's going on for a while."

"Pyanfar." The voice was calm, quiet, reasoning. *"I understand. I make problem, a? You got protect you crew. I make 'pology. I lot embarrass', Pyanfar. Long time with kif make me crazy. Now I got time think—I know what you do. We be long time ally. We be friends, Pyanfar. Same interest. You unlock door, a?"*

"I tell you there's nothing you can do up here. You got a while to rest, Jik. Take it. You may need it."

"Pyanfar." Thump. Impact of a hand near the pickup. Hard. So much for patience. *"You in damn deep water. Hear? Deep water!"*

"We got another expression." She flattened her ears, lifted them again. "Told you. After we dock. We got enough troubles, friend. I want your advice, but I got enough to deal with right now."

"It be war," Jik said, and sent a chill up her back. War was a groundling word. *"Fool hani! The ships go, they go ever' damn place, not got stop, not got stop!"*

"F'godssake, this is open *space!* This is the Compact, we're not talking about some backwater land-quarrel!"

"No. No harus. New kind thing. Not with rule. We talk 'bout make fight all kif, all hani, all mahendo'sat, make ally, make strike here, strike there. This new kind word. Not like clan and clan. Not like go council. Here we got no council. War, Pyanfar, all devils in hell got no word this thing I see."

Colder and colder.

"I see it too. So what are the mahendo'sat going to do about it? What *have* they done about it? Play games with the kif til we got 'em all at each others' throats? Shove Akkhtimakt off toward hani space? My world? How'm I supposed to be worried about you and yours, rot your conniving hide, when you doublecrossed my whole *species!* You doublecrossed the stsho, f'godssakes, and *that* takes fast dealing! You doublecrossed the tc'a, gods help us, you doublecrossed them and the chi and maybe the knnn!"

"We got humans. We got humans, Pyanfar. Same got hunter-ships, got way shove these bastard back *from out hani territory, you got listen, Pyanfar. Pyanfar, I got timetable!"*

Her finger was on the cutoff, claw half-extruded. She retracted it.

"Do you? Way I hear, you got something else too. Like a fancy new maneuver your ships do, just like humans."

Silence from belowdecks then. Profound silence. Then: *"Open this door, Pyanfar."*

"At dock."

"Soshethi-sa! Soshethi-ma hase mafeu!"

Thump.

She cut him off. Looked Haral's way. Haral studiously lowered her ears. "Not too happy," Haral said. "*Timetable.* What's he mean?"

"By the gods I bet there's one. At our expense. Mahen gifts. 'Got a present for you.' Jik, turning up at Kshshti. Us, miraculously getting our papers cleared so we could turn up back here."

"I'd sure like to know what was in that packet Banny took on, I tell you that."

"Eggs to pearls that Jik slipped something into it. Gold-tooth's version, I got a copy on. The stuff that didn't take a translator to dupe, at least. Which won't be the sensitive stuff. But anything might be helpful. Downgrade the nav functions: we'll run that packet of his with the decoder."

"I'll start it," Hilfy said. "My four."

She keyed the access up and sent the packet over, while *The Pride* started freeing up computer space.

Jik had held out on Sikkukkut. And on her. It was certain that he had. He had been dead silent on that gibe about mahen ship capabilities.

The archive in question blinked into Hilfy's reach.

And they slipped closer and closer to dock.

"Might have some lurker outsystem," Hilfy said. "I've been thinking about that. Might have a strike here most any time."

"Cheerful," Geran said. That sounded almost normal, crew bickering and muttering from station to station.

"Station's on," Hilfy said. "Docking calc."

"That's sot it." Haral said, and sucked them into nav. "Auto?"

"Might as well. Nothing problematical here." Pyanfar sat and gnawed her mustaches, gnawed a hangnail on her third finger. Spat. "Hilfy: send to all hani at dock, hani-language, quote: *The Pride of Chanur* to all hani at dock: we are coming in at berths 27, 28, 29 consecutive. Salutations to all allies: by hearth and blood we take your parole to assure your security. *Industry,* salutations to your captain in Ruharun's name: we share an ancestor. Let's keep it quiet, shall we? End."

"Got that," Hilfy said.

Haral gave her a look steady and sober, ears back-canted. "Think the kif read poetry?"

"Gods, I hope not."

Five decades ago. Dayschool and literature. When she had ten times rather be at her math. *Stand and recite, Pyanfar.*

"I hope to the gods this younger generation does."

> *On a winter's eve came Ruharan to her gates*
> *beneath black flight of birds in snowy court.*
> *White scarf flutters in the wind, red feather*
> *the fletch of arrows standing still in posts*
> *about the yard and the holy shrine where stands*
> *among a hundred enemies her own lord,*
> *no prisoner but of her enemies foremost*
> *seeming. But Ruharun knew her husband*
> *a man with woman's wit and woman's*
> *   staunchness.*
> *So she cast down her bow and spilled out the*
> *   arrows,*
> *on blood-spattered snow cast down defense,*
> *bowed her head to enemies and to fortune. . . .*

"*Industry* answers," Hilfy said. "Quote: *We got that. 27, 28, 29. We have another kinswoman here in Munur Faha. Greetings from her. We are at your orders.*"

"Gods look on them." Pyanfar drew a large breath. Message received, covered, and tossed back again under kifish noses. Munur Faha of *Starwind* was kin to Chanur. But not to Harun. Harun had no ties of any kind.

And Faha had a bloodfeud with Tahar of *Moon Rising*.

A small chill went down her back. It was response to her own coded hail. It was just as likely subtle warning and question, singling out Faha for salutations: *strange company you keep, Pyanfar Chanur, a mahen hunter, a kifish prince, and a pirate.* The Faha-Tahar feud was famous and bitter.

At your orders, smooth and silky. It was kifish subservience, never hani; it was humor, bleak and black and thoroughly spacer. *Let's play the game, hani. You and your odd friends. Let's see where it leads.*

It took a mental shift, gods help her, to think hani-fashion again, and to know the motives of her own kind. Like crossing a gulf she had been on the other side of so long that hani were as strange as the stsho.

"Reply: See you on my deck immediately."

*   *   *

Grapples took. *The Pride*'s *G*-sense shifted, readjusted itself. Other connections clanged and thumped into seal. They were not the first ship in. *Ikkhoitr* and *Chakkuf* crews were already on the docks. *Harukk* was in final. But no kif came to help non-kif ships dock. Pointedly, they handled their own and no others. They were *Industry* crewwomen risking their necks out there on the other side of that wall.

"I've got business," Pyanfar said, and unclipped the safeties.

"Aye," Haral said. "Routine shutdowns, captain. Go."

She got out of the chair and saw worried looks come her way. Tully's pale face was thin-lipped and large about the eyes, the way it got in Situations.

Thinking, O gods, yes, that this might be the end of his own journey, on a station where the kif had won everything that he had set out to take; and where humans were still a question of interest to Sikkukkut an'nikktukktin. He had reason to worry. The same as Jik did.

Queries were coming in, com from *Moon Rising* as it docked, operational chatter. *Aja Jin* was a minute away from touch.

Still playing the game, Kesurinan trusting that her captain was consenting to this long silence.

"Stay to stations," she said to all and sundry. "Khym, monitor lowerdecks."

"You going down there with him?" He looked at her with his ears down, the one with its brand new ring.

She flattened her own. He turned around again without a word. "Tirun's down there," she said to his back and Tally's face and Skkukuk's earnest attention.

I would go, hakt', that kifish stare said. *Tear the throat out of this mahendo'sat, I would, most eagerly, mekt'hakt'*.

"Huh." She made sure of the gun in her pocket and walked on out, wobbly in the knees and still with the sensation that *G* was shifting. She felt down in her pocket, remembering a packet of concentrates, and drank it in the lift, downbound.

The salty flood hit her stomach and gave it some comfort. Panic killed an appetite. Even when panic had gotten to be a lifestyle and a body was straight out of jump. She ate because the body said so. And tried not to think about the aftertaste.

Or the ships around them, or the situation out there on the docks.

Jik was on the bed, lying back with his head on his arms. He propped himself up as the door opened, his small ears flat, a scowl on his face.

" 'Bout time."

"I'm here to talk with you." She walked in and let the door close behind her. His ears flicked and he gathered himself up to sit on the edge of the bed, with a careful hitch at his kilt.

"You been listening to ops?"

"A." Stupid question. But an opening one. He drew a large breath. "You do damn fine job, Pyanfar. We sit at station, same like stsho. We got kif go blow Compact to hell. *Now* what do?"

"What do you want? Run out of here? I got hani ships here, I got ten thousand kif on their way to Urtur, right where you wanted 'em, gods rot you."

"Listen me. Better you listen me now."

"Down the Kura corridor. Isn't that the idea?"

"He be kif, not make connection you with these hani. They got be smart, save neck all themselves— Better you do own business. You don't panic, Pyanfar. Don't think like damn groundling! Don't risk you life save these hani. You get them killed, you make damn mess!"

She laid her ears back. "I got kifish ships headed at my homeworld, Jik. What am I supposed to do, huh? Ignore that?"

"Same me." Muscles stood out on Jik's shoulders, his fists clenched. "You let kif make you plan for you? They shove, you go predict-able direction? Damn stupid, damn *stupid,* Pyanfar! You lock me up, take kif advice now? You let be pushed where this bastard want?"

"And where does that leave my world, huh? I got one world, Jik. I got one place where there's enough of my species to survive. Hani men don't go to space, they're all on Anuurn. What in a mahen hell am I supposed to do, play your side and lose my whole species? They got us, Jik, they got us cornered, don't talk to me about casualties, don't talk to me about any world and any lot of lives being equal, they're not. We're talking about my whole by the gods species, Jik, and if I had to blow every hani out there and three hundred thousand stsho to do something about it, I'd do it, and throw the mahendo'sat onto the pile while it burned, by the gods I would!"

The whites showed at the corners of his eyes. Ears were still back, the hands still clenched.

"Why you here?"

"Because," she said, "two freighters and a hunter can't stop it. Because there's a chance I can turn Sikkukkut to do what I can't. Now you tell me about timetables. You tell me about it, Jik, and you tell me all of it, your ship caps included!"

He sat silent a moment. "You got trust."

"Trust. In a mahen hell, Jik. Tell me the truth. I'm out of trust."

"I got interests I protect."

"No." She walked closer, held up a forefinger and kept the claw sheathed with greatest restraint. "This time you trust *me*. This time you give me everything you've got. You tell me. Everything."

"Pyanfar. Kif going to take you 'board *Harukk*. They try question me, I don't talk. My gover'ment, they make fix—" He tapped the side of his head. "I can't talk. Can't be force'. You whole 'nother deal. They shred you fast. Know ever'thing. They know you got me 'board, a? Know you got chance make me talk. Maybe they give me to you for same reason—they can't, maybe Pyanfar can do, a? Maybe block don't work when you ask, I tell you ever'thing like damn fool."

"*Can* you tell me? Can what they did to you, can what your Personage did to you—make you lie to me, even when you don't want to?"

A visible shiver came over him. Hands jerked. "I ask not do."

"Jik—you got to trust me. However they messed you up. Jik, if it kills you, I got to ask. *What timetable?*"

The tremor went through all his limbs. He hugged his arms against himself as if the room had gone freezing. And stared her in the eyes. "Fourteen," he said past chattering

teeth. "Eighteen. Twenty. Twenty-four—First. Seventh."
Another spasm. "This month. Next. Next. We g-got
maneuver—make jump coordinate with same."

"You mean your moves are aimed at certain points at
certain dates?"

"Where got th-threat. Don't fight. Move back. Make
'nother jump-point on focus date."

"So that somewhere, tracking the kif, your hunters are
going to coincide and home in on them."

"Co-in-cide. A." He made a gesture with shaking hands.
"More complicate', Pyanfar. We push. We pull. We make
kif fight kif. We make kif go toward Urtur, toward Kita."

"Toward Anuurn!"

"Got—got help go there. Back side. We not betray
you, Pyanfar!"

Her legs went weak. She sank down where she was, on
her haunches, looking up at a shaken mahendo'sat on the
edge of the bed. "You swear that."

"God witness. Truth, Pyanfar. You got help." The hands
clenched again. "Ana—me *Aja Jin*. He got chance. Got
chance, damn! And he run me out from this place, leave us in
damn mess! Got 'nother plan. He got 'nother plan, got way
push kif on kif, damn conservative."

"Or he suspects deep down his human allies aren't to be
trusted. What if he knows that? What would he do?"

"He be damn worried. Same got worry with tc'a." Another convulsive shiver. Jik wiped his face, where it glistened with sweat. "He maybe listen to me too much. Take
my advice. I come into his section of space. I damn surprise' see me at Kefk. I tell him—I tell him we got save
this kif, make number one. True. He be confuse', he pull
out." He slammed his hand onto the bed beside him. "I
don't send code. You understand. I not on *Aja Jin,* I don't
send code, he don't attack!"

"Kesurinan doesn't know all this."

"I not dead. She got file to read if I be dead, but I be
on friendly ship, a? She take you instruction, she think I
be on bridge—she not know. She don't send the damn code
and Ana don't move on this kif!"

There was sickness at her stomach all over again. She
stared up at him. *And have you told me the truth even yet,
old friend, my true friend? Or have you only found a lie*

that'll keep me moving in the direction you want? Or are you giving me the only truth you've been brainwashed into believing? Would they do that to you, your own people?

Would they stick at that, when they got into your mind to do other things?

Gods save us, I almost trust the kif more.

"The kif would have blown us, Jik, before we could help anybody. We could've lost it all. I don't think it would've worked. We still got a chance, don't we? Where's our next rendezvous point? When?"

"Kita. Eighteenth next month."

"Can't make it. Give me the next *we* could reach. Or is it *here?* Is Goldtooth just waiting a signal?"

"Two month. Twenty-fourth. Urtur. You got. Maybe be there. Maybe not. We got now six, seven ship go out from here."

And a single incoming ship at extremely high *V* had a killing advantage. If it turned out to have position as well, its high velocity fire could rip slower ships to ribbons.

"When's Goldtooth come back?"

"I not say he come back. Don't know what he do. *Not get damn signal!*"

"Gods-be *lie*, Jik, you got to coordinate this somehow. You know what he's going to do. My information says he can short-jump and turn. That maybe all those ships can. Is it *here*, Jik? Is Meetpoint the place we have to be? Was that message he didn't get from Kesurinan—aimed to catch him a few days, a few hours out from this system, was *that* it?"

Terror. Never before in Jik. Raw fear.

"Scared I'll tell the *hakkikt?* Scared I guess too much?" She was sitting vulnerable and too close. She stood up and looked down at him, mindful of the gun in her pocket. "Scared they'll get it out of me?"

"You damn fool."

"I want your help. You want mine. You want to figure your chances without the hani? If it was you and nothing else, alone with the kif, with three human governments all doublecrossing each other, and the tc'a and the chi, gods help us, running lunatic? You refigure it, Jik, hear? You got some authority of your own. You got authority to take up a Situation and settle it, I got that figured. And I'm giving you a Situation. I'm giving you the fact we got this bastard going to take my species out, going to kill all of us, which loses you an ally, which loses you a major market, doesn't it, which loses you *friends,* about the time you need 'em most, you and your Personage. Humans aren't half your trouble. *I* am. The *han* is. And you don't give me orders. *I* got the influence, *I* got the thing in hand, and all of a sudden I'm dealing with a threat to my *planet,* Jik, which means I'll do any gods-be thing I got to and I'm not kiting off in any gods-be direction you want. I got *one* direction. And you got no choice but my choice, because I'll shoot you down before I let you do something that'll stop me. I love you like kin and I'll shoot you with my own hand, you hear me, mahe? Or you help me and give me the truth at all the right spots and maybe you still got an ally left."

Muscles were still clenched. Hard. He took a long time. "Got," he said finally. "You open door, a?"

"No deal. *Not* your terms, you hear?"

He stood up, gave the kilt a hitch, and stared down at her. Made a sudden move of his hand, a strike. She skipped back, ears flat.

"First thing," he said, "you got learn not trust ever' bastard got deal. You damn fine trader. But kif not be merchant."

"Neither are you. I'm proposing something else. I'm telling you you're not going to break my neck because you got more sense."

"You got right," he said, and sniffed and drew a large breath. The fine wrinkles round his eyes drew and relaxed and drew again in an expression very like Tully's. "Love you like kin. Same. Got tell you you going to bleed." He touched his heart. "Same you win, same you lose. You number one fine woman. Got lot haoti-ma. Lot. I make deal, honest. You get me smoke, I give you whole time-table."

"You gods-be lunatic."

"Sikkukkut not only source. You got whole station. You got ask *Aja Jin.* Same bring."

"Drug's scrambled your brains."

A little light danced in his eyes. "You want me stay 'board, you got find me smoke. I be number one fine pilot.

Same better when I got relax. You maybe need. You, Haral,
you number one too. Not too many."

"What are you talking about?"

"Same you." He gave another hitch at the kilt. He had
lost weight. "You got deal." More wrinkles round the eyes,
a grimace. "My Personage damn me to hell. Same be old
territory for me. You want me, you got. Long as Sikkukkut
not got us all. You got trade sharp, hani. Number one
sharp. This be hard deal. Maybe he take me. Maybe take
you: you got no knowledge. You want plan you got get me
back. Safe."

"He hasn't asked for you."

"He do. You wait, see. *Know* this kif."

"How's your nerves?"

"You not forget get smoke, a? Same time you get me
out."

"Captain," Hilfy said over com. *"Harukk's coming in
right now. They're insisting to pick up all the captains. With
appropriate escorts. They want Jik and Tully too."*

Jik lifted his brows. "See?"

"Gods rot that kif." But she thought: *He could strip every
ship here of its senior command. Couldn't he? Me. Dur
Tahar. That'd leave Haral Araun, but he doesn't know her
that well.*

*I need an escort. Not Haral. Gods, I can't take Haral off
this ship.*

Not one of my crew. Just my translator.

"Hilfy. Tell Skkukuk he's going with us. No other but
the ones they asked for. Send my gear down here. Send an
AP for Jik too. We got a point to prove."

Gods send the rest of the captains have got some sense.

Gods send they understand old epics.

"Aye," Hilfy said after a second. *"Captain. Tahar's here.
We got others coming. Haral asks: let 'em through?"*

Not happy. No. Sikkukkut's not going to like this.

And, no, niece, I'm not crazy.

I just got no choice.

The lift worked. That was Tully coming down. Or the
kif. She walked along the corridor with Jik for company,
spotted Tirun coming the other way about the time the

lock cycled with its characteristic whine and thump and let someone into the ship.

That and a cold lot of air with the smell of Meetpoint about it. Nostalgia hit, and left an ache after it. Old times and rotten ones, but that smell was familiar in a mundane way that made the present only worse by comparison.

Tully and Skkukuk arrived together, Skkukuk a-clatter with weapons, his own and what he had gathered on Kefk dock: maybe, she reflected dourly, it was sentiment.

Tully had her gun slung over his shoulder, and an AP at his hip: that took no claws to operate—shove in the shells and pull the trigger. He was steady and able to use it. He had proved that at Kefk.

And from the airlock corridor, Dur Tahar arrived with Soje Kesurinan.

Pyanfar drew in a large breath.

So how stop her? If hani were going to hold a meeting under the *hakkikt*'s nose, what stopped Kesurinan from joining it?

And what stopped Jik now from joining her?

"We got a problem here," she muttered. "Jik, don't you do it."

"Lo," he said, "Soje. Shoshe-mi."

"Shoshe," Kesurinan said. And something else, in dialect.

While other figures came down the white corridor, several hani-bright and equipped with weapons. And one dark and tall—as a foreign kif walked right into *The Pride*'s lowerdecks.

Countermove.

Do what, Pyanfar? Throw it out? This is a friendly *conference we're going to, that's likely* Ikkhoitr *crew, and that bastard's one of Sikkukkut's own special pets.*

Her heart set to beating doubletime. *Fool. Twice a fool. Do what? Do what now?*

"Gods be," Hilfy muttered, "we got Kesurinan and a kif past that lock. Gods *rot!* Haral—"

"I'm on it, I'm on it." Haral's voice rumbled with vexation. They were observing from the bridge. It was all they could do.

"I'll go down there," Khym said, a deeper, more ominous rumble.

"Easy, easy, stay put, the captain's handling this. Let's don't make it worse."

And from the com: "*Pride of Chanur, this is* Vrossauru's Outbounder, *our captain should be arriving at your lock. Please confirm.*"

"Affirm that, *Outbounder.* No difficulties." With more confidence than she felt.

"I've got the lift under bridge control," Haral said. "We're sealed up here. They're not going to try anything on us, I don't think."

"Faha's going to be gnawing sticks with Tahar in reach," Hilfy said.

"At least they're not siding with Ehrran," Geran said.

"Spacers," Haral said. "You want to bet young blackbreeches stopped to consult these crews before she kited on out of here? They've had their backsides to the fire here, and it's sure she didn't help their case."

It made sense. That the hani insystem had not fled meant that they had not had the chance; there was, gods knew, no profit in this crisis for a trader.

Now the resident hani had a further insanity to contemplate: kif in control of the station: and with those kif a mahen hunter-ship, and with them, Tahar and Chanur, who were blood enemies to each other.

But if these ships had been stuck at Meetpoint through all the troubles, they must be used to lunacies.

"*Pride of Chanur,*" com said, "*this is* Faha's Starwind. *Request explanation at your leisure. Standby signal for tight-beam.*"

Cagy old spacer, playing it very careful. Lifetime of experience with the kif. And taking a bigger risk than she knew.

"*Starwind,* this is *The Pride,* stand by your query." The board signaled acquisition of the impulse against *The Pride*'s receptor-dish, and confirmed their own pulse sent back; all discreet and hope to the gods the kif did not pick up that furtive exchange. "Haral, we got a ship-to-ship—"

"Break it," Haral said, and Hilfy shut down at once, thwarting the contact. Then over a station-system relay Haral appropriated: "This is Haral Araun, duty officer, *The*

Pride of Chanur: all com will go on station relay. The *mekt-hakkikt* Sikkukkut an'nikktukktin is an ally, and beyond that we aren't authorized to say anything—is that Junury I'm talking to?"

"Gods-be right it is. Haral, what in a mahen hell is going on between you and Ehrran? Can you at least answer me that one?"

"Bloodfeud, that's what's going on. Which is no part of anything going on in this system, excepting some deals with the stsho. Excepting deals in the *han.* I'll fill you in on it later. Junury, anyone else who's listening: we've been doubledealt in the *han,* every spacer clan's been done up inside and out by a few gods-be graynosed groundling bastards with full pockets. We had bloodfeud with Tahar; we paid that out; gods know Tahar's paid in blood. Right now I got a cousin lying gut-shot from back at Kshshti thanks to Ehrran and thanks to that bastard Akkhtimakt, and we got trouble loose that we got to settle—we got *hani* interests at stake, like we never had. And thank the gods you stayed, Junury. Thank the gods, is what I say: we can use the help, and I don't know if you'd have gotten through the way you were headed. Hear me?"

A long pause. *"I hear. I hear you, Haral Araun."*

For Haral it was outright eloquence. Hilfy drew a long breath when Haral did; and tried to think whether Haral had shot any messages into it between the lines—nothing but *caution, caution, caution, we're being monitored,* was what she heard.

"Starwind," Transmission came from another source, *"this is* Moon Rising. *Our captain's gone same as yours. We're under parole to Chanur. We'll stand trial. Araun's too polite. We're coming in for that. We haven't got a choice. So we surrendered. We're still armed and we're under Chanur's direction. End statement."*

Transmissions ceased. Discreetly.

Hilfy switched back in on the intercom channel Khym was on, leaned back in her chair and tried not to think at all. She worked her hand and extended claws and tried to keep her ears up and her expression matter-of-fact as Tirun's down the row, while Khym *nef* Mahn sat there beside her with a new-won ring in his ear—a man, with a spacer's ring; with his scarred face grim and glowering at the trouble belowdecks, and the certainty Pyanfar was bound for the kif.

What kept him in that chair and what kept the pressure-seal on that temper of his gods alone knew; Hilfy felt his presence at her right like a boding storm, like something ready to erupt, but which never did.

"Fry Ehrran," Khym muttered to himself. "Gods-be Immune. I *want* a few of them."

Khym *nef* Mahn was not a swearing man. Hilfy turned a second misgiving look his way and saw the set of his face and his ears, which was a male on the edge. With not an enemy in reach.

"Health," Pyanfar murmured—other salutations had loaded connotations in main-kifish. As more of the captains walked in on *The Pride*'s lower deck and joined the conference. With one of Sikkukkut's kif to witness. Her own kif took up a wary stance with rifle in hands. Prudent; and ignorant and naive in his own kifish way, gods knew. "It's all right," she said in pidgin, and in hani: "Kerin, hau mauru." *Clanswomen, there's no worry.* "Haaru sasfynurhy aur?" *Everyone understand the pidgin?* She gave a meaningful glance up and about the edges of the ceiling. *We're being monitored. So you know.* "This is Tully. And *na* Jik. Nomesteturjai. And his first officer Kesurinan." No need for more than that. Since Gaohn, *Aja Jin* was famous among hani. Ears were up in respect, among these armed and vari-shaded hani, who came from every continent of Anuurn, mostly graynoses like Kaurufy Harun with younger escorts; Munur Faha being the exception, a red-gold smallish young woman with a graynosed and scarred old cargo officer beside her: that was Sura Faha, and a good and a steady old hand she was.

She knew most of them from docksides from one side of the Compact to the other, and the sight of familiar faces ought to have been a comfort. It was a mortal jolt, that sense of disconnection, how far she had come from civilization; it was like looking at it all through a window.

And Dur Tahar stood there to complicate it all, in a company that had individually and severally sworn to have her piratical hide, and carrying a heavier complement of weaponry than the rest of the captains, whose sidearms were all legal in the Compact.

"This is Skkukuk," she had to say atop everything else, smooth and never stopping, with a gesture to her left hand. "He's mine. *Sha mhifj-shau.*"

My vassal-man. She bent the language to make a word that had never existed: and called a kif a man, into the bargain, because so far as she could figure, he was not female. *Mhifj* was a word for a woman who came to link herself to a more powerful clan. Women could do that. Men just fought their way in, with their lives at risk and in the greatest likelihood of being driven off by the clans-women before they ever got as far as challenging their lord for his place. Male vassal, indeed. Ears flicked and flattened all around the room; and frowns grew darker.

"He was a present," she said. "The *hakkikt,* praise to him—" Another glance aloft: *we're not alone, friends*— "I couldn't explain anything when I sent that message out; but we've got a delicate situation in progress here. I'll be honest with you: the *han* has signed some kind of treaty with the stsho: Rhif Ehrran may have been carrying it—she came through here. She may not have stopped."

"Didn't," said Kauryfy, and drew a large breath, setting her hands in her belt. "But she blasted out a warning." Kauryfy's ears went all but flat, lifted, flattened again nervously. "Said there were kif coming; and us up to our ears in aliens. Gods-rotted late news. We got caught here—I gather this *hakkikt* isn't friendly with the other one."

"You might say." She flicked her own ears. *Careful, Kauryfy. You're no fool; don't begin now. Watch the mouth.* "Glad to see us, were you?"

"Crazy around here. Gods-be aliens. Mahendo'sat feuding with the kif. Stsho Phasing all over the place. Never know who you're dealing with from one hour to the next. Gods know who's maintaining station's lifesupport. This Akkhtimakt—not a friend of yours?"

"No."

"Well, none of ours either. A rotted mess, that's what we've had here. Got stuck here with Urtur shut down, just kept running up dock charges and mortgaging our hides with the gods-be stsho, and everything going crazy— Five months, five *months* we've been stuck in this godsforedoomed lunatic port, Chanur! Then we get the kif. Came in all peaceful, and us knowing, by the gods, *knowing* what he'd done over by Urtur, and these gods-rotted fool stsho putting it out over the com that they'd asked him in, that it was all treaty—"

"It was. Treaty with the *han* and faceabout, treaty with Akkhtimakt. All to save them from humanity."

"Well, they got a gods-be poor bargain."

"You got stuck here."

"We got stuck here. That son moved in and interdicted traffic, got himself onto the station and did about what you'd figure. We went along with him while it looked like everything was going to be blown to a mahen hell and then the mahendo'sat showed and the humans came in and the kif cleared the station, we just sat still and hoped to all the gods it wasn't our problem. Now it is, I'm figuring."

Kauryfy's face underwent subtle changes, the tightening of her nose, the slight and timely tightening of a muscle by one ear—a wealth of signals a kif might miss. *I'm trusting you only halfway; and there's a lot I'm not going to say out loud.*

"Yes," Pyanfar said, with a like set of signals back again, and thrust her hands into her belt. *So humans arrived here out of the dark. Couldn't be a coincidence of timing. They were short-jumped and parked out there. By the gods they were waiting. Goldtooth knew they would be.* "It *is* our problem. The whole Compact's coming apart, and the *han*'s policy has got us in a mess. I need you. Hear? Never mind the aliens. The *hakkikt* is going to ask you where you stand. And I'm telling you: we've never been worse off than we are right now. You can believe me or you can believe Ehrran; that's the sum of it. I'm trusting she messaged you more than just the news. Must've had plenty to say about us."

There was prolonged silence. Ears moved, flattened, halfway lifted.

"It got here," Munur Faha said. "We got it from the stsho and we got it when she kited through. Urtur-bound."

"Gods fry her," Tirun said.

"There's a real strong reason," Pyanfar said, "she doesn't want to see us again. That's a *han* matter. Meanwhile we've our own business to tend to. Yours and ours. Very critical business."

"Specifically?" Kauryfy said.

"Settling things among ourselves. This isn't over. Far from it. I want you to take my orders."

Kauryfy's pupils did a quick tightening and redilating. Her mustaches drew down. "Known each other a few years, haven't we?"

"There was Hoas."

Kif dust-up, back in the small-time pirate days. Another flicker of Kauryfy's eyes.

"Yeah," Kauryfy said, and looked from her to the kifish shadow that stood at her back; and back again. "Well, we got along then."

"I'll go with it," said Haurnar Vrossaru, in her deep northlands accent.

"Same," said Haroury Pauran, dark as some mahendo'-sat, and with one blue eye and one gold. She thrust her hands into her belt and scowled, looked aside at young Munur Faha, who sullenly lowered and lifted her ears: "Aye," said Munur. She was Hilfy's cousin, remote. "I'm with you."

That left two. Vaury Shaurnurn gnawed at her mustaches and turned her shoulder to the lot of them: the other (that would be Tauran, by elimination, of *The Star of Tauran*) turned and looked Shaurnurn's way. And then Tahar's.

"Kin of ours died at Gaohn," said Tauran.

"Here is here," Tahar said.

And: "Kkkkt," from Skkukuk, who had antennae for trouble. That long jaw lifted. So did the gun. And the other kif stiffened.

"Pasiry died at Gaohn. Your allies shot her in the gut. She bled to death while we were pinned down."

"Here is here," Pyanfar said. "Argue it later. For godssake, *ker* Vaury. I'll tell it to you later, where we got Tahar. Right now we've got an appointment. An important one. In Ruharun's name, cousin."

They were not kin either. Far from it. Vaury Shaurnurn looked her way with ears flat. *Cousin. Listen to me, ker Vaury. Believe nothing I say, do everything I say, make no false moves. Cousin.*

She stared Vaury Shaurnurn dead in the eyes and thought that thought as hard as she could. Vaury's ears lowered and lifted again. "Cousin," Vaury said ever so deliberately. "We've been in and out of the same places, haven't we? Never been other than courteous with me; all right. That's all I'll say. All right." Vaury gave a glance at Tully, up and down. "This the same one?" The glance lingered at the AP at Tully's hip and traveled up again to his face. "Same human as at Gaohn?"

"Tully," Pyanfar said. "Yes." She looked aside to the stranger-kif. "Who this visitor of ours is, is another matter. *Ikkhoitr* crew, I'm thinking."

"Ikkhoitru-hakt'."

"Captain." The hair bristled down her back. "Honored, we are. I'll trust your people are going to escort us over to *Harukk.*"

Ikkhoitr's captain turned and stalked down the hall in that direction, kifish-economical. And without hani courtesy.

"Kkkkt," Skkukuk said, warning.

It was not friendly, that captain's move. He was, kifish-like, on the push, looking for chinks and advantages; and one little lapse into hani courtesies had achieved unintended irony. She had ordered him.

She had invoked the *hakkikt.* And being kif, he dared not demur or hesitate. She had scored on him, who had come in here looking for fault, fluent and deadly dangerous.

Gods hope he had failed to find it. Or that kif did not have the habit of lying in certain regards.

"Skkukuk says watch him," she muttered to the others. "Tirun, you stay aboard. Hear?"

Tirun did not like it. But crew did not argue these days. Not in front of kif, even their own.

The personnel lock cycled, letting the party out. And closed again, audible from the bridge over the steady bleep and tick of incoming telemetry and com. "That's seal," Haral said to Tirun belowdecks. "Get up here."

"Station com's still gibbering," Hilfy said. "Gods-be stsho're going crazy. I can't make out anything except how glad they are to have the noble *hakkikt* back a—" She blinked, as Geran suddenly turned her head, and blinked again, seeing Chur wobbling into the bridge, Chur without her rings and dressed in a towel, the implant still in her arm and secured with tape. Her mane and beard were dull, her fur thin in pink spots where skin showed through, and her ribs showed prominent above a hollowed belly.

"Geran—" Hilfy said, but Geran had already grabbed her. Haral turned her chair and took a look. "Geran, for godssakes—"

"Got to walk a bit," Chur said, the merest ghost of Chur's voice, but she passed a glance around at monitors and displays. "Got a mess, do we? Lock working down there— Y'don't expect a body to sleep. Geran, set me down, I've got to sit. Who's covering you?"

"*He* is." Meaning Khym. "Sit."

"You're an emergency," Haral said. "Gods rot it, *sit down*." As Chur wilted onto Skkukuk's seat. "We're up to our noses. Could have an attack from gods know who come screaming through here any minute, we got to be able to move, how do we move with you wandering around?"

Chur save a ghastly grin. "Hal, cousin, if we've got to move without the captain, I'm sitting a chair, no way I'm not. What in a mahen hell is going on out there?"

"The captain aboard *Harukk* is what's going on out there. We got kifish guns to our heads and gods know what else about to come in here for a piece of stsho hide."

"Figured." Chur drew a large breath as if breathing was hard. "Gods take 'em. What's our cousin up to?"

"*Sfik*," Hilfy said. "She's got three species for an escort and a half-dozen hani captains following her moves. She's running the biggest gods-be bluff of our lives, that's what she's doing. Trying to buy us time."

"If we got two hani walking sequential it'll be the first time since we went on two feet." Chur leaned her head back on the headrest and rolled it aside to look at the displays. "Not mentioning the mahendo'sat." Her breath was coming harder, and for a moment Hilfy tensed in her chair, thinking she might go unconscious; but Geran had Chur's shoulder, and Chur got her head up again. "Haral, I want a pocket com and I want ops-com run back there to my cabin. All right?"

"You got it," Haral said. "Geran, get her out of here."

"Hilfy," Khym said, "you want to cover me?" —preparing to get out of his seat and help. But: "I'm doing

all right," Chur said, and caught hold of the arm and levered herself up like an old woman, where Geran could
steady her. Then she walked, slowly, slowly, back the way
she had come, past a startled Tirun Araun, just arrived up
from lowerdecks.

"What's that?" Tirun asked when she and Geran were
out and down the corridor. With a look backward. "She
all right?"

"Wants to know what's going on," Khym said. "She's
fighting."

"She's got her way again." Haral said in the same low
tone. "Too." And swung her chair back around.

"Priority," Khym said suddenly, which set a lurch into
Hilfy's pulse.

"Scan-blocking," Tirun said, slipping into place while
Hilfy cast an anxious look at the scan display on her
number-two monitor. A vanished ship reestablished itself
in the red of projected-position. One by one other ships
went red, the blight spreading in an orderly way. Then:

"That's friendly of them," Haral murmured as their own
position at station vanished from the other display. "At
least they're catholic when they blank the scan."

The ramp access doors opened, above the once-teeming
docks: deserted now, mostly. Bits of paper. Trash. Abandoned machinery. Burn-scars on the paints. And cold,
which the Meetpoint docks always were, too much size and
too little free heat from the dull, dead Mass about which
the station orbited. There were abundant kif—not far away,
black shapes in robes. *Skkukun,* likely, quasi-slaves on *Ikkhoitr.* Expendables and dangerous as a charged cable.

And there were stsho, fragile-looking pale figures huddled over against the far side of their own docks, scurrying
like pale ghosts, out of doorways and shelter, the dispos-
sessed owners of Meetpoint. A mass of them surged toward
the foot of the ramp, indecisively retreated, bolted again
toward them in utter chaos, a crowd all spindle-limbed and
gossamer-robed in opalescent whites and pearl, stsho of
rank, with their feathery, augmented brows, their moonstone eyes struck with panic. They gibbered and wailed
their plaints, their effusive pleas for protection—

And they came to one collective and horrified halt, and gasped and chittered for dread. Of the kif, perhaps.

Or perhaps it was the first sight of Tully that did it.

"Stay close," Pyanfar muttered to Tully. "Not friends."

"Got," he said under his breath. And kept close at her elbow as they descended, Jik trailing behind her; and Tahar; and Harun and all the rest. Kif waiting below formed a black wedge as they went down into that mass of stsho, and the stsho gave way before that like leaves before a wind, gibbering as they went, down a dock on which many of the lighted signs, indicating ships at dock, showed stsho names. Too timid to break dock, helpless in the advent of armed ships sweeping in out of Kefk inbound vector, which was unhappily also the outbound vector for the nearest stsho port, at Nsthen—they could do nothing in their unweaponed state but cower and wait, while their appointed kifish defenders did the smart thing and ran like the devils of a mahen hell were on their heels.

"Lousy mess," Pyanfar said; and hitched the rifle she carried to a more conspicuous attitude, while they walked along an aisle of kif with *Ikkhoitr*'s black-robed captain, and stsho retreated and stared at them from concealment with terrified, moonstone eyes.

Then a kifish name showed in lights above a berth: and the ramp of *Harukk* gaped for them.

She hitched her gunbelt up and tried to calm her stomach. Her nose had begun to prickle and she searched after another pill in her pocket, never minding the timelapse. Metabolism did peculiar things after jump. She was strung tight and getting tighter, on the raw edge of fatigue.

Walking up that ramp was very much not what she wanted to do, if her body had had its choice in the matter; but brain began to assert itself as cold terror ebbed down to a different kind of wariness.

Gods, we got to think, Pyanfar Chanur, we got to think about all those stationfolk, dithering stsho though they be, and gods help any hani and any mahendo'sat—the hakkikt's *just taken himself another space station, and this time he's got his blood up and he's got a point to make. Gods help 'em all,* think, *think, get the mind wide awake.*

Gods-be pills make you sleepy, curse 'em.

*I haven't got the strength for this. I'm not any kid any-
more. The knees are going to go. I'm going to fall down
right on this godsforsaken rampway, and if I do it's all unraveled, we're all going to die and the gods-blessed Compact
is going to go all to pieces because I can't keep my knees
from wobbling and my gut from hurting and my eyes
from fuzzing.*

*Ten more steps, Pyanfar Chanur, and then ten more, and
we get to rest a while, we can lean on that lift wall, can't
we? They won't notice.*

Down the corridor, the bleak, black, ammonia-reeking
corridor past *Harrukk*'s airlock; and Jik and Kesurinan
walking side by side behind her— *No knowing what signals
they've passed, gods rot the luck*—

Tully, where's Tully, f' godssakes—

She caught sight of him, shouldered back by Skkukuk
as she entered the lift with *Ikkhoitr's* captain and Jik and
Kesurinan and Tahar. "Tully!" she snarled, and he dived
forward and made the door before it closed on the first
group, leaving the others for a second lift, and gods only
hope they ended up in the same place.

Herself and Jik and Tully and Skkukuk, with Tahar and
the kifish captain and his lot: the lift let them out in *Harukk*'s upper corridor, in a chill, damp closeness and the
stink of ammonia and incense.

*They'll die if we foul it up. All these people on Meetpoint.
My crew. Us on this ship. How do you reason with a kif?*

Kif waited for her at the other end, kif dressed in skin-
tight suits and robes modified for freefall work. Sodium-
light glared and tinted gray-black skins, the glitter of
weapons, of wet-surfaced eyes as they waited to welcome
the *hakkikt*'s guests.

In a hospitality both Jik and Tully had abundant cause
to remember.

Chapter 7

The *hakkikt* waited for them in his audience-chamber, deep within *Harukk*'s well-shielded ring, and, thank all the gods, there was a place to sit, a chair at a low table, the captains and Jik and Tully all offered chairs at the table with Sik-kukkut, and the captains' escorts left with the *skkukun*, standing about in the dim sodium-light and the smoke of incense. Pyanfar took the little cup of parini they offered her as she sat: her hand shook when she did it, and if the cup was not drugged, it was as dangerous on her queasy and pill-shocked stomach as if it had been. She had rather food, she had far rather food at the moment.

But not on a kifish ship.

And: "Tully," she said. "Be careful of that. *Hakkikt,* I don't know if he can drink."

"Kkkt. Indeed. *Can* you, *na* Tully?"

"Yes," Tully said in perfect hani. And answered the *hakkikt* face to face, after all his evasions and his stratagems. He sipped a bit from his cup, and what went on behind those strange, shyly down-glancing eyes was anyone's guess.

So with Jik, who drank his own cup, carefully. And if there was raw hate inside him, if there was shock and a still-raw wound, it did not surface. Kesurinan sat beside him, at this different, jointed table with the hollow center, in which a kifish servant squatted ungainly with a serving-flask and waited for someone's cup to empty. Harun and Tauran, Vrossaru and Pauran and Shaurnurn, Faha and Kes-urinan and Jik and scar-faced Dur Tahar; Tully and Skku-kuk side by side; and the captain of *Ikkhoitr,* if she had not lost track of the kif in the shuffle, sitting by his (her?) prince's elbow.

Gods save them all from the *Ikkhoitr* captain's talebear-

ing. The long-snouted bastard had indeed been whispering
and clicking away, nose to Sikkukkut's hooded ear.

"Kkkkt," Sikkukkut said then, and looked at his senior
captain with—it might be—curiosity. "Indeed." He turned
then and extended a thin tongue briefly into the metal-
studded cup which rested like a silver ball in his black hand.
"Is there unanimity among you?"

"Enough," Pyanfar said; and in coldest blood: "Hani
methods, *hakkikt*. Hani will always dispute. Even when
they agree. A *sfik*-thing. Mine and theirs. It's satisfied and
they're here. In fact they're glad to see you."

"Kkkkt. *Are* they?"

"We weren't fond of Akkhtimakt," Harun said in a low
voice, before Pyanfar could mull it over.

*Gods, be careful. Speak for yourself and you become a
Power, Harun. He may ask what you don't know how to
answer. Watch it, for godsakes watch it, you don't know
what that sounds like in kifish.*

"Hani understatement," Pyanfar said. "Akkhtimakt, a
curse on his name, moved in here and dealt with the stsho.
That was one thing. He disturbed hani interests. That was
another."

"There were, of course, the mahendo'sat. And this other
group of ships. Humans? Were those humans?"

"Yes," Harun said.

"Interesting." Another sip at the cup, a glance Tully's
way and back again. "Close but not close enough. The mahendo'sat have pulled off, doubtless to try again. Hence my
watchers about the system. A fool would linger on these
docks. We might have another Kefk here. In an emergency.
There might even be sabotage, kkkt? Did the mahendo'sat
touch here?"

"No," Harun said.

"Who is this captain?"

"Harun of *Harun's Industry*," Pyanfar said.

"Ah. Your cousin."

Cold went through her nerves. "Distant," Pyanfar said.
"Our clans have a distant tie." *O gods, I hope he doesn't
have our kinships in library.* "Ceremonial." The lie wove
itself wider and wider. "Hani place *sfik* on kinships. And
blood-debts. Harun has ties to some of these. I have ties
to Harun and Faha, there. It's really quite simple. And

blood-debt to Jik and Kesurinan." *Not to forget that business. Add it in. Secure Jik much as I can.* "We can have that even to non-hani." *Change the subject. Hold out possibilities to the bastard.* "There's *sfik*-value on that too."

And if hani around the table did not know now that every other word she said to the kif was a lie, they were deaf and blind.

"Has he talked to you?"

"Somewhat." She took a chance, reached and took a sip of parini. "I'm going to keep him on my ship as adviser. I'm sure Kesurinan understands, ummn? But he misses the smokes, *hakkikt*. He truly does."

"The smokes," Sikkukkut repeated in a flat tone, as if she had gone quite mad. "Do we still have such a thing?"

The *skku* in the center of the tables searched anxiously among its robes. Efficient, by the gods. Foresight covering all sorts of hospitality. It brought out the little sack, eyes aglitter with triumph.

"Your *skku* is amazing," Pyanfar murmured, making a low-status kif very happy in its neurotic zeal; and took another minuscule sip of parini.

"I might bestow you another gift," Sikkukkut said. And scared two kif and a hani at the same time.

"Huh." She kept her calm. With difficulty. "We hardly have formalities enough to keep another *skku* occupied. Nothing so splendid, *hakkikt*."

"But you want another gift."

Bluff called. She looked up, lowered her ears and got them up again, heart hammering. "Is the *hakkikt* disposed to talk policy?"

"Ah." Sikkukkut set down his cup, hands in his lap as he sat crosslegged in the insect-chair. "Shikki," he said sharply; and the *skku* eeled its way over to lay the smoke-pouch on the table in front of Jik.

Jik picked it up carefully, felt of it and carefully extracted a smokestick and a lighter. "You mind?"

Sikkukkut gave a wave of his hand and Jik put the stick in his mouth and carefully lit it. His hands were shaking, but only a little, limned in the fire that lit his face. The light died. He drew a long breath of smoke in as if it was life itself.

"Foul habit," Sikkukkut said as the smoke went up to

mingle with the ammonia-stink and the incense. He rested an elbow on the raised insect-leg of his chair and leaned his chin on that hand. "But you and I remain friends. Kkkt. Good. That is very well. Kotgokkt kotok shotokkiffik ngik thakkur."

—*prisoners?*

All round the table backs stiffened. Except Jik's, to look at him; he sat there concentrating on his smoke, with a cloud of it round his head.

"Sit still," Pyanfar said in hani; and Haunar Vrossaru and Vaury Shaurnurn turned their heads to look toward their escorts, the only two who did.

But maybe they knew their crew.

"Is the *hakkikt* disposed?" Pyanfar repeated.

"The hani captain may push too far," *Ikkhoitr*'s captain said out of his silence. "Be careful of it."

"Makes me nervous," Pyanfar said. "This place. We're exposed sitting here at station. If I were Akkhtimakt—" She rested her elbow on her knee, easy pose, though her heart was hammering away fit to take her breath: thank gods for the incense that masked the sweat. Her nose itched and ran. She ignored it. "This place smells of trap, *hakkikt.*"

"In what way?"

"I'm an old trader, *hakkikt.* And stsho may cheat you one way and five more, but I never knew them to plot violence." *Phrase it so the bastard has salve for his pride. A trader can know merchant-things. He isn't expected to understand grasseaters, is he?* "But they'll buy violence, without understanding what they've bought. They've made mistakes before. This is a big one. They've involved the *han.* Technically, hani are allied with Akkhtimakt, because of the stsho treaty, which gave him what he never would have had. Support on the far side of the Compact. All of a sudden you don't hold the majority of Akkhtimakt's territory. He's just quadrupled his holdings. And he's on the other side of an uncrossable gulf. No jump-points, *hakkikt,* no bridge between hani space and here. It's a narrow neck and one where he can interdict you if hani abide by that treaty."

There was deathly quiet in the room. No kif moved. Then a nervous shift from the Faha. Ears were flat, all in that section of the table.

And Jik shot her a carefully frowning glance. Sucked in

a great deal of smoke and let it go. "A." Drawing Sikkukkut's attention to himself.

"Is it so."

"He go Urtur. Damn sure not go Kita."

"You have ships at Kita."

Another slow draw at the smoke. "I don't swear. Good
guess. We send message Maing Tol. My Personage make
move on Kita. Where he go? Here? Got no cross-jump but
Tt'av'a'o, damn bad choice. Methane-breather, human, lot
mahendo'sat. Damn bad choice. You no do. He no do."

"Should I wonder that that is then precisely what I
should do?"

Go off toward Tt'av'a'o and possible ambush, and involve
himself with everything Jik had listed? Go home to Akkht
and consolidate his hold? Or to Llyene and terrorize the
stsho in a raid every kifish pirate must have dreamed of?

They were all good choices for the Compact as a whole.
If they cast themselves totally on hope of rescue from the
mahendo'sat.

Who had their hands full already, saving their own hides.

"Masheo-to," Jik said. And something more involving
Akkhtimakt and ship IDs, rapidly. While Sikkukkut's black
eyes fixed on him.

"Kkkt," Sikkukkut said. "Interesting thought. Do you
follow that? No? Keia proposes that Akkhtimakt may have
faked identification in his ship ID. That he may not be
among that group we dispersed, but already at Urtur. We
will both have taken precautions: my ships will reach all
the jump-points that lead out from here in time to prevent
escape from insystem or to prevent any ships not already
launched from arriving here. But Keia favors us with another interesting proposal. I tell you I value you both."

*Gods, he means it. The absolute, thorough-going bastard.
He's dead inside. He doesn't know what he's done. He
doesn't know Jik's his enemy. Or if he knows it he doesn't
know it, from the gut. He hasn't got the equipment. He theo-
rizes. You can revise a theory, but never gut-knowledge,
never instinct.*

*He's naïve as Skkukuk in some ways. He mimics our
ways. Even friendship. And he can't feel it. He can't ever
understand us: just logic his way through our motives; and
that won't always work for him.*

"Not know where he be," Jik said. Another puff of smoke. "Maybe even hani space."

Hani bodies all about the table stiffened.

"Maybe already there, a?"

Gods look on us all. Let it go. Let him think his way into it. Slowly, slowly.

"Kkkkt. Kkkkt." Sikkukkut's tongue flicked in the gap of his teeth.

Can we go too far? Make him lose sfik *in front of his servants?*

And beside the *hakkikt* the captain of *Ikkhoitr* leaned over and spoke rapidly and quietly. Sikkukkut answered a word or two back.

Gods rot him. That one's no good news.

Worse and worse.

Ikkhoitr's captain got up from table. And left. While Sikkukkut looked their way again. "You will have noticed the dispatch of certain ships. They are not the first. From Meetpoint, from Kshshti, from Mkks and Kefk. Continually my messengers have gone to inform my ships. And ships have moved. You have never seen all I have. Nor is this all of Akkhtimakt's company. You are quite correct. Kkkkt. From you, Keia, I expect a certain astuteness in such matters. But the hani are also hunters. And you've talked to them, have you, Keia?"

Jik frowned. And said nothing at all.

"Not quite by his wish," Pyanfar said. "Say that friendship has other uses. He was confused when we got him. He talked rather too much to us. That simple." *We're lying, Kesurinan. Trust me. Sit still.* "It's what I said. Nothing *Jik* wants. He knows something Goldtooth doesn't. *That* made the difference. Tully doesn't know what the humans are up to, but a thought occurs to me that I don't like, *hakkikt.* That the trouble inside the Compact is weakening us as a whole. That the humans may not wait until the trouble's settled. Just delay their attack till the most advantageous moment. Because they will push at us."

"Is this so, Tully?"

Tully made an uncomfortable shift of position. A shrug. Turned a worried look Sikkukkut's direction, hers.

"He has trouble understanding sometimes. Tully. The *hakkikt* asked: will the humans fight the mahendo'sat?"

"Not know." Tully's eyes fixed on hers, shifting minutely as if they hoped to read a clue.

"You told me. Tell him what you told me. *Do* it, Tully."

"Human—" He looked back toward Sikkukkut. Toward this kif who was more than all others his personal enemy. "Come. Got three—" He held up fingers. "Three human—"

"Governments," Pyanfar said.

"Three," Tully said. "Fight. Push one humanity to here."

"Kkkkt."

"I belong *The Pride.* Crew-man!"

Keep your hands off me, you bastard.

And implicit in a glance her way: *Captain, don't let them take me.*

"He doesn't know much more than he's said, *mekt-hakkikt.* But he understands methane-breathers. I don't think the rest of his people do. He had no importance among his people. They got what information from him they wanted to hear and they shoved him aside without listening to the rest of what he had to say. They didn't *want* him to say the rest. We think. Gods know *he* might not understand as much as I think. We might not understand him. I think he's tried to tell the truth, but I don't think he was in on the planning. Just a crewman. That's all he ever was. That's what he still is." Her hands wanted to shake. If the kif took him, there was nothing she could do to stop it. *I got their attention on him. Gods, get it off!*

"But," Sikkukkut said, "we have other sources to question. The stsho will not hold back information. They bend to any wind. And I have sufficient of them to gain an excellent picture of what happened here—they will lie to a mahendo'sat, they will lie to a hani, but they will not lie to a kif. And they have very large eyes. Two of my least *skkukun* are on the station at this moment; and so are three hundred thousand stsho." Again Sikkukkut lifted the cup and drank, a quick dart of his dark tongue. "They are apprised of the possibility that I will decide to remove this station. And that they will not be allowed to leave—"

My gods.

"I have told my *skkukun* the same. They will find information. They will cause the stsho to find it. We have already identified responsible individuals. My enemy destroyed the station datafiles. After doubtless sucking them into his own records. So there is nothing to learn there: I expected as much. But we have direct resources. Ksksi kakt."

A servant moved. Fast. Hani shifted anxiously as an inner door opened, as kif rearranged themselves, arustle like leaves in a midnight forest.

"Sit still," Pyanfar said again. In case any of them forgot. Her ears were flat, her muscles had a chill like fever in them that was going to start her shivering. She reached, ears flat and scowling, and picked up her cup and drank.

The parini went down like fire. And held her caught in that minor, eye-watering misery when a gibbering outcry rang out from the opened door.

A gleam of white showed in the doorway, where kif parted, where dark-robed kif shoved stsho forward, through the shadowed rows of their own kind. Stsho white, stained with sodium-light, marked with darker smears, their pitiful, spindly limbs all bruised from kifish handling.

So fragile. A breath could break such limbs.

Jik turned his face in that direction, slowly. The smoke curled up from the stick in his hand. He did not move, himself, beyond that; the other captains turned in their chairs; and Tully—on her other side—she had no way to observe. She guessed.

"Now," said Sikkukkut, "let us ask some questions."

"Translator's not making sense of it," Hilfy murmured, gnawing her mustaches and monitoring kifish transmissions. *Harukk* was talking to its minions off-station. Talking a great deal. "I don't like it, gods, I don't like this."

"Takes a decision somewhere," Geran said, "to get that ship that talkative. You'd think Sikkukkut'd be busy. You'd hope he'd be."

"Calling more of them in?" Khym said.

"They got a worry about something," Geran said. "No. They won't pull ships in while there's a chance of something coming in and catching them nose to station. That's some kind of bulletin. Instruction. Gods know what."

"Still talking," Hilfy muttered. And remembered *Harukk*'s dark bowels. The transmission went on at some length.

Likely Haral remembered *Harukk,* too. She had seen it, when they pulled the Tahar crew out of there.

"Hostages," Hilfy said. "That's what he's got Gods-*be,* Haral, I could make a routine query over there, take the temperature."

"Just sit still," Haral said. "Captain's got enough trouble. Let it be."

They flung the larger of the two stsho at the table, between Pyanfar's chair and Haroury Pauran's. *Gtst* collapsed all in a nodding huddle of white, delicate limbs, of swirling pearlescent draperies at the table edge. *Gtst* shuddered and shivered and bubbled.

While Pyanfar looked at the designs of pastel paints on *gtst* brow and her heart thudded in shock.

It was Stle stles stlen. Or it had been. Gods knew what personality the wretch had fragmented to when the second wave of kif invaded *gtst* station.

"You recognize this creature?" Sikkukkut asked. "Or do they still look alike to you?"

"I know *gtst.*"

Gtst—or *gstisi:* it might well be Phasing—wrung *gtst* hands and wailed something about noble kif and noble hani. Moonstone eyes looked her way, liquid with pleading, and Pyanfar's stomach turned over. *Gtst* stank of oil and perfume and something indefinable, doubled when the kif flung the other stsho down beside it.

"Talk," Sikkukkut said to the stsho. "Or we begin to hurt something, perhaps one of these others; perhaps your translator. And then if you don't, we will hurt *you.* Do you understand, creature?"

The stsho bubbled and babbled at each other; the one clung to the person which had been Stle stles stlen, fingers locked in *gtst* robes. *Do it, do it,* the translator was crying, and the erstwhile Stle stles stlen poured out a sudden flood of wails and words.

"—The Director is not responsible," the translator cried then. "*Gtst* was another person—"

"That's very well. We don't care which of you we skin."

"—*But!* But! noble, esteemed friend—this wretch Akkhtimakt—"

"You begin already to make a lie. Tell us about the treaty and about what happened here."

More babble. The translator turned *gtst* face about again,

moonstone eyes wide, *gtst* mouth a tiny, trembling *o*. "It was a mistake, it was—"

"Report what you did!"

"We are not a violent people, we had need—"

"This translator is useless. We can send for another."

"—*but!* but! in our foolishness we listened to agents of the other *hakkikt,* we had need of ships to defend us and in our foolishness—"

"What of your bargains with mahendo'sat; with hani; with the methane-folk; with *humans?*"

"Mahendo'sat are with these creatures, these—" The translator looked Tully's way with a visible shiver that made all *gtst* plumes tremble. "Creatures! We ejected them. We sought accommodation with the hani. But hani have no great ships. What can we do now but shelter with the most powerful? We were fools to think this was Akkhti-makt: we see very well now: we will make treaty with you, at once, at once, estimable! Defend us!"

"Kkkkt. What an offer! And what will you do for me, little grasseater?"

"We have science! We have—unique objects—"

The whole of stsho culture—open to kifish piracy.

Pyanfar coughed, and the stsho mistook it and trembled the more, lifting *gtst* hands to the kif.

"Save us! Estimable!"

"This thing is a fool," said Sikkukkut. "Where is Ismehanan-min? What bargains have you made with him and with his Personage?"

Jik, Jik, for godsakes don't make a move, gtst'll talk, O gods, we can't help it and we don't need craziness right now, we need wits, we need the sharpest gods-be dealing any trader ever made.

The stsho once Stle stles stlen waved *gtst* hands and babbled.

"*Hakkikt,*" the translator lisped. "*Hakkikt,* Ismehanan-min dealt with us, he is the other side of a conspiracy, pernicious, pernicious, most honorable *hakkikt*—" The stsho waved *gtst* hands, rocking and tearing with nervous fingers at *gtst* robes; *gtst* cast an anxious look back where the kif stood with guns all about them; toward Jik, who had no restraint on him. "We are not a violent people. What are we to do? Mahendo'sat crowd upon us, they force their way into our offices—we need guards to secure our privacy, but we are not a violent people—"

"And we are not a patient kind," Sikkukkut said, and Stle stles stlen said something lengthy and urgent.

"—The mahendo'sat left us. They left these few they said must close out certain business, menials, functionaries, persons of no import— Lies. They attempted bribery—"

"To which you surely listened."

"—Akkhtimakt had betrayed our agreements!"

"What are the mahendo'sat up to?"

"—They are making you fight each other, *hakkikt*. One mahe aids you; the other dare not aid your enemy, but he leads and lures him."

O thank gods.

"Kkkkt, is this so, Keia?"

Jik was relighting his smoke, which looked to be reluctant to stay lit. He capped the fire. "Sure. Same we always like you best. You win, *hakkikt,* we glad deal with you. I think maybe you do win. Right now I not much happy 'bout humans. So same I convince Ana, he switch tactic fast. Maybe come you side, a? Meanwhile got this hani problem."

"A ship of mine has gone to Kshshti. If it finds no resistance it may find other sympathetic kif and send them out from there. I tell you that we will cover all of space. We are already close to encounter with your partner. At Tt'a-v'a'o. Or wherever he is."

Pyanfar sat still, forced herself to sit still. *O gods, gods, how much does he know? How much can these hunter-ships do? If kif can match the mahendo'sat, all bets are off, what Akkhtimakt may be doing, what he's doing— Would the kif ever have started this mess, with inferior ships?*

"We sit here," Sikkukkut said, "attempting to preserve three hundred thousand fools. Why this is, I wonder. Perhaps I shall lose patience with it. In a very little time any outsystem spotter will be receiving our early movements down his timeline. Once he knows *Harukk* has docked, he will know it is too late: I will not have stayed here overlong. Or if he is a fool and does not know that, still I will not be here, kkkkt?" Sikkukkut took a sip from his cup. "As for incursions from system-edge in general, that is all anticipated. *If* some of Akkhtimakt's ships exist out there, which

I still doubt. Only a fool would annoy me and pen himself into the system with me, a fool or a very formidable enemy. Or my friends Keia and Pyanfar, kkkkt? But I am not vastly worried. On the one hand I am not anxious to lose the station itself; on the other anything that brought Akkhtimakt's ships within my reach would please me, and likewise," Sikkukkut said, and turned a glance on the two stsho before which they wilted like grass in the fire. "Likewise anything that brought the perfidious Ismehanan-min to an interview with me. Do you understand me, kkkt?"

"Yes. Yes, honorable."

"He dislodged Akkhtimakt. And the hani ship with him?"

"—Yes, yes. He hung off and waited, the hani went to Urtur. Discovering Akkhtimakt here, these perfidious scoundrels abandoned us, each, yes, honorable."

"And sent you nothing?"

"—Nothing, nothing, O, Honorable, we would tell you. They waited and then these *creatures* came out of hiding! Waiting at the limits of our system! We were shocked, we were dismayed, we cannot understand how they penetrated our net—"

"Akkhtimakt here," Jik said lazily. "Ana know you come. He do thing I say. He wait. Wait you come. Maybe you fight these bastard kif, he come in. He got these human on short chain."

"And you?"

Jik drew a mouthful of smoke and let it out. "What I do, a? What do my ship? My First, she don't fire. We make quiet, wait. I be you friend, *mekt-hakkikt.* Not po-li-cy fight you. Po-li-cy my side want you win. What we got, we come in, hit both you *hakkiktun,* a? Damn mess. Ten, fifteen week got new *hakkikt,* whole different game." There was a stirring in the hall, ominous movement against the lights. Jik lifted a hand. "I not dis-courteous, a? Long time neighbor, you, me. We do fine. I know these thing, same Pyanfar know these thing. Same time I got big worry what we see here not real honest. Maybe bait. Maybe Akkhtimakt sudden smart, want bring us here, hold us here, make us fight Ana while he go do what he want."

Safeties had gone off weapons. "Kkkkt," Skkukuk said anxiously, with a furtive wave of his hand.

"No. Long time the *mekt-hakkikt* been patient with truth. He ask question, he still be patient."

"I am still patient, Keia." Long jaw rested on black, retractile-clawed fist. "Pay no attention to them. I am listening."

"This got big danger. Tully say don't trust human. What happen, a? You got fight Ana, fight human, fight maybe other mahen ship, few; then come some bastard out from Akkht, want make self *hakkikt*—same all time happen, you know you people real good: first time you got trouble you got some bastard want make suicide. All same take time, take ship, take you attention. Same time got Akkhtimakt settle in real good in hani space, same time far from methane-breather—*you* got methane-breather trouble, a? You be real close over here. But Akkhtimakt not got. Maybe he make good friend with mahendo'sat over by Iji— same join with them, come fight human when human make trouble—now where we be, a?"

"That is an elaborate possibility. Very elaborate."

"Same. But two kif want fight, my people always help." Another lifting of a finger. "This time you got luck. Akkhtimakt damn fool, all time push mahendo'sat, mahendo'sat never like help that bastard. A? So you got *no* mahen help to you enemy. Maybe change. That bastard get rule in hani space, he be whole different bastard."

"Can it be you're trying to maneuver me, Keia? Or do you agree in this move, hunter Pyanfar?"

"I think it a real possibility, *mekt-hakkikt.*" While hani captains and Tully sat and listened to this; while kifish hands rested near weapons and the two stsho retreated into a small, soiled ball, glad to be forgotten. Her heart beat to the point of hurting. Her stomach ached and weakness came and went in tides. "I see one way Akkhtimakt could go from here. One path. Mahendo'sat occupy Tt'av'a'o; you have Meetpoint. Either you've got Kshshti or the mahendo-'sat have, by now; or they'll be headed there like chi to a hot spot; on that, I wouldn't predict. The third path Akkhti-makt assuredly has, open all the way behind him." *Do you see, sister captains, do you see yet what we're dealing with, what we're trying to do? For godssakes don't twitch, don't distract this kif, don't make a slip.*

"Kkkkt. One path. Yes. Why do you think I've favored

you as I have? That area of space which lies like a penin-
sula amid a gulf without jump-points. That unfortunate circumstance which has made hani isolate. And kept them
pinned between that gulf and mahen ambitions. Do you
understand me, hunter Pyanfar? Do you know now why I
have given you so much?"

"Hani space." The pain was back in her chest. She found
breathing difficult. "A pocket in which Akkhtimakt can be
contained. Uncrossable space on two sides, unfriendly mahendo'sat on the third, yourself on the narrow fourth."

"Mahendo'sat will be quite busy. I want Akkhtimakt
kept busy. I know you have self-interest in that. Do you
recall our debate on self-interest?"

"I have one there. Yes. A considerable interest."

"Name what you need."

So easy? My gods. So easy. "These captains. All these in
my company. Their ships."

"Do you include *Aja Jin?*"

*Gods, gods. Be calm, Pyanfar. Don't lose it all. Don't let
the voice wobble.* Her nose was running. She sniffed and
tried to focus. Ignored the itch. "I wouldn't put Jik to a
choice between you and Goldtooth. Not twice. With *me*
he's got clear reason to cooperate. With me he'll be fighting
something that's clearly his enemy, and a threat to that
whole border. Self-interest. He won't bolt and go home till
he knows hani aren't going to collapse. I *know* the mahendo'sat, and everything he's done is perfectly reasonable. So
is his going with us now. You want hani ships to fight
against Akkhtimakt, they will, and a lot safer with *Aja Jin's*
guns with us."

"Kkkkt. Merchants. Against hunters. I will give you reliable ships of my own. *They* will give you that chance."

"And Jik, *mekt-hakkikt.* I'm going to have to make a
show of power with both the mahendo'sat and the *han:* call
it hani psychology, call it *sfik,* but it works that way. You
need no ornaments. I do, to prove what I've got. I need
Jik and *Aja Jin;* I need my human; I need your ships—"
All right, I accept them. Worry about my motives, bastard.

Sikkukkut's jaw lifted ominously. And sank again. Dark
eyes glittered in the sodium-light, beneath the hood.

"*Skku* of mine, you look to make yourself a *hakkikt.*"

"I look to hold hani space, *mekt-hakkikt.* I'm securing my agreements."

There was profound silence. Her heart beat hard, every thump a pain in her chest; her limbs went cold and hot and the edges of the room went in and out of focus around the one darkness that was the kif; and life or death, then and there, if the kif took suspicion, if one of the hani captains reached her tolerance, if someone moved or sneezed, they could all die.

And worlds would.

O gods, O gods of my mothers, gods greater and lesser, littlest and far away, gods of my world—hear an old reprobate: can you move a kif . . . even a little bit?

"Kkkkt. Take all you have named. Dispose of Keia as you will. On his ship or in your hands. Now. Go. You are dismissed, *skku-hakkikt.*"

She drew in a breath; a second one. Not *skku-hakkiktu* but *skku-hakkikt.* Not *vassal of mine* but *vassal-prince.* Her heart beat and skipped. Then she gulped air, grabbed the insect-leg of the chair and thrust herself to her feet. "Up," she said. "Move. The *hakkikt's* order, gods rot it, don't sit and think about it!"

Hani moved as if galvanized; Jik was slower, but only to put out his smoke and to pocket the pouch.

And the stsho huddled there at her feet gibbering and wailing in pain. A chill went over her. She hesitated, turned back toward Sikkukkut, opened her mouth.

"If the *hakkikt* has no use for these—"

"Enough!"

She stepped past the stsho. One caught at her trouser-leg. "Help," it cried. "Esteemed hani, help, intercede—"

She walked past. She had to. The kif had made an aisle, directing everyone out.

No further risk, I can't, I daren't, gods, don't let me fall on my face here and now.

I can't do more than I've done.

"That's another," Hilfy said. "*Harukk's* talking again. Encoded. Names—that's orders to ships. *Chakkuf. Sukk. Nekkekt.* I can't make anything out of it, but they could be moving-orders."

"I don't like this." From Tirun.

"What's going on?" From Chur's channel, over the main speakers.

"You know everything we know," Khym said.

Which summed it up well enough.

If there was a spotter, something they had constantly to worry about, it would lie more than a lighthour out, maybe three or four. And it would move when it felt like it. When its own criteria had been met. One of Goldtooth's ships, maybe. Maybe one of Akkhtimakt's. Or more than one. They sat here with nose to station with the chance, however remote, that some attack might come in, some mass of ships might be sitting out there dead silent and so lost in the immensity of the spherical search-zone that they were virtually invisible. Like the spotters. There was no way to find that kind of lurker either, except by that same blind luck, or its own error. The entire perimeter of Meetpoint's dark-mass influence, at a spherical radius of one to four lighthours—was an impossible area to search for any single ship. Station obscured part of their sweep and rotation complicated matters, with station not sending, the buoys on but erratic, and the kif deliberately censoring their own scan output. There was not even a star close enough to light an object, little help that that was: the dark-mass radiated, but with a sullen, dying heat, a spot their instruments regularly scanned, looking for any anomaly that might be a ship trying to mask itself; Meetpoint's own mass gave off a quiet white noise to their most sensitive instruments, the several system navigational buoys screamed their false information into the dark, emissions of a vast number of ships churned and dispersed in a maelstrom generated by other traffic; while their best chance of seeing a hidden ship lay in the computer's memory of the starfield continually overlaid on its present reception. Any star occulted, anywhere about the sweep, might signal that presence, and they had had two such occultations, which buoy-information called planetesimals—

"—Library," Haral had said on the first such: "does the Meetpoint buoy correlate its input with archives?"

Meaning did the buoy-system ever check itself to see if a cold, silent object it spotted was a known planetesimal? Affirmative. It did. But it reported it out as a planetesimal even while it was relaying a query: it was defaulted that way. The AI of the buoy *knew* nothing else to call it. The stsho who built it built no contingencies into it: or they had made them and did not put that information into the navigational ephemeris.

If something was out there hours out it had not *seen* recent developments in any of its timelagged reception: depending on its line of sight, it might only now be watching *Harukk* arriving at station . . . in the confused, digital way of distance-scattered passive. It might not know what ship; or be sure how many were out here.

And gods only knew what would trigger it.

Hilfy wiped her eyes, shifted the com plug, and kept focused. For their very lives.

"Abort linguistics search," Haral said suddenly, out of profound silence. "We need the room in nav."

Hilfy hesitated. And did it. Haral started running calc and never saying what it was for; but if Haral aborted one of Pyanfar's orders it was desperate. She pulled out the print she had, which was all gibberish. Lost. Utterly.

Then com beeped:

"*Harukk-com to all ships at dock: praise to the* hakkikt, *stand by departure.*"

"What are they doing?" Khym exclaimed. "They can't be putting out!"

"We're going live," Haral said sharply. And started throwing switches. Systems thunked and started coming up.

"We keep those connectors?" Tirun asked, businesslike, while Hilfy sweated in panic and punched buttons on her own: "*Harukk-com*, this is *The Pride of Chanur.*"

"*This is* Harukk-com, *praise to the* hakkikt, *report your status.*"

Her mind blanked. She sorted wildly, found the standard reports, shot them over. "Praise to the *hakkikt,*" she muttered, "status on our personnel."

"*Returning,*" the kif said. "*We are in receipt of your data,* Chanur-com. *Provide data on your subordinates.*"

She shut the channel down to hold. Kifish courtesies, abrupt and rude by any other standard. She punched in on Haral, whose information-request light was flashing priority. "They say they're coming back. *Harukk* wants stats from the rest."

"Subordinates," Haral said. "Get the stats on *all* those ships."

Haral was right, gods, entirely right: it was kifish, it was a matter of protocols, claim everything the captain claimed, have all those stats in hand, permit no ship they claimed to report on its own. Her fingers stabbed at buttons, opened com to the mahendo'sat, to Tahar, to every other hani berth.

Claim it or lose it.

Down to the docks again, herself and all her company, and no kif but Skkukuk with them. Pyanfar drew one great breath of burn-tainted air and drew a second, and ventured a glance about her as others overtook her at the bottom of *Harukk*'s ramp. Jik and Tully, Harun, Tauran, Vrossaur, Faha— The faces blurred and hazed: she went lightheaded in the change of air. "Did what we could," she muttered. "We got a chance. Whatever we got to argue among ourselves we do it on the way. Jik, Jik, my gods—" She bit it off, with the sight of the kif in the tail of her vision and remembering Skkukuk's interested ears. "Come on. Let's move it. We got to clear this dock." The departure light was flashing on the wall over their heads, *Harukk* preparing to move out. Across the dock, stsho huddled in forlorn panic—foolhardy of their kind. The prudent were locked in other levels, hidden deep in station interiors.

Where kifish crews searched for records and raided central in search of names and data.

"We're ready to move," Harun said. "We've been ready, waiting the chance for months. And we've got questions, but I'm not going to ask any. Any way we can get out of this godsforsaken place I'll take the ticket."

With an ears-down, troubled look. No fools in this group. Oldest to youngest.

Though Munur Faha looked at her with her anxieties plain and the whites showing round her eyes.

What are you doing? What kind of deal are you making? You were lying but how often and where and for whose sake?

As for Dur Tahar, she walked along in her own world, her scarred face grim, never looking at other hani. Scars were everywhere about her. Inside and out.

Skkukuk brought up the side and clicked and muttered to himself; Tully walked along with his hand on his gun the same as the kif.

And Jik asked Kesurinan quiet, rapid questions, the two of them talking dialect as they walked.

Do what about it? Jeopardize his life and everything else? Pyanfar fretted and gnawed her mustaches, and walked along near the pair, her heart speeding as she saw other departure lights start flashing all down the row. Their own ships.

"Word's out," she said, and glanced at the hani walking on the other side of her. "We do it the way you heard it. Adjustments and amendments when we clear Urtur. We've *got* to clear Urtur. We'll be thanking the gods for that kifish escort and I hope to gods Urtur is as far as Akkhtimakt gets, but I doubt it. We have a long run and a hard one ahead of us. We're fast enough to keep pace with the hunters. We've had some modifications: say we've been running courier for the mahendo'sat and we've got a hunter-rig. There's a *lot* been happening, but you heard some of it in there. What I'm worried about is getting us through systems fast enough and holding together long enough to get home in time. I can slow down; so can *Aja Jin;* and I can argue the kif into it; but nothing's going to slow Akkhtimakt down, and they're all hunters. Days can count in this. We're bypassing Hoas Point. What're your unladed caps on the Urtur jump and what on the brake and cross to Kura vector? Who's low?"

A low mutter of stats and capacities. *Industry* was far and away the strongest; little *Starwind* was fast enough, engines large enough with its light mass to send her right up into *Industry*'s rating. *Shaurnurn's Hope* put them only a little down, and *Pauran's Lightweaver* only a shade under that. But *The Star of Tauran* was far under. Likewise *Vrossaru's Outbounder.*

"You know," Pyanfar said, "Tauran, Vrossaru. We can slow down and make your rate; it'll cost us. You understand what we're facing. I'm going to ask you—I got to ask—"

"We'll get there," Sirany Tauran said. "Our own way."

"No. Power down. Mothball at dock. I know it's risking your ships; so's the trip home. Listen. My crew's blind tired, strung out. Tahar's little better. I can take Tahar on *The Pride*—" Instant glower from Dur Tahar, but no word. "Or one crew can go with me and work alternate; other with Tahar. Get us all there alive and precious days faster."

Work alternate with a pirate? Bloodfeud and outlawry. She all but heard the scream. But:

"You can keep an eye on us," Tahar said in a low voice. "Split shift or whole. Whatever suits you."

"All right," Vrossaru said. "*We'll* take you on."

Tauran looked at Pyanfar's direction. Thoughts went through her eyes. *Aliens. Gods know what.* And maybe on the other side: *That Chanur ship's got priority protection from the kif. And it's fast. It'll get us there alive. And we'll be sitting where we can do some good if they're lying, won't we?*

"All right," Sirany Tauran said. "Soon as I can get my crew off. We got seven. You got berths?"

"We'll find 'em." *Does she know about Khym?* Pyanfar's muscles clenched up and let go again. *Gods be, we got worse problems than hani prejudices.* "Thanks." They had reached *Moon Rising*'s berth. And *Aja Jin* and *The Pride* beyond, all with departure warnings blinking urgently above. "We get those stats relayed ship to ship, right down the line, direct transmission. We have to share specifics with our kifish escort, no choice. Let's get ourselves out of this port, we don't want anything intervening and we got gods know what going we don't know where."

"Understood," Harun said. "Luck to us."

"Luck," Faha said. "Gods look on us." And with the appearance of a shudder, she looked at Tully and his dark-robed partner. Perhaps in that instant of afterthought she wanted to take that pious wish back. But that would have been an embarrassment. "Hearth and home," she added, and with monumental charity: "and whatever." With a physical effort.

Then Munur Faha started on ahead, her own ship farther on; other captains followed, Harun and Vrossaru with a backward look, Vrossaru's ears flat in dismay.

"Tahar," Pyanfar said: and Tahar stopped there at her own dock. So did Tully and Skkukuk. "Jik," she said. Jik and Kesurinan stopped, too, within an easy sprint of *Aja Jin*'s berth. "We got it worked out," Pyanfar said. Which

Jik and Kesurinan might not have heard, they had been talking too intensely and too urgently all the way back. Passing instructions, fomenting conspiracy. Gods knew what.

But Jik left his First and came back to her, his dark face all sober. "Where I go, a?" He held up both hands. "Want back? Or you tell me go?"

"Gods rot you, what are you likely to do? Leave us? Get us all skinned? Kill my world with your conniving?" Sikkukkut's kifish ignorance had let this hazard loose: *Dispose of Keia as you will.*

Now it came to a bluff she could not call, force she could not use, persuasion she knew would not work. To haul him aboard *The Pride* even by strong pressure now would set Kesurinan off, trigger gods knew what contingency orders.

"I do number one good back there."

"I got no way to trust you!"

"I got interest like I say." He reached out and laid his hands on her shoulders. Stared into her eyes, and she stared up at him, looking for something to rely on. *Liar. Ten times a liar. Your gods-be government won't let you tell the truth once a day.* "Hani got importance, Pyanfar. I swear. God witness."

"More than your own? Don't tell me that!" Her knees felt weak. The face looming over her was alien, the eyes as unreadable as Tully at his most obscure.

"We be neighbor to hani more than kif, a? That be backside whole mahen space, I don't doublecross you."

"Gods be, we're reasoning like the kif. Self-interest!"

"Politic all time reason like kif. Damn mess. I best pilot you got, hani. You want lock me up? Or you want trust?"

"When did it ever work?" Panic rushed over her. "No, gods rot it, I don't want to trust you."

"Work in there number one good. You get me out, got me smokes, a?"

"Same time we got Sikkukkut going to come in behind us! You know he is! He's appointed *me* to do his work for him, you think he's not going to follow up on it?"

"Damn sure. You be no fool, Pyanfar." He waved a hand toward *Aja Jin*'s berth. "Number one fine ship in whole Compact, you got. Got number one fine pilot. Me. We go keep promise, a?"

"Get! Go! Give your orders! And get your rotted carcass back aboard my ship and give me that data before we undock. I want it, Jik, I want it in plain language and plain charts!"

"You beautiful." A touch at her face. She flinched and spat; and he gave one of his maddening humor-grins, then turned and sprinted for his own access-ramp, Kesurinan running with him stride for stride.

For their own ship. Their own choice. Gods knew if he *would* come back. The docks were dangerous. Kif might intercept him even on that short a crossing between ships. Sikkukkut might discover something in his questioning of stsho to change his mind. Stle stles stlen might have secreted damning records, being a trader through and through.

She looked at Dur Tahar. And had no doubt at all of the pirate, of her enemy, of a hani she had been willing to kill.

"That may have been a mistake," Pyanfar said.

"Could be."

"Tahar, if we get through this, anything between us. . . ."

Tahar's face went hard, her ears flat. "Yeah. I know."

"You don't know, gods rot it! There *is* no bloodfeud, between you and Chanur. You've paid it."

The ears came up. "Paid it on your side too," Tahar said with Tahar's own surly arrogance. And stood there a breath longer before she turned abruptly and headed for *Moon Rising*'s ramp.

It left her Tully and Skkukuk. A bewildered and nonplussed Skkukuk, Tully close at her side and the kif standing there as if his orderly world were all disarranged.

The great captain let his enemy lay hands on her. The great captain believes she has these for subordinate. The captain is wrong. Can the great captain be such a fool? Beware these hani. They are not subordinate either.

She lifted her chin. Come-hither. And Skkukuk came, all anxious, not without a suspicious glance toward the vanishing mahendo'sat. "Hakt', that is dangerous."

"Friend," she said. And in perversity reached out and laid a hand on Skkukuk's hard arm, from which touch he flinched out of reach.

"Kkkt!" As if she had attacked him. Very like her own

gut reaction with Jik. And she had not perceived Jik's touch as lifethreatening.

"I teach you a thing, Skkukuk. You're traveling with hani. You'll hear things that may disturb you." A second time she reached, and this time caught him. The arm was thin, hard as metal. She felt a tremor there. "*Scare* you, *skku* of mine? Power among hani is a different matter. Power among hani is a handful of clans that just decided to go along with me because I handed them the only way out of here they're ever going to get. And because as long as there've been clans on Anuurn, there's been Chanur, and our roots go deep and our connections are complicated, and we're calling in debts they have to pay for *sfik* reasons and self-protection. We're connected to Faha; Faha's got ties of its own. Gods know I'd have to look up library to see where the others run. That's the way we are. Clan is *one entity*. You're *skku* to Chanur. Do you see? You behave yourself with these strangers aboard. And they won't gain a bit on you. Their relation is all with Chanur as a clan, do you follow that?"

Dark eyes glittered. She stared at a kif's face a handspan from hers, closer than she ever wanted to be. He made her nose run. And she made him shiver.

"Yes, hakt'." he said. "Power."

She let him go. And wanted a bath. Wanted clean air. Wanted—gods, never to have tried to reason with a kif. Or to have dealt with one.

"Come on," she said, shoved him and then Tully into motion and turned and hurried to *The Pride,* faster and faster, Skkukuk close after her, Tully panting along beside her, his breath hollow and hoarse from the thin air and the chill. *Get you out of this, lad, before you catch a cough. Get me out of this. Gods, I'm too old for this kind of stuff.* She took the pocketcom from her belt. "This is Pyanfar. Open up, hear me? We're coming in."

"Aye," Haral's voice came back.

Up the ramp. Into the chill ribbed yellow of the passageway. Around the bend and toward the white light, the safety of the airlock. She came across that threshold weak-kneed and with her side one mass of pain.

"Lock it up," she yelled at com. "We're all in."

"Aye," Haral said. *"Everyone all right?"* The hatch whined

and hissed shut; and they were as free of the kif as they were
able to be.

She shut her eyes and hung there, bent over then to get
her breath while Tully did the same.

"Captain?"

"Fools, fools!" Skkukuk cried, and an alien grip closed
on her arm. "The *mekt-hakt'* is starved, is fainting for your
incompetence!"

Tully snarled something at him. Pyanfar rescued her own
arm, blinking dazedly as it became almost a matter of keeping two men apart. Neither one hers. And both being hers,
in a way which had nothing to do with being male. She had
never seen that look on Tully's face. Tully's teeth bared
without humor at all, teeth no match for Skkukuk's, which
were all too close. She straight-armed them apart, hard.
"Manners, gods-be, *shut it down!*"

"Captain?"

"I'm all right," she said, and shook her head, dazed,
dizzy, and with a rush of fight-impulse going through her
veins that turned her giddy. Human sweat and kifish mingled in her nostrils with her own. *So much for human/
kifish cooperation.*

*Gods, no time, we got our orders, I got no time to go
away like this.*

"I'm coming down there," Khym said.

"No need." She felt totally disconnected, blinked back
and forth between Skkukuk and Tully. Her husband in it
was the last thing she wanted. "We got more coming. Tauran's crew is boarding as soon as they can get locked up
and back here. Working alternate with us. They tell you?
We got a trip to make."

The door to the inside corridor opened. *"Where, cap'n?"*
Haral's voice took over com again. *"Where are we going?"*

They had not known. "Home," she said; and felt a momentary rush of triumph for her own cleverness.

Until she thought again of Chur, and the cost it might
be to them all in more terms than one. The triumph faded,
left only an ache and a vast and mortal terror. "They've
turned us loose. We're going home."

Chapter 8

"Go," she said to Skkukuk outside the airlock. "If you want to get to quarters for any reason, get to it. You're going to be standing watch out by the ramp in ten minutes. We got too much traffic coming in here to take any chances. *And be polite!* Hear?"

"Yes, hakt'!"

"Get!"

He ran, a flurry of black robes and rattle of weapons, down the corridor toward his own quarters.

That left her and Tully; and Tirun coming to meet them, welcome sight. "You all right, captain?"

"We got Tauran coming in, we got nowhere to put them, we got data up to our ears to process into nav, but things could be worse—" Another figure turned the corner, tall and wide-shouldered and hani: her husband was coming her way in a hurry, and she flinched to the very bones. "Haral, you listening up there?"

"Aye, captain."

"Lay us course for Urtur on our old capacity: we got some slower ships to take with us. Have Hilfy line up our direct transmission with *Aja Jin*, we got specifics to get. Then relay the result to Tahar. Have *Aja Jin* run our backup check."

"Won't take long; I got us course plot already on our present cap. I got their caps. We got this fancy mahen computer and I figured we were going somewhere. We doing the sequencing for the whole convoy?"

"You got it." Miracles from the harried bridge. She did not even question them. "Do it, cousin. And get kif stats out of *Harukk*, we got an escort."

Khym intercepted them and fell in to walk with her and Tirun and Tully. "You all right?" he asked. That was all.

"I'm a whole lot better." She discovered she could breathe again. The tightness in her chest let up a bit, and a sneeze startled her. "Gods-be kif." Her eyes watered. She wiped her nose. "Khym, you and Tully want to go up there and get us some sandwiches and get us rigged for a run? We're getting out of here."

"They're letting us go?" Khym asked, ears half-back. Worried-looking.

"You're right, we got troubles. Even the kif are worried. We got to get through Urtur, remember? We got to get past Akkhtimakt to get home. Got to clear out the opposition all the way to Anuurn, that's what we've got. Go do the galley. And give Tully a chance to get off his feet, he's exhausted."

Me, I got to take this ship through jump. We got to move, I got no time to be resting—

"Tully," Khym said. "Galley."

"Aye," Tully said, and quickened his pace and got through to join him; the two of them went off up ahead at a fair walk, Tully staggering a little as he went, muscles undone by fatigue and exertion and cold. Her own felt like rubber.

"Tirun, we got seven of Tauran clan coming in. We got to bed 'em somewhere. Run protocols for me. My brain's mush. Got to figure out where to put Tully and their captain. No, b'gods, put Sirany Tauran in Jik's cabin. Tully—"

"He's with us."

"They're not going to like sharing sheets with 'im on offshift. Gods-be. Our attitudes. We got the world going down and we got to worry about sheets and our gods-cursed prejudices."

"Let 'em gripe. He's crew, captain."

She gnawed her mustaches and heaved a breath. "Let 'em howl, then. We're going to split-shift with a couple of them if I can get it out of Sirany. Do the best we can and hang their sensibilities. If Khym doesn't send them into frothing fits—"

"Aye," Tirun said.

"Let's get at it, then." She waved Tirun into faster motion as they came to the turn for the lift. "We don't know what's going to break loose here. I want us out of here. Fast. We could have a hundred ships all round us."

Three hundred thousand stsho, Pyanfar. Vulnerable and helpless, whatever breaks around them.

Ask the kif to let them go?

What reason? What reason can I think of?

"Better restock that downside freezer, huh? How close are we to full tanks?"

"Three quarters, last I looked. Haral's running checks on systems. She had to cancel that linguistics run in favor of the course plot, cap'n; sorry about that."

"Sorry. My gods. Get. Go. Out of here is all we got time for; tell her I want that course sequence as tight as she can shave it down, no waste time, everything up to cap. Time's what we can't buy."

"Here, here, here," Jik said, using a light-pen to mark the moves on the computer monitor, and the 3-D rotating model obligingly paced itself through its level-changes: he had brought both fiche and software key aboard when he came, and the mahen-installed comp suddenly displayed unguessed virtuosities. "Same come in maybe Tt'a'va'o, maybe V'n'n'u."

Geran made a sound deep in her throat, slow and full of omen. "We got the whole mess shoved off into hani space is what we got."

Jik said nothing at all to that. He had a mouthful of sandwich. He had not stopped for food on *Aja Jin* and arrived opportunely for a handout from *The Pride*'s galley. Pyanfar gulped a mouthful of gfi and blinked with the heat of it while she watched the display run its paces.

Tauran clan was on their way down the docks, with everything they could carry. Tirun was down there in the airlock with Skkukuk on guard at the foot of the ramp, preparing to receive them with their baggage. An eerie quiet hung all about them, *Harukk* and its chosen few bound out from dock on whatever business it chose, the station itself subject to kifish piracies she had no wish to think of; and saw every time she shut her eyes—the wretches on *Harukk,* pale and fragile and physiologically incapable of violence, not even to save their minds or their lives.

A destruct mechanism on the station might be set to blow on a signal sent from outsystem. That was possible too, if someone were totally ruthless: if someone like Akkh-timakt, with no sympathy for three hundred thousand stsho, had mined the station exterior, the whisper of a transmission arriving at lightspeed to some receptor could blow the station's vulnerable skin. On certain vectors they would never know it till it blew, even if they were listening. Gods knew she had no wish to give Sikkukkut any ideas he did not conceive of on his own, by warning him of the possibility. Neither did she want to stay connected to the station any longer than she had to.

In the meanwhile she sat drinking gfi and watching a wobbly-tired mahe trying to reconstruct diagrams out of his memory and a computer's help, and listening to him make misidentifications once and twice and catch himself.

They both needed help. Food was no substitute for rest. And they had soon to move out and start ops for a long, risky jump. Pumps were filling the tanks to capacity. Khym was wandering about readying all the duty stations, setting up everything they had to have to keep them going.

Thank gods for a backup crew on this one.

We're laying ourselves wide open, Tahar and Chanur both—to mutiny and murder. You'll understand us at close range or you'll kill us on the way home.

That was what she implied in that offer. And all the captains knew it; while presumably Sikkukkut and even Skkukuk just thought she had all her compatriots sufficiently bluffed.

Gods hoped they understood, because one hani ship would not be able to talk anything but ops with another of their ships so long as they had their kifish escort; and that meant all the way home.

She watched the red and green marks grow on the screen as Jik built the patterns, and sipped her drink and ate her sandwich.

And slowly the wider implications of what Jik was constructing dawned on her.

Longtime moves. Very longtime moves.

The kif had not lied: the mahendo'sat scheme had been aimed at the kif from the start, a series of operations stretching back to the days when Akkukkak had been the threat. And even before that. Mahendo'sat owned far more than the few hunter-ships they were supposed to have, which meant shipbuilding and secrecy—heavy secrecy, to have kept the whisper of that construction out of the rumor mill.

Gods knew what the kif had been doing during that time. Or what the mahendo'sat knew and what the kif knew about their own intentions that they were not telling and that even Jik might not know the truth of.

Gods knew too, what both kif and mahendo'sat knew about humanity; or how long ago they had known it; and how much truth anyone was telling in that department.

And right now and to this hour, if Jik could get his hands on Tully, she feared, in some dark corner of *The Pride,* Jik would ask him some very hard questions; and perhaps Goldtooth had done that, when he had had Tully aboard *Mahijiru,* and, irony of ironies, gotten distrust. Likely Tully had done his don't-understand-you act. He was very good at it. And gods knew—perhaps Tully's instincts about when to use that silence were better than any of them believed.

Tully had asked her once, with distress wrinkling up his smooth brow, whether Goldtooth was on their side or not. She had not suspected the full implications of it then, or the extent of the pressure Goldtooth might have been putting on him. Or why Goldtooth had jerked him alone away from the human crew that was traveling on the mahen ship *Ijir,* before it fell into Akkhtimakt's grasp.

Being taken off that foredoomed ship was Tully's good fortune; indisputable. But she remembered his face when he had seen her aboard *Mahijiru,* remembered an expression she could read a little better now in retrospect, the terrible stress and the relief with which he had flung himself toward her and wrapped his arms around her, shivering and smelling of fear.

Friend, he had said over and over, said it repeatedly, with a worried look, during that early part of the voyage; but he had kept what he had known behind his teeth . . . while dissension among them, the normal stresses of the crew, any hint of violence—had sent Tully into a panic that was not at all reasonable in their old friend. He had become afraid of them, in the isolation of his translator-interpreted environment, missing virtually all the nuances and the subtleties of what was said around him. He had lived in doubt of them right down to the moment he betrayed his own kind with a warning not to trust humanity.

Tully's was a treason unlike Jik's complicated diagrams. But not simple at all. She watched Tully sitting at scan-monitor, his face—gods, she had even gotten used to it—intent on that screen, seeming lost in his autistic world while the alien babble went on. He *was* listening; she would bet a great deal on it. He was a great deal *like* Jik on some levels. That was the anomaly. He did his work. He came with her time and again onto a kifish ship, which had to be terrible to him. But kif were not his greatest fear. She sensed that in a thousand little moves, little twitches of expression, the way his face and his whole body reacted when there was some momentary false alarm.

It's something not here present. Akkhtimakt's only another kif. He hates Sikkukkut but Sikkukkut doesn't panic him. There's Goldtooth and the mahendo'sat for him to worry about. There's his own kind.

We might end up in a fire-or-die case of mistaken identity: that's certainly to fear, if humanity comes breaking in here.

Or is it something he knows they'll do? Or that he'll have to do?

Or does he see a day—no matter who wins—that someone might take him into that dark corner and start asking questions he won't want to answer?

Gods, why'd he do it? Why'd he help us, even when he's afraid of us, over his own kind? He knows loyalty. He knows friendship. He commits himself to us like kin. It doesn't make sense. What kind of people could create him, and still make him betray them?

A people varied as we are. A people in internal conflict.

A chill went through her. A bit of sandwich went down hard. She washed it down with gfi and focused on Jik's dark, red-rimmed eyes. He had asked her something. *Got?* she realized belatedly. She glanced at the diagrams, at the instructions inbuilt to the comp. She had followed him, followed maybe more than Jik thought. The data and the model were both in their library now, and connected to Nav, the probability of mahen ships being anywhere in this zone.

"Backside," she said. Meaning the hinder side of hani-mahen space. "Where's the stats on that, huh?"

"Not got. Not mine."

A fool would believe this mahendo'sat. But he had shown her too much, confirmed too much, admitted too much. And he knew she could put it together.

The whole mahen–hani treaty was in rags with what he had handed over. And as much as she could ever believe him, it had harm enough in it to be most of the truth he had.

"No way we can make that rendezvous with your ships at Urtur," she said. "And remember, we got two of Sikkuk-kut's ships running hours in front—days, with these merchant rigs dragging at us, if they don't keep the pace we tell them."

"Cost us five day. We got five day?" A weary blink. "World can die in five hour. I got crew shoot message out."

"You mean when we go through there? You got a beeper?"

"Silent till got mahen ID. 'Spensive. I try. Mahen ship come through there, they get, if we don't get kif notice."

Truth, something said again. "Jik. Truth about those short-jumps. Can you do it? Can the kif do it?"

"Got limit like maybe two day light, precise. You try farther you don't come down ever."

"Two days. Then Goldtooth is short of that. Out there turning around."

"Same." A flicker of dark eyes, a little withholding of truth. "We try fix other end, a?"

"You going to run on me?"

"No," he said, and looked her in the eyes when he said it. Reached and grasped her wrist where it lay on the counter. "You, me do lot work get inside this business. We got high priority stay there. You understand? Ana be outside. We be inside. He *use* us way we want to be use', number one good deal. Best. I tell you I damn smart." Ghost of a grin. His hand squeezed her hand. She tolerated it. Gods-be mahendo'sat never figured what pressure did to retractile claws. Same as Tully. "I tell you. You valu'ble. Damn valu'ble. You don't take chance. Hear. All spacer hani be precious stuff."

She retrieved her hand. "You better get back. While you can. Before I change my mind."

"You got good nerve," he said. "Mahendo'sat got no better."

"Same you, gods rot you." Mawkish sentiment overcame her. She laid her ears down. They burned. Crew was witness. But it occurred to her she might never have the chance. "That was quick thinking in there, on *Harukk.*"

"A." He tapped his head. "Number one stuff." He levered himself blearily to his feet and caught himself on the cabinet. "See you otherside, a?"

"Get. Geran, walk him down."

She watched him go, tall black mahe and smallish red-maned hani, off the bridge and down the corridor. A shiver came over her. She drank the last of the gfi and got up to toss the cup. Haral got it from her. They treated her as if she were glass.

"Captain," Haral said, "you want to go lie down, catch a nap, I'll get Tauran settled. I've had my off-shift, you're—"

"I'll take you up on that," she murmured, and wandered off, toward the corridor. There was a thump from below. That was the airlock cycling, too soon to be Jik. Tauran was arriving. They were about to take boarders. They had about time to get them settled in and then they started their outsystem run. It was discourtesy to Tauran, not to be there to meet them.

But to dump her ship into system at Urtur, into kifish fire and Urtur's dust, herself helplessly groggy, she could not do that either.

Neither could she trust a strange pilot at Urtur. It had to be her or Haral. Tirun at a pinch. No one else. *Not with The Pride's new rig, either. O gods. I've got to brief Tauran on systems, she's not used to that much power. Haral's got course auto'ed in, gods know all we have to do is persuade Tauran's pilots to keep hands off the autos and ride with it, O gods, I hope they take orders.*

She turned and trekked the weary, staggering way back to the bridge, over to com, leaned there, over Hilfy's shoulder. "Give me lowerdecks main." And when the light lit: "Tauran. *Ker* Sirany?"

"I'm here," the answer came back.

"Pyanfar Chanur here. Welcome aboard. I'm about to

go offshift awhile. I'd do briefing myself but I'll be taking us through jump. I want you to sit topside during undocks; Meetpoint system is the best chance we have for you to check out our boards, on the run out. Appreciate it if you'd make a quick settle-in and come up to bridge, let my on-shift crew show you the rig."

"Understood."

"We're running wobbly, *ker* Sirany. Out on my feet. Pro-foundest apologies."

"We'll be up there directly, ker *Pyanfar."*

"Thanks." She clicked them out. Shoved back from the board and wandered off with the sour, distressed feeling of proprieties slighted and gods know what she had just said or how it sounded or whether it did any good or not. And no one had explained to Tauran clan about Khym's crew status.

No. They would have heard. Everyone at Meetpoint would have heard plenty about Khym and the riot and the kif. *The Pride* and Chanur had become notorious. They would have heard about Khym, about Tully, even before they saw him. Only Skkukuk had startled them.

They were spacers, not groundlings. Not Immunes, black-breeched and arrogant with power like Ehrran and her ilk.

She stopped by Chur's cabin, shot the door open a moment. Chur was awake, there in her bed with the silver machinery there by the wall and all the tubes going into her arm and out. "You doing all right?" she asked as Chur lifted her head. "We're going home, you hear that? Got crew from *The Star of Tauran* coming on board. You're going to hear strange voices on the bridge. Didn't want you to worry."

"Aye," Chur said. "Been keeping up with things, captain." A difficult wrinkling of her nose. "You look like you could 'bout as well trade places with me."

"Hey, we're all right, we got Jik out. Got his charts and some cooperation for a change. He's back on his ship. We got the whole lot of kif backing us. We're going back home, to make sure nothing of Akkhtimakt's gets that far. Minor matter to the kif, but it may be just our size, huh? We got this one turn at Urtur. Then easier. How are you doing?"

"They threw me back in here. I was up walking, captain." Her ears pricked up. "Want you to think about that one double-jump, about getting to the other side of it. It's all easy after that. Home. You hear me?"

"Promised my sister," Chur said. The voice grew strained with the effort of lifting her head. "Gods-be machine trying to put me out again. No sense of proportion. No sense."

"Cousin." She shut the door and went on, next door to her own cabin, leaned on it and pushed the open button. It let her in. She left it on autoclose, crossed the floor to her bed and flung herself onto it facedown and fully clothed. She reached blind and fumbled after the safety net. It hummed across.

Chur.

Jik could still be setting us up.

Tauran—got to make them understand.

We got Skkukuk down there lunching on little animals, we got Tally stark scared and sitting next Armaments, if he could read the keys; we got Urtur—

—O gods, Urtur.

"Py. Py." A gentle shake at her shoulder. She gasped air and blanket fluff and came out of it with a swimming-motion, a wild flailing of her arm for the bed-edge. It would be an emergency. Everything was an emergency.

She clawed her way to the edge and a hand helped her upright, two hands held her there by the shoulders. She flicked her ears with a chiming of rings she had not taken off; and blinked into her husband's face.

"They need you," he said. "It's all done, we're inertial. I'm one of the ones going offshift. Haral said they need every experienced hand they have up front for this one. They got two Tauran-clan at the boards. I'm just going to have a nap myself. All right?"

He was so calm. She stared at him stupidly. She had slept through undock? Slept through all the clank and thump and the shift of gravity? Haral had handled the ship gentle as eggshells.

Then Haral had evidently told her husband to give up his post and get off the bridge: more, to shut himself up alone in here and wait out the worst jump they had ever made; so her Khym just came back and explained it all calmly? He was terrified. He had to be. *She* was.

Of a sudden she felt a great tenderness toward him; she

reached up and touched his face, nosed him in the ear. "Huh. Good job. Real good job." Nothing more than that, no compliment for following orders; he deserved having that part taken for granted.

Going home. If they lived to get there it was no good place for him. If they lived past Urtur.

"Don't do that," he said in his lowest voice. "You don't want to be late."

"Uhhn." She scrambled past him.

She came onto the bridge still raking her mane into order, still with sleep fogging her brain.

Everything done, the man said. Haral had let her sleep, that was what; Haral had gone and run everything her own way, the competency of which she trusted with her life, high and wide and inside out. But there was more than a handful of lives riding on it this time. And she had wanted her hand on it.

There was Tauran crew in Chur's seat. Skkukuk was in place. Another young Tauran sat at the com, in Tully's place. Haral and Tirun, Geran and Hilfy; and strangers. Sirany Tauran rose from her seat, forward. Her gut knotted in spite of everything.

"Tauran," she murmured, offering a dip of the ears by courtesy to the tawny-hided westerner. "Sorry, dreadfully sorry. I meant to be up here long before this."

"Your First told me you'd run without sleep." Tauran lowered her own ears; they stayed half-down, an attitude of reservation, jaw jutting. She swept an arm about. "My cousin Fiar Aurhen at com. Sifeny Tauran at scan: call her Sif. I'll be heading down."

"Haral explained—"

"As well as she could." Tauran gave a hitch at her breeches. "I took you on credit, *ker* Pyanfar. I'm still doing that. I'd better get moving. We're coming up on our jump."

"Right," she murmured. "*Ker* Sirany." At Sirany Tauran's departing back. The Tauran went off in some haste. The whole bridge crackled with necessity.

"Entering count," Haral's voice said over the intercom. "That's five minutes."

Pyanfar went to her chair and settled into it. The food and the water was in the appropriate clip. She powered the frame into position, adjusted the restraints, swung the arm-brace up, and locked it.

"Four," Haral said, flicking switches. They were by the book on this one: too many strangers aboard. "You want it, captain?"

"You got it, do it." She was checking displays. Tirun was switching at the moment, Haral having her hands full with the count and the last-minute power-ups. *The Pride* upped her rotations a bit, a little more *G* dragging them into the seats, for comfort's sake when they made drop at Urtur.

"We got our escort," Haral said. "That's *Chakkuf, Nekekkt, Sukk.* None I know."

"Me neither."

"Message sent," Hilfy said. "They're on final to jump, on schedule."

"My captain's secure," said a strange voice from across the bridge.

"Clear to go," Tirun said.

"Mark," Geran said. "We got everyone on the mark back there."

They were moving, a field of blips going with them, while another field, stationary, shifted color downward. They were leaving Sikkukkut and company behind. Gods help the station and the stsho.

"Steady on," Haral said. "How're you doing, captain?"

"You going to take it amiss if I ask what in a mahen hell we got set up?"

A dip of Haral's ears. "Same as you planned, captain. I got a checklist, your four." Haral pushed a button and two screens flashed and changed displays. "Tauran asked questions, I answered as I could, no apparent problems. We're shift on and off with Tauran down in crew quarters; sent Tully down to ride it out in ops. Tauran was going to get upset about him. He said it was all right. And *na* Khym, by your leave. I figured we needed senior crew up here on this one—"

Haral let her voice trail off. *And men and aliens were an issue,* was the unspoken part.

"Did right," Pyanfar said. Gods rot them, Tully all by himself down there, contrary to her orders, because a prig-gish lot of hani balked at having him in in crew quarters even with opposite shifts. Same sheets and blankets. Gods rot them all.

Couldn't put him with Khym. Or in Skkukuk's stinking quarters. Sirany Tauran got Jik's, captain's privilege, private cabin.

No room with Chur. Except in the same bed. Gods, and the protection might be worth it. Chur—

Gods, let her make it. This is the hard one, gods. Get her through it.

Let me get her home. She's so small a matter in the balance. One hani. While you're doing all the rest, gods of my mothers—can't you just keep her with us?

You want my cooperation, gods?

No, no, not the way to go about it. The gods traded too sharp.

She scanned the list, flicked a glance over at number three monitor on her board, where augmented scan showed nine ships moving with them. Five hani, *Aja Jin,* and three kifish ships. The list showed tests run, checkout made, Tauran's agreement to crew assignment and quarters, status on Chur, and the fact that ops-com was open all over the ship for anyone who wanted to access it.

Course plot: affirm.

She affirmed. Plotting came up, splitscreen with data.

It was an illegal course, skipping to Urtur's zenith, braking hard, and jumping again from the incoming range. No passage through the dust-and-gas soup of the accretion disc at the ecliptic. No high-V passage through *that.*

It was also where trouble would be waiting. Best of all if they could have skipped directly nadir; but few stars had such a relative axial tilt that made that maneuver possible. The Meetpoint Mass and Urtur were not two of them; and trying it would probably pull them at high-V right into the worst of the disc.

If it did not drop them instead right into the heart of the well, into the bosom of Urtur's sullen yellow sun.

"We running calc on our collective?" she asked, while the chronometer ticked down. "Where is it?"

"We got it," Haral said. "It's going. We're sequenced two minutes apart, you want it closer?"

"Gods, no." They were going to make one long streamer

through hyperspace as it was, which was going to put some additional push on all of them, and that meant being very careful on the braking capacity. There was fuel-mass to worry about. They could not afford wastage. Little *Starwind* had particular trouble in that regard. *The Pride* had large fuel cap, but also a larger mass with that new engine pack; and as for the rest, freighters were designed to haul, not do stop-and-turns under fire, even if the super-sized tanks and small unladed mass were in their favor on this run. *All* tanks and engines and hollow holds. But no extra shielding. It was going to be touchy. In all departments. She pulled the figures up—telemetry was flowing between ships now, fast and furious, catching up on status advisements. Their weakest was *Lightweaver,* with *Star of Tauran* and *Vrossaru's Outbounder* both left behind at dock. *Lightweaver* had to trail them; no other position for a ship with that mass/engine ratio.

The three kif ran ahead, indubitably with live armaments and kifishly intent on the business in front of them. A chance for distinction. For advancement. A proof of the *hakkikt*'s favor.

And doubtless having their own instructions: the ops log had a separate note from Hilfy: a great deal of kifish chatter had gone on between *Harukk* and the ships of the escort.

Coded, to be sure.

"Give me Jik's map."

"Your three," Haral said, and it displaced the display on that screen.

She studied it, watched it flick through its dated changes, the moving and spreading of kifish power over decades; and mahen actions; and the sudden intrusion of humanity. . . .

. . . the slow ebb of hani influence.

Gods rot you, Jik—

Her pulse quickened, watching it through again. It was truth, unpalatable, plain, and simple. Jik had made a political statement, telling her more than she asked, more than timetables: the information went into history as well as the imminent future.

"*Ker* Fiar. *Ker* Sifeny." Her mind had two spare moments, amid the scramble to catch up. "This is Pyanfar Chanur; welcome aboard."

"Captain," a double murmur came back. Gods knew

what their captain had instructed them—before she abandoned *The Star* and they boarded. Things like: keep an eye on the bastards? Wait my orders? Keep your heads down and be polite?

We'll take the ship if we have to, and mahen devils take the kif and all foreigners?

"We're not a by-the-book ship," she said. "You can guess that, the way things have been running. The second you get something my First better know about, you sing out *Priority-priority* and you get it; interstation com's usually free for crew chatter, meanwhile, station-station or all-stations, same as my own crew, no differences on this deck. We got non-hani aboard, same rules, and men on this ship get no special courtesy, no discourtesy either. We got a long trip and a hard one and Chanur's grateful for all the help we got; we need it at the other end too. You want to know anything, you ask, we'll answer; you have any trouble, you come to me same as your own captain. You won't have any trouble. If you do, I want to know about it. Hear?"

"Aye," the double voices came back.

Probably unconvinced.

"There's *Chakkuf* jumped," Sif Tauran said.

"Got that," Haral said.

"Priority," Geran snapped, and scan flashed to monitor one. "We got movement incoming, bearing 05, 35, 19, point zero zero 3 by 5 *G*s—"

An object was out there, coming out of concealment and accelerating as if devils were behind it.

"Time we got out of here," Pyanfar muttered. "Gods and thunders, it *had* to be on our side of the system—"

"Priority," Geran said, "Sikkukkut's moving."

Scan showed the color-shift.

"Tirun—" Pyanfar said. "Intercept calc, all along that vector."

"I'm on it," Tirun said, "coming up. They can't do it, can't do it, nowhere along our line, beam or missile, b'gods, the incomer's lost us, but it's gods-be close."

Close for intercepting fire, pegged anywhere along their track; sweat broke out all over her.

"Priority." Geran's voice, booming out over the com on override. *"We got another incoming—"*

Pyanfar overrode with a priority master and a button on intercom. "Priority, priority," from Sifeny. "That's two more."

"Got that," Pyanfar said "Tirun: recalc."

"They're farther down, we're all right, I'm checking it anyhow, cap'n."

"Priority!" The monitor screen blinked alarm: space was blossoming with ships.

"Kkkkt!" Skkukuk cried over station-to-station. "Priority, this pattern is *gktokik!* This is methane-breather, this is tc'a and chi! Avoid output!"

"F'godssakes—" —*Shut up on my bridge, you gods-be lunatic!*

"Clear on our vector," Tirun said, "we got it, we got it clear, go, go."

"Sikkukkut's got visitors and we're not waiting for this to unfold around us. *Out* of here, as the schedule goes. Stay by it!"

"Priority," Hilfy said.

Comflow was coming over from Tahar, hani and obscene. Her heart lurched. "Hilfy, I got it, I got it. Send. Tahar! This is Pyanfar, what's happened back there?"

"Chanur," the answer came back, *"we got a glitch in final-check. We're trying to fix it. You got to go, go. We'll come in as we can."*

A sick feeling hit her stomach. Irony, maybe. It was a jump-lost ship that had started the Faha-Tahar feud. And it was a Faha-kinship crew and Tahar riding together on a ship that might not make it this time.

"Yeah, I hear that, Dur. How much lag?"

"Feathered if I know. We're tracing it. Give us a quarter hour down if we're lucky. If not—"

"If not, yeah."

"Hey, I speak kifish real good, Chanur. I'll turn 'round and hail 'em all. Got a message?"

"Luck to you. *Luck,* Tahar, hear?"

"Same to you."

Moon Rising cut communications. Dur Tahar had her hands full, with her own crew doing well to be working at all.

She dropped her head against a shaking hand and drew a deep breath and tried to get herself in order.

Gods and thunders, the best we got—the ones I could

trust— The best and the only friends we got except Jik—that gods-be pirate—and Vrossaru with her. Gods, don't let us lose 'em now.

I'll go religious, I swear I will, get 'em through jump with us!

"Coming up on mark," Haral said, while com crackled and sputtered with advisements from the rest of the group: *Moon Rising* had to be subtracted out of jump equations all the way down the run, a contingency that was all too close to happening. From his own limited board, Skkukuk rattled off a string of kifish exhortations and instructions, something about his captain; the *hakkikt*, praise to whom; and their destination.

Another thought froze her heart. "Tully. Has Tully got his drugs?"

"He's got them," Hilfy said. "He just reported on com; Chur's under; we got clear from all our passengers, in and secure."

Ten thousand things to come undone, ten thousand ways the whole business can go wrong—

The scan-projections were a shifting mix of color, Geran and Sif Tauran working feverishly to keep some semblance of accuracy in ship actions, with system scan blank and tc'a popping in at high-V: they had only their own knowledge, passive-scan; and their long-established, dopplered realscan; passive-scan and longscan leapfrogged, projection and factual report, older and older as their time-packet left the arena.

It was riot back there. Other ships appeared out of system fringes. The *hakkikt* had not fallen into the trap, had not sat there nose to station in the safe interval he might have thought he had before outbound ships could have faked a jump, braked beyond system edge, and turned around.

Bastard has the luck.

Gods help the stsho.

"Ten to mark," Haral said, seeming unperturbed. "You want to take it on otherside, captain, or take her out?"

"I'll take it otherside." That meant mind in order. A precise knowledge of the coordinates and the parameters for error. "Eggs'll get you pearls we don't get system scan at Urtur either."

"Huh. *Akkhtimakt's* been through there, not too certain we even got a station there. If he ever got there. If *he* didn't short-jump and turn. That's eight to mark."

"Secure for jump," Hilfy's voice rang out over general com. The warning sounded early. For the strangers.

"We couldn't hope for that much," Haral commented. "Seven."

"How's *Moon Rising?* What's their status?"

"They're not talking," Hilfy said. "*Ker* Fiar's trying to raise them."

"Gods," she said. "Ha—"

"Priority!" Geran screamed across the bridge.

Instruments broke up. Cleared in wild retreating doppler. Com wailed in the earpiece. Pyanfar yelled to drown the sound and the pain as *something* passed them at *C*-fractional inbound, ran right down on them and whisked away into system. Her heart all but stopped; and lurched into action again in heavy thumps as someone sent the com-output to her.

It sang, it wailed, it moaned and howled up and down the scale like a lunatic; and its retreating image showed the perilous yellow of knnn-ID.

O my gods—

"Mark!" Haral cried.

And flung them. . . .

   . . . outsystem. . . .

      . . . into jump. . . .

        . . . tranquility. . . .

     . . . returning. . . .

   . . . . *down* again. . . .

  . . . . *emergency.* . . .

Chapter 9

. . . emergency. . . .
. . . emergency. . . .
   . . . Siren shrieking, auto-alarm from scan. . . .

Pyanfar reached, rolled her head to get view of the chrono and blinked to clear her eyes on the display. It was not at fault. They were on mark. On schedule. Urtur arrival.

   . . . "Message," Hilfy mumbled, "message . . . kifish. . . ."

It came blasting out over the com, general. *"Proceed!"* came a kifish voice from Pyanfar's own back, their interpreter, live and with them. *"Our escort ships are laying down a pattern of fire, they are proceeding on!"*

"We stay on auto!" Pyanfar yelled at Haral. "We got ships at our tail—" Lest old habit take over.

Slow down and they had ships racing up their backside. They kept on, hurtling into Urtur system with all its debris of dust. . . .

   . . . a star more like a black-stained, broken egg, sullen yellow at system heart, all bound up in a black, flat mist of dust and rock through which a couple of distant gas giants and a host of moonlets plowed rings. It was a scientific wonder. . . .

   . . . a hellhole for inbound ships, where dust and rock could break down a starship's defensive bubble and strip away its *V*. Hit the thick of it at their present velocity and they would make a UV glow, particles accelerated by the contact with virtual particles they brought with them, exotics shooting off in richochet fashion and creating an accelerated maelstrom of reactions that would bleed away their energy. Ships had to dump when they reached a gravity well; but a cloud like Urtur's had ways of doing it for a ship. . . .

. . . getting through the *V* shield, chewing away bit by bit in pyrotechnic decay, until it got to vulnerable realspace metal and quasimetals, and got the vital vane-surfaces, and gnawed away at the hull till it began to glow. . . .

Not yet for *The Pride*. Instruments jumped and flared as dust and larger debris met the bowshock of particles they carried with them and flared and came apart to join the stream and fly off in discharges at collision with still other particles.

They were a cometary fluorescence, if any living eye could track them, if any ship moving at that *V* dared be close to any other ship doing the same or had the time to look to anything but their own survival.

The trailing ships would be popping into system and running into their backturned message and the kif's as Hilfy relayed it on: *We're here, so are the kif, keep going, stay on auto.* And wide of their entry point, three kif launched precautionary fire before enemies could get organized, plowing through the medium as an irregular flutter of telemetry out of the maelstrom they were meeting, creating more hard radiation trails with the passage of their fire.

Their escort was not going to stop. It had to blow a hole for them through anything that might be in the way and keep going, they had agreed that much. But the kif had their own idea what precaution meant.

It was not saying that a contrary-coursed enemy could not come flaring bow-on toward them, to unintended collision.

Or that there might not be one of Urtur's rocks out there too big for their shields.

"We're not getting buoy telemetry," Haral murmured; and Pyanfar swallowed hard against the upwelling of nausea in her throat and fought the blurring of her eyes. Her hands were numb. It was the brace that held her right hand near controls; she shoved with a heave of her shoulder and swung it woodenly over, pushing Confirm to comp's automatic warning that they were blind.

"Bad habit hereabouts," she said between her teeth. And tried to remember what to do next, which was to read the advisements comp was programmed to hand her, data and detail matches to check against the autos.

Enemies might peg them by sheerest luck. A rock was

more likely to do it for them. Sikkukkut's earliest ships had come through here and gods knew what had become of them, whether they still existed, whether they had not gone on to a kifish rendezvous at Kita or Kshshti.

—a knnn had grazed past them, otherside.

—hallucination?

Gods, no, it was real, it had been real—attack pouring into Meetpoint off several vectors, including Urtur . . . Sikkukkut's enemies had come out of Urtur and Tt'av'a'o and Hoas and V'n'n'u vectors—or space corresponding to those points—

Realtime months ago.

Your doing, Jik? Your gods-be contacts with the tc'a? Gods, gods, have you ever told the truth in your life? What have you done?

Had it been Goldtooth coming in at Meetpoint? Could he marshal methane-breathers to his aid—along with humans?

Could anyone guarantee the methane-folk?

Whatever had begun to happen at Meetpoint had played itself out already, while they existed only as a probability in the gods' intentions, an arc in hyperspace, a bubble with a slender stem to Somewhere shooting along in Nowhere Reasonable on the whim of *V* and vector and the dimples stars made with their mass—while they did that, ships had battered away at each other, and ships which might have been at Urtur might well have leapt out again days ago, with the kind of hyperspace arc hunter-ships could cut— sleek, power-wasting hunter-ships who could cut days off a freighter's time—

—but not *The Pride*'s, except they were encumbered with a handful of freighters who had to make it through to give them a chance at all where they were going.

—*Moon Rising,* O gods, where?

System buoy gave them nothing. *Industry* existed back there in that timelag; and *Starwind* and *Hope;* and *Lightweaver* to bring up the rear, unless *Moon Rising* made it on some miracle—

There was a sick feeling at her gut that had nothing to do with the after-jump queasiness. The numbers ticked away; warnings flashed all over the board, approaching mark, have to make it on schedule or lose it all—

"Coming up on dump," she said. And let the autos take them, as instruments blipped and flashed hazard warning.

—Easy then to drift away, give it up, quit trying after the figures that glowed ghostly green just beyond her reach, just out of focus. Survival was in those numbers. It was just inconveniently far, everyone so godsforsaken tired and home so far and so fraught with disasters—

Wake up, Pyanfar Chanur, focus, make the fingers feel, the hand move, the mind work—

—long way home. Someone else's job. She was already there, the pale golden dust, the deeper gold of grainfields and the fleet herds that raced and bounded and soared for the sheer exuberance of running, sharp hooves and sharper horns—

Blood and hani hide. No uruus was calved that could get a horn into Kohan Chanur, except for young Hilfy's mistake, wide-eyed youngster caught right in the path of one that should have gone the other way.

"It's all right," Kohan said. *And sat down, plump, right where he stood, with his hand pressed to his ribs and his nose gone pale. "It's quite all right."*

While Hilfy stood there in horror, only then catching up to what had happened, when all the rest of them had reached their peak of panic when na *Kohan had, and moved; but Kohan was nearer, saw young Hilfy's danger, and hit the uruus like a projectile. It lay dead, its quickness and its beauty all still in the dust; he sat there with blood leaking through his fingers and a sick look on his face that was none of it for himself, only for what could have happened. And the rest of them, chagrined and self-disgusted that he had had to do what he had done, a skilled hunter caught like that, and none of them in position to help when a young girl's mistake near killed herself and her lord. Hilfy stood there thinking, they knew later, that she had killed him, killed her father, her lord she should have died for, the dearest thing in all her protected young life. She had never taken a scar. Never did.*

Till a dockside brawl on Meetpoint; till the kif laid hands on her; till she was their prisoner for much too long—

Kohan would not know his daughter.

She's grown up, brother. She's not a girl anymore. Not anything you can understand anymore, your pretty Hilfy; you, tied to the world; her, a spacer, with a spacer's ways, like Haral, like Tirun, like me.

I don't want your world.

I've ruined her for it, taken her out of it, changed her in ways I wouldn't have chosen, brother; but I couldn't keep her prisoner myself; couldn't hold her, wouldn't try.

I hate it. I've always hated it. Not the fields, not the feel of the sun. It's the confinement. One world. One place. A horizon too small.

Minds too small to understand me.

I'd rather go anywhere than home. Rather die for anything than fat old women and empty-headed men who love their walls and their wealth and their privilege and never know what's out there—

Khym knows. Maybe you almost do. But I'm coming back for them. Hilfy and I. So gods-be many have bled for you. Or frozen cold in space. Or gone to particles, not even enough to find. You don't know the ways you can die out here.

I don't want to get there. Don't want to see the look on your face.

But by the gods I won't leave you to Ehrran and the scavengers.

—Aren't we coming out of it? Has something malfunctioned? Are there red lights? Gods, do you ever stop thinking when you lose it and the ship doesn't come down again, do you just go on—

—out again, and back to realspace, with V lower and the telemetry flicking past numbers in mechanical agony, red lights flaring—

"I got it, I got it," she mumbled to save Haral the effort. Not malfunction lights: it was gas out there, thick enough to glow and flare off their shields. The shield-depletion curve was rising, fluctuating as they swept up gas and hit a bare spot, where the shield recovered a little strength. The kifish escort was far away now. On auto, relying on numbers alone and not even in direct control, they achieved a kind of tranquility. Warning lights flickered, reminding them of laws and lanes they overrode. Haral swore and disabled them for the duration of Urtur passage, to be rid of the beep.

She fumbled after the nutrients packet, bit a hole in it, and drank it down—and Tully, Tully was alone belowdecks, his poor teeth always had trouble with the packets and

there was no one to help him, alone because the gods-be
Tauran were too squeamish—

—behind her Skkukuk would be seeing to his own meal.
Her stomach heaved at the thought. But his kifish voice
came through now and again, delivering some information
to Hilfy and Fiar at com, translating off those kifish ships
up front.

Kifish transmissions everywhere; and *Chakkuf* and *Nekekkt* and *Sukk* were doing their job, the point of a spear
that had to drive straight into Urtur before it stopped, re-
vectored, and ran up the *V* sufficient for a jump out of this
hell. That was the worst of it, that dead-relative-stop they
had to do to line up that next jump, or slew through hyperspace askew from their target and depending on the next
star to pull them in, loss of realspace-time, loss of everything if they miscalculated. . . .

Those hunter-ships were aware of their schedule, were
able to make up that time and distance on sheer power,
and rendezvous again, elsewhere. They claimed. It was their
idea. A merchant pilot would have laughed, disbelieved it:
and suffered a chill up the back at the thought of ships that
could do that, knnn-like, as far off their capacity as they
were off that of an insystemer.

She had no doubts. Clearly the kif would not have shown
them everything they had.

And, gods, she would have given anything to find that
fire answered, Akkhtimakt *in* Urtur system, resisting. He
was not. That meant he was elsewhere. The terror reas-
serted itself, habitual and consuming.

"Chur," she heard Hilfy say. "Time you woke up.
Chur—"

Persistently. She cut in on that channel herself. "Chur,
gods rot it, answer, we're coming up on braking."

No answer.

"Geran," Pyanfar snapped. "You got backup, we're stable; get back there."

There was a snap from a released restraint. She did not
look around to see. Did not try to talk to Khym, had no
doubts of his safety, or Tully's. They were no different from
other crew, probably had reported in to com monitoring,
as the Tauran would report, from crew quarters, going
through frantic prep for shift change while they had this

small inertial stretch for the generation systems to recharge. The machine was keeping Chur quiet. That was what it was. It was supposed to. That was all it was.

"No gods-be hope of Akkhtimakt being here," she muttered to Haral.

"We ever expect it? Hope to all the gods those first ships of Sikkukkut's cut 'em good. We got station output, no buoy, no ship-com. No tc'a, f'godssakes, tc'a miners don't notice kif stuff. They're not talking either. Something big's been through here like thunder. Something that bothered *them*."

"And a knnn comes in at Meetpoint. I want out of here. I want out of here real bad." Pyanfar took another swallow at the bag, another listen at com off Chur's cabin. There was the sound of the door opening. Geran's voice desperately calling Chur's name. She swept an eye over scan. All the ships behind them had dumped down. "We're all on. How're you doing, Haral?"

"I'm holding up." The voice was hoarse as her own.

Then: *"Chur's coming out of it,"* Geran said over com. *"Tell the captain."*

"I got that," Pyanfar said, punching in. "How is she?"

"Weak," the answer came back, which was not the answer she had wanted, not with what they had coming.

If Geran admitted that much, it was bad back there.

Pyanfar took another drink, emptied the noxious liquid into her mouth, and swallowed hard. She threw com wide to all-ship. "We're stable. We're doing all right, high over the soup. If the two kif have jumped past us back to Sikkukkut, he's welcome to 'em. . . ." She cut it off. "Gods," she said to Haral. "Gods, I hope. What in a mahen hell's keeping our backup crew? Query 'em." The weakness came and went in waves. Her muscles had no strength left. They had a while yet to run before they reached their turn point. *The Pride* would query for a Confirm; but if it got no Abort it would make that final dump on its own, reorient, find its own reference star and head out to Kura, would do it if they were all dead or incapacitated, taking its log records and everything it had into hani space, to brake at Anuurn and wait to be boarded . . . by hani, pray the gods. The chance that the automatics could do all that flawlessly was about fifty-fifty; but it was their third-backup, failsafe to feeble living muscle and overtired brains. Haral had run all that calc, even had it plugged into one contingency course-plot for Kshshti to Maing Tol; and one for Tt'a'va'o as well, all while she had been tied up with the kif. Brain-bending, meticulous checks, run fast and by the gods accurately. And Haral like the rest of the crew, like Geran back there trying to keep her sister alive, had far overrun her physical limits.

"Tully's on his way up," Hilfy said. Internal-com was not her proper assignment; but it was a fair bet Sifeny had not understood him. "*Na* Khym's up and headed out upper sec. Tauran crew is on its way."

"Thank gods," Pyanfar murmured. Things started to sort out. She could just about hold on that long. "Skkukuk."

"Hakt'."

"You're offduty." *No, gods, no, can't send him down the lift with Tauran crew coming up, they might shoot him.* "Soon's Tauran crew hits the bridge, you can go to quarters. See you at Kura."

"Kkkkt. Yes, hakt'." Exhausted as the rest of them. "Hakt', there is not adequate resistance here. *Chakkuf* has advised subordinates of this. Akkhtimakt has gone elsewhere. The two advance ships will have gone on. I queried regarding those courses. Our escort does not know."

"Thanks," she said. Calmly. There was no course but what they were following. It was academic information. That was all.

While all the agreements that held the Compact together had been shattered.

"On the other hand there a possibility both may have turned and gone for Kita," said Skkukuk. "Akkhtimakt, defilement on his name, might circle back to Akkht. If he had Akkht he would be formidable again. Homeworld could not stand against him if it were not aware that he is severely challenged."

"And not to Kura? Leave Akkhtimakt free to go to Kura?"

"*We* are that contingency, *mekt-hakt'*. Certainly the *hak-kikt* has sent a message to Akkht. But that we are not aware of the course of these ships indicates that they are not part of our business."

"Or, of course, that our escort has separate orders."

"Assuredly. Should I have mentioned that? The *mekt-hakt'* is no fool."

She tasted bile. Her heart labored and skipped like something moribund, on its last strength. The lift-door light reflected in the monitor at her right hand. A group of figures exited, shadows in a dimly-reflected corridor. *Tauran, thank the gods. And where in a mahen hell's Tully?* She was not mentally fit for problems. She knew that. *For godssakes get up here, Tauran, I can't handle anything, I'm not sure I can walk across the floor.* Her chest was hurting again, a persistent pain. She violated her own rule, powering her chair about on a working station. But Tauran was there, Sirany and all the rest of her crew, and—dull shock—Tully was with them, Tully had ridden the lift up with strangers and gotten out unscathed, points to that crew's nerves and decency.

She unbuckled her restraints and groped after the chair arm. She was in that kind of condition. She heaved herself to her feet as Tully went off the back way to the galley, on duty; and Sirany Tauran and her crew headed for their change-off. "We got it easy," Pyanfar said, though ops-com had been open for monitor the while. "Escort's been laying down fire ahead of us, we got no sound out of Urtur station, we got no sound out of kif insystem. We got an hour to run before we hit our last dump and turn. We're still missing Tahar and Vrossaru. They didn't make the jump."

"Understood," Sirany said. "I've been on your com feed since before we dropped. Knnn. Knnn, for godssakes."

"Knnn_and trouble of some kind back there at Meet-point. Whether that's good news or bad for Tahar or for the kif I don't know. I hope to all the gods it's Goldtooth's bunch, but they weren't running IDs." She passed a glance aside as Skkukuk unbuckled. "Kkkt," Skkukuk murmured, and got up to his full, if unsteady, height. *"Hakt'."* That was only one captain he saluted; he bowed and turned and walked off the bridge, bound below, while Tauran crew took the briefings, the critical situations, from Chanur crew on the last of their strength.

Pyanfar straightened her shoulders and looked at Sirany. "You got a real good crew," she said of Sif and Fiar.

"Yeah," Sirany said, but the flick of the ears said immensely pleased. And said something else she could not read. "We got it, go."

Time then to step out of her way and let another captain to *The Pride*'s boards, the codes stripped to master-unlock, even the log and their private files. Fire-codes, data-codes, the whole ship. "All open," she said to Sirany, and turned and collected Haral, who left the boards like she was leaving a lover, with a second and a third look. She put a hand on Haral's shoulder and shoved her galleyward, paused to shepherd Hilfy through, and Fiar too, offshift with Chanur crew; but Sif Tauran went to hang over the back of Sirany's seat at the main boards and deliver a quiet report.

My compatriot. My maybe-enemies and allies of necessity. My crew of men and aliens and reluctant, ambiguous hani. Clans were more absolute in the old days; the hani tongue had nothing native to express halfway loyalties. A hani had to come to the deep wide black to find it. Among kif and mahendo'sat. And humans. "Tirun," she said out loud, and gave an irritated jerk of the chin at Tirun, who delayed with her opposite number, on her feet and physically clinging to the seat. "Come on, gods rot it, cousin, time's running."

Tirun came. Geran arrived from down the corridor, bleary-eyed and staggering. "We're relieved," Pyanfar said. "Come on. How's Chur?"

"Alive," Geran said, and her mouth went hard shut, as if that was the only word that was going to get out. But: "Going to get something down her," Geran muttered in passing. "Going to sleep there this trip."

"Huh," Pyanfar said, venturing no more than that. The two of them crowded into the same bed, that was what Geran meant: there was nowhere else in that lifesupport-crowded cabin. She said nothing about it, tried not to think of anything at all, but the bridge and the galley corridor went strange in her sight, all near and far at once.

Dark and stars and the monstrous shape of a knnn ship bearing down on them as if they were a minnow in the deep.

Kif ships putting down a steady barrage of fire into nothing at all, because there might be something out there. (But there might equally be helpless bystanders. Mahendo'sat. Hani. Tc'a.)

Strangers with their hands on *The Pride*'s controls, delving into Chanur records—

Kefk docks, all lit in fire—

Three hundred thousand stsho dying in sudden vacuum, delicate, gossamer-robed bodies frozen and drifting, with horror on their faces.

Human shapes, tall and mahen-like, pouring by the thousands into a hallway, Tully times infinity, armed and hostile—

"Captain—" Tirun had her arm. Held onto her, as the hall went dark in her sight and the wall suddenly ended up in the way of her shoulder.

"I'm all right," she snarled, and shoved the hand off.

"Aye," Tirun said, in the tone it deserved.

She made it as far as the galley, dropped into a seat as her sight went dark again. Someone shoved a cup of gfi into her hands and her vision cleared on it; she got it to her mouth and forced a nauseating swallow down. Grimaced then and nearly heaved. A sandwich arrived in front of her, in a hairless human hand, Tully and Khym in better shape than any of them who had been on duty since Kefk. But the mingled stink of them all was enough to turn a kif's stomach. It was more than enough for a hani's, and mixed with the godsawful smell of gfi and food and the ammonia-stink that had somehow gotten onto all of them. She had always run a clean ship, an immaculate ship. Now this.

While the Compact was trying to come undone, and, gods—

"I'm worried about the kif that went out of here," she said. "Sikkukkut's. Not just Akkhtimakt's lot. The pair of Sikkukkut's that went out on this heading before he came into station—" Remember. Remember it. Mind did strange things when jump shook it and set it down again. There had been such kif. She and Skkukuk had discussed it. There had been methane-breathers. There had been Jik, on their bridge, spilling an incredible sequence of evidence into their computer. She forced a mouthful down. "I got to tell you, *ker* Fiar, and you can tell your cousins, we got a Situa-

tion aboard: we can't always say what we'd like to say.
Skkukuk's real stable, but we don't tell him we're not the
hakkikt's loyal friends. Wouldn't bother him in some ways.
But he'd think we were crazy. Kif thinks you're crazy, he
won't do what you say. So we just don't fill him in on
everything. You got to understand him—"

"Aye," Fiar murmured in a guarded tone, because, perhaps, it seemed incumbent on her to say something to that
insanity, surrounded as she was by Chanur and Chanur's
odd crew. Khym attracted as much of her attention as Tully
did, little nervous moves of her ears, following sounds.
They came desperately forward. "You think one of those
lead ships went on to Anuurn, captain?"

"Could have," she said, and Haral:

"Our escort's in a way to cover anything they choose to
cover. Emissions all over the godsforsaken system. No telling what's here. But *they* know what they found before
they churned it all up. That's for sure, whatever they've cut
out of what they send us."

"You're not working for them."

"Gods, no," Pyanfar said. Maybe Tauran clan had believed her assurances from the start but Fiar wanted to be
reassured in words she could hear. "Skkukuk was a present.
One I didn't choose. But I get the feeling his alternative
was worse. Kif serve the ship they're on and he's on this
one. Fight for us like a maniac, he would. And has."

"He any trouble?"

From a young and worried hani who was about to bed
down and sleep on lowerdecks, with a kif down the corridor. Humans, Fiar seemed more able to take in stride. Even
one handling the food she ate. But her shoulders were
bristled.

"He gives you any, tell him I'll skin him. With a kif that's
literal." Gods, when had she gotten so callous? Another
gulp of sandwich, on a stomach that was taking it better.
Little talk. Little problems. What about the kif, captain, he
going to go crazy and cut our throats? What about the
human, captain? What kind of thing is it, your husband and
this alien rubbing shoulders and making nothing of it, and
this human handling the food we got to eat? "We're going
home, Fiar Aurhen. Home and gods know what else waiting for us. Got no passengers here."

"I heard—" Fiar said, and whatever she had heard waited when Sif Tauran showed up late and edged her way past Khym in the little galley. Not without a look.

"Heard what?" Pyanfar asked.

Fiar swallowed a choking bite. Her ears went back, her eyes blinked, watered, and fixed on hers dead-on and wide. "Word is—what happened at Meetpoint last year, how you came in there and took it apart when they got—particular. Captain. How you set to with the Immune. How you had a run-in with the kif and that mahen hunter. Whole Compact has the rumor the humans are coming in and you're involved in it." Her voice went hardly audible. "To get trade, maybe. Maybe something else."

"Who said?"

"I don't know who said. It's all over. And the treaty and the *han*— What're we going to *do* when we get to Anuurn, *ker* Pyanfar?"

An edge of panic there. Of outright fright.

I don't blame you, kid. Not at all.

"Mahendo'sat are moving to cut this off," Pyanfar muttered. "We got the plot on it. This is one godsforsaken mess. But we got that hope. Fact is the kif that moved on Meetpoint is about as worried as we are—that's what we were working on. That's all that got us out of that port."

"Does our captain know this?" Fiar asked.

"About the mahendo'sat? Dunno."

"No," Haral said. "I briefed *ker* Sirany on ops and course and the fact we and the kif aren't cozy. Mahen business I didn't say."

That was right. It had been in the report. Otherside of jump. She was losing things. She stuffed more sandwich in her mouth. Waved a hand at Haral, who took that signal and started spilling what else she knew; Tauran ears sagged, flagged, flattened. And:

"You talk to your captain," Pyanfar said, to Fiar, to Sif Tauran, "before you head below. Tell you another thing. You're on my crew shift. Tully here's crew. Shares quarters on this shift. My orders."

"Work," Tully objected. "I wake, work."

"Shut up. You're on my shift and you stay that way. Give me trouble I'll bed you with Skkukuk." She swallowed another mouthful of gfi and shuddered. "I got no

time, we got no time." While Geran staggered off with a
pair of cups Khym had given her, for herself and Chur.
"We got to get there, is what. Our guns may be all Anuurn's got, you hear me?"

Tauran ears pricked and half-flattened again in dismay.
And maybe, maybe an increasing bit of belief.

One of their number was lost already. *Moon Rising* arriving late or in any condition was a sight she would give a
great deal to see. And there was less and less hope of it.

She shoved herself away from the table, shoved sandwich
wrapper and empty cup into the disposal. She was working
on autopilot, same as *The Pride*. Programmed stuff. Lower
brain functions.

In the same way she turned and wandered through the
bridge, where foreign crew sat working, as strange to see
there as if they were mahen. Or human. Sirany Tauran
acknowledged her presence, and Pyanfar flicked her ears
back and nodded in return, before she wandered out and
down the corridor.

Nothing else was wrong. If it were, Sirany would have
said. Tauran crew was going to do something about in-
tership communications, try to relay a coded do-watch on
mahen ships. Or whatever they might manage to get across
of their situation. While *Aja Jin* rode beside them.

She paused at Chur's open door. Geran was there, at the
bedside. " 'Lo," she said, and was not sure if Chur responded; her eyes were blurring out on her. "Hey, we
about got the hard part, cousin, just hang on, huh? We're
all right. We'll make it."

She got into her own room, made one trip to the head,
fell face-down into bed and coordinated herself enough to
jab the bedside console and power the safety rig over, never
forget that, gods, never forget, an old spacer never lost that
reflex, move down the corridors right smart, stay out of
open areas, get to safe small places in case the ship had to
move. Broken bones and smashed skulls else. Spacers died
of bad luck like that, a ship moving to save its steel hide
and some poor bastard of a spacer smashed to pulp down
a corridor become a three-story drop—epitaph on many an
acquaintance: *the luck ran out*. On a ten-ring spacer it could
happen—

Luck out on Tahar and Vrossaru. Gods help 'em.

After a dark space the restraint hummed, a large and warm weight settled onto the same mattress and a warmth settled about her. "We're about to brake," Khym said; and woke her up just enough to feel a drunken panic.

"Restraint," she said. "I've got it," he said, and she opened her eyes blearily on dim light and the arch of the safety web going over them, on a familiar face, a large arm going over her like the arch of the safety, a huge body shaping itself to hers, awful and stinking as they both were, straight out of jump and headed in again without respite. She hugged him back, hard.

The vanes cycled again, blowing velocity in a dizzying pulse of neither here nor there, right down to the lowest energy they could reasonably achieve. It was a hunter-ship maneuver. Honest freighter never had the reason to do a thing like that.

Urtur dust screamed over the hull, shields downed during the low-*V* of their turn and reacquisition, dust abrading the vanes. The whole ship wailed and keened in sound that hurt the ears.

Gods let Tahar make it after all, gods save the rest of us, where's the kif?

"Unnnh." Khym clenched his fist in her mane. "Claws, Py, gods—"

Realspace acceleration started up, the unsettling *G*-shift of rollover.

"We're going," she said, "we're going all right." Which might or might not be true. There might be enemies after all. Or a big rock the shields would fail on. It was all Tauran's problem now. Not hers. Not hers.

The dust wailed away, changing pitch.

"Py—"

He burrowed in closer, arm stretched above her. "I'm holding on," he said; and did: his weight kept her steady and comfortable, so that her groping reach after the handgrip became too much effort. He stayed like that forever, in a position that could not be comfortable for him. She tried again to move and get a foot braced against the safety-rim. "I've got it," he said again, "it's all right, Py."

"Sprain your gods-be shoulder," she muttered.

He breathed into her ear and tongued the inside of it, like in the dark of off-watch, like the two of them twenty and brand new again. "Good gods." She caught her breath and lost it again. "Not now, Khym."

"Think of a better time?"

He couldn't, under the strain they were under. But he amused himself. While they hurtled on toward oblivion and it was clear he was in pain.

"Gods be fool man," she said. "Love you like my sister." It sounded stupid. It was the only way she knew to say it to him, in hani, so he would know what she meant. "Always have."

"Man's got no brother," he said. He was breathing hard. Strain was in his voice, while the scream of the ship went on and he kept up his lackadiasical attentions. "Man's alone. Man never even knows what I've got exists at all. Not alone anymore. Never alone anymore. You were right. You were always right."

"Gods, I wish I were." *I wish I was right about what I'm doing, what I've done. We're going to jump and they haven't got that gods-be com on, they cut the gods-be com, we don't know when—*

She hazed out. She came to and realized *G*-stress had shifted and Khym had come down on her limp as a dead man, breathing hard. That was no matter. He was warm, and without him she would shiver; she felt it.

"*Mark,*" a sudden voice came over com, not Haral's, stranger-voice. "*We're outbound.*"

—into jump.

—falling.

"*Hello,*" *said the young man, sitting on the rock, beneath blue sky, above a golden valley; and she took him for a Wanderer, up to no good on Chanur land. She set her jaw and drew a deep breath and made herself as tall as she could:* No nonsense, man, take a look at the spacer rings and figure you're not dealing with any young fool; I'll shred your ears for you.

"*Hello,*" *she said, on her way up from Chanur lands, on the road. She had chosen to walk, when she might have made a landing here, created a little stir, coming in like that. But she was romantical in her youth.*

What it got her was a young bandit, that was what. Real trouble, if he was also crazy. And worse trouble if he carried a knife. Some did.

"You're on Chanur land," she said. *"Wise if you'd move along."*

"You're Pyanfar," he said. And, gods, he was beautiful, his eyes large and gold-amber, his mane thick and wide. He stepped off his rock and landed on his feet in her path. *"Are you?"*

"Last I checked. Who in a mahen hell are you?"

"Khym Mahn," he said. *"Your husband."*

—down.

—alive. By the gods alive.

—and where? Gods, where? Kura. Kura. Got to get up, get to the bridge—

No. First dump. Got—remember interval.

"We all right?" Khym murmured. His weight hurt her, hurt her all the way to her bones. She was smothering. "We at Kura?"

"Move," she said, gasped. Gasped again when he tried, and fought and moaned her way to the edge of the bed, reaching for the console, involved in the edge of the safety net. "This is Pyanfar. We all right? Where's that gods-be com? Give us com, hear?"

There was delay. *"Aye, captain,"* a strange voice said. And waited, by the gods *waited* during some on-bridge clearance, while a rag-eared bastard of a Tauran com officer asked *her* captain for clearance to report, that was what was going on.

"Gods-be—"

Khym moaned in that way he had when he was about to be sick. And rolled over to the other side of the bed.

Com came through, a busy crackle of voices.

Khym was not sick. But she did not bother him either. She lay there listening to the data-chatter and the heavy machine-sounds of the ship.

"We're not getting buoy-output, from Kura," someone said. And sent icewater flowing through her gut.

Someone swore over com.

"Standby number two dump," a voice said then.

And the ship cycled down again, a lurch half into hyperspace—

—no buoy at Kura.

—in hani space.

"I came here to wait," Khym said, on that path, beside

*the way she would have had to take. Perhaps someone had
just phoned. He was perhaps another romantical fool, having
come this long trek to sit alone and wait on a prospective
wife. His face had a kind of wistful vulnerability: she had
not known it then, but when she remembered that look afterward, she knew what it was, of experience. It was hope. It
was Khym's gentle and earnest self, open to everything, en-
tranced with her.*

*And he had escaped his sisters and his wives and gotten
away alone. Or they did not care for him the way they ought:
that had been her first thought when she believed he was
who he claimed to be:*

"*You alone?*" *Anything might have happened to him.
Some bandit might have attacked him. Some Chanur hunter
might have taken him for a bandit and asked questions later.
Or he might have fallen in with a group of Chanur herders
who might have taken a fancy to him, and precious much
they would have believed his claims to be their neighbor. A
lord never got out in public. Except at challenge. And Chanur and Mahn, old allies, would never challenge each other.
In those days.*

Gods, *she had thought atop it all,* I'm betrothed to a fool
in a house of rump-sitting fools who can't keep track of
their own lord.

"*It isn't far,*" *he said, pointing back toward Mahn land.*

Gods if I don't keep you better, *she had thought; and then
knew she could indeed do no better. Home was not a place
she stayed. She had to trust the other wives and his sisters
and his female cousins, who clearly could not handle him.*

I'll have to knock heads in this house. Do I really want
to get into this? If I weren't a fool I'd go home right now
and leave him out here.

Gods, he's good-looking, isn't he?

But so're a dozen more I could find in the bushes.

"*I don't do this all the time,*" *he said earnestly. "*I told
them—*" A gesture back toward the heart of Mahn land.
"*—I was going to the garden. I guess no one's looked. I
wanted to see you—*"

*He knew he was in the wrong. He knew he had made a
bad impression. He knew he had even made a dangerous
mistake, if she had a notion to take offense and go back to
her clan, figuring a fool of a man was an easy mark for her*

lord; then he might die a young fool, and Mahn was in danger, if she were either unscrupulous or truly outraged. He knew this and he worried, now, when it was too late. Break her neck, he might, if he could get his hands on her. But it was not likely that he could. She was fast, in those days, and looked it; and might have a knife or even a gun (she had); and had the advantage of her clan, who could kill him under any circumstances for being where he was, but under felony charges, could dispossess his sisters and his kin and send them out homeless. He knew all of this. ("I thought you would go back," he had said to her in after years. "I thought if you did I would have to challenge. And you would hate me. And so I couldn't do that either. I'd spend all my life trying to get you back.")

She set hands on hips and looked him up and down. Here in this isolated place where only they knew what might happen. And flattened her ears at him and slowly pricked them up again when his drooped. "Huh," she said. "Well, you got your border wrong." Even a man would know where that *was. The flick of his ears showed he had indeed known. And deliberately trespassed, by the difference of two hills. The one in Chanur land just happened to have better vantage. And she came up close to him and up next to him and laid hands on him, which only his wives and his sisters could do without offense.*

They were husband and wife before she walked him home. Out there on the border of Chanur land, as if she were some landless scoundrel and he some equally landless lad with hopes. She knew what she had married before she got there. A romantic, who, gods help her, asked her ten thousand questions, what was it like in space, where did she go, how long was she staying, would she come to see him every time she came back to the world?

He was ingenuous and reckless and a veritable encyclopedia of trivialities and natural science. He loved poking about under logs and into ponds, as devoted to hunting out curiosities as he ever was in hunting the game in which Mahn hills were rich; he could study a flower for whole minutes. Or the color of her eyes. She was not sure she liked being studied, there under Anuurn summer skies. She had come up to Mahn after a husband for politics, for finance, because they had dealt with him indirectly and believed his sister, that he

was a decent domestic administrator and a man with some
legal sense and no disposition to quarrel with Chanur; a fast
few days in Mahn, a satisfaction of certain urges that were
about to come on her, and which were misery on shipboard—
and she ended up with a shy-smiling young man who did a
fool thing like trespass and let himself be led off into the
bushes and who spent whole minutes telling her how unusual
her eyes were and (being Khym) what the statistical frequency of gold-and-bronze was with her ancestry.

She had known then she had gotten herself an odd one.

> *—aren't we coming out?*

> *—Gods and mahen devils, what are they doing*
up there? Is that the drop?*

It was. *The Pride* came down with a vengeance; Khym
moaned; and she did; and heard the curses over com about
the inlaid program in Nav, about the fools who had laid it
in and the condition of Tauran stomachs.

Got to get up there. Second dump, I got to.

They had laid in food stores in the room, pinned to the
console. She groped after them, packets the same as they
used on the bridge. Dared not retract the net. Not till she
got an all-clear.

Then over com: *"Gods fry it to a mahen hell! What is
that thing?"*

She jabbed the com button, fighting with the net. "What
is it? What's going on up there? This is Pyanfar Chanur,
gods rot it, what's going on?"

Delay.

"Gods blast you, don't you give me authorizations on my
own ship! Give me Sirany! What in a mahen hell's going
on up there?"

"Chanur. We're stable. Proceed with crew change."

"Gods be." She retracted the safety restraint, rolled over
and got her stiffened legs off the edge and hauled her sore
torso upright. "Oh, gods." *Never, never make love in jump,
oh my ribs, my back, O gods.* She got herself upright, swallowed down a rush of nausea and reeled and staggered,
limping, toward the door.

A black streak shot down the hall, about ankle-high,
squealing as it went.

"Gods and thunders!"

The Dinner was loose again.

*   *   *

She came reeling and limping her way onto the bridge with the crew-call sounding out over the general address, and grabbed the back of observer-two seat to steady herself while she got a look at the monitors, at scan, at a situation that looked tranquil enough, except for the kif running silently ahead of them. No firing here. No output from station either.

They were in hani space, and Kura, the second-largest station in that space, was dead silent at least as far as buoy output went.

"Kif've tripped a warning," she surmised suddenly, and staggered her way toward Sirany Tauran, grabbing the back of her seat to hold herself steady. "That's where buoy went. Shut itself up the moment it got kifish ID. *Which* kifish ID it got and how long ago, that worries me. Has our escort made it in? Did they overjump us?"

"Neat and sweet, they did, about two hours' worth. Got plenty of power on those ships, and their emissions trail's strong and clear. Covering up everything."

"Have we got a message going out? I auto'ed a message for Kura."

"Aye, captain," the com officer said. "We're three minutes out of response time."

"It tells Kura what we can. Advising any ships here to get home. Fast."

"Same I sent," Sirany said. "Same all the others been sending, their own ships' wrap on it. The mahe's been transmitting coded stuff, long burst just before we left Urtur."

"Huh." More than *huh*. But not with Sirany. Worry broke out all over again. *Jik's still with us. Still on our side.* She scanned the monitors and saw the positioning of ships, the still-broken pattern, the hole where Tahar ought to be and was not. "No sign of Tahar."

"No sign."

She gnawed her mustaches and waited, eye on the chrono. "We get any response?"

"Negative."

"We got some gods-rotted vermin run through here," Sirany said.

"I know it. We cleaned it out once. Skkukuk's gods-cursed food supply. Something's got loose again."

"F'godssakes. What are the things eating?"

"The ventilation filters."

"Lifesupport?"

"We got an electrical screen on the main systems from last time. We got it covered. Don't worry about it. The problem's in our watch. Just a stray, more'n likely. We'll get it."

"You thought of sabotage? That gods-be kif—"

"Is crew."

"Not in my watch, captain. That door of his is locked from the boards."

Question my judgment! On my bridge, in my chair, rot your hide! It was also a sane and reasonable suspicion. She restrained herself and got her voice quiet. "That kif," she said, "is our translator. *Protocol* officer and a gods-be decent one. Crew." It half-choked her. *Get your backside out of my chair, Tauran.* "He takes orders. Takes 'em fine. He's had a lot of chances to kill one or the other of us. Saved my hide back at Kefk." *And I don't let him loose either, but he's not risking his neck in those corridors hunting vermin.* "Shift. I'll spell you, work with yours and spell 'em off as mine come in. You did a marvel, Tauran, got us here through that soup, real fine job and strange boards—" *Compliment the graynosed bastard. Keep us friendly. It was a good job. We're alive. We still got all our ships behind us, Jik and Harun and the rest, and all three kif out to front, and she's trying real hard to be polite, isn't she, Pyanfar Chanur? More suspicious than young Fiar. Wiser and harder and she has to be. She's got to push me a little. Got to keep her eyes clear and play the hardnose and try to get at truth, that's what she's after. She didn't fail us. Hasn't failed us.*

"Fancy stuff," Sirany said, still sitting. "Mahen-make. Real fancy. That comp's a wonder."

What'd you pay for it, Chanur? What buys equipment like this, state of the art, class one stuff, when Chanur's broke and bankrupt and all space knows it?

What's this we hear about you and mahendo'sat and the Meetpoint stsho?

Before we go to sleep again—what kind of ship are we on?

"We got our tail shot up. Emergency patch at Kshshti.

The mahendo'sat wanted us out of there real bad. It's this passenger of ours."

"The kif or the human or the mahendo'sat?"

Pushing hard now. Her pulse hammered and her ears flattened as Sirany turned in her seat to look up at her.

Out in the dark places too long, maybe, Chanur?

"I'll argue that in the *han*," Pyanfar said. "But our records are unlocked. Had a look, have you?"

"I've been busy," Sirany said. "Real busy." Her ears were flat. "Interesting stuff. But the important thing's still to get home, isn't it? We do it your way. Your rules. You want that kif in on com, that's fine. We got two more jumps to go. You want us to bed down with the gods-be kif, if you want to vouch for his manners, I'll take your word on it."

"Listen. I mean this. Don't expect him to be hani. He'll take your hand off if he thinks you're pushing me. Tully's quieter, but he's scared of you and he's got troubles you don't know about; let him be. And my husband—let me tell you, *ker* Sirany, since you've said not a word on it, let me tell you: my husband's steady as anybody at the boards, and gods help him, you won't shock him, not after this trip, he knows what ship life is; he knows how to take orders, and you don't have to worry about him. Or Tully. They work together in galley. No problem with tempers. They *like* each other."

Sirany's ears went down and struggled bravely erect. "I saw the ring."

"Didn't win it in a fight. Won it sitting the boards doing his job while Haral Araun had her finger on a destruct button. And he'll take your orders, or mine, or any senior's. That's how it is. I want your help, *ker* Sirany. It's *good* we've got someone aboard who doubts us. And every word in that log is true. You understand me?"

Sirany's ears went half-flat. White showed at the corners of her eyes and her jaw was hard. Then the ears came up. "We'll worry about that when we're through this alive."

"I'm fighting for the *han*. They'll call me a traitor. They'll put that on my tomb if I get one. You understand me yet? It's one thing to be a gods-be hero. If we get through this alive, I want someone, I want one hani else to know this crew's not what they'll say we are."

Fear snowed in Sirany's face. Undisguised. "What do you want, *company?*"

"I want your influence. We got two fights. *One's* in space. The other's with that fool Ehrran and all her ilk. The *han* tucks its collective head down and the kif have got the axe hanging over it. You hear me, Tauran? I'll do whatever I have to. If you see what I see, you'll be with me. Whatever else you think about me."

"You're a lunatic!"

"I'm doing something. What in a mahen hell has the *han* done right lately? What has anybody done about it?" A claw popped through the seat-leather as her hand clenched tighter. A second. "Tauran, how long do you think we can sit still while the Compact's blown to a mahen hell? Humanity's coming in on us. Mahendo'sat've done something stupid, they've done something that's touched off humans and got something started that they don't understand and I'm not sure the humans do: Tully's witness to that, and he warned us. Jik's tried to do something to save us all, and it's cost him. He at least knows his people've been fools. Like the stsho. Like hani. *And* the kif. And maybe the tc'a, gods save us. And even the humans may know by now. Most of 'em are fools by doing something. Ehrran just got *us* a brand-new treaty with the stsho, did you know that? And look where they are. Look what we're into. The kif just took 'em. We got kif backing into hani space. We got Kura not answering here. We got Akkhtimakt in such a mess that hani space is the only thing left he can get to, because Sikkukkut's sent out ships to every jump-point in reach and blocked his other routes. Meanwhile there's a major mahendo'sat push coming down out of Kshshti, which if Akkhtimakt's spies are worth anything, he knows and Sikkukkut doesn't—*he's* been at Kita and up by Kshshti. That bastard's going to let Sikkukkut take the hit from the mahendo'sat while he pulls off into hani space and comes up again at the mahen underbelly, straight up at Iji. You *know* the mahendo'sat, you know they'll fragment if the Personage goes out. They won't have a defense. And humanity's going to be right in the middle of mahen territory with a whole lot of ships, ships that can jump short, just like our friends the mahendo'sat and just like the kif, ships that can shorten the time between strikes like nothing we want to imagine. But we won't worry about it. We'll be lucky to have a world left. And we'll belong to whoever wins. With nothing to say about it. If we survive at all. We got *one* of our men in space. One, and you know how safe this ship is, with half the kif in the universe hunting us and the other half about to. The whole rest of our species is on Anuurn. And it takes one big rock, Sirany Tauran, one *C*-charged rock, and we're all widows and brotherless. Forever. You hear me? You know what I'm saying?"

Tauran said nothing. The ship hurtled on, crossing planetary diameters in every few heartbeats. In silence, all about them, inside the ship, inside the space between them.

"Tauran."

"I hear you. This is all crazy."

"Tauran's a spacing clan. Three generations. You know what I'm talking about. That mess you got into at Meetpoint. Could you even explain to those old old women in the *han* why you couldn't take out running? What chances you had getting up to *V* or what those distances are like? How many of 'em *understand* a stsho?"

"*Who* understands a stsho?"

"How do they formulate policy with them, make a treaty with them, tell *us* who live out here that we're supposed to stand off the kif, do I guess—that they expect us to dispose of the kifish problem, because it's going to take them ten, twenty years to change their concept of the way kif behave, or what the mahendo'sat are likely to do, and gods save us when they start dealing with the humans and their three governments, all fighting each other? What in a mahen hell are they going to do right now when Akkhtimakt comes into system? Order the Llun to bar them from station? Put hegemony sanctions on them? *Study* the problem?"

"It's too much—"

"I'm asking another clan to damn itself. With me. I'm asking all the rest of you. I'm asking those who know what I'm talking about to do something about it. We're not dealing with scattered pirates anymore. Hani out here'll do the right thing. I'm betting all we've got on that. Traders'll have stripped down, some go home, some scatter like seeds on a high wind. Everywhere. They're warned. But it won't save us from a rock. It won't protect us if some kif decides to

take our species out. I can't get to the *han* to tell them
what I'm telling you. I can't explain what happened at
Meetpoint—gods *know* what's happened at Meetpoint. Or
what's going to follow us. Or when. If Sikkukkut sent a
ship out we don't know about, and some bastard's tailing
us, they might pick up our directional transmissions. We
can't do anything but what we've done."

"I read your running orders. I got your message from
Sif. And I'm not a fool."

"I never took you for one. I got that impression early
on. And I've got to go on walking the track I've been
walking. Inside. Same as Jik's done. Till we've got Akkhtimakt stopped. There aren't enough hani ships in all space
to do what we have to do, against hunter-ships and gods
know what. We *need* the kif's firepower, even at the risk
we're running. That's the game I'm playing, Tauran, and
you know what I'll hear from the *han* if I can even get to
'em. *Illegal contacts. Violation of treaties. Illegal personnel
for the eternal gods' sake, on my ship.* If somehow we live
through this and the *han*'s still operating, they'll probably
hit us both with a charge of *registry* violations. That's how
much they understand. You *know* who we're dealing with.
Those old women are up with every twitch and power shift
in the insystem markets, they know who's leaning where in
the vote, they know every move and current in Anuurn
affairs, and every dustup in history between the River Hegemony and the Amphictiony of Pesh and every other
gods-be particle of past history that isn't going to matter a
whole lot, Tauran, if one incoming rock kills every living
thing on the planet back to the bugs and the worms, is it?
A whole lot of expertise that's by the gods *useless* in the
only question that matters, which is what are we going to
by the gods *do,* Tauran, with what we know and where we
are, and what we got behind us and ahead of us that we
know about and they don't?"

"I'm hearing you," Sirany said. There had been a quiet
stir about. Chanur crew was up. Tauran crew was still in
place. But it was very quiet now. "I'm hearing you. I'm
agreeing with you. But I've still got to think about this,
Chanur."

"Think all the way to Kura Point. I'm going to send you
Sifeny and Fiar back to your shift; let you all work it out.

Take my own back to the boards. Human and my husband and the kif and all. With my thanks, *ker* Sirany. They're good. I don't like to mess with teams that work. Yours or mine. And we need some crew rested full. For contingencies."

"You got it." Sirany released restraints and climbed out of the chair. "Get you a sandwich back here," she said then, and gathered up her crew, galleyward bound. Pyanfar stared at her retreating back, still hanging onto the seat. In case. The way any spacer held onto things in a moving ship. She looked at her own crew, at sober faces of Chanur who had arrived around her.

Ears lifted. "Good," Haral said.

"I hope," she said, and slid a glance Geran's way, at a face that showed trouble. "How is she?"

Geran shrugged. The woman had gone so gaunt herself that her ribs showed. Her worry was tautly held, made a darker spot above her nose, an indentation in her brow that had gotten to be part of her expression.

"You're a mess yourself. We need you. Get in there with Sirany's crew, get some food down you; Tully'll run some back to Chur. Don't argue with me, gods rot it, I'll have your ears. Chur'll have mine if I get her there without you. Hilfy, get the rest of us up here." The assigned crew was all there, all settling in as Hilfy's voice began calling Tully and Khym and Skkukuk on the general speakers.

"Mess," Pyanfar said, and flung herself into her chair. Haral was beside her, already in control of things. "No sign of *Moon Rising*."

There had been a chance. There was less and less. It was four months back at Meetpoint, as hyperlight ran down the starlanes, but not by the way they traveled; whatever had happened there was four, five months old and about to get older.

"Long time back," she said, while the data flowed past her.

"Kura's alive," Haral said. "Just not talking. Kif's scared them plenty. They shut down everything. They got no ships here or they're all lying silent."

They had been a long time away from home. And far from the *han*. "Gods know what the stsho taught us, huh?"

Years the way homeworld saw it. That was the way of

spacers. To stay young while the worlds aged, and groundlings connived and contrived their little worldly plots and
made their gains in the intervals when spacers were strung
out between the stars, lost in dreams.

"Kif's not having any trouble out there. Real fine piece
of navigation, that."

"*We* got troubles, Skkukuk's gods-be dinner's loose again.
Got careless with his door open."

"Or we missed a couple of 'em."

"What's it eating, that's what Sirany wanted to know.
That's what *I* want to know."

"Maybe it's gotten *acclimated* to electric shock," Hilfy
said, breaking in on station-to-station. "*Adaptive*, Skkukuk
said they were. Akkhtish life."

She looked straight across at Haral with a sinking feeling
about her stomach.

"Lifesupport," Haral said.

"Check it. Those godsforsaken things eat plastics."

"We'll get it." Haral was out of her seat and headed.
"Hilfy, get the menfolk on it. Get Skkukuk!"

"We can't leave our gods-be schedule. Can't. We got no
way to recalc this thing and get word to all the ships back
there fast enough. Gods rot it—" They were off auto-pilot
see-and-evade while crew was coming up. It put the ship
at some risk of damage. Not doing it was worse in terms
of fragile flesh and bone. They had lives at stake back
there. She punched a button to usurp com. "*Ker* Sirany,
we're staying stable a good half hour. I'm taking your advice on the vermin. We're trying to track them down."

"*Understood*," Sirany's voice came back, clear above the
quiet of other voices in the galley. And, politic, not one
other word.

Second jab of keys tied into com. "Skkukuk, this is the
captain speaking, you hear me, son? Your gods-be dinner's
loose again, I want 'em counted, I want to know where it
is, I want it out of our way, or I'll have your hide for a
wallhanging, you hear me?"

"*Kkkkt*," the answer came back, dopplered from pickup
to pickup. "*Hakt', I let nothing escape, this is not my doing,
not my doing, mekt-hakt'—I am on my way, at once, at
once— Fools, fools, hold the lift!*"

He doubtless believed it about the wallhanging. She

ducked her head between her hands and raked her claws through her mane. Tell the Tauran they were sane and this cut loose. It was ludicrous. It was deadly serious. No telling what systems the things could take out. The whole ship was infested. She had lost her reputation already. She stank, the whole ship stank, was acrawl with kifish vermin and gods knew what else, the whole clean, well-ordered universe was turned inside out and the vermin were the last, grotesque insult. The gods' own dark humor, that was what it was; just a final, ugly joke on the species. Take out the ship that might save them, with a mucked-up lifesupport, filters ruined, gods knew where they could get in and short something out with their wickedly sharp little teeth.

How many of them?

Breeding during jump? Something that lived so gods-be fast it just went on living and breeding even in hyperspace, generations upon nasty, squealing little generations?

Nothing could do that. Most animals did well to breed at all on shipboard, with all the noise and the clatter and clank that kept them upset; *nothing* could shift its metabolism like that and live realtime in hyperspace.

Even kif couldn't.

Could they?

She stared at the situation on the screens in front of her, she kept the ship on course while one crew had its necessary meal in the galley; and Geran came back to tell her she had just reassigned Khym and Tully from galley to the hunt and she was, by the captain's leave, taking a cup of soup to her sister, by the captain's leave. Please. In spite of her specific orders.

"Gods. Yes." Pyanfar took another desperate swipe at her disordered mane and part of it came out on her claws, the way a body always shed during jump, but no one on ship had had a bath in over four realspace months and six or so subjective days. "How is she?"

"Just real still. Says—says there's a trouble at home. Says there's kif going there. Says *Moon Rising*'s behind us. Akkhtimakt's ten days up on us. She says."

A chill went up Pyanfar's spine, and right down again to the gut. "She could be right." For a moment she had a conviction Chur could well be right: crack scan tech and sometime navigator, Chur *knew* how much time determined hunter ships could gain on a band of freighters. Then she saw it the way Geran had to see it. Chur was a practical woman. And she was babbling prophecies across lightyears. Jump could do that to a mind. There were casualties who never came in out of the dark. She had seen them, sitting in the sun at hospital, with Anuurn's blue sky above them forever and not a realization in the world where they were.

They were everywhere, that was their delusion. They would always be everywhere. If there was anything mystical about it, the thing that was themselves had just reached infinity and stayed there, like a machine with a broken cut-off switch.

"She wants to work," Geran said.

"Tell her—" Pyanfar drew a breath. "*Can* she?"

"No."

"Get her fed. We got an hour insystem here. I'm taking you offshift; you stay with her."

"No." Geran's ears went flat. "No, captain."

"You want one of the Tauran? Tully, f'godssakes? You do it. We got Tirun to take scan. We can run this one short or I can haul Sif back in. *Stay* there."

Geran's face went hard and desperate. Ears flicked and struggled up again. "Tully," she said. "I mean, he's not going to *do* anything, is he? Sleeps with us below. They're friends. Aren't they?"

"Yeah." Less said on that the better. "The good of the ship. Good of—a whole lot of people. Yes. I want you on the boards if you got your mind there."

"It'll be there," Geran said. "Do her good. She can't argue with Tully. I'll feel better about it." And she went, with a solid purpose in her stride.

Pyanfar settled into her place, listened to the chatter in-system, ran checks, took a cup of gfi when Fiar came bringing cups round. Charity. Out of their own galley.

The hunt went on, upper decks and lower. And the system they were running through stayed far quieter than it ought to be.

"They got the upperdecks filter changed out," Hilfy said. "Caught three of those things. Skkukuk swears they didn't slip from his collection. Old stuff, he says. They're coming from somewhere."

"Great. Wonderful." She clicked through changes on the comp. "That's fine news." *Ought not to snap. Crew has enough on their minds.* "Sorry."

"Aye, captain."

You've grown a lot, Hilfy Chanur. Can't tell you that. Grown woman never wants to hear that. Can't tell you anything anymore.

"First escort's jumped," Tirun said. "We're on—"

The fifteen-minute warning sounded, a double pulse. *"That's fifteen,"* Hilfy's voice rang out through the halls.

Pyanfar punched in on the same channel. "Leave it, whatever it is. Give us an easy trip, get yourselves to stations and quarters, wherever they are, forget the gods-be mess, I want you where you're going on the five. Tully, you go to Chur's room. Now."

"Got," that lone human voice came back. And other acknowledgments. Perhaps no one had broken it to Tully until now where he was spending the jump.

He would not object. He understood. Would do anything for Chur. *Friend,* he would say.

What Chur would say about Tully in her bed was another matter.

Annoy her. Make her mad. Get her mind *back.* That was what might work. Of a sudden she saw Geran's logic, clear and plain.

"He's what?" Chur murmured, and blinked at her sister, and at Tully standing all diffident at the foot of her bed.

"Taking care of you," Geran said. "Mind your manners. You take advantage of him the captain'll skin you. Hear?"

Chur blinked again, deciding finally that this was funny. The worried look on Tully's face was funny. There was a time she would have worried. Had been a time—yesterday, it seemed—when she had wanted no more of anything but hani. It was strange how all that had washed away, as if jump had left it behind, left her washed out, new, all things and everywhere. A god would feel this strange sensation, as if all space was her body and her brain, the stars so many particles. She might be a god. She laughed at them both, and flexed the fingers on the arm so long stiff it had gone beyond pain. Machinery ticked away. She had learned how to cheat it, how to keep her heart quiet and not trigger its anesthetizing flood through the tubes. She felt the pulse increase and settled it down again, deliberately.

"Brought me a handsome lover, have you? I must be better. C'mon, Tully. It's all right. They got one hand out of operation."

"I stay with," he said. Innocent of everything.

He stank. Everyone did. She did. There was no help for it, though Geran tried to keep her clean. That was all right too. Geran went off and left them together, Tully standing there lost-looking, and the com crackling with reports.

The reports confused her. They had hunted the black things out at—wherever they had been.

They were back again at Kura. Little slinking evils. A god might have worse things to deal with. They were only nuisance-nightmares.

"Go soon," Tully said, and sat on the edge of her bed. "I be with you." He patted her knee under the blankets. That hurt a little. All her joints ached. "You be fine, Chur."

It was nice to be told that by someone other than Geran, who was biased. She drew a larger breath.

"We go to Anuurn," he said, and held up two slender, agile fingers. "Two jump. We got—" Another rearrangement of the fingers. "Nine ship. Make safe."

"Against the kif?" For a moment space went inside and out. "No. Tell the captain—tell the captain—trouble. They'll be waiting off Tyar."

"Geran tell," Tully said. "She tell, all right?"

"Logic," Chur said, and waved the free hand, a loose, limp failure of a gesture. "Logic—position. The geometry of the thing—" She stared at him in despair. Geran had looked at her as if she were crazed. Tully simply blinked, beyond his vocabulary.

"Danger," she said. "*Danger,* gods rot it."

"Understand," he said. And looked at her with fear. With Geran's look.

Crew returned. Pyanfar ran the checks. They were still on the mark. They had no communication with the other ships excepting the necessary crosschecks of position and exchange of navigational data. It was not politic or wise, considering possibility of spies overhearing them, to do more than they had done. Their messages would be reported, as often as they were detected, and some they had sent were already pushing the limits of prudence.

Hakkikt, she would say, such arguments were necessary. They won us allies. Isn't that the point?

If she got the chance.

The five-minute warning sounded. The ship started procedures. Data started coming up. Tauran crew and their mahen passengers reported themselves secure.

"*Sukk* just made jump," Geran said.

"Coming up on mark," Haral said.

They left behind a scrap of message, to persist after them. *Danger to Anuurn. Assist.*

Chapter 10

. . . Down. . . .
   . . . one more time. . . .
     . . . *"Kura Point, Pyanfar."*
She was young. Back in Urarun's day. Green kid on her first trip back home again. Looking forward to Anuurn and swaggering about the estate.

See me. Ring and all. Got this scratch dockside at Meet-point, I did.

Difference of opinion, me and a Jesur crewwoman.

Gods bless. What were we fighting about?

No matter. We healed fast in those days.

"Meet you at the door, Hal." With a slow and heavy-lidded look, while a graynosed spacer (that was the name: Pura Jesur) Pura Jesur thought she could push a couple of Chanur kids and have a bit of fun. Herself and Haral, insubordinate and full of young arrogance toward a rival ship's crew. And drunk. That too.

Gods save us.

Urarun Chanur being the captain on the old Golden Sun. *She retired as captain two voyages after. Chanur clan took the ship out of service, sold it finally to Thusar, where it ran under the name of Thusar's Merit, a little ship. A lot of ship, for a little clan like Thusar, new to spacefaring. Chanur retired the shipname. Transferred the crew eventually, as many together as they could, to the newbuilt* Pride. *Urarun Chanur died in her sleep one night planetside.*

   . . . "Captain."

"I got it, we're on, aren't we?"

"We're running smooth."

How's Chur? Calm down, she won't answer yet. Can't answer. Gods-be drugs. No. Tully's with her. "Tully. Report. How is Chur?"

A long pause. Muzzy human. Tully was always hard to rouse after jump.

"Tully? How's Chur, Tully?" *Is she alive, Tully? F'gods-sakes, answer back there.*

"She sleep."

"Are you sure? Is she all right?" With Geran listening. But it was what Geran had to know.

"She sleep," Tully's voice came back again.

"We've got acquisition on our escort," Geran said, dead calm, onto business. "We're still doing fine, captain."

I have no nerves, captain. The job gets done. For the ship and all of us.

"No buoy here, either," Haral muttered.

"No sign of anything." She drank down the concentrates. Her hand shook. She wadded up the foil packet and thrust it into the bin after, and wiped her face. An appalling lot of hair came away. Teeth were sore, when she pushed them with her tongue. One felt loose. That more than any wound she had ever suffered made her afraid; not of dying. Of time. Of the inevitable wall that said this far for a body and no farther, courage and wit and skill notwithstanding.

Where are we? Is what I remember true?

Gods, how did I get here? Get this old?

Kif. Kif out in front of us. It's all true. No hallucination. Gods, if it were a hallucination, if I was back there with Urarun all this time, if I never knew these things, if these friends, this ship, this terrible mess—were all illusion—

Earflick. A weighty number of rings chimed and rang against each other.

Old graynose. Yourself, Pyanfar. Here. In this gods-be mess. Wake up. Come back. You're fuzzed and drifting. . . .

. . . when did I get old?

Haral beside her. A flash and flicker of monitors at her board. Scan information vanished for a checklist, one critical moment. Reappeared again. Haral had missed a switch and changed all the priorities in a rippling flicker of screens. *Haral* had missed. That never happened.

"You on?"

"I got it, cap'n. Sorry. That's confirm on *Aja Jin.* They're in on schedule."

Vermin. Little vermin.

drop again. . . .

> . . . *reform.*

". . . got us stable."

"Hilfy. Relay that. Tell our relief we're looking for 'em up here fast as they can do it. Skkukuk, you're discharged. Get some rest."

"Hakt', I should check the filter traps."

"Do it fast, then. Go to it."

"Yes, hakt'."

Long hour til jump-out.

And still days down. She did not want to know how many. The figures were lost in her jump-mazed brain.

Akkhtimakt's ships were indisputably in front of them, already gone, in transit toward Anuurn. Of the two missing probes, nothing. Their own escort was there, that was all.

She forced another nutrients-packet down. Swallowed and listened to an eerily deserted nowhere, the dark mass of Kura Point, its little beacon extinguished. Not a place hani had ever found it economical to put a station, it was just an astronomical oddity, Kura Point Mass, a lump of rock that just incidentally made hani an independent species—making a route to Meetpoint and other species through *hani* space only, and not through mahen Ajir, to the sure annoyance of the mahendo'sat.

An accident of nature that had cut four months off the Anuurn-Kura run and saved the whole hani species from becoming a dependency of the mahendo'sat.

It just sat there radiating away, dead and quiet. A chancy, spooky place where hani met and hailed each other, glad of another voice in the tomblike silences. Have a breakdown here and a ship just sat and waited for rescue. Which might bankrupt a running ship. Weeks waiting on help and months getting a repair crew out from Anuurn or Kura star.

She made the count on those coming in behind them. "Send," she said to Hilfy. "*The Pride of Chanur* to all ships. Status check."

Because the silence oppressed her, because of a sudden, this last, this perilous last jump, she wanted a voice or two out of the dark. She wanted Jik's most of all, wanted it to come across the way she was used to hearing it, deep and humorous and reservedly friendly.

Crazy. Crazy impulse. Why him? Ought to want his ears, I should, I ought.

Lying bastard that he is. He's not suffering on that ship of his. Got enough crew to rotate shifts with no pain at all.

They're built *for this kind of run. A ship like* Lightweaver, *or* Starwind, *back there, they're going to be feeling it near as bad as we are, gods help 'em.*

Kifish advisements came in, cold and exact. No pain there either. *We are running well,* one sent. *Glory to the hakkikt.*

Hani ships: *"We're hanging on."*—Harun's *Industry.*

"We got one system on backup."—Pauran's *Lightweaver.*

"We counting? We got four." That was *Shaurnurn's Hope,* a youngish voice. *"We're patching, this lay-through."*

"We're doing all right. We've got a few red-light conditions. We're seeing to them." Munur Faha, on *Starwind.*

And last of all: *"We all time good condition, friend. I be here, no worry. What you 'spect, a?"*

Hilfy made acknowledgments, passed advisements, in a wan, tired voice.

And from Geran, quietly, speaking to someone: "How is she?"

"Geran. You want to get back there? That's an order, cousin."

"Aye."

No argument this time. Tirun signaled she was covering that station. A belt clicked, and Pyanfar gnawed her mustaches and fought the hypnosis of the blinking lights, the wash of green on the board— *Going to lose her,* was the thought that wanted through, and she would not let it.

Bone and muscle. Vital organs. Nutrients. Steel and plastics could last the trip. Living bodies needed time to rebuild, and there was no recovery in their schedule.

Do kif suffer this?

Image of a black bundle of rags, Skkukuk collapsing in her arms, virtually moribund in the first jump they had made.

Image of black, ravenous lengths of fur and muscle and sharp little teeth gnawing away at *The Pride's* vitals, fatal, voracious stupidity destroying the vessel which kept them from the cold of space.

Like the *han* and the stsho.

We learned the lesson: the kif must have learned it. The law of controlled predation: neither predator nor prey can survive alone. Intelligent predators manage their resources.

Do you recall that lesson, Sikkukkut?

Burn the land? Lay waste whole ecosystems?

Suicide, *na* kif. Kill the stsho and you will die. Take out hani and mahendo'sat and the economy the stsho live on collapses, same result.

A predator needs his rivals as much as he needs his prey. Ecosystems interlock. One predator, one prey, can never sustain itself.

Her eyes hazed out. She knew the signs. Forced herself back again, arched her shoulders. Withdrew her arm from the brace and hissed at the pain.

"You all right?" Haral asked.

"Gods," she said, short of breath from the hurt. *Old age, cousin. It's old age for sure. You and me. It's not fair this should happen to us. We were immortal. Weren't we?* "We got one more jump to make. One more." That reassurance was for herself. *Not that much more to go, Pyanfar, not that far. Done it time after time, haven't you, lived days while Anuurn lives a month. Two months out and back.*

But the gods of the Wide Dark gave time with one hand and took it with the other. Wore a spacer out from the inside, strained the heart, took the steadiness from the hands. Kohan was graying, last she saw him. Graying in earnest. But he sat on his cushions in the stability his wives provided him in Chanur's lands, and hunted his preserves and had the best of care. He never knew hunger, only a lunch delayed in the field, his wives and daughters and nieces and cousins and juvenile sons all slogging along with the makings of a small feast. Rough living, the groundlings thought. A hunt burned off the fat and quickened the blood and a little hunger put an edge on a body.

O gods, Kohan. Late lunch. A tragedy.

Never been jump-stretched, never had your fur falling out so thick it left a shimmer of bare skin beneath it, never had your backside hurt because the bones hit the seat, never wake up from jump and find the bones and tendons all prominent, your hand like a stranger's at the end of your arm, your teeth sore and your joints aching like the stab of a knife between the bones.

Another food packet. Something on the stomach.

"What in a mahen hell's keeping Tauran?"

"They're in the lift," Hilfy said. About the time the lift door opened, bright and spreading reflection in the right-hand monitor, and dark figures came down the hall, resolving themselves into hani silhouettes and hani presence.

She turned the chair around and saw Sirany Tauran, saw her face change and her ears flatten in dismay at what she saw. Like looking in a mirror. *Am I that bad?*

She reckoned that she was.

"We're stable, everything clear," she said to Sirany. And levered herself up from the chair, caught herself on the arm and on Sirany's suddenly offered hand. She had a close view of Sirany's face then, wide, shocked eyes. She shoved herself upright and tried to find equilibrium.

"*Ker* Pyanfar—"

"Want to rest," she said.

"Go to it," Sirany said. "We'll bring you something. You, your whole crew. Get to bed."

Pity, Tauran?

She resented that. Resented it with an irrational touchiness and knew that it was irrational. It was concern the Tauran offered her. Was belief in them. Was what she had been trying to rouse in Tauran in this long alternate life-death they were locked in.

How long? Months on months now.

How long have the kif had to do harm at Anuurn?

Gods, were they gone from Urtur long before us? Was the force at Meetpoint only a part of what they have? Were they already weeks ahead of us?

Are we running into a trap meant for Sikkukkut?

Chur seeing visions.

Black vermin in the ducts.

"Pyanfar—"

A hard grip settled onto her right shoulder. Claws bit. She stared into lambent, hani eyes. "I let Jik go," she mumbled, knowing she was rambling, but suddenly it seemed to matter, it seemed something that Tauran had to know, part of the puzzle, the jagged pieces that resulted when someone dropped the universe and it shattered, scattered, made new patterns that a ship had to navigate. "It's important." But that was not enough to say. "The mahendo'sat are the key. Neither predator nor prey. They're important. Always prying into things. Like Tully. The humans are like them. Both predator and prey. Be careful. The mahendo'sat didn't know that. Humans are trouble. They'll confound us like the mahendo'sat. Like the methane-breathers. The kif know that. Even the *han* had instinct on their side in that one. We were right."

"Captain," Haral said. Haral's face this time, displacing the other. "Captain, here's *here*. Watch the time, cap'n."

She blinked. Jolted back to physical motion again instead of all-movement, particle-dance and star motions. Blinked again. "Yeah," she said. Blinked a third time and things hurt again. Her legs felt unsteady. "I'm going."

("Is she all right?" someone asked, not a Chanur voice. Young voice. Fiar.)

Pyanfar turned around, flattened her ears, fixed the young tech with a stare. "She's *fine*, youngster." She drew a larger breath, continued the sweep of her eyes on back to Sirany. "I've preset us to drop close in. May have been a mistake. We do the best we can."

Doubt. Plain and clear on Sirany's face. *This is what we've got to rely on, is it? Woman's been through too much. Too long, too far. We're bound to sit duty on this leg and we have to hand off the ship at Anuurn to a lunatic. With all that may be at stake.*

"Sirany, if you think I'm not tracking right, you're mistaken."

"Didn't say that." Not a bristle at the familiarity of first names. Not a twitch of irritation. It *was* pity. The ship crossed planetary diameters at a breath or two, and a fool wanted long arguments on the bridge, distracting the crew from their business.

"Get to work," Pyanfar said. "Eyes on those boards!" Ordering the wrong crew. "*Somebody* get their eyes on those boards. I don't care which." *So much for inattention, Sirany Tauran. Which of us is wit-wandering?* "I'm telling you," she said, trying to dredge gnosis up from the free-association where it was wandering. Dark territory. Nowhere. Numbers and lines spread wide through the Compact. "Jik is the best we've got. Rely on him and his First. And I want com through to allship this time. The kif too. We can't afford to come out the other side wondering where we are."

No, Pyanfar Chanur, we certainly can't afford that. Still the doubt. Below the surface now, like a fish gone into deep waters. Surface smooth, a relief to have the proprieties back again. But the doubt was still cruising along down there, all sleek and dark and quiet.

To flare up at the wrong moment, and turn and bite you, yes, Pyanfar Chanur.

"We're still on auto?" Sirany asked. *"Still?"*

"Good computer," Pyanfar said. "Good crew. I told you those nav figures are *right*. I'm not a liar, *ker* Sirany."

"No," Sirany said, quiet against her heat, "I really don't think you are."

"What I was talking about. Think on it, you said. *Think on it.* *See, I remember. Do you, Tauran? Your mind that clear? Or do you still think I'm crazy?* "I'm asking again. Here and now. Before we get make drop at Anuurn."

"Join you?"

"That's what I'm asking. You're supposed to give the rest of the captains out there some kind of report before then, aren't you? Sure you are. But you haven't, yet. Jik would have reported it to us. Unless you coded it real clever." She leaned hard on the chair back, eased the weight on her legs. "What are you going to tell them?"

Long hesitation. "That you're no pirate. That we're convinced of that."

She stood there a moment. Blinked, trying to run it through her brain. "But not that we're right."

Sirany's ears went down. Not anger. Profound distress. "I'm still figuring that out for myself."

"How long are you going to think about it, huh?" Her pulse thumped in her ears. The bridge fuzzed in one long smear of lights both white and green. "We got no gods-be time left when we come out. You understand that?"

"You've set the comp that way. I know."

Black closed in. Cleared again. "I set it," she said carefully, "to get us in there as close in the well as we could get. We got one lousy lot of Akkhtimakt's kif in our way. We're not going to have time to sit and talk about it. We don't have the guns to hammer our way clear across system from far out. We aren't fit for a long fight. This ship has *seen* fighting like that before, at Gaohn, captain, and I don't want to do it again. Odds get up to you, fast."

A hand descended on her shoulder, ever so gently. "Cap'n. Time."

"I'm onto it, Haral, I'm gods-be onto it." She drew herself up on a deep breath. "We're one ship down, we're up to our noses in kif, and I am not, by the gods greater and lesser, *ker* Sirany Tauran, a raving lunatic." A second breath, speech clear and spaced this time. No shouting, no hysteria. "I am giving you my sane assessment of the situation: we're aiming one set of kif at the other set and hoping to the gods we have enough left to push them outsystem. If we don't, we are going to die there, collectively and gods hope, without seeing what else will happen. And I am not having my plans tampered with and my communications setup interfered with and myself and my crew deprived of necessary information *or of control of this ship at the last moment* do we understand each other, *ker* Sirany? I'm going to take controls at Anuurn. My shift. That's the way I set it up, that's the way it's going to be, don't play hero with me. You want to fight, you'll get your share. Not on the drop!"

Sirany's ears were down. Not anger. That fright-doubt expression again. They lifted and twitched and flattened and lifted again. *And what will you do about it, you and your crew, none of you fit to stand?*

Someone moved. More than one someone out of a chair.

Khym's gusting breath. Khym looming like a shadow over in the peripheries of her vision.

Male and crazy. It was in the sudden nervous flick of Sirany's eyes.

"He's on our side," Pyanfar said hoarsely. She was disarmed by that threatening move of his. There was nothing left to say. Sirany doubted her husband's sanity if not her own and they had just lost all hope of reason. Clock was running. The ship was headed for jump and they had crew to take care of. She made a despairing wave of her hand, not sure she could find equilibrium if she let go of the chair. Everything swam in a blur. "See you otherside, *ker* Sirany. Gods hope." She let go, resisted the urge to grab Khym's arm, managed to keep the deck stable and the exit steady in her vision.

"Pyanfar." Sirany's voice, name unadorned.

She managed to turn around. Steadied herself, Khym's shadow to her left, Hilfy and Tirun over there somewhere. Haral still beyond.

"It's concern, understand," Sirany said. "It's not—doubt, *ker* Pyanfar."

"I'm going to fall on my face," she said calmly, rationally. And stared as much at the level line of the control boards beyond Sirany's back, to keep something level in her vision. The bridge was trying to tilt. "Send us something to eat for godssakes and let us go, *ker* Sirany."

She managed to turn, still keeping the counters level in her sight, walked out without the use of her internal equilibrium. One foot in front of the other. Khym was behind her. Others were. Chur's door was shut as she passed it. Where Geran was—she could not remember, whether Geran had gone to the galley, whether she had heard her pass that corridor.

She reached the door of her own quarters. Fumbled after the lock and got it, and staggered in and fell into bed.

"I'm going after food," Khym said in a voice hoarse and deep.

"They'll do it."

"Me," he said. "I make sure it gets done. We're time-critical."

And came back out of a confusing darkness and shook at her till she sat up and wrapped her hands around the cup he gave her. Whole jug of the stuff with him. Awful. Full of sickly spices. Tofi. "Gods, you got to put that stuff in?"

"Way I cook. Shut up and drink it. It's got calories."

She drank it, drank another cup because he insisted. Ate the dried stuff. Her hands just fell away limp and dropped the packets. He fell in beside her. Out of some terrible reverberating tunnel the intercom was ringing with strange hani voices: *"Rig for jump."* Operations noises. Strange crew. The words echoed and twisted in and out of her brain, losing focus. She felt after the security of the restraint webbing, found it, and all the while the room kept coming and going.

Khym had remembered the safeties. Half conscious as he was, he had remembered that.

"They're all right," some real voice said from the doorway. "Excuse me, captain."

It confused her to a mahen hell. The door shut. Tauran security check.

They had had a door open.

Black things. Might *feed* on a body while it was helpless. Kifish life, active in jump, when they lay inert and unable to move, to feel pain. Might wake up with fingers gone. Bleed to death. Gnawed to a rack of bones, aswarm with slinking vermin.

A siren went.

"We're going," Khym mumbled against her shoulder.

She grabbed him and held tight. Trust their lives to Tauran. And her programming and the Nav-comp, and the lock on that door.

"Last jump," Hilfy murmured, in her bunk beside Haral's and Triun's and Geran's, down in crew quarters. Two beds were empty. Chur's and Tully's. She clenched her claws into the mattress, counting breaths. Tully had stayed topside with Chur. She had been shocked when Geran showed up to join them. But: "I got to work otherside," Geran had said. As if she had turned all emotion off. Their lives and more than their lives rode on Geran, otherside. That was true. And Geran came down to rest with them, face cold and set, leaving her sister to Tully's care a second time. "He's good with her," Geran had said. "She wanted him."

And sent you away? Perhaps Chur had done that. Gods *knew* what Chur's condition was. Geran kept her mouth shut.

"How is she?" Haral had the nerve to ask. The same question. Forever the same question, as if it was going to have some better answer.

"Holding," Geran said. "Holding." No optimism. Geran had stayed up there a long time and come down at the last moment of stability, with the alarms ringing.

"She able to eat?" Tirun was merciless. Trod right in where even Haral did not dare.

Long silence out of Geran. Then: "Yeah. Did pretty well." In a flat and hopeless voice.

Last jump.

"I programmed that son to take us right in close to Anu-urn," Haral said between her teeth. "Forty-five and eight by six. Lay you odds we get it inside point five."

"We'll string it a bit," Tirun said, all matter-of-fact calculating the drag and push of entering and already-arrived ships on the gravity slope. Deformation calc. Keeping the mind busy.

It was Geran and Chur who always laid the bets. Even that was offkey. Geran refused to take the bait. She remained in dire silence. It was not money Tirun and Haral were betting. It was drinks in the nearest bar.

Hilfy stared at the overhead. Terrified.

We're not going to make it, we're not going to make it, we're too few and the kif too many, we can't push them. Sikkukkut's ships are a throwaway—we're all throwaways.

What's a kif care, how many ships he loses?

Cheap annoyance to his enemies.

And we were pushing him too hard.

"Otherside," Pyanfar murmured, "we got to move. We'll run stable right after the first cycle-down. You got to count. First pulse, then get up and go even if we got an alarm going. I don't know if Tauran's going to call us. I don't trust that."

"First pulse," Khym said against her ear, all indistinct. "Right. Got it."

"Got to—"

—down.
—the wide dark again.

She struggled to remember her own name. It was important to recall. She lay with an alien snuggled tight against her, his strange smooth hand holding hers ever so loosely. He had drugged himself before this, and lay helpless, as his kind had to be, in order to face the deep.

Chur, the name was. She stayed, tied by that loose grip on her essence. She could not have left him alone.

Left my son. Lost him. Never find him again, never know. Not leave my friend out here helpless. No.

She was aware. It was not normal to be this hyper-stretched. She knew this. She had time, in this long waking

of subjective days, to sort through things, not in the waking
dream of time-stretch, the dim haze with which minds got
through the deep, slower than bodies, but wide-awake in
the twisting dark. She stretched out like the ship, and ran
calculations in her head with one part of her brain, and
kept the tether of that strange, fine-boned hand.

Not leave him. She thought of Tully and remembered
why they were here, remembered aliens, and the ship, and
the situation, Situation, the captain would call it. She forgot
about time with Geran, Geran being forever, like the stars
and the movement of the worlds. But Tully came from
elsewhere; was more lost than she was. Tully had period
and limit. There was a time when she had not known him.
There was never a time but this that she had lain so close
to him. She tried to tell Geran this, explaining why she
wanted Tully to stay. "Get out," it came out of her mouth.
Not the way she had meant it, but speaking with her mind
that full was a surreal experience. Calculations. Numbers.
One could spill out too much. "Gods rot it, get. Go. I don't
want you here. Him. He's enough. You got work, Gery.
Get to it. You want to kill us at those boards?"

I'm sorry.

She wiped that scene. Built another. She sat in bed,
propped with pillows.

"We got troubles," she said, which was what she had
meant to say. "Gery, I want my place back."

"You'll get it," Geran said, gently (she knew Geran would
say exactly that thing, knew the precise cant of the ears, the
pained look, the soft, quiet tone). "Come on now. We got
relief aboard. Tauran. I told you that. You want to go to
the galley, have a sit? Something to drink?"

"All right," she said; and let herself be led there, slowly.
Seated, in familiar surroundings. Tully was there. He came
and laid his hand on her arm.

"You scare me," he said.

"I'm sorry," she said. (Back in bed a moment. Tully lying
there asleep, drugged senseless. Pretty mane he had. Prettiest thing about him. The gods could have fur like that, all
sunlight. She scared him sometimes. But he snugged down
against her: maybe she kept him warm. *Friend,* he had said
just as he was going out. A little pat of his hand on her
shoulder, a smoothing of her fur. Friend.)

They were all there, all the crew, at the galley table, which made no sense with things as they were, at risk. Only the captain was missing. And the kif. Someone put a cup in her hands. Geran shaped her hands around it and nudged them, helped her carry it to her mouth. It was hard to get back again. Hard. She was aware of heat in the liquid. It tasted of nothing at all. It was hard to focus small enough, to adjust her ears to hear the noise of their speech, to concentrate her mind to sort this kind of detail and not raw calculations of the sort she had been running.

She blinked at movement, at the captain's voice. Pyanfar had shown up, sitting between Haral and Tirun. Khym was meddling about in the cabinets, on galley duty again.

". . . I'm not easy about this," Pyanfar said. "Some reason, I'm just not real easy about this next jump. We're going into it close to Anuurn as we can. I don't know what we're into. But it's been too quiet, all along the way. Kura had no time to get us a message. I wish we'd come closer to the station."

Chur blinked. Blinked and found Jik there, when she had remembered only dimly why he was there at all. Their little galley table held more places than usual. Space folded itself. A lot of things fit.

"Push them out of the system," Chur said then "That's what we have to do. Cut them to ribbons on first encounter. The *han* knows they're coming. The mahendo'sat have told them. Haven't you, Jik?"

"A," the mahendo'sat said, and shrugged.

"There was Banny Ayhar. Ayhar went on to Maing Tol. You gave them a message, Jik, when they shot me at Kshshti. I've figured their course home. That's where they'd have gone. Nothing would stop them. Not with what they knew. Not with what you gave them to carry. Isn't that so, Jik?"

"Good guess," Jik said, in better hani than he usually spoke. He leaned his elbows on the table. "Bad luck at Kshshti dock. How you know 'bout Maing Tol?"

"I told her," Geran said. "Told her the message was all right. Gods, she got a hole in her gut defending it, you think I wouldn't tell her that? It *was* important, after all."

"Better be. I got a hole in my gut to prove it. You think I'm going to lose track of something like that? Banny Ayhar went on to Maing Tol and I know she went with something

*of yours. I know what I'd have done in Banny Ayhar's
place. I'd have gotten out of there fast. I'd have run for
home the safest, shortest way. And the Personage at Maing
Tol would have a thing to say to the* han *about then,
wouldn't he, knowing he had to arrest that whole crew or
let them go. Let them go with a message. Let them go with
a whole mahen company to see them home."*

"I'm not at controls," Pyanfar said. "I've been thinking
about something like that. I've hoped it was so. But this isn't
my shift. Not my watch."

"I told you that," Geran said.

"Hey, you think I don't keep track of things? I'm better
than that. I know where I am. I've known all this time. You
think it's easy running calc in your head? I know where
every ship could be. And how long. I know their mass and
their cap. I know what their drop time is. I got gray hairs
in this game. I know our competition, don't I? Not competition this time. Our help. All the help we got. Trust me, captain. I got it figured for you."

"Not my watch," Pyanfar said again.

And left the table. Was gone.

So did others. "I'm sorry," Jik said. "I'm not here."

Then she was alone with the crew again. Khym left. Then
she did.

There was deathly quiet. Tully was anchor, in a long
dark sea.

She reached out and carefully, in motion that took the
better part of a day, perhaps, in timestretch, disconnected
herself.

. . . down again.
. . . gravity slope.

It was hard to move at all. But Chur did that, levered
herself to the side of the bed and remembered—she could have
forgotten nothing—to put the safety back. For Tully's sake.

Longer still down the corridor, which reeled and snaked
and kept going into the lighted bridge. Perhaps it took a
day to walk it. Dark things skittered and moved, ran like
black, rapid serpents in the corridors.

New logical track: moving and breeding. Feeding where
they could. Insulation. Plastics. Ignoring barriers.

Akkht-bred. Like the kif.

Alert within jump.

. . . down and still falling. . . .

She made it as far as the captain's place. And leaned there. "Captain," she said, perhaps another day in the saying of it: "The mahendo'sat. A message has gone to them. A message can have reached from Maing Tol to Iji. Ayhar of *Prosperity* will have come home. From Kirdu to Kita is one jump. A ship can have gone to Iji from there. From Kirdu to Ajir, one; from there to Anuurn. Our ships will have heard. They'll come home, captain. As we are, coming home at the earliest possible. The mahendo'sat will not have resisted this move. The quarry goes to the small valley, but hunters cross the hill. That is only reasonable." Words slurred. She watched the slow twitch of a listening ear. *Not* her captain, but this stranger. Tauran. She knew that too.

"Believe us," she said to that captain. "Believe what we've told you."

Other calculations. The solar system danced in her memory, swung through two years of positional changes. Lanes threaded like moving spirals of color through this maze of rock, converging on Anuurn.

Cover a ship with mass and emissions-noise, a gravity well it could stay in, concealed in dancing fragments, in the thunderous emissions of a gas giant. Akkhtimakt *knew* there would be attack coming in at him. He had had time to plan and research the moves he hoped to make, and attack could not possibly take him by utter surprise.

She crossed to the com board, reached the slack hand of a Tauran crew woman, punched in a channel. "Kif. Do you hear me?"

"Kkkt," the voice came back, slow and slurred. *"Who calls? Who is this?"*

She reached—it was terrible effort—to the board. Sat down in a vacant chair. Tully's. Between two Tauran crewwomen. She freed up armaments from that master board and set her hand on that control, preprogramming fire on the Tyar vector from their entry point.

Black things ran and squealed. There were red lights on boards, systems failures. She went to the main board and carefully switched to backups, system after system, where automation had failed.

. . . down again. She staggered, held to the board, blinked with the jolting *here* of the bridge about her, where she spent her life. The crew woman beside her was turning her head in confusion, the whole of the bridge was real for the moment before it began to darken.

"My gods," someone said. As *The Pride* fired on its own.

The dark folded round again, but it was only a dimming of the light; and there was pain, the bite of the strap against her sagging body. She pushed herself upright again. She reached for the com-switch again, threw it on wide. "Captain. This is Chur. Get up here. Emergency, emergency."

"How in a mahen hell'd she *do* it?" a young voice cried; and another: *"Captain!"*

As space sorted itself into sanity, as alarms wailed, advising of systems gone backup; as they ran into a wavefront of information that said ANUURN, ANUURN, ANUURN—

"My *gods!*" someone yelled, seeing something.

And their own ship answered, automatic: *The Pride of Chanur.*

They were well into system. *Close* to the star. To the sun that had warmed their backs as children and beaconed them home trip after trip.

Anuurn buoy was out. No help for that. "Watch out for Tyar," she said to the scan operator by her, tried to say. As *The Pride*'s weapons fired again.

Pyanfar ran. She had never moved so hard, straight out of jump. She hit the door with her whole body, triggered the lock and staggered into the hall and ran it with the thud and thump of Khym running behind her. A blurred figure came out of Chur's room and collided with her, embraced her, stink of human, half-naked and all but falling. "Chur—" Tully said, but she sorted out from him, already on her way, and left him to obstruct Khym's path.

Bridge loomed, lit and swimming in and out of focus. She grabbed the doorframe, safetywise hand-over-handed toward the nearest console and lurched for the next, heading for the captain's seat, grabbed the back of it and hung there. "I'm here," she gasped, and Sirany twisted in the seat and began to get out of it. "Get to observer one. Too far to go below."

"We're still firing," a youngish voice said. "Do I stop?"

"*Priority,* we got no buoy here."

"What are we firing at?" Sirany snapped. "Gods and thunders, what are we doing? My gods, we're high-V— those guns—"

"Not sure," that one said; and: "She's fainted—" Another voice. As Pyanfar grabbed Sirany's seatback. "*Out!*" she yelled at the Tauran; and Sirany cleared it as she threw herself into it, a collision of bodies. "Tyar vector," someone said; and: "Stay your posts," Pyanfar snapped, blinking at a blur of lights, and felt blind after the general hail: "Chanur, get your backsides up here! Run for it! Tauran, cancel fire, cancel."

"*My door, my door! Fools!*"

"Unlock the kif," she said to the Tauran copilot/switcher. Confusion behind as Tully and Khym tried to ascertain Chur's state. "Khym! Get her to the galley, emergency secure. Get liquid down her if you can." They had run that drill, galley-secure, smallest fore-aft space next the bridge. Close the corridor-access and hit the padded benches, collapse the table to use for auxiliary brace, and belt in and tie down. In the tail of her vision they took Chur out that way. Sirany moved and came on over intercom from the seat Chur had left. "I'll aux switch, Chanur."

"You got it," she said, ripped a nutrients packet loose and downed it, her eye to the chrono and the red numbers flashing on the screen. "Gods—" Into the general com: "Make that lift, gods rot you, *run,* we got thirty seconds to dump, *run, run, run!* Ride it out in the lift!"

"*We'll make it!*" Haral's voice. Dopplered and moving, from the com. "*Let it go!*"

Images got to her screen. She jammed a com plug into her right ear and listened with one ear to that flow, kifish jabber.

Fifteen seconds. Noise from the intercom, wide open from both ends. Shouts and curses at a recalcitrant door. "*Open the gods-be lift!*"

Then: "*We're in.* Different speaker. Tirun this time. And: "*Wait, wait, wait! Kkkkt-kkt-kt! Wait!*"

"*Hurry!*"

"*Kkkkkkkkkkkkkk—*"

Dump.

—down. Velocity drop.

—red lights. Breaking out like plague.

O my gods, don't let us lose it here.

Not now. Not now.

Normal space. Anuurn and kif. She swallowed down sickness and flicked switches while the Tauran switcher next to her fed her images.

"Position, position, where in a mahen hell are we?" Not Haral beside her. Fire was going on out there, their kifish escort hammering away at something forty-five degrees off and low. Haze blossomed on the scan as it cleared. They had no clear way to know *what* the kif were firing on. "Com, gods rot it, where's ID on those ships?"

"No ID," the young voice answered. "I'm not getting ID."

Captain, we got hits out there, Tyar vector!

"Targeting."

"We don't know who we're shooting at," Sirany objected.

"*Targeting,* gods rot it, did I say fire? *Get us a gods-be lock on it!*"

"Gods rot yourself, did I say I *wasn't?*"

Not a crew up here. A collection. Left and right hand tangling. In the monitor a light-reflection showed, widened. Lift door opening. She looked at the time and saw fifty seconds to next dump. *"Fifty to dump, clear those seats, number two, three, five, seven—Chanur crew's in upper main, we got a fast shift, bail out and go, move it!"*

"*Get!*" Sirany yelled at her own crew. "You heard her. *Galley!*"

Every regulation in the book was fractured. Crew bailed out and fled in mid-ops, a scramble for the galley corridor. Running footsteps hit the bridge deck and seats sighed and hummed and belts clicked, new crew in. New voices reported over com.

"Your sister's all right," Pyanfar said.

As the chrono ticked over and they went down again—

—programmed dump.

More red. Red, red, red.

O gods, not the main boards—

Lifesupport out.

Gods fry those slinking things!

Over to backup on three more systems. Final backup on another.

Out again, with telemetry coming in, Chanur voices delivering information.

"Affirmative: Akkhtimakt. Tyar vector, breaking for nadir."

"Fire."

As another disruption streaked past them, disrupting scan.

"That was Jik!" Geran said.

"Go for 'em!" Tirun cried, and: "Kkkt! Sgot sotikkut pukkukt'!" from Skkukuk.

More disruptions. A welter of high-*V* projectiles, passing by them.

They added their own, lower-*V*, and a burst of beamfire from their small bow projector. Hydraulics whined and thumped, reloading the chambers on the launcher, tracking. The source of the fire was off—gods, in the ecliptic. A chill went up her back. Chur and premonitions. The first fire they had thrown out was the most damaging kind, high-velocity, aimed blind.

Someone had keyed the guns.

Whump and groan. Another missile round off. More loading.

"Stand by braking." *Gods hope the systems hold.* As she threw them into rollover, the guns still tracking and firing under auto.

She threw the mains in. Her hand was shaking on the board, even with her arm thrust through the stress brace. Her vision fuzzed under the strain, and something small and black flew past her head and hit the forward bulkhead beyond her panel, squealing and yelping. Three story drop, where it had come from. "Gods!" she yelled in revulsion: it ran right back over the boards and chittered and squealed as it went, tiny claws scrabbling as it climbed against the *G*-force and ran right over the counter along the bulkhead, the course of least resistance.

Then colors blossomed all across the scan.

"We got company!" Geran yelled, and pounded the board. "Gods, O gods, they're ours, hani IDs—hani ships lying off-system ecliptic, they're coming in!"

Chapter 11

"Hani ships!" Hilfy cried. "Waiting—O gods, someone got 'em the word! They're coming in on our escorts' wavefront!"

"Ayhar," Pyanfar said. Her heart again. It was a good hurt. As if the universe itself were not large enough to hold it. "Gods look on her, Banny Ayhar got through!"

While *The Pride* hammered down its *V* and Akkhtimakt's kif picked theirs up, faster and faster shifts. Comp subtracted their *V*-drop out of that relative *V* increase and still came up with a plus. "The bastards are running!" Haral exclaimed. "They're getting out of here; they got Ajir for an outbound—"

"They got Jik on their tail," Tirun exclaimed. While on com, Sif was trying to explain it all to the crew in the galley. A cheer racketed out of that section, weak and wobbly in the strain of decel, but a cheer all the same.

"They are lost!" Skkukuk cried, and a string of something else in kifish.

His former associates. Akkhtimakt and all his minions, and Skkukuk was not with them in their debacle, but in the lead ship of the winning side. It was surely a sweet moment to a kif, all his maneuvers justified. He chittered and hissed and all but chortled. "Give me a channel," he cried. "Hakt', give me a channel, praise to my captain, *mekt-hakt'*, they will not turn, they dare not turn, give me a channel!"

"Affirm," she said. It seemed little enough to keep a kif content. And having gotten it he sent out a steady burst of clicking main-kifish.

Fools, was the burden of it. *Join my captain, join us in success, turn and rend the doomed and hapless fools who lead you!*

"Com," Hilfy said. "*Harun's Industry* says their compliments and they're wanting instructions."

"Come about and stay after them and for the gods' sweet sake let the comp do the shooting, we got too many allies out there that look like the other side."

"Kifish signal," Hilfy snapped. "Skkukuk."

"*Notiktkt* has begun to fire on its fellows!" Skkukuk cried. "It signals its loyalty, *mekt-hakt'!*"

O my gods.

She stared, appalled, listened as Skkukuk rattled off more and more names. As kif hindmost in the whole retreating force began to add their fire to the attack on their own forces, and hani ships swept in like a wave, hammering at the ships that were attempting to flee.

Hammer and anvil. More and more kifish defections, and the Ajir vector, the only way out at their velocity and on that heading—barriered suddenly with yet another wave.

"My gods, what's *that?*"

More breakout of plague on the com, this time nadir, ships lying emissions-silent suddenly having picked up velocity and started to run.

Howling out mahen IDs.

"My gods, we *got* 'em," Haral yelled. And laughed aloud and pounded the console. "You hear that? That's the mahendo'sat! We got the kif between us, Akkhtimakt's forces are defecting right and left, they're chewing each other to bloody rags!"

Pyanfar stared at it with her mouth open. With bits and pieces of things sorting themselves into vague order, as they had been ordered for longer than she had wanted to look at them.

She did not cheer. There was an obscenity in what was happening in front of them. And yet not obscene or unfit. No more than the little vermin that had multiplied and succeeded against all odds.

It was kif out there, surviving again.

Doing the best they knew to do.

Murder is possible here. Ours, committed, against kif innocent by their own lights.

In one stroke, I can order it, clear our system of kifish ships till we can get organized in defense. Wipe the aliens out of home system.

It's prudent to do. It's only prudent.

But gods help me, I'm not a butcher.

"Send: *The Pride of Chanur* to all ships. Cease fire, cease fire on all kifish IDs that signal surrender."

Then com reached her down the other vector, backflung from Jik.

Requesting that same message that she had anticipated and just sent.

Braking continued. Fighting diminished. There were still casualties. Solid mass became drifting clouds. Scan attempted to track misaimed projectile-fire and confused itself with the sheer magnitude of the problem till Geran gave it a Disregard on non-intersect-potentials.

They reached lower and lower *V.* "Take it," Pyanfar said, and Haral slewed *The Pride* around to use the mains on acquisition in a new vector.

Headed for Anuurn.

Vid came up. Haral had been too busy for that till now. The homestar, Ahr, shone brilliant yellow. Lifebearer. Hearthfire to the species. And the paler, nearer light that was Anuurn.

Home again.

With a straggle of battered, stress-damaged merchant ships slewing about in disordered break out of the rigid formation they had kept so long and so far, Harun and little Faha, Pauran, and last and limping, Shaurnurn, reporting damages, talking to each other over com.

"This is Sirany Tauran." Sirany had gotten herself an output channel. *"Affirmative on the linkup, inquiry affirmative, all ships. They're all right. Chanur's clean and clear. Thank the gods."*

"Gods look on us all. Here and otherwise." Harun was talking, Harun always the leader in that group.

"We've got that," Faha said, and other acknowledgments came in.

While the slaughter went on, while a hard burn shoved at them and made breathing difficult, and a lightspeed message proliferated through ship relays.

"We've got contact with Gaohn," Hilfy said. "They ask for a report."

"They know by now," Pyanfar muttered. "But answer them. Send: *The Pride of Chanur* to Gaohn. We claim navigational priority. Clan business. End message. Put a call through to Kohan. Ask him how things are down there."

On Anuurn. At home. On that small shining sphere in all the wide dark.

It would take a long time. Question and answer went slow at this range. Conversations were all one-sided.

"Where in a mahen hell is *Vigilance?* Did we pick up Ehrran's ID anywhere?"

"Affirmative. Affirmative," Geran said, all business. "Five ships are putting out from Gaohn. We got a pickup on Ehrran. They're moving now. Make that six ships. They're not talking."

"I'll bet she's not. Where's Ayhar? Gods rot it, where's Banny Ayhar and *Prosperity?*"

The burn stopped. Her vision cleared, her voice no longer had to force its way out of her throat. A wave of giddiness came on her. Depletion. Fight-flight reflexes let go and the body had dues to pay. She clamped her jaws against nausea and fumbled after a packet, dropped one and got another. Bit down on it and swallowed and swallowed, which was the only thing else she could do but retch. *Going to faint. O gods. I don't do this.* "Haral—Sirany. I'm not—"

"Cap'n? *Cap'n?*"

She drifted. Lay still under a ceiling which was not the overhead of the bridge. Blinked at it and at Khym's anxious face.

"You fainted," he said.

"Gods rot." She drew her hands up to locate her head, which seemed drifting loose and all fuzzed. "Who's running the ship?"

"*Ker* Sirany. We're inbound for Gaohn. It's all right, Py. We did it."

"Jik. . . ."

"The kif jumped, such as could. A lot surrendered. They've attached to the other kif. To *Chakkuf.* Skkukuk's been talking to them, telling them—Hilfy says—that they'll do well to hold still."

"Where's Jik?" Fear set her heart to hammering. *"Did he jump, gods rot it, did he jump out?"*

"We aren't tracking him. It got—pretty confused, Py. Not

Geran's fault. Sirany says so. We—lost some ships. His ID just cut out."

"He's lying. Gods-be, that bastard's pulling another one." There was an obstruction in her throat. She wanted to break something. Anything. There was dark around her vision, a pain all through her gut. "We need him." All quiet and hard to get past that knot. *Oh, Jik, Jik. Another gods-be doublecross.*

What do I do now? What am I going to do?

"Cap'n?"

It was not a voice she expected to hear. Not loose and wandering around in places like her cabin. She lifted her spinning head and looked at the worn, wan hani clinging to the doorframe. "Chur? F'godssakes—"

"I'm doing all right," Chur said.

"Huh," she said. "Huh." And fell back into the pillows. It was all she could manage at the moment. The whole cabin was going into slow rotation. It felt like tricks with the *G* force, a little acceleration this way and that way, but if she asked was that going on she would look the fool. It was her head. Her equilibrium.

Gods. Sikkukkut. Where? When?

A weight depressed the end of her bed. A hand touched her leg. "Cap'n." Haral's voice, ragged with fatigue. "We got a little rest now. *Ker* Sirany's arguing with Gaohn, telling 'em we got right of way and they can by the gods quit quibbling. She's all right, captain. Swear she is. Never shot at anything in her life, her and her crew, I think they're a little shook. Us—we're falling-down and gone away. Whole crew. Thank gods for the Tauran, thank gods, I say."

"I say too," she murmured. Felt a touch across her brow, her ears. Khym's hand. She opened her eyes and stared at the uninformative ceiling. "Was that Chur in here?"

"Not walking too good, but she's put on weight. Turned a corner somewhen and started storing it up instead of burning it. Skkukuk's having lunch—"

"O gods." Her stomach heaved.

"We got to get those things cleared out somehow. *Skku-kuk* says Chur got to the bridge in jump, went into some kind of hyperdrive, started telling the Tauran what to do when they came out, got us all waked up— Cap'n, *somebody* threw a bunch of relays on manual, got us over on backup

systems, or we wouldn't have made it: those gods-be black
devils had got into the works, chewed stuff up good. And
somebody aimed the guns. Chur doesn't remember, but I got
my guess who did it. Or we'd be on the long trip for sure."

She blinked and absorbed that. Remembered bailing out
of bed and running the corridor. Was not too clear on how
she had gotten into her own seat. Or how anything had happened. The mind did not function well on the trailing edge
of jump.

Did not function well after too many jumps, either.

"Call to home," she remembered. "We on response-
time yet?"

"Gaohn refuses to relay."

"Gods and thunders, *politics,* politics and we got a system
full of kif—"

"They've got Ayhar under arrest, cap'n. We're still on
course. We got *Vigilance* in our way and we got three other
big freighters just hanging off and not doing anything.
They'll have fire position on us if we keep coming. They
warned us. Have to ask you what you want to do."

She lay there and breathed quietly a moment, ran that
situation through her aching skull once and twice and a
third time.

Vigilance positioning itself where it could go head on
with them or strike at their tail if they docked.

You gods-be fool, I got thirty, forty kif out there!

Bring kif against the han? *O my gods, my gods. That
fool's going to call bets and I can't bluff, those kif back
there don't know where to stop and I can't hold them else.
I can't bluff, Ehrran! Don't try to call it.*

"Mahendo'sat. Where are they?"

"They're braking. Holding steady relative to the kif.
Keeping an eye on 'em."

"And no sign of Jik." That pain was back again. It hurt
to blinding. "Gods *rot* the luck." *He's got to be alive. Out
there somewhere. Preserving his options. Saving his own
people. He has no choice. And I did it, I, I gave it to him.*
"Ayhar arrested."

"Aye, cap'n. We inquired. We got a communication from
Llun, onstation. They're real sorry, they got no choice."

Old friends, the keepers of Gaohn station. Old allies.
Under a lot of pressure. "That all they said?"

"Says plenty, doesn't it, cap'n?"

There was a time they were Py and Hal and Tirun. Across every accessible dock in the Compact. Here they were, graynosed and at wits' end and Haral was sticking by formalities. Haral had held that line ever since the day she got set upstairs, command post, being heir to Chanur; and Haral, equally qualified, being sub-sept, got the second seat. It was the System.

"Captain?"

"Yeah. It says plenty. It says every gods-rotted thing *wrong* with us." She shoved herself up on her hand and an elbow, flung her feet for the side of the bed. Blood was moving in her veins again. Her vision cleared. "I'll have Ehrran's ears, b'gods if I don't. My own hands. In the condition I'm in, I could take that blackbreeched prig! I'll kill her!"

"We got other word," Haral said, and braced her back, setting her down with both hands. Held onto her. "Rhean sent on com—says Chanur's fallen. Kohan's exiled. Mahn's got the estate. Rhean's broken with the blockade out there. She and Anfy—coming in hard behind us with *Fortune* and *Light*. Pyruun—Pyrunn got Kohan to safety somewhere. They swear that. So it's not all lost onworld, and we got help on the way if we just hold and wait. Sirany's up there trying to keep the thing from blowing to a—"

"Mahn." She shook her head, blinked. Tried to focus on it. *"My gods-rotted conniving son?"*

"Our godsrotted conniving son," Khym said at her back, his voice a low rumble. "And our twice conniving daughter."

"With *Ehrran!"*

"With their own interests, Py, when were they ever anything wider?"

"Gods. *Gods!"* She flung off Haral's hands and slapped Khym's interference aside. Hit the floor with both feet wide and swayed there till she had shaken the fog out of her eyes. Then she headed for the door.

The corridor.

The bridge, where Tauran crew filled the seats.

"Give me com," she snarled, coming up over Sif Tauran's shoulder. Sif hesitated, throwing a startled glance her way.

"Captain—"

"*Give* it to her," Sirany said. "*Ker* Pyanfar, I'll give you your chair."

"Keep it. We got troubles." She slipped into the vacant post between Sif and Fiar. "Get me Gaohn station. Are armaments still live?"

"We're shut down, captain." Nasany Tauran, down at Tirun's post. "Reactivate?"

"Do it." The com light signaled available and she punched in on the frequency.

"*Pride of Chanur* hailing the station," Sif was saying. Trying to raise a response. Another light was blinking, another channel active. Sif punched it in, on a momentary pause. "That's a call from *Vigilance,* captain. They advise us we're under arrest."

"Tell Ehrran there's a threat to Gaohn and we're not it. Standby. That's all."

The message went.

"Gaohn station," she said on her own. "This is Pyanfar Chanur, *The Pride of Chanur.* Stand by to record and relay." Gaohn was hearing: that was beyond doubt: every official on that vulnerable and threatened station would be prioritized onto their transmissions. "Llun, you've just seen the first and smallest wave of our assault on Akkhtimakt's ships. The next one is incoming. Naur, there's no time for your politics. Your treaty with the stsho may have destroyed the whole species, hear me? Your relations with the mahendo'sat are tottering. Attack on our own world is possible and imminent. It is possible that no life will survive on Anuurn surface. I appeal to you, I *beg* you, anyone who can get their menfolk off world right now, *do* it, get us a chance, for the gods' own sake, get to shuttles and get to shelters. There are still three large groups of ships unaccounted for and one of them has threatened attack on Anuurn itself."

Static. Sputter. *"Pyanfar Chanur, retreat from this course."*

"Is that Ehrran? Gods rot you, is that Rhif Ehrran?"

Static and squeal. *"This is Rhif Ehrran, Chanur. Take your kif and go deal with your owner."*

"Is that what you're going to tell the next attack that comes rolling in here? Are you going to arrest it? *You absolute and total lunatic, get that ship out there on Kura-*

incoming where it can do some good and stay out of my
way before I blow you out of space! Deny my crew medical
attention! Turn tail and run at Kefk! What do you write in
those gods-be reports of yours? By the gods nowhere near
not the whole story, not the part where you take stsho bribes
and connive with the kif against the han! *Get that ship out*
where it belongs!"

No response. From anyone. Not Ehrran, not Gaohn Station. Not from Anuurn itself, while lagtime ran on.

"They're Immune," Sirany said, a low voice from her other side. "You're challenging an Immune, Chanur."

"Arm. Target."

"*Ker* Pyanfar, they're hani!"

"They've arrested Banny Ayhar. They've arrested the courier that just risked her by the gods neck and Ayhar clan's whole livelihood getting word to the mahendo'sat and getting word back here again, bringing back the captains and the crews from Maing Tol all the way home— *Where do you think those ships out there with the mahendo'sat came from?* They've swept in out of mahen space, that's where! *With* the mahendo'sat! We got the gods-be *hakkikt* coming in here, we got this blackbreeched prig quoting rules from Naur and all their godscursed pets downworld—"

Sirany spun the command chair about, facing her. "I said I'd surrender this. I'll do it. I don't agree with what they're doing. But let me talk to Harun. Give Ehrran a chance to back up, for godssakes, Chanur, back off! Give 'em time to react, they have to have a way to save something!"

She clenched her hands on the leather of the chair arm, hit the control, and turned it to face Sirany. *No.* Muscle reaction jerked her mouth. Stopped breath. Put a black ring around Sirany's taut figure. *Time, for the gods' sakes, the godscursed fool, the fatherforsaking bastard—Pride, pride above the* han, *Ehrran's precious face—* A breath then. A sane breath. "All right." Another. "All right. Let's talk to the *spacing* clans. Let's talk to Harun and Pauran and Shaurnurn and my sisters out of Chanur, and all the ships back there. They've arrested Banny Ayhar. The ships back there—they know what got them home. Tell them about Ayhar, tell them the rest of it, b'gods, we got it for them, the whole gods-be thing!" She spun the chair about, activated comp at that station and exhumed a log record. Accurately, first try. No one on *The Pride* was going to forget that date, that hour, that time.

Kshshti station: Ehrran trying to take Tully by force, kifish attack coming from two sides on the station docks, Akkhtimakt and Sikkukkut, Banny Ayhar's dispatch to Maing Tol carrying a message from a threesided conference: herself, Jik, Rhif Ehrran.

Ehrran agreeing to go with them into kifish territory.

Second log segment: another date, another moment: exchange between *The Pride* and *Ehrran's Vigilance,* kinrequest for medical aid, denied, made contingent on surrender of Tahar crew from Chanur sanctuary. Granted when they logged a false emergency and got in touch with *Aja Jin.*

"Capsule it," she told Sif. "Every hani ship out here. Then capsule the whole gods-be log and shoot it over to Gaohn hard afterward. Tell them beam it down to Anuurn archives. File petition for Ayhar's release. Let's see if for once, one time, the *han* can understand what's going on out here. Put our wrap on that log transmission. There's a lot we can't say in front of kifish witnesses, but there's by the gods enough there to hang that fool. Brake to standby reply."

"B'gods there is," Sirany said. "Sif. Send: *Industry* and all the rest. Slow to standby. Transmission follows."

Alarm rang. The take-hold. *The Pride* prepared itself for braking. Other bodies hit the seats, Chanur crew, Haral and Khym and Geran, on upper decks and close enough to make it to vacancies. Blind-tired. Gods, yes. Her own head was too heavy to hold up. Her hands shook on the boards. There was not a critical control she would trust herself to handle.

Thank gods for Tauran.

"Captain." Tirun from the com, voice strained by the decel. *"Give us a window, we'll get up there."*

"Negative, negative, stay down there. You want scan on monitor down there you got it. I want you rested. Hear?"

"Captain—"

"Do it, Tirun. Don't fight me. Trank out if you got to. I need you later, hear me?"

Delay.

"Trank. I mean it, Tirun. I got to come down there?"

"No, cap'n. Loud and clear. We don't need the trank, though. Can I ask—"

"Gods help me." Her voice faded and breath all but failed her. "Get off the com, f'godssakes, cousin, give me a rest."

"Out, cap'n." Short and quiet and off the com. Instantly.

She ducked her head into her hands. *Was I short? I didn't mean to be short. Call 'em back. Tell 'em— O gods. Tell 'em what?*

Brain won't work. That's all. I can't think. Call 'em back, they'll know I'm off.

That'd make 'em rest real easy, wouldn't it, Pyanfar?

Professionals down below there. Not kids. Not stationsiders. Tirun knows what I mean. She'll trank if she has to. Professional.

Got to sit on Hilfy and Tully. My young fools. My devoted young fools.

Where's Chur? Where's Chur in this shaking-about?

"Geran, is somebody with Chur?"

Dip of the ears. "They took her downside. Crew quarters."

Safe, then, and not alone. One detail not on my shoulders. Then:

"Transmission from *Vigilance,*" Sif murmured. Data flowed onto her number one screen. Wordage abundant.

It was what she expected. Selected log entries. Two ships firing log segments back and forth like beamfire. Truth and counter-truth. "Gods-be fool," she murmured. Some of it was potentially explosive with the kif.

"We sot that interview with Sikkukkut," Haral said.

"Save it," she said. "We got kifish ears out there. If Sikkukkut loses face here, we may have troubles we can't handle."

"*Sfik,*" Khym said. "It's *Chakkuf* we have to worry about, isn't it? That's the leader."

"You got it." A chill and a warmth went through her. Her husband, on target and calm and having picked up more on the way than she gave him credit for, the way he always did. On the bridge, in a seat beside Tauran crew, and no Tauran twitching an ear at it. *Do you know what you're hearing, Tauran? It's change. It's power tilting and sliding. And there's one way in all the universe I can out-*

do that bastard over there commanding Chakkuf. *Take and hold. Grab with both hands.*

A kif well understands this exchange of messages.

A kif understands what I'm asking the spacer clans to do, and he understands Ehrran's position, that it's eroding, fast. The kif aren't meddling in this, thank the gods, they know this is a situation they can foul up if they lay a hand on it and they don't want to do anything. They're waiting for me. Of course they're waiting for me. Thanks, husband.

"Message: priority." Data leapt from Sif's monitoring to monitor one, a flood of mahen log output, off a ship named *Hasene.*

Mahendo'sat. My gods. They're affirming Ayhar's story.

"Priority, priority."

Color-shift had begun on certain ships on far-scan, positions relayed and matrixed via continuous dopplered interlink from ships in position to pick them up. Certain ships were disentangling themselves from that welter of dots out there where the kif-kif-hani battle had wound down to stasis.

Stasis no longer.

"Priority."

Six of the spacing clans were moving. Coming in behind *Chanur's Fortune* and *Chanur's Light.* Faha kin and Harun clan were among them.

"Inbound," Haral murmured. "Gods hope they're on our side."

"Stand by armaments. We don't know what that lunatic Ehrran's going to do."

"That's spacers at Ehrran's back," Haral muttered. "Those five ships out from station behind her. I'd worry, in Ehrran's place. I'd worry right fast."

"Priority! That's a burn, Ehrran's maneuvering—"

Unmistakable on the passive-scan, the little flicker of the directionals; then mains cutting in, a deluge of energy from *Vigilance,* while the ships behind her stayed still.

Ehrran kept on with the burn, accelerating on an insystem vector, while information continued to shoot this way and that through the system. Then Ehrran shut down to inertial: they were leaving, but not at any great pace. *Vigilance* still had plenty of option to turn around. Or roll and fire.

"Bastard," Geran hissed.

Still dangerous. Very.

Sudden, heart-stopping flares showed from one of Ehr-ran's backers. But that was rollover, turning nose toward Gaohn and home, the same direction as the incoming ships.

"That's *Raurn's Ascendant*," the Tauran First said.

Hares from the others, one and the other, and the next and the next. Rollover in each case.

Pyanfar clenched her hands and flexed the claws and gnawed her mustaches. *I haven't got the strength to stay on the bridge. I can't do this. I can't last it. My gods, what am I going to do?*

When it was most critical. When hani existence rode on it.

"Medkit," she said, fighting down a wave of nausea. "Fiar. Get me the medkit. Stimulant. I'd better have it."

"Captain," Haral said hoarsely, in hardly better shape.

"Don't. Don't. Get me the stuff, get me a sandwich. I got to, Hal."

"You got it," Haral said. While Fiar was off at the cabinet getting the kit.

"I'll get the sandwich," Khym said. "Gfi. Whatever you want."

His cooking. Gods. Not the tofi. She turned a dull and helpless glance his way. "Thanks. Hold the gods-be sweet stuff, huh? Just make it fast and simple."

"Fast and simple." He got out of his seat, grabbed the seat back for balance and headed up toward the galley, about the time Fiar came back with the kit, laid it out on the counter, and pulled a syringe out.

She held out an arm. Held it there while the needle went in, while Sirany's voice whispered out of the distance, talking to other ships.

"You can't do this twice," Haral was saying. "Hear me. I'll put you out, cap'n."

She gave Haral a bleak stare. It was an honest threat, meant to save her life. The stimulant hit with a wave of giddiness, sending her heart thudding. For a moment her own pulse was all she could hear, and if she moved she would drift free off the floor, disoriented.

Harder and harder pulse. She drew a great breath. A second. "I'm all right," she said. And knew she had better not get up. The bridge spun and swung as if ship rotation had gone totally erratic.

Food arrived. Sandwich first. Cup of water. Fiar ran courier. The water went down best. She forced a single bite of the sandwich.

"Worse shape than Chur," Haral muttered at her side.

"Gods, go off, we got running time, take it."

"Get some food yourselves. You. Geran. Get. We got everything covered. Get, hear. Want a tour with the kif?"

Haral's ears flattened. Old threat. Old joke. Not a joke, nowadays. She cleared the chair and took hold of Geran's arm when Geran got up and staggered. Both of them were out on their feet.

And leagues and leagues to go for Anuurn's sake.

It was a knifing pain when she let her mind shift to home, and Kohan, and a refuge which did not exist any longer. The bright blue world was there. Chanur was not. Dissolved. The estate legally in the hands of her son Kara Mahn.

And her son firmly under the influence of her daughter Tahy, who was groundling to the depths of her short-sighted, narrow heart.

I never knew you! Tahy's voice, Tahy's face, nose wrinkled in anger. *That ship, always that ship—*

And Kara, big lad, inheriting height from both Khym and herself.

And brains from neither.

The gfi arrived, in Fiar's careful hand. She sipped it. It was overstrong. It hit her stomach like acid. But the warmth comforted. That much.

"Send to Gaohn," she said. "Pyanfar Chanur to the Llun. We call on Gaohn station to release the Ayhar ship and crew. The ships out here constitute sufficient of the *han* to make a temporary quorum. You have that authority. Officers of the *han* will respect this order or deliver themselves to the protection of Llun Immunity. We take possession of the station in the name of the *han.* End message. List the clans out here. Put all of them signatory to it."

It was a drunken, arrogant move. It was also fast, and it gave the down world *han* no time to organize or decree.

"Good bet the *han*'s in session," Sirany said. "Down there."

"They would be. Yes. Let 'em debate what to do. Let 'em debate till the sun freezes. Dither and stew and argue. We've got an emergency out here. Send my apologies to the other ships for using them on signature, we got no time for transmission lag. We're operating under stress out here. Ask them to send a confirm and back me. Tell them we've got to get into Gaohn and get Banny Ayhar out of there.

"We're already getting confirms on that quorum call," Sif said.

It hit slowly. Like a wave of cold and heat. *My gods, it's going to work. What do I do?*

Jik! gods rot you, Jik, what do I do?

"Call the clans in front of us. Ask them would they return to Gaohn and secure Ayhar's safe release."

"Aye," Sif said. "Sending." And a moment later: "Llun responds. Ayhar crew is in process of release already. *Prosperity* is being serviced. Llun sends its compliments, *ker* Pyanfar, and asks what about the kif, quote, *What are we facing?* End quote."

The relief was giddy. She probed it a moment, replayed the statement that echoed in her skull, whether it was real or stim-induced hallucination. *Good news, my gods, it's still working.*

"We're coming in. Tell them that. Tell them I'm coming in for conference and if any of the *han* downworld want to get themselves up on the next shuttle, they're welcome. Tell them no danger from forces with me, repeat, *with* me. End message. Just that way, *ker* Sifeny."

"Understood. Re-request on order to the ships in front of us?"

"Tell them stand by. Does Llun need help onstation? Query them that while you're at it." *I'm muddling. Not thinking of things. I'm dangerous up here.* "*Ker* Sirany. I'm resigning operationals. Policy I'll handle. Refer to yourself and the other captains—all other—" She gave a desperate wave of her hand. "—stuff." And fumbled after the belt and tried to stand up.

"Help, cap'n?" Sif reached and grabbed her arm. "*Ker* Haral!"

I'm doing quite all right, thank you.

And the whole bridge went gray and dark.

Operations chatter. Quiet stuff. She got to her feet hanging onto the chair and held to the back of it.

All in gray. Dark a moment. And the blood rushing in her ears.

Someone got to her. Someone held onto her. "You want to walk," Haral said.

"I'm walking." Legs insensate as dead meat. Equilibrium gone. Haral had one side, Khym had the other.

It was a long, long walk to her quarters. The corridor lights writhed like the spine of a glowing snake.

"Just gone too far," Haral said. "Knew her like this once at Ajir."

Liar. I was drunk then. I'm scared, Hal. I haven't got anything left and they need me.

"I got her." When the whole universe did a sharp and sudden tilt. Khym hauled her along with an arm about her. Might as well have been flying, upside down and sideways.

Bed then. Mattress. Sheets. Pillow.

"Chur's room," Geran's voice said, hoarse and panting and utterly exhausted. "Haral, tell 'em. We can fall in there."

A body landed beside her. Thump. The safety restraint hummed and clicked.

Dark then.

Till the gravity shifted and she came awake with a reflexive clench of the claws into what was not mattress, but her husband; he hissed and shifted and jerked as he came awake weighing less than he ought and with gravity not where it ought to be.

"Uuuh!"

"Docking. It's all right, it's all right, we're at Gaohn." Mumble. Even that was not sufficient goad to get the body moving. The brain dimmed down again, with too great a load to push. More *G*-shifts. Clang and thump. Not safe to stand, in the condition she was. Prudent just to lie there and catch the few extra moments of drowse she could. Before the clangs and thumps of contact told her the grapples were secure. Then was time to get on her feet and clean up.

Safety hummed into retraction. It was Fiar standing over them, with a tray in her hands and an ears-back worried look on her face. The ship was miraculously stable and quiet. "Captain. M'lord. You want to try to eat something?"

We aborted dock? Backed off?

I slept through the grapple-noise? The connects? Gods, we're not on rotation.

She levered herself up on her arms. Khym stayed unconscious beside her. The place smelled. They did. Everything did. Her eyes were sticky and her mouth felt awful. "Situation," she said.

"We're in, captain. Berth thirteen. Got a solid line of our ships out there beyond us. Just everybody sitting, except us, except our lot—Harun and Pauran and Faha and all, we're in dock right together. So's *ker* Rhean and *Chanur's Fortune.* Ehrran too. Anfy Chanur held 'em under her guns on the way to dock, she's still got *Light* standing out right nearby, but Ehrran's still talking for Naur and them, but spacers are mad, captain, they're not having any of it. They want to see you. We told 'em you were in no fit condition. But my captain asks, she says maybe you should get up there and see 'em soon as you can, captain—we got a whole lot of kif and a whole lot of hani eyeball-on out there around Tyar; but she wants you to have a breakfast and take it slow, her word, captain."

"Gods." She shut her eyes with force and opened them again, trying to focus. Fiar looked exhausted, ears flagging in a curious, lopsided way that made her look younger than she was. Stable at dock. Other ships having had time to make it in. Anfy and Ehrran in standoff. She reached and took the offered cup. Biggest they had. Full of savory soup, steam going up like a wish to the gods. "Unnnhh." She took a sip. Blinked the kid back into focus. "Ayhar. Where in a mahen hell's Ayhar?"

The ears sank. "They still got them hostage, captain."

"Where?"

"Up in station. *Ker* Rhean and Harun and my captain, they're working on it, but there's some holdup, and they got fighting at the shuttleports downworld, some on our side and some on theirs, and they can't launch, except a couple got away— The Llun are mediating that, captain says, trying to get the shuttles clear to launch, and some of the Immunes onworld, they're trying to negotiate—"

"A mahen hell with that."

"Meanwhile your crew is coming on, captain said they

should take their orders from *ker* Haral, and *ker* Haral said—"

"The kif. Where's the kif?"

"They're just staying out there. That kif Skkukuk wanted to talk to them. My captain said no. *Ker* Haral said no."

"No," she said, and took a careful mouthful of soup as Khym moaned and rolled over and lifted himself on his elbows. "Food," she said. "Khym." The soup was hot as Ahr's fires. Instant stuff. Wonderful stuff. They were still alive and the cabin was staying still and the worst things were far from as bad as they might be. No major confrontations. Kif staying where they belonged. Everybody where they belonged. Excepting Ehrran and a set-to at the shuttledock. And Ayhar; and gods knew where Sikkukkut was. Alarm bells kept going off all down her nerves. *That bastard Sikkukkut pulled a surprise arrival at Meetpoint. Does he need originality?* She shivered convulsively, blinked, and guarded herself as Khym shook the mattress getting himself propped up. "Here." She gave him her cup and took the other, the tray more convenient for her, then glanced up at Fiar's anxious, dutiful face. "Llun's fending rocks, is she?"

"Lots of rocks," Fiar said. And dipped her ears in nervous respect. Embarrassed, now that Khym was awake. She was young. "But my captain told them on station lines, about the kif, about the methane-breather we saw. About all those stations shut down. About the humans and the mahendo'sat. Everything. Figuring they might not have had time to sort the log out, they better know."

"Good. Thank her. I'll be there fast as I can."

"Yes, captain. You want anything—"

"You want to turn that monitor there on, on your way?"

"Aye, captain." Fiar hugged her tray under her arm, flipped the switch on the wall monitor mounted next the bath, and dived out again. The door shut.

"Uhhhn," Khym moaned around a swallow of soup.

The system schema on the monitor showed what the young spacer had said: a lot of hani ships within spit of Gaohn station and a lot of kif and hani and a scatter of mahendo'sat staring at each other farther out on the fringes. All at relative stop.

No Jik. Not showing himself. He wouldn't.

Not dead, not dead, gods rot it. He jumped and got him-self after those bastards or he's out there calling the moves and waiting for Sikkukkut. Has to be. We got too many mahendo'sat in this system just sitting there cooperating. He's going to use my whole by the gods solar system for a mahen battlezone.

She reached to the console and punched the com. The tick and chatter of bridge operations invaded the cabin. Quiet talk. Reassuring in its monotony. Llun clan was in charge of the station, fair and sane: trouble in the corridors, but Llun had central, and sanity was making progress out there. Against Ehrran's best efforts.

"We're all right," she said.

All right. My gods, Pyanfar. Where's Kohan? What's hap-pening out on dock, onworld, what are we going to do?

"Uhhn," Khym said again. Drinking soup in constant lit-tle sips as if it was going straight to the veins, direct transfu-sion. They had both shed all over the sheets. Fright. Exhaustion. Depletion.

"Bath," she said. It was the thing she wanted most, more than food, more than sleep. She set the cup down on the table console, crawled out of bed, and left her breeches on the floor on her way.

Straight into the shower cabinet and on with the water and the soap. Lots of soap. A deluge of soap and hot water.

A shadow showed up against the transparent door, tall and wide and hani. She opened the door and let him in.

Both of them then, soaked, soaped, and by the gods clean, just standing propped against each other under the warm water jets until she found her eyes shut. Falling asleep again. "Gods. We got to go, husband."

"Uhhhn." Like mornings downworld. Incoherent for half an hour at best.

She got out, cleaned her teeth, dodging sore spots, dried halfheartedly with a towel and hunted up the last pair of clean breeches in the drawer.

And the pocket pistol. Gods, yes, that.

Out into the chill of the corridor still tying the cords, the deck cold under her feet.

"Captain," she said.

Sirany was still at her post, on a mostly deserted bridge, just herself and her First. The place smelled of unwashed hani. And Sirany's face as she swung the chair about, was marked with fatigue and strain. "*Ker* Pyanfar." The voice was hoarse. "We're doing all right, but we have a lot of questions backed up. Whole lot of people want to talk to you. *I* want to talk to you. What do we expect?"

"We expect another wave of kif in here. Meanwhile I'm wondering where in a mahen hell a certain pair of mahen hunter ships have got to and where we misplaced about half a hundred human ships that are doubtless armed and meaning things we don't want to think about."

It was maybe more than Sirany wanted to think about. Her face had that kind of look.

"Yeah," she said. "I've been wondering these things. Maybe I've been hoping you didn't. But in a way I wish you did."

"Different truth once we got to dock, once we threw Akkhtimakt on to the mahen side of the line?"

"I don't mean I thought you were lying." Ears lowered in apology and rolled flatter as the jaw took on a harder line. "*That's* a lie. I still don't know. But I don't think so. I'm betting everything on it. But what choice have I got? There aren't any sure things out here. I tell you something, *ker* Pyanfar. They tell all kinds of stories about you. Since Gaohn. Since you took out the way you did and kept—" Ear-twitch. "—kept *na* Khym and all. And wouldn't lickfoot to the *han*. I heard a lot more stories on Meetpoint, while we were stuck there. Stsho are scared of you. They call *you* changeable, the stsho do."

"They'll call me worse than that. I figured a crew that had the nerve to come aboard this ship had the nerve to handle the boards under fire. Way we'll have to yet, maybe. Even against hani, if you had to. I'm telling you the truth now. I'm working only our side. The mahendo'sat have doublecrossed us so many times you need a chart to track it. But they're the best allies we've got all the same, and I'm hoping that conniving friend of mine is still alive out there beyond system edge."

"Waiting for the rest of the kif?"

"I think b'gods sure he is. That ship's equipped. *Lots* of com equipment. I've never been onto that bridge, but I got the idea it's not a small place. *Lot* of crew and techs. Ability to short-jump. Goldtooth's *Mahijiru* has a lot more facilities, but I don't think it gives much to *Aja Jin* in abilities. We lost track of more than one ship in that flurry out there, and I'm not sure any of 'em are dead. Kif have this concept. *Pukkukkta.* Revenge. Destruction. That kif Sikkukkut has launched ships down all the lanes. Into all sorts of space. He's prepared to take civilization out. He says. He gives the impression it's no use to him. I think otherwise and I think he knows it, but I don't want to put it to the proof. We've lost track of kifish ships too and it worries me. I want a count if anyone can get it."

"Maybe they met each other out there. Maybe that's where *Aja Jin* is."

"If we were lucky." She tightened her mouth. Headache still bothered her. "If we were real lucky. But whatever happens we've got to handle what's coming in from Meetpoint, whoever survived that set-to back there. If it's the kif we're dealing with it's got to be one voice talking here. One."

"I understand you." Sirany's hand trembled on the arm of the chair, jerked in a small tic. She gripped the chair arm till the tendons stood out.

"You want to bring the captains aboard?"

"We got no room in dock. Have to stack 'em in lower main. No. I'm going outside and hope to all the gods I live through this. I'd be expensive to lose. Real expensive. *I* can talk to that kif. My kif can talk to those bastards out there. Where is he?"

"Lowerdecks. Well-fed, I might add. I wonder he can move."

"Gods." She walked over to the com console and punched in the number. "Skkukuk. What's this you want to tell those kif out there?"

"Is this you, hakt'?"

Hani voices. Different voices. "Gods-rotted sure it is, *skku* of mine."

"Kkkkt! I am delighted!"

"*Worried* about me, were you?" Gods, a change of captains aboard, possibility of mutiny in the air, the kif like a lit fuse and she had never picked it up. "I told you hani are a peculiar lot. You asked contact with the kif out there. What were you going to do, in particular?"

"Call them in, hakt', to take this ship."

Gods, gods, and gods. Perfectly logical. Her own crew exhausted, in his eyes perhaps acquiescing to this threatening change of authority on the bridge. Ships were moving and threatening everywhere. And here was one little constant light of kifish loyalty, a kif who knew no other hani would tolerate him and who planned to serve her interests through his.

"I'm in command here. No problems. What do you think ought to be done, regarding those kif out there?"

"Kkkt. Put me in command over them. That is your best action, hakt'. I am a formidable ally."

"Skkukuk. What rank did you hold? Is it proper to ask that?"

"Kkkkt. Kkkkt."

"Not proper. All right. Let me point out something to you, Skkukuk. Sikkukkut is a bastard, a real bastard, with a sense of humor. I think if he ever did get his hands on you again you might never get out with a whole hide. Despite your cleverness. *He's* too clever not to know you're clever. Do you understand me?"

"Hakt', you are completely correct. What will you do?"

"Why, I'm going to give you all those kifish ships out there, and a treaty with the mahendo'sat and the hani, *skku* of mine, and tell you that if you will take my orders very closely you may fare very well. But first you have to take those ships and hold them."

"You will see, you will see, *mekt-hakt'*."

She leaned over the First's panel and unlocked doors. "There you are. You can just go down to ops, down to the auxiliary command right down the corridor to your left, and you can use com in there. You call yourself one of those ships for transport, and you pack up your Dinner and any weapons you think you need, and you get yourself out there and remember how far you are from kifish territory, and who your *friends* are. Hear me?"

"Kkkkt. Kkkkt. I will give you Sikkukkut's heart!"

"You take orders! Hear me?"

"What you will, what you will, Chanur-*hakkikt*."

Promoted, by the gods.

There was a deep, gnawing cold at her gut. Raw terror.

Just made my will and testament. To Sikkukkut, should some fool stationer pick me off out there. To my beloved enemy: a new and kifish *problem.*

Enjoy it, bastard.

She looked at Sirany, who was staring at her in dismay. "One thing about the kif. When they're on your side they're on it. And they're on it as long as they're profiting by it. That's a real happy kif down there."

"I hope to the gods you know what you're doing."

"I'll tell you. If something happens to me, if you have to take charge of this mess, rely on my crew and threaten Skkukuk within fear of death, then turn him loose. Best insurance in the world. He'll respect you for it." She had an impulse toward the weapons locker, for one of the APs, remembered it was Gaohn out there, civilized, home; and then went and did it anyway, pulled the heavy piece out and belted it on. "Tell my crew meet me belowdecks. Tell the captains I'll see them in dock offices."

Off the open docks, out of the way of snipers. She had gotten wary in her new profession. *Learned the hard way, like any fool.* "Khym stays aboard. So does Chur. You can tell them that in the appropriate quarters, too. Tell 'em it's an order. Skkukuk's calling a kifish ship in. We don't want any more hani ships sitting at dock than we can help."

"Relay that," Sirany said to her First. And glanced back again. "Take care, for godssakes."

"Huh." She leaned over the com console, punched in on station. "Llun. Want to talk to you."

"Chanur. Pyanfar." The station-Immune's voice was calm and quiet. "It's a trap, *Pyanfar,* it's a—"

Something hit the mike at the other end. And silence, then.

Sirany rose from her seat. The First turned in hers.

She stood there paralyzed a moment, then turned and started punching codes. "Rhean! *Fortune,* are you hearing me?"

"Com's dead," the First said; she could see that, the telltale not lit: the dockside com relay was cut off. Pyanfar half-knelt in the seat, reached and put in the ship-to-ship as her incoming com board lit and the First started taking calls. Other ships had gotten that sudden cutoff. "*Pride of Chanur* to *Chanur's Fortune, Chanur's Light, Harun's*

Industry—all ships relay: trouble in central com, we've got troubles—"

"Pyanfar!" A familiar voice, her own sister's, out of two years' absence. *"This is Rhean, they got somebody into central, that's what they've done, they've cut Llun off—"*

"I know that! Bail out of there! Get 'em out!"

And in the same heartbeat: *Gods, the kif. Pull off, Pyanfar, let the station stew in its own troubles, deal with it later, we got kif incoming.*

No, gods, no, if there's no control here, Sikkukkut will take it himself, he'll come in shooting. We've got to get Gaohn in hand, get our ships repositioned if we can.

"Pyanfar." It was another voice, coming from the speakers, deep enough to shake the speakers. A male voice. Off *Chanur's Fortune.*

"Kohan? My gods! Is that Kohan?"

"Pyruun sent me. Llun just called Immune Sanction, did she not? I distinctly heard it."

Hani answers. Hani matters. From a voice she had never looked to hear again.

"My gods."

"Pyanfar?"

"Immune Sanction. Yes. By gods, yes. Tell Rhean I'll see her out there."

"Ehrran," said Tauran's First, impeccably and crisis-wise serene at her post, "has just called Sanction from her side against Chanur and taken possession of the station in the name of the *han*. She says we are all under arrest. They have taken Llun clan under Ehrran protection."

"In a mahen hell they have! Message: transmit: *Spacerclans!* Get to the docks and get to central! Arm and out!"

Acknowledgments came back, some mere static sputter. Gods knew how many were following. Or who would.

"Pyanfar," came another voice, clear and familiar and cold. *"Anfy, on the* Light: *we're positioning ourselves over station zenith: any ship fires, we'll blow it to blazes. Go for 'em!"*

"We're going!" she said back, and grabbed Tauran's First by the shoulder, cast a desperate look at Sirany Tauran's dazed face. "Take care of my ship, hear me!"

And dazed and aching as she was, she ran for it.

Chapter 12

She was wobbling when she reached belowdecks, staggering with the weight of the gun; she ran face-on into the others as she came off the lift and into the corridor—regular crew, with Tully and Khym. "I sent orders," she said to them both. "*No.* Stay here."

"It's changed out there," Khym said. "Py, for godssakes—"

Panic set in, facing that obdurate desperation, that look in his eyes, which met hers and asked, O gods, with a desperate pleading for his own place. If she never got him back alive . . . if she lost him out here; if, if, and if. She saw all the crew in the same mind, all thin-furred and haunted-looking, ghosts of themselves, but with weapons in hand and ears pricked up and eyes alive though flesh was fading.

"We've got to hit fast," she said, and saw Chur come round the corner from crew quarters, leaning against the wall for support, Chur with a rifle slung at her side. "You—" she said, meaning Chur. "And *you,*" meaning Tully, who was provocation to any hani xenophobe and a class one target. "You—"

"Tully and I hold the airlock and cover the rest of you, right." Chur's voice was a hoarse whisper, befitting a ghost. "Got it, cap'n. Go on."

That was the way Chur worked, conspiracy and wit: Chur cheated at dice. So would Geran. For cause. Pyanfar drew a ragged breath, threw a desperate look at Geran Anify and got no help: silence again, now that Chur was back in business. "Then for godssakes keep Tully with you," she said, and jabbed Tully with a forefinger. "Stay on the ship. Help Chur. Take Chur's orders. Got?"

"Got." With that kind of Tully-look that meant he would argue to go with them if he thought he could. Language-barrier worked on her side this time. "Be careful."

"Gods-be sure. Come on," she said to the others, and shoved off the wall she was using to lean on for a moment, and trotted for the airlock.

Alert began to sound, *The Pride*'s crew call: not their business, though muscles tensed as if that alert were wired to Chanur nervous systems. There was the thunder of steps in the corridors, additional crew running to the lift behind them as they reached the airlock corridor. More footsteps behind. She looked back. Skkukuk appeared, coming from the other direction. "Orders!" she yelled at him, *get!*" and he vanished in the next blink of the eye. Then: *"Sirany!"* she yelled at the intercom pickup, her voice all hoarse, "open that lock—" because it was not Haral up there, Haral was beside her; and she had to depend on strangers to get their signals straight.

The airlock hatch opened. She threw the safety off the illegal AP, and inhaled the air as a wind whipped into their faces: *The Pride*'s pressurization was a shade off; and that wind out of Gaohn smelled of things forgotten. Of hani. Of cold and hazard, too, and the chill reek of space-chilled machinery. She jogged through the lock and into the passageway, yellow plastics of the access tube and steel jointed plating, and sucked up a second wide gulp of the air her physiology was born for. Something set into her like the stim, a second wind, a preternatural clarity of things in which the whole tumble of events began to go at an acceptable speed.

"These are hani," she said, drymouthed and panting as they ran along the tube, trusting her crew around her as she trusted her own reflexes, knowing where each would dispose themselves, that Chur was where she had said she would be, that she had Tully under control, that Tirun, hindmost with her lameness, would be watching everything they were too shortfocused to see up front, that Haral was at her side like another right hand and Hilfy and Geran were with Khym in the middle, Khym being the worst shot in the lot, and not the fastest runner, but able to lay down barrage fire with any of them if it got to that. *Hani,* she reminded them as she came off that ramp and headed aside for cover of the gantry rig and the consoles. Down the row another crew was hitting the docks about as fast: that was Harun. And Sif Tauran arrived: Pyanfar spun around to stare at Sif in some confusion, saw Fiar coming at a dead run down the ramp. "We're offshift," Sif panted. "Captain says get out here and help."

"Come on," she said, seeing Fiar's youth, the grudging frown on Sif—sent along for Tauran's honor, then. Another Battle for Gaohn. Everyone wanted in on it.

Fool, Sirany, this is hani against hani, don't you see it? No glory here—

There were others arriving on the docks and running up the curved flooring toward them. Some of Shaurnurn, a trio each of Faha and Harun, not whole crews, but parts and pieces. That meant that those ships were still crewed, enough hands aboard to get them away if the kif came in; enough to make them a visual threat if nothing more. She had not ordered that. Perhaps Harun or Sifeny Tauran had. It was sane. It was prudent. She still wished she had the extra personnel on dockside, with their firepower. No other crew had the APs or even rifles: it was all legal stuff. Most of them that had run the long course from Meetpoint looked exhausted already; it showed in their faces, in the dullness of coats and the set of the ears. And Harun and the rest had only come from four jumps back.

But others were coming to join them, glossy of coat and in crisp blues; in vivid green; in skycolored silk: crews and captains of other ships from farther down the docks, ships which had run their own Long Course getting in, perhaps, but which were at least clear-eyed and fresh from their time on blockade. Banny Ayhar's contingents. The ships in from mahen space. Pyanfar drew a breath, blinked against dizziness and an insufficiency of blood and in a second hazed glance at that one in sky-blue, recognized her own sister. Rhean Chanur, looking much as Rhean had looked two years ago; with a tall figure coming up behind Rhean amongst the girders and hoses and machinery of the dock, a male figure conspicuous amid that large crew of Chanur cousins and nieces. The man had too much gray on him to be her brother, but no, they were indisputably Kohan's features, it was Kohan's look about him, and he wore a gun at his hip, a pistol, which gods knew if he even knew how to use—

His Faha wife was with him, Huran, Hilfy's mother. So were others of his wives: Akify Llun was one, on his side and Chanur's and not with her own kin. "Pyanfar," Kohan said when they came to close range. They stared at one another a moment, before Kohan blinked in shock at what else he saw, the thin, scarred woman his favorite daughter had become, Hilfy Chanur *par* Faha, who came across to him and offered her left hand to touch, because she was carrying a black and illegal AP in the other. Hilfy Chanur touched his hand and her mother Huran Faha's, giving them and her aunt Rhean and her cousins the nod of courtesy she might give any comrade-under-fire, with a quick word and an instant attention back to other of her surroundings, taking up guard with crewmates who shadowed her: she signed Geran one view toward the open docks and took another herself, all while everything was in motion, crews were taking positions of vantage, so there was no time to say anything, no time at all. Kohan looked stricken, Huran dismayed. Khym coughed, a nervous sound, somewhere behind her.

"We've got to get through to central," Pyanfar said. "Get Banny Ayhar out of there, get the Llun free—"

My gods, they don't know what to do, they're looking at me, at us to do something, as if none of them had fought here before this, as if they didn't know Gaohn station.

There was a time and a rhythm in leading the helpless and the morally confused; a moment to snatch up souls before they fell to wrangling or wondering or asking too keen questions.

"Come on," she yelled at them, at all the lunatic mass of hani spacers that was persistently trying to group round her like the most willing target in all the Compact; and yelled off instructions, corridors, crews, her voice cracking and her legs shaking under her as she started everyone into motion—in the next moment she could not remember what she had sent, where, when, as if her mind had wandered somewhere back into hyperspace and she had the overview of things but not the fine focus. . . .

. . .battles fought at ports and in countrysides on a little blue pearl of a world where foolish hani thought to prevent a determined universe from encroaching on their business. . . .

. . .Pyruun bundling Kohan onto a shuttle, smuggling him aloft to Rhean, gods knew how they had managed it

or at what risk; but, then, mahendo'sat had once smuggled
a human in a grain bin, right through a stsho warehouse. . . .

. . . .Banny Ayhar racing home with a message
which proliferated itself across all of mahen space, sweeping up hani as she fled homeward: and alerting mahendo'sat
as well, from Maing Tol to the mahen homeworld of Iji, so
it could not then be taken by surprise by any kifish attack,
try as Sikkukkut would. The incoming and outgoing ranges
of solar systems would be mined: the mahendo'sat would
have had time for that laborious action, especially up near
Iji and Maing Tol, so nothing could have gotten in the back
door. They *would* have done that, while hani ships were
moving home like birds before the storm. Mahendo'sat
would have pulled every spare ship borderward in defense
and offense, set in motion agreements with the tc'a, so that
the elaborate timetable of mahen ship movements would
have functioned as a spreading communications net, news
streaking from jump to jump and spreading wide with every
meeting of affected ships. . . .

. . . .even to hunter captains far removed from the
inner reaches, captains like Goldtooth, no longer operating
on their own discretion, but receiving information and
reinforcements. . . .

. . . .Goldtooth had been vexed beyond measure
when *Aja Jin* had violated the timetable by showing up at
Kefk; *that* had been his anger, that, the reason of his fury
at Jik, *that* the reason why Goldtooth had rushed away: his
orders had dictated it. And what might he have told to
Rhif Ehrran to send her kiting out of there with a message
for homeworld? Look out, he must surely have told her:
beware the consequences when the push *he* knew was coming rammed the kif right down hani throats. He had sent
Ehrran where *The Pride* was supposed to be, and where
Banny Ayhar was already headed, Jik would have told him,
in a much slower ship but with a message he had given *her*,
if she had lived to get to Maing Tol. Goldtooth's plan had
worked till *The Pride* blew a vane coming out of Urtur and
had to go in for repair, till Sikkukkut stole Hilfy and Tully
and lured *The Pride* off to Mkks and then (Jik following
his opportunity and a hani's desperation, and seeing only
one way to make his schedule *and* keep his position on the
inside of things) to Kefk, where things went even more

grievously awry; where hani proved intractable and divided by bloodfeud, and Chur lay dying, preventing *The Pride* from making that critical dash homeward by the Kura route, to warn of disaster at Meetpoint. . . .

. . . .Goldtooth had given them that med equipment to make a long run possible, gave it to them the way mahendo'sat had spent millions upping *The Pride*'s running capacity, last-ditch try at sending updated information on to Anuurn and spacer hani. . . .

. . . .because no ship could get through the kifish blockade at Kita; and in the end they had to rely on the slim hope of Banny Ayhar's ship. Jik had failed to convince Ehrran to veer from her stshoward course and *The Pride* had involved itself deeper and deeper in the heart of Jik's schemes; Ehrran had not budged till Goldtooth confronted her with more truth than Jik had yet told any of them.

Pyanfar blinked, brought up against a brace and hung there while the dock spun in her vision. Her brain wanted to work for a change, and the white light and gray perspectives of the dock were chasing visions of dark and stars and tiny ships in wheeling succession. Her AP was in her fist. Steps thundered past her as others secured the other corner and the neighboring corridor turned up empty of everything but scattered paper and a closed windowed door that said DOCKSEAL in large letters. KEY ENTRY ONLY.

"Gods rot them all!" She fired. Thoughtlessly, because an AP was as good a key as any; and fired again through the smoke and the deafening thunder as shrapnel off her own shot peppered her hide. "Gods-be *fools!*"

The door was never armored to withstand that kind of blast. The window-seal went. She was not up to running, just walked behind the fleetfooted youngsters and the foolhardy who went racing up to step gingerly through the shattered pressure-seal window.

She stepped through: her own crew stayed about her, and Rhean's lot, as if it were a walk up a troubled dockside, back in the days when a winebottle was the most fearsome missile and an irate taverner the greatest hazard a hani crew on dockside had to deal with. She trod on something sharp, winced and flinched, walking into a corridor her followers had already taken possession of: Fiar and Sif jogged out to the fore.

"Slow down!" she yelled. "Rhean, hold it back!" —As the whole thing became a faster and faster rush forward; she could not keep up, had no wish to keep up there with the young and the energetic. They had to take the stairwells beyond this long corridor, they had to go up the hard way, not trusting the lifts that could be controlled from the main boards: Gaohn was too big to take quickly, except by overwhelming force. And time was on other sides. Time was, O gods, on the side of Sikkukkut. . . .

. . . .who arrived at Meetpoint to drive his kifish opposition against the anvil of mahen territory, knowing that there were limited routes Akkhtimakt could take: down the line into stsho territory was one, where there would be no resistance—but Goldtooth and the humans had sealed that route.

. . . .the second to methane-breather territory, but that was a deadly trap: *no* one wanted to contest the knnn.

. . . .the third course lay past Sikkukkut to Kefk, which would have put Akkhtimakt at psychological disadvantage, though ironically not a positional one: there was no worse place for a kif on the retreat to come, than into kifish territory, a wounded fish into an ocean of razor jaws. . . .

Think, Pyanfar, it's late to think. The enemy either has one choice more than you've thought of, or one fewer than they need.

Sikkukkut knew that some message had gone with Banny Ayhar—knew that someone would have carried it, and where mahen forces would come—he had used the mahen push, anvil and hammer, but he never trusted the mahendo'sat, not Jik, manifestly not Goldtooth. He obviously didn't stop Ayhar.

Or he didn't try because he wanted it to happen.

Gods, could Jik have told him? No. No. He surely wouldn't. Not to someone that smart and that canny. They cooperated with limits. It was convenient for both sides. For separate reasons.

But why did Sikkukkut value me from the beginning? Why did he and the mahendo'sat both value me enough to keep us alive and set me here, with this much power?

Is Sikkukkut a fool? He was never a fool. Neither is Jik. Nor Goldtooth.

If Sikkukkut lost too many ships fighting for power, my

gods, he'd find some other kif gnawing up his leg the moment he looked weak. That's what the mahendo'sat are doing to him, whittling away at him. It's the kif's chief weakness, that aggressiveness of theirs. Does Sikkukkut know that? Can a species see its own deficiencies?

Look about us at ours, at this pitiful spectacle, hani against hani, spears and arrows flying in the sun, banners aflutter—

I see what keeps us from being what we might be.

Can he?

Can—?

"Look OUT!" someone yelled; and fire spattered from the end of the corridor.

"Any word?" Chur asked. She had left the rifle in lowerdecks. To carry the thing was more strength than she had, and there was no enemy aboard. She arrived on the bridge with Tully close behind her and clung to a seat at her regular post. It was a strange captain who turned a worried face toward her. "I'm taking orders," Chur breathed, to settle that, and clung to the chair with her claws, the whole scene wavering in and out of gray in her vision, her heart going like a motor on overload. "Any word on them?"

"Ehrran's threatening to back out of dock and blow us all. *Light*'s threatening to blow *Vigilance* where she sits. We're supposed to have a kifish ship in here picking up—that. Skkukuk. I've told him that's all we want it to do." There was a fine-held edge to Sirany's voice, an experienced captain at the edge of her own limits. "Handle the kif."

"Aye," Chur said, and crawled into the vacant chair between scan and com and livened the aux com panel. With Tauran crew on either side of her. Tully sat one seat down. Other seats were vacant. Fiar's and Sif's.

Handle the kif. Indeed.

Skukkuk thought of himself as crew. He was loyal. Geran had said that much with a grimace. And Chur had gotten her own captain's instructions to the kif on open com. That and the encounter belowdecks was all she had to go on, while the kif waited below in lowerdeck ops, for transfer arrangements to be finalized. But she had been in the deep too long to panic over the unusual or the outré.

One of the black things skittered through the bridge and

vanished like a persistent nightmare, long, furred, and moving like a streak.

On scan, one of the kifish ships nearest had just flared with vector shift.

Skkukuk's tight-beamed request for transport had had time to be heard and was evidently being honored.

"Tully," she said, leaning to look down the board where he had settled in. "We don't know when the humans come, right? You record message: *record,* understand? We send it to system edge, wide as we can, and constant—" She remembered in dismay she was not dealing with Pyanfar. "Your permission, cap'n."

"What?" the snapped answer came back. She had to explain it all again. In more detail. And: "Do it," Sirany said. "Just keep us advised *what* you do. You got whatever you want."

She drew a larger breath, activated com output and set about explanations, alternately to kif and to human and to *The Pride*'s interim captain. Then there was the matter of communicating with their mahen allies out there, whose disposition and intentions were another question: not many of the mahendo'sat ships had stayed insystem, but such as had were out there face-to-face with the kif, and nominally linked to the hani freighters who were also holding position out there in that standoff. So far they were letting the kifish ship move out where a kifish message with *The Pride*'s wrap on it had indicated it should go.

Blind acquiescence was asking a lot, of both mahendo'sat and hani. And even of the kif.

But things had to stay stable. More, they had to sort themselves out into some kind of defense, both internal and external. The next large group of ships to come in, at any given moment, could be Akkhtimakt's kif in a second strike, which would swing the whole kifish allegiance in the other direction; or it might be Sikkukkut, having disposed of Goldtooth; or Goldtooth and the humans. Or either without the other. Gods knew what else. Panicked stsho, for all they knew. Or tc'a.

Far better that whatever-it-was should meet an already existing wavefront of information designed to provoke discussion instead of indiscriminate fire.

Handle the kif, the woman said.

She sent it wide. In half a dozen languages and amplified via whatever ships would relay it, to all reaches of the system, continuously, since Gaohn station relays and apparently those of the second outsystem station and both buoys were not cooperating. She was talking to more than those insystem and those arriving; she was talking also to a certain mahen hunter, who had lost himself and gone invisible.

Chanur is taking Gaohn station. This solar system is under control of Chanur and its allies and its subordinates. You are entering a controlled space. Identify yourselves.

"Hold fire!" Pyanfar yelled, turning, her back to the side wall, the AP up in both hands where it bore on a flat-eared, white-round-the-eyes cluster of hani blackbreeches, Immunes, who were framed in the corridor opening and vulnerable as stsho in a hailstorm. A shot popped past her, high; one streaked back. *"Hold!"* Khym yelled, and: *"Hold it!"* Kohan Chanur echoed, two male voices that rumbled and rattled off the corridor walls in one frozen and terrible instant where slaughter looked likely.

But they were kids who had run up on them. Mere kids. Their ears were back in fright. None of them was armed except with lasers and they were staring down the barrels of APs that could take the deck out. They thought they were going to die there. It was in the look on their faces.

"Don't shoot!" one cried, with more presence of mind than the rest, and held her little pistol wide.

"Are you Ehrran?" Pyanfar yelled back at them, and one of them bolted and ran.

The others stayed still, eyes wide upon the leveled guns.

Prisoners we don't need.

Gods-be groundling fools.

"Get out of here!" she yelled at the rest of them. "*Out,* rot your hides!"

They ran, scrambling, colliding with each other as they cleared that hall, no shot fired.

She turned again, saw weary faces, bewildered faces, saw dread in Rhean Chanur and the rest, spacers who had come home to fight against kif and ended up fighting hani kids. That was the kind of resistance there was. That was what they had come down to, trying to take their station back from lunatics who threw beardless children at them.

"Gods save us," she said, and drew a ragged breath and shook her head and winced at the thump of explosion, which was Haral with their allies blasting their way through another pressure door that had been, with hani persistence, replaced with another windowed door after the *last* armed taking of Gaohn station. Nothing bad would ever happen twice, of course. Not at civilized Gaohn. Not to hani, who had no wish to become involved in foreign affairs. Gaohn station prized its staid ways, its internal peace, maintained by ceremonies of challenge and duel.

"Gods curse Naur," she said aloud. "Gods curse the *han*." And shocked her brother, and surely shocked *ker* Huran Faha, whose shoulder-scar was from downworld hunting, who knew little more of kif than she knew of hyperspace equations. Pyanfar shoved off from the wall and kept going, stepping through the ruined doorway.

"Stop," the intercom said from overhead. *"You are in violation of the law. Citizens are empowered to prevent you."*

There were no citizens in sight. Everyone with sense had gotten out of the section. Those on Gaohn that were not spacers outright, excepting folk like Kohan and Huran, and red-maned Akify who had lived so long downworld with Chanur she had forgotten she was Llun, were all stationers, who knew the fragility of docksides, and knew there was a Chanur ship and a flock of kif and mahendo'sat looming over them. There was a way to slow station intruders down. Anyone in Central might have sealed and vented the whole area under attack, had they been prepared. Had Gaohn station ever been set up for such a defense. But no, the necessary modifications had been debated once, after the first taking of Gaohn, but never carried through: the Llun themselves had argued passionately against it.

There would never, of course, the Llun had thought, never in a thousand lifetimes come another invasion. The very thought of it disturbed hani tranquility, the acknowledgment of such a calamity was against hani principle: plan for an event and it might well create itself. To prepare Gaohn for defense might create a bellicose appearance that might cause it to need that defense. To provide Gaohn corridors with windowed pressure doors (which permitted visual communication between seal-zones in some contamination or fire emergency) was a safety measure and a moral statement: there would never come the day that the station would have to take extreme measures.

So it had fallen to Ehrran quite simply.

And the foreign forces that were coming in had never heard of such philosophy, and cared less. How could one even translate such a mindset to a kifish *hakkikt?*

How could a kif who planned across lightyears comprehend the Llun, let alone the groundling Naur, and the mind of the *han,* which decreed all on its own that hani would be let alone?

. . . .a kif who planned. . . .

. . . .a kif who let loose a mahen hunter-ship and a hani force to accomplish a task for him which he—

—could not do himself?

—did a kif ever believe force insufficient?

Could a kif be so subtle?

Gods-rotted right a kif could be subtle. But not down any hani track. A kif wanted power, wanted adherents, wanted territory—

—Sikkukkut knew, by the gods, that Goldtooth was not done, and being capable of tricks like short-jumping himself, he knew what Goldtooth might have done at Meetpoint, a trick that *she* had only discovered when they pinned Jik down and wormed it out of him.

Knnn and gods-knew what had come in on Sikkukkut at Meetpoint, and what would Sikkukkut have done back there? Stayed to contest it? Run home to Kefk and Mkks, or Akkt?

One wished.

But that was not Sikkukkut's style. The wily bastard would have put more and more of the mahen puzzle together, the same as they, Jik's determined silence notwithstanding. Since Kefk, there was less and less left that Sikkukkut had to know.

That intrusion which had nearly run them over on their outbound course had been attack coming in again at Meetpoint, that was what it had to be, with the methane-breathers coming in the Out range as methane-breathers were crazy enough to do; and right before Sikkukkut launched his own pet hani toward Anuurn, he had been couriering messages right and left to other ships. . . .

. . . .Sikkukkut was planning something, and *he* had that babbling traitor Stle stles stlen aboard: the stsho would have told him anything and everything about Goldtooth he knew to tell.

Small black creatures stayed active during jump. They were from the kifish home world. So could the kif? Were they plotting and planning all the way, was that the secret to kifish daring and fierceness in their strikes, that they came out of hyperspace clearheaded and focused, revising plans such as hani and mahendo'sat and humans and anyone else would have to make well beforehand?

My gods, my gods.

She slogged along after the others, her own group lagging farther and farther back. Flesh had its limits. Even Hilfy flagged. Her pulse racketed in her ears like the laboring of some failing machine. There was that pain in her chest again, her eyes were blurred.

We may not have even this time. We shouldn't be here. I should turn this back, get back to the ship, prepare to defend us—

—with what, fool? This vast armament you have?

—turn kif on kif? Can you lead such creatures as that, can you even keep a hold on Skkukuk if you can't get control of Gaohn?

Jik, gods rot you, where are you?

Another doorway. An AP shell took it out, just blew the window out, leaving jagged edges of plex. The youngsters and then the rest waded on through the wreckage that loomed in her vision like an insurmountable barrier, the gun weighing heavier and heavier in her hand. Kohan had gone ahead with Rhean. Khym was still with her. So were all her own crew. "Looks like we got rearguard," Haral gasped, a voice hardly recognizable. "Gods-be fools not watching their own backsides. Groundlings and kids."

"Yeah," she murmured, and got herself through the door, walked on, and wobbled in her tracks. A big hand steadied her. Khym's.

The PA sputtered. *"Cease, go back to your ships immediately.* Vigilance *has armaments to enforce the decree of the* han. *It stands ready to use them. Do not endanger this station."*

"*Ker* gods-be Rhif's safe on her ship," Geran said.

"Patience, we got the *Light* up there over her head, she's not going anywhere."

"We got a kifish ship coming into dock," Haral said. "*There's* trouble when it comes. Gods know what that fool Ehrran will do."

Another agonizing stretch of hallway. The first of them had gained the stairwell. There was much yelling of encouragement, inexperienced hani screwing up their courage before a long climb that meant head-on confrontation with an armed opposition.

They were out of range of the pocket-coms. Too much of the station's mass was between them and the ships at dock.

"M'gods." Footfalls came up at their backs, a thundering horde of runners. Pyanfar spun, on the same motion as the rest of the crew, on a straggle of hani in merchants' brights, with a crowd behind them all the way down the corridor, a crowd a lot of which was blackbreeches, strung out down the hall as they filtered through the obstacles of the shattered pressure doors. *"Over their heads!"* She popped off a shot into the overhead, and plastic panels near the shattered door disintegrated into flying bits and smoke and a thundering hail of ceiling panels that fell and bounced and paved the corridor in front of the onrush.

"Stop, stop!" the cry came back, with waving of hands, some of the merchants in full retreat coming up against the press behind, and a dogged few coming through, holding their hands in plain view. "Sfauryn!" one cried, naming her clan, which was a stationer clan: merchants, indeed, and nothing to do with Ehrran.

"We're Chanur!" Tirun yelled back at them, rifle leveled. "Stay put!"

The press had stalled behind, tide meeting tide in the hallway, those trying to advance through the broken doors and those in panic retreat. The few up front hesitated in the last doorway, facing the guns.

"Ehrran has Central!" the Sfauryn cried.

"You want to do something about it?" Pyanfar yelled back.

"We're trying to help! Gods, who're you aiming at? People all over the stations are trying to get in there!"

"Gods-be about time!" Her pulse hammered away, the

blood hazed in gray and red through her vision. "If you can get the phones to work, get word to the other levels!"

"Llun's with us—Llun've got portable com, they got some rifles— It's Llun back there behind us, Chanur. They don't want to get shot by mistake!"

"Bring 'em on," she cried. Gods, what days they had come on, when Immune blacks meant target in a fight. She leaned on the wall and lowered the rifle. Blinked against the haze. Rest here awhile. Rest here till they had the reinforcements organized. Llun! honest as sunrise and, thank the gods, self-starting. They had been doing something all the while, one could have depended on that.

But they could still get shot, coming up behind the spacers up front. Someone in spacer blues had to get up there and warn the others in the stairwell that what was coming on their tail was friendly. "Who of us has a run left in her?" she asked, and scanned a weary cluster of Chanur faces, ears flagged, fur standing in sweaty points and bloodied from the flying splinters.

"Me," Hilfy gasped, "me, I got it."

"Got your chance to be a gods-be fool. Go. Get. *Be careful!*"

To a departing back, flattened ears, a lithe young woman flying down that corridor while the shouting reinforcements got themselves organized and came on.

The tide oozed its way through the shattered door, over the rattling sheets of cream plastics that had been the ceiling. It swept on, past a bedraggled handful of heavy-armed hani that hugged the wall and waved them past.

"Time was," Pyanfar said, and hunkered down again as the last of them passed, the heavy gun between her knees, Haral and Geran and Khym already down, Tirun leaning heavily against the wall and slowly sliding down to her haunches, "time was, I'd've run that corridor."

"Hey," Khym said, tongue lolling. He licked his mouth and gasped. "With age comes smart, huh?"

"Yeah," Haral said, and cast a worried look down the corridor, the way Hilfy had gone. Hilfy with a ring in her ear and a gods-awful lot of scars, and a good deal more sense than the imp had ever had in her sheltered life. Hilfy the veteran of Kefk docks and *Harukk*'s bowels. Of Meetpoint and all the systems in between and the circle that led home.

"Kid'll handle it," Pyanfar said. "We hold this place awhile. Hold their backsides. Got to think. We got *Vigilance* out there. We got kif to worry about."

Station poured out a series of conflicting bulletins. Events were too chaotic for Ehrran to coordinate its lies. "They're still threatening to destroy the boards up there," Chur said. And: "Unnn," from Sirany Tauran. There was nothing for them to do about it. But there *was* a steady pickup of information from Llun scattered throughout the station, static-ridden, but decipherable. It gave out a name. "They've met up with the cap'n," Chur cried suddenly, on a wave of relief, and pressed the com-plug tighter into her ear to try to determine where that meeting was, but Llun was being cagey and giving out no positions. "They're saying they've linked up with Chanur and the rest and they're headed with that group."

There was a murmured cheer for that. ("Good?" Tully asked, leaning forward to catch Chur's eye. "Good?" "Gods-be good," Chur said back. "The captain's found help.") While Tauran crew stayed busy all about them, stations monitoring scan and outside movements, keeping Tully's recorded output and her own going out on as wide and rapid a sweep of the sphere as they and *Chanur's Light* could achieve in coordination, snugged against a rotating station, and sending with as much power as they could throw into the signal. Especially they kept an eye on *Vigilance* at its dock, *Vigilance*'s image relayed to them by *Light*, as a kifish ship headed for them, conspicuous now among all the others and coming the way a hunter-ship could, by the gods *fast*. While on a link all his own from belowdecks ops, and without a need to sweep the available sphere, Skkukuk maintained communications with his fellow kif.

"*Chanur*-hakkikt *skkutotik sotkku sothogkkt,*" his news bulletin went out, and Chur winced. "*Sfitktokku fikkrit koghkt hanurikktu makt.*" Other hani ships were picking that up, and there were spacers enough out there who knew main-kifish: *The Chanur* hakkikt *has subordinated other*

clans. Something more about hani and a sea or tides or
something the translator had fouled up. Skkukuk was being
coded or poetic, was talking away down there, making his
own kifish sense out of bulletins he got. She considered
cutting him off. She thought of going down there and shooting him in lieu of ten thousand kif she could not get her
hands on.

But the captain had given her orders. Pyanfar Chanur
had asked it, and asked it with all sanity to the contrary,
which meant it was one of the captain's dearly held notions,
and *that* meant Pyanfar Chanur intended her crew to keep
their hands off that kif and let him do what Pyanfar had
said he should do.

This kif had saved the captain's life. Geran had told
her so.

This kif was Pyanfar's kifish lieutenant. Pyanfar herself
had told her so.

For Pyanfar's reasons. If they were to go down, as well
be on the captain's orders, where they had lived forty years,
onworld and off. If Pyanfar Chanur said jump the ship they
jumped; if it was on course for the heart of a sun, they
objected the fact once to be sure and then they jumped it.

It was a catching sickness. The Tauran captain was doing
much the same, obeying orders she doubted.

While one of *The Pride*'s black, verminous inhabitants
boldly sat on its haunches in the aisle by the start of the
galley corridor and stared in wonder at the fools who ran
the ship.

Up the stairs, up and up until the bones ached and the
brain pounded for want of air. Hilfy Chanur had gotten
herself up to the fore of the band, *after* dispersing parts of
the Llun contingent down every available corridor as they
ascended, to round up other stationers and get them moving down other corridors. There was one advantage to holding the heart of a city-sized space station, which was that
one had all the controls to heat and light and air under
one's hands.

The Ehrran had that.

But there was also an outstanding disadvantage to holding Central: that it was *one* small area, and that a city-sized
space station had a lot of inhabitants, all of whom were

converging on that point from all corridors, all passages, every clan on the station furiously determined to put the Llun *back* in control of systems the Llun understood and the Ehrran interlopers patently did not.

If there were Llun working systems up there at gunpoint, they were doing it all most unwillingly, and Ehrran had only the Llun's word for it just *what* they were doing with those controls.

Fools, Aunt Pyanfar would say. A space station was a good deal different than a starship's controls; if there were even experienced spacers in the Ehrran contingent up there. Mostly it had to be groundling Ehrran, blackbreeches whose primary job was trade offices and lickfooting to Naur and others of the Old Rich and the New.

Aunt Rhean was beside her as they climbed. Her father was just behind, grayed and older by the years *The Pride* had been away. And somewhere they had picked up two other men, young Llun, who had come in somewhere around level five and charged in among them in a camaraderie quite unlike men of the common clans—Immunes, free from challenge all their lives and having not a hope in the world of succeeding their own lord except by seniority, they came rushing in, stopped in a moment of recognition, likely neither one having known the other was coming, and surely daunted by Kohan's senior and downworld presence. Then: "Come ahead, rot you!" Kohan had yelled at them. And they had paired up with a great deal of shouting and bravado like two adolescents on a hunt. There were Llun women, armed and experienced in the last desperate battle for Gaohn. And it was all headed right into Ehrran's laps.

If the captive Llun up in control had been willing, they could at least have killed the lights and put the station reliant on the flashlights the Llun and the station merchants and some of the spacers had had the foresight to bring with them. They could have vented whole sections of the docks, with enormous loss of life. They could have fired the station stabilization jets and affected the gravity. They could have thrown the solar panels off their tracking and used some of the big mirrors to make it uncomfortable for *Chanur's Light*. Perhaps the Ehrran urged them to these things at gunpoint.

But none of them had happened.

The level twelve doorway was in front of them. Locked. Of course that was locked. One of the Ehrran had probably done that on manual. They surely held the corridors up here, between invaders and Central.

"Back," Hilfy yelled, and those in front of her cleared back and ducked down as best they could on the stairs, covering themselves. An AP threw things when it hit. And this door went like the others—the window was down, when she opened her eyes, her face and arms and body stung and bleeding with particles. The broken doorway let in a swirl of smoke, and a red barrage of laser fire lit the gray, exploding little holes off the stairwell wall up there.

For the first time panic hit her, real fear. This was the hero-stuff, being number one charging up the stairs into that mess. It was where her rashness and the possession of that illegal AP had put her.

"Hyyaaaah!" she yelled in raw terror, and rushed the stairs, because running screaming the other way was too humiliating. She fired one more time and got plastic-spatter all over her as the shell blew in the corridor and ceiling tiles hailed down in front of her. For a terrifying moment she was alone going through that doorway, and then she felt others at her back, blinked her burned eyes wider and saw blackbreeched hani lying in the corridor, some moving, some not; saw laser fire scatter in the smoke and aimed another shell that way.

There were screams. She flinched.

They were hani. They were downworlders. They had no experience of APs or what it was like to have a body blown apart or walls caving in with the percussion of shells. The survivors scrambled and fled and left guns lying in their disgrace, while outraged Llun charged after that lot, the two stationer-lads yelling as they went.

"Door," Rhean said, having arrived beside her, and she pointed to where the Llun were already headed.

"No problem," Hilfy gasped. She was cold all over. Her hand clenched about the grip of the gun as if it was welded there: she had lost all distinction between herself and the weapon, had lost a great deal of feeling all over her splinter-perforated skin. She cast a look back to see how many of their own had made it through, and it was a sea of their own forces in that corridor.

She walked now, over the littered floor, past the dead, where the others had run; and up to the sealed door their charge had secured, near where a shocked handful of Ehrran prisoners huddled under guard. It was the last door, the one that led into Central. "I'll blow it," she said. "You got to take it the hard way—" remembering only then that it was a senior captain she was telling how to do things. It was so simple a matter. It was hurtfully simple. Near Rhean Chanur, near her father, were hani who surely knew. There was Munur Faha, for one. And the Harun. They had to charge in there hand to hand against guns that might destroy fragile controls and kill fifty, sixty thousand helpless people.

Fools. She could have wept over the things she saw. *Poor fools. My people. Do you see now? Do you see what we've done to ourselves, what a plagued thing we've let in, because we tried to keep everything the old way?*

There was information coming in, finally, scattered reports booming out over the PA as Llun portable com began supplanting the reports out of Central: *"Ehrran is in violation of Immune law,"* one such repeated. *"Llun has appealed to all clans to enforce its lawful order for Ehrran withdrawal from station offices and enjoins Ehrran to signal its intent to comply."*

That announcement was becoming tiresome, dinning down from the overhead. Pyanfar wiped her bleeding face and flicked her ears and looked up at the wreckage of the speaker, which gave the advisories a rattling vibration and garbled the words.

"I'd like to shoot that thing," Geran muttered. Which was her own irritated thought.

"Gods-be little good we're doing here," Pyanfar said. "That's sure." Her throat was sore. Her limbs ached. She put effort into getting onto her feet. "Hilfy can take care of herself. Whole station's in on it. Better to get back to the ship, get Chur off her feet."

"Not putting her in any station hospital," Geran muttered. "Safer on the ship."

Which was what Geran thought of Gaohn's present chances, with kif incoming. Or Geran echoed Chur's wishes, if they all went to vacuum and there was no real difference.

"Yeah," she said, noncommittal, and pushed herself off the wall she had braced on. "Gods. What'd I do to stiffen the arm up?" The AP weighed like sin. The debris in the hall was an obstacle course, stuff that stuck in the feet, up in the sensitive arch of the toes. Broken plastics and bits of metal mingled indiscriminately on the deckplates. The mob that had come through had left bloody footprints, but they had seemed crazy enough not to feel it much. Pyanfar limped and winced her way over the stuff, the crew doing the same.

"We got that kif incoming," Tirun said.

"Gods, yes. Llun's not going to like that much." It was about the first thing the Llun partisans were going to learn when they got back into contact with whatever Llun personnel were keeping the station going under Ehrran guns. *Crazy Chanur's bringing kif in.* And Llun at that point had to wonder what side Chanur was on. So did the others, up there with Hilfy.

It was a fair question.

She caught her breath, wiped her nose, seeing a red smear across her thumb. No wonder she was snuffling. And how had *that* happened?

Down the corridor, past one and another of the shattered doorways, over debris of broken plastics, the stench of explosion and burned plastics still hanging in the air, cleaned somewhat by the fans: things were still working.

And Pyanfar was in a sudden fever, now she had begun, to get back to *The Pride* and get out to space again, to deal with the kif she had in hand before she suddenly had more kif than she could deal with.

They reached the corridor end, where the last shattered pressure door let out on the open dock. She stepped over the frame, swung the AP in a perfunctory and automatic sweep about the visible dock, right along with the glance of her eye, which had gotten to be habit.

An AP thumped: her brain identified it as one of that category of dreadful sounds it knew; knew it intimately, right down to the precise sound an AP made when it was aimed dead on: and the twitch went right on to the muscles, which asked no questions. She sprawled and rolled as the world blew up around her; rolled all the way over and let off a shot with both her hands on the AP, in the maelstrom of her crew shouting and shots going off.

My gods, into the doorway, thing hit us dead center— O my gods!

Second shot, off into the cover of the girders.

"You all right?" she yelled back at her crew, at her husband. "You all right back there?"

"Get back here!" Khym's voice, deep and angry.

Third shot. *"Are you all right, gods rot it?"*

A shot came back, hit the wall. She made herself a part of the deck.

"Py!"

"Get out of the gods-be door!"

"Chanur!" a voice came over a loudhailer. *"Leave the weapons and come clear of there. You want your crew alive, we have you pinned! We have women coming down that corridor at your backs—"*

"Ehrran?" she yelled out, still belly-down. "Is that Ehrran?"

"This is Rhif Ehrran, Chanur. We have crew behind you. Give up!"

"She's the same gods-be fool she ever was." Haral's voice, somewhere behind her, something in the way of it. Door rim, Pyanfar earnestly hoped.

"You got to match her, Hal? F'godssakes, get out of that door!"

"Hey, she just told us we got company to the rear. You want us to go handle 'em, or you want help out there to fore, cap'n? She's a godsawful lousy shot."

"Chanur!"

"I'm thinking!" she shouted back. And to Haral: "Is everyone all right back there?"

"*Na* Khym caught a bit in the leg, not too bad. You want to back up, or you want us to come out there?"

She looked out toward that line-of-sight where structural supports gave cover. And up. Where a gantry joined that area, with its couplings and its huge hoses and cables. A grin rumpled her nose and bared her teeth. "It'll be for'ard." As Ehrran yelled again over the loudhailer. *"Chanurrr!"*

"You gods-be fool." She flipped up the sights, aimed, and sent the shell right into the center of the skein. That

blew some of the huge hoses in two and blew the ligatures
and dropped the whole ungainly snaking mass down behind
Ehrran's position, hose thick as a hani's leg and long as a
ship ramp dropping in from the exploded gantry skein, hitting, bouncing and snaking this way and that with perverse
life of its own. Pumps screamed, air howled, and safeties
boomed; and blackbreeched figures scattered for very life,
in every direction the bouncing hoses left open.

She scrambled up. "Come on," she yelled to her own
crew, to get them clear in the confusion, out of that exposed position; and: "Captain!" Tirun yelled.

She whirled toward the targets, got off one shot toward
the one figure who had stopped in the clear and lifted a gun.
It was not the only shot. APs and rifles went off in a volley
from the door behind her, and there was just not a hani at
all where that figure had stood. The shock of it numbed
her to the heart.

"Still a fool," Geran said, without a qualm in her voice.

And Haral: "Couldn't rightly say who hit her, cap'n, all
this shooting going on."

"Move it!" she snarled then, and shoved the nearest
shoulder, Geran's. The rest of them moved, covering as
they went, Khym limping along and losing blood, but not
overmuch of it. *The Pride* was a short run away, *Ehrran's
Vigilance* out of sight around the station rim; it was *Harun's
Industry* that might well have taken damage in that hit on
the gantry lines, if its pumps had been on the draw. Still
spaceworthy, gods knew, the pumps were a long way from
a starship's heart. They ran across the edge of a spreading
puddle of water and mixed volatiles: the toxics, thank gods,
ran their skein separately, in the docking probe in space:
those were not loose, or they would have been dead.

They could all still be dead if *Vigilance*'s second-in-
command decided to rip her ship loose and start shooting.
That little stretch of dock loomed like intergalactic distance, passed in a dizzy, nightmare effort, feet splashing
across the deck in liquid that burned in cuts and stung the
eyes to tears, that got into the lungs and set them all to
coughing. Pumps had cut off. On both sides of the station
wall. Gods hope no one set off a spark.

"Chur!" That was Geran's strangled voice, yelling at a

pocketcom. "Chur, we're coming in, get that gods-be hatch open!"

They reached the ramp. She grabbed Khym's arm as he faltered, blood soaking his leg. She hauled at him and he at her as he struggled up the climb, into the safety of the gateway.

Then they could slow to a struggling upward jog, where at least no shot could reach them, and the hatch was in reach. She trusted Chur's experience, *The Pride*'s own adaptations: exterior camera and precautions meant no ambushes—

"We got that way clear?" Haral was asking on com.

"Clear," Chur's welcome voice came back. "You all right out there?"

All right. My gods!

"Yeah," Haral said. "Few cuts and scrapes."

A numbness insulated her mind. Even with eyes open on the ribbed yellow passage, even with the shock of space-chilled air to jolt the senses, there was this drifting sense of nowhere, as if right and wrong had gotten lost.

A hani that sold us out. A hani like that. A kif like that gods-be son Skkukuk. Which is worth more to the universe?

I shot her. We all did. Crew did it for me. *Why'd I do it?*

Hearth and blood, Ehrran.

For Chur. But that wasn't why.

For our lives, because we have to survive, because a fool can't be let loose in this. We have to do it, got to do something to stop this, play every gods-be throw we got and cheat into the bargain. Got to live. Long enough.

What will they say about us then?

That's nothing in the balances. That there's someone left to remember at all—that's what matters.

Chapter 13

The lock shot open and it was Tully on the other side, Tully alone and armed and out of breath, his lively pale eyes widening when he saw them, shock and worry at once. He holstered the gun and reached for Khym as he limped over the threshold, and got a snarl for his trouble: "Let be," Tirun said; and: "I'm all right, gods rot it!" from Khym. "Gods! Let me alone!" And: "Shut up," from Tirun. "I got a lame leg from that kind of stuff. Down to the lab and move it."

While Tully shoved a bit of paper at her. "Chur send. Kif ship come send take our kif gods-be quick now. Got Central fine. Now got ask question from station hani what we do. Lot worry. Sirany captain got smart, let Chur do."

More human babble, mingled good and bad news. *Urgent,* Chur's message said: *Courier* Nekekkt *is braking. Lighter is enroute to pick up Skkukuk back at E-lock. I have transcript of all his communications to the kif. They seem clean. Communications from station indicate Ehrran holed up in Central, attack ongoing; no mention from Llun regarding kif;* Vigilance *applying to* han *for instructions, captain's whereabouts unknown. . . .*

That was a message a few moments old. Long as it took for Tully to run down the topside corridor and down the lift and down another passage to meet them. There was more than that happening. *I am transmitting messages to system edge, Tully assisting; Tauran cooperation excellent—*

Thank the gods for Chur Anify. And everyone else involved.

"Come on." She swept Tully up, Tirun having snatched Khym on through; Geran and Haral limped along with her.

Was altruism possible? Had Ehrran come at her in defense of the station itself, tried to arrest Chanur crew in hope of seizing control of the situation, knowing that kifish ship was incoming?

Sorry about it if that's so. Real sorry. All I got time to be. She hurt everywhere. Her eyes blurred with particulate dust and her nose still bled. She stank of sweat and volatiles.

There was no time to wonder about it. She headed for the lift.

Two of Sifeny's crew and one of her own were still out there in the shooting. And her husband was down in sickbay to let an exhausted, shaking spacer hunt a piece of shrapnel out of him.

Those were the things she wanted to worry about, the things a hani could somehow manage.

It was not what was waiting for her topside.

There were casualties. One dead. Three likely to be. The dead one was one of the lads from Llun; and Hilfy stood over him and looked down at a boyish, simple face. Nothing much. A boy who had been too brave and a little foolish. Playing at hero.

Gods. Gods. He never knew it was real.

Did he? This boy? Could he imagine Harruk's *black gut? A kifish dockside?*

Or did he have to?

A hand touched her shoulder. Her father, sweaty and bloody and breathing hard. And safe. She looked up at Kohan Chanur: he towered, huge and kind and perhaps no longer or ever as innocent as she had always thought him.

She looked at him and saw he was also hunting someone who no longer existed. His daughter. The unscarred one. Perhaps he wanted her to show some emotion. That made her saddest of all, that if she softened it would be a lie. Sadness was all she could muster. She only looked at him.

Her mother was more practical. Huran Faha stood by, with perhaps a little amazement, a hard and reckoning look between them when she turned away, a warning look, because there were Llun taking back this control center as Ehrran clans women were rounded up and led away. It had not been that hard at the last. Poor groundling fools who melted away in hand-to-hand so fast it was over in a couple of shots and a tangle of bodies, Ehrran struggling up close and intimate with spacers who learned their infighting in

dockside bars. Not a chance in a mahen hell, after that.
Easy stuff.

Only the boy, who had never dodged. Who just plunged
ahead in his simple bravery because that was what men
were supposed to do, wasn't it?

"Gods blast 'em!" Suddenly the anger was too much, and
there was nowhere to spend it. She had no wish to stay
and answer close questions from the Llun.

She was not known the way her aunt Pyanfar was. She
was only another spacer, thin and scarred and unremark-
able, except that she had stood for a moment with Chanur
clan, except for a moment the lord of Chanur—*ex-lord! O
gods!*—had laid his hand on her shoulder. It was time to
be gone back to her ship. She gave a look to Fiar and Sif,
caught their eye in one sweep and slanted an ear toward
the door. Time to be out indeed, before Llun caught on to
who she was, and what crew she belonged to.

But a brusque presence swept into the center, graynosed
and haggard and accompanied by a band of hani in hardly
better shape—the look, Hilfy had gotten to know it, of
spacers off a brutally hard run. Dulled fur, thinned patches.
She knew them, had seen this lot last on a Meetpoint dockside with police closing in on all of them.

Banny Ayhar and her crew filled the doorway, blinked,
and stared at her closer than a chance encounter warranted.
"Is that young Chanur?" Banny asked. "Is that Hilfy
Chanur?"

Hilfy's jaw refused to work. The wits that had done quite
well up to that point, turned to butter.

"Chanur for sure!" Banny drew a deep breath, and her
ears slanted back and up again. "They told me what you
did." Down again. "Got us free, b'gods! Gods-be fools! But
what's this with you and the kif?"

There was profound silence at her back, and profoundest
attention to the question.

"Chanur," another voice said at her back. "*Ker* Hilfy."

She started out, past Banny. But that obstacle was not
moving.

"Kif," Banny Ayhar said. "That's what I want to know.
What's going on?"

It was stop or fight. A fight now could do Chanur no
particular good. She glared at Banny Ayhar with flattened

ears and the power of the AP in her fist which was right now worth nothing at all.

My gods, I can lose it all. Everything. If they get wind of what we're doing, they'll throw it wide and high and we'll all die, the whole world will die for it. O Banny Ayhar, you godscursed fool, you're about to throw away everything you won.

"You got the message here," she said to Banny, quiet and urgent, ears up now. "You want to lose it all? Or you want to stand with me here?"

She was talking to a captain; and a hardnosed one; and flatly forgot the *ker* and the respects: she threw her whole life and self into it.

Banny's ears twitched this way and that in the deep hush. Everyone in the whole center must have heard that appeal, as if Ayhar and *Prosperity* were part of all that tainted Chanur. There was Harun back there. And Munur Faha. She was *not* alone. Even in the matter with the kif. There were senior captains to rely on. There stood Fiar and Sif, co-conspirators off the same bridge.

She saw a sudden guardedness in Banny Ayhar's eyes, the look of an old trader and an old hand in rough places. The old woman knew when she had gotten a high sign, by the gods she caught it up; and it was suddenly spacers and stationers in the control center, spacers and Them, which was only slightly less foreign than the kif.

"Chanur," that Llun voice behind her said, a woman's voice of some age and authority.

But before she turned, Ayhar lifted her chin in that way that from Anuurn docks to Meetpoint, said *Ally, till I find out different.*

"Cap'n, they got into Central, they got it."

Pyanfar crossed the bridge in the wake of a cheer from both crews, to lean on Chur's seatback. "Clear?"

"Not officially confirmed yet." Chur did not look around. Her ears backslanted as she flicked switches and punched buttons. "Gaohn station, this is *The Pride of Chanur,* we got an incoming lighter, we'll handle that. Appreciate word on casualties at your earliest." Pause. Flick of the ears. "Captain, we got a general announcement: *Remain calm. Llun has retaken Central.*"

"They'll have every clan in reach of there asking casualties. We've got to sit and wait, I'm guessing."

"I'd like it better if they got some operators on output. We just got that same message cycling over and over. Nobody's handling anything. We got what we got from a ship-to-snip off a Moura freighter. *Somebody's* got com in there."

Pyanfar gnawed at her mustaches, spat and gnawed again. "We got no favors coming. Those with bad news get it first, that's the way of it. They're all right. Just keep after 'em."

While Tauran crew methodically handled the approach of the kifish lighter, which was coming in toward the docking boom aft. And a certain kif was standing there with bags and Dinner packed. One hoped.

("Skkukuk," she had said lately, over com. "This is the captain. Just want you to know I'm back and we're quite well in control.")

(*"I had absolutely no doubts,"* the kifish voice came back to her, tinny the way E-deck pickup always sounded. *"I will give you the hearts of your enemies."*)

Literally. It was not a thing she wanted to contemplate at the moment, with the possibility of casualties up in Central and the dire memory of Ehrran out there on the docks. She flinched from that every time the image came back to her, and it came time and again.

Nothing left. Nothing, O gods.

An Immune. With all the trouble she was, she was still an Immune.

She listened while the sorting-out of com and the docking of a kifish lighter proceeded.

"You want your chair," Sirany offered her a second time.

Meaning: command of this situation. Everything that went with it. She looked at the Tauran, saw the exhaustion and the anxiousness of a woman who feared every moment she sat there and feared equally to abdicate that chair and turn it back to Chanur.

"I'll take it," Pyanfar said. "I want to get my second up here; you mind to sit observer? Fit both our crews in here and galley: we got need of all the expertise we got."

"I'll sit it," Sirany said, and hauled herself out of the number one place. "Two minute break and I'm back here."

"We have touch imminent," the Tauran working that docking said, never pausing: the interface between crews went through smooth as the shift of a few bodies, and never a missed beat.

Not a jolt as the kifish lighter made its contact with the boom. Retraction whined away, a moan throughout the ship as the boom swung down and dragged lock and lock into contact.

A hani might wish to say goodbye. Even to a kif. It was not the way of kif. The presence quit *The Pride* with never a word and never a report, just the abrupt communication from the lighter pilot that they were ready for undock.

Then the lighter took off, rolled and left with all the speed it could muster, a little sputter of its engines against *The Pride*'s hull.

That was, she reckoned, another ambitious kif, the captain of that so-quickly moving ship out there, the one which had appropriated the responsibility for picking up the hani's kif.

Not the foremost among the ships out there. She knew that much by now. It was about the third-subordinate, not in contention for primacy in Sikkukkut's favor; so it was taking a calculated risk, maybe to do in its passenger, maybe to listen to him, depending on how things developed. And right now there were probably some very worried captains on the number one and two kifish ships. There were worried captains *everywhere* among the kif out there, Sikkukkut's highest captains sweating sudden adjustments in hierarchy: they had just gained a lot of Akkhtimakt's ships.

Good luck, my skulking shadow. Good luck. To both of us.

She drew a deep breath and flipped switches.

"We pulling out?" Haral wondered, beside her.

It was what she ached to do, get *The Pride* out of station, away from dock where it was less a target. "Want to get our people back." There was a cold lump at her gut. *I want to hear something out of Central, gods rot it. What kind of a hash have they got going up there? Station's stable. No damage alarms. They can't have shot it up too bad.*

Kohan's too reckless. Gods, don't let him have rushed in there.

Hilfy, now, Hilfy can cover herself.

* * *

"I don't credit that answer," the Llun said quietly. "*Not tip off our enemies.* I don't see any enemies here, *ker* Hilfy Chanur. I see alien ships moving out there, I see this station in jeopardy, I hear talk about a threat to the planet. I'm wondering where it comes from. I'm wondering what else we don't know about."

Hilfy kept her ears up, let them dip a bit in displeasure, brought them up again. Kohan was there, Kohan stripped of his title and his courtesies, the whole clan—gods, the whole clan must have deserted Kara Mahn's takeover and exiled themselves with their lord rather than submit to the Mahn and his sister. The powers of Chanur were most likely here: like Rhean. Like Jofan, who must have connived at getting herself and Kohan and the rest up to Rhean.

She was never prouder of her clan and her kin. "*Ker* Llun," she said, quietly, steadily, "I can tell you this. It's not numbers that'll win this one. We can't match numbers with what's out there. We haven't got the ships or the guns. Best thing we've got on our side right now is a mahendo'sat we've lost track of out there and the deep-spacers. My aunts are three of them. Ayhar here. Harun and Faha and Shaurnurn and Pauran and Tauran. And all the rest. Whatever men and kids are onstation, we'd be safer to get them off, out of here: every ship that hasn't got the guns to fight—take the men and the kids far as they can run into mahen space, and we just hope to the gods they'll get the word in a few months that Anuurn's still here. If it's not— there'll still be hani. That's what we're fighting for. The worst place in the whole system to be right now is one of our armed ships: second worst is the space stations; third is the world down there. You've got to turn the spacers loose, *ker* Llun, it's not Chanur I'm talking about, I'm not asking favors; I'm asking you turn the spacers *loose* and let us have a chance." She held out an arm, turned a shoulder, where kif had left scars that would last all her life. "That's the kind of treatment kifish guests get. Never mind what they do to the ones who aren't hostages."

"Are you," the Llun asked in a slow and level voice, "are you that now, Hilfy Chanur?"

"Hearth and blood, Llun. We're our own."

"We're on that ship." A young voice, talking out where seniors were silent. It wavered and all but died. Then Fiar Aurhen *par* Tauran edged her way past two captains and faced the Authority of Llun, flat-eared and with her voice pitched too high. "They're r-right. They ran clear from Kshshti—"

To station-bound Llun, Kshshti was only a place on a map, remote from all experience. Mkks was beyond their imagining. For a moment Hilfy felt a profound terror, the gulf between them uncrossable.

"We got a mess out there," Banny Ayhar said in her rumbling voice, and sniffed and hitched her pants up before she flung an arm out to gesture. "F'godssakes, you got your house afire you ask them as have buckets, Shan Llun! You don't lock 'em up and call 'em traitors! To a mahen hell with the gods-be *han* deputies and the notebooks and that trash! You can't call any referendum from the kif and they don't have any study committee! You godsforsaken fools, you listen to the likes of Ehrran till they take your station over and you *don't* listen to them that's had their shoulders to the dike. Look at 'em, you say! They got mud on 'em, must be they brought the flood! And you never seeing they've been propping up the gods-be timbers!"

There was profound silence. The Llun's ears flickered minutely in restraint. The eyes were gold and large and black-centered.

She waved a hand at the Llun who was taking furious notes.

"Record that a quorum voted. The Llun have heard the vote. The Llun call civil emergency: the amphictiony is space-wide." The hand fell. "Which captain do you want in charge?"

The silence went on several breaths. "Pyanfar Chanur," Kauryfy Harun said.

"Banny Ayhar," another said.

"Gods and thunders, not me," Banny said. "Pick someone who's got some idea what's out there. Chanur's stayed alive this far. I'd go with their knowhow."

Quiet muttters then. "Chanur," Munur Faha said. And: "Chanur," from Shaurnurn and Pauran and a scatter of others.

"Chanur," the Llun said, with another wave of her hand.

"Implement the orders. Tanury: evacuation operations. Nis: communications interface. Parshai: spacer logistics. Open the boards. Get it moving."

Hilfy stood there with her muscles cold and uncooperative. It had all changed course. She was free. The ships were. She cast a grateful look Banny Ayhar's way, but Ayhar was already moving; and beyond that consideration she knew where she belonged. Fast.

She was into the rush for the door and collected Fiar and Sif before she recalled she owed some glance toward her father and her mother, some apology for having set herself forward: but the Llun had cornered her, they had wanted *her* answers, and Rhean had stood there in the silence an accused clan had to maintain. With dignity. The little dignity that Chanur had left, with its land gone.

I'm sorry, she wanted to say. But the rush carried her through the door and there was no time to spend on goodbyes and regrets.

Gods hope they talked Kohan into going refugee with the other men. Gods hope.

She doubted that they could.

Where are the rest of us, the old aunts, the kids, my sisters and cousins?

On Fortune *and* Light? *How many could they get aloft? If that's so, if we lose those ships, Chanur will die here.*

She did not wait for the lift. There were too many waiting. She joined the impatient ones that ran the stairs, all the way down again to dockside.

". . . earnestly hope," the voice out of Gaohn Central Control said, precise and patient, *"you will remember the lives on this station; but we realize that this is not the greatest priority under the threat that exists. Therefore we do not encumber you with instructions of any sort. Take what actions you see fit. The citizens of this station are carrying out all domestic safety precautions. We will not issue any further order to you until this emergency is past. Gods defend us. You'll have other priorities. End statement."*

"Thank you, Llun." Pyanfar kept the voice cool, the hand steady over the contact. "We'll be putting out as quickly as possible. Can we have all dock crews on line?"

Gods, where had she learned such short courtesy? The

kif? She got the acknowledgment and punched out of the contact. But there were no promises that meant anything. There was nothing she wanted to say, that might not get to one of the other ships and have one of those captains second-guessing her. That was not kifish manners: it was hani good sense, hani levelheadedness. So the whole gods-be system defense was in her lap. So they were sending men and children out to the far quarters of mahen space, to be sure something of the species survived. It was what the Llun ought to have done days ago, instead of waiting till disaster came in on them. Rage boiled up in her and shortened her breaths as she kept the pre-launch checks going, one and the other switches, while Haral ran those on Tirun's board. Armaments.

There was another ship coming into Gaohn's traffic control, up from the world itself: shuttle-launch, out of Syrsyn. The information trickled out of Central to *Light*'s query: an unauthorized lift. An escape. A junior pilot and a single flight tech. The story came in from a ground station: the little Syrsyn Amphictiony had heard the warning out of space, and gotten the menfolk and the teenage boys and girls of at least six clans all onto a commandeered shuttle, the men and the boys all drugged beyond argument, and that whole fragile, precious package presently climbing out of Anuurn's atmosphere.

That terrified her more than Gaohn's danger. Syrsyn was taking the monumental risk of an action she had asked them to take. And it was so small a ship, and so helpless, and a fool thing to do, under-crewed and gods knew, with no flight plan but up. Use the engines, get course *after* they were in space, trust someone would take them in: lifesup-port adequate for—gods, what kind of figure? how many on that ship? Six clans' kids, the menfolk, a couple of women to handle the emergencies and keep down panic—

Four, five hundred lives?

How many of Chanur were still ground-bound?

Gods, get us away from this dock. Give us a chance.

Let us get at least to system edge.

There were no mines laid, gods-be nothing done, to forestall invasion. The *han* directed: the *han* had no grasp of mahen tactics, gods help them, no *knowledge* what the universe was shaped like above their day-sky, how ships and

objects incoming and dropping out of hyperspace went mis-
silelike to a sun, and coincidentally the near planets, of the
habitable kind, at velocities that made them undetectable
until they arrived. And the farther out from the system
center the defense was set, to prevent such strikes, the
larger the sphere of defense, and the wider the gaps in it,
even if a body was reasonably sure what jump point it was
coming from, and whether it was sticking to standards like
system zenith entry, or whether the cant of the local star
and the origin-well permitted something like a nadir arrival.
It was a good guess where anything incoming from Meetpoint might arrive via Kura. Which was, gods knew, the
shortest route.

But it was a lot of space. And if the kifish bastard did
some fancy maneuvering at Kura they might just come in
nadir.

Or they might already *be* there, having short-jumped.
That thought set the hair on end all down her back: Sikkukkut or gods-knew-who might be out there and by now inbound, well knowing the position of everything in the
system.

"Take the count. Mark."

"Mark." Haral started the clock running. "Tirun. *Na*
Khym. We're on the count."

"We're on our way," Tirun's voice came up from
lowerdecks.

Put Khym in his cabin? It was where he belonged.

No. *Give him that. We're not going to get out of this one
the same as we got in. The last time, husband. I think this
crew knows it.*

"Hilfy's just called," Geran said. "She's on her way to
the ramp. With Sif and Fiar. Not a scratch on 'em."

"Got that." A muted murmur of relief across the bridge.
The lost were found. Hydraulics sounded below, as Haral
opened up the lock from the board.

*I ought to wish she missed the ship. I wish she had.
Gaohn's got a better chance than we have.*

The airlock sealed again. *The Pride* took back its own.

"We're on count," Geran advised the new arrivals. "Get
up here."

Six minutes.

"Captain—" From the Tauran comtech. "We got contact with *Ehrran's Vigilance.*"

"Give it here." Pyanfar punched the button when it lit; and her gut knotted. "This is Pyanfar Chanur."

"Captain." The voice that came back was cold and neutral. *"This is Jusary Ehrran. Acting captain. Vote has been taken on this ship. We will act in system defense. We will go to Kura vector."*

She looked aside at Haral, at a flat-eared scowl.

"Gods-be earless bastard," Haral muttered. Bloodfeud: there was no doubt of that. With an Immune clan. They could not decline that, or their offer of help. "Covering their gods-be ass."

"We got no graceful way, have we? You want to leave 'em docked at Gaohn?"

"Captain—" The tech again. "Ayhar's on. *Prosperity.* They're aboard."

Bad news and good, like opposite swings of the pendulum. The whole universe was confounded. She punched in on the indicator, the first one still blinking. "This is Pyanfar Chanur. Banny, I owe you a drink."

"You owe my whole crew drinks, you notch-eared old dockcrawler, first we get back to port."

"You got it, Banny. Take care, huh? I'll get you sequence in a minute here." She cut out and punched the other. While quietly, a little murmur among the crew, the rest of them arrived. Tirun and Khym, Hilfy and Fiar and Sif. There was sorting-out going on, Chanur crew prioritied to seats. "He's got ob-2," she heard, Geran's voice. Definitively. A murmur from Khym. A Tauran voice, quietly. And Tully and Hilfy. It was all getting arranged over there. "We got a prelim sequence here," Haral was saying, likely to her sister Tirun. "Central's passed control over to us, we got the say." And into the microphone: *"Vigilance,"* Pyanfar said. "This is Pyanfar Chanur. Stand by your sequence."

"Understood," the acknowledgment came back. And: *hearth and blood,* she heard unsaid, under the chill, precise voice. *Later, Chanur.*

"We'll cover you same as the rest," Pyanfar said.

A small delay. *"We appreciate that, Chanur."* Grace for

grace. The woman had some positive qualities. Then: *"This is your fault, Chanur."*

"We'll see you in the *han*, Ehrran."

The com-telltale went out.

The power came up, the undocking sequence initiated. Familiar sounds. There was a great cold in her gut and an ache in her side. A sequencing flicked up on number one screen. She keyed affirm, and it flicked off: flashed out to all the ships via Central.

Fortune and *Light* were going wide out on either side of their formation; her own group contained the ships she had come with: *Industry* and *Shaurnurn's Hope, Starwind* and *Pauran's Lightweaver.* And ships that had run with *Fortune* and those that adhered to *Ayhar's Prosperity* each to those captains' discretion—a great number to *Prosperity,* with more on the way. *Ehrran's Vigilance* took farthest sweep, nadir. Not the hottest spot. The catcher-point. The one to take the strays.

It was the second time for some of these crews, the second time they had ever uncapped the red switches on the few armaments a freighter carried. Two years ago. Or whatever year it was, currently. Gods. She had lost track. Four? More than that? Kohan's face flashed to mind, Kohan grayed and time-touched. The world changed. More of the people she had known in her youth onworld would have died. Of old age.

How old am I? How many years did we lose out there?

The month, two-month jumps added up to years fast, with so little dock time between. She suddenly tried to think what her son and her daughter might look like, Kara Mahn and Tahy, down there ruling Chanur land, sitting in the *han*, for the gods' sake, *Tahy* senior enough to sit in the *han* and talk for Mahn, and vote against Chanur interests. Of a sudden the baby faces leapt to adolescence, to adulthood, to broad-faced maturity, Kara's sullen, broad-nosed face gone more sullen still, Tahy's furtive look gone to something pinched and unpleasant—a smallish teenager become a smallish, surly woman whose ears were always flicking about as if she suspected conspiracy. A mother's imagination painted these things and touched her children's manes with gray. Kara's ears would be notched up right proper. Kohan had gotten the ears the first time Kara made a try for Chanur land: it was a good guess Kohan had gotten him again. In return for his own scars. *Gods. So fast. Life's so fast. How much of it I've missed.*

Grapples withdrew. Undocking jets eased them out, under Haral's careful hand. Com babble came to her, three operators at once, on their separate channels, each dealing with procedures some of which went to Tirun back there at the aux panel.

She used her own comp, sorting the data that sifted past Tirun. *The Pride* backed hard; and something black and furred and angry shrieked and scrabbled across the decking, crack! against the bottom of the panel. It squealed in rage and scrambled sideways under the acceleration.

"Gods and thunders." She kicked at it, hardly sparing attention for the little bastard. Figures were more important. What it had done to systems back aft, gods only knew. It escaped, off galleyward. "Have to purge the ship to hard vacuum to get rid of those things."

"I'm not sure," Haral muttered, "that *that*'d do it. Standby rollover."

The Pride rolled, *G*-shift and re-shift; and six of the mains cut in, a moral shock this close to Gaohn. Laws and regulations were fractured. But Gaohn was under disaster-rigging, population snugged to the inmost sections. They made speed. They passed the zone where the aux-engines were permitted and slammed the mains in full.

They were free. Moving. Bound for the system rim.

Gods knew what was already out there, inbound.

"Communication from *Mahaar's Favor*," Chur said, "bearing off Tyar. They're AOS on our earlier transmission and say they're holding position."

Standing nose to nose with the kif.

She cast a wary eye at scan, where a dot that was a kifish ship stood all too close to Gaohn with the lighter-ship in its gut.

Too gods-be close to Gaohn and Anuurn.

It's a mistake. I'm a fool. They'll kill Skkukuk, poor bastard. They'll take him apart and they're in position to take the station out.

Fire on 'em? Gods-be kif hunters bury their personnel sections deep inside, got twenty feet of stuff to blast through to get a hit on the things, godsforsaken missiles we got won't dent it that deep without us throwing 'em at V *and we're near sitting still even yet. Fool, Pyanfar, fool.*

While acceleration went on. There was a stuffiness about the air. An unpleasant taint, like chemicals. Like dust in the air. Ozone. Filters were out. They had a redlight condition on the lifesupport board. They ignored it.

She blinked her eyes. For a moment it was *Harukk*'s dark gut, the flare of sodium-light. Dark-robed kif and the smell of incense and ammonia.

Kifish ships at dock at Kefk, lean and wicked and massive-vaned, bristling with guns. Like that thing out there.

"Priority," Hilfy said, and froze her heart. "Captain, it's *Nekkekt*. They're asking instructions."

Gods, of course *it won't turn now. Things are too uncertain. It's in crisis they kill their officers.*

And their allies.

"Have 'em put Skkukuk on."

A pause. While the mains blasted away, squaring the *V* and bringing them at an angle to the kif. Kif could fire from any angle. *The Pride* and the rest of the freighters had their limits.

It's godsblessed suicide. Bluff from one end to the other.

"They're sending for him," Hilfy said. "Captain, there's a Situation over there. That was the captain who asked instructions, I think, by their comtech."

"I think you got it," she muttered. *Push the bastard. Make him get your own* skku *to the mike. Gods. What're the* han *doing, what are they thinking, the ships out there? Chanur's talking to the kif, we got a kif right into Gaohn, we got kifish and human transmission going out of this ship. . . .*

It's Harun and the rest they're watching. The ships that came with me. Spacers. That's what they're taking their cue from—they know Chanur could be crazy, but not Chanur and five other clans and the mahendo'sat. They're holding steady so far—gods, they know *the kif, they know this whole mess is unstable.*

If they knew how much—

"Skkukuk to your com one," Haral said. A light blinked.

She punched it. "*Skku* of mine. We're taking Kura vector. See to it."

There was a pause. *Is he on? Gods, let's not have a mistake.*

"*Chanur*-hakkikt." In a voice cold and clear and clipped. *Skukkuk? Is that Skkukuk?*

"*Pukkukt' on your enemies, hakkikt. I will give them to you.*"

"*Skkukuk?*"

A pause. "*Of course, hakkikt-mekt. Skkukkuk.*" An edge to the voice. The tone was different. "*Pukkukt' on* all *your enemies. Rely on me.*"

What in the gods' name is he up to? Is that him? What's going on with him?

Is this some gods-help-us kifish test?

Or a kif gone important?

"Get those gods-be ships into line and get it organized. First one makes a wrong move, take it out!"

"*Yes.*"

The light went out. Like that. A little chill went down her back.

"What've we created? Migods, what've we created out, huh?"

Haral looked her way. Mirrorlike. "*Mekt-hakkikt*, was it?"

She blinked. The chill got no better. And no questions came through com from hani ships. Or station. Or the few mahendo'sat keeping their post out there with the kif Skkukuk had just appropriated.

Not a word from Sirany Tauran, sitting a duty post like crew.

It's out of control.

Crew's not talking. Stations are too quiet. What are they thinking, for godssakes?

Last run we make, and we know it, don't we? It's not what we used to be. None of us are that.

She coughed. "We got one of those gods-be black things loose somewhere up here, gods know where it'll land when we maneuver, just want you to know that."

"Gods," someone muttered. And it was as if the whole crew drew a collective breath and loosened collective muscles. "What say?" Tully asked plaintively, lost as usual. "What say?"

"Captain said—" Khym began.

"Movement on *Nekkekt*," Geran said monotone, deliberate monotone. As Haral prioritied scan up. No emergency. That was where it had to be.

"Transmission," Hilfy said. "Skkukuk's passing your orders to the kif. Ordering the clans and the mahendo'sat to clear out of their way."

"Confirm that to our allies."

A pause. A longer-than-one-breath pause. Then: "Aye." And compliance, rapid pushing of buttons.

"Captain." Chur's voice, quiet, very quiet. Strain was in it. "I got this idea—"

"Spill it.'

"The kif. They know their enemy. They turned round here. Akkhtimakt's ships—" The voice faded out, restored itself. "They knew it was sprung, the trap— They've been here—how long? Jik went on—but there's others—"

"Timetables. Gods. The mahendo'sat know there's a second wave, they knew it. Hilfy. Transmit: *Hasano-ma*. My gods, we've been sitting on that code program—Jik's letter. Run the coded parts through. Spit it on at them. Send it out on the Ajir vector. Put our wrap on it and get the mahendo'sat—gods, gods, gods, the man gives us a key and a coder and we sit on it."

"That'll worry the kif some."

"Good! They love it. Jik. Jik, gods rot it—no, he hasn't gone on. He doesn't have to jump all the way to Ajir, b'gods, he can *stop* out there, stop, turn, and get back here, and the kif know it, they know it, *that's* why they're stalled. Akkhtimakt's run into a trap, and his ships saw it coming, by gods, he was already pinned here thanks to Ayhar— We came in and his ships panicked; and defected; and now they don't know what to do."

"Kill their captains," Haral said grimly. "*That's* what they're doing, you want to lay odds to it? One place they're not going is back to Akkhtimakt. That bastard's gone. Run to the deep for sure, and his crew will kill him and turn that ship around if they can stop fighting mahendo'sat long enough: they'll be out of there and back through here like a shot if they get half a chance."

"Tirun. What's the mahen AOS?"

"Good eight minutes."

She gnawed at her mustaches. A good hour Light to the

nadir range. Maybe two out, if there was a mahen force out there lurking.

Gods blast you, Jik—throw the hani at it again, do you? Use us for a decoy. Set us up. Unless you're already on your way. And you won't be, will you? It's a trap the kif understand. The lurking kind. That's *why the kif flinched, why I've got me a dozen kif out there trying to figure out whether to listen to me now and turn on me later—*

They don't know what might come through out there first. Anything could. If it's Goldtooth they better have joined me. If it's Sikkukkut they better not have. Poor bastards. What's a kif to do but stall?

And Skkukuk, that gods-be conniving son is out there risking his neck because it's logical. *He's mine. He senses I'm against the* hakkikt *and Sikkukkut's going to kill him right along with the rest of us, that's what's going on in that earless head of his—he's taking all he's got and charging the bastards headon with the widest bluff he can run—*

Gods, can you call a kif brave?

"We got a—"

"Priority!" Geran cried. "Blip's in, bearing zenith ten, twenty two, ten. . . ."

The scan image flashed red-rimmed, flashed red on the newly arrived blip—

"Knnn!" Hilfy said. "That's knnn output—"

"Vector, vector—"

A line popped onto the course diagrams, the whole perspective shifted, rotated, showed it passing through system on a trajectory right past them, while the dopplered image flashed to yellow: "Going right through system fringes," Geran said, "passing within—Tyri orbit to nadir range."

"Gods, I don't like this." That was Sirany. Quietly.

"All sorts of strange fish," Pyanfar muttered. "Goldtooth. They ran right before Goldtooth at—"

"Priority, priority, we got another one—"

"It's here," Haral said. As the scan image acquired another blip that blinked and came ahead. The knnn kept dopplering, the image rotating to show relative position: comp had the hazard warning blinking all round the edges. "Same course."

"Not knnn," Pyanfar said. "That thing's might not be knnn, I got this terrible feeling—"

"*Fake* a knnn ID?"

"Who'd dare fire on it? Put the armaments on track. Warning to all ships: Hilfy."

"Aye."

"Armaments locked," Tirun said. "And tracking."

"It's just gone kifish; it's *Harukk!*"

"Gods *rot*— To all ships. Inertial!"

"Slow him down?" Haral was mind-reading again. *The Pride*'s mains cut out abruptly, an abrupt feeling that *down* was no longer aft, bodies were suddenly *not* lying flat on backs but attracted weakly seatward under the slight rotation—the whole board went blurred a moment in her eyes and a feeling of vertigo and panic came over her—

"We've got—got to play it step by step. Hope to gods Sikkukkut's being smart again, smart'll hang him—*no*body understands the *han*." A screen flashed change. More kif were dropping into system. IDs multiplied. *Harukk. Ikkhoitr.* Others of the old association.

It was very quiet for a moment. Just ship after ship dropping out of hyperspace.

And hani ships biding in prudent silence. Even Ehrran. No moves but the cutting of thrust, instant and undisputed. Keep the formation. They were still ripping along at more speed than insystem navigation rules permitted.

Think, fool. That kif's either fired or talked out there, the other side of Light. Do one or the other.

"Com to my board." The readylight flashed link to com one. *Gods, they got our message wavefront out there, everything Chur's sent out, kifish and human: and they can't crack the human stuff.* "Get scan relayed out there, give 'em everything we know. Fast." She punched the mike in. "*Harukk*, welcome to Anuurn: this is Pyanfar Chanur, aboard *The Pride of Chanur*. Akkhtimakt is defeated, his ships have defected, praise to the *hakkikt*. If enemies follow you we are ready."

"*That's* by the gods sure," Haral said under her breath, when she punched out. Haral's ears were flat. Pyanfar found her left hand clenched on the seat, claws right through the leather.

So what's he done? Fired or talked?

Farther and farther.

"*They're dumping!*" Geran yelled, and a yell and a collective breath and a gasp went through the bridge. "Thank gods," someone said. Tully muttered something humanish and faint.

"Keep transmitting that message," Pyanfar ordered. "Repeat, repeat."

"We've got it going," Hilfy said.

Five ships. Five, six ships in the system now. *Harukk* and *Ikkhoitr*. And another one. Seven.

How many? Gods, how many? Did he get away free? Run early and save his ships?

He's got to have lost some. At Meetpoint. At Kura, if the mahendo'sat got there from Ajir. They've got to have done that. Run them through that gauntlet and peel a bit more flesh off them. Give us some help, *for godssakes!*

Eight now. Nine and ten, widely separated.

"Priority," Hilfy said, "from *Harukk*-com: gods, it's code, we got some kind of code, it's for those ships back there. . . ."

"Keep our transmission going."

The ache grew around her heart, grew and grew. The blood pounded in her temples. Not a sound from the ships around them, nothing from the ships behind, yet . . . yet. Light had a little lagtime for them.

"*Nekekkt*'s answering," Hilfy said. "All code."

So what are you doing, Skkukuk? What are you up to? Who's in charge on that ship?

Twelve. Thirteen ships. Fourteen.

"*Priority.*" Com came through direct to her earplug. "*Instruction from the* hakkikt, *praise to him. Restore buoy output to our ships. Surrender this system and all its ships instantly. It will exist under the authority of my* skku *Pyanfar Chanur, whose orders come from me. Cease all hostilities. You are dealing with the* mekt-hakkikt *Sikkukkut an'nikk-tukktin, who allots the rule of this system and its adjuncts to his vassal Chanur.*"

She let the breath hiss softly. *Gods-be, what must they think now, Rhean and Anfy and Harun and Banny and the rest—what in a mahen hell do the kif back behind me think, and what kind of a move have I made with Skkukuk?*

Then: *Gods help me, I've got it, I've got it all, everything in my hands to protect, my people, my allies. He's not shooting.*

Now what do I do?

"Reply: Pyanfar Chanur to the *mekt-hakkikt* Sikkukkut an'nikktukktin, praise to his foresight, his enemies are under my hand."

Ambiguity. *Gods save us all.*

Haral had looked her way. And there was that little black thing slinking back from the galley, in a hurry, as if Tauran crew in there had done something violent.

"Smart is all we got," she said to Haral. "I remember what Goldtooth said. We get this situation calmed down a little and then I go for a little visit to *Harukk*. That's what. We take Goldtooth's suggestion. Snuggle up to this kif and get him."

"The two of us," Haral said.

"No. *You* got a ship to run. Get our *V* and *Harukk*'s matched, that's what we got to do. I'd hit him now if we had the angle and his *V* to use, but we can't break through those shields, slow as we are."

Haral kept looking at her. She was talking about suicide. Haral knew it. Haral also knew the other plain fact, that their armaments were nothing against hunter-ship armor— unless one or the other in the encounter had *C*-fractional velocity to add to the impact, virtually head-on. And Sikkukkut, praise to his wily kifish heart, was not obliging them.

" 'Bout the only thing we can do, don't you think?"

"You mean just board and shoot him pointblank."

"Hey, they never have been too fussy about us carrying weapons. Kifish etiquette's on our side, isn't it?"

"Yeah," Haral said.

"He'll ask me aboard. You wait and see. I get my chance, and then you blow his vanes if you can. I don't have to tell you. You know what you're doing." A look aside at Haral. Old partner. Old friend. The one who just as well could have captained *The Pride* a long, long time ago. Who right now looked at her with that stolid calm behind which was a great deal of pain. "Long time."

"Yeah," Haral said again. "Watch out for *Ikkhoitr*, that's what I got to do. But that's not your job in there right now. No one but you's got the credentials, hear me?"

"Nobody *else* can get close to the gods-be kif—"

"He's going to be expecting a move like this. That's *why*

no one else can get close to him. This is why it doesn't work for the kif. No percentage in it. You do it, Py, and we got ourselves a kif ball-up right here in the system."

"We just got to get me inside there, that's what we got."

"We got those mahendo'sat hanging off system. We still don't know where Goldtooth is—he could come tearing through here any minute, f'godssakes, him and the whole clutch of humans. We got that message going out to the mahendo'sat. Jik's coming in here—don't do it. Don't throw yourself into that mess. We just stay tight here, we talk to that bastard as long as he wants to talk, we got to hold our *nerve,* captain, that's what we got to do. We got to just bide our time and hope to—"

"Captain," Hilfy said. "We got a query from *Vigilance.* Query, query, query, quote. That's all they say."

"Gods *rot* that nest of lunatics. Tell 'em shut it down. My gods, they'll blow this up yet. Tell 'em— No. Tell 'em what I said. Shut it up. Next ship transmits out of turn I'll have some ears for it, say that. Tell *Harukk* again the system is stable and his enemies are in retreat. Say that we have a contingent of mahendo'sat insystem in support of Jik, who's gone on in pursuit of Akkhtimakt. Say that we're ready to meet and arrange things."

Eighteen ships in. The range out there was a confusion of ship IDs and colors as ships downshifted their *V* and others kept arriving.

"Aye," Hilfy said.

"Captain," Tully said. "Wrong. Ship wrong."

"Gods." Geran's voice. "No ID on that last ship. It's not outputting. We got an anomaly out there."

Her heart sped. "Track and target. Get me vector on it."

"Working," Sif said.

It was behind the others. The line popped up, projecting course right with the rest of the mass.

Chapter 14

It kept coming, a ship on which ID squeal had malfunctioned.

But that kind of malfunction was a kifish trick.

A pirate trick.

"My gods. It's not theirs. It's not theirs, they know it—
stand by, stand by armaments!" Pyanfar shoved her arm
into the brace and gulped air in starkest panic. "Haral!
Control to me!"

"Aye," Haral said on the instant, went over to switcher-
one while Tirun busied herself with the tracking of the
armaments.

"What *is* it?" Sirany wondered from her vantage.

"A stray," Pyanfar said. "It's a godsforsaken stray, Goldtooth's or—"

"Priority!" Geran yelled, but it was already clear on the
screen: the interloper had not dumped, and something else
had come out from it: missile fire, projectiles launched *C*-
fractional at ships that were relativistically stationary targets dead ahead of it.

"Priority!" Hilfy cried. "It's Tahar! That's *Moon Rising!*
My gods, she's going to run right through them!"

"Track on *Harukk!*" Pyanfar yelled, and slammed the
mains in. "All ships, fire at will—tell 'em that's an ally
coming through!"

The armaments were tracking. Missiles launched with a
thump and a shock against their own substance. Dead
against *Harukk*, everything they owned to throw, hard as
they could throw it.

"Ikkhoitr!" Pyanfar yelled over the whine of reloading.
"Tirun, get their vanes. Never gods-be mind the others!
Hilfy, give me output!"

"You got it," Haral said. "Tully, output! Talk to humans, got it?"

In the case there was anything back there to talk *to*. All kinds of com ready-lighted, human channel, mahendo'sat, kif, hani, while that dopplering ghost that was *Tahar's Moon Rising* came ahead pouring fire at a single target, savvy and deliberate.

"This is the *mekt-hakkikt* Pyanfar Chanur: Akkhtimakt is fallen and Sikkukkut has run here pursued by a thousand enemies who are my allies, hammered between mahen forces and the unity of *han*. In this *pukkukta* I give you a chance, *Chakkuf, Nekekkt!* You've served us well on this voyage. You have my favor now! Hani ships and mahendo'-sat, be sure of your targets! *Harukk* is your target, and any other ship which fires in our direction! Make no mistakes! Kifish ships, run from this system and my agents will hunt you down even to Akkht! Join us in this hunt and become among the first of my *skkukun*, all of you strong enough to maintain your place! Hani, fire your loads and scatter!"

This while *The Pride* belched out all the missiles and all the fire it had; while a deluge of fire converged from the ships in formation. Something came over com, overhead, general address: a hani voice, a familiar voice:

"Here's from us, you godsforsaken motherless son of a nightwalker! Hearth and blood! from me and my crew!"

"Tahar!" Pyanfar cried. "Gods rot you, *I forgive you!*"

A timelag off in messages. The kif had only limited fire-sweep aft, because of its own vanes, and it had to track a ship whose missiles were only scantly lagged behind its com-wave, the difference between realspace *V* and light-speed. Tahar's missiles hit: others were still incoming from all points of the sphere.

"*Chanur,* mekt-hakkikt!" another voice came blasting into her ear. *"I am here, behind you, praise your foresight! Our ships are coming!"*

"Whose in a mahen hell is that? Is that *Skkukuk?*"

"It's coming from *Nekekkt,*" Hilfy said.

"Time to get out of here," Pyanfar cried, "transmit, hani ships: Scatter, scatter." She reached and rang the collision warning for the Tauran crew off in the galley, kicked *The Pride* bow-nadir and threw in the mains with all they had.

It was all they could do to evade return fire, some ships rising, some going wide, some diving systemwise, like the blooming of some vast flower, each as they finished their load of missiles and got down to the beam guns. Tirun kept the guns tracking as they dived, firing for all they were worth.

It was still forward motion they made; but it was angular, kiting along skewed and hurling all the energy the mains had to give to that slew toward nadir.

Gods grant—

"Hai!" The whole ship banged and slewed violently, so that the course was different than it had been— "What'd we lose?" she yelled. "Gods rot it, what blew?"

"Vanes—" Tirun started to say.

Second impact, like the loudest thunder that ever cracked: the ship jumped sideways and a whole panel started flashing red. A small black body went hurtling and hit the wall, a black blur til it hit: it scrabbled right across the top of the control panel and Pyanfar swallowed and spat a red spatter that shocked her as much as the sound, only then feeling what her teeth had done to the inside of her mouth. "Gods *fry* that kif bastard—you all right?" The cursed black thing was as terrified as the rest of them, fellow in misfortune. It ran and screamed in rage: she did not even hit at it when she had the chance. There were too many switches for two hands, too many systems over to backup and third backup and past. *"Damage report, gods rot it!"*

"Chur," Tully's anxious voice came. "Chur!"

"We lost the whole vane, I think it slewed down into the mains." Tirun's voice, hoarse and breathless. And the firing of the guns resumed, realigned to the new track, while gods knew where they were going.

"Priority," Geran said, "we got fire over us—our kif are moving, the mahendo'sat are moving—we're clear of it—"

"Industry's bad hit," Hilfy reported. "Khym—Chur—"

"I'm with you." Chur's own voice, weak as it was.

"Cease fire, cease fire."

While the mains slammed away at them. Then it was a matter of finding their bearings, getting the skewed *V* shaved down. She got a screenful of garble out of Tracking, reoriented to bring the dishes and receptors to optimum—

no matter which direction *The Pride* was physically headed: coherent data started coming up.

And camera image, an area of flares in the battle zone as *The Pride* began rollover to brake.

She looked round at her own bridge, still swallowing blood, saw all the stations still working. Wiped her mouth and glanced back again at the images Haral sent her way.

It was still happening out there. But more slowly. There were ships in wreckage out there, blown in those flares. She earnestly hoped one of them was *Harukk*.

She remembered Stle stles stlen. And felt a chill as she hit the com-button, the contact still live. "This is the *mekthakkikt* Pyanfar Chanur. Report."

"*Praise to the* hakkikt," a kifish voice came back eventually. "*We give you your enemies.*"

And others began, a flood of ship names, *Nekkekt. Chakkuf. Ikkhoitr* itself, declaring fervent loyalty.

Not a hani voice. Not a one.

Or a mahendo'sat.

"This is *The Pride of Chanur* to all hani ships: acknowledge status; hold other transmissions pending. Thank you."

She sat there staring after. And shaking, little tremors which had nothing to do with the stench of dead air in the ship and the ozone and the fact that the bridge fans had stopped working. Or that there was a periodic and rhythmic shock against the hull which was some piece of debris trailing and still in motion while the mains hammered away at their drift.

Just the bridge sounds and the distant thunder of the mains. And a great loneliness.

"Everyone all right? Is everyone all right?"

"I got a patch on it." Khym's voice. "It's all right."

"Galley." Sirany's voice on general com. "You all right in there?"

"I think I got a broken rib," the answer came back. "But we're all right, how's it going, captain?"

"Going to go stable in a while, hold on."

Stable. My gods, they're killing each other up there. Kif are butchering each other in the corridors of those ships out there, kif are doing what kif do when they win and others lose, and how many ships have we lost out here? What do we do, hit the kif now while they're confused?

*The kif would. If they had our options. Poor naive sons.
They don't understand what's all round them. They don't
understand what hani are capable of.*

Fire on them—and change us forever.

Do that—and be sure there is a forever.

"You want me to trim us up?" Haral asked, while several
channels of com talked away, getting damage reports out of
other ships, ascertaining casualties. *Fortune* reported minimal
damage. *Light* was going to have to limp into dock. There
were others. The information came up on the screens.

Ayhar's Prosperity: damage: no casualties.

Harun's Industry: heavy damage: braking and maneuvering positive. Casualties: four.

Faha's Starwind: heavy damage: casualties: two.

Pauran's Lightweaver: vane gone: casualties: minor.

Ehrran's Vigilance: no damage: no casualties.

Nirasun's Melody: minor damage: no casualties.

Shaurnurn's Hope: lost.

Tahar's Moon Rising: out of contact.

Suranun's Fairwind: out of contact.

The list went on. More and more names. They blurred
in her sight. As *The Pride* braked, and the stress hammered
away at them.

Then: "Priority, priority," Geran exclaimed. As scan
started blinking furiously. "Breakout zenith."

Ships were coming in. A lot of them. One; and three
more. And five.

"O my gods," Sirany breathed.

"If it's Akkhtimakt—"

Then the ID started flashing. Mahendo'sat.

Mahijiru.

"Goldtooth," Pyanfar muttered, and slammed her fist
down on the console rim. "Goldtooth, gods rot him— *Now*
he shows up. Now, by the gods, now he comes chasing in
here, comes in here with by the gods bastard frigging
mahen interests, to sweep up the poor godsforsaken hani
they've done it to *again,* b'gods greater and lesser, one
more frigging time we bleed for them, their godscursed
meddling selfish gods-be-feathered interests! *Tully!*"

"Aye, cap'n!"

"Get on that com, hear, *com!* Fast. Tell the humans no
shooting, understand, *don't shoot!*"

"Don't shoot, I got, I got, cap'n!"

It started going out.

And hard on it: *"Mahijiru,* this is *The Pride of Chanur.* Cease fire, cease fire. These are allied ships. Dump and brake and hold off. Do not transit the system. Other mahen ships hold the approach to Ajir: nothing passed here beyond their capacity to deal with and mahen authorities in that direction are forewarned. Repeat: the Ajir approach is defended by mahen ships. Stay where you are. All mahen ships anywhere receiving: this is Pyanfar Chanur on *The Pride of Chanur:* cease all hostilities. End. Repeat that." She slumped back then, at the end of her energies. "Till response."

"We have a transmission from *Vigilance.* They register protest."

"Tell 'em—tell 'em we note it. Tell them—" It was easier and easier to think in kifish mode. "Stand in line, gods rot it. And consider where they are."

There were more and more ships arriving in the range. It was nightmare. If it had been an hour earlier it would have been a rescue.

By that much, you cursed bastard. By that much you missed it.

By that much Tahar was almost with us. Across all that space. Goldtooth must have held Sikkukkut—must have pinned them down good. The kif must have thrown something at him again at Kura. Must have—gods know what they did. Keeping Sikkukkut from overjumping us. When he came in here he was desperate. Needing me, for godssakes. He couldn't fire on me, I was the last hope he had.

We got ships out there—needing help.

"Human ship!" Tully cried. And talked to someone a steady stream of babble, as if they were on the same timeline. It was Tully's old message those incoming ships must have picked up. It was the old message they had responded to.

The same as Goldtooth must have gotten their own former chatter, and known well what ships were out to meet the enemy. She cut the mains, let them go inertial on what they still had, on the rotational *G.*

While Tully poured out something, rapid and urgent. And went on saying it. One assumed it was friendly. One assumed nothing nowadays.

She felt a hundred years older. And turned herself and her chair and looked over the bridge, at a crew worn and tired beyond clear sense, at more gray hair than she recalled a few weeks ago. Or maybe it was the stark lighting. Or maybe it was that they all looked older, thinner, abraded away by distances and a load they had carried too long.

I want to see Chanur again.

But Chanur land was Mahn territory. Nothing could change that, unless Kohan could take Kara Mahn; and the weary, grayed man who had met her on Gaohn docks had not the strength left. The wit, yes; the wit and the will and the canny good sense that had been more than figurehead in Chanur these many hard years. A real power. A mind and an insight shrewder than many a woman's. But time bore down on Kohan, that was all. The only hope was Hilfy Chanur, who might find herself a man to take care of Kara Mahn: there was nothing Pyanfar Chanur or Rhean or any of the former powers could do about it any longer.

She saw Hilfy sitting there, talking to someone, likeliest one of the nearby hani. *Up to you, kid. It all is, from now on. Our time is done. You think you've grown up. You're Chanur now, have you figured it out? I don't envy you.*

Except your youth. I wish I'd known you and you'd known me forty years ago. They looked like rough years then. But the years you've got ahead—I can't see into them. Like there was something in the way of me and this ship, like a curtain I can't see past.

I always used to know where I was going. And now all I can see is aliens. And all I can think of is the mistakes I've made; and how to get this straight somehow.

Her eyes drifted to Tully. To him. The alien among them. *It's an enemy at his back, isn't it?*

I got to be, Tully, poor Tully, I got no choice. You warned me, and I see it clear, I see everything down that way with no trouble at all, and I'm going to do you hurt, I can't turn back from that.

You gods-be knew it, didn't you? Knew it from the time you came to us. Always thinking, never talking. Afraid of me and not afraid. For two good reasons.

What'll they do to you when I'm through? Where'll you go? My friend.

"Hilfy. Get me Banny."

"I got *Prosperity* right now. You want Banny in person?"

"I want her." She turned the chair back square to the board and punched in. "Banny. Banny, you hear me?"

"Such as it is, Chanur. It looks like we got help out there."

"I don't know how much the mahendo'sat told you, Banny, but we got some other visitors out there and I can't talk about it real clear just now: we got politics here. I'm asking hani ships to form up; I'm going to ask the kif to do the same and they're going to do it, Banny, they're going to do it. Then we're going to have to do some talking—you want to take charge of the hani ships for me, just keep it kind of quiet and trust me. We're not out of this yet. We got a real problem here. A real problem. Banny."

There was prolonged silence.

"Banny. Haurosa naimur f'fhain'haur murannarrhm'ha chaihen." *Ambush in the trees, Banny. . . .*

More of the long silence. "Accepted."

That was the first thing.

The next was harder.

"Message, Hilfy: tell the kifish ships to put themselves in order and stand by for instruction. Stop all forward drift."

"Aye."

"Chur: transmission to *Mahijiru.* Quote: This is Pyanfar Chanur. Hold your ships where they are. Your Personage is aware of the kifish advance; mahen ships were in position to prevent escape by the Ajir corridor. Ajir corridor, repeat, is secure. We ask you dump all *V* and wait. This situation insystem is still extremely volatile. The kif remaining here are under my personal direction and within *han* jurisdiction. I ask you instruct your allies to total dump and recall all other mahen ships to your group immediately. Cease all hostile operations. All ships are in *han* jurisdiction. Repeat, request immediate total dump and hold pattern. Endit and repeat at intervals. Transmission to *Nekkekt:* This is the *mekt-hakkikt* in person. Permit withdrawal of mahen ships from center system. Continue to reduce all *V:* cease all drift toward mahen position. Take no action against mahendo'sat. Wait orders. Endit." She slumped back in the chair. Waited with her claws clenched.

"That's a dump," Geran said finally. And she began to breathe freely again. More when they saw the second one.

But attacking ships might do as much.

Then *Mahijiru* took the third dump, coming down to in-system velocities.

"Thank gods, thank gods," she muttered. And over com: "Banny, we're gaining on it. We got it stopped." Out on that channel. "Hilfy. Get me Goldtooth."

"Working. Lagtime ten nine."

Twenty-two on the roundtrip of messages. Far out in the range still. But Goldtooth had to be AOS on the initial message now. Ten minutes ago. Other ships incoming were observing the same sequence; and that was all but certain to be pre-arrangement.

Humans, migods, humans drug themselves senseless. We got doped-up pilots out there. Robotics. Gods know what.

They have to stop with the mahendo'sat. Stop and get their bearings. Or plan to blow the system to a mahen hell.

They wouldn't. Couldn't. Gods save us. They have to take Goldtooth's lead till they figure things out.

It's not over.

She drew a shaky breath. "We're going stable," she said on bridgecom. "Free to move about, arrange your own covers, five minutes, maybe longer: maybe ten, fifteen gods-be *days* out here, I dunno." She lifted shaking hands to her face, just shut out the sight of things if not the sound, and rested. Quietly some of the crew saw to themselves. "I'm all right," she heard Khym's low complaint. "Gods rot it, I can get to the gods-be head."

From her husband. Who had a hole in his leg and a plasm patch, a deep wound that had to be swollen and hurting if it was not worse than that. *She* wanted a trip to the head. Desperately. She decided to take the chance and unbuckled.

"Captain," Hilfy said. "*Nekkekt:* stand by replay."

"Uhhhhn." *It starts. Kif have sorted out. Who am I dealing with?*

And from the earplug. "Mekt-hakkikt, *I have all these ships in my hand, praise to you. We will strike at your order.*"

"Who am I talking to?"

"Mekt-hakkikt, *to your faithful Skkukuk. I have carried out all your orders. I will deal with all your enemies. Name them to me.*"

"Right now, Skkukuk, I'm just real glad to hear from you. You keep those ships of yours under control and you don't make a move without my direct order. Hear me?"

"I will give you your enemies' heads and hearts."

"I'm real fond of you too, Skkukuk. Just do what I said. You get your com linked up to mine and you stay in constant touch. Anyone twitches, I want to know about it. These hani with me are allies. They won't cause any trouble."

"And these mahendo'sat and these invaders?"

"Wait for my orders. That's all." She punched the contact out. She was trembling. She set her elbows on the counter and dropped her head a second time into her hands, wiped her mane back. Haral was still by her. Someone else was moving about. It was all distant. She had no wish to talk to anyone.

"Captain." It was Nifeny Tauran holding out a sandwich and a container of something liquid with a null-cap. The sight of it turned her stomach and attracted her shaking hand. Gfi. She took a sip of it, and felt another urge unbearably strong.

"I got to take a break," she said to Haral. "We got the gods-be kif, don't we?"

"Go," Haral said.

She spun the chair about and took her own way to the galley corridor and the head. The air everywhere seemed stagnant. *Three days and we'll have the whole gods-be life-support in a mess. We can't go that long. Crew's got to get that system up.*

She passed Tauran crew in the galley, one with wrapped ribs, sitting white-nosed at the table, the other capping up food as fast as she could. "We got a while stable. Get the slinkers out of the godsforsaken filters, get that lifesupport up."

"Aye," the Tauran said, a distracted, exhausted look till she realized who was talking to her. Then the ears came up. "Aye, cap'n."

She made the trip, into the closet of a head, came out and shouldered past Tirun on the same mission.

"Captain," sounded in the com-plug in her ear. *"We got Mahijiru. They're indicating that they want us to pull back to Gaohn. They're waiting for reply."*

"In a mahen hell," she muttered, and went through the galley, down the corridor with a hand to either wall, onto the bridge where she had sight of Hilfy and the rest. "Tell them hold that perimeter. We'll accept *Mahijiru* only. That ship can come in for conference, and we'll draw back to Gaohn. We're not having any others."

"Aye," Hilfy said. "We've got query from *Vigilance*," Sirany said. "Ayhar is telling them shut it down."

It was one more thing than she wanted to know. She hand-over-handed herself back to her own post, fell into it, and sat drinking at the gfi in minute sips that did not agitate her stomach.

It was a long wait for messages. Goldtooth and the humans were a long distance out.

She drank. She wiped her blurring eyes and leaned back against the seat in as much relaxation as she could take. While *The Pride* slewed on, inertial. The hani formation was spreading itself around the kif. *Vigilance* was far to nadir now and out of her way. Ayhar was considerably off to sunward and beginning to take some of the way off. So were others of the merchants, trimming up. Kifish ships were in hard decel, those going in both directions until they could take the speed off and achieve a coherent pattern.

But *The Pride* was going where it belonged. Out into the open. Where it formed no part of any group.

One of the calls Chur had handled, listed on monitor three: from Rhean: *Do you need assistance?* Reply: *Negative: fully operational; thanks.*

Another, from Ehrran: *Query, query, query.* Reply from Fiar: *All queries deferred. Your patience appreciated.*

One more, from Ehrran: *Protest lodged.* Reply from Hilfy: *Sink it in your own datafile; advise you kifish allies are monitoring your transmissions and misunderstandings are possible. For your own safety and safety of those near you maintain com silence.*

Tully's, through the translator: *This is # # Tully # # # call # # # # do not # # this is # # hani # # with # #. . . .* No reply listed.

From *Shanan's Glory*, far to the rear of the combat: *Shall we come in or hold position?* From Banny Ayhar, monitored: *Hold relative position. Maintain full-sphere surveillance.*

From Gaohn station: *This is Gaohn Central: general inquiry.* From Banny Ayhar, monitored: *Firing has stopped. Situation uncertain but improved.* Harun's Industry *will be making return to Gaohn with casualties for medical assistance and will courier details. Possibility of strike in your vicinity still exists but is less probable. Reserve other inquiry for* Industry. Chanur *remains in contact with various allied ships. Ayhar is directing hani ships in the zone of contact. . . .*

From Ayhar: *We have computed trajectory on missing ships. All vessels along these lines be alert to evade or assist as needed. . . .*

"Captain," Hilfy said. "Message from *Mahijiru*."

It had already hit the screen: *Ana Ismehanan-min advise you we got talk number one urgent.*

"Reply: Quote: *Mahijiru* is welcome alone. All other mahen and foreign ships must hold position. We will not support violation of our system borders by any agency however friendly. The approach of *Mahijiru* is clear and velocity should not exceed normal limits. Please convey to all your ships our thanks for their support, and proceed without escort to a point where we may conference without appreciable timelag. There is no urgency. I repeat the earlier advisement: few ships passed our system borders and there were more than adequate mahen forces on the outgoing vector to have handled the problem. Akkhtimakt is finished. Sikkukkut likewise. End. Repeat that at five till acknowledgment."

"Aye," Hilfy said.

She rested a moment then. Just rested, eyes shut, head against the seat back. It was all the rest they were going to get.

While around her, crew moved carefully about on necessary errands or took a chance to stretch. Chur Anify and Khym went offshift to the galley, their two walking wounded, while a pair of exhausted Tauran risked their necks trying to clean the lifesupport filters. Fans went on, highspeed, shut down again. Went on yet again, with a decided ozone smell in the air.

"*Mahijiru*'s moving," Tirun said finally, on cover for Geran. "*Priority, priority,* we've got a general movement all along their formation."

It was already on monitor, a sudden and ominous blinking all along the mahen front that sent her heart speeding.
"Message? Gods rot it, is he *saying* anything?"—while
crew, away from seats, in the galley, wherever they had
strayed to, came scrambling unordered: in-ear coms, and a
fine sense of disaster when it started.

"Negative. He's just started to move. All of them— We
got—got an inquiry from *Nekkekt,* quote: *Shall we attack?*
Advisories—"

Other crew hit the seats, low murmur of exchanged information, the passing of duties, briefings in two words and a
key punch that logged in: Geran, Hilfy. Others were already there. "I tell human stop," Tully protested. "Give
com."

"General output," Pyanfar snapped, as Haral hit the seat
beside her and logged on. "Hold steady. Message to *Mahijiru:* Hold position. Keep your ships back. We will not be
bluffed. Reply to query at once and brake. Endit and repeat. What's our lagtime?"

"Fourteen nine," Tirun said; and a hani message turned
up on channel two. *"Chanur, this is Ayhar. What in a
mahen hell is going on?"*

"Ayhar. Hold firm. Hold firm."

*"Hold firm! We got a half a hundred ships gone stark
lunatic! What do they think they're doing?"*

"They think they're getting through, they're pushing us,
that's what they think they're doing. Those are human ships
out there. Stand firm—"

"Mahijiru," a voice broke in on her into her left ear.
"Same Goldtooth. H'lo, Pyanfar, old friend!" Cheerful as
any dockside. *"Good hear you voice, same good find you
one piece. Long time chase, damn good job stop these bastard. Got you number one message, good news. You number
one fine, a? Same. Plenty ship. Same you tell these fine kif
they stand by, we make deal 'bout how they get home."*

"Mekt-hakkikt!" Into the right ear. *"We are tracking this
advance. Give us the order! We are your allies! This mahendo'sat is a devious and a ruthless liar! Take him!"*

"Goldtooth, I got a real anxious kif here. Now it's seven-
odd minutes ago, and if I don't see those ships of yours
start braking in thirty seconds from the time you get this,
I'm going to take some serious measures. I'll clip you good,

friend. *Your* ship. Now you stop, and you get ready to talk this out, you don't push your way here. You want an incident, you want trouble that's going to echo all the way to Iji, I got to serve you notice these hani ships aren't moving. I'm timing this real close. I know you, old friend. If I call your bluff like this, you'll shoot if I don't. So you better be doing what I say by now, because if you aren't, you got a fight coming. Endit. No repeat. *Time* that bastard. *Skkukuk!* You keep those ships of yours in line."

"Yes."

"Jik!" Hilfy's voice, between two beats of a panicked heart. "Jik's transmitting, incoming—"

"Negative scan," Geran said.

Lightspeed wavefront, inbound, the buoys not reporting and no one in position to pick him up.

"Pyanfar—" the thin voice reached her. *"We follow you fast we can, damn, you not engage, not engage—"*

He was talking about the kif. She realized that finally. He was that far away. Hours out.

Hours ago, when he had fired off that message, he had known Sikkukkut incoming and that a few fool hani were in a lot of trouble.

About his own partner, he could not know.

Nor could Goldtooth know that he was there. For seven more minutes.

"Goldtooth. I'm in contact with your partner now. Ismehanan-min. My friend. There's a lot of data you don't have. Critical information. It's Iji at stake. It's your border. We've got a kifish *hakkikt* here willing to talk borders. What we've got left at Meetpoint you know and I don't. But I've got a passenger, an old mutual acquaintance, who has some real important information. And I'm not talking to a fool, Goldtooth. I want a face-to-face meeting. You, me, a few old friends."

"One minute," Tirun said, timekeeping.

"At Gaohn. Dockside."

Chapter 15

The docks at Gaohn were deserted, with the profound chill that came of seals cutting off the air circulation, the deck-plates so cold they burned the feet; and Pyanfar limped a bit—had been limping since she rolled out of bed stiff and sore and knowing what there was yet to face.

There had been a little leisure, on the way back to Gaohn, a little time for *The Pride* to run at a decent, safe rate; for aching crew to tend their own needs and the ship's, and to catch a nap and a hot meal.

She went in spacer's blues. It was all she had left, and that was borrowed. She went with her own crew about her, and left *The Pride* in Sirany's capable hands.

Another lostling had turned up. Dur Tahar had quietly showed up on-scope, blinking in with an ID signal and turning out not to be a piece of hurtling wreckage. "Friggin' hell," Tahar had said when they got her on com: "you don't think I'm going to run my ID, *us*, while we got you standing off half the Compact and most every hani ship out here ready to blow us to dust and gone. I'm not coming in yet, Chanur. I'll meet with you or one of your ships, I'll let Vrossaru and her crew off, but I'm not going to go in to dock . . . not this old hunter. I'll just watch awhile."

"You running with Goldtooth? Or Sikkukkut?"

"Me? Gods upside down, Chanur, you got an exaggerated idea how fast we are. I got out on your tail, been following your emissions trail like a highway clear from Meetpoint, trying like hell to catch you up, but I blew two more systems making that gods-be Urtur shift: sorry if you had any fondness for that kif. Me, I owed him. Plenty."

"You godsforsaken lunatic! You could have blown us all."

This during two hours of timelagged exchange. And after

a longer than usual pause, in which she had thought Tahar might have quit talking: "Chanur, if you ever trusted that kif, you got something yet to learn. He made you too powerful, haven't you got it yet? So did the mahendo'sat. Do I have to tell you?"

She had sat there then, after Dur Tahar had in fact quit talking, a decisive signoff. She sat there receiving the information from Gaohn that a half dozen little light-armed freighters had scattered down the Ajir route with a precious cargo of hani lives, the men and children of the Syrsyn clans.

Seeds on a stellar wind.

And she looked Khym's way, her husband sitting backup duty at a quieter time on the bridge, taking his time at scan while exhausted senior crew took theirs at washup and rest. He did not notice that glance: his face, dyed with the light from the scope, was intent on business.

Whatever we lose here, she had thought then. *For all we failed in, one thing we did.*

There was one other man there on the bridge. And he did look her way. She thought she had seen every expression Tully's alien face had to offer. But this, that all the life seemed to have left him, no more of fight, as if something in him had broken and died. Except that the eyes lighted a moment, glistened that way they did in profoundest sorrow; and looked—O gods—straight at her. While Hilfy, leaving the bridge, paused to put her hand on his shoulder. For comfort. For—

"Come on," Hilfy had said. "Tully."

You know, don't you? Pyanfar had thought then. *You know she'll leave you now. Her own kind, Tully. She's Chanur now. The Chanur. And you're ours; even when you go back, your people won't forget that, will they? Ever.*

Gods help you, Tully. Whatever your name really is. Whatever you think you are and wherever you go now.

Like Tahar. They don't ever quite forget.

I'm no fool, that look of his said back to her. Neither of us are. We're friends.

And perhaps some other human, unfathomably complicated strangeness she could not puzzle out.

Tully came with them onto the docks this time. It was the second time for him onto Gaohn station, among staring and mistrustful hani, in a confrontation where he was a

showpiece, an exhibit, a pawn. They gave him weapons. The same as themselves. So he would know another important thing in a way the sputtering translator could not relay.
. Last of all she had caught hold of him in the airlock, taken him by the arm and made sure he was listening: "Tully. You can go with the human ships. You're free, you understand that. You know *free?*"

"I know free," he had said. And just looked at her with that gentle, too-wise expression of his.

Down the docks where a line of grim-looking Llun had set the perimeters of this meeting, the towering section seals in place on either end of this dock. There were stationer clanswomen, spacer clans. And a delegation from the *han* had come thundering up from the world, only just arrived. There were weapons enough. And Llun guards enough to discourage anything some hani lunatic might try.

The Llun marshals were no protection against the huntersships which had come in, snugged their deadly sleek noses up into Gaohn's vulnerable docking facilities, and disgorged their own guards and their own very different personnel. Three mahendo'sat, a human ship, and a trio of kif: besides *The Pride* and *Harun's Industry:* that was the final agreement. *Aja Jin, Mahijiru,* then one other mahen ship named *Pasarimu,* that had come in after Jik; *Nekkekt, Chakkuf, Maktakkt,* and finally something unpronounceable that Tully said for them three times and they still could not manage. The Human Ship, they called it by default.

The gathering on the dock was very quiet, and all too careful. Even Jik, who had on a dark cloak and kilt so unlike his usual gaud it took a second look to know it was Jik. Only a single collar, a solitary bracelet. An AP on his hip and a knife beside it. That was usual. Soje Kesurinan was there, brighter-dressed and no less armed. And with them some Personage walked with the captain of *Pasarimi,* complete with Voice, with all the appropriate badges. Official, yes. Indisputably.

There was Goldtooth, in the same dark formality. And his own escort. Not a flicker of communication passed between him and his partner.

Harun and Llun, a tired crew in spacer-blues, with Kauryfy herself in green and the Llun all in Immune black.

Another lot came in black: a mass of shadow drifted out from the perimeters, all alike in their robes, their hoods, their utter sameness to hani eyes, all bristling with weapons. One of them would be Skkukuk, but she could not find him by the clues she knew, the gait, the small gestures. There was a tall kif evidently in charge, one the others evidently gave place to.

Who is that? Is it my *kif?*

She feared it was altogether another. In one sense or another.

And the humans, from whatever-it-was. She had seen the like once before: different kinds of humans; different shapes; any species had that. But these varied wildly, some handsome in a Tully-way; some just strange. They all wore dark gray, all glittered with silver and plastics, body-fitting, skin-covering suits: even the hands covered. Not one was armed with anything that looked like a weapon. Com equipment. Plenty of that. They remained an enigma. And stopped, at about the distance everyone else had stopped, like points of a star.

Fear grew thick on this dockside: it was evident in the set of hani ears, in the way kif and mahendo'sat moved. In the way that Tully stayed right at their side, and no human advanced beyond the mahen perimeter.

There was another thing in the system. There was a very real knnn and a tc'a out there, singing to each other in harmonics of which the computer-translators which were supposed to handle such things made no sense but positional data. It was significant and ominous that the matrix of the harmonics had the position of Gaohn station in it.

The knnn were interested. That was more than enough to account for the fear.

But the representatives from downworld would hardly comprehend that much: they would, most likely, be getting their first look at a mahendo'sat, let alone kif or humans. And perhaps they had a resolution in their hands; or perhaps the debating was still going on, and Naur and Tahy Mahn *par* Chanur and others of that worldbound mindset were still arguing protocols and policies. Gods knew. If she let herself think about it she grew cold, killing mad.

They had set out a huge table, for godsake, a table and chairs there on dockside, the Llun's council furniture

moved out, that was what it was, hani council furniture, as
if all these factions could be gotten together, as if in all the
chaos and amid ships moving in with major damage and
injured, some fool (from Anuurn surface most likely) had
time to insist on tables and chairs which would hardly even
accommodate the anatomy of some of the invaders. With
knnn running around the neighborhood, and ships still at
standoff out there in the zenith range, over fifty of them
determined to force an issue and get passage through, others determined to move kif who would literally die of the
shame, and kif who were as doggedly determined to resist.

*Gods-cursed groundling fools. If that knnn out there
comes calling, we won't survive it. Do your resolutions understand that?*

Humans have fired on them. Tully says.

*Jik's played politics with the tc'a. Gods! does he know
what that is out there, is it something that's come for him,
for the mahendo'sat?*

*Tables. My gods, we're lucky to get these species within
shouting distance of each other! The kif never do anything
without the scent of advantage, they're here on a thread, on
the least thread of a suspicion that I'm their best way out.*

*And Jik and Goldtooth aren't talking, they're not looking
at each other, the crews don't mix—and who in their own
hell is the Personage Pasurimi came in with?*

*Came in with the ships out of mahen space, not the Kura
route. Came in, my gods, from Iji, that's where he's from.
That's someone from the homeworld.*

*That's Authority. That, with the Voice and the badges and
the robes. And he hasn't introduced himself. The Voice
hasn't spoken a word. The han's been insulted and they
don't even know it.*

*They're frozen. No one's not moving. It's the kif they
distrust.*

"Skkukuk," she guessed, taking the risk. And the foremost kif lifted his face the least degree, then lowered it,
belligerence and manners in two breaths. Even amiability.
For a kif.

"Mekt-hakkikt," that one said. So she knew it *was* Skkukuk. But he took it for a summons, and a panic seized on
her, instinctive aversion as that band of kif crossed the deck

plating and got between her and the mahendo'sat and the humans. And swung their weapons into line as they went.

"Weapons *down,* for godssake." The panic made her voice sharp. Skkukuk instantly hissed and clicked an order to his company. Weapons lowered. She grabbed the chance two-handed. "There's not going to be any shooting. On *any* side." One of the Llun came too close and she flattened her ears and rumpled her nose. "Get back, gods rot it." But the mahendo'sat had come closer too. Suddenly there were a great many guns, her own crew with their own rifles slung conspicuously toward level. "Back off!" Haral snapped at a graynosed hani who moved in with foolhardy authority. And shoved with the gunbutt.

"Chanur!" that hani shouted.

And faced three kifish rifles.

"Hold it! Sgokkun!" Her heart all but stopped. She physically struck a kifish rifle up, out of line; and that kif got back and stood clicking and gnashing its inner teeth, its fellows likewise confused.

"Mekt-hakkiktu sotoghotk kefikkun nakt!" Skkukuk snapped; there was quick silence.

Quiet then. Even the down world hani had it figured how precarious it was.

"We don't need any shooting," Pyanfar said, her own heart lurching and thumping and her knees shaking. Her voice gathered itself somewhere at the bottom of her gut. Khym was by her, *close* by her; between her and the hani, thank gods for his wits and his instincts. She waved a hand to clear the kif back and get a view of where the humans were, where the various mahendo'sat had gotten to; and the humans had stayed where they were, a good distance back. Goldtooth and his armed group had followed up all too close and Jik maneuvered to the side, both of them between the kif and the Personage. "Use your gods-be heads! Skkukuk, just stand there. Just stand. Goldtooth. Ana. We're all right here. You're not going to be using those guns; let's just all calm down, can we?"

"We come here talk. Same settle this mess." Goldtooth's dark brow was knit. He waved a hand indicating the perimeters. "We got knnn out there all upset. You got lousy mess, Pyanfar. Now I talk with you, you make big mistake."

"Yeah. I found out about that. Nice of you to tell me what you were doing. Nice of you to tell Jik, too."

"Jik got no choice. Got important hani, got human, all same mess at Kefk. Try to pull you out. You got go pull Tahar out, we don't 'spect same. Bad surprise, Pyanfar. Bad surprise. All same come out. We got Sikkukkut, got Akkhtimakt, both. We got no more worry with kif, a? So you let these fine kif go back to ship. They want go home, we let go. Best deal they got."

"Have no dealings with this person," Skkukuk said, beside her. "Our ships are the defense of this system. We are faithful, *mekt-hakkikt.*"

No threats, no untoward move. The hair prickled down her back. It was not subservience in this kif. Just quiet. The intimation of power, but not quite enough power: the kif was here, talking. It was a move Sikkukkut excelled at, but this kif was smoother, and Goldtooth was giving good advice, O gods, if there were a power that could shove the kif back to their borders and keep them there.

That power was standing right in front of her. A mahen-human association.

If she did not know what she knew, from Tully, about what humans stood to gain. About human powers currently at each others' throats, and spread over an area that would, could! (a single look at the starcharts told that) dwarf the Compact.

"I have to know," she said, quietly, reasonably, to Goldtooth, "what happened to the stsho." Like it was gentle concern. It was desperation. It was suddenly their bulwark on that side, their trading-point. Without them—

Does he see? Does he suspect why I ask? He's no fool, was never a fool, O gods, this is one of half a dozen minds that rules the whole godshelpus Compact, he always was, he's one of those the mahendo'sat just turn loose to do things on the borders, things that echo years across civilized space. He still is. Even with a Personage here.

"We do fine." An unlooked-for voice. Jik had pulled out one of his abominable smokes and was in the process of lighting it, as if those dark eyes of his were not alert to every twitch from hani and kif. "Ana tell me he get there number one fine, three, four day fight. Chew up Sikkukkut good. Fine for us here. Our friend Sikkukkut—" He capped the lighter and drew in a second lungful of smoke. "He know then damn sure he got trouble. We owe damn lot to Banny Ayhar. Same you, friend. Same all hani come spread alarm."

"The stsho—"

"Little damage. Lot confuse. Methane-folk take care real good." A gesture with the back of the hand with the smokestick, vaguely outward. "Same knnn. Offi-cial, a? With tc'a interpreter. Same be tc'a been long time with."

"The same from Mkks?"

"A. Same all way from Kshshti. Tt'om'm'mu been real co-operative."

"Then it *is* your agent."

A wave of the fingers, amid a hani and a kifish murmuring. "Same talk lot people, a? I tell you, Ana—shoshi na hamuru-ta ma shosu-shinai musai hasan shanar shismenanpri ghashanuru-ma shesheh men chephettri nanursai sopri sai."

Dialect, thick and impenetrable. It had as well be coded. But Goldtooth's face went guarded, his eyes darker, with the least small shift toward the left.

Toward Tully. Just that little twitch.

It was a guess what Jik had said. Or how much. A second shift of the eyes, that little degree that showed a white edge around the brown. Back to her this time. "Nao'sheshen?"

"Meshi-meshan." Jik tilted his head back, a gesture behind him. "Meshi nai sohhephrasi Chanuru-sfik, a?"

It did not please Goldtooth, whatever it was. "Shemasu. We talk. We talk plenty. We tell Personage. You tell these kif go. Now. We deal with methane-folk. You fix stuff here."

"*Fix* stuff!" She caught her breath and her wits in the same gulp after air, saw backs stiffen left and right and lowered her voice instantly. The *han* was back there. The Llun. There was a deafening silence.

"Kkkt," Skkukuk said. "Kk-kkt. This mahe does not dictate here. There will be *no* escort. There will be *no* mahen ships in our territory. Do not be deceived."

"We talk later," Goldtooth said, and got one step.

Weapons came up. In one move. So did mahen weapons.

"*Hold* it!" Pyanfar yelled, and shoved a rifle barrel. A kif's. It was momentarily safer.

"Chanur," a hani voice began.

"Shut *up*," Tirun said.

"Let us begin it here," Skkukuk said. While Jik put himself between the kif and Goldtooth. Carefully.

"Let's not." Out of the peripheries of her vision she saw a human movement, a quiet melting away of certain of that group toward cover. "Tully! Stop them."

Tully shouted out, instant and shockingly alien and fluent. With an uplifted hand. And that motion stopped.

"Cease this!" the Voice snapped, and said something else in mahensi, too fast and too accented to follow.

"Withdraw them," a hani said. Downworlder, graynosed. Elderly and overweight. *My gods, Rhynan Naur. That gray, that old.* The voice rang with something of its old authority in the *han.* "We will not have our space violated. We will not countenance—"

Skkukuk's rifle swung that way. "Don't," Pyanfar said sharply. "Gods rot it—shut up, Naur. Everybody. Don't anybody move."

"You Personage," Jik said at her left, at Skkukuk's. "You want stop, *you* got stop. Shemtisi hani manara-to hefar ma nefuraishe'ha me kif."

"Trust that we will do that," Skkukuk said, all hard and with jaw lifted ominously. "We do not intend to take any voyage in your company."

"We got solution." Jik winced and pinched out the smokestick that had burned down to his fingers. "Pasuru nasur. Kephri na shshemura, Ana-he. Meshi."

"Meshi ne'asur?"

"Lot better. Same I say." Jik looked her way. "We got *spacer* hani, same. Sikkukkut be damn fool doublecross you, a? Damn fool. All time I say you lot smart. Got whole lot *sfik,* whole lot stuff, Pyanfar Chanur—same like I say. Same Ana here find you, same Sikkukkut want you—damn good. Now you got say like Personage, you got make decide."

"Decide, *decide,* f'godssakes, there's no *decide.* We got you and the kif trying to blow each other to the hereafter all through our solar system—"

"You Personage. You got kif. You want deal for the *han?*"

"I don't deal for the *han!* I'm telling you, me, Pyanfar,

you talk to your Personage and tell him what Tully told us."

"I do." Jik looked at her in a strange and maddening way. "You not be *han.* You be Personage. Send *hakkikt* back to kif—how you guarantee, a? Stoheshe, Ana." With a glance at Goldtooth. And back again. "The *han* decide this, decide that. You do what you want with *han.* But the *han* be for Anuurn. You be Personage for hani, Personage for kif, same Tt'om'm'mu want save you life. You got the Person-thing. Born with. You understand this?"

"What are you talking about, for godssakes?"

"You no damn fool. You see. You see clear. Sikkukkut get power by create little *hakkikt* and take what they got. Let them do work. He lot smart kif. Till he make you *hakkikt* and try take what you got. You got the Person-thing. He think he got more, he damn lot mistake. We don't mistake. This kif here don't mistake. You got whole thing in you hands. Me, *I* recognize. Same like this kif. Long time."

"No. My gods, no!" She waved her hand, cast a look at the hani behind her, at her crew and back again.

"War, friend. What I tell you happen? Not war like ground war. War like new kind thing. Like crazy thing."

"Then send your gods-be human friends home! *Out!* Turn those ships around, restore the balance, for gods-sake!"

"How you guarantee Anuurn be safe, a? How you heal stsho? How you 'splain these human we got change mind? How you deal with knnn, a?"

A sense of panic closed in on her. Not alone because it was all logical, and the pieces were there. She looked around again at the hani lines, at her own people, at some faces gone hard and ears gone flat. At others, spacers, who just looked worried. Like her crew.

Like Goldtooth.

And not a sound from the kif.

The politicians would hang her, eventually, when all the furor died down. It was the last shred of Chanur's reputation they asked for.

"Yeah," she said. "Well, it's clear, isn't it? We just tell these humans they have to leave. That you consulted with some high Personage and there's a lot of trouble and they just have to turn those ships around and get back the other side of that border. Which we can do, can't we? It just might give Skkukuk here a good chance to go home in style, number one fine—a whole shift in policy, a new *mekthakkikt,* a new directive. I'm not real interested in going *into* kifish space, Skkukuk my friend: I'm just real pleased for you to be *hakkikt* over all the kif you can get your hands on. And all you have to do is hold that border tight once the humans cross it outbound."

"Kkkt." Skkukuk drew in a hissing breath. "*Mekthakkikt,* you justify my faith in you."

"You won't cross into mahen territory."

"They won't cross into ours."

"They won't." Looking at Jik. And Goldtooth. Goldtooth lowered his small ears and bowed his head slowly, with reluctance.

"I hear," he said quietly. And made the same gesture to Jik, and to the Personage as he turned away.

Something's wrong with him. Something mahen and crazy, and something I don't know: I've done something to him. I've beaten him.

Two plans. Two treaties. The mahendo'sat rise and fall on their successes; and they disown the failures.

"If I've got to run this business for a while," she said to Jik, "I want him. What would he think about it?"

Jik's eyes flickered and something lightened there. "He tell you you got damn fine fellow."

"This Personage of yours—" She tilted a careful ear toward the robed mahe with the Voice. "Iji?"

"Same. I talk for him. He don't got good pidgin. Same his Voice. He also Personage, see you got same Personthing, lot strong. He say—God make Personage. He—" Jik gave a helpless gesture. "He say God make lot peculiar experiment."

She laid her ears back, trying to put that on one side or the other. "Tell him—gods, just tell him I'll do what I have to. First thing—" She put her hands in the waist of her trousers. They were icy; her feet were numb from the decking. And it was still raw fear. "Tully."

"Captain?"

The humans were first. She kept her shoulder to the *han* representatives and to the Llun; and felt a dull shock to find Skkukuk's armed presence a positive comfort on her left, where it regarded breaking that news.

"What we do, we talk a little trade, talk up all the trouble they got to watch out for. I figure maybe they've seen enough to worry about. Maybe we just tell them it gets *worse* up ahead."

"They go," Tully said finally, coming out of that small fluorescent-lit room on Gaohn dockside, where mahendo'-sat and kif and humans and hani argued. Armed. Every one of them, since the kif were worse without their weapons at hand than with. And they went at it in shifts, till Tully came out in a waft of that godsawful multispecies stale air, and leaned against the doorframe. "They go." He looked drowned. Sweat stuck his hair to his forehead and his eyes looked bruised. After three days at this back-and-forth, herself out of the room for clean air and a new grip on her temper, agreement was like the floor going away.

"Go? Leave? They say yes?"

Gods, who threatened them? What happened? What went wrong? Belligerence was not the strategy she chose. Discouragement was. She had hammered this home with Skkukuk until the deviousness and the advantage of the tactic slowly blossomed in his narrow kifish skull, and his red-rimmed eyes showed a distinctive interest, which, gods help them all, might turn up as something new in kifish strategy.

"They say yes," Tully said, and made a ship-going motion with his flat hand. "Go way home. Kif and mahendo'-sat go with. First mahendo'sat, then kif, with few hani. You got find hani ship go. Make passage 'long kif territory."

"That bastard." Meaning Skkukuk, who had ulterior motives in running a parade of exiting humans right through kifish territory. It was also the shortest route. And Tully just hung there against the wall blinking in his own sweat and smelling godsawful no matter how much perfume he dosed himself with. He picked it up off the others. They all did. But overheated human still had its own distinctive aroma.

"Good?" he asked.

"Gods." She drew a deep breath and took him by the shoulder on her way to the door. He had to go back in. They still needed him. The mechanical translators were a disaster. And he looked all but out on his feet. "Yes. Good. Thank gods. Can you go a little longer? Another hour?"

"I do." Hoarse and desperate-sounding.

"Tully. You can go with them. You understand. Go home."

He blinked at her. Shook his head. He had that gesture back. "Here. *The Pride.*"

"Tully. You don't understand. We got trouble. We're all right now. After this—I can't say. I don't know that Chanur won't be arrested. Or worse than that. I have enemies, Tully. Lot of enemies. And if something happens to me and Chanur you'd be alone. Bad mess. You understand that? I can't say you'll be safe. I can't even say that for myself or the crew."

He did not understand. The words, maybe. But not the way the *han* paid off people like Ayhar, like Tahar, who was still not in a mood to come in. Gods knew what they reserved for Chanur.

"I friend."

"Friend. Gods. They owe you plenty, Tully. But you got to get out of here with somebody."

His mobile eyes shifted toward the door, the same as a hani slanting an ear. *They.* "Not good I go with."

It made sense then. Too much. "They got the *han*'s way of saying thanks, huh? Same you, same me with the hani. Gods-rotted mess, Tully."

He just looked at her.

And they went in one after the other. To get down to charts and precise routes.

Across the table from a tired, surly lot of humans.

Tully talked again, from his seat halfway down the table. In a quiet, colorless tone.

What came back sounded heated. But not when Tully rendered it. Simply: "They go. Want us come home with."

"No," the Llun said, before the mahen Personage got a word in. Skkukuk just sat and clicked to himself.

"This isn't a good time," Pyanfar said. Being an old trader. Tully rendered that in some fashion. "Knnn out there." And he rendered that, which got surlier frowns.

"Kkkkt," Skkukuk said, lifting his jaw, which they probably failed to understand.

Tully said something. It was probable that Tully *did* understand.

They were disposed to go to their ships after that.

"We've got it," she said to the Llun, after, herself and Tully outside in the corridor again with the Llun guard, when it was all adjourning. They were somewhat kin, she and the Llun senior. They kept it remote: the Immunes cherished their neutrality.

"We expect," the Llun said, "that the mahendo'sat may come up with some reparations."

Pyanfar's ears went down. Her jaw dropped. "My gods, we just *got* the kif and the mahendo'sat settled—"

"You have a peculiar position."

She went on staring at the Llun.

"Unique influence," the Llun said.

Trading instincts took over. In a blinding flash. *My gods. They* need *something, don't they?*

Gods save us. The mahendo'sat.

I can get The Pride *running again. Maybe get clear of this port. Bluff them out of arresting us.*

"It occurs to the *han* and the Immunes collectively," the Llun said, "that if you can do this, you can do other things. You have an extreme influence with the mahendo'sat."

My gods, my gods, they don't see yet! The mahendo'sat, the mahendo'sat are all they can see. The stsho and the mahendo'sat. Their precious trading interests. She walked away, stared off down the corridor where her own multispecies escort waited, rattling with weapons. Like the knnn and the tc'a out there, which Jik and Goldtooth swore was a tolerably friendly presence. And a pirate ship which was lying very quiet, but assuredly listening. She knew Tahar, that she would go on listening till she knew it was time to run for it. *I'm dangerous. I'm a plague and a danger to them. But they're mistaken what the danger is.*

"Chanur. The *han* is offering you your land back."

She turned around, blinked and stared at the Immune. "You mean my son is giving it up. Surrendering the land? Or the *han* is just confiscating it?"

"They'll work something out. They're disposed to work something out."

"Gods-be greedy eggsucking bastards! What are they asking? What are they buying? *Who in a mahen hell do they think they're trading with?*"

"I don't think they know either. I don't think they imagine. *I* do. The spacer clans do. They're saying they'll fight if the *han* lays a hand on you. They know what it would mean with the kif and the mahendo'sat. I know."

"They're crazy!"

"You're in a position. What will happen if you aren't? Tell me that."

Skkukuk being what Sikkukkut wanted to be. Jik discredited. Shakeups in the mahen government. More craziness.

It was not what she wanted to think of. It lay there day and night in her gut like something indigestible.

So did the solution.

"So the *han* just wants me to come down there and play politics and pay the bar tab, huh? Cozy up with the Naur."

"I didn't say that. I don't say the Naur won't try." The Llun looked as if she had something sour in her mouth. "I don't say you'll have to listen to them. You've got friends. That's what I'm trying to say. Unofficially."

"Because I won in there."

"I'll be honest. Some clans would have stood by you. The Llun couldn't have. We have other considerations. I'm not talking to a political novice. I'm not one either."

"Meaning you know what I *could* do."

"You're hani. You came back here. You came back here like Ayhar did. Like all the rest. That's some assurance what you'll do."

"The land's the rest, is it?"

"Some accommodation can be worked out."

Her heart hurt. Acutely. It took several breaths to dispel enough of the pain to talk. "I'm too honest, Llun. I'm too gods-be honest to take that deal. I'm too honest to do that to the *han,* and I mean *us,* not what sits on its broad backside down in that marble mausoleum and tries to play politics in a universe it doesn't by the gods *understand.* I'm the best education they're ever likely to get. You're right. You and your guards don't lay a hand on me or mine. You *know* what it would set off."

The Llun's ears had gone flat. "Is that a threat? Is that what I take it for?"

"Don't worry about me. I'm not Ehrran. Or Naur. I don't keep notebooks. And I'm going to be a lousy houseguest. You understand that? I can't drag that kind of politics into the *han*. I can't sit in the *han* and handle the kif. Or the mahendo'sat. Or the stsho. That isn't what the kif and the mahendo'sat created. I don't have any kin anymore. I can't have. I can't pay those kinds of debts. Come on, Tully."

She walked past the Llun, away from her and down the corridor without a backward look. She hurt inside. There were only foreigners waiting for her. And the crew she had to face. And explain to.

"Wrong?" Tully asked.

"No." She felt better, having said that. Having decided it. She laid a hand on his shoulder as they walked. "Friend," she said, and discovered that felt better too.

"Pyanfar." He stopped, faced her, pulling something from his hand and, taking hers palm up, pressed that something into it. She opened her fingers. It was the little gold ring. The one from lost *Ijir*. From some other friend of his. "You take." He reached out and touched the side of her ear. "So."

It was the most precious thing he owned, the only thing he really owned, the only link he had with his dead. "My gods, Tully—"

"Take."

She clenched her hand on it. He seemed pleased at that, even relieved, as if he had let something go that had been too heavy to carry.

"You want to stay or go? Tully?"

"Stay. With *The Pride*. With you. With crew."

"It's not the same! It won't be the same! Gods rot it, Tully, I can't make you understand what you're walking into. The crew may leave. Hilfy will have to. I don't know where we'll be. I don't know how long this will last before it gets worse."

"Need me."

She opened her mouth and shut it. Of all the crew she reckoned might be steadiest, she had never even reckoned him. Like the ring, it was too profound a gift.

"Come on," she said.

"We're doing all right," she said, on a full stomach, in the crowded galley—the Tauran had gone, with Vrossaru,

aboard *Mahijiru,* trailing the humans out. There was a matter of getting back to Meetpoint and picking up their ships
and cargoes. *Ayhar's Prosperity* had a guaranteed run in
that direction too, with a full hold, which Meetpoint might
direly need. And, good or bad news, one never knew, the
knnn had disappeared with the tc'a, off on a vector which
ought to get it lost in limbo, if it were not a knnn, and
capable of making jumps that other ships could not.
Toward stsho space, it looked like. At best guess.

"We got word from Tahar," Haral said. "They got the
message."

"What'd they say about it?"

"Said thanks. They said they'll believe in a *han* amnesty
when they get it engraved, but they say they plan to shadow
us awhile. Till the word gets around."

"Huh." It was prudent. Dur Tahar was that. She let go
a small sigh. "*We* got some business at Meetpoint too, soon
as they get our tail put back together." She took a sip of
gfi. There was a vacancy at table. Hilfy was off doing Chanur business. Which was the way it had to be. Married,
within the year: that was what Hilfy had to do, find herself
some young man strong enough to take her cousin Kara and
pitch him clear back to Mahn territory.

In that choice she had burned to give advice; but what
was between her and Hilfy had gotten too remote for that,
too businesslike. It was her own hardheaded, closemouthed
pride. She saw it like a mirror. Hilfy knew everything; more
than Hilfy might ever know when she was a hundred.

Then: "Hey," Hilfy had said to her when she left, not
captain-crew formal, but a level, adult look eye-to-eye. "I'm
not going hunting round in Hermitage. I'm just putting the
word out I'm looking. Me. Heir to Chanur. And the winner
gets a shuttle ticket up to Gaohn. I don't care if he's handsome. But he's by the gods going to have to have the nerve
to come up here and meet my father."

"Huh," she had said to that. Since she had resolved to
disentangle herself from clan business as long as the Personage business persisted. She did not, likewise, offer advice to Rhean or Anfy or any of the others.

"I'm telling you," she said now, to the crew, to her cousins, her husband, and a human, "you don't have to go out
on this one. You want some ground time, gods know you've

got it coming." With a look under her brows at Chur, who
had it coming doubly. "Or station. Or discharge. To *Fortune;* to *Light.* Anywhere. I'm the gods-be Personage of
Anuurn, I can get you any post you want, it ought to let
me do *some* things I want to do."

Long silence. "No," Haral said. And: "No," like an echo
from Tirun.

"World's not safe," Chur said, and shrugged uncomfort-
ably. "But I met this Llun fellow. Immune. Quiet. Real
quiet."

"You want your discharge. Or just some leave time?"

Chur sighed, a heave of her shoulders. "Gods, I want till
we get the tail fixed, that's all."

Geran had looked worried. Terrified for a moment. The
shadow passed.

Khym looked Chur's way. And back to her, with a quiet
and considerate expression. Sometimes the thoughts went
through his eyes so plain she could read them. After all
these years.

Epilogue

The docks reeked of foreignness, of metal and oil and machinery, and they echoed with announcements and the snarls of monstrous machines; it was a frightening place for a boy from a land of blue sky and golden grass. Hallan heard the PA thundering advisements the cavernous gray spaces swallowed and gave back garbled in echo. He looked about him and saw groups of black-trousered Immunes moving down the docks in a cordon across the whole dockside: what little he did catch from the PA was alarming, snatches of advisories to clear some area, but he had no idea what section four green was or why the lights were flashing blue down there and red where he was.

It was a confusing arrival for a downworld lad, laboring along with his pass and all his worldly possessions in a brand new spacer's duffel. He had spent two bewildered hours in immigration, then taken what turned out to be the wrong lift up from the shuttle dock; then into an administrative office for directions, and down another lift, then, which went sideways as often as it went down and came to dead stop on the main docks, resisting all his attempts to get it to go up. So he had ventured out into the docks of Anuurn, which dazed him with echoes and its true size and its reality after so many dreams. It was a dangerous place, his sisters had warned him; it was wonderful; it overloaded his senses with its noise and its echoes and its foreign smells. It was too huge a place, its few people too hurried or too rough-looking to bother with a newcomer's foolish questions. The docks ran all the circumference of the station: he was sure of that, and surely, if he started walking in the up-numbers direction, section four could not be too far from the section seven he was hunting. He walked along where there was no traffic at all, in the shadow of the gantries, and went from berth 14 where he had come in to berth 15; 16 was a working berth, all its lights lit with a glitter which stirred his sense of the beautiful—white and gold, a hundred lights to shine on the lines and the gantry and the whole surrounds. The ramp access looked to be open. The dockers were driving their vehicles away, and no one noticed if a boy kept walking, so he might pass by as close to his dreams as he had ever come in his life.

But now—*CLEAR THE AREA* the speaker overhead said while he panted along at the foot of the towering machinery, there by the lights. *CLEAR THE AREA,* and something more that he could not hear in the garble. He looked around desperately and saw the Immunes moving and the docks suddenly deserted. His heart began to beat in panic: he wondered was it a decompression warning, whether something had gone dangerously wrong on this dock or somewhere near—he had heard horror tales from the war years.

But in his casting about for direction he spied a spacer, a graynosed woman whose ears had, gods, a whole fistful of voyage-rings, who sat on the skirt of some huge piece of machinery, just sitting, observing the whole furor, arm around one knee, her ears backslanted in the racket; suddenly she was looking straight at him.

He dropped his ears at once in politeness: and in outright awe at the spacer rings and the easy assurance of this veteran who was everything he was not and longed with all his heart to be. He would never have come her way on his own; but she was staring at him as if he were somehow more interesting than the chaos and the goings-on with the Immunes. He thought he detected an invitation, a summons in the twitch of a many-ringed ear: and he hitched up his duffel and all the courage of his seventeen years.

"H'lo," he said, walking up—his smile and his friendliness had won him a great deal in his life, and he relied on it now, when he was afraid, slanting an ear toward the commotion behind him. "Lot of noise, isn't it?"

The spacer nodded.

Not a word. Not the least ear-twitch of friendliness. He was left a fool, twice desperate. His blue breeches were brand new. His ears were ringless. His duffel still had package-creases and he swung it back behind him and dropped it where it was less conspicuous, figuring he had mistaken her invitation: he was suddenly anxious only to get his directions and go, before he found himself in something he could not handle.

The eyes raked him and down in lazy ease, flickered with some kind of interest. "Wrong side of that line, you know."

He cleared his throat, looked nervously over his shoulder. "What are they doing down there?"

"What are you doing up here?"

"I—" He looked back again full into the spacer's lazy stare, that stripped him down to the bones and the truth; there was not even a lie he knew how to tell. "I'm new here," he said; and dropped his ears in deference when her mouth pursed in dour amusement. "What's all the commotion down there?"

"*The Pride*'s in port."

He could not help himself; he looked back again toward the distant lines and drew a large breath. The *station,* for godssakes, he had truly come to the station, where fantastical species came and went; where fabled ship-names were ordinary on the freighting lists, and many-ringed spacers sat about ordinary as could be. And on the very day he came up from the world, *The Pride of Chanur* just happened in, with no advance notice in the newsservices, nothing at all to tell the world it was coming. He saw nothing for his looking but a solid line of black-breeched Immunes in the distance, practically no one on the docks there or near at hand; and nothing at all of the ship-boards down there: gantries obscured the view. He looked back and tried to catch his breath. "Gods, I'd like to see it."

"You don't *see* a ship, son, they stay out there." She was laughing at him, all dour-faced. "But you could go up to the observation lounge, the cameras'll give you a view."

"I want to see *them.*"

"Who?"

"*Them.*"

"The Personage? Gods-rotted lot of nonsense."

He caught a quick breath. His ears went flat. *Nonsense. My gods!*

"Nonsense," the spacer said again. "No different than you and me. What d'you think, boy? Blackbreeches scurrying around like chi in a fire, shut down the whole gods-be dockside—"

"Well, oughtn't they?" He was indignant. *One of the old ones, this, one of the surly old-timers, just blowing off. She doesn't like a boy being up here, doesn't like me being on any ship, ever. Walk off, that's what I ought to do. She probably has a knife somewhere, even a gun in that pocket, gods know what.* "I'm going to go have a look." He grabbed up his duffel again.

But the spacer patted the machine-skirt. "Tssss. You won't get anywhere through that line. Just a lot of trouble. Have a seat, boy. All bright-eyed and new, are you?"

He was off his stride. He delayed. And knew himself a fool when the old spacer took on a friendlier, amused look. Turn about for his pretense of being what he was not, that was what she had given him. Fair and fair.

"Sit. Crew's going to be down here in a bit. What ship are you going to?"

"Not to a ship. Yet. School. I'm Meras. Hallan Meras. From Syrsyn." Confession once started, tumbled out in the old spacer's unchanging stare, and his ears burned with embarrassment; she had known even when she asked, but she did not ridicule him. "I *want* to be a spacer." It was his dearest dream. He saw it coming true and she did not laugh when he said that either. *One of the old ones.* "Have you—" He cast another look down the dock, leaning forward, and saw nothing of ship names at this angle either. "Have you ever seen the Personage?"

"Lots of times."

He looked back in awe. "Are you a friend of hers?"

"What's the matter with you, boy, what do they teach you nowadays, all this fuss to see some Personage, what's *seeing* do, anyway? Makes me worry, that's what. Hani I knew'd spit in the eye of somebody that wanted all that bowing and guarding. You ought to."

He understood then. "She got me here," he said. And when the old spacer blinked: "That's why I want to see that ship. I wouldn't *be* here without her, without what she did. That's why."

"Huh," the old spacer said. "Huh." And: "Uhhnnn—" With a gesture outward, toward the sudden flashing of a strobe light and the arrival of several official cars. "Llun."

"Are we in trouble?" Hallan got anxiously to his feet as his spacer companion stood up. He snatched up his duffel and held onto it. Immune officials and weapon-bearing marshals were getting out of the car, coming their way, while suddenly, adding to the confusion, there were other spacers coming down the ramp out of the ship, one of them a man, one of them—"O my gods," Hallan said, having seen humans in old pictures, and having seen a picture of this one.

"Cap'n," one of the spacers said, scar-nosed and broad-faced; and coming their way. "My gods, you going like that?"

"Too much fuss," the old spacer said, and dusted off her trousers. "Drives me berserk, this whole business. They want a decree, I'll give 'em a decree. Haral, meet a nice kid. Hallan Meras, meet Haral Araun. Sorry we can't stay and talk right now. Luck to you."

She walked off with the crew from the ship, the human Tully and all. And *na* Khym *nef* Mahn, who was the first man in space.

One of the crew lingered a moment, a small woman who looked him up and down with eyes that for a moment seemed to see—gods, inside him and around him with a force that left him all but shaking. Chur Anify. The strange one. She was the one that had charted the new Points off beyond Minar, and probes had found them, a bridge to other stars. She was almost as famous as the Personage.

"Who is this boy?" A Llun officer asked, all hard and threatening.

"He has a right to be there," Chur Anify said, and the officer looked at her and dropped her ears and let him alone.

"Are you some relative?" that officer asked when the cars had left the dockside and grim Llun marshals stood double guard outside *The Pride of Chanur*'s ramp access. "Are you Chanur?"

"No," he said, holding his baggage and still dazed as if all the stars in space spun about him. That had been the Personage, the *mekt-hakkikt* of the kif, the Director . . . there were as many names as there were species in the Compact. She had talked with him, this power that could move a thousand ships and mediate affairs among species.

With him, as if he were truly someone who mattered.

Or as if he might be that someone, someday.

CHANUR'S
LEGACY

Chapter 1

Meetpoint was in one sense the center of Compact space: in another sense, this place where all the Compact met for trade was the hindside of every species' separate territory, and, along with its cosmopolitan character, it had that chancy watch-your-back kind of feeling on its dockside, even in these days when weapons were discouraged and peace governed the dealings of species. Meetpoint's oxygen docks were redolent of cold and oil and volatiles, its dockside shops and bars echoed of trade and business and offered a selection of vices. Its methane side—the methane-folk had to answer for, in their multiple-brained thoughts and stranger songs: but on the oxygen side, the stsho, who were the landlords of Meetpoint, traded in what pleased them. Among those spindly, white-skinned merchants one could find hani, mahendo'sat, kif, and (at least when a certain ship was in dock) a stray human from a world named, unenterprisingly, Earth.

That certain ship had been here. That certain ship had departed twenty-odd days ago in pursuit of its own business, a circumstance which completely satisfied Hilfy Chanur, captain of *Chanur's Legacy,* newly in dock at Meetpoint and besieged by her aunt's unreceived mail—beset also by every hanger-on, would-be, and might-have-been politician, inventor, and academician with every offer of favor, every piece of influence-peddling, every crackpot idea and complaint for forty light-years about.

Being niece to the President of Compact space, the elected President of the spacefaring amphictiony of Anuurn, the *mekt-hakkikt* of all the kif, the Personage of Personages of the mahendo'sat (gods only knew about the methane-folk) . . . in short, entailed a few liabilities.

It remained to be seen, with the *Legacy* past the initial

formalities, whether Aunt Pyanfar's latest dealing with
Meetpoint's governor was about to become another of
those liabilities. It remained imminently to be seen, because
at the top of the message stack which had landed in the
Legacy's files at the instant of their docking, sat a message
from *gtst* excellency No'shto-shti-stlen, requesting the presence of "the august niece of the most distinguished (untranslatable) Pyanfar Chanur in the inner most hospitable
(?) administrative offices," and so on and so on, "omitting
customs formalities which this office will be delighted to
obviate," and so on in that vein.

One *didn't* trust that those formalities were going to be
ignored, by the gods, one didn't. One set one's second in
command to handling them, in case the honorable or excellent No'shto-shti-stlen changed *gtst* mind and charged one's
ship with smuggling.

So Hilfy put on her administrative-offices best pair of
black satin trousers, and (acutely aware of her youth)
combed the mane until it crackled with static (and looked
fuller) and the mustaches so that they somewhat covered
the youthful scantness of beard. Hilfy Chanur's ears at least
had no scarcity of rings to signify her voyages. Her red-
gold coat was brushed to a sheen. Her mood was even
cheerful as she took the lift down from topside to the main
lowerdeck corridor and put her head in at lowerdeck ops.

"I'm off, cousin. You're in charge. How's it going?"

"Smooth so far. Are you sure you don't want one of us
to go along?"

Tiar was harried, hurried—they were a small crew, in a
strange port, dealing with officials they didn't personally
know. The crew was eager to go on liberty, which they
couldn't do until the forms were filed and the cargo was
delivered.

"I'm fine. I know this place. I know exactly where I'm
going."

"You've got the pocket com."

She patted the pocket of her trousers. "No problems.
Just a walk down the dock to the lift. You get those forms
filed, make *sure* we're clear of customs . . . make them sign
the forms anyway. Refer them to the governor's office. I'm
not taking any chances."

"Aye, captain," Tiar said, and Hilfy walked on and into

the lock, cycled it through to Meetpoint's biting air, and walked the frost-rimed yellow tube of the ramp to the wide open docks.

It was a world of gray steel gantries, towering up into an overhead obscured by blinding light, an overhead so tall it made its own weather, had occasional haze about the lights, and rained condensation puddles on the utilitarian decking. Neon glared from storefronts and bars, oxy-breathing species rubbed shoulders in disregard of differences, and nowadays one could trust there were no weapons—

One could at least carefully hope there were no weapons. She carried none. Since the Peace, guns on dockside were strictly for the police: all species were civilized now. Law decided controversies, ships refrained from piracy, as a historic source of provocation, and from cargo-pilfering, a clear violation of treaties every known species but one now respected.

So Hilfy Chanur didn't hurry on her way—or worry about the attention she drew here. She cut a fair figure, red-gold hide and black silk breeches in a world of dreary grays and garish neon light. Hani were fairly scarce at this end of space, but most of all, the Chanur name on the *Legacy* would not have passed unnoticed. She could imagine the whispers: the Personage's relative, the *mekt-hakkikt*'s niece, what's she up to?—justified, since Chanur had a habit of being up to things.

But, credit to Meetpoint's new ordinances, there was not a single interception on her way across the docks, only ordinary traffic; and the lift coordinates she punched in with the number *gtst* excellency's request had provided her were a priority destination: no waiting for the car, not even fellow passengers to deal with, just a *G*-shifting express ride into the great body of Meetpoint station, to a debarcation into that area the stsho landlords reserved unto themselves, white halls draped in shades of nacre and pastel, and ornamented with the writhing alabaster shapes the stsho called art.

She abandoned cautions, abandoned concerns for untoward encounters: this was a safe place; quiet and peaceful, so harmonious that she no more than blinked in dismay when black-robed kifish guards turned up in her path.

So the stsho were back at *that* foolish practice: uncombative themselves, so fragile a single blow could crush them—they engaged species who could defend them against individuals who might do them violence, the most likely to do violence, unfortunately, being the very species that they hired. One thought that they might have learned that most expensive lesson about the kif—but the stsho made the choices the stsho made: the experiment with mahen and hani guards had apparently not satisfied them, although Hilfy herself had not heard about it; and the fact that the hair rose on a hani captain's nape and that her vision hazed about the edges at the mere sight of these tall, black-robed figures, the fact that a hani of otherwise peaceful intent instantly entertained violent thoughts at meeting these creatures, did not matter to the stsho. It was so polite. So civilized. The kif bowed; she bowed; they said follow, and she followed these thin, long-snouted shadows, these creatures that always, no matter what the circumstances, reeked of ammonia, if only in her memory.

"Chanur captain," they called her, with their peculiar clicking accent, the sound of double, deadly jaws, making consonants that no hani could exactly duplicate. They spoke to her respectfully, for her aunt's sake, for their employers' sake: they showed every sign of fearing her displeasure—as kif might, who had reason to think she had power and influence with their employers. So these were no danger. They were not high in kifish rank or they would not be working here, in alien employ. Kick them and they would estimate you the higher for it.

But she was profoundly relieved to meet a stsho at the end of the corridor, beyond the blowing gossamer curtains, and to leave the guards behind. The spindly, fragile stsho, who was the personal aide, *gtst* told her, to *gtst* excellency the governor No'shto-shti-stlen, drifted in draperies of almost pink and almost gold, fluttered agitatedly along a corridor of blowing drapes of almost-white—wherein a gold-coated, red-maned hani, unsubtle intrusion in a realm of faintest distinctions, refused to be rushed. The aide had not deigned to come in person. She was in no imminent need of the governor's approval. So in the game of diplomatic tit for tat, Hilfy Chanur walked at her own pace into the governor's vast gossamer-curtained audience hall, where multiple bowl-chairs, pastel cushioned depressions in the floor, defined the stsho's sense of elegance, decorum, and, thereby, social status.

In one of these bowl-chairs governor No'shto-shti-stlen waited, plucking pale green leaves from some sort of fruit and eating them one by one.

But the governor set down *gtst* lunch as they approached. Manners improved. The aide, bowing, declared the presence of 'the great hani captain, the birth-bond-relative of the estimable *mekt-hakkikt* and so on and so on, worthy of *gtst* attention, and so on.

"Sit," the entity lisped in the Trade, with a wave of white, long fingers. *Gtst* excellency seemed half-transparent, hardly a touch of color in the body-paint, to hani eyes, white on white. *Gtst*—not precisely he or she, since stsho had three genders, and two indeterminate states if frightened—called for something in *gtst* rippling planetary language. The attendant scurried to comply, while stsho music played softly in the background, the occasional chime of a single, same note.

Hilfy folded down into the bowl opposite *gtst* excellency No'shto-shti-stlen, knowing better than to rush matters with the governor, as she had refused to be hurried. But very quickly a servant showed up with a tray of crystal bowls and a colorless, exquisitely flavored liquid in a crystal pitcher.

Thereafter, five tiny bowls, savored in silence. She knew the protocols—and knew the giddiness that could set in for a hani partaking of too much stsho hospitality. She kept her ears up and her mouth pursed in hani pleasantness, evidencing the right amount of cultured pleasure in each serving, all the while she watched the minute flutter of feathery lashes and feathery brows, the minute shifts in expression as No'shto-shti-stlen made slow estimation of *gtst* guest and tried (it was second nature to the stsho) to guess her current rank, her mood, and her expectations by her selection of jewelry and her composure in the meeting.

"Do you find it pleasant?"

"Delicate," she said, *in* the stsho's own trade-tongue, and feathery eyebrows went up. "Very delicate. Very pleasant."

"We are astounded at your commendable fluency."

"Your excellency flatters me. And this *is* very fine."

"Please accept a case lot in appreciation."

Ye gods. Appreciation. Of what, one wondered. It was no mean gift. But the obligatory response, with precisely the right degree of gratitude: "Your excellency is most kind. Please be understanding when a gift from my own ship arrives: after seeing the grace and discrimination of your establishment, I can only hope my personal token of admiration finds favor."

"I could not possibly."

"Honor it with your ownership. Your discrimination is of wide repute."

"Your graciousness is most extravagant."

"Your excellency's delicacy and sensitivity amply justify our admiration."

It went on like that for two and three more rounds of compliments and deprecations.

That case of tea was worth about 3000 on the market. A good merchant had her figures in her head. The stsho certainly did.

"There is, however—" said No'shto-shti-stlen (there was always the "however") "—a way in which we might favor ourselves with an opportunity to amplify our association. More tea?"

Gods, the convolutions. One suspected a stsho was trying to lose an upstart foreigner in the verbal underbrush. But one did not decline an offer of further negotiation, not if one wished to remain on good terms. One only hoped one's good sense held out and one's tongue did not trip.

"Of course."

Another round of platitudes, another period of quiet assessment, in which, ample time to reflect on one's capacity for *shis* tea and on the extent of a stsho's connivance. No'shto-shti-stlen was a stsho whom Aunt Pyanfar called moderately stable.

That meant both reliable for trade . . . and dangerous by reason of *gtst* long-term personal interests.

"I would wonder," she said, setting down the third emptied cup of the second round of *shis-thi-nli.* "I would ask why my illustrious and esteemed aunt was not foremost to help such a deserving person, if your excellency would enlighten me. Surely your trust in my junior self cannot exceed that you would place in her august person."

"I hope that my request does not cause any—" A flutter

of the hands, a hiding of the mouth behind a napkin, "—awkwardness."

Kftli. "Awkwardness." Cognate relationship to "foreignness." Perhaps *gtst* excellency was making a joke. Perhaps *gtst* excellency had not studied the evolution of the trade-tongues.

"The august Director left here, perhaps you are aware—deep—into a territory—ahem—of utmost secrecy. Yes, she might oblige us, she is so extravagant in her good offices toward persons in distress. But we are extremely fortunate in your arrival. We were searching records to find a captain of sufficient—mmm—standing and respectability. Your arrival insystem is a most delightful surprise."

One did *not* want another round of tea. And one could now regret one's youthful enthusiasm for dealing in the other's language. Avoiding a request at this point was something only a stsho could finesse—and one suspected, not at this disadvantage of rank. Did you want your ship to leave on time, your goods to stay unpilfered, most of all, did you want your manifest *not* to display some flaw four and five solar systems away that would cost you days and bribes to straighten out?

Gods rot the scoundrel. She wished this one *had* landed in Aunt Py's lap. Or possibly it had been about to, and Aunt Py had suddenly decided on a course numerous light-years away.

"And how may we merit your good opinion?"

"I have a cargo," said No'shto-shti-stlen, "an object actually, which must get to Urtur, time being of the essence."

"A precious object."

"Most precious."

"The favor of your trust overwhelms me. But may I ask? The nature of this object."

Hands fluttered. Brows wavered. "An artwork."

"Not living. Not animate."

"Oh, no, no, no, nothing of the sort. But—"

Here it comes. They might have an offer. She was by no means certain she wanted it.

"—its delivery is, understand, *liiyei.*"

A guess, based on the Trade. *"Ceremony."*

"Just so. Just so. But it must go immediately to Urtur."

"Immediately."

"Immediately. What will you charge? By no means be modest."

"Its mass?"

"Oh, very small. I could lift it. Of a dimension . . .". Long, white fingers described an object about the size of one's head.

"Fragile?"

"No more nor less than the cup you lately held. You are so modest. And perhaps have other cargo. Let me name a figure. A million in advance."

Her throat stopped working. She extruded a claw and nudged the cup. The attendant hastened to fill it, and No'shto-shti-stlen's.

"Is there some difficulty?" No'shto-shti-stlen asked.

"By no means. If—I hesitate to impose upon your excellency's already considerable generosity, but I have consignments to pick up here for Hoas port. —I might perhaps arrange a transfer of those orders—I've no contractual problems. . . ."

"No difficulty. None at all. I take it these were open market contracts."

"Open market, nothing illegal about an interline, but your excellency must understand, I have bonds requiring that delivery . . ."

"A trifle, a trifle. My personal guarantee. I personally will put a bond on the interline carrier for your entire and unexcepted protection."

Too good to be true. "My ship certainly has the engines to make the jump, at low mass. But a million, while most generous as an offer . . . does the contract enjoin us from carrying other cargo?"

"Absolutely not. Whatever you can carry safely. And certainly—certainly we can assist you with priorities. Even—hm—information on low-mass stsho goods. I have a contract already drawn up." From an alabaster box by the side of the bowl-chair No'shto-shti-stlen whisked a sole spot of blackness, a data-cube. "This has both the contract for transport and the authorization for the disbursement."

"Cash at undocking."

"Cash at undocking. The whole sum to be paid to the bank on signature of the contract, with no restriction on withdrawals once the *oji* is aboard." A waggle of long fingers. And a tightly sewed-up set of conditions. "Of course one so honorable as yourself would need no contract. But for our mutual protection."

"Of course."

"Please accept *three* cases of the tea, to salve the inconvenience of diverting your ship."

"I do not of course guarantee signing the contract. Please make the gift contingent on our agreement!"

"Your honor is impeccable in my eyes. No such stipulation. Please. Take it for your help in an additional difficulty."

A sip of the tea. Definitely. Two sips. "Additional difficulty."

"A matter in which your honor might, if you will, be a solution."

"In what way might I be the solution of a problem so difficult?"

"A matter of delicacy. A member of your species is stranded here at Meetpoint—clearly an oversight on the part of the ship in question. But we are most anxious to see this resolved."

"They left her."

No'shto-shti-stlen took a sip of tea, and fluttered eyelashes. "Him, if I may be so entirely forward."

Him. Gods. Hilfy did a rapid resorting, with a distinct sense of alarm. "A hani ship? Left a crewman?"

"There was—your honor will please be understanding—a slight intoxication, a breakage of insignificant items of extremely bad taste—most of all—an altercation with a foreign national of—em—higher status—which I assure your honor had been harmlessly resolved."

"The nationality offended, excellency?"

"Kif."

Gods.

"A simple misunderstanding, a few hours detention and filling out of forms . . . but through some inadvertency, his ship—simply claimed a cargo priority and left without our office—em—aware of the oversight. We are excruciatingly embarrassed. We believe that perhaps they believed he was already back aboard, as did—em—an individual in traffic management, who cleared the undock."

"Did no one advise them?"

"They were unalarmed. They sent back word that it was unfortunate, but they had a contractual commitment and they urged us to send him along by the first hani ship that might consent. Your esteemed aunt, of course, had already left. *Handur's Rainbow,* which came in afterward and preceded you out . . . did not have a berth available."

A *contractual* commitment?

Read that *Rainbow* had refused to burden itself. Damn their down-the-nose attitude.

But—gods—hit a kif of rank? Did one *want* to take aboard a hani with that kind of grudge?

"Can we prevail upon your extreme generosity? His presence here is an embarrassment. How do we care for him? How do we lodge him?"

"I quite understand." Think fast, Hilfy Chanur. "What was his ship's course?" Fifty-fifty it was . . .

"Hoas, as happens. But everything passes through Urtur."

"In any case—" Gods, how did I get into this? But, damn it to a mahen hell . . . you don't even ask his clan. He's hani. He's lost. He's been *dumped* here, gods rot them—if the kif claim him, the stsho can't resist that pressure. Small wonder they want him out of here before there's an incident.

"We can *pay* his passage," No'shto-shti-stlen said.

"No. No. Forgive my unseemly distress. I could not possibly accept payment. This is a question of . . ." Stsho had no equivalent for species-honor. ". . . Elegance."

"Another case of tea."

"Please." On the other hand. At three thousand the case. "On the other hand—"

A flutter of distress. No'shto-shti-stlen wanted this lad gone very badly. *Very* badly. And feared he would have to pay heavily for it.

Which he might deserve to do . . . except Hilfy Chanur was not dealing in hani hides, under any circumstances.

"Your esteemed and wise influence might clear any legal obstacles, any defect in his documents, that sort of thing. That would expedite matters."

"We are delighted to assist. There will be *no* impediments."

"No entanglements. No pending charges."

"You have my word. I have so enjoyed this meeting. Please give my regards to your esteemed relative. Advise her that No'shto-shti-stlen admires her exceedingly."

"I shall." There was a civilized way and a barbaric one to quit a bowl-chair: the left foot on the unpadded line, the right onto the rim, no trick at all. She made a small bow, the data-cube in hand, and No'shto-shti-stlen nodded with a graceful swaying of *gtst* white center-crest and *gtst* feathery, cosmetically augmented brows.

"Most, most pleasant," No'shto-shti-stlen said.

"A memorable hour, most memorable."

Never underestimate a stsho.

So, so, she had a passenger—but he was an inconsequence; the other question, what was in the contract, took momentary second place to the heady thoughts of a million credit haulage fee for some trinket she could juggle one-handed, and with the hold, after discharging their cargo, altogether free for what she could buy outright at Meetpoint for resale in a port whose fairly recent futures and shortages list *Legacy* had in file?

Far too good to be true, was what it was. She had gotten too far into this. Her disclaimer that she might not sign had not been early enough or forceful enough, and it needed no kifish guards to upset her stomach on the way out.

"All went well?" one had the temerity to ask her.

"Ask the one who feeds you," she retorted, and the kif who had presumed, retreated, hissing.

No love lost, no. The kif knew an implacable enemy; but they had to let her pass back to the dockside.

And how did one at this point refuse the governor who sat at the junction of virtually all trans-sector trade—even if one's aunt *was* the *mekt-hakkikt* of the known universe?

Appeal to Pyanfar's influence?

By the gods, no. Not Hilfy Chanur. Not if she wanted to face herself in the mirror. Not if she didn't want the story spread on every ship that dealt with No'shto-shti-stlen.

And the stsho would spread it. Not strike a blow in anger, oh, no, not the stsho. Their daggers were all figurative and theoretical. Or wielded by kifish hire-ons.

But, dear, featherless gods, if the offer was on the up and up . . .

*　　*　　*

Legacy was spitting up cans—had at least one truck full already, with the bright red stamp that meant warm-hold goods, and the trucks lined up that would take them to their various destinations, some for the station, some for interline to Kshshti, some on for ports no hani nor mahen ship could reach; and some of them were even destined for the methane-side—fifty more cold-hold cans: hani goods—bound for the t'ca. New markets. New prosperity—for ships that would take the risks and go the far and alien distances.

Competitive ships. Ships that carried clan wealth and clan business where hani clans had no on-world referent. Ships that brought back new ideas to Anuurn. Like the Compact itself. Like making the old women on Anuurn look up instead of inward, and making senior captains hide-bound in their ways admit that Chanur was *not* in exile, Chanur that had respect in every gods-be-feathered port of call in the Compact: make the nay-sayers believe that Chanur *had* more than a proxy head-of-clan in her, and that the head-of-clan had a right to replace *The Pride* and replace Pyanfar Chanur *and* survive by honest trade.

This run could be the break-even that would prove it. This contract could put them at a profit for the first time in the *Legacy*'s existence: the *Legacy*'s construction was entirely paid for and they were running free and clear, if they could take this break and go with it—a million for a ridiculously light haul and a 500,000 current clear take off the cargo, here, against a remaining indebtedness of 14,000,000, plus a turnaround with a mil and a half origin-point purchase for low-mass luxury goods and palladium offering a pay-out of 500 percent at Urtur above running costs; with, moreover, a price break on cargo guaranteed by No'shto-shti-stlen *gtst*self . . . not to mention the flat-rate hauls they could manage: she was already figuring what they *could* haul on that difficult long-distance jump including express mail; and trying over and over to admonish herself to caution as she walked up and took cousin Tiar quietly by the elbow.

"We have an offer. It involves a turn-around for Urtur. I'm inside to read the contract. If some station guards show up with a passenger, take him."

"Passenger," Tiar echoed. Chihin had stopped work, ears

pricked. Veteran spacers, Tiar Chanur, Chihin Anify, both out of Rhean's crew when Rhean retired. And "station guards" and "him" got Fala's ears up.

"Him?" Tiar asked, wiping her hands. There were two other puzzled frowns.

"Why us?" Tiar asked. "Begging the captain's pardon, of course."

Meaning if "he" was mahe, there were mahen ships to take him, and if "he" was kif there were kif enough, not to mention the stsho.

"Because," she said quietly, "he's hani."

"Gods . . ." Chihin's ears went flat.

"I want him out of here. I want the hide of the captain that dumped him. Most of all, I want him away from the kif. If he shows up—when he shows up—check his papers. Make *sure* of those papers, if you have to keep him waiting to do it: get into station comp and make sure there's no proliferating taint of any kind on his record, you understand. Above all, don't take him aboard until they're clear. The governor wants him out of here, and once he's aboard we don't have that leverage—*immigration* does, you understand?"

"No question," Tiar said.

"Ship *left* him?" Fala asked, her young face all seriousness.

"It's a long story. We're taking him out of here, is all we can promise. Catch his ship if we can. Just be nice. Be nice."

She clapped Tiar on the shoulder, Chihin second, and deliberately did not hear Chihin say, "That's what comes of letting men into space . . ." Chihin was conservative, so was Tiar, and you didn't change her overnight.

But things had changed. They had changed so far a hani ship could bring a hani lad forty lights away from home and *leave* him to a station where kif were the guards and stsho were the only justice.

She walked up the ramp and into the yellow-ribbed access tube, trod the chilly distance to the lock, and locked through. In the lowerdeck ops station, she found Tarras working comp on the loaders, and she snagged Tarras for the computer work.

One did *not* drop a strange cube into the ship's main computer or any terminal in touch with it. Not that one didn't trust *gtst* excellency. Of course not.

So it was the downside auxiliary, the computer that suicided and resurrected on command.

"I want a printout," she told Tarras. "One original, one through the translator, stsho formal, but first I want you to diagnose the source. I don't want the thing changing, erasing, or cozying up to our navigation. *Ma'sho?*"

"*Sho'shi,*" Tarras said, ears pricked, all enthusiasm.

"Fast. Inside the hour."

Tarras' ears went to half. "Captain, . . ."

"You can do it."

Tarras muttered another word in mahen trade, gave a shiver, and took the cube, looked at it on one side and another—for obvious things like inbuilts.

"I need a laser on this."

"Check for more exotic contagions after we get the print. I need the print, Tarras. All of us need this printout."

"What's up?"

"Only our operating budget. Only a major contract I don't know if I want and I don't know if we can get out of, on which the governor's good will happens to be riding."

"I'm on it," Tarras said, and went.

The sounds and smells of the cells were dreadful. Hallan slept when he could, a sleep disturbed by distant sounds of doors, attendants coming and going. It went on constantly, but you could never see anything: just a blank door and blank gray walls, and the sounds to let you know you were not alone. He had long since lost track of the time. He amused himself by adding chains of figures. They had said when they arrested him that his captain would have to get him out. And then, days and days ago, the kifish guard who brought him his breakfast had said his ship had left without him.

That had been the absolute depth of despair. He had asked the guard what would they do then, and the guard said, oh, probably keep him here for the rest of his life.

The kif had said, When we want rid of someone we kill him. Hani sneak away and leave him. You're half again bigger than your females. They say you're a fighter. Why didn't you kill them and secure your place?

He had been appalled. But the kif as kif went was a talkative one, and more friendly than he had expected of that dangerous kind. He had had trouble understanding it at first. It interrupted everything with clicks. It smelled of ammonia. It complained that he stank. It had naked, black skin that was gray where the light fell on it, and velvety soft and wrinkled, although in kif that didn't seem to be a sign of age. It had long jaws and a small mouth and what he had heard said it had to have live food, which it diced into a fine paste with a second set of jaws, far up toward the gullet—after which it spat out the bones and the fur. If it bit you, those teeth could get a crippling mouthful. It ate its own kind and it did not feel remorse. Such statements were not prejudicial: its psychology was different, utterly self-interested, and one had better believe so and not judge it by hani standards: that was what he had learned about kif in his books.

But that kif was the only one who spoke to him, the only living being he had seen besides the mahen doctor, who had not had much to say to him, except what he knew, that he was in trouble. He had come even to look forward to the kif in the morning, because it did stay to talk; and he had stopped thinking it was going to take a piece out of him without a reason.

But it had not come this morning nor the morning before. And when the door opened, he thought it was lunch, which he wasn't interested in, because his stomach could only tolerate the breakfasts, and no one cared, and no one changed the menu.

So he thought he could lie there on the bunk and not pay any attention and it would go away.

But it didn't. Whoever it was didn't make the ordinary sound of setting down a tray and leaving. Whoever it was just stood there.

He turned over and looked, and saw a kif like every other kif, except its black robes glistened and the border of its hood had silver cording. He could not see all of its face, just the snout. But he had the impression of its fixed stare as he sat up.

"Sir?" He had no idea of the proprieties, whether he

should bow or stand there, but he decided on bowing. He
thought it might be a station officer of some kind. It was
even possible it was the kif he had hit, which had gotten
him in here. He hoped it didn't want a fight. He was considerably at a disadvantage, and besides, he had gotten in
trouble that way in the first place.

"They tell me you're refusing your food."

It was an official of some kind. "It doesn't agree with
me, sir. I'm sorry."

"A very respectful hani. Males of your kind have a reputation for violence. For strength—one can expect that. But
they say you're such a quiet, cooperative prisoner."

"I didn't mean to hit anybody. If it was you, I'm sorry."

"No, no, not me. I assure you. In fact I've taken the
liberty of contacting the governor in your case. A hani ship
is in port. I thought it might agree to help you get home."

All at once his pulse was racing. Everyone said never
trust such a creature, and it had to want something—kif
didn't *do* you favors. Everyone said so. There had to be
a catch.

"Who are they, sir?"

"Relatives of the *mekt-hakkikt.* Chanur clan. And they
have agreed to take you in custody. I hope this is agreeable
to you."

Agreeable. He folded his arms to keep from shaking.
"Yes, sir. Absolutely." Chanur. Gods, O gods, if it could
possibly be true . . .

"You wonder why one of my rank would be interested?"

"Yes, sir."

"My name is Vikktakkht. Can you say that?"

"Vikktakkht."

"Can you remember it?"

"Yes, sir."

"You understand gratitude."

"Yes, sir."

"Then do me a favor. When it occurs to you . . . repeat
my name where it seems appropriate."

"I beg pardon—?"

The kif came close to him, and laid a black-clawed hand
on his arm. It was as tall as he was, and he had a most
uncomfortable look within the hood, into narrow, red
rimmed eyes that gazed deeply and curiously into his.

"Go with the officers. Cause no trouble. Remember my name. Never forget it. At some time you will want to ask me a question."

Sheets dropped into the printout tray. One . . . two . . . three . . .

. . . ten . . . eleven. The thing was a monster.

. . . forty nine . . . fifty . . .

My *gods,* was the printer on a loop?

. . . one hundred . . . one hundred one . . .

Out of paper. Tarras reloaded the bin and Hilfy sat and stared glumly at the stack. She *refused* to start reading until it was done.

. . . two hundred twenty-six . . . two hundred twenty-seven.

The ready light went off. The binder whirred. She extracted from the bin a contract almost as heavy as the cargo it represented and flipped through the minuscule print.

The computer started into the translation program then, and started displaying the result. She was looking at the stsho script, page after closely written page.

The intercom blurted out: *"Security is here, captain."*

"Get outside," she said to Tarras. "Get a check on those papers. Tiar knows what I mean."

"Security?" Tarras asked, ears up again.

"Delay the offloading for an hour. You're going to query station on this one."

"What's security got to do with it?"

She was trying to read stsho script. On this screen it was a challenge to the eyesight. "I committed an act of mercy. The gods' penance for fools." The translator was already querying for conflict resolution. And *she* had to do it. Tiar knew enough stsho to handle customs. Tiar didn't read the classical mode. Which this was.

And when you had a contract, you by the gods read it. Demand it in hani? Better to pin down the contract-giver in native expression—or *gtst* could claim deception on your part. Better to be able to claim deception by them against you. The courts did give points for that.

Was there a non-performance clause? And on which side was the penalty?

Was there a contingency for breakage? For war and solar events and piracy?

Did it cover personality alteration? And gender switching? Stsho *did* that, under stress, and in trauma.

Did it cover death or change of the designated recipient before accepting the object?

Did it provide a sure identification for the object?

The translator kept interrupting, begging resolution. She foresaw a sleepless watch, and irritably split-screened the display, stsho and hani versions.

One did *not* translate a formal stsho contract into Trade tongue: it only developed ambiguities. One did not tell the translator to solve its own conflicts. The first wrong logic branch could start it down the road to raving lunacy.

"Captain. Sorry to interrupt you. They say we can't access the legal bank without an authorization from admin—"

"Get it. Call the governor's aide. Tell them the difficulty. Tell them I've just spoken to *gtst* excellency and been assured this would not happen."

"Aye," Tiar said cheerfully, and the com went out.

Did it stipulate a deadline for delivery?

Did it set damages and arbitration?

"Captain."

Gods. "Tiar?"

"The station office won't put the call through without an authorization from you."

An addendum to the contract. Access. For every last member of the crew.

"I'm going to shoot the kif. Tell them that. Tell them . . ." No, she was not going to invoke Aunt Py's name or her perks or her reputation. "Tell them I'm putting the call through. Personally."

"Aye, captain."

She did it. Very patiently. She resolved a conflict for the translation program, then punched through to station com, and drawled, "This is captain Hilfy Chanur, *Chanur's Legacy,* to No'shto-shti-stlen, governor of Meetpoint, and so on—fill in the formalities. Excellency: some individual in lower offices is obstructing your orders. —Relay it! Now!"

"Chanur captain."

"Yes?"

"Chanur captain, let us not be hasty. Can this person assist?"

"Possibly." She took on far sweeter tones. "If you can

get a copy of that entire dossier my crewwoman just requested, *and* relay us an affidavit that the case in question is settled as of this date . . . in case something proliferates through files at some other station. Should we be inconvenienced by this, in doing a favor for the governor? I think we should not."

"Notable captain. —A matter of moments. A formality only. Every paper you want."

"In the meanwhile—hold that message ready to send. One quarter hour, to have those papers on the dock, at our berth. This should have been done, do you understand that? This was No'shto-shti-stlen's own order!"

"Esteemed, a quarter hour. Less than that!"

"The quarter hour is running now, station com. Good luck to you."

There was the clause regarding payment. One million haulage and oversight. And there was the clause regarding delivery of the cargo, to a stsho in the representative office on Urtur Station.

So far so good. She read through the succeeding paragraphs.

"Captain. We got it."

"Good. *Thank* station com."

"Captain. His clan is Meras. But he's off a Sahern ship."

Her head came up. The translator was stuck again. She ignored it. She had ignored the situation with the boy—not wanting to walk out that hatch and deal with a party of kif and a hostage. It wanted a cooler disposition than she could manage at the moment.

But *Sahern,* was it?

Not friends. A clan with whom they had a centuries-old, formally filed feud.

Thank you, gods. Penance for mercy indeed.

"I'll see him."

She solved the translator's problem, let it run and read until she heard the hatch cycle. Then she leaned over and killed displays, swung the chair around toward the door.

Boy, she had said. So many were, that had gone to space. But he was older than that. He had his full growth—at least in height; had to duck his head coming through the door. His shoulders were wide enough to put the consoles in jeopardy. *Handsome* lad—a statue had to notice: and a spacer crew months out on a run was going to notice. Shy, scared, all those things a young man might be, dropped in the midst of a strange clan, and him in the wrong—it took a moment before he decided he had to look at her.

"*Na* Meras. Welcome aboard."

"Thank you, *ker* Chanur. I'm very grateful to be here."

"I don't doubt. I hesitate to ask why your ship found it necessary to leave."

"I don't know, *ker* Chanur."

"Captain will do. And don't you?"

Ears lowered. The boy found a spot on the deck of interest. "I don't remember what I did. They say I broke some pottery. And hit a kifish gentleman."

"A kifish gentleman." The boy *was* delicately bred.

"I don't remember that part," he said. Add *new to drink and bars.*

"You weren't in communication with your ship."

"No, captain."

"Not since?"

"No, captain."

"And you've no notion why your captain suffered a lapse of memory either."

"No, captain."

"*Na* Meras, that answer could get very tiresome over the next several months. Possibly even by tomorrow."

"I'm sorry, captain."

"What's your *name, na* Meras?"

A glance up, ears half-lifted. "Hallan, captain. From Syrsyn. —I—I met your aunt once, on Anuurn dock. And *ker* Haral . . ."

Her ears went down. She remembered a dockside, at Anuurn, too, a parting with the crew. A handful of bitter words.

There was absolute adoration on the boy's face—not, she was sure, cultivated on any Sahern ship. And sensitivity enough to realize he had just trod on dangerous ground. Bewilderment . . . confusion. He had the sense to shut up, give him that.

"Are you married in Sahern, lateral kin, . . . what's the relationship?" It was a measure of how often and how long she had been downworld that she did *not* track the lineages any longer. He could be related to the Holy Personage of Me'gohti-as for all she knew.

"No relation," he said, managing to locate that spot on the deck again.

So a tasteful person would stop asking. Look at the boy. Figure a kid wanted a berth. And Sahern gave him one.

She shot a glance up at Tiar. "I think the lad could stay in passenger quarters."

"I can work maintenance. I have my license."

"That's to prove. In the meanwhile—" Practicalities occurred to her. "I don't suppose you came with baggage."

"Everything—" The boy made a despairing gesture. "Everything's aboard the *Sun*."

"*Sun Ascendant?* —*Tellun* Sahern?"

"Yes, captain."

More bad news. "We'll get you caught up to your ship, or drop you where you can make connections . . ."

"I want to stay *here*."

"On Meetpoint?"

"No, captain. On this ship. I want to stay with *you*."

"The *Legacy* has a full complement. No berths." She saw the ears go flat, the frowning attitude of not quite resignation, and ticked down a Watch this boy, a little sense of resistance there. Of . . . one was not certain what. "You want *my* long-term advice? Ship home. Go back, work in-system cargo if you're so dead set on space."

"*No*, captain."

A little flare of temper. A set of the mouth. Gods-rotted fool kid, she thought, and glared. What did I do to deserve this?

Chapter 2

The stack from the translator was 532 pages thick . . . counting the alternative translations successively rendered. That was the first pass the comp had made. The legal advisement program advised that its analysis of the translation would be 20,588 pages in length and did the Operator want it simply to summarize?

"Apparently the thing is a vase," Hilfy said. Four hani faces, four worried hani faces, stared back, and blinked in near unison.

"A ceremonial vase," Tiar said. "Somebody's grandmother buried in it?"

"Not from what I figure. I've run *oji* through every cognate and every derivation I can find. It means 'ceremonial object with accumulated value' and it's related to the word for 'antique' and 'relic.' Its transferred meanings and derivatives seem to mean 'ceremonial object with social virtue,' 'communal high tea,' . . ."

"You're kidding."

". . . and 'inheritance.' "

"No'shto-shti-stlen's going to die?" Fala asked.

"Who knows?" A shrug was not politic, but it was close company, here. "Maybe *gtst* is designating a successor. Maybe the old son *is* going home to die."

"They do that," Chihin said. "Stsho won't die in view of strangers. Bad taste."

"It's pay in advance. *Gtst* can't change *gtst* mind."

"That's for certain."

Hilfy stared at the stack. "Pay in advance. Gods, it pays. You just keep asking yourself why."

"What can go wrong?" Fala asked, and got a circle of flat-eared looks and a moment of silence.

"There's an encyclopedia entry," Hilfy said, "under *oijgi,* related substantive, to the effect that an object like that can't be paid for, that it just transfers, and money can't touch it directly. Mustn't touch it directly. It's all status. Of some kind. It could account for the extravagance."

"We could outright ask somebody," Tarras said.

"No. Not when we don't know what we're dealing with— or how explosive it is. No'shto-shti-stlen has ears in every wall in this station."

"Electronically speaking," Tiar said.

"I certainly wouldn't bet the contract against it."

"So you're leaning toward signing?"

"Once every quarter hour. Elsewhen I'm inclined to take our cargo on to Hoas and forget I ever heard about it. Why in a mahen hell does this thing have to go rush-shipment to Urtur? Why not a slow trip via Hoas in the first place? Does the governor have to be difficult? Does the thing explode on delivery?"

"You want my opinion?"

"What?" she asked.

"I say *if* we take the contract, we get all our cargo buys nailed down in advance. And stall signing to the very last moment. Gossip's going to fly the moment that check hits the bank. They'll jack the prices on us."

"Give the old son *no* time," Tarras said, "to frame us for anything. Because you can bet the next trip's take that bastard No'shto-shti-stlen is thinking how to get that money back before it hits our pockets. On *gtst* deathbed *gtst* would make that arrangement. *Gtst* isn't the richest son this side of space for no reason."

"Trouble is," Chihin said, "we've got to take certain cargo *for* Urtur if that's where we're going. And unless old No'shto-shti-stlen's been uncommonly discreet, there are stsho on this station who know what the deal is; and if they know, security's already shot. If we're going to deal, we'd better deal fast, because I've got a notion if this thing is that important to the stsho, it could be important to No'shto-shti-stlen's enemies, too. If it is, figure on spies reporting what we buy, and what we deal for, and what we've got contracts on—if we sneeze, it's going into somebody's databank and right to No'shto-shti-stlen's ears for a starter."

"And elsewhere simultaneously," Hilfy said. Aunt Py

had dealt with the stsho. And still did; what was Aunt Py's expression? Never trust the stsho to be hani? They weren't. They wouldn't be. No more than hani would play by stsho rules; or mahen ones; and the stsho had been cosmopolitan enough to know that single fact before the *han* or the mahendo'sat ever figured it out. Add to it, that a hani who happened to be fluent in stsho trade tongue and its history might deceive herself in special, personal blind spots related to the interface between languages and world-views.

"I want," Hilfy said, extruding claws one after the other to signify the items: "an estimate on a list of things I've left on file, under 'Urtur.' I'm betting on goods that originate from beyond Meetpoint, that no one's going to bring in from the other direction. Things we know Urtur's short on. And I want a search on the manifests for ships going out of here. We can't account for what might come in from Kshshti—so let's concentrate on stsho and t'ca goods."

"Gods, not another methane load."

"It pays. It pays and they have their own handlers."

"It's who else might be interested in it worries me," Tiar said.

"It's a straight shot to Urtur. If we just do a fast turn-around here, and get ourselves out of port . . ."

Tiar made a visible shudder, and waved a hand in surrender. "It pays."

"So we agree?"

A murmured set of agreements. Hilfy watched the expressions, wondering whether they might be agreeing against better judgment, because of kinships, because of loyalty.

"I want *opinions!*" she snarled. "I want someone to disagree if they're going to disagree!"

No one moved. She waited. And no one said anything.

"No opinions to the contrary."

"No, captain," Tiar said, with a flat, unmoved stare. And added: "I'll check methane ship departures. See what their trade's been. If it looks like there's a niche for us, aye, we do it. We'll pay out the ship on this run. That's worth a chance."

"Do it tomorrow," she said, with the weight of the day on her shoulders. "I want that Hoas cargo done, too, who's going out we can dump it on. Again, quietly."

"I'll check on that," Chihin said. "We'll just pull a big general dataload from the station . . . costs, but nosy neighbors can't tell anything out of one big request."

"Do that," Hilfy said. Specific records-searches *would* tip off the curious. Fifteen thousand credits. Minimum, for that datadump. But they could re-sell it at Urtur, get back five, six thousand, as moderately comprehensive information. Maybe ten thousand. They stood to own the highest currency of information coming in. With a full dataload. She found herself thinking, with increasing solidity: *at Urtur.* Not Hoas, as they had been bound. At Urtur. They had the advantage of having just been through there, they had the uncommon situation of having the funds to buy their own cargo. That meant the profit was *theirs,* not some shipping company's.

And Hallan Meras still had a chance to catch his ship. Gods. One more problem than they needed.

"You're not staying on watch," Tiar said.

"No."

"I'd better."

"Get some sleep, I said. I want a crew with brains tomorrow. Good night."

" 'Night, cap'n." From Tiar. At the door, hindmost. Still registering objection, in that backward glance. But Tiar went.

Tiar was right. If they were half practical they would keep one of them on watch from now on until they parted company with Meetpoint. If they had enemies, things would develop in files on their off watch and proliferate through their sleep. Anyone who had prospects had trade rivals here, and they could have plenty, if No'shto-shti-stlen's shipment was general knowledge . . . which, of course, they could not ask to find out.

But all that had proliferated into their files thus far was mail, the stack of which, even from ships that had long since left port, equaled the translation. And with the comp set to rouse them for fire, collision, and interstellar war, she reckoned they knew enough. She added one more alarm word from her console: *contract,* and on a stray thought, added *No'shto-shti-stlen.*

And headed for her own quarters and for bed, tired, gods, yes.

Until her back met the mattress and her head hit the
pillows. Then every detail of the day wanted to come back
and replay itself behind her eyelids.

Kifish guards. That brought her eyes open, and she tried
to think of something else, anything else, bright things, full
of color, like the clan estate on Anuurn, with the golden
fields and green forest and rolling hills.

But that did no good. She wound up thinking about family
politics, remembering her father, *wishing* that the time-
stretches that spun out her star-jumping youth had somehow
reached planetside, and extended Kohan Chanur's life. But
the years had caught up with him—not a fight with some
upstart, thank the gods. His daughter and his sisters and
his nieces had kept the young would-bes away, had given
him a peaceful old age. No one but time had defeated him.
He had just not waked one morning.

Meanwhile *her* husband, *na* Korin nef Sfaura, thought *he*
was going to move into Chanur. Pick a husband with brains
and muscle and you got the hormones that went with it,
you got a husband with ideas, and Hilfy Chanur had spent
sleepless nights telling herself there were reasons to abide
by the old customs, that shooting Korin Sfaura, while a
solution on the docks at Kshshti, was not a solution on
Chanur's borders, with a neighboring clan.

Not unless one wanted to crack the amphictiony wide
open, and see war on Anuurn.

Gods-rotted bastard he had turned out to be. But the
male-on-male fighting men learned for territory had a few
things still to learn from Kshshti docks. Korin had limped
out of Chanur territory, half-wed and vowing revenge, and
by the time he'd made another try, cousin Harun had come
in as lord Chanur . . . big lad, Harun. Rhean had searched
the outback to find him and get him home, out of his wilderness exile. Best fighter they could find, best lord of
household, for a clan taking a lot of challenges. Of all the
lads that had come home at Kohan's invitation, and some
of them even settled inside Chanur walls, Harun . . . was
not one of that liberal, easy-going number. Ask any of the
males he had sent packing, including the ones born to Chanur. A hani of the old school—hair-triggered—thick-
skulled . . .

But it had taken him to rid the clan once for all of what

she had brought home, and detest and despise *na* Harun Chanur as she did, and know, as she did, that Rhean had brought him home precisely to counter Aunt Py's influence . . . she had to think that he might be the right hani for the times; because Pyanfar's gallivanting about and Pyanfar's naming *her* head of clan had certainly raised the hair on a number of conservative backs. Change happened and you thought it was forever, and immediately there were all the enemies of that change making common cause and meeting in the cloakrooms.

And there were all the victims of that change—dead, like poor bookish Dahan Chanur, who had died for nothing more than wanting to collect his notebooks. Gods-rotted thick-headed Harun had ordered him out, Dahan had said something about his notes, headed back for his room, and Harun had flung him into a wall.

That was the lord of Chanur now. And she had done Rhean's daughter out of the *Legacy,* and some didn't forgive her for pulling rank and spending her ascendency as clan head as an absentee.

Truth be told, she was guilty of everything they said at home. Aunt Rhean was disgusted with her. High and wide she'd fouled it up, mate-picking and house-running . . . parted company with Aunt Py, that day on Anuurn docks. And Aunt Py . . .

Ex-clan-head Pyanfar Chanur had said, being lately hailed grand high whatever of everywhere civilized, and leaving Anuurn's dust for good.

Aunt Py had said, *Responsibility, Hilfy.* Jabbing her with an attention-getting claw. *I can't go down there again. It'd be war. And every enemy I have—listen to me!*

Another jab, and a grab, because she'd tried to walk out on Pyanfar, and nobody did that.

Every enemy I have on Anuurn will try to break the clan. That's the only revenge they can get on me. I want you to go down there, take the responsibility I gods-rotted carried, do your marrying . . . Kohan's not going to hold out forever . . . and get somebody in his place that can hold on to what he helped build. Do you hear me, Hilfy Chanur?

Gods-rotted right she'd heard her. Pyanfar talking about Kohan as if he was already dead, just to be written off; Pyanfar telling her to go down there and make a baby or two, when Py's own offspring in Mahn had been trouble from birth . . . tell *her* about handling her responsibilities to the clan, when Pyanfar was off with her ship and her crew and everything in the universe that mattered to her.

Py wanted her off her ship and away from Tully, was the bare-faced truth. Go fall in love with your own species, kid. Tully's all right for Chur and Geran, and Haral and Tirun and anybody else who wants a roll in the bunk, but don't even think of the heir of Chanur in that picture.

Go make babies downworld. Go find some muscle-bound, ambitious son of a clan you trusted, that you have to get some other muscle-bound dimwit cousin to get rid of. It's a tradition.

It's a gods-be tradition we kill the ones like Dahan and keep the ones like Harun.

And all the lost young lads who believed in Chanur's taking men onto ships, all the hundreds of young lads who with stars in their eyes had begged and bribed their way up to space, where they'd be free of tradition . . . what did they meet, and where were they, and what became of them, on the ships they'd gone to?

She tossed over onto her face and mangled the pillow, thinking about a human face and a place she didn't want to think about, ammonia-stink that she still smelled in her dreams. Sodium-lights and kifish laughter. And Tully'd collected the worst of it, because Tully was a novelty. Tully'd escaped them once and they had something to prove. . . .

They'd come through that, and come through war and fire, and Pyanfar had said . . .

You'll only do him harm.

Damned if Pyanfar knew that. Damned if Pyanfar cared whether she knew what had gone on between them: Pyanfar had cared whether she took up the burden of the clan, and Chanur's politics downworld said there'd been scandal enough—Chanur's heir had to be something the old women downworld could deal with, and accept, and politic with.

She couldn't deal with it. She wouldn't deal with it. The hypocrisy gagged her. And the hypocrisy of *We have to change our ways,* and *Men aren't educated to make decisions,* and *This generation has to pass*—

So Dahan was dead and Harun was lord Chanur, and a

hani ship took a naive kid aboard and *left* him, at the farthest point hani traded, because he wasn't *educated* to think and wasn't *educated* to handle strangers, and because every species in the Compact believed that hani males were helpless, instinctual killers.

Gods *rot* the way things worked! Gods *rot* the old women who made the rules and the captain that had pulled a ship out with a crewman in kifish hands! Gods *rot* Pyanfar Chanur, whose powers extended to every godsforsaken end of the Compact and beyond . . . and who couldn't do justice in her own clan!

She pounded the pillow shapeless, she thought of the kid she'd received out of the hands of kifish guards, she thought of a big, good-looking lad who'd probably paid the obvious for his passage, and she thought bitter thoughts of what was probably going through her crew's heads . . . months away from home port and the sight and sound of a male voice.

She hated to make an issue. She probably should give a plain and clear hands-off order: Don't scare the kid. Don't crowd him. Where he's been—

She flung herself out of bed, crossed the room in the dark, and found the bathroom door cold blind. Washed her face in the dark, washed her mane and her neck and her hands and stood there with her ears flat and her nostrils shut and told herself it was her cabin, her own ship and she had no need to *think* tonight about that place, or to remember the stink and the look on Tully's human face.

She did not need the light. She felt her way to the shower and shut the cabinet door behind her, turned on the water and let the jets hit her face and her shoulders, hit the soap button and scrubbed and scrubbed, until she could smell nothing but the soap and her own wet fur, until she was warm through and through and she could stand a while against the shower wall while the heated, drying air cycled.

She could forget them, then. She could forget that place, and tell herself the lights if they came on would be the spectrum of Anuurn's own yellow sun; and the voices if she should call on them would be those of the *Legacy*'s crew, cousins and kin she could rely on, kin from Chanur itself, and Chihin and young Fala Anify, Geran's and Chur's cousins, of the hill sept.

Not unreasonable women. Not fools, not political, not planetbound in their thinking, not any of those things she had met downworld. Believers in Pyanfar's ideas . . . gods, could she ever escape them? But trust her crew? With her life, with her sanity. Lean on their advice? Often.

Risk their lives, on this wild hope of proving Rhean and the rest of them wrong, paying out the *Legacy*'s costs and putting the clan on a footing financially that owed not a gods-be *thing* to Pyanfar Chanur? If she signed that stsho contract, there was a chance that she might go back to Anuurn solvent and independent of debt.

A chance, too, that she might so compromise herself that Chanur could not redeem her, not financially, not in reputation.

Hilfy Chanur did not intend to come home begging for resources, Hilfy Chanur did not intend to make her way on her aunt's influence, her aunt's reputation, or her Aunt's decisions. That was what she decided.

Sign the contract. Take the chance. What would Aunt Pyanfar do?

Far more foolish things. Far crazier chances. Aunt Pyanfar had risked Chanur and everything they owned for a principle.

Was that not mad . . . when no one else of her acquaintance gave a damn—and hani did as hani had always done?

He had not slept, truly slept, in very long; and having a comfortable bed and only the whisper of air from the ducts, he had hardly needed do more than lie down and shut his eyes before he was gone.

He tried to think about things, but they escaped him. He tried to worry about where he was and where he was going, but he simply fell unconscious.

He waked after that in the disorientation of some unfamiliar sound and an unfamiliar cabin—he found he had left the lights on, and wanted to do something about it, but his eyes shut again and he burrowed under the covers and forgot about it on the instant. The next time he waked, he lay thinking about it, and realizing his eyes were tired of the light, and thinking that he ought to get up and do something, but he threw the covers back over his head and was gone again.

The third time he realized someone was in the room, and he took fright and lifted his head.

"Sorry," the crewwoman said—one of the senior two, his scrambled wits could not recall her except as Chanur clan. His fright did not go away. She seemed friendly enough, but he was in strange territory, with strangers he had to get along with.

"Go back to sleep if you like." She opened the closet, took his breeches off the hook and took a quick several measurements while he blinked stupidly at the embarrassing proceedings and decided it was something about the clothing he didn't have.

"Going to need a special order on this," she said. —Tiar was the name, he could recall it now. Tiar. Chihin. Hilfy Chanur. Someone else he couldn't recall, the small one, the young one . . . "Do you some kifish outfits, stsho, whatever you like, no trouble. Even mahen stuff. Not hani. I can't even swear we can find blue. I'll do the best I can."

"Thank you," he said uncertainly. Something seemed called for, however awkward the circumstances. And it got a pursing of the mouth, a twinkle in the spacer's eye.

"Hey. You're safe here. Relax."

He wanted to think so. He remembered Pyanfar Chanur. He remembered every time things got truly bad, that *she* had taken time to talk to him, and *she* had encouraged him.

It was a Chanur ship. That was the realization in which he had fallen asleep, and the reality to which he waked. It had all the attributes of a dream, that it was improbable, it arrived out of nowhere, and it promised him everything he couldn't likely have and couldn't hope for.

He truly wanted Tiar Chanur to like him—most of all, to think of him as a spacer. He watched the door shut, and thought that he shouldn't lie here like a lump, he should get up and make up his bunk and be ready to do something around the ship. He wanted to make the best impression he could on Hilfy Chanur. So he got himself out of bed, hoping no one would open the door unannounced, and showered and dressed in the only pair of breeches he had, everything else being on the *Sun*. He made his bed meticulously.

But when he went to go out, the door was locked.

He tried it a second time, to be certain. His heart sank,

and he debated whether to try the intercom and appeal to be let out, but they knew he was here and they surely knew why they had locked the door.

So, with nothing to do, he sat down on the carefully made bed and stared at the furnishings, listening to the sounds that a ship had even when it was at dock, the rush of air in the ducts, the thumps and occasional cyclings of hydraulics. He had no breakfast. Which he supposed they might omit, thinking he was still asleep. But he had looked forward very much to familiar food. He had thrown up most everything they had given him in the jail, and there was nothing available here but water—which at least did not smell of ammonia, there was that to be glad of.

He listened to the sounds of the cans moving out of the hold. He heard the hatch cycle more than once. Finally he lay down and stared at the ceiling, trying not to despair. He did not want to think about his situation. It was like the jail. It was better if you didn't think there, either, or wonder about things.

He did not need to wonder about his ship. He had every certainty where it was, in hyperspace, bound for Hoas. He had every certainty why it had left him, and he supposed now he should not have been surprised. If he were back on Anuurn, he would have had to quit the house, because when boys grew up, they had to leave. They had to go out into the outback to live, learn to hunt and to fight each other and if boys lived long enough they could come back and try to drive some older man out into the outback to die. If the man's wives and sisters didn't beat him to death before he got a chance to challenge one on one.

That was what he had been headed for. That had been the order of things forever. There were always too many boys and most of them died. But Pyanfar Chanur's taking Khym Mahn into space, her moral victory over the *han* and its policies, and her outright defiance of the law and the custom . . . had given him a chance at the stars, at . . . freedom.

Well, it was freer than shivering in the rain and killing to eat and to live. Freer than getting beaten off and driven off and told he was crazy because he was male.

He didn't think he was crazy. He thought he did a fair

job of holding his temper. He hadn't *meant* to hit the kif. He'd only wanted away.

Probably, though, the captain had heard the story from the police and the station authorities, and that was why the door was locked. So he could get out of this. He just had to be quiet and patient and not cause any trouble, and prove to the captain that he'd learned something in his apprenticeship aboard the *Sun*.

Hilfy Chanur was Pyanfar's niece. She was one of the crew that had fought at Anuurn. She was one of the ones that had changed the world. She wouldn't do what wasn't fair. She wouldn't judge him without giving him a chance. She wouldn't just put him off somewhere, or send him home.

He would rather die than go home. Not after . . . after all he'd learned, and worked for, and seen existing just outside his reach.

Granted he hadn't fitted in. The crew of the *Sun* had accepted him, slowly—well, they were on the way to accepting him. He tried to outlast their opinions, and they were almost, sort of beginning to take him for granted once they'd gotten used to the idea of having a male aboard. He'd gotten them to show him things, he'd done the best he could, he'd studied everything he could get his hands on, and he'd been getting better, in spite of the growth spurt he'd put on.

He hadn't lost his temper. They'd played jokes on him, but that was just to see how he would react, it was just because he was there and he was different, and he'd proved he could take it. He'd only slipped up the once—

On the docks. Which was bad. That was really bad, and the captain had a right to be mad. But he'd gotten control of himself. He'd not hit anybody else, not even when they arrested him.

Truth was, he'd been scared, not mad. He'd been dreadfully scared. And that feeling was back with him as if it had never left.

The translator was on the fourth from-scratch pass. The legal program was on its second. If this kept up, Hilfy thought, they were going to have to put in an order for another carton of paper. She *hated* the hand-slate. You took notes on it and it just got messier and spread the information you were working with farther and farther apart. And you couldn't punch marks in it or turn down the corners or take notes on the back.

Paper, she keyed to the Do List. The thick stuff. It massed more but it didn't fold up while one was reading or note-making. And she had done a lot of reading this morning, while the loaders were clanking and thumping away under Fala's and Chihin's supervision. Meanwhile Tarras was tucked down with the datadump from station files, looking for information—who might take the transship cans, who had what for sale and what the futures list and the methane-folk routings looked like.

The party initiating the contract requires of the party accepting the contract that in the event of the activation of Subclause 14 Section 2 the party accepting the contract shall perform according to the provisions of Subclause 14 Section 2, notwithstanding this shall not be construed as negating the requirements of Section 8 parts 3–15, provided that the party receiving the goods be the person stipulated to in Subsection 3 Section 1, and not a Subsequent of said person; if however the party qualified to receive the goods be the Subsequent of said person or Consequent of the Subsequent named in Subsection 3 Section 1, then the conditions set forward in Section 45 may apply.

She had a headache, and sipped gfi and put a purple clip on the side of the paper for *performance* and a blue one for *identity,* took another sip and winced as something hung up in the *Legacy*'s off-loading system. A new ship had glitches in common with an old one, systems with bugs in them.

One of the bugs was in the out-track, the very simple chain-driven system that should take one of the giant container-cans smoothly from the hydraulic lift to the hydraulic loader-arms. They had tried lasers to find a fault in the line-up, they had tried carbon-coated paper to turn up an imprecision in the teeth, they'd marked the places on the chain that jammed and the places on the wheel that jammed, and no joy. She had preferred the system because it was what *The Pride* used, it was old, it was tested, it was straightforwardly mechanical, cheap to repair, but that gods-rotted chain was going to break and kill somebody someday. Every time it jammed like that she flinched.

A small problem, the outfitter swore. Easy to fix. Just pinpoint the problem, and we'll make it right.

The loader started up again. So nobody was killed. Hope it wasn't the mahen porcelain they were hauling. But the chain was intact. She heard it working.

If the party receiving the goods be not the person stipulated to in Subsection 3 Section 1, and have valid claim as demonstrated in Subsection 36 of Section 25, then it shall be the reasonable obligation of the party accepting the contract to ascertain whether the person stipulated to in Subsection 3 Section 1 shall exist in Subsequent or in Consequent or in Postconsequent, however this clause shall in no wise be deemed to invalidate the claim of the person stipulated to in Subsection 3 Section 1 or 2, or in any clause thereunto appended, except if it shall be determined by the party accepting the contract to pertain to a person or Subsequent or Consequent identified and stipulated by the provisions of Section 5 . . .

However the provisions of Section 5 may be delegated by the party issuing the contract, following the stipulations of Subsection 12 of Section 5 in regard to the performance of the person accepting the contract, not obviating the requirements of performance of the person accepting the contract . . .

Another sip of gfi. A chase through the stack of paper after Subsection 12 of Section 5. She could Search it on the computer but that meant moving the output stacks, the notes, the reference manuals and the microcube case that was sitting in front of the screen.

Somewhere in Library there was a reference work on Subsequents, at least as far as mahendo'sat understood stsho personality changes. She would have the computer look it up. When she found the monitor screen.

She took another sip of gfi.

The Rows were the open market at Meetpoint—anything you wanted, you had a chance of finding scattered on the tables of a hundred and more small-time merchants, stsho and mahendo'sat . . . stsho and mahen hucksters shoving things into your attention and claiming miraculous potency for unregulated vitamins and curious effects for legal and peculiar compounds, offering second-hand clothes and trinkets, carvings by bored spacers and erotic items peculiar to mahendo'sat and curious to everyone else.

But to a hani in a hurry, with specific measurements and business already in the hands of a mahen tailor in a real established Rows shop, with a pressure-door and every indication of permanency and respectability, the glitter and gaud and traffic of the market were an obstacle—and Tiar tried to make time against it.

Though an honest hani watching her waistline *could* get distracted here, because among the glitter of cheap jewelry and real gold, the echoes of argument and the twittering of doomed kifish delicacies—came the smell of baked goods and spice; mahen pastries. And a number of worldbound hani might turn up their noses at sweets, but she was cosmopolitan in taste: truth was, there was a good deal about mahen sweets she found to like.

And maybe the kid did. And certainly Tarras had the habit.

Well, maybe a dozen. The captain liked some sweets. Fala might. Chihin favored salted things. She could manage that.

And if they were in a mortal hurry and did not get back to the market on this rare stop at Meetpoint (she had asked the tailor to deliver, at soonest) . . . she could take a small detour.

She bought two dozen of the sweets. And decided, well, there were the fish done up in salt crystals, a crate of those, deliver immediately. And the smoked ones. Practical, and a welcome change in the menu aboard. The stsho merchant offered samples, and, well, a box of those. And there was the herb and spice section, right adjacent, where a hani could inhale her way along, collect a bottle or two—she did no small bit of the cooking, and she felt inspired, here.

Then she thought, with her arm considerably weighted with parcels, well, the poor kid had come aboard with nothing in hand. He could use a few toiletries—such things as a young man might like. Brushes, yes. A couple of combs. A mild cologne, something clean and pleasant.

A pair of scissors. A file—it was absolute hell to be without that, and have a claw that snagged. Toothbrush. Of course. Creme for hands and feet—Meetpoint air was dry by hani standards, and he had been in it for days. A good conditioner for all over, while she was at it, not spicy, something like sweet grass. Any young man would like that.

A kit-case to hold it all. Second-hand, with real silver ornament. Never mind the inscription was in mahen script, and probably some love sentiment, it was a nice piece and if nobody but mahendo'sat could read it, who cared?

"Hani officer. A word?"

She looked around, at a brown mahen belly; and up, quite a distance up, at a sober mahen face.

"Legacy?" the mahe said, laying a hand on his chest. "Friend to Chanur, I, long time, follow the Personage."

Gods, another one.

"Look . . ." Tiar shifted the packages in her arms and suddenly realized she was far along the Rows, she had spent longer than she intended collecting her odd items, and a mahendo'sat with religious enlightenment or a crackpot scheme either one was not going to get her home any sooner.

"I know, I know, too many come you ship talk crazy. Not me." A hand larger than her head applied itself to approximately a mahen heart. *"Good* friend, name Tahaisi-mandi Ana-kehnandian, ship name *Ha'domaren,* dock right down there—"

"I'm late. Cap'n's going to skin me as is. Send a message."

"No, no." Said mahen hand landed on her arm, and it was drop the packages or listen. As a third alternative, she laid back her ears and stared up at the owner of said hand, who protested, "Important you listen."

"Important I get back, mahe."

"Call me Haisi."

"Haisi. Get the hand off or I'll give it to you on a plate."

"Very serious! Listen. What you name?"

"Never mind my name! You got a message for the Personage, save it for her! My captain's got her own troubles!"

"You take stsho deal?"

She shouldn't have reacted. But she had, she did, and she stood staring at the mahendo'sat.

"Where'd you hear that?"

"Got ears."

"Got ears. Great. You want a word with the captain? I'll *get* you a word with the captain, you just go right down to berth 23 and use the com, like any civilized individual."

"What you name?"

"Tiar Chanur."

"Ah! *Chanur* officer!"

"Chanur officer, gods-rotted right, Chanur officer! You want to *stay* friends with the Personage, you get down to 23 and say what you've got to say—"

"I carry package for you."

"I'm doing fine! Get! Don't walk with me! We got enough gossip!"

"You lot worry, Chanur officer. All fine. Name Haisi. *Respectable,* long-time come and go this station."

"Get!" She aimed a kick. Haisi escaped it. But Haisi went.

"So where did you hear about this deal?" Hilfy asked, as the mahe sipped expensive tea and lounged in her shipboard office, foot propped. "*When* did you hear it?"

"What deal you want know?" A large mahen hand balanced a tiny cup, and the mahe regarded it closely. "Nice porc'lain. Tiylcyn province, a? You got good taste."

"What do you want?"

"You so ab-rupt. So ab-rupt. How you deal with stsho?"

"I don't think you know anything. I swear to you, if you've talked your way onto my ship for some gods-rotted sales pitch, you can take yourself right out—"

Hand on throat. "You insult me?"

"I'm too busy to insult you! I have a ship to turn around, I have cargo all over my dockside because I can't get enough gods-rotted transports! If you know something, spill it!"

The mahe leaped to his feet. "I leave! I don't sit be insult!"

He might be serious. She regretted that, just long enough for him to reach the door and look back.

"You stupid hani let me walk out."

"I stupid hani let you sell me some damn deal! All right, all right, sit down, have another cup of tea."

"You say nice."

Rubbing salt on it. She pursed her mouth in pleasantness, pricked up her ears and made a gracious gesture toward the abandoned chair. "Do sit down, Ana-kehnandian."

"Nice." The mahe, gods rot his hide, sauntered over to the chair and sat down again, leaned far back and crossed his foot over his knee. "Nice you ship, hani captain."

"What deal?"

"You so sudden. I like more tea."

"Sorry. My entire staff of servants jumped ship at Hoas. The pot's right beside you."

A mahen grin. Only humans and mahendo'sat did that. It was life-threatening on a hani ship. And Tahaisimandi Ana-kehnandian took his time.

"So," Ana-kehnandian said, with a sip and a sigh. "You want know how I know?"

"I want to know *what* you know."

"You got fat deal, stsho with stsho. No'shto-shti-stlen got kif work for him. Same Urtur stsho. Lot big thing with kif. You tell Personage she need take quick look."

"Easy to propose. Not so easy to do. Why should the Personage be interested?"

"What word *hotai?*"

"Bomb. Explosion."

"Explos'. Damn right. Explos' like hell. I tell you, make good deal with you, you let us look this cargo."

She had felt a skip in her pulse from the instant the word *kif* came into the conversation. And this mahe was probing for information, playing a little information as if he was in it up to his ears. Let him look at this cargo indeed.

"Where did you learn about it, Ana-kehnandian?"

"Call me Haisi. We friend."

"Haisi. Where did you learn about it?"

"Cousin on Urtur."

"So this isn't exactly unexpected."

"No. Long time expect."

"Tell me."

"You let me see cargo."

No spacer. Not any merchant captain, if he was a captain, which she suspected: *Ha'domaren,* Tiar said. And that fit: top of the line ship, fire-power concealed by panels, capable of dumping cargo and moving fast, with all the engine capacity of a freight-hauler. She'd seen mahen agents operate when she was with *The Pride,* and she folded her hands now easily on her middle, assuming a studied relaxation.

"Which Personage are you working for? Not my aunt. She'd not be so coy about it. And if you aren't working for my aunt, why should I let you look at anything?"

"You assume lot."

She pursed her mouth into a smile. "Gods-rotted right I do. Who *are* you working for, and is it anyone I should trust?"

"Absolute." Give him credit, cornered, presented with the case, he shifted directions. Which meant he had some authority from someone.

"Name?"

"Paehisna-ma-to."

Didn't tell her a thing. And if the mahe had good research on Aunt Py's clan, he might know she had a slight sore spot about kif in general. So tell her the kif were interested.

But if the mahendo'sat were interested, and kif got wind of it, they would be sniffing around the situation. It was their nature. Like breathing.

"So who is Paehisna-ma-to?"

"Wise woman."

"I'm glad. Tell her Hilfy Chanur keeps her contracts. Tell her if there's anything untoward about this contract, her representative should tell me before I sign the thing."

"You not sign yet?"

"Maybe I have, maybe I haven't."

"Don't do!"

"Maybe will, maybe won't. Right now I'm busy. No more time. Unless there's something else I should hear."

"My ship *Ha'domaren.* You want talk, you send. Don't call on station com."

"I gathered that." She stood up and walked the mahe to the door and down the corridor toward the hatch, her crew being otherwise occupied—listening, and armed with a stranger on board, but occupied. "You give my regards to your wise woman."

"Will," the mahe said, and bowed, and strolled off down the corridor to their airlock.

She stood there until she heard the lock cycle.

"Is he gone?" she asked the empty air.

"Down the ramp," Tiar said via com from the bridge. *"Watching him all the way. Sorry about that, captain. I thought you'd better have a face-to-face."*

"No question," she said, and stared at nothing in particular, thinking how the most secret plans couldn't remain a secret once anybody talked to anybody at all. Suspect anyone. The aide, the kifish guards, most especially them. Stsho refused, since the war, to take their ships out of stsho space, or to trade anywhere with the younger species, except only at Meetpoint. But there was a stsho ambassadorial presence on Urtur. There was a stsho presence even at Mkks nowadays. There would be one at Anuurn, if the *han* would permit it, but the *han* let no one in, secretive and protective of the homeworld, with recent reason.

Certainly whatever was going on between No'shto-shtistlen and the stsho supposed to receive this whatever-it-was at Urtur had attracted someone's attention, or leaked at one end of the deal or the other.

Point: Haisi was here. He had come here from elsewhere at sometime—and Urtur was as good as anywhere. While chance and taking advantage of a local leak of information might have brought him to their ship, it was just as possible he was telling part of the truth—and he had known it and come here knowing it.

Which meant others might.

They were offloading canisters as fast as the *Legacy* could cycle them out; and by tomorrow they had to be taking others aboard. They had to know as early as next morning whether they were going to pass over the Hoas cans and let another ship take the Hoas load. And that meant making a decision . . . that meant signing or not signing.

That meant solvency after this trip . . . or *still* being involved in the deal even if they turned it down, dammit, because being Pyanfar's niece, if she took the stsho object aboard, it said one thing; and if she refused, and it was some crazy stsho religious thing that brought down a friendly governor at Meetpoint—that was disaster.

For once she wished she *could* ask Pyanfar.

But if leaks were happening, they would proliferate. If the mahe agent knew, his crew knew something; if his crew knew something, it could get to the docks; if the kifish guard knew, the kif they might be in collusion with knew; and if things had gone out over station com, then the com operators in station control might know, and so might their associates. . . .

In which case if she didn't sign it and didn't take the deal, and left here for Hoas, there were die-hards who would never believe they hadn't the object aboard, and that it wasn't all a ruse. So the minute one Haisi Ana-whatever knew anything about it—they were tagged with the stsho deal and the stsho object whether or not they actually had it.

At least if they signed the deal and took it, they got paid.

"Who we got to take the Hoas stuff?" she asked on com, when she got back to her office.

"We taking the deal, captain?" Chihin asked.

"Looks as if. Who do we have?"

"Mahen trader. Notaiji. Just in, reputable ship. Regular runs to Hoas. Plenty of time to make the schedule and looking for a load. They don't usually bid, just take what's going and ship when they're full—but this is up to their cap. Good deal for them."

She considered that an unhappy moment and two. Of course a mahen ship was all there was. Where was another hani ship, when a little obfuscation might have served them?

"There are kif outbound. And a t'ca may be. But I didn't consider them as options."

"No," she said. Almost she had rather the t'ca. But getting the address and the disposition of cargo straight with a matrix brain was an exercise in frustration.

And it might send the cans to O'o'o'o'ai, for all any of them could tell. It didn't bother a t'ca shipper, so far as anyone could figure out their economics. But it played hell with one's reputation with oxy-breathers.

Chapter 3

The kid *hadn't* had breakfast. He attacked the meat and eggs like a starveling, between trying to appreciate the kit, and the personal items.

"Thought you could use them," Tiar said, standing by the door, and due to be on other duties. But Hallan Meras was alternately shoving food in his mouth and opening packages. She had brought in nothing contraband, so far as she could figure, nothing he shouldn't be let loose with. The captain hadn't said anything about any restrictions, or given any impression she feared the kid would sabotage them. The captain hadn't thought overmuch about the kid, by what Tiar could tell, not delegated anybody to get him breakfast, even if the captain had remembered about the torn trousers and sent her off to the market to do something about his wardrobe. Small wonder—but still . . . where the kid sat, it hadn't been a good morning.

"Everybody thought you were still asleep," she said, by way of apology.

"I got up to work," he said, and swallowed a hasty mouthful, looking at the silver-trimmed box. "It's beautiful. What kind of writing is it?"

"Mahend. Formal. Probably lost in some dice game. Maybe in a mahen bar. Then down to the Rows. Somebody needed cash. Anything you want, you can find it in that market, that's what they claim anyway. Anything you ever lose—ends up here eventually."

"I got to see it," the kid said.

"Got to see it, huh?"

Hallan's ears dropped by half. "That's where I got in trouble."

"Swung on somebody, what I hear."

"I didn't intend to!"

"Yeah. The police probably hear that one a lot here."

"I didn't! *Ker* Tiar, . . . I wasn't drunk. They said I was drunk, but I wasn't. Somebody just started swinging, I don't even know who."

She found herself disposed to believe the boy—at least that he believed what he was saying; many the hani novice that had lost count of the cups. She could recall such a time. Or two.

"I want to work," the boy said. "I do. I have my license. I used to fix the farm equipment. . . ."

"That's not exactly qualification."

". . . before I shipped on the *Sun.* I mean I learned mechanics. I can run the loaders, I can do anything with cargo. . . ."

"Not that we can't use a hand, but part of the deal with the stsho was getting you off and out of here. I don't think the captain wants you on the docks attracting attention."

The kid's countenance fell, his shoulders slumped. More than disappointment. It was a need of something, there was no time, and Tiar told herself she was a fool for asking.

"Upset you. Didn't mean to. How?"

The kid shook his head. Interest in breakfast and the packages seemed gone. He didn't seem articulate at the moment, so rather than embarrass him she answered her question with a question.

"You want *out* there for some reason? Kid, it's romantic, but it's hardly worth your neck. There'll be other places."

He gave her a hurt look. So it touched on the nerve but didn't quite press it.

"Somebody you want to meet out there?"

Shake of his head, no.

"Something you want to find out there?"

Another shake of his head. Further and further from the sore point.

"You want to talk to me, kid?"

Third shake of his head, and a stare at the wall.

She never was able to walk away from a problem. She stood there, set hands on hips and looked at him a long, long time, figuring he'd collect himself.

"I want to work," he said finally, without looking at her. "I'll do anything."

"I hate to bring this up," she said, with the feeling she

still hadn't heard what she was after, and might not, now. They had circled somewhere away from the substance. "But you know we're sort of ancestral enemies."

"Not with Meras!"

"But with Sahern."

"I know," the kid said faintly.

"Hey, it's not as if it's active. A couple hundred years since. We've got no present grudge. We'll get you back to your ship. We can be real civil to them, just let you off and wish them well. If we can't do that, we'll drop you at some station where they're due."

"How could I live? And I don't *want* to go back to them!"

It was a question, how they were going to install a hani male on anybody's quiet space station. Never mind he was a quiet, mannerly kid, the reputation of hani males for violence was well-established and the fear was there. And if anything did happen . . .

"Well, we'll think of something. Don't worry about it."

He did worry. He looked at her as if he faced an execution. Then looked down and shoved his breakfast around the plate.

They'd locked the door on him. They hadn't been certain of his disposition to stay put, or to take orders. They hadn't been certain his sojourn in the station brig hadn't been justified and they still didn't know that.

But she had some judgment of the situation. And the captain might have her hide, but . . .

"What's your skill entail, son? Your license says tech. You do anything else?"

"Cargo. Maintenance. Galley. —I want to stay with Chanur."

Stay with Chanur. An unrelated male. Nobody's husband. —Same mess he'd been in on the Sahern ship, to tell the embarrassing truth, and she wasn't going to ask. Young kid like that, too anxious and too gullible, who knew *what* his skills had entailed?

"I can *prove* I know what I'm doing," he said.

"I haven't said you didn't know what you were doing. I'm sure you do."

"Then let me work!"

Plain as plain, his hope to impress hell out of them, to

prove himself in some dazzling display and have the whole
crew beg him to stay. And who wouldn't rather a Chanur
ship than Sahern? Perfectly reasonable choice. Perfectly en-
gaging kid. She'd had two sons—had cursed bad luck, that
way. They were probably dead. She hadn't stayed planetside long enough to make it worse than it was. Had had
them, one and the other, but the disappointment was there
from the time the tests had shown they were male. Lot of
women wouldn't have carried them. She didn't know why
she had, tell the truth, but she was old-fashioned, and she
had problems about *that.* Had regretted it for years. And
here came this kid, about the age of her younger boy, in
space, trying to overcome what Pyanfar Chanur and a lot
of her own generation called stupid prejudice, and what a
whole string of other generations from time out of mind
called nature.

She wasn't sure where she stood on that. If Pyanfar was
right her boys had gone out in the outback and died for
nothing.

If Pyanfar was right—it still made problems. Because the
kid was unattached, he had a face you wouldn't forget,
particularly when he looked at you like that and stirred
feelings that weren't maternal at all. She tried to think
about her own boys, telling herself it was Pyanfar's new
age and she was not supposed to think thoughts like that
about lost, scared kids some clan had let stray out of a
cloistered life to deal with people who hadn't had to exercise their moral restraint in a long, long time.

"Tell you what," she said, because she *was* ashamed of
herself, "we got some mop-up to do, and if that fits your
notion of work . . ."

"Anything that needs doing."

"You finish that breakfast. Door's unlocked, I'm right
down the corridor, in the operations center. We're calc'ing
trim and we're going to be taking on a fuel load. Sound
familiar?"

"I can learn." The animation that had left his face was
back, his eyes were bright, his whole being was full of anxious energy. He looked strung tight, probably so scared he
hadn't been eating, scared now, too, of the word no.

"Eat your breakfast. Take a right and a left as you leave
the room. You'll know it when you see it."

*   *   *

"Back again," the kifish guards observed.

Hilfy had no comment for them, except, "I'm here to see *gtst* excellency."

"Of course, of course, fine hani captain. This *way,* hani captain. We would never give offense to the great—"

"Shut up," she said. And regretted losing her temper that far. But she had a bad feeling all the way to the audience hall.

"Tlsti nai," the secretary said, with a lifting of augmented, plumed eyebrows. It might not be the same secretary. The pastel body paint looked subtly different. But it was hard to tell. *Gtst* gathered the contract and the requisite gift into *gtst* long fingers and performed three increasingly deep bows.

"Tlistai na," Hilfy said, bowing once. "I send it by your undoubtedly capable hands. There is no need to disturb the excellency."

"So gracious. Bide a small moment, most honorable."

She bided. She felt her stomach upset—felt an insane and thoroughly impractical urge to charge after the secretary and retrieve the contract before *gtst* passed the curtains.

But the deed was done. She thought after a moment that she might successfully escape back to the ship, but in that moment the secretary returned through the curtain to wave at her and to beckon her to come ahead. No'shto-shti-stlen wanted to see her, perhaps to hand the object into her keeping on the spot, for all she knew; and she was not eager to have the responsibility crossing the docks. An order to move the bank to action, on the other hand . . .

She had far rather the million on credit in her account, because there were cargo cans irrevocably destined for the *Legacy*'s empty hold; while the Hoas cans, already on their carriers, were scheduled for *Notaiji,* a very happy, very grateful *Notaiji,* who could not quite believe the good fortune that had landed in their laps, from "the good, the great hani captain."

So they had stepped over the brink. Figuratively speaking. As she walked into the audience hall.

"We are exceedingly pleased," said No'shto-shti-stlen as she seated herself.

"We have concurred with your excellency. We are pleased at our agreement on the contract and look forward to continued association with your illustrious self."

"Your response is gracious. The elegance of your utterances and your circumspect behavior is a credit to your species."

Then why are you back to using kifish guards? occurred to her, but stsho had rather elegance than truth.

"I am honored by your confidence," she murmured instead; and bowed; No'shto-shti-stlen bowed, everybody bowed again, and No'shto-shti-stlen inquired whether she had time to take tea.

Two teas was a monumental sign of favor.

"Of course," she said, with lading piled all about the *Legacy*'s cargo bay, with transports in scarce supply, thanks to the Hoas load, with a mahendo'sat scoundrel and probable agent of some power swearing to her that the contract was a supremely bad deal, and offering, of course, his services.

A tea in full formality, in the audience hall, in the bowl chairs, with stsho servants this time, and No'shto-shti-stlen reciting poetry:

> *White on white.*
> *The distinctions thereof are infinite.*
> *Upon white snow the eyes dream in pink and gold and*
>   *blue.*
> *Nothing is.*
> *Everything might be.*

Or something of the sort—in classical mode. Hilfy sipped tea and pricked up her ears and laid them flat in deference when it was done.

"Extraordinary view of a delicate perception," she said. "How extraordinary to be afforded such an honor. Are you the poet, excellency?"

No'shto-shti-stlen positively glowed . . . for a stsho. Painted lids fluttered over moonstone eyes and long fingers made wave patterns. "I have that small distinction."

"I am touched to the heart by such an honor. Would it be indelicate to ask your excellency for a copy?

"Not in the least!" Fingers ripped at the aide, who fluttered off in a cloud of gossamer drape and nodding plumes. "You inspire me to thought. And . . ." No'shto-shti-stlen produced the gift box from among *gtst* gossamer robes, and delicately lifted the lid, on a little item she had brought from Anuurn—from Haorai, a carved alabaster box, and within it a single carved *ua* stone ball. And within that— another ball and another and another.

No'shto-shti-stlen opened it; and *gtst* crest flattened and lifted.

"An *oji* of sorts. The ball and box have passed hand to hand for a hundred sixty-three years since it left the artist, of Tausa, in Haor, in Sfaura's eastern sept, on Anuurn. There's a small card that traces its provenance, if your excellency finds it of interest."

"Extraordinary!"

"Each is unique. One bestows the stone on ceremonial occasions. This stone came into the hands of Chanur and thus into mine as clan head—a Sfaura clan object, as the design indicates. Luran Sfaura had it made for her fifteenth birthday celebration; and it passed at her decease to her daughter, and so down to the end of that line in Haor; thus to Sfaura's western sept, part of the unsecured gifts—the explanation is on the card—which has gone back and forth between Sfaura and its tributaries at weddings, oh, a hundred years before it came to me, as a birthday gift from my prospective husband." It was white and it had a history, which she had written up in florid and dramatic detail. It had last been her late husband's, and such historical trinkets impressed the stsho.

Clearly No'shto-shti-stlen was pleased. The creature bowed numerous times where *gtst* sat. Hilfy felt constrained to bow.

And there was, necessarily, yet another round of tea, after which she bade farewell for the second time, and walked out with the kifish guards and out into the foyer and took the lift down to the docks.

Feeling rather pleased with herself, truth be known. She had scored with that gift. She knew the stsho, in a way most hani did not. The governor had given her something monetarily valuable and ceremonially valuable in the cases of tea. But she had given *gtst* something ceremonially and personally and *historically* valuable—so there, she thought, walking out onto the dockside. So there. Remember *me,* stsho, remember *me* and my crew.

She was in such a good mood she decided against taking the public transport. It wasn't that far, down to the *Legacy*'s berth. She was still in a good mood when she threaded her way through the maze of loaders and cargo transports to reach the *Legacy*'s personnel access. She walked on up the ramp way into the yellow, uncertain tube, with its coating of frost, and she walked into the *Legacy*'s lower decks and operations area in an expansive, happy mood, after what she had had to do. She had at least an assurance it was going to work.

Then she put her head into ops and saw Hallan Meras.

"What in hell is he doing here?"

"Captain," Meras said, standing up at once.

"Not bad, actually," Tiar said; and Chihin, managing the number two console, said, "Begging the captain's pardon."

"Get him back to his quarters!"

"Aye," Tiar said. "But he is a licensed spacer. And we are short-handed."

She was not in a mood for reason. Disasters were still possible. "He's not been out on the docks, has he?"

"No, captain," Hallan said at once, and got up from the chair he was occupying, very respectful.

Which made her the villain in the case.

"Gods rot it, he's not crew! He goes back to quarters!"

"Aye," Tiar said. "But he's a help, captain."

"Not right now!" she said. Gods, they had outside messengers likely coming aboard. They didn't need Hallan Meras underfoot. Even with that soulful look in his eyes.

"Captain," he said.

"Don't 'captain' me! You're a passenger on this ship. Chihin, take him back where he belongs."

"I—" he was still saying.

"Kid's done all right," Tiar muttered, as Chihin took him by the arm and drew him out the door. "He's not had a good day, cap'n, go easy."

"He's not had a good day. We're going with the number 1 load. Skip the alternates. Berths full of kif. Snooping police. I want the gods-rotted deck clear out there, I want the fueling done—we've got three loads coming in tonight and we're going to be working straight through the watch!" She was on nervous overload, on her own way to the door. "I'm going to run the nav-calc, I want it checked and triple checked—we're hurrying, if you haven't noticed. We haven't got time for shopping tours and mahendo'sat with a deal and stray boys who'll be reporting our ship cap to Sahern, next thing we know, keep him the hell out of stations!"

"He doesn't want to go back to Sahern."

She swung around, hand on the door frame, finding herself in the middle of somebody's completely foreign dealings, that possibly went against her own. "He says. Don't cut him any deals, cousin! You don't know what he did, you don't even know he isn't a total mistake—'Take this poor lost boy,' the stsho say. In the same gods-rotted conversation with their deal—and *I* don't know what connection if any the two have, I don't know why they didn't give this deal to Sahern except their boy was out breaking up the station market, I don't know what connection it has to anything, and maybe it doesn't, but gods rot it! let's not complicate matters. We get to Urtur, he goes off the ship, he waits for whoever he likes, his ship, somebody else's ship, a passing knnn trader, I don't care, but we don't need to activate the feud with Sahern, and we *will* if we keep him—"

"How's he going to live?"

She had not gotten that far. Not at all.

Tiar asked: "What's he going to do? Urtur isn't going to let any male hani aboard. Do we give him to the police to hold till his ship gets there? That's no better than he had."

She hadn't exactly put *that* together either, in her concentration on the contract. "They can't arrest him without cause."

"They'll find one."

"Hell. —There'll be a hani ship there. There always is. . . . Don't make him any promises, don't let him near our boards, don't complicate our lives, d' you hear me? He's going off this ship!"

"Aye," Tiar said, which didn't mean a thing, except Tiar heard her.

"I have to lock the door," Tarras said, looking apologetic, and that was better than had been this morning, at least. Hallan told himself so, and told himself that politeness was obligatory.

Even when he was shaking mad. He kept his ears up and murmured a thank you.

"Ship's just real busy," Tarras said. A smallish hani with a wavy mane that said eastern blood, from the viewpoint of someone from west of the Aon Mountains. Tarras had one ear notched, and a lot of rings that meant a lot of major voyages . . . you only got those when you'd risked your neck on a trip. Which meant Tarras for all her slight size was a person to respect. "Captain's a little quick-fused just now. We'll sort it out with her."

"I appreciate that," he said, and tried to quit shivering and most of all not to have Tarras see that he was. Women were allowed to have a temper. If he did, he was unreliable and a danger to everyone around him. "I'm not Sahern. I'm not related to them. Even by marriage."

"Wouldn't matter. Captain took you aboard. She would have if you'd been Sahern head of clan. So would we. *Don't* try to talk against Sahern. You won't impress us."

"I'm not!" Gods, everything got twisted. "I never said that. I never said anything against them."

Tarras just looked at him a moment, making him wonder if she believed him.

"How'd you get arrested?" Tarras asked. "The straight story."

He wondered how much *was* in whatever report they had gotten from the kif. "I was fighting."

"That's nothing new. Doesn't always get you arrested. What was the fight about?"

"Me. Being there. In this bar."

Surely she could get the idea. Maybe she had. He didn't want to volunteer more details and he hoped she wouldn't ask. He didn't want to remember them.

"Captain wouldn't leave you in any foreign jail," Tarras said. "She's pretty brusque sometimes. But you being here was her idea. Wouldn't leave anybody where you were. You copy that?"

He had, already. He wasn't willing to think badly about Hilfy Chanur. He knew that, being Chanur, she was inclined to believe he had a right to be here. Chanur was the clan that stood up for his right to be here. Only, even in

Chanur, the attitudes weren't universal, the change hadn't changed every mind; and he was used to that. He had to be used to that. Things as they were gave him no better choice and no court of appeal.

He said, while Tarras was there to listen, "I'd not do anything against Chanur. Ever. Tell the captain that."

Tarras didn't say a thing, just shut the door. And locked it.

Pumps were thumping away, pouring water and other liquids into the *Legacy*'s reservoirs. Fueling was in progress. Tiar slid a cup under Hilfy's inert, poised hand. And reaching the fingers after it seemed a move too much. Hilfy extended a claw, snagged the handle, and dragged it into her weary hand.

"We made it," Tarras said, dropping her bulk into a chair, gfi in hand. "Every gods-blessed one of those babies."

"Course comped," Tiar said.

"Got to be the one that makes it. Pay the ship off and go into the profit column."

"Somebody feed the kid this time?"

"Fala's seeing to it."

"What's our launch, cap'n, we ever get 'im clear?"

"First watch, topside. We take her through, we get our rest at Urtur."

"Gods, that's brutal."

"Mahendo'sat sniffing around us, this hardship case turns up and No'shto-shti-stlen just happens to want him out of here. I don't like it. I don't like it and I wish I hadn't agreed to take him on."

Tiar's ears flattened. "What do you think, he's some deal of No'shto-shti-stlen's?"

"I think the old son knows more about why he's here than *gtst* is saying. I'm not doubting *gtst* wants him off this station: the stsho don't want trouble and he's trouble. I don't know whose, that's the problem. I don't know who's behind him."

"There are coincidences, captain."

"They become increasingly less when the mahendo'sat show up with deals. *That's* what I don't like. 'Let us look at it!' That bastard's on someone's payroll."

"Not *ker* Py's."

It was a thought that had occurred to her. "If he was hers, why not say so?"

"Good question," Tiar said. "But I don't think the boy's involved. It's perfectly understandable."

"What? Leaving him in the brig?"

"Understandable that he doesn't *like* Sahern clan."

"That's what he says. Sahern is *not* our friend. Other interests aren't our friends, for my aunt's sake, for reasons that have to do with decisions she's made that affect things we have no way to know about. We don't know who could have hired her, we don't know who could have hired him, we don't know what side this Haisi person is on, we don't even know that No'shto-shti-stlen's on the up and up or what *gtst* is up *to*. The news got to Urtur and this Haisi person had a chance to get here and offer us a bribe for a look at the object. So why hadn't the news the time to get to Sahern clan, and maybe Sahern lay out some game that would inconvenience us? Ha?"

"Why would No'shto-shti-stlen give you the boy?"

"Because hani aren't as frequent here as they used to be. Because if *gtst* has had a political object dumped in *gtst* lap, No'shto-shti-stlen is going to want rid of it in the way most guaranteed to absolve *gtst* of responsibility. *Gtst* couldn't dump him on Aunt Py, *gtst* couldn't return him to Sahern, and here we come, Pyanfar's close relatives, just so convenient to hand him to . . . I don't know that's the case, but thinking about it is going to cost me sleep, this trip, it's going to make me uncomfortable until he's off our deck and out of our lives, and I *don't* want him loose gathering data at our boards, hear me?"

"Let me understand—you think Sahern *planted* him here?"

"I think it's a possibility. Maybe to create an embarrassment, maybe it's something else. I think it's a possibility there's something more to him than he's showing us . . ."

"Captain, he's a kid!"

"I don't like where he was, I don't like anybody dropped into a kif-run jail and I don't like Sahern dragging him clear to this pit on the backside of the universe to drop him, where, if they wanted rid of him, they could at *least* have dropped him at Urtur. It smells to me like a captain with a god-complex, but I don't swear that's the case; there are all the other possibilities, some of which aren't pretty and aren't conducive to good sleep, but that's the way I see it, that's the way I know how to call it, and that's the only way I know to keep this ship out of trouble. We've got enough problems going, let's not take any additional chances, shall we?"

"Trouble?" Fala asked from the doorway to the little galley.

"No trouble. I trust you locked that door."

"I locked it. I don't see, begging the captain's pardon, why he's—"

Hilfy leaned her forehead on her hand.

"Tell you later," Tarras said.

"We're in count," Hilfy said, leaning back and looking at the clock. "Load's got to be finished by 2300. Gods, I want out of this port."

"Have we got a problem?" Fala asked.

Something ticked over, like a piece in a game falling. A roll of the dice. "I want an instrument scan."

"What?" Tiar asked.

"I want a thorough read-out, I want a camera scan on the hull, I want to know if any skimmers have approached us during our stay here."

A solemn stare from several pairs of eyes.

"Is something going on?" Fala asked.

The camera scan turned up negative. Nothing had approached their hull. Station skimmers always came and went, on such business as external inspections, catching the occasional chunk of something that escaped a ship's maintenance systems, things nobody wanted slamming into their hull or catching on some projection, to be accelerated with the ship and boosted to lethal v. Trouble was, such skimmers had legitimate business back by one's vanes and engines and up near one's hatches; and if a ship with legitimate reason to worry didn't have cameras to prove where such little tenders had access, that ship had far more reason to worry.

But being the Personage's niece had convinced her before the *Legacy* was outfitted that the camera-mounts were a good idea and that motion-sensors and tamper-alerts were mandatory. So they didn't have *that* to worry about—at least so far as they opted prudently to use them.

There wasn't, of course, a way to monitor everything. But they were sure it was water that had gone into their water-lines and that that water was Meetpoint ice-melt, the sensors above the valve had proved it or that valve would have shut. *Being* Pyanfar's niece and having shipped aboard *The Pride,* she had been in ports where one had good reason to wonder about the lines; absolutely right, being sure was worth the cost.

Unfortunately having solved all the high-tech means of sabotage, one still had to worry about the low-tech means at an enemy's disposal. Certain things one could solve by carrying all supplies aboard, and by not refueling and not taking on water at certain ports: but carrying extra mass cost a ship, if one wasn't paying somebody else's freight plus station-cost getting it to the station. If it was local, you were financially ahead to buy it. If it wasn't, and it massed much, you were ahead to freight it, and that was the sum-up and payout of it: if you operated otherwise you weren't competitive, in a tightly competitive market.

But even if you did all of that, and even if you absorbed the cost of being as self-contained as possible, you were still vulnerable to your own cargo and to the legal claim of your ship to use a port and the station's legal right to charge you for being there and, after that was said, to a bank's obligation to honor the claim of other banks on the funds you had in that all-important record you carried that the bank alone allegedly could access.

But banks themselves were not without their compromised accesses, where stsho were concerned, since stsho had set up the banking system, all through Compact space: stsho technology, stsho procedures, stsho rules of accounting, and the stsho system of transfers and debits.

Hilfy Chanur preferred an old hani tradition: cash . . . and cargo; and as little as possible of the former, since it was not going to be drawing interest for the month you were in transit, but your goods were acquiring value during that transit, simply by moving closer to where they were in shortest supply.

Which left you vulnerable to piracy, but you always were;

and at least that answer was in your own hands, and in the quality of the armament you carried and your skill to use it.

The hose connections clanked free, and that was one less problem on Hilfy's mind. The *Legacy* was on its own power, cargo in its hold, and the cash from the station bank was on its way . . . hand-carried, the bank insisted, since the bank did not trust any outsider either, and wanted a signature *at* the *Legacy's* lock *by* the *Legacy* captain that said the money had transferred, all outstanding debts were paid, and the bank was legally absolved of claims against Chanur clan.

And at the same time, they were conveying the Cargo, the *oji,* No'shto-shti-stlen's precious object, along with the funds. Logical enough.

So . . . about time to get one's self down to the lock, looking presentable.

She dusted off her breeches, clawed her mane to be sure no hair was standing on end, and took a wet-fingered swipe at the mustaches and the (cursedly) juvenile beard. Impressions counted, especially with the banks, *which* one could need some dark day. Knees were clean, belt was straight. She picked up Tarras and Tiar for escort, and was still fussing with the beard when they cycled the lock and a blast of chill air from the temperature differential came rushing up the ramp-way and blew her fur and fluttered the fabric of her silk breeches—

Just as a kifish guard was about to punch the call button outside, within the tube, a scant pace from the *Legacy's* own deck. She did not snarl, did not acknowledge the presence, which she vaguely registered as bowing respectfully in realization of her arrival, she simply focused on the stsho approaching in the frost-coated tube and ignored the dark-robed guards . . . fancy, the stsho were, the group from the bank, with the tablet the nature of which she recognized at a glance, and the group with boxes and cases, in one of which might be—surely was—the precious Object. One could hardly pick out any outline, so extreme were the garments in that lot, a drift of pearlized gossamer, of white fronds and feathers. She bowed, they bowed, her crew-women bowed, everybody bowed again, even the kif. It was supremely ridiculous.

"Of course the esteemed captain's word would suffice," the banker was constrained to say, in pidgin.

"We can only regret that your honor did not have sufficient time to take tea," she answered, *not* in the pidgin, and augmented eyebrows shot up and the stsho in question clutched the signed tablet against *gtst* heart, or thereabouts, within *gtst* robes.

"Your most esteemed honor is inadequately recompensed in the press of time which requires our most distressing haste. At another moment we would achieve distinction by accepting your honor's offer."

"Your honor has impressed us with outstanding courtesy."

"Allow us however to present the honorable Tlisi-tlastin, most esteemed adjunct of *gtst* excellency No'shto-shtistlen. The excellency has afforded us the most extreme honor of conveying *gtst* adjunct and the preciousness of *gtst* entrusted burden to this ship and into your most capable hands. We are abundantly satisfied of your honor's most excellent character and elegance."

The leader of the second band of stsho came fluttering across the threshold into the airlock, with an engraved case clutched to *gtst* heart—anxious, by the pursing of *gtst* small mouth, and the three increasingly agitated bows.

"We are so inexpressibly relieved, most honored captain, that you speak the civilized language. We have far less anxiousness to entrust ourselves and this preciousness into your ship."

"What's this 'ourselves'?" For an instant all command of stshoshi language deserted her; but Tiar and Tarras hadn't understood a word thus far. Only that. She said it in stsho: "Would your honor clarify the matter regarding one's illustrious self and one's presence on my ship?"

Another bow. "As *gtst* excellency's most honored representative, of course, as guardian of the preciousness which foreign hands must not touch." A wistful curtsy. "I do hope the excellency did not omit the doubtless inconsequential matter of this absolute necessity, and that some provision has been made for my lodging and my meals of sufficient taste and decorousness not to offend my status as the excellency's emissary."

Possibly she did not control her surprise. Certainly her vision suffered that tunnel focus her ancestors used in hunting, and at the same instant the stsho officials and escort backed an identical number of paces—while in the gray fringe of her vision the kif reached for weapons. Consequently so did Tiar and Tarras.

But she did smile, a hani pursing of the mouth, not to show the teeth. And her ears did not flatten, nor her claws extend. Nor did her escort or the kif, fortunately, open fire. She said, sweetly, because they had the contract, and they had a hold full of cargo bought with its proceeds, "How extraordinary the excellency's trust in our ability to adapt to unusual situations. How much baggage do you have?"

Chapter 4

There was an amazing lot of coming and going next door, when Tiar had called down on com maybe an hour ago saying they were going to undock soon. Hallan put his ear to the wall, then backed off as someone began hammering and banging. It sounded as if someone were tearing into the paneling, and maybe taking the whole cabin apart.

That was a peculiar kind of thing to do, on a ship that was supposed to be in count to undock. He began to wonder if they had a malfunction of some kind, and if maybe the access to the conduits or something more critical was there.

But it was certainly an odd place to put an access.

Something had leaked, maybe? The plumbing had given way?

It kept up a very long time. He heard them moving equipment in, he heard thumping and banging and hammering and hissing. He listened again, thinking maybe the whole compartment had flooded. Maybe—

His door opened. A very dusty, contamination-suited Tiar Chanur put her head in and raked her hood back. "Kid?" All of Tiar came in and shed white dust on the floor. He had had his ear to the wall and could find no plausible excuse for himself standing in the corner.

"Captain's compliments and we got a very important passenger right next. She really wants me to impress on you be careful."

He shoved his hands in his pockets. "I understand." He was used to the idea foreigners were afraid of him. Every foreigner he had met was.

"Kind of short on space," Tiar said. "We'd like to sort of move you. Except it's not quite as comfortable. But there's facilities."

"All right," he said, wanting to be accommodating. Really

it didn't matter that much. It would be nice to have another set of walls to look at.

"It's kind of—minimal," Tiar said.

"That's fine. —There's nothing to do here. There's nothing to look at. I'd really like some books or something."

"We can get you books," Tiar promised. "I—don't suppose you have to pack."

"This is it. Except the kit."

"The clothes came. We have those. We just haven't had time—"

"That's all right." Anything was all right if it made them happy. And if it proved to the captain that he was obliging and knew how to take orders.

"You want to come with me? We're between coats. I can set you up."

"Sure," he said, and went and got the kit she had given him. When he reached the corridor, Tiar had shed the contamination gear, and there was still a great banging and clattering coming from the closed door of the cabin next door.

"Stsho passenger," Tiar said. "Important deal. Got to change the color, change the sleeping arrangements . . ."

It must be an important passenger, for sure. He followed Tiar past that area, and into the main downside corridor, and to a door there, which Tiar opened.

He truthfully had expected more of a cabin. At least a cot. It did have more to look at. And a blast cushion, with a swing track against the after wall. Otherwise it was a kind of a—laundry, he supposed. Or bath. There were facilities. That was about all. Bare conduits. Water-pipes. Whatever.

"Gods," Tiar said, and pulled his shoulder down. "Watch your head."

"It's all right." He was used to being tall, on ships built for women.

"There's blankets," Tiar said. She opened the wall locker and there certainly were, the whole ship's supply, it must be. "I'll get you a reader and some tapes. Gods, I'm *sorry* about this."

"It's all right," he said. "It really is."

Tiar stood looking at him, and finally shook her head. "The captain's got a lot on her mind. She honestly does. You don't understand."

"*Ker* Tiar, I *understand.*"

"Then *I* don't," Tiar snapped. And went and locked him in.

The blast cushion was one of those arrangements that let down and changed angles, according to which axis the ship might move, one of those emergency station affairs that you had to have in every corridor, in case. So he pulled it level with the deck as was, and got himself a couple of blankets to prop himself with, and one to throw over him, because the thermostat must have only just been reset, and breath frosted. He was not actually uncomfortable once he settled down with the blanket over him. There was more to look at, all the lockers and pipes and such. He could keep his mind busy figuring out all those. He supposed he could warm the compartment up faster by showering, but it might not warm it that much, and he was not sure they were through coming and going in here. So he sat and tried to read the locker labels from here, hearing the thumping still going on that meant they were redoing things for the stsho.

Stsho wouldn't like to meet him at all. People wouldn't, everywhere he went. That was the biggest shock he had had when he got beyond Anuurn's atmosphere, that it was the same Out There as it was at home, that no matter what Pyanfar Chanur said and no matter how you really acted, nobody waited to find out if you were the way they thought, they were just afraid. Even Hilfy Chanur didn't know what to do with him. And he was glad to hear from *ker* Tiar that things were going on that didn't give the captain time to consider his case. That was reasonable. He could understand that. He really could. It was just so important to him, and he told himself that Hilfy Chanur wouldn't really sweep him aside without listening, he just had to be patient and quiet and prove his case by that. If he was patient and quiet they would notice. If he cooperated they would be appreciative. *Ker* Tiar had noticed.

But he waited and he waited, and the thumping and the carrying of things down the corridor went on, but Tiar didn't bring the books. She didn't even bring lunch. It would be easy at this point to feel really sorry for himself, but that got no points, either.

Just be patient when you wanted people to notice you. That was what his mother had always told him.

(But she always noticed his sisters, who weren't. She always gave his sisters what they wanted. Which was natural, he supposed. Daughters stayed with the clan, and sons went away and didn't come back unless they were attacking the lord of the clan or stealing something. So it was good advice, the Be Patient thing, because he hadn't attacked his father; and he hadn't come back and stolen the livestock. His sisters had thought enough of him to talk him onto an offworld shuttle, which had led to everything hopeful in his life. He just wished patience got better results in the universe outside. Because nobody had ever taught him any other way to be. Just crazy mad. Or patient.)

The stsho aide put a satin-slippered foot into the newly-paneled room and wiped long fingers on the door frame. This passed. *Gtst* ventured further, onto the newly elevated white decking, to the white bowl-chair sunk into it.

Gtst crest lifted and sank several anxious times and lifted to half. *Gtst* looked all about, turned full circle, making little flutters of *gtst* hands.

"Adequate," *gtst* said in Trade-tongue. "I will inform the honorable."

Whereupon *gtst* retreated from the room and up the corridor, with *gtst* own stsho attendant.

The crew said not a word. Ears were flat. But they had said not a word about the contract.

Neither had Hilfy Chanur. She escorted the stsho out and up to the topside lounge, where the honorable Tlisi-tlas-tin sat sopping up cup after cup of tea and giving orders to Fala, whose ears were valiantly upright.

The stsho conferred, informed *gtst* honor the quarters were adequate, they now dared leave the honorable alone in hani keeping and could assure *gtst* excellency No'shto-shti-stlen that Chanur had taken at least austere care of their charge.

Whereupon the honorable Tlisi-tlas-tin wearily aroused *gtst*self from a chair ill-suited to *gtst* spindly legs, and with a flourish of voluminous gossamer, announced *gtst*self willing to go below with the Preciousness.

Which traveled in that box, apparently, which had its
appropriate customs seals as, simply, *oji*, and no *hint* of its
shape or nature.

"Honorable," Hilfy said, with, she hoped, an expression
as diplomatic as Fala Anify's . . . "may I ask your honor
to favor this person whom *gtst* excellency has trusted with
your person with a viewing of this most distinguished . . ."

"No!" Tlisi-tlas-tin said. Which might be the most direct
sentence she had ever heard from a stsho. *Gtst* gathered
up the small box and wrapped it within the gossamer folds
of *gtst* robes. *Gtst* gave them collectively and sundry a burning look of *gtst* moonstone eyes. "The Preciousness is not
for display."

A practical *and* an academic education in diplomacy did
not encourage one to seize *gtst* by *gtst* skinny white throat.
Being Pyanfar's niece did; but Hilfy recovered from the fog
of anger and her ears were still up and her mouth was still
smiling. "Please convey yourself and the Preciousness to
your cabin before some incident offends you. My aide will
escort your honor to your quarters and show your col-
leagues to the airlock."

And lock the gods-be cabin door on *gtst* honor afterward,
she thought. The crew was exhausted. They *hadn't* let mahendo'sat workmen do the job, invade their ship, look at
their interior, take notes on their systems. Gods-rotted certain they hadn't had kif. And stsho of the *laboring* class
didn't exist outside stsho space. So that left themselves—
and they had blisters on their hands and panelboard dust
up their nostrils, they had broken claws and were missing
fur, not to mention the captain had dropped a large panel
corner on her ankle and taken the hide off.

The captain was not, consequently, in a good humor. The
captain was sweaty and ached from head to foot. They were
two hours past their scheduled undock, and presented an
enigmatic silence to Meetpoint docks, hatches sealed (once
the supplies had arrived) hoses uncoupled, com completely
silent, their own power plant supplying their needs while
they underwent "technical adjustment."

Tarras came up from downside, saying something about
the shower downside being occupied, and her having to use
the one topside, poor put-upon dear, and Hilfy glared at
her, thinking it could be the end of a family friendship if

Tarras opened her mouth on the matter of subclauses at the moment.

"Do that," Hilfy said sweetly, with as great a control as she had left. "I've a few things to see to. We've got to recalc our outbounds."

Tarras took the hint. "Want help?"

She thought about it, a second run-through. Thought about particles floating through the filter systems. "Shower first. We *all* will. We'll just give station last-minute notice of our undock." Satisfying notion. "Let *them* do the scrambling. The *oji* has priority. Doesn't it?"

The banging and hammering had stopped. The hatch had cycled. For a long time there was quiet. Hallan decided the ship might be headed for undock, but people tended to forget him. So he decided it was a good idea to put the blast cushion in order, just in case, and to take a couple of blankets out of the storage lockers, because the heat still had not caught up, and also if they went out very hard or very long, one could want something to stuff in the unsupported spots. They didn't make flight cushions his size either. Or chairs. Or most anything on a ship.

But the ship didn't go, for a long time. He tucked up with his blankets and tried to calculate what he knew about Meetpoint and exactly what *V* they were going to carry if they were loaded full and going, the way the captain had said, to Urtur—which, as he understood, most ships couldn't do without going to Hoas, unless they dumped all their cargo. And they were carrying cargo, he'd heard the loaders, which he was relatively sure sounded inbound. So the *Legacy* must have the engines for it, or they were in a lot of trouble—like lost in hyperspace, forever. Truth be told, he was scared, and a little suspicious that even Tiar had been having a joke at his expense.

If it really was Urtur they wouldn't come in fast or close to the star, because of the dust. Urtur was a dreadfully dirty system, most of it in the disc, but not all of it—

And a pity they couldn't see their own fluorescing trail. Riding on light. Bathed in it. At home, he had had a picture on his wall, a photo someone had caught of a mahen ship coming into Hoas. And he liked to imagine them doing that, every time they made system drop. But you couldn't see it yourself. He had asked about it; and the *Sun*'s crew said it was a stupid question. Everybody was busy when you were coming in, and if you ever did see something like that they were too close and you were real busy real fast.

He had ridden through jump himself a lot of times, the last two years in the *Sun Ascendant*'s ops center. He thought through all the moves Dru would be making, if he were in ops, if Dru were sitting by him. Dru said he knew what he was doing. Dru was the one who'd gotten him a license, so she could take a break and leave him with the boards, she said—which was undoubtedly true, but she also said he really deserved a license, in a way he could never get the rest of the crew to admit. Yet.

"Hallan?"

Tiar, he thought, on the intercom.

"Yes?"

"Just checking. Are you all right down there?"

"Yes. I'm fine."

"Gods in pink feathers! The books!"

"That's all right."

"No, it isn't. Look. We're about to go into sequence. Are you all right?"

"I'm fine, *ker* Tiar."

On the *Sun,* they didn't use words like Tiar used to him then. He'd never heard them put together that way—and from a very old, very proper clan like Chanur. He didn't understand why she was upset.

But Tiar sent Fala running down the corridor from ops with the nutrients pack he desperately needed for jump and a book, a real, battered, tag-eared book . . . of Compact Trade Regulations.

He was quite touched by that. He really was.

The *Legacy* achieved *V* at a gentle burn. No more energy, in the long haul, to put a push on it—*V* was *V*, and you paid for it, until you ran past your capacity; but the *Legacy* had a stsho aboard, a creature that couldn't take more than 1.5 *G*'s without cracking its mostly hollow bones.

Which might be tempting, but they had Tlisi-tlas-tin in charge along with the "Preciousness," whatever it was, and the reason doubtless that No'shto-shti-stlen hadn't put the Preciousness aboard a kifish ship was the very well-known

habit of kif changing loyalties when unthreatened, un-
watched, and seeing a point of advantage.

And likewise for the mahendo'sat—if the Preciousness
was in any sense religious, keep it away from mahen hands:
the mahendo'sat knew that game too well—and some of
them were crazier than others.

The methane-folk? Who knew? The stsho, maybe, knew,
who had dealt more with the methane-breathers than anyone. And if the honorable Tlisi-tlas-tin had to go with the
Preciousness and the honorable had to breathe oxygen,
then maybe that answered that question in a very practical way.

Which left hani—since stsho traders refused to take their
own ships beyond Hoas. Stupid hani. Credulous hani. Hani
who hadn't been in space until the mahendo'sat (with no
one's leave) landed on Anuurn and pitched them from
wooden exploration ships into star-faring trade.

For mahen reasons, of course, some of which were sane
and some of which were not.

She flipped switches to check working stations, heard
Meetpoint's thin voice in her right ear. "Coming up on
jump," she was able to declare at last, and opened channel
3 and said in stshoshi trade, "Your honor, kindly take position for jump. We trust you have your medical kit at hand."

Silence.

"Your honor. Kindly advise us if you have done what
we request for the preservation of yourself and the Preciousness."

Fry that dimwit!

"Honorable captain?"

"Are you ready, honorable?"

"We are ready."

"Steady, cap'n." From Tiar, at her right elbow. "Murder's not in the contract."

"Don't say that word."

"Hey, we'll be free of it. Shove the Preciousness and *gtst*
honor right out the chute and be damned to them."

"Not allowed. Subclause three."

"They tell you about this Tlisi-tlas-tin character, cap'n?"

"No."

"Didn't think so."

From Tarras: "Do I get to pitch *gtst* out the lock?"

"Negative. Negative. Subclause three point two. No pitching of the Preciousness."

"What *is* this thing? Do you figure?"

"Not a bit. Religious or something. Who knows?"

"That's a blip." From Tarras at scan. "We got somebody away from station."

"Ha'domaren."

"How'd you know that?" Tarras asked.

"How could I not guess? I want a readout on every ship that's left Meetpoint since we've been there."

"No problem. I got it. You want it now or otherside?"

"Any kifish ship?"

"Two kif, one t'ca. All Hoas-bound, last few days."

"That son's going to move. Lay you odds."

"After us?"

"Lay you any money you want that's a mahen agent, for some gods-rotted Personage we don't know who, with an empty hold. It's politics, it's politics, it's some one of Pyanfar's rivals . . ."

"Possible," Tiar said.

"It's going to come," Hilfy said. "They'll try. There's never been a dearth of Personages. . . ."

"Coming up on mark," Tiar said.

"Advise our passengers."

"Got that," Fala said from belowdecks.

The numbers ticked down, everything automated, more so than *The Pride.* Progress. And more things to go wrong. She still watched the lines, and compared the numerical readout, scary large numbers. She'd done it on *The Pride,* with her aunt's hand or Haral Araun's on the controls. These days it was Tiar's. She wasn't a pilot, never would be. She could just ride it through.

"Here we go. Suppose we got that mass calc right?"

Ship dropped. Everything went hazed.

—You could dream in jump.

—Sometimes you even knew you were dreaming, if it was an old dream, an often dream.

Dream of gold hair and a human face.

Waiting there. He always was. Even if he was on a ship fifty lights away. Hello, he said, most times, though he was always distant. He had been, since they had parted com-

pany at Anuurn. Clearly Pyanfar had talked to him. Told
him the practicalities of things. Laid down conditions.

Hello, kid.

But she wasn't the kid any more. Things had changed.
She'd been married. And widowed. Thank the gods there
were no offspring to promote permanent ties with Sfaura.

Give No'shto-shti-stlen the gods-be puzzle egg. And good
luck to *gtst* with it.

Meanwhile there was a human face, a human presence,
distant and shadowy, a comfort in her traveling.

You have to take care, Tully said to her. He had never
gotten that good at hani speech, that she knew of. But that
was years ago.

I always take care, she said.

You trust this deal you're in.

Let's not talk about business. She knew what she wanted
to do. Exactly what her aunt frowned on her doing. But
Tully was evasive. He walked away from her, with his
back turned.

And the lights dimmed, and there were bars about—
ammonia, and sodium-light.

She took alarm. "Tully?" she said, and he looked at her,
scared as she was. She didn't want to be here again. She
didn't want this part.

He came and held on to her. He had then. He did until
the kif came and then he went with them because they
threatened her. The whole thing passed in a kind of haze,
the way the hours had in that kifish cage. There were
sounds to hear. She chose not to hear them. She could
govern the dream now—she had learned to do that, and
she kept saying, over and over again, Tully, come back.
Tully, listen to me. I don't want to remember that. What
do you go there for? I don't want to see that—

Come back and talk to me.

"Tully!"

He came back then, just a shadow. And wouldn't talk
to her.

"He knows better," Pyanfar said, out of nowhere and
uninvited. "He had his choice, go or stay. He understood.
You wouldn't. You still won't."

She did. That was the trouble. She loved him, enough to
make them both miserable. Go have babies, Py had said.

Thank the gods that had failed. And maybe Korin had never had a chance, maybe he'd sensed that, male-wise, sullen, quarrelsome, and unwisely set on running domestic affairs. Maybe that had set up the situation from the first day he moved in. Maybe—

Maybe in some remote way that had set up everything else, because *she* had come home with violence, with anger, with the habit of war and the indelible memory of a kifish cage. Korin couldn't have imagined that place. He'd made assumptions, he'd made assertions, he'd struck out to make her hear him—

And she couldn't have cared less . . . what he thought, what he wanted, who he was. The only thing she'd wanted—

—was kif in her gunsights. Korin dead. And Tully, on her terms.

"He's not your answer," Aunt Pyanfar said, in that brutal, blunt way Py had when she was right. "Look past your gods-cursed selfish notions, niece, and ask *him* what's right to ask of him, and don't tell me it's helping you outgrow him."

That day she'd swung on Py. Not many people had done that and gotten away unmarked. But Py had just ducked, and faced her, the way Py did now, hand against *The Pride*'s main boards.

"Meanwhile," Aunt Py said. "Meanwhile. You have a ship to run."

That wasn't what Py had said. Maybe it was her own mind organizing things. The brain did strange things in jump. It dreamed. It worked on problems. At times it argued with itself, or with notions it couldn't admit wide awake.

Most people forgot what they dreamed. It was her curse to remember. Mostly, she thought, she remembered because she wanted to be there. She wanted to be back on *The Pride,* before the kif, before anything had happened.

"Time to come back," Pyanfar said.

—Alarm was sounding. Wake, wake, wake.

They were in Urtur space, with the alarm complaining and the yellow caution flashing. The computers saw dust ahead.

"You there?" she asked. "Tiar?"

"I'm on it. We're close in. Going for secondary dump."

—You can be a gods-be fool, Aunt Py was hanging about to say. Because there's no way you're not being followed.

"Ship out there," Tarras said, on scan.

"Ha'domaren?"

"Sure the right size and vector."

She reached after the nutrients pack, bit a hole in it, and drank down the awful stuff. They were, as their bodies kept time, days away from Meetpoint. On Meetpoint docks, on Urtur station, it was more than a month. As light traveled, it was years. And the body complained of such abuses. You shed hair, you lost calcium, you dehydrated, your mouth tasted of copper, and you wanted to throw up, especially when the nutrient liquid hit your stomach and about a quarter hour later when the iron hit your bloodstream. But you got used to it and you learned to hold it down, or you didn't, and you didn't last as a deep-spacer.

"You all right?" she heard Fala ask of Meras, below, heard him answer, brightly, *"I'm fine."*

Like hell, she thought. It wasn't fair if he was. The stsho would be coming out from under . . . stsho and humans had to sedate themselves for the trip, whatever *those* completely different brains had in common—though Tully could survive without; had had to prove it . . . once, at least; and was still sane. . . .

Woolgathering, Pyanfar called it, and damned the habit. She didn't have her hands on controls. She'd been ship's com tech, protocol officer, and that didn't have a thing to do with running the ship. But she followed the moves, she knew in her gut when it was time for Tiar to kick in the third *V* dump, and lip-synched the order, tense until Tiar gave it, and then satisfied.

She *could* do it herself. She was tolerably sure of it. But she never bet the ship on it. And certainly not on this jump.

"Fine job," she said to Tiar.

"We're in a little closer than I wanted."

"Still," she said. First class equipment, first class navigator in Chihin and first-class pilot in Tiar. It wasn't any run of the lot ship *could* single-jump as they'd done. The older pilots, the navigators of Chihin's age . . . they'd done it in the war years, they'd the kind of reflexes and system-awareness that could come out of it with a critical sense where they were.

So, most clearly, did *Ha'domaren*'s crew. That told you something. That told you, at least, the quality of that crew and equipment, that it carried no cargo, and that whoever was at the helm had done this before.

That they were overjumped, that somebody had actually overhauled and passed them in hyperspace, that said that was one bastard who didn't mind the navigation rules *or* care about the dust hazard in Urtur system.

Chapter 5

Urtur was a smaller port than Meetpoint—heavily industrial. Its star was veiled in murk and dust, a ringed star, with gas giant planets sweeping the veil into bands of crepe and gas and ice; with miner-craft both crewed and otherwise running the dusty lanes in the ecliptic; with refineries and mills and shipyards operating at the collection points—

And the main station, under mahendo'sat governance, devoted itself to manufacture, shipping, and entertainment for the miners and makers of goods. You wanted culture? Go to Idunspol. You wanted religion? Go to forbidden, gods-crazed Iji. You wanted iron and heavy metals, you wanted sheet and plate and hydrogen, you wanted a raucous good time and a headache in the morning? Urtur was the place for it.

You said Chanur here, and certain authorities' ears pricked up and twitched—by an irony of things as they were, there were outstanding warrants here that could not quite be forgotten, by mahen law: every situation was subject to change and every administration could be succeeded by some new power diametrically opposed to the last. So charges stayed on the books, something like reckless endangerment, public hazard, speeding, unlawful dumping, and damage to public property. *The Pride of Chanur* had had its less popular moments.

And supposedly the charges included the name of Hilfy Chanur, crewwoman. But she paid no more attention to them than Aunt Py did, coming and going as she pleased these days in regal empowerment.

So she ordered the *Legacy* shut down and the hatch opened to Urtur; and she completed the formalities with station control, signing this and signing that—advised station control of the existence of their full-scale dataload and its date of provenance from Meetpoint; and got a bid of 3,000, which wouldn't go higher-counting that rag-eared son of a mahen outlaw had beaten them in by eight hours.

But with their fragile passenger and *gtst* fragile object, they couldn't have made it in at anything like that speed.

"That's five thousand that son Haisi's cost us," she muttered. "Maybe eight."

"Couldn't have done better," Tiar said. "Better take it."

"Out of his hide," she said, signaled acceptance, and switched channels to *gtst* honor Tlisi-tlas-tin. "Honorable, we're ready to make contact with your party on Urtur. We're pleased to announce arrival and opening of station business. We will have the distinction to contact the excellency immediately and advise *gtst* of your presence and mission."

"We acknowledge. We are in preparation. We would like our meal now, if your honor will instruct her aides."

"We will, honorable. Stand by." A sigh as she cut the connection.

"*Gtst* could have eaten it when we fixed it," Tarras muttered.

"*Gtst* mission is to be a pain," Hilfy said. "Check on the other passenger while you're at it. Make sure he didn't crack his head."

They'd been up and about for hours. They had had their lunch, but the stsho had been too exhausted and too sick to, as the stsho put it, "burden the stomach with uncertain and foreign preparations."

Hell.

Meanwhile she had been putting together a message to advise *gtst* excellency Atli-lyen-tlas to contact her on an urgent basis.

To the most excellent Atli-lyen-tlas, emissary of gtst *excellency No'shto-shti-stlen, the honorable Hilfy Chanur, captain of the hani ship* Chanur's Legacy, *head of the ancient and honorable Chanur clan, sends her respectful greetings and has the distinction and honor to advise and inform your excellency that she has a message of extreme importance for the attention of your excellency personally, which can only reflect well upon the achievement and elegance of your excellency for the future.*

It went out on the push of a button. It would probably

take time for a response. The computer was set to listen for a message from *gtst* excellency.

Meanwhile the messages were pouring in. From customs. That had to be answered. From routings. Had to be answered. From the stationmaster. Had to be answered. From name after name of ships and individuals she had no idea who. Anything that contained the name Pyanfar Chanur automatically routed over to the auxiliary stack—otherwise their operations could drown in the deluge, and important operations could stall.

The Pyanfar stack had hit 105 messages and added four more while she checked it for bombs and known names.

Somebody had to read them. After customs. After the stationmaster. After dealing with the freight office and getting on the lists for goods. The futures market had already reacted to the arrival of a ship out of Meetpoint, to the arrival—the sharper traders had surely figured—of a ship that had just come from Urtur round trip; and the knowledgeable types were basing their bids on what they thought she might know, what they thought she might carry, and whether or not they thought by the way the *Legacy* had entered system they were carrying mass. And *she* had the definitive answers, which mahen rules let her give *before* customs—figuring that if a captain didn't like the result of customs, it was only a matter of sufficient fines or sufficient bribes, or court, all of which was fodder for the gamblers on the market. Old mahendo'sat lounged in their station apartments and bet their retirement checks on the system. Hustlers bet on it in bars. Businessmen prayed for it and burned incense to whatever fad religion they thought guaranteed their luck.

And, having that answer, she keyed it through and watched on separate screens as the futures market reacted, as bids started coming in, as customs notified her that she had inspection officers on the way to expedite her cargo in what was clearly a move to stifle disruptive speculation on the reason a hani ship came straight in from Meetpoint.

Tiar's job, handling the inspectors, going through the forms. Meanwhile the bids were looking good. Hard not to let the pulse quicken and the fever set in. But the hani captain that took to gambling on the market herself—that was marginally legal, and ultimately foolish. She watched.

She had the computer set to analyze the trend—and she could interrupt at any moment by taking the bid of a particular company; with a bond, before customs, without one, after.

Historically speaking, she preferred after. The market knowledgeables would know that too, and play their serious bids accordingly.

"Felicitations," came a message from the stationmaster, on the more private communications possible now that they had a station communications line physically tapped into their interface. *"You come back much soon than expect, Legacy. You got trouble?"*

"No trouble. Personal choice. Felicitations, stationmaster. Chanur's compliments."

"You wait customs before exit."

"I understand they're on their way."

"You come big emergency?"

"No problems, thank you. All fine. On an express run."

"Express run. Who?"

"No'shto-shti-stlen." It was no more than *Ha'domaren* was going to tell them. *"Gtst* excellency wanted a message carried, diplomatic privilege." Freely translated, not legally your business, stationmaster.

"Expensive."

"Yes."

"Congratulation' you safe arrival, Chanur ship. Felicitate you pilot."

"Thank you, sir. I have."

Station seemed satisfied. Meanwhile there was a bleep from the computer, which had found a trigger word in an incoming live communication.

She keyed it in: got:

"H'lo, you, Legacy! What delay you?"

Grinning bastard. It wasn't worth an answer. Not one she wanted to give over station com.

"Got talk you, Legacy."

She wasn't about to.

"You clear paper with that haul, Legacy? I got rumor customs got question, back at Meetpoint."

At *Meetpoint.* In a mahen hell there was a question! "That's the oldest scam in the book, *Ha'domaren!* You try to tie me up with some gods-be lie, I'll have your ears!

You know gods-rotted well we have clear papers on everything aboard!"

*"On what they see. I got rumor not ever'thing seen. Got
stsho arti-fact no papers."*

"Diplomatic! It doesn't need papers, you—" It wasn't
politic or productive. She shut up. Fast. "Cute joke. Cute
joke, Haisi. You still got those charges pending at Mkks,
or what?"

*"Lot funny, Chanur captain. You want meet for talk busi-
ness now? You want talk Atli-lyen-tlas, a? I got bad news.
Real bad news."*

The stationmaster hadn't said that name. She hadn't said
that name to anyone at Meetpoint, nor to anyone at Urtur
until a scant few moments ago, that she'd keyed out a message for that individual. She had never so much as heard
the name aloud on this leg of the trip—but she knew *gtst*
as the well-reputed stsho ambassador to Urtur, the addressee in the contract, the intended recipient of the
Preciousness.

"You want meet for drink?" the mahe said. *"You going
need same."*

"Atli-lyen-tlas quit," Haisi said, taking a puff of one of
those cursed mahen smokesticks. And exhaling, what was
worse. "Same quit, go—" A move of Haisi's large, bare-
palmed hand, a glance of dark mahen eyes about the in-
definite perimeters of the lounge—the lounge next the
trade office, as happened. Hilfy was not about to go onto
Ha'domaren, or take Haisi Ana-kehnandian's hospitality,
or be subject to whatever esoteric truth-seekers Haisi might
have installed. Haisi's eyes roamed the implied infinite and
came back to solidity, to her—the poetic hand returned to
lie above Haisi's heart, and Haisi smiled.

"So, so difficult figure alien mind."

"So where did *gtst* go?" Hilfy's ears were flat. She made
no pretense of pleasantness.

"You do me small favor."

"What favor?"

"I tell you," Haisi said, "I do work in files, all hours I
wait talk with you, you know? What for you got arrest
here? I curious."

"I never got arrested here."

"You all same got police record. File on list. Hilfy Chanur. That you? Sound like you."

"Then you just better let it lie there. You go digging in that dirt, you're going to need the bath, because it's nothing Urtur station wants to find. And how patient is your Personage with foulups?"

Maybe she scored one. Haisi took another puff and seemed to think about it, blowing smoke from his nostrils like some brazen image.

"I might call your Personage," she said, "and tell her— it is *her,* isn't it? We got one mahe being damn fool. Call him home before he embarrasses you."

"Personage might say, Who you talk fool, Hilfy Chanur? You got thing aboard you don't know what is, you don't know what does, you got stsho play politic, use you name, use you ship . . . Big fool."

"What do you want? Outright, mahe, what do you want?"

"You bring me 'board you ship. You let me talk stsho."

"You want to send a message, I might take it. You let the stsho ask to talk to you. If *gtst* wants to, I'll bring you aboard."

"I tell you no good you come here. Stsho you look for—gone."

"Gone since how long? Since you found out about the shipment? Since you were here last and you learned about it?"

"You not bad guess."

"What is it to you? What do you care what the stsho do with each other?"

"Ask why stsho care what I do."

"Why, then?"

"Maybe rise and fall Personages."

"Which Personages? Stsho? Mahendo'sat?"

"Maybe so. Maybe."

"Gods rot you, give me a plain answer!"

"No more you give me, Chanur captain. Which side you?"

"I'm on the side of making a living, I'm on the side of running an honest trade and shipping operation! If somebody's got cargo going, and it's not live and it's not illegal,

CHANUR'S LEGACY

457

I haul it, that's all! I'm not a Personage, I'm not a fool, I'm a ship captain."

"You think that, you be number one fool, Chanur captain. Wherever you go, politic. All time politic. You want tuck head under arm not see what is, you do. But maybe all same Urtur find old arrest warrant. Maybe search ship . . ."

"You want an incident with the stsho, you go right on and try that. You want an incident with Chanur, you want an incident with the *han*, you want me to sue you clear back to your ancestors, you earless bastard—"

The lifting of an empty mahen hand. "Want no incident. Want know what thing No'shto-shti-stlen send Atli-lyen-tlas."

"What in your ninety-nine hells difference does it make what *gtst* sent?"

"You not know that?"

"I have no interest in that!"

"Then why you ask?"

Murder occurred to her. Most vivid murder.

"Because I got a large hairy fool being a fulltime pain in the—"

"You *know* what No'shto-shti-stlen send? Or you take *gtst* word what you carry? Sloppy way pass customs."

"Until it comes *off* my ship, customs can wonder."

"Unless it univers-al contraband. Like run guns. Like run—"

"I'm bored. I'm leaving."

"You not know."

"Goodbye."

"You want know where Atli-lyen-tlas go?"

"Where?"

"What you give me?"

"I'll look it up in station records."

"Kita. Go Kita Point. Easy jump. You want data on Kita market? Got. Real cheap. Great bargain. Give you break. Get you futures reports maybe two month back."

Futures in a deeper mahen market where the mahendo'sat knew best what they had and didn't. Speculation there was asking for trouble, hired hauling was the only sure thing, and information at the narrow downside end of mahen trade routes wasn't going to tell you what goods might already have arrived there from points upstream.

And there was a worse problem with Kita.

"You want deal?" the mahe asked.

"I'll think about it." She stood up and walked for the door.

"Not real long time think," Haisi said. "You got stsho deal, not good you break promise. Cargo get lost, stuff screw up at Meetpoint . . . Personage not real damn happy with you, Chanur captain. Big mess. You go ahead. You do. You make. Talk me later I see if rescue you worth while."

"You captain?"

"Me? Not."

"*Ha'domaren* your ship?"

"Not. Belong cousin."

"You got cousins everywhere, don't you?"

"Big fam'ly."

"I'll bet." She did walk out, shoved her hands in her pockets and thought how this had more and more the smell of trouble, such that she wasn't seeing Urtur's garish lights, she was seeing what used to be, and missing the weight of the pistol she had worn in those days before the disarmament agreement, before the peace.

It didn't feel like peace. Not at all.

"We got check," the mahen customs agent said, and Tiar jabbed the slate in question and said, politely, "It's on our ship. Until it comes off our ship it isn't your province. That's in your regulations. Until it's offered for sale it isn't merchandise. It's an item in the possession of *gtst* honor under *diplomatic* privilege and it stays on this ship until we find the addressee. In which case you can work out the problems with the stsho delegation. It's not our problem!"

"Got consult stationmaster," the agent said, and flipped his slate closed and walked off. Tiar stood staring after him, and turned and stalked back into the access, up the rampway to the hatch and the lower main corridor.

"Trouble?" Fala asked.

"Gods-be right we have trouble, we have bids breeding like crazy and we can't get the gods-rotted customs to fill out the gods-rotted forms and clear the gods-be-feathered—"

It had been quiet for a very long time. And *Trade in Agricultural Goods* might be informative, and Hallan was willing to learn anything that gave him expertise in anything whatsoever to do with space and trade; but it was uninspired and highly repetitive.

Still, he read on, having had his shower and his lunch and all. He heard crew members going up and down the corridor outside, he listened hard, thinking that he might hear something, but most of all he heard a voice he thought was Tiar's yelling about mahendo'sat and customs and blackmail.

So he thought something bad must have happened.

Then he heard the captain's voice, he was relatively sure, yelling something about mahendo'sat and blackmail. So he didn't think things were going well.

Probably it was not a good time to ask to be let out of the laundry. Probably he should read *Trade in Agricultural Goods* very slowly and thoroughly and make it last, because it might be all the entertainment he had for a while.

Home again, to read the gods-forsaken contract. To consult the legal program. The translation. The transcription of the original into mundane type, and into phonetic rendition.

Seven thousand ninety-eight pages. Of which the computer identified twenty clauses as of particular application, regarding *Unproven Subsequents*.

And the pertinent dictionary and legal dictionary definition: *Subsequent: a person who in substance whether in whole or in part may be in tenure of the same rights and legal entity as a named individual. See: Subsequent in Identity; Consequent.*

Subsequent in Identity: a Subsequent who has the same physical identity as a named individual.

Consequent: an individual who in substance whether in whole or in part is in tenure of legal rights and legal entity as a direct result of contact with or the actions of an individual or gtst subsequent.

. . . If the party receiving the goods be not the person stipulated to in Subsection 3 Section 1, and have valid claim as demonstrated in Subsection 36 of Section 25, then it shall be the reasonable obligation of the party accepting the contract to ascertain whether the person stipulated to in Subsection 3 Section 1 shall exist in Subsequent or in Consequent or in Postconsequent, however this clause shall in no wise

*be deemed to invalidate the claim of the person stipulated
to in Subsection 3 Section 1 or 2, or in any clause thereunto
appended, except if it shall be determined by the party accepting the contract to pertain to a person or Subsequent or
Consequent identified and stipulated to by the provisions of
Section 5 . . .*

*However the provisions of Section 5 may be delegated by
the party issuing the contract, following the stipulations of Subsection 12 of Section 5 in regard to the performance of the
person accepting the contract, not obviating the requirements
of performance of the person accepting the contract . . .*

"We have a problem," Hilfy said, over *gfi*, in the *Legacy*'s
galley. She was maintaining, she felt, extraordinary control
over her temper. Sober faces were opposite her, the whole
crew—since no offloading was going on. Meanwhile *gtst*
honor was lighting up the com board with requests to go
out into the station, and whether Haisi had messed them up
with station officials or whether Haisi had only fairly warned
them what they were facing—customs had a hold on them.

"Have you told *gtst* honor?" Tiar asked, elbows on the
table opposite her.

"Not yet. Haisi *could* be lying through his teeth."

"If he isn't? What about that contract? What's it say, if
we can't *find* the bastard we're supposed to give this to?"

She truly hated to say that. She did hate it. She leaned
her own arms against the cold surface and regarded a table-
ful of more experienced traders—give or take Fala.
"There's a clause in there about Subsequents and Conse-
quents. That we're still bound to get it to the right party."

"You mean that son of a stsho has transmogrified?
Switched personalities? Disintegrated *gtst* psyche?"

"We don't know that exactly."

"We don't know it, so we're not responsible if *gtst* has
gone crazy and shipped out of here."

"We aren't responsible if *gtst* does. But we do have a
clause in there about finding out if there's a Subsequent."

"Oh, gods," Tiar said, and her hand slid over her eyes.

"It said Urtur," Fala Anify protested.

"It also said—find out if there's a Subsequent. And we—
I, I'm not passing the responsibility. I should have considered the possibility of *gtst* not staying at Urtur."

"What possibility?" Chihin asked with a rap on the table-top. "Stsho don't travel once in a—"

"Lifetime," Hilfy said. "Which only holds true until someone spooks it into a new personality."

"So what spooked the ambassador? We were through here, we dealt with *gtst* excellency at least indirectly to get our clearance for Meetpoint, we didn't see anything wrong, did we?"

"I didn't," Hilfy said. "But I'm willing to bet Haisi has some remote thing to do with it. He was at Meetpoint when we came in, he was in a position to know what No'shto-shti-stlen knew . . ." A thought came to her, a summation, a time-table, that sent an outrageous anger rolling through her veins. "That son of an earless mother!"

"Haisi?"

"No! No'shto-shti-stlen!"

"You mean *gtst* knew we weren't going to find *gtst* recipient here?"

"If *gtst* didn't know, *gtst* had a gods-rotted good idea there was trouble here! *And* wrote that bit into the contract about obligating us to go on a Subsequent-hunt! Gods *blast* that skinny, painted, conniving—he wants us to go running around the immediate universe looking for this character!"

"Where would *gtst* go? Where would *gtst* be?"

"*Who* would *gtst* be? That's the question! Haisi says Kita. But that won't be *gtst* stopping-place—it hasn't got amenities for them. And the mahendo'sat are all stirred up, or Haisi's Personage has got a lot of pull here, a *lot* of pull."

"You don't think it's Pyanfar behind his Personage."

"I don't know! I don't know not! That's the trouble getting involved in politics, nobody wears a name badge!"

"So what are we going to do, captain?"

Run for it? Haul their load clear to Kita, with no guarantee there was a profit there?

Hope the mahen stationmaster had traded heavily into the futures market here, and took a soaking when they yanked their cargo off the market and ran for it? Break a few regulations that made the speeding violation look like a mahen commendation?

Good way to make lasting enemies, in either case.

But *deal* with Haisi? He might be Pyanfar's bosom

friend. He might be working for her overthrow and with a
mahen sense of humor, using her help to do it.

Get the truth out of Tlisi-tlas-tin? *Not* outstanding likely.
And there was no way to consult No'shto-shti-stlen.

Continuing silence at the table. It was the crew's moral
refuge and her moral dilemma: the captain was thinking.
The captain was going to get them out of what the captain,
who was young enough to be Tiar's daughter, had gotten
them collectively into.

"We can pull out. We can stay. We've got two other hani
in port with us. That's *Padur's Victory* and a Narn hauler,
both slated for Hoas. But they're marginal ships, they're
not up to this. If we involve them, they could be in big
trouble, so that's no help."

"No threat to them."

"None so far. We could get the kid aboard—"

"The kid's in potential trouble."

"The kid's ship is at Hoas."

"The kid's ship is probably on its way here right now, if
we put him on one of them, he'll miss his ship."

It was true. And beyond Hoas, either ship might be on
to Meetpoint, where he wasn't welcome—and consequently
they might not be.

"Tell you something else," Tiar said. "Captain. That
kid's been *on* this ship."

She understood what Tiar was getting at. She didn't particularly want to listen to it.

"If you turn him out on the docks," Tiar said, "the mahendo'sat are going to pick him up. There's no question.
They'll assume he knows what they want to know."

"He's also not Chanur, *not* involved with us, he's Sahern
crew, they're coming here, and if we're holding him . . ."

"He doesn't want to go to them. He wants to stay with
Chanur."

"He's in love with my gods-forsaken aunt! He's a fool
kid, light-years from home on a notion—"

"A gods-forsaken ticking bomb," Chihin said. "We have
a stsho aboard this ship, a stsho that we daren't upset. We
have a kid with healthy hormones right around the corner
from *gtst* honor and the Preciousness *we're* now supposed
to get to Kita—beyond which, there's precious few choices
where we're going, captain."

"If they're Pyanfar's, she'll sort it out. If they're not—and we help them, they'll cut our throats."

"What happens if *our* stsho fragments and decides *gtst* is the queen of the gods?"

"We have a problem," Tarras said, which brought them back to point one.

"Honorable," Hilfy said, not cheerfully. "I have news."

A languid wave. *Gtst* was restoring *gtst* body-paint, carefully brushing a pattern down a white forearm. *Gtst* completed it with a flourish.

In strictest courtesy, Hilfy invited herself into the bowl-chair and sat down.

"There has been a complication," she began.

"Then your honor can surely solve it. Are you not hired to do so?"

"Would your honor care for tea?" She made a slight wave of the hand toward the door, and Fala, with tea-service in hand.

"If your honor sees fit." *Gtst* looked anxious, waving the newly painted arm, arranging *gtst* draperies.

With a species that tended to dissociate psychologically at grievous upsets—five rounds of tranquilizing tea seemed perhaps a good idea. Especially since it was their stsho and their contract, with the Preciousness enthroned in its case above their heads.

Five cups, in which Fala contrived not to spill anything on the white cushions, in which their juniormost acquitted herself with commendable self-possession.

"We hope your honor has been comfortable such as our hospitality has been able to provide."

"We have survived. We are composed. The Preciousness in our possession is unmolested. We could not ask more of your meager circumstances."

Snobbish son.

"May your honor," *gtst* asked, "choose to inform us of the matter which troubles your peace?"

"Regarding the intended recipient of the *oji.*"

"The Preciousness."

"The Preciousness. Would it surprise your honor in the least to know that the intended recipient has—em—quit *gtst* post?"

Shocked pale eyes lifted and centered on her face. "Impossible."

So *gtst* did not know in advance. Perhaps her surmises were unjust and mistaken.

"Quit *gtst* post so far as the mahendo'sat have been willing to inform me. Should they have reason to lie? One of them has been quite forward in asking me to allow him access here."

"No! A thousandfold no! This is insupportable. This is *unthinkable!*" Paint spilled as *gtst* jostled the bottle. "Oh, where are my servants? The paint, the precious pigments, —oh, my predecessors, oh, my honor, oh, my reputation, oh, I am wounded! I perish, wai! I perish!"

It was blotting furiously—impossible to tell whether the migration of Atli-lyen-tlas was the shock, or the paint, or the reference to mahendo'sat, but *gtst* was highly agitated, breathing in great gasps, and Fala came running, cups rattling on the tray, all the while the honorable was fighting for breath and clear as clear was the possibility of a dissolution before their eyes.

"Be calm!" Hilfy said, unsure whether to lay hands on the creature or not. "Be calm! Your honor is not in question, most honorable, most excellent! Calm yourself, breathe quietly—"

The stsho did listen. Moonstone eyes gazed at her in shock, a paint-spattered hand clutched a paint-stained fold of *gtst* robe to *gtst* breast, and it shook and trembled and lifted and lowered *gtst* plume-augmented crest in high agitation.

"We are empowered to search further!" Hilfy said, reaching for vocabulary. What *was* the ceremonial deferative singular for "personality disintegration" and was it appropriate to use it? "You are in no wise responsible for this, honorable! There is every possibility *gtst* excellency foresaw such an event—we find it in the contract!"

"In the contract."

"In the contract, honorable."

"But *gtst* excellency should have confided in me, *gtst* excellency has dishonored me—"

"*Gtst* excellency has entrusted you with the Preciousness. Has *gtst* not? Or should we not question that? Should we ask what is in that box?"

Moonstone eyes went wide and horrified. And *gtst* looked up and up and around, where the shipping box sat within its braces.

"Must we not be certain? Would you *recognize* the Preciousness if you saw it?"

"Of course! Of course! Oh, the villainy in your mind!" Tlisi-tlas-tin scrambled to an undignified exit from the chair, trailing paint-soaked robes over the white cushions and the tiles of the floor, *gtst* long fingers sought the shipping latches and undid them, waving Fala's offered help away in indignation. *Gtst* undid the latches of the box itself, and Hilfy held her breath, unbearably driven to reach out restraining hands in case it should fall.

But there in the plush white liner sat a white, carved—vase, one supposed. Is this it? Hilfy wondered; Fala looked puzzled; but Tlisi-tlas-tin sank down with a sigh and fluttered *gtst* fingers, held a hand to *gtst* chest, and muttered.

"I am vindicated. I am vindicated, *gtst* excellency has not lied to me."

"We had no doubt of your honor," Hilfy ventured to say, and stood by as Tlisi-tlas-tin picked *gtst*self up off the pastel-smeared floor, in the wreckage of *gtst* finery. *Gtst* struck as belligerent and proud a pose as a creature could, that a gust of breath could shatter.

"But this is a pen for *animals!* I cannot possibly abide these circumstances! Look at me! The Preciousness cannot abide in this wreckage! My honor! My reputation!"

Hilfy thought of another word, but she bowed with great courtesy and smiled. "We are of course concerned. We will act instantly to rectify this unfortunate circumstance."

"Immediately! I cannot abide this! Oh, the injustice, oh, the cruelty, oh, the perfidy!"

"*What* perfidy, honorable?"

"I *demand* to see the next highest stsho authority, I *demand* to have access to this individual!"

"Honorable, —"

"I am wronged, oh, predecessors and antecedents, I am wronged, most grievously!"

Fala made a glance toward the overhead. But in space there was no direction for heaven.

And the gods were probably busy with Aunt Pyanfar.

Chapter 6

Potential spies everywhere, Haisi blackmailing them for access to the stsho *they* had contracted to protect, and the stsho in question wailing and moaning and lamenting betrayals on the part of the stsho ambassador to Urtur, *and* of the staff of said ambassador, who did not return calls.

And the honorable Tlisi-tlas-tin's quarters were a shambles, *gtst* person was a shambles, *gtst* affairs were a shambles, and in a species that Phased under stress, into new and unpredictable psychological configurations. . . .

The Preciousness might end up in the hands of a completely different individual, for which—Hilfy hesitated even to send the legal program on another search through the contract and the handbook of Compact law looking for legal responsibility. *Gtst* honor was tottering on the edge of dissolution and *gtst* wanted the damage to *gtst* quarters repaired, *gtst* wanted the colors changed, *gtst* wanted new clothing, and a better diet, and entertainments and amenities.

Which meant scouring the market for stsho items, checking through what *they* had in cargo cans; *and* dealing with customs one more time.

"You got problem?" a mahen voice said; and Hilfy turned to find the scoundrel on her track—*following* her, gods rot him. Maybe not even doing the watching himself . . . just have some underling do it, and call him for the intercept.

"What do you want?"

"Want make deal. Hear you look for stsho stuff. Hear you want make buy stuff like deck tile, like *'vuli* cloth, like . . ."

"How *nice* you got all these things to sell me! Good price, huh?"

"You funny. Amuse stsho?"

She started to walk away. He got in front of her.

"Hear you try talk stsho embas-sy. Not possible. Stsho shut down. Some go Meetpoint. Some Kita."

"You've had yourself a main proper disaster here, haven't you? You try to break off trade with the stsho? Try to screw up politic for my aunt?"

"I *friend* Pyanfar." Hand on chest. "My Personage friend with Pyanfar, number one try do good for you." Haisi Ana-kehnandian glanced about as casual traffic passed, and he made an unwelcome catch at her elbow. "You want stsho stuff, I get for you. Easy done. Stuff all over embassy. Nice stuff, number one stsho furniture."

"Breaking and entering? Pirated goods?"

"Shush, shush, don't make noise ever'body hear. You come. I fix, you get."

"You drove the whole gods-forsaken stsho embassy off Urtur, and you want to help me? No thanks! Go talk to the kif, they appreciate a pirate!"

"Don't be fool. You want clear customs? You want get stuff *on* ship, same deal you got get customs stamp. Customs don't let you trade till you cleared, hani, you got figure how things are."

One could figure how things were. One could figure somebody was in tight with the officials at some level.

"You want stop whole deal for redecorate stsho cabin?" Haisi asked. "That funny."

"Who said?"

"Funny thing you got real white shopping list. Stsho emissary not happy with decor? Maybe lot stress on this person?"

"Go to hell," she said.

And walked off, walked and took a lift and a transport bus to the dockside customs office.

And got the official no. No onloading if there was a hold on offloading.

"So what if a ship pulls in here and doesn't want to sell to you? You're not going to let them buy?" Her fist landed on the counter. "I don't believe that!"

"Not same. Not same. You got hold on you cargo. Not same legal situation. You want deal, you let custom inspector see contraband."

"It's not contraband! It's stsho diplomatic property!"

"Make you appeal stsho mission."

"There *is* no stsho mission on Urtur! You scared it off!"

"Not us scare off. Maybe this object you got scare them."

"No way! News of it got here with *my ship!* No way
they know about it. You ask Haisi Ana-kehnandian what
spooked them, you ask him what in your seventh reprehensible hell he knows about our cargo and who's pockets he's
got access to. I want to talk to the stationmaster, I want to
talk to the personage of this station, I want a legal accounting of every paper you've brought against us, and I want
my ship cleared!"

"You not yell in this office!"

"I by the gods yell in this office, I yell until somebody
contacts the personage of Urtur and *gets my customs slip
cleared,* and no more of this talk about invading a stsho
emissary's privacy and searching his baggage!"

There was a disturbance at the door behind her. A
mahen voice registered protest in some mahen tongue, another joined it before she could even look around. She did
look, and there was a handful of mahen spacers *and* Haisi
Ana-kehnandian shoving other business out the door.

He shut the door and held it then, with a wall of large
mahendo'sat.

She *missed* carrying a gun. Gods, she did. Claws came
out. Haisi twitched and she went over the counter, scattering customs personnel left and right. Chairs went over,
clerks jammed up in an inner office door and shrieked in
panic.

"Hani!" Haisi shouted. "You stop, stop now! You
listen!"

Nobody had guns. But they had the door. There were
clerks under desks. The group behind her squeezed into
the room and shut that door.

"Where's your authority? Where's any proof you're not
a pirate, Haisi Ana-kehnandian? Unblock that door!"

"All right, all right." Haisi made calming gestures. "You
not break furniture, Chanur captain. You got important
relative, no reason break place up. Don't be damn fool!"

"I got important relative, same time got real distrust of
people who get pushy, mahe. You want I charge piracy?

You want I say you try damn underhanded trick with customs? I want to talk to the stationmaster, I want to talk right now, and no more tricks!"

"Stationmaster indispos'."

"Indisposed like the stsho ambassador? Indisposed like run for Iji?"

"You talk wild, hani. No. Indispos' like not take time talk with every damn' fool got problem."

Damn' fool was close to the point. Something was seriously wrong at Urtur, and the more they suspected she knew the less likely she was to get out of this room, much less out of the port. Far better to have played outraged trader.

"I want my ship cleared! I want customs clearance, I want my record cleared, I want to sell my cargo when and if and at what price I choose, and I want an end of interference with my business."

"You want tell what sort object you carry?"

"No, I don't. It's none of your gods-rotted business! You get out from in front of that door, you get yourself and your crew out of my way! This is a public office. If I don't see a badge, an authorization, or a personage, I'm not giving you anything. And if you try to hold me, my ship—a *Chanur* ship—is going to carry a complaint to the Compact."

"You be calm, be calm, hani. This get to very silly point. You listen to me. You walk 'round station talk about dangerous business, name dangerous stuff, you come in this office make demand in front of witness you don't know by damn who, you try get throat cut?"

"Open that door!"

"A' right, a' right. —Rahe'ish' taij meh, jai."

The mahendo'sat with him moved aside from the door.

"Against the wall!" she said.

"You got damn poor idea who give orders in this room, hani!"

"I got damn good idea you got no authority to give orders. Or *you* can clear the papers. You want big blow-up you just keep going."

"Clear papers. I clear papers. All right!" Haisi spat out a torrent of mahendi instructions, only half of which she

could understand, but which got the clerks cautiously out
from under the desks and brought the customs agent back
from the office in the rear.

The door opened, from the other side. Station police
stood there, armed with pistols and ready for trouble.
Someone had called them. Probably from the back office.

Fine, Hilfy thought. Great.

"Small misunderstanding," Haisi said, with a wave of his
hand. And said something to the police, low and fast. Stationmaster, she caught that word: stsho; and ambassador.
And trouble. But she could guess that one.

The Personage of Urtur was ruffled. Highly. The Personage of Urtur found the business too evidently distressful,
and abandoned it to her Voice, a towering mahe with a
furious scowl.

"You disrupt whole office, you got clerk scare' like bunch
pirate, what for you damn' fool action?"

"Ask him! He blocked the door, wouldn't let honest citizens in or out!" You didn't yell at the Personage of Urtur.
The Personage of Urtur didn't debate such matters. The
Voice did. And Hilfy found her ears persistently flattening.
She made every effort to keep a pleasant look on her face,
and to keep to logical points, when at the same time the
Voice tried to provoke gut level reactions. She wanted to
make mincemeat out of Haisi Ana-kehnandian—who sat
smoking like a factory, with a frown on his face.

The Voice did ask Ana-kehnandian, evidently. The two
of them talked back and forth in one of Ijir's numerous
languages, in which the Voice grew quieter and quieter,
and even good-humored—which suggested, first, they had
no wish for the hani foreigner to understand; and second,
they were out of the same district of Ijir, and *therefore*
Haisi Ana-kehnandian must be a good upstanding fellow.

This went on and on and back and forth, and in the
meanwhile the Personage sat surveying the potted plant on
her desk and frowning mightily.

"You make mess in customs office," the Voice then said
in the pidgin. "Personage not happy. You make lot public
mess, scare people—"

"I take it the Personage understands the Trade. Ask the
Personage whether she has given any authority to this per-

son to harass my crew, threaten me, create a riot in customs, hold my cargo for ransom, and ask personal questions about a stsho passenger who's never set foot on this station nor applied for local customs clearance. I feared firearms were present. I went over that desk in protection of my life! This advised innocent persons to take cover, for their personal safety! This fool committed the aggression, by blocking the exit in an aggressive manner, in the clear intent to do violence!"

That prompted another conference, a lengthy one. And more frowns from Haisi.

The Personage then took to pinching leaves off the plant on her desk, and paying no attention to either of them.

"Personage not like speak pidgin. Say 'pologize for distress you. Say customs cleared. All fine."

She had to replay that again to believe she'd heard it. But Haisi looked far from happy with the situation.

"Then thank the Personage on behalf of my ship and my passenger."

"She understand fine. She say, Be careful with stsho. Good luck on you deals on station. You need all luck you got."

"Ask her why."

"Not need ask. Ask you: why be fool? Why make damn lot racket, attract notice? Ask you: what benefit you this stsho thing?"

"Money. *Money,* like making a profit on this trip, like getting hired like any merchant captain—"

"You not merchant. You *Chanur.*"

"Gods-rotted right I'm a merchant! What do you think, I'm rich? I travel from station to station for a hobby?"

"You got aunt."

"The gods-be *universe* has got Pyanfar Chanur, but I don't! She can't be head of Chanur any longer, she can't sit in the *han,* she can't hold property and she can't vote on Anuurn— Your informers have been lying down asleep if you think I'm on her payroll! My ship hauls freight to pay the bills and keep our clan's taxes paid. That's all, no politics, no secrets, and no *interest* in secrets. I'm paid to transport this thing and transport it I will, until I can get the thing off my deck to its legitimate owner. But *don't* expect my aunt knows. We don't speak!"

Evidently it was not the answer the Voice or the Personage expected. There was another sharp exchange between the two of them.

Something—she understood two of the mahen languages—about relatives and assumptions and another Personage of feminine gender.

And Haisi was not pleased. "All you papers cleared," Haisi said. "You go. You put stuff on market, quick as you want. Stsho you want go Kita. Wish you luck find same. Suggest you make nice thank you to busy Personage."

"Thank you," she said, and made two successive bows, to Haisi, and to the Personage who had never once looked her in the eyes. There was a small pile of leaves below the miniature tree. The Personage raked them together with a nail, and seemed perfectly absorbed in this activity. The Voice did not exist when the Personage was speaking for herself. And the Voice stood to the side of the room, hands behind his back, with no more to say to her.

So she left. And hoped the Personage of Urtur had more intense words for Haisi Ana-kehnandian once the door closed.

There was all this banging and sawing again. And the loaders were taking things off the ship, finally. Hallan was puzzled by the former, found the latter comfortingly ordinary, and had himself another snack while he read the tail end of *Love in the Outback.*

They had moved in a minifridge full of food and snacks and drinks, a microwave, a viewer, a tape player, and a stack of somebody's tapes and books . . . some of them really embarrassing. But interesting. He really hoped they hadn't known those were in the stack. Tiar had been in a real hurry when she brought them in, and said something about the captain having been in some dust-up with customs, but everything was all right now, and she was sorry, and she wished she could let him out, but they had a very upset stsho on their hands and if the stsho ran into him *gtst* would Phase on the spot. So please forgive them.

With which Tiar ducked out again. And the banging and sawing went on, and the loaders proceeded.

Clank-clank. Clank. Bang and thump.

It would have been very tedious, except if anybody was

going to come after him he hoped he got to the end of the book first, and he hoped they didn't catch him actually reading it.

If he were on the *Sun* the book in the stack would have meant one thing.

Here—he was having thoughts he'd never exactly had before . . . or not thoughts, exactly, but feelings. Not about Tiar, actually. Just about belonging. Dangerous thoughts— like fitting into an ancient pattern that he didn't want, that he'd rejected for his dreams of traveling and being free, and here he was reading this stupid book, increasingly confused about what was going on with his hormones and his thinking processes. Try to be independent and put up with any crude thing the crew did, and sometimes go along with what they wanted, and he could do that without letting them really get to him; but now here he was, guiltily reading what he really hoped they hadn't meant to be in the stack, and thinking thoughts that meant maybe Mara Sahern was right and instincts were too strong, and he couldn't depend on using his brains—that ultimately, when he got all his size and hormones kicked in for good and earnest, he wasn't going to be worth anything but one thing until he was as old as Khym Mahn and hormones had stopped making him crazy.

That reputation for violence was why the stsho was afraid of him. That reputation was why everybody on Meetpoint had panicked when he had panicked and swung on the kif. And that reputation scared him, because there wasn't just the kif to deal with, there was *the* Chanur, lord Harun Chanur, who would break his neck if he caught him in Chanur territory, the same as there was lord Sahen to object to his presence on the *Sun.* It was one thing to go to space before he was old enough, quite, to have his adult growth, but after three years he was about *there,* banging his head on the doorways built for female crews, and finding instincts he'd thought he was immune to—worst of all, to think that, over the next few years, he might progressively lose his self-control and his reason. It just was not true. It would not happen to him, it didn't need to happen, it was, what had Pyanfar Chanur said, that so outraged the *han?* —an unscientific belief system; and conforming to it was custom, not hardwiring.

But here he sat on a Chanur ship having thoughts he didn't even want, and wanting to finish the cursed book, and not wanting to, and scared and drawn at the same time.

Was that being crazy? Was that what happened, and was that what had started when he came on board the *Legacy,* among female people he could really want?

He kept reading. He got to the end and he sat there staring at the wall and wishing he knew what was ahead of him, and whether he was a fool or not, being out here, in this foreign place with a crew he . . .

Really, really wanted to belong to, in a very absolute and traditional and gut-level way that that book was about.

Which could very definitely get him killed. Which was stupid, intellectually speaking. But not—not when feelings cut in.

The incoming messages were stacked up.

From Haisi, Hilfy presumed, since it had *Ha'domaren*'s header: *You better think who you are. Dangerous you not know.*

From Customs: *Customs approved.* For the third time. They were overcompensating.

From *Padur's Victory* and *Narn's Dawnmaker,* a joint communique: *We are in receipt of troubling news regarding difficulty with customs and station authorities. We request a briefing at earliest.*

That had to be answered, urgently and in the most courteous way, hence the presence of a Padur and a Narn captain in the downside corridor, plain trader captains in workaday blue trousers, out of the midst of their work. And it certainly behooved the bone-tired hani captain in question to meet them personally at the airlock, and invite them into her downside office, and sit down and explain the situation, in spite of the fact she and her sleepless crew were again facing no sleep and snatched meals. Tarras was down there alone, no one was on the bridge, and the offloading was going to go on until the *Legacy*'s holds were empty.

Meaning about twelve more hours.

"There's a ship to watch," she said. "*Ha'domaren.* If you want my guess what's going on, there's a Personage with an agent on that ship who's fairly high up in the hierarchy;

that Personage *assumed* I have a direct line to my aunt—which I don't—and somebody on this station tried to blacklist my ship by bringing up old records about *The Pride*. I wasn't interested in a secret game, I raised a racket, this agent didn't want the publicity, and when the police got involved it bounced the case right where I couldn't get anyone else to send it—straight to the Personage of Urtur, where I said very definitely I hadn't any contacts with my aunt and all I wanted was trade. After which they gave me my customs clearance and the Personage of Urtur gave the agent a reasonably dirty look. That's the sum of it."

"We hear," Tauhen Padur said, with a discreet cough, "there's some sort of politically hot stsho cargo."

"Where did you hear that?"

A shrug, a lowering of one ear. "From my crew, indirectly from the market. Where, specifically . . . I think they'd have said if the source was unusual. Probably just the merchants."

"Same," said Kaury Narn. Old spacer, Kaury was, lot of rings, pale edges on the mane, and a right-side tooth capped in silver—ask where and on what kif pirate she'd broken that one. The Narn captain came from far wilder days. "Whatever the chaff is, it's drifting up and down the market."

"We didn't talk to anybody in the market. There's only one way that information flew in here ahead of us."

"This *Ha'domaren*."

"And one Tahaisimandi Ana-kehnandian, nickname Haisi, who's operating out of that ship."

"Eastern hemisphere Ijir. At least by ancestry." This from Kaury.

"You know him."

"No," Kaury Narn said. "But the name is eastern. I'll remember it."

"Haisi," Tauhen said. "Which Personage?"

"Not the Personage of Urtur. Somebody named Paehisna-ma-to."

"Not familiar."

"Not to me."

"Is there any way," the Narn asked, "you *can* get in touch with your aunt?"

"No. That's the truth." Touchy question, under other circumstances; but this was with obvious reason. "What I hear, she's somewhere . . ." She censored that. ". . . inconvenient; and I don't know where. Possibly Ana-kehnandian's Personage is shaking the tree, so to speak, to see what falls out; certainly somebody wanted to use me to get to her, and I couldn't if I wanted to. So if your trail and hers should cross, let her know. But meanwhile I *hope* I've settled this mahe and got him off my tail. What I want to know—*are* there any stsho hiding on this station?"

"Gone when we got here," Padur said. "And Padur was here before Narn. Rumor is they just boarded ship and took out of here. I won't bet on any holdouts, but by my experience, they'd Phase if they had to hide: they wouldn't do it."

"Which ship took them? Where?"

"The general staff, on *Pakkitak,* to Meetpoint via Hoas. A rumor—a rumor about certain ones going to Kita on *Ko'juit.*"

One kifish ship. One mahen ship, to Kita Point. Not unheard of, for stsho to use either species' transportation. But Padur said it: it was rumor. Everything they knew, was a report they had *from* the mahendo'sat, namely from the Personage and from Ana-kehnandian.

"We've got to find Atli-lyen-tlas. We have a package with that address. Hear anything on that score?"

"The ambassador?" Kaury Narn said. "That *gtst* excellency and one of the staffers went with the mahen ship."

"How sure are your sources?"

"Market gossip, no more, no less." Kaury twitched her ring-heavy ears and settled back, arms folded. "Which means nothing. And if I knew anything else that bears on it, I'd be quick to tell you. I don't know."

Information appearing without source, in a hotbed of gossip both true and false, in a market that sailed and fell on rumors and accusations and public perceptions. Wonderful.

"We're outbound tomorrow," Padur said. "Fueling in the next watch. You're on to Kita, then?"

"Not willingly. Certainly not where I'd like to go. If you do run across my aunt's track—"

"I'll pass it on what's happened, where you've gone." Small movements, twitches of the ears, shiftings in the

chairs, said that two busy captains were anxious to get back
to work: news was welcome, but sparser than they had
hoped, and it threatened none of their clan interests.

This captain was the same—at least busy and anxious to
get back to the market reports—to safeguard her clan interests. Their on again, off again entry into Urtur market and
the (by now) famous encounter in the customs office had
sent the prices of goods in their hold up and down, up and
down, and (more than one could play that game) she had
had Chihin and Tiar buying current entertainment, fine-
grade composites supplies, grain, and a handful of mahen
luxuries on the market, saying, if asked, that the *Legacy*
might just go on to Kita to sell its load. Which was an
honest possibility—until she had gotten a fair offer and a
fair buy option.

Not that she'd have deceived other hani captains: they'd
already concluded their deals before the *Legacy*'s cargo hit
the boards; besides that they were coming from the other
direction, with different goods; and one being in process of
loading and one set for undock, already in countdown.

Dirty tricks on the mahen traders and the handful of kif
in port, but traders who relied solely on the rumors that
ran the docks were asking for surprises; and those who
asked what all of a certain species seemed to be acting on,
and how they were selling and buying learned far more. It
was the way the game was played, that was all, a stsho
game from top to bottom.

Except they had a direct barter offer on the methane
load, gods rot the luck: that was the trouble with dealing
with the methane docks—they too often wanted to barter,
you couldn't always handle what they wanted to give and
you couldn't talk to a matrix brain to explain your constraints.

Hani, thank the gods, were much more straightforward.

"What's the situation at Meetpoint?" Padur asked on the
way to the airlock.

"Chancy. You want my opinion, if I weren't carrying
what I'm carrying, for a rate I can't tell you, I'd do a turn-
around at Hoas back for here. Something's going on with
the stsho, you've guessed that the same as I have, and I
don't have the least idea what, but it would keep me out
of Meetpoint if I wasn't paid real, real well. *Possibly* the

administration there is in some kind of crisis. Possibly the crisis is here. Possibly . . . ." The idea occurred to her on the spot, and she might have censored it, but these were allied captains, of nominally friendly clans. "Possibly it could be a crisis much farther into stsho territory. And someone wiser than I am should consider that possibility. I've no way to get a message anywhere, except by you."

Kaury Narn gave her a particularly straight stare. And nodded and left. Padur walked with her down the yellow, ribbed tube, around the curve, the two of them talking together and doubtless more comfortably, with an associate decades older in her friendship than a young upstart Chanur.

Seniority was what they had lost, with Pyanfar out of the picture, and doubly so with Rhean retiring to manage the situation at home. From senior, and important, Chanur had descended to a Who are you? from captains who honestly had to see Hilfy Chanur to know whether they could trust her word or her judgment. Oh, they *knew* her: they'd recall her as one of *The Pride*'s crew, once upon a time; but no few of the captains and worse, the crewwomen, gave her that second look that remarked her youth, and wondered what deals she'd cut to obtain of her clan, at her age, the post they'd worked a lifetime for.

Working *for* her aunt, certain mahendo'sat evidently thought—running the *mekt-hakkikt*'s errands and serving as decoy.

Having notions, the old women in the *han* would say of her and of Pyanfar. Delusions of deity. A disdain for Anuurn. A blurring of self—what was hani and what was not. Herself, yes, defiantly she blurred those lines—but blurred lines were definitely not Pyanfar's attitude: that was the first and foremost of the problems between them.

The loader clanked. She held her breath, stopped in her office door, wondering was it going to balk and stick. It kept on. Tiar passed her, paint-spattered, towing a large carrier full of plastic-wrapped cushions, all white.

"For the gods' sake watch the—whatever-it-is. Don't spatter it."

"Won't, cap'n," Tiar panted. Chihin and Fala brought up the rear, with a lamp trailing connections, like some sea creature rudely uprooted. A trail of white dust tracked down the *Legacy*'s corridor, while *gtst* honor sat in sheet-draped splendor in the lounge, making personal purchases on the station market and demanding to be back in *gtst* quarters as soon as possible.

The loader balked again, cl-unk. She looked at the deck as if she could look through it, beseeched the indifferent gods of trade, and the thing limped onward. It worked better on incoming, for some reason known only to those gods. They had the cursed thing on auto at the moment, and trusted mahen passers-by and dockers not to fling themselves gratuitously into the gears and sue while Tarras was working inside.

Impossible. Impossible to get out of here with any dispatch. And a tired crew was asking for accidents to happen.

Wasn't, however, the only source of brute muscle they had aboard. The stsho was topside and little likely to stir.

She walked down to the laundry, hit the door once, and opened it.

Hallan Meras stuffed something away in a hurry, ears flat, face dismayed, and she surveyed the laundry, that now contained pieces of the crew lounge, the galley, and somebody's personal library.

"Captain," Hallan said, scrambling for his feet. He *was* respectful, commendably so.

"Crew says you say you can work cargo."

"Aye, captain."

Sounded sane. Sounded like someone who could take basic orders.

"We've got a problem," she said. "We're in a crunch, Tarras is working the loader solo, inside, we've got nobody keeping the local kids' fingers out of the loader—I don't suppose you brought a coat, did you?"

"No, captain." Ears flagged. "But I could sort of wrap a blanket around—"

"Unworkable. No boots, no coat, no cold suit, no hold. Can you *behave* yourself on the dockside? We're going late. We're nearly twelve hours behind, we're unloading and we're loading, fast as I can get the buy made and the cans on our dock. Nobody's getting any sleep."

"I'd *love* to, captain. I really would!"

She truly didn't trust enthusiasm in a kid who'd broken up the Meetpoint market. She refused to soften her expres-

sion, only stared at him with ears flat and nose drawn.
"Hallan Meras, have you lied? *Can* you work cargo? *Do*
you know what you're doing?"

"I swear to you, captain."

"You foul up, you break any seals, you scare *anybody*
on this station, Hallan Meras, I'll sell you to the kif."

"Aye, captain."

She hated when people she threatened were overanxious
to go ahead.

"At ten percent off," she said. But she failed to kill his
enthusiasm. And it made her remember what he *really*
wanted, which she wouldn't give, wasn't about to give, gods
rot him. She had a smoothly functioning crew, they understood each other, they were relatives, they had everything
they needed.

He was also too gods-rotted handsome and too feckless
and too *male,* confound him, which was the main reason to
get him out of here before more than the crew lounge and
the galley found its way down here.

"Get!" she said, shoved a pocket com into his hand, and
he got, down the main corridor toward the airlock, at a
near run.

Couldn't fault that. She looked for ways. She went into
the laundry, looked around for signs of mayhem or misdeed,
found nothing out of order except one unfolded blanket, the
viewer, the *Manual of Trade,* for some gods-only-knew reason, and . . .

She bent and drew from under the blast cushion the
printed book Hallan Meras had put there.

And who gave him *that?* she wondered.

Chapter 7

You didn't run on the rampway link, you respected that perilous connection, that icy cold passage that gave a ship pressured access to station.

But Hallan walked it very fast, and, via the pocket com, called Tarras to report in: he figured that was the first test, whether he could use it and whether he knew what to do next.

"What are you doing out there?" Tarras snapped at him, probably cold, certainly surprised.

"The captain said I should, she said you could use some help."

"Gods-rotted right I could use some help, but don't scare the dockers! Are you on pocket com?"

"Aye."

"You keep near the access ramp. And don't be sight-seeing!"

"I'm at the bottom now. Have you got a cam-link?" That, he figured, would tell Tarras he had some notion what his job was. "We've got space for one more can on the transport, we've got a fourteen canner moving up. Have we got a destination list?"

"Your display, code 2, check it out. Docker chief's a curlycoated fellow, and just hold it, I'll call him and tell him who you are. For godssake, bow, be polite, you'll scare him into a heart seizure."

"Aye, I do understand. Tell me when it's clear." He used his time taking stock of the surroundings, *feeling* the cold near the access and wishing that he could move away from the draft. The pocket com had a display: keyed, it scrolled the offload, 142 of the giant containers gone to their various buyers, the loader with, one reckoned, 10 more in its grip, outbound, and the transport sitting there with 15, which meant that particular hold was probably approaching empty, and Tarras was going to have to initiate the number two hold, which—

"You're clear," Tarras said. *"His name is Pokajinai, Nandijigan Pokajinai, he speaks the Trade, mind your manners."*

"Got it." He spotted the mahe docker chief, flipped the com to standby, and strolled over. He saw the apprehensive expression, too, and made his most courteous bow. "Sir." In case they thought hani males went homicidally for anything of like gender. "Hallan Meras. *Na* Pokajinai?"

A nervous laughter from the rest of the dockers.

"Name Nandijigan, call Nandi. You Meras."

"Meras is fine." His father would have his ears. "*Ker* Tarras is working inside, I'm her eyes out here."

"Not hear Chanur ship got male," somebody muttered. He was undecided whether to hear it or not. He decided not. He simply flipped the com to active and advised Tarras he'd made peaceful contact.

It was wonderful. It was the best thing in all the universe, being out here, trusted, with the smells and even the cold, and the noise of foreign voices—the clangs and bangs of machinery, and the romance of the labels that the docker chief had to give mahen customs stamps to, and write on, and sign for.

They were a lot less likely to have a miscount with one of the *Legacy* crew out here. It was a real position of trust the captain had given him—she *had* listened to the other crew on his case, so there was still hope of pleasing her and becoming indispensable and permanent.

"How's it going?" Tarras asked, breathless, teeth chattering, he could hear the rattle over the com.

"Everything's clear," he said. "*Ker* Tarras, are you all right?"

"Cold. Just cold."

There were transports coming, a *lot* of them, and there was nobody else loading at this section of the docks. The sixteen-carrier moved out with a whine of its motor, and the fourteen moved in. Another sixteen-carrier moved into the waiting line and the automated handlers moved can after can out, instantly frosting on the surfaces, internally heated, but the insulation was so efficient they could sit in a cold-hold and keep their necessary conditions within

parameters. Tarras had been scrambling about the lattice-
work of walkways in the hold unhooking the connections
and the hoses from the temperature-controlled cans. Alone,
the captain said. No wonder she was out of breath.

Where had everybody else gone? He had no idea what
time it was. He didn't think it was a good idea to ask
questions, especially on the comlink, outside—just do his
job.

Maybe Tarras would get some relief in there.

Meanwhile he consulted with the mahendo'sat and relayed Tarras' suggestions about sequencing the offload, to
minimize shifting the cans about from loader arm to loader
arm. *He* was cold. He didn't want to think how it was for
Tarras.

Cl-ank. Cl-l-l-l-

Tarras said a word over com you weren't supposed to
say on com.

The loader chain had stopped. The loader arm was half
extended.

"Can you back it up?" he asked Tarras. "If you can sort
of rock it—"

"I know that!"

"It's those fourteen-can transports."

"What?" Tarras snapped.

"The fourteen-can—"

"What's that to do with the gods-forsaken chain?"

"The loader arm. When it extends full out."

"What's that to do with anything?"

"It has to. The fourteen-can jobs, the old ones are a little
low. The loader arm has to extend out, it cramps the leads,
and it just—ties up. You back the loader arm up."

"Are you serious?"

"It works with the *Sun's* loader, *ker* Tarras. The loader
arm tells the driver the chain's hung. But it isn't. The loader
just thinks it is. Back the arm up and set it down about a
hand short. —Wait a minute. You're going to—"

Bang.

Into the carrier cab.

"Not that far," he said.

"That's where it goes!"

The mahen driver was getting out, yelling in his own
language, and when people did that it scared him, like at

Meetpoint, like when the fight started, and he didn't want to fight anybody. He made a fast approach to the docker chief, but all the mahendo'sat were yelling, and the docker chief screamed, "Move damn cart! How for park there?"

He thought the chief meant him. He was by the single-can cart, it was no more than a lift vehicle they had to hoist the inbound cans, but they didn't need it yet. He just stepped aboard and backed up out of the can-transport's way so *it* could adjust position with the arm.

"Move damn thing!" the transport driver yelled at him. "Damn stupid park there!"

He didn't know who had. He wanted to save his ship fault in the matter. He whipped it smartly around; and *bang!*—

Brought up short, with a transport there filling his view that just hadn't been there before, a transport that was flashing yellow lights and shrieking alarm, with a writhing shape inside the purple-lit glass.

Methane transport. . . . Explosive as hell.

He tried to go forward. The bumpers were hooked.

He cut the motor. He had that much presence of mind. Lights were flashing everywhere. Sirens were shrieking. The ten-story-tall section doors were moving shut, walling off their whole area of dock.

"*Ker* Tarras?" he said into the com. "Help."

"*Captain?*" came the call on all-ship.

"Lower main," Hilfy said, got the message, and something like three seconds later was on the downward access.

Colored lights were everywhere, sirens were blowing, there was a tc'a vehicle and a cargo lifter clearly in mortal embrace, with rescue techs swarming over the scene, and a knot of Urtur station police clustered about Hallan Meras, who was out of his vehicle and answering questions with the gods only knew what legally complicating admissions.

She drew a breath and strode down into the mess, answered the inevitable, "You captain this ship?" with the lamentable truth, and fixed Hallan with a flat-eared look. His ears twitched downward, and he winced, but he did not look down.

"Is the methane truck leaking?" she asked. If the tc'a vehicle was leaking its atmosphere into flammable oxygen this was a bad place to be standing. Procedure was to evacuate the passenger into a rescue pod, pump the methane atmosphere into a sound container, and get the victim methane-side for medical treatment, rather than to pry the wreckage apart—but nobody had told the docker who was bouncing on the oxy-vehicle bumper trying to disengage it. "Stop that!" she shouted. "Fool!"

The police and the rescue workers started yelling, and maybe the tc'a in the cab was distraught too: it started writhing about, its serpentine body bashing the windows of the cab with powerful blows, and wailing—wailing in a tc'a's multipartite voice its distress. Its companion chi was racing about—a wonder that the convulsions didn't smash the sticklike creature to paste, and the whole cab was rocking, rescue workers were shouting at the tow-truck, something about come on, hurry up.

Then the thrashing grew quiet. The rescue workers climbed up on the cab and peered inside, and Hilfy held her breath. There was a lot of dialectic chatter, a lot of muttering and one of the workers got down off the cab and began motioning the tow-truck to move in.

The police yelled at the rescue workers, the rescue workers yelled at the police, Hallan said, "I'm sorry, captain."

"What," she said in a low voice, "happened?"

"The loader jammed. I backed the truck. It just—turned up in back of me."

Tc'a didn't exactly drive a straight line. It was the nature of their nervous systems. "Do you have a license to drive on dockside?"

"No, captain."

"Do you suppose there's a reason why you don't have a license to drive on dockside?"

"I think so, captain."

The police were coming back. They had the tow-truck hitched. "Watch your mouth," she said. "Let *me* do the talking." Out of the tail of her eye she saw Tiar and Tarras on the ramp, and Fala behind them.

And the police were on their way back to them, with their slates and their recorders. Lawyers would be next—if it was an oxy-sider Meras had backed into. One could only wish it was lawyers.

"It reproduce," their chief said, with an expansive gesture involving his slate. "You responsible. Urtur station not."

She drew a long careful breath. "You write your report. I write mine."

"We got take him."

Tempting thought. "No."

"He not list with you crew."

"He's on loan. He's a licensed spacer. I put him on the dockside. I take responsibility for accidents."

"Captain," Hallan objected, brim full of noble and foolish objections—her claws twitched out and her vision shadowed around the edges.

"Shut *up,* Meras. —I'll need a copy of your report, officer, and I'll pay charges on the alarm."

Don't even ask if anybody was injured when the section doors moved shut. Disruption of business, inconvenience to traffic, time and services of rescue workers and police . . .

Say about 200,000 in damages . . . give or take.

She signed the report as Reserving the right to amend or correct, and so on, due to language barrier and lack of legal counsel, etc., and so on. She thanked the officers, thanked the rescue workers, gave the eye to her crew lurking up in the ramp access, and smiled sweetly at Meras.

"He try fix loader," the docker chief said.

Grant the fellow a fair mind and an inclination to speak out. She delayed for a look up at the mahe, and gave a bow of the head, and put the name in memory, Nandi, in the not unlikely event they needed a witness. "He thanks you for your support," she said, in her best mahendi, and gave a second bow, before she took Meras by the arm and headed him up the ramp.

"I feel awful it was pregnant," he said on the way up, and she threw him a disbelieving glance.

"They *reproduce* under stress," she said. "You're a *father,* gods rot you, to a tc'a! What's lord Meras going to say to *that?*"

He looked horrified. Appropriately. About the time they reached Tiar and Fala and Chihin.

"It spawned," she said, shortly. "Probably so did the chi. —Tiar, get up to the bridge. See to *gtst* honor!"

"Aye, captain."

Tiar went, at top speed. That left two. "Fala, down there

and take over for Meras. —Chihin, you're on your own with the guest quarters. Get!"

The com was trying to get her attention with periodic, when-you-have-time beeps. She waited until she had gotten Meras into the airlock, and keyed into the ship's internal system. "Tarras. You all right?"

"Aye, captain." Chattering teeth. *"Captain, the kid was giving me a fix on the loader."*

"Fix on the loader." Two and two weren't making four. "You get that gods-forsaken cargo out of there. I'll hear it later." She grabbed Meras by the elbow and steered him through the lock and down the corridor toward her office.

"Captain, I'm really sorry. I'm really—really sorry you had to take responsibility . . ."

"We are in one gods-rotted *mess,* you understand that? You understand me?"

"Captain." From the com again. Tarras. *"I'd really like to talk to you about what happened. . . ."*

"Later!"

They reached her office and Meras followed her in. She sat, he sat, disconsolately, his big frame somewhat over-flowing the chair that was designed to accommodate even mahendo'sat. She stared, he looked at the front panel of her desk, or somewhere in that vicinity. The loader had started again. Presumably they had the go-ahead from the port authority. Clank-clank. Clank-thump.

"Meras."

"Yes, captain."

"Do you know what you've *cost* us in fines?"

"If there were any way I could take responsibility—"

"Would Meras like a two hundred thousand credit bill?"

"I don't think so."

"I thought your captain was reprehensible for leaving you at Meetpoint. I begin to feel a certain sympathy for her, you know that?"

"Yes, captain."

"I don't have a license to drive that cart. Tiar's been out here for forty years and she doesn't have a license to back that cart up. Do you understand me?"

"Yes, captain."

"I want you to understand something. We have a stsho passenger who's already in delicate health. They are *not* a robust species. This stsho is occupying the cabin around the corner from here. If *gtst* saw you, it could tip matters right over the edge. Do you understand *that* fact?"

"Yes, captain." A visible wince. "—Captain,—"

"*Yes,* Meras?"

"I really—really want to do right. I can *do* a good job—"

"Two hundred thousand worth. That's a gods-rotted steep hourly wage!"

"I didn't know about the license! The loader was jammed, and they couldn't move the truck till somebody moved the cart—"

"Until a licensed driver moved the cart!"

"I didn't know that!"

"Well, there's a gods-be lot you didn't learn in your apprenticeship, Hallan Meras, and you're not doing it at our expense. We've got to go on out of here to Kita, from Kita the gods only know where the gods-forsaken addressee has gone to, but *gtst* is on a mahen ship, and from Kita our choices are Not Good. Do you follow my logic? This is no trip and no place for any gods-rotted apprentice!"

"I'm not an apprentice—I've got my license—"

"Got your license—I'd like to know how in a mahen hell you got your license, I'd like to know doing what you got your license, because it sure as taxes wasn't on any dockside ops board, and it gods-rotted sure didn't entitle you to back a cart the length of this office! You're a papa, Hallan Meras, you're a papa to a methane-breathing five-brained colony entity and probably to another chi who's crazier than it is—and mama or whatever you call it when you reproduce when startled is just capable of asking his, her, or its matrix what gods-be *ship* its offspring's papa is working on! Methane-folk have this way of turning up in the deep dark empty and saying hello when you don't want to see them. Methane-folk have this way of navigating that doesn't respect lanes in space any more than they respect lines on a dock! I've had them come near my ship when they weren't after anything, thank you, Hallan Meras, and I don't want to deal with them when they are! I by the gods sure don't want to meet that mama or its offspring in deep space! Do you remotely understand why I'm upset?"

"I could—I could try to have station get a message to them, station can talk with them . . ."

"That's a myth. That's a thorough-going myth. Station can approximate things like 'Open the hatch,' and 'That's a fire hazard!' It doesn't do gods-be well with, 'Hello, I'm Hallan Meras, I'm responsible for your offspring.' They've been in space long before we were, and we *still* don't know how to say 'Stop it you're in my lane,' and: 'My ship can't perform that maneuver.' You want to see a matrix brain communication? I can show you one. . . ." She got into comp with two jabs of a key and voiced it: "Matrix-com!"

Matrix-com came up, with the typical grid. Five rows across, output of each of five voices of its multiple brains. She hit vocal and knnn-voice wailed over the speaker, like a wind-organ, like pipes, and deep, deep bass vibrations.

Hallan winced, ears twitching with the assault, nostrils working. He shivered visibly. *Then* she remembered she was dealing with adolescent male hormones, which ought to give a sane woman pause—but gods rot it, he insisted he was one of the girls, that he was cool-headed, he wanted to play the game on their terms; and she slammed her hand down on the desk, *bang!*

"Off-comp!"

Sound stopped. And Meras was still twitching, but he hadn't left his chair, his eyes were dilated, but the ears were trying to come upright—he was paying attention, he was listening, he wasn't crazy.

"Captain." Tiar—on the bridge. Magnificent timing.

"I'm in my office, Tiar. What's the problem?"

"Just got a blip on station feed. Sun Ascendant's just entered system."

The answer to prayers, it might be.

Hallan looked upset. Shook his head and shaped No with his mouth. Said something else.

"Thanks, cousin. Glad to hear that."

"I don't want to go, captain. I don't want them—"

"You signed with them. You sat at their table, you slept in their shelter, they got you your license, and I don't know what made them leave you at Meetpoint, Meras, but so far as what I've seen they may have run for their lives."

Made him mad, that did. Good.

"If you want to go back to the laundry, you stay there. If you want to go back to the passenger cabins and help Chihin paint and patch, feel free. I'm not turning you over

to station police, and being the righteous fool I am, I'm
not identifying *Sun Ascendant* to the tc'a. We'll handle it.
But I've done everything I'm obliged to do for somebody
I gathered out of a jail he by the gods got himself into.
I've got 41 messages in ship's files for my aunt at this station; I've got 156 for *me,* most of them from people trying
to use me to get *to* my aunt for favors they want; and here
comes one of my aunt's devoted admirers who just really
badly wants into my crew, because he just really badly
wants it, that's why. —Well, so does half the universe,
Meras. And I'd suggest you give up and go home if meeting
my aunt is what you want; or if being a spacer is what you
want, focus down and use your head on problems before
you kill somebody. I'd suggest you give up on the *Manual
of Trade* and start reading the licensing and operations
manual. It may keep you out of the next hot spot you land
in. —And give my regards to Tellun Sahern. Minute your
ship makes port you're going over there."

Ears were flat. Really mad. Better. Maybe he'd *survive*
in Sahern, in far space.

"Go on," she said. And he got up and bowed and left.

Which didn't make her happy. Nobody could be happy,
who had a 200,000 credit charge pending against her ship,
a cargo half unloaded, a distraught stsho dignitary in the
crew lounge, and a course change pending to Kita Point, a
gods-forsaken dot in the great empty, after which, as she
had said to Meras—limited options.

"*Ker* Chihin," Hallan said, hesitating in the open doorway. "The captain suggested I help."

"I don't need anything backed into," Chihin said shortly,
and Hallan winced. The room was all white. The furniture
was gone. You walked up steps to the floor and there was
a depression full of white cushions.

Beside which there was a pedestal with braces going out
to it, but nothing on it.

"You can vacuum," Chihin said. "Floor, walls, everything. Steam vac. All the dust. Height could help. Are your
feet clean?"

He looked. They weren't, exactly. "I'll go wash," he
said meekly.

"Packaged wet towel, right there by the steps." Chihin

frowned at him as he sat down on the steps and reached for it. He tried not to look at her face. He felt sick, he had felt sick ever since he had backed into the tc'a, but he couldn't go back to that closed room, he couldn't stand it. So he washed his feet off so no one could complain of a smudge and he looked for a place to dispose of the towel.

"Over there," Chihin said, indicating a plastic bucket. He went and dropped it in. "You know how to use the steam vac?"

"Yes, ma'am." He was too well acquainted with it. It was all Sahern had let him do for his first weeks aboard the *Sun.* He went and checked the prime, checked the water and pulled the filter screen, which he figured he ought to clean before someone else found fault with him. "Is there a sink, ma'am, or should I—"

"Bath's in there. Sink works just like ours—it's the fixture on the left."

He went and washed the filter. It *was* different plumbing. Ordinarily he would have been intrigued, but the lump in his throat would not go away and he just tried to go moment by moment and not to think about what the captain had said, one way or the other. The captain had a right to be mad, gods, he couldn't pay back the damage he'd cost— probably nobody in Meras clan history had ever fouled up so egregiously, so consistently.

But the docking chief had *said* to move the cart.

He put the vacuum back together. He took it to a corner and started there, with a racket that made conversation impossible. But he was aware of Chihin staring at him from time to time: maybe she expected the vac to explode or something; or him to do something she could fault. Of all the crew, Chihin was not in any way friendly, and he supposed by now the rest of the crew was ready to kill him. Except maybe . . . at least Tarras had tried to speak for him. Fala and Tiar had looked upset, as well they might, but they hadn't hated him. Chihin—didn't want him here. Which was why the captain had sent him to work with her, he supposed. But it was still better than sitting alone in the laundry and remembering backing into that truck, and that *thing* snaking back and forth in pain and battering itself against the windows, leaving bits of skin and fluid on the glass. . . .

At least it hadn't exploded. Nobody had gotten killed. Quite the opposite. Somebody had gotten created. He wondered how the tc'a felt.

"The kid was trying to straighten out the loader," Tarras said. There was still ice in her beard, melting and glistening in the heat of the downside office—Hilfy had called her up, ordered her to trade places with Fala, and the way to the dock lay through the lower main corridor and past her office. So she had both of them, Tarras *and* Fala, arguing with her, the loader was in temporary shut-down, pending the switch, and no cargo was moving. But she figured she might as well listen and be done with it.

"All right," she said. "Voices on Meras' behalf . . . while we're at it." She pushed the call button. "Cousin. Listen in."

"Aye," Tiar answered from the bridge. *"What's up?"*

"The loader jammed," Tarras said, and sat down, while Fala edged a half a step farther into the office, in the doorway. "The kid knew the equipment—*Sun Ascendant* must use the same model. Anyway, it pulled its usual stunt, and the kid said it was the fourteen-can truck, when the arm positions itself: he says it's a false signal, there's nothing to do with the chain, it's the arm overextending. This one model of truck has a slightly lower bed. It reaches down to get it, the arm jams, jams the chain, you back the chain— it fixes it. So if you move the truck a little farther—"

"The docker chief said he's heard of it," Fala said. "It's something they say on the docks but the companies won't investigate. Doesn't happen until the equipment gets a little wear on it, and then it'll happen if the play that gets into the joint works far enough to the right where the sensor bundle runs through, and *that* bias only happens when you get a whole lot of fifteen-year-old Daisaiji fourteen-canners in a row. Which you get on Urtur, they got more of them than anywhere, because they made them here. And it only happens if some driver parks short. That's why it comes and it goes."

She couldn't help but be interested in the purported solution to the loader glitch, if it was the answer—it sounded iffy to her; but most of all she didn't want to hear it was Meras who had the information. She'd worked up a perfectly good, justified fit of temper, from which Meras could learn something that *might* keep him alive, and she didn't want any extenuating circumstances.

"So the thing jammed," Tarras said, "and the docker crew wanted to move the truck, and somebody'd parked a can-hoist in the way—"

"Probably why the truck parked short," Fala said.

"And the kid said it was the truck, so the chief started yelling about moving the truck," Tarras said. "He was pretty hot, so the kid—just got in and backed it up."

"Without a license."

"Captain," Tarras said, "the length of the truck, it had to move. Isn't a spacer working freight hasn't stepped aboard and moved a hoist a few—"

"I haven't. I don't want my crew doing it. You *let the dockers* do their job, you don't lay a hand on their equipment, we got a special handicap, f' godssake, Chanur's got too many enemies who'd like to sue the hide off us, you understand?"

"Understood," Tarras said sullenly.

"But," Fala said, "it was only cosmic bad luck the tc'a was back there—"

"Luck! Methane loads come in on oxy side all the time at Urtur, and we got tc'a going back and forth on business oxy side, and it had business which is now complicated by an offspring! We can only hope we don't get *company* our next trip out. Luck be damned!"

"Aye, captain."

"Captain," Tiar said, *"begging your pardon, but he's young. Haven't any of us made mistakes?"*

"He can make them on *Sahern's* deck, and welcome to him. Enthusiasm is one thing. We can't afford his enthusiasm. Besides, his ship is here—"

"They didn't do him any favors, cap'n. That's their teaching? They take a kid on for an apprentice, and he's got a little of this, a little of that? I asked him stuff on ops. He knows this board real well, doesn't know how it relates to the main board. That's 'Sit here and watch the colored lights, kid,' that's what they gave him."

"It's not our problem! He's not signed with us, he signed with them."

Silence from Tarras and Fala. Glum stares.

"Aye," Tiar conceded from the bridge, not happy.

So no one was. She wasn't. Meras wasn't. But neither, one could suppose, was the tc'a.

Meanwhile *Sun Ascendant* was inbound, in contact with Urtur control. "To work," she said; and, in peace, composed a polite message for merchant captain Tellun Sahern, to rest in her message file.

From Chanur's Legacy *to* Sahern's Sun Ascendant, *the hand of Hilfy Chanur, to Tellun Sahern, her attention:*
We are pleased to report that—
No, scratch that. Sahern would find a way to take it wrong.

Meetpoint authorities, having dropped all charges against Hallan Meras, requested us to ferry him as far as Urtur where he might rejoin his ship. We will be glad to escort him to your dockside at your earliest convenience or to turn him over to your escort here if that is your wish.

From Sahern's Sun Ascendant *to* Chanur's Legacy, *the hand of Tellun Sahern, to Hilfy Chanur, her attention:*
We trade for a living, we don't take secret money or run without cargo.
It's clear you had a motive in buying him free of the stsho. As you've surely learned by now, he has no data on our ship to give you. I doubt he could even falsify credible numbers. Chanur has made its bargains. We will not rescue you from your folly.

The message slipped into the tray in printout. It burned on the screen. Hilfy pushed the button to capture to log, took the printout and slipped it into physical file.

The message she thought of sending was: *Earless bastard, I thought your reputation had hit bottom.*

The message she sent was:

From Chanur's Legacy *to* Sahern's Sun Ascendant, *the hand of Hilfy Chanur, to Tellun Sahern, her attention:*
We require a release from apprenticeship signed by you, under Sahern seal, and we will seek passage or assignment for him elsewhere.

From Sahern's Sun Ascendant *to* Chanur's Legacy, *the hand of Tellun Sahern, to Hilfy Chanur, her attention:*

Too late, Chanur. We've been following the news since we entered system. We accept no legal liability for the actions of a fool we left in stsho custody and you conveyed here and let loose on Urtur docks. You bought him. He's yours.

Although I thought your personal preferences lay outside your species.

From Chanur's Legacy *to* Sahern's Sun Ascendant, *the hand of Hilfy Chanur, to Tellun Sahern, her attention:*

Daughter of a nameless father, if this young man wishes to file a complaint against you for desertion in a foreign port, I will swear to particulars.

As to my personal tastes, at least I have preferences.

Possibly she had made a mistake. Temper had gotten the better of her. She should not have offered legal backing. She sat contemplating the screen, and thinking black and blacker and blackest thoughts.

"Captain?" Tiar asked from the bridge. *"We got all that on log."*

"Good."

"Kid never got a fair break, captain."

"The universe doesn't guarantee fair breaks, and I don't want any apprentice under *any* circumstances! Something's gone wrong with this whole business, we've got a nervous stsho on our hands and Kita is no place to take a novice. I want you to contact Narn and Padur—no, never mind. *I* will."

"Captain. Can I say a word?"

"I know what you're going to say, and I'm not listening."

"Captain, on behalf of the crew . . ."

"We're not taking any apprentice! His apprentice papers are over on a Sahern ship, they're not going to give them to Chanur, they're out to cause us whatever trouble they can, the whole radical right is looking for a Cause against Chanur, and I was a fool ever to agree to take him aboard—I *thought* Sahern would be reasonable, but clearly not."

She beeped off the contact, and composed another message—thought about couriering this one over to avoid public commotion and public pressure, and thought about the hazards of sending *Legacy* personnel alone and within reach of station police, angry merchants—or Ana-kehnandian.

No. *No* such chances.

From Chanur's Legacy *to* Padur's Victory, *the hand of Hilfy Chanur, to Tauhen Padur, her attention:*
We have advised Sahern of the presence of their apprentice crewman, Hallan Meras, on our ship. They have refused responsibility for this young man, who has been cleared of all charges which caused him to be detained by stsho authorities, and further, they have refused him access to their ship in harsh terms, preferring to recall an ancient feud with Chanur, no fault of this young man of Meras clan, a licensed spacer, who has traveled under our protection.
While Padur has no obligation, Chanur would be obliged if Padur could take this young man under its protection and possibly find a berth for him.

From Padur's Victory *to* Chanur's Legacy, *the hand of Tauhen Padur, to Hilfy Chanur, her attention:*
Padur while friendly to Chanur and altogether desirous of maintaining Chanur's good will, under the circumstances of the recent accident on Chanur dockside must regretfully decline to incur the possibility of legal liabilities under mahen law.

From Chanur's Legacy *to* Narn's Dawnmaker, *the hand of Hilfy Chanur, to Kaury Narn, her attention:*
We have advised Sahern of the presence of their apprentice crewman, Hallan Meras, on our ship. They have refused responsibility for this young man, who has been cleared of all charges which caused him to be detained by stsho authorities, and further, they have refused him access in harsh terms, preferring to recall an ancient feud with Chanur, no fault of this young man of Meras clan, who has traveled under our protection.
While Padur has declined our solicitation, we hope and Chanur would be obliged if Narn could take this young man, a licensed spacer, under its protection in any sense whatsoever.

*　　*　　*

From Narn's Dawnmaker *to* Chanur's Legacy, *the hand of Kaury Narn, to Hilfy Chanur, her attention:*

I have my sister's young daughter aboard: I could not in good conscience expose her or Meras clan to the consequences of taking on this young man. Nor do we have passenger facilities. However, Narn is willing, under appropriate safeguards, and at Chanur's request and assumption of all consequent responsibility to Meras, to convey the young gentleman under close supervision as far as Hoas, where he may await a ship with familial connections.

Read that: lock him in the laundry and turn him over to Hoas authorities. At least no worse accommodation than he had, and a station where (gods hope!) he had no legal problems. But going to Hoas took him *back* toward Meetpoint, and he would have to come back through Urtur again.

Where that ship might find legal problems waiting for them, unless they could get a release, and she *knew* the mahen politics waiting for them.

Hilfy sat and contemplated the screen; and sent back:

From Chanur's Legacy *to* Narn's Dawnmaker, *the hand of Hilfy Chanur, to Kaury Narn, her attention:*

Thank you for your offer. We fully understand. We will hold your proposal in reserve while we seek other safe disposition for—

—him.

The pronoun itself was unaccustomed out here. Ten, fifteen years ago, you didn't by the gods *use* the male pronoun in a message between clans. It still felt queasy and indecent. It felt indecent to have one's decades-senior aunt ahead of one's self in pushing the conservative limits. When had *she* become the defender of hani propriety?

—*the gentleman,* she finished. *If we don't get back to you, we wish you a safe voyage.*

And to Padur:

From Chanur's Legacy *to* Padur's Victory, *the hand of Hilfy Chanur, to Tauhen Padur, her attention:*

We are seeking other solutions. Please bear witness that we have attempted the honorable discharge of our reasonable obligations to Sahern and to Meras. Safe voyage.

She sat. And sat.

She *wished* she had not used the com in the approach to Sahern. Aunt *never* used com for clan to clan business if she could help it. Good, on the one hand, that the initial business with Sahern was on public record and overheard by two other clans. She did *not* regret that. But ... . mahendo'sat who did not speak hani certainly had translators. So did the kif, of whom there were fifteen in system.

She had a prickly feeling all down her back, the same feeling the whole atmosphere at Urtur gave her—since the dust-up in customs, and the Personage's too-easy dismissal of Ana-kehnandian, and every gods-be stsho on the station running for elsewhere when *she* had the Preciousness just itching to be delivered to somebody.

It had the feeling of powers at war, somewhere. And powers at war always went for the soft spots, the joinings between uneasy allies, the bribes, the coercions—the cooperations.

The feuds.

Chapter 8

Ker Chihin passed finger-pads over the panel surface, stooped and passed the same inspection over the floor, and evidently she found no fault with the job. Hallan put the vac away; and *ker* Chihin inspected that, too, then told him to take it to the laundry and stow it in the number 3 locker.

Then Chihin said, "Good job, kid."

He looked back from the doorway, and bowed, hands full and all. He didn't think he was called on to say anything, just to keep quiet and do what he was told; so he went and stowed the vac.

But *ker* Chihin hadn't said about whether to come back or not. He thought he should; and came quietly back and stopped in the doorway, because Chihin was fixing a case back in the traveling brace, on the pedestal, and it might be fragile.

He waited until she had tightened the bolts and slid the cover off the box, which proved to hold a simple vase. Then he cleared his throat.

"Gods *rot* you!" Chihin cried, with a start, and knocked back into a bucket of construction trash and another of panel clips.

"I'm sorry, *ker* Chihin."

"You didn't see this thing."

"Yes, *ker* Chihin." He honestly wished he hadn't. He thought maybe he was meant to get out, immediately, but Chihin started picking up loose bits and pieces of the scattered debris. He went to help, tentatively, and grabbed up loose panel clips as fast as he could find them, until he had a double handful.

"You be careful you don't miss any of those. If one of those goes whizzing around here under *V,* you don't want to know what it'd do to a body's head."

"I know, *ker* Chihin. I'm sorry."

"It was my foot," Chihin muttered, which was fairer than most ever were to him. He went back after more clips, and searched all around the edges of the cabin, and around the cushions and down in them, no matter how remote the chance.

No more of them. He came back and dumped what he had.

"Boy,—what got into you, wanting to come out here?"

"Captain said I could help . . ."

"I mean *here.* I mean going to space."

That question. It always came up. "I *wanted* to."

"I know that. But what's a nice kid want to come out here and run over tc'a and get arrested for?"

Ker Chihin didn't think he belonged here. He was used to that. And you couldn't argue with it. He shut up and kept his head down, already knowing the captain was going to throw him off the ship, so there was no use in arguing.

"Kid?"

"I wanted to go to space, that's all."

"Think you couldn't have found yourself a spot on Anuurn? Don't think there's some niche you could have carved out? You're a good-looking kid. You'd have gotten somebody's attention."

"I guess. Maybe. I don't know." He'd been through this too many times, with every ship he applied to, with the one that had taken him, with every member of the *Sun*'s crew, in one form or another. Sometimes he'd given answers to make them happy. He'd caught himself lying and sworn off it. But he didn't want to argue with Chihin either. The day had already gone wrong enough.

"So what d' you think?" Chihin asked. "Is space what you expected?"

"I don't know." Same stupid answer. He found a piece of debris and brought it back, thinking, and he said it: his back was to the wall and he couldn't lose any more than he had. "But I don't want to go back. And I'm getting better."

"At what? Parking?" Chihin said, straight to the sore spot. He kept his head down and picked up the container of debris. "You know where to take that?"

"To 'cycling. I guess it's out by the lifts."

"You guess right." Which let him go, so he went out

down the corridors and sorted the trash into the right chutes, plastics and metal bits apart, then wiped the bucket down and took it back to the only place he knew to take it.

"Goes in the maintenance locker," Chihin said. "That's—"

"Lower Main 2. Next the lift. I spotted it."

Chihin frowned at him and flattened her ears. He didn't know whether Chihin was annoyed at him or not. "Sharp eyes we have."

"Shall I put it up, *ker* Chihin?"

"Get," she said. He got, back to the area he had just been in. The lift was working. One of the crew coming down, he thought. He opened the locker, stowed the bucket, and was just latching the door when the lift door opened. He looked up, to say hello to whatever of the crew it was.

It wasn't.

He saw the stsho in the same moment it saw him. He stared in shock; it let out a warbling shriek and ducked back into the lift.

He ducked back down the corridor. Fast. And around to where its cabin was.

"Chihin!" he stammered. And when Chihin looked at him: "I think it saw me. The stsho. It was in the lift."

Chihin blasphemed in a major way and told him to go to his quarters. So he went there, and shut the door and sat down on the cushion.

He hadn't thought things could get worse, or imagined that he could find another way to foul things up.

Oh, *gods,* he hadn't thought so.

"Perfectly safe," Hilfy said in her best stshoshi Trade. "I do assure your honor, this is a person who came aboard with references from *gtst* excellency *gtst*self . . ."

". . . who lied!" Tlisi-tlas-tin said from the speaker.

Hilfy leaned against the panel, kept her voice calm. "Your honor, occupying the lift is against all safety regulations designed for your comfort and well-being . . ." She was down to quoting the primer lessons in the Trade. "Kindly bring the lift car back to lower decks and open the door."

Gods rot the creature for taking it on *gtet*self to wander about the ship.

"Your honor, do you hear me? This is a civilized and well-mannered young person who was assisting a member of the crew in maintenance."

"An immature male person? This ship has immature male persons performing life-critical maintenance? This ship has entrusted vital junctions to persons known for irrational behaviors and distasteful tendencies toward violence toward uninvolved bystanders?"

"This young male person was disposing of refuse. *Kindly* bring the car back to this deck."

"We have been betrayed by all pertinent interests. How do we know if anyone is telling the truth regarding anything? How should we have anticipated this desertion? How can we survive this devastation? We are the prey of strangers and persons without discrimination!"

"Your honor, as the captain of this ship I require you to come to the lower level, for your own protection, your honor, as if there should be an emergency on-station the lift is not a safe place to be."

There was no response. But stsho were not a valorous species where it came to bodily injury.

"Broken bones are possible," she said, "should this station encounter some emergency."

The lift thumped and whirred into motion.

"I think we got the son," Chihin said.

"Don't push our luck," she said.

The lift reached lowerdecks. The door opened. Hilfy pushed the hold button, and bowed to the pale, tremulous creature at the back wall of the lift.

Gtst bowed. She bowed.

Gtst edged outward. And peered past her, cautiously.

"Will your honor view the quarters? Your honor certainly will not want to leave the *oji* unattended."

A slippered toe edged across the line and into the corridor. Hilfy stood well back as *gtst* honor looked over the corridor.

And retreated.

"Your honor . . ."

And advanced again, with a fluttering of *gtst* long fingers about the vicinity of *gtst* heart. Moonstone eyes looked toward the corridor, under feathery brows, and *gtst* honor advanced a pace.

"We are not certain, we are far from certain we can bear this stress. We have been affronted, we have been transported far from tasteful and familiar places, our presence has been assaulted by strange persons of male and violent gender—"

"If your honor please. You will be most favorably impressed by the tastefulness of your quarters. And the Preciousness is absolutely inviolate. Have we not promised?"

Step after step. Chihin backed aside. Hilfy gestured the stsho further and further and around the corner into the appropriate corridor, which *gtst* was willing to enter only after an advance look.

As far as the doorway at least, *gtst* advanced. *Gtst* craned *gtst* long neck around the doorframe to look left and right, and took a step inside.

And another.

"Spare," *gtst* said. And advanced another pace, into a white, white, white cabin with white treelike shapes and the Preciousness enthroned in its case.

"Elegant," *gtst* said, and sighed and walked farther, from object to object, fluttering *gtst* hands and sighing and sighing again.

"A success," Chihin muttered at Hilfy's shoulder.

"A triumph," *gtst* breathed. "How can a colored species have achieved it?"

One hardly knew whether to be complimented or not.

"Is your honor then comfortable?" Hilfy asked.

Gtst turned full about, staring at all of it, no little of which was gotten at bid, from an abandoned stsho embassy and abandoned stsho apartments. And two mixed lots of white paneling, the only white paneling they had been able to find.

"Does this . . . male person share nearby quarters?"

"By no means," Hilfy said.

"Moderately acceptable," *gtst* said. "Our sensibilities are relieved."

The door shut.

"Put him in the lounge," Hilfy said.

"Captain?" Chihin said.

"I said put Meras in the crew lounge! The crew can socialize in the galley! We can't afford another incident!"

"Aye," Chihin said quietly. And went.

* * *

"No question now," Hilfy muttered, over gfi, at supper. "Hoas. Narn's not happy about taking him, but they will. Leaving him here's not a good idea. Let them think about it and somebody'll think up a lawsuit."

Faces weren't happy. "I'm against it," Tiar said, foremost. "We have a responsibility, captain, we didn't exactly ask for it, but this isn't an experienced spacer we're talking about. . . ."

"We're *all* against it," Hilfy said. "We'd all *like* to leave him in better circumstances. We'd all *like* for Sahern to behave like a civilized clan and take care of its responsibilities, but that's not going to happen. The only question is whether we throw him off our ship or we send him to Hoas where Narn will throw him off theirs. Maybe I can get a legal release out of the station office that'll make it safer for him coming back through here—I'll try that, in what time we've got, while we're onloading . . ."

"Dangerous," Chihin said. "Rattle a lawyer's door and you get more lawyers, that's what I say."

"I know that. But we've at least got some influence to bring to bear, at least I've got a foot in the door with the Personage of this system—not mentioning Aunt Py—and the questions we can settle are questions that have to be answered, by any other ship that brings him back through here from Hoas. And Hoas it has to be. We can't alter distances. There's no way he can get back except through here."

"He's still safer with us," Fala said, her young face earnest as might be.

"We're *not* taking him."

"I've backed a loader now and again," Tarras said. "The docker chief was yelling to move it—the boy moved it. There's not a one of us—"

"That's fine. So we're all occasionally guilty. We're leaving the boy with Narn!"

"What if Ana-kehnandian thinks he knows something?" Tiar said.

And Chihin: "There's—ah—a complication."

"What complication?"

"The boy's seen the vase."

"What do you mean, 'seen the vase'? Wasn't it put away?

Didn't I order it taken down until we'd absolutely finished knocking around in there?"

"We were. I thought he'd gone back to quarters. I sent him there. I thought he'd stay. He didn't."

"Chihin, —"

"I'm sorry, captain."

"He disobeyed orders?"

"I didn't exactly order him to stay there. I sent him there. He came back."

"Gods. What else? What possibly else can he get into?"

"I don't know," Chihin said. "But—being fair, it wasn't as if he was deliberately doing anything wrong."

"He's never doing anything wrong! I've never met anybody so gods-rotted innocent. Gods in feathers, *why* is Meras wherever you don't want him?"

"It's a small world down there."

"Small world. Small gods-rotted one corridor he was told to keep his nose out of!"

"The stsho took an unscheduled walk too."

"The stsho is a paying passenger. The stsho wasn't picked out of station detention! The stsho didn't create an international incident on the docks and have the section doors closed!"

"What I can't figure," Tiar said, "is why this Haisi Anakehnandian wants to know what the object is. What possible difference could it make?"

"Evidently a major one, to someone." She stirred the stew around in her bowl, stared at floating bits as if they held cosmic meaning, and thought back and back to this port, and days when one went armed to dockside. When accidents that happened weren't accidents and you didn't trust anything for face value. It felt like those days again and she felt trapped.

Fool, she said to herself. Fool, fool, fool. One grew accustomed to high politics, one grew used to breathing the atmosphere at the top of bureaucratic mountains, and one's vital nerves grew dull to signals of high-level interest and dangerous associations.

One just didn't by the gods think of it as unusual . . . when any freight-hauler else would have said Wait, go back, why me?

"If we leave him," Tarras said, "somebody's going to grab him for questioning. Or try to."

Of course they were. Give them sufficient cause for curiosity and local authorities might trump up some charge to get the boy off any ship that was carrying him: figure that too. She had rather not have that ship be *Legacy*. But honorably speaking, she could not wish it to be Narn, either.

And *customs* had come asking about the nature of the cargo. Maybe Ana-kehnandian's questions had put them up to it, and maybe the Personage of Urtur was innocent as spring rain. Or maybe she wasn't. Maybe that angry scene with Ana-kehnandian had been only because Ana-kehnandian had produced no results. Because it had gotten noisy, and public, and Ana-kehnandian had had his bluff called in a way the Personage of Urtur didn't like.

She found herself still stirring the stew, like an idiot. And asking herself what Meras could actually say that could do damage. "It's a white vase?" Stupid piece of information. And what did it mean? What in a reasonable and occasionally logical universe did Ana-kehnandian know or not know about the stsho that could make it valuable or life-threatening or politically important to his Personage, or what in a mahen hell was going on among the stsho? Meras could know something useful or he might not have seen any detail the mahendo'sat could remotely find useful. It might not be *that* it was a vase. It might be the carving on the vase. It might be that it wasn't a doorstop, a bag of dried fish, or an antique teapot, for all they could possibly know.

She looked up at four sober faces, four sober stares. Fala's ears went down, Tarras' did; then Tiar's did, one ear at a time. Chihin was the only exception, eye-to-eye with her.

"My fault," Chihin said. "I thought he'd stay. I *didn't* expect the stsho down the lift. —If we could transfer him to Narn secretly—"

"And say somebody gets onto it, they get him anyway, and they've got help. Say they *might* be within one jump of doing something with the information, straight back the way we came. But the ambassador went to Kita so we have to go to Kita. That's more than one jump from Meetpoint. I wish I knew what in all reason it matters it's a vase."

Chihin shrugged perplexedly.

Hilfy took a spoonful of stew, wondering if history would forget one Hallan Meras if she sent him on a spacewalk, say on their way to jump.

"I'll talk to him," she said, and ate another spoonful. "With any luck whatsoever, divinely owed us these last five years, there'll be a hani ship through here outbound from Hoas on its way to somewhere useful. I've got a hundred lots of cans, a general mail shipment, twenty cans of medical supplies, the luxury goods, the dupe-rights on the entertainment tapes; and that's about the best we can do on short notice. High value shippers are spooked. Can you blame them? Lucky we can get better than pig iron this run. Industrials and a load of foodstuffs and a ten can lot of spare parts for some construction company at Kita. Mostly cold-hold stuff. I know you've been going shift and shift; and we could carry more. But we need to get out of here. I want us out of this port before somebody files suit."

"I'll go with that," Chihin said. "The sooner the better."

"I'll get down to cargo," Tiar said. "I've had the easy stint last watch."

"We're going to push till we're loaded," she said. "Sleep when you're off, do anything we can to get turned around. I'll work hold. Meras can stay in the lounge, *in* the lounge, I don't care if it catches fire, he's not to leave it except on my personal order, do we agree on that?"

Nods. "Aye, captain," from Tiar.

She shoved the bowl back and got up. "I'll talk to him. And I don't care how persuasive he is, I don't care how pretty his eyes are, I don't care how polite he is, I don't want that son out of the crew lounge until we're sealed and we're sure our paying passenger is staying put! Do I hear Yes, captain?"

"Yes, captain," the answer came back.

So she left the galley for the lounge.

The captain came through the door with her ears down and her face scowling. Which might mean something else had happened that was his fault, although, before the gods, Hallan had no idea how or what. He stood up in proper respect and ducked his head.

"*If* the gods are good, a hani ship will come through here

at the last moment bound directly for hani space and take
you off our hands. If the gods are less well-disposed, you'll
be on to Kita with us. And if—" The captain's first claw
extruded. "If you do one more thing to screw up, if you
walk out of this lounge without my express permission, if
you startle our passenger again, if you *assume* any gods-be
need to go anywhere, if you bat your eyes at one of my
crew or land in anyone's quarters, you're going to find
yourself *chained* in the laundry for the duration of this voyage, which may last another year! Does this order get
through to you?"

"Yes, captain."

"Do you believe I'm joking?"

He looked the captain in the face, a very pretty face it
was, and a very serious and dangerous one. "No, captain."

"Do you *want* to spend a year down there?"

"No, captain. But if I could help in any way—"

"You don't help!" She jabbed the forefinger in his direction and he backed up. "You don't offer to help me, you
don't offer to help my crew, you don't offer to help our
passenger. You never saw anything, you will never remember that you saw anything in the stsho's cabin, and if you
ever do remember you saw anything you'll forget it forthwith. Do you follow that?"

"Yes, captain."

"With luck someone *will* come through here and I can
send you home."

He hoped not. He truly hoped not. He knew that the
captain was angry and that she had absolutely good reason.

"I want more than anything," he said, "to help. I don't
want to go back to Anuurn. I never want to go back to
Anuurn."

"We can do better," she said, "without your help. *Stay
out of it,* do you hear me?"

"Yes, captain."

With which she walked out. And shut the door. He sat
down again. It was not an uncomfortable place to be. And
he didn't get his hopes up. She'd said—there might be another ship. He truly hoped not. He hoped he would have
another chance.

He sat down and thought and thought how he might have
done differently about the accident; and the stsho; and how

he could, still, if he could just get one break, prove to the captain that he was qualified—if they would just let him work cargo. He *wouldn't* back up any more trucks. But they wouldn't believe that. He wouldn't be in any corridors he wasn't supposed to be in. But Chihin had told him go there. So he'd thought it was safe. . . .

Maybe Chihin had set him up. But he didn't want to think so. She'd been fair, about him startling her. She'd taken shots at him, but everybody did. He didn't want to think Chihin had done it to him. And she certainly hadn't been responsible for the truck. That was all his doing.

Tiar brought him supper soon after, which was stew. Tiar asked him if the captain had explained things to him and he said that she had.

Tiar said don't take the captain too seriously, and said that the captain yelled when she was upset, but that she was fair when she calmed down.

"I'm sorry about scaring the stsho," he said, and Tiar said it wasn't hard to scare the stsho, the harder problem was keeping it happy, which they had to do. And Tiar said he'd done all right, except not to take any chances, even if it seemed people were yelling at him—don't let them rattle him or make him move faster than he could think.

In other words, he thought, Calm down. It was what women said to misbehaving boys, stupid boys, who at about thirteen started having shaking mad temper fits, and their sisters said, "That's all right, just calm down, Hallan," and papa got irritable and refused to have him around any more, and youngest sister said, "*Try* to think, Hal, just use your head about things, everybody feels like that."

(Then oldest sister said, after he was sixteen, "He thinks too *much.* He can't survive out there." Or at home either: papa had told him get out, the girl his sisters had tried to fix him up with said he wasn't a match for her brothers, and his sisters had spent all their savings to get him a ticket to station, to a place they'd never seen, and hadn't any interest in going to; but it was everything he wanted, and they gave him that very expensive chance—for which he adored them. He couldn't come back and be sent down in disgrace they'd know about, to an exile he'd die in, because he'd trained himself to be *here,* that was all, and he'd rather die here than there.)

He didn't have much appetite for the stew Tiar left him. But he told himself that was male temper too, upsetting his stomach. He told himself stop it and think how he was going to feel in an hour or two; and how if they were going for jump this soon, he *had* to get the food down, as much as he could make his stomach take.

So he finished it down to the last, and set the dishes by the door.

There were vid tapes to watch. There were books to read. He wished they would let him bring his things from below.

But he didn't ask. He didn't use the com. He didn't make himself a problem to them. He found himself a blanket in the storage locker in the lounge and he tucked up and watched bad vids while the loader worked. Clank. Clank-clank.

It didn't stall. So they *had* listened to him. And Tarras at least knew he'd been right.

Chapter 9

The *Legacy* eased out of dock and away—put her bow to solar nadir in the dusty environs of Urtur system and took a leisurely start-up, a leisurely acceleration at *G*-normal for their stsho passenger. The *Legacy*'s hold was not full, the cargo was light-mass, the crew on watch was minimal to the safety requirements, and as soon as they hit their assigned lane for the outward run, the crew was snug in beds, sound asleep, except for the captain, who had the sole watch, who was propping her eyes open and seeing ghosts in the shadows of the bridge.

She never had done such a turnaround since she came to the *Legacy,* never hoped to do another. And when they had gotten out past the worst of the dust, and the rocks that attended the planetary vicinity, the captain set autopilot, tilted the cushion to flat relative to the accel plane and wrapped herself in a blanket for a rest.

Musing on tc'a and outraged stsho, wandering in a mental wilderness of white on white. . . .

Thinking of *The Pride* and the human aboard her, thinking of a friendly face and eyes of unhani color. Tully wouldn't have turned on her, Tully wouldn't have attacked poor cousin Dahan and broken his head. She hated her late husband; and *hated* cousin Harun. If she'd had her way, Harun Chanur wouldn't be lounging his oversized body in her father's chair, sitting by her father's fire, and slapping the younger cousins around; Rhean would be back in space aboard *Fortune* where she wanted to be; she, for her part, would be on *The Pride,* with Tully, clear of all of it: the gods only knew who'd be managing the clan's business, then. Which showed how impractical it all was.

But she wouldn't be thinking of the Meras kid, then, and thinking how his expression had reminded her all too much of Dahan's, kind and confused, and upset and hurt when she'd yelled at him. She had never thought she agreed on principle with Chihin, she'd stood more with Pyanfar on the question of culture versus instincts; but she found herself with Chihin this time: Meras didn't belong in space, Meras didn't think, didn't think *first,* at least. Like backing the truck, because some mahen foreman yelled do it. That the foreman hadn't meant him just hadn't tripped a neuron in his brain.

Imagine cousin Harun in a position of responsibility. Imagine Harun having to use his head rather than his hands.

Men that did think had gotten killed, for thousands of years, that was the way biology had set up the hani species. Other species were luckier, maybe, and other species might be better at handling politics between the sexes, but hani hadn't been civilized long enough to sort out mate-getting by any other means. Nobody had told her when she was growing up that every attitude and opinion she had learned was going to be obsolete when she was twenty-five. Nobody had told her the whole world was going to be set on its ear and the way hani did business with outsiders was going to change. Evidently nobody had told the rest of the home planet, either, because they were still doing things the old way. Same with the kid in the crew lounge . . . nobody had told him things were going to change, until Aunt Pyanfar had lured him off in the promise of a miraculous change in the universe.

(Wrong, kid. It doesn't work that way. Narn won't have you. Padur won't have you, we don't want the complications you pose and the crew that took you aboard in the first place wasn't looking at your resume, were they, kid? Hani are hani. People with power aren't going to give it up. Fair isn't fair, not among hani, not elsewhere. And no sister ever taught you to think before you jump.)

Nice-looking boy. That's all anybody had thought. That's all anybody would ever think. She had no personal illusions about changing the way hani were, or worked, or thought: that was Aunt Pyanfar's pet project, not hers, she had never asked to carry any banner for reforming anything, or anyone, except that hani shouldn't be so gods-be xenophobic and so set on their own ways.

And don't say Pyanfar Chanur got beyond biology when it came to personal choices either. Pyanfar had dumped Chanur in her lap and run off to do as she pleased, free as she pleased, with *na* Khym— It's your turn, niece. You go be responsible.

Nothing in her life she had planned had ever worked and no living person she had ever trusted or wanted had ever come her way. Tell that to the jealous rivals who thought Hilfy Chanur got everything she ever wanted at no cost and no effort.

She was on a self-pity binge. She recognized it when she hit the chorus. She tried to get her mind out of the track and stared at lights reflected in the overhead, listened to the small constant sounds of the ship under way, and thought how so long as they were out of ports and so long as she had the *Legacy,* she was safe—how she didn't have to go back to Anuurn ever again if she didn't want to, how space was all she wanted, all she ever had wanted, and to a mahen hell with planets and the attitudes that grew up on them.

So occasionally she ran into other hani ships and had to meet the world-bound mindset out here, in people like Narn, who ought to know better, who ought to be free enough to spit at the *han* and the old women back home— but she didn't, and wouldn't: you couldn't expect it of most of the clans, and you didn't see it taking rapid hold of the spacerfarers. Quite to the contrary, there was a conservative backlash. That was the disappointment.

Which told her how badly she personally wanted to crack heads and knock courage into Narn and Padur, and how badly she wanted the universe to be different, and play by civilized rules, and not by the gods *care* whether a young fool wanted to fight biology and go to space, but things didn't work that way either.

So Meras hadn't asked for what had happened. Neither his upbringing nor his apprenticeship had taught him what he needed to know, and maybe she hadn't been fair with him, either: she hadn't exactly given him any parameters, just a general instruction to go out there and do what he claimed he knew how to do, as if those papers of his really meant more than a license to sit and watch the boards while a licensed spacer took a break.

There were ships that treated apprentices like that. There were ships that treated female apprentices like that—a lot of them, more the pity. *The Pride* had turned her out knowing what she was doing—and most ships never met what *The Pride* had on her tour: there wasn't much she hadn't met or done or seen in the years of running communications on Pyanfar Chanur's intrigue-bound dealings.

The kid hadn't had any such break. The kid was in the lounge watching vids, the only one of them who wasn't falling down tired; they were stuck with him for a little while; and the more she thought about it, the more she felt uneasy with herself for the family temper and an extravagant expectation of an apprentice she'd *sent* onto that dockside, thanks to the lack of a coat—rather than down in the hold, also true, where he could lose an arm or a neck in the machinery. But the dust-up with the Urtur authorities hadn't been entirely the lad's fault . . . he hadn't known his limitations, he'd probably imitated a bad habit he'd seen somebody else do—Tarras was right in that.

And he'd go off the *Legacy* no smarter and no better than he was if nobody knocked the need-to-knows into his head. He'd been the *Sun*'s responsibility; somehow he'd gotten to be theirs, and by the gods, she had a certain vanity where it came to the *Legacy*'s operating and the *Legacy*'s way of doing business.

Her papa hadn't been stupid. Uncle Khym wasn't stupid. *Young* men were stupid, while their hormones were raging and their bodies were going through a hellacious growth spurt that had them knocking into doorways and demolishing the china. Then was when young men left home, and went out and lived in the outback, and fought and bashed each other and collected the requisite scars and experience to come back formidable enough to win a place for themselves. Seven or so years and a gangling boy all elbows came back all shoulders and with muscle between his ears.

But Hallan Meras didn't seem to have as much of that as, say, Harun Chanur. Light dose Meras had been given. Illusions he was a girl. Trying to act like one and use his head, at his age.

She angled the couch upright, straightened her mane and flicked her earrings into order with a snap of her ears. She punched in the lounge com and called Meras forward; so he came, diffidently, as far as the middle of the bridge, darting glances here and there about the crewless stations.

"Used to the environment, are you?"

"I've—seen the bridge, yes, captain."

"Seen the bridge. You're a licensed spacer and you've seen the bridge? That's remarkable."

"I mean I've seen the bridge on the *Sun*."

"Not worked it?"

"I got my papers in cargo management, down in—"

"You're a specialist, then. A real specialist. —What's that station?"

"That's scan, captain."

"Congratulations. Ever read the screen?"

"Not actually."

Figured. "Who in a mahen hell gave you your papers?"

Ears flagged. "The authorities at Touin."

"Did they speak the Trade? Did you take a test? Did they interview you?"

"I think they took *ker* Druan's word."

"Druan Sahern."

"Hanurn, actually. *Ker* Druan Hanurn nef Sahern. She helped me. She showed me things."

Aunt Pyanfar had had no patience. Under her captaincy, an apprentice sat every board on the bridge, somewhere before Aunt Py signed any application for a license. Emergencies don't wait for the experts, Aunt Pyanfar had used to say. Gods-be right you learned every board, every button, and every readout. You could be the only one that could reach the seat. The whole ship could depend on you in a station you didn't ordinarily work.

"I haven't changed my mind. I'm still kicking you off this ship first chance I get. But I don't think we're apt to find a thing at Kita, it's not a place I'd leave anybody, and, by the gods, nobody's going off my ship and having the next crew say we didn't teach him anything. You understand me?"

Ears were up, eyes shining. "Thank you, captain."

"Thank me, hell. Keep me awake. We've got six hours to jump, my eyes are crossing, I'm sore down to my fingertips, I'm out of patience with fools, and I want you to sit down over there at the scan station and read me off what you see happening on that board and on that screen."

"*Yes,* captain!" He went and dropped into the seat, and started rattling it off, the numbers and the names and the lane designations.

Not by the gods bad, actually. Most critical first and right along their laid course—which was plotted there, for somebody who could read the symbols.

"Who taught you the codes?"

"I had this book."

"You had this book. What book?"

"The general licensing manual. *Ker* Dru let me study it."

"She let you study it. Nice of her. So you read up on more than cargo operations."

"Everything. I read all of it."

"You remember everything you read?"

"I read it a lot."

Her pulse ticked up. It sounded familiar, sounded by the gods familiar; in the same way, she'd had the manual downworld, Aunt Py had slipped her the copy, and she'd studied and studied and kept it out of her father's sight, because *he* had gotten upset about her studying. *He* had wanted her to stay downworld and be papa's favorite daughter; but *she'd* memorized every bit, every chart—memorized boards she'd never seen and operations she'd never watched.

Because she'd wanted it so much it was physical. And some gods-be hormone-hazed boy thought he could want something that much?

"What's in quadrant 3?"

"That's a buoy."

"What buoy?"

"That's the insystemer code."

"Quadrant 4?"

"That's an ore freighter."

"How do you know?"

"Its prefix is a mining designation. A lot of letters."

Brilliant. A lot of letters. But the kid was, essentially, right. That was how the peripheral vision made the sort-out. That was what the system of IDs was set up to do.

"Captain, something's just away from station. I think it's mahendo'sat."

Her thoughts left young fools and proceeded immediately down darker tracks.

"Can I ask comp?" he asked. "Is this the toggle?"

"Below the screen, left bank? Punch it."

"Ha'domaren."

"Of course it is. On our heading?"

"I think so, captain. It looks like it."

"Approximately. Anywhere headed out, Kita vector."

"I think it is. Yes. I'm pretty sure."

So here sat the two of them, watching a mahe up to no gods-be good. Alone, on a mostly darkened bridge. Witness to collusion, intrigue, things that smelled like Personages at war.

But Hallan had no least idea. Hallan Meras gave her a puzzled, worried look and didn't exactly ask what was up, but he must have caught something from her expression. His face grew troubled.

"This isn't a mahe I trust," she said. "This one's been on our tail since Meetpoint."

"Why?" he asked faintly. "Do you know?"

"Meras, do you know what we have aboard?"

"No, captain. A stsho person."

She had to smile. She, gods help her, had to smile. And so few living souls could make her laugh. She gazed at his sober, foolish face, and thought, How in the gods' sweet name could he hope to make it out here? Could a naive boy learn the control boards from a book, and not learn where the power was that runs the Compact, or what betrayal was?

No. He already knew what betrayal was. Betrayal was a ship that left him stranded in a foreign jail. Betrayal was a ship that had signed him on without his best interests at heart, and used him for the menial work, the work somebody had lied about to get him licensed.

And he must not have made the captain happy. The captain had had to make the decision that had stranded him.

"You shouldn't look away from the boards when you're on duty," she said. "You don't do that on this ship."

"Yes, captain. I'm sorry." He turned around immediately, and watched what she had told him to watch.

And she watched him, thinking . . . she was not even certain what. Not thinking about him. Thinking about one Ana-kehnandian, and what he possibly had to gain. And about the stsho belowdecks who had said something about betrayals.

A white vase. A vase carved over all its surface with non-representational bas-relief, that made sense to stsho, one was certain. Maybe even ancient writing. There was a lot the stsho kept secret. And one was certain not to get any sense out of Tlisi-tlas-tin.

Meras kept at the scan image for the next hour or so—kept at the post so reasonably competently that she began to believe if anything did turn up he might beat the autoed alarm giving the warning, and do it with at least some sense that certain ships were reason for worry even if they weren't on a collision course. She let her eyes drift shut, dangerous business, against all regulations, considering what she knew about Hallan Meras and his license. But they were autoed. And she did sleep—dropped right into a deep and resting oblivion, so that it was Tiar's shadow that waked her, passing between her and the light.

"You all right?" Tiar asked.

"Fine," she said, blinking at the screens, the five that automated ops delivered to her working station.

"He all right?" Tiar asked.

"Ship hasn't blown up." The rest of the crew was arriving on the bridge, for the last stint before jump. Hallan Meras was ceding his place to Chihin, with apologies that weren't at all in order. Hilfy punched buttons to pass the active boards to Tiar; and, thinking about dismissing Hallan Meras back to the crew lounge, decided otherwise. "Meras can take the observer seat," she said, before she quite thought that that seat change put him with Chihin, at scan.

So, it put him with Chihin. Not the happiest pairing, but not one *na* Hallan could blink his pretty eyes at and overwhelm with stupidity, either.

"Meras, you stay out of Chihin's way."

"Aye," he said, "thank you, captain."

Chihin shot her a reproachful look; and probably took it for revenge for the stsho incident. But *na* Hallan settled in, and Chihin settled at nav and scan; Tarras on his other side, at general ops and cargo; and armaments, if the *Legacy* had ever needed them. Fala Anify slid in at com; and the captain—the captain sat backup to several posts, a selection of inputs to her screens.

"We've got company out there," Chihin said. "That son's still with us."

"Noticed that," Hilfy said. "I don't credit him with any good wishes."

"Not him or whoever sent him," Chihin said.

Switches went to On, lights and more screens flared up, and changed displays at Tarras' switching. The computer locked onto the guidance point. Fala advised their stsho passenger to take precautions and got an acknowledgment. Hilfy took the leisure of being momentarily out of the critical loops to pull up Kita charts and the latest trade figures, figuring that if the gods were good they could do a jump for Kirdu and mahen space, once they'd delivered the *oji*. They had the requisite clearances. No question on that. And Kirdu wasn't a bad destination out there. Most ships were going the other direction, and you could pick up a major load of mail, bank shipments, and the occasional high-paying passenger, not to mention the items out of stsho space that were fairly scarce at Kirdu port.

Only granted the faint, fair hope their addressee was at Kita and not elsewhere by now . . . or about to be elsewhere. Atli-lyen-tlas seemed to have had a fair head start.

"Set for jump," Tiar said. "Boy, are you all right over there?"

"I'm fine," the answer came back, but he was doing something that wasn't regulation, she could see the activity in the tail of her eye as the numbers spieled down toward a convergence of V and distance from mass.

"Kid," Chihin cautioned him.

"I'm trying to get ops echoed," he said. "I want to see—"

"Just enjoy the ride," Chihin said.

"Can we get attention to what we're doing?" Hilfy asked. It wasn't a time for a side issue. "Tiar."

"I've got it, I've got it. —Kid, punch in your 3. Leave that gods-be board alone, it's live!"

"There it is!"

"Gods-rotted distraction," Chihin muttered. "This is a working station. The kid had better learn not to punch buttons."

"I'm sorry, *ker* Chihin."

"Learn it!"

"Yes, *ker* Chihin."

"Belong at home, is where."

"Ease off," Tarras muttered.

"I want to know if he understands about that board!"

"I'm not pushing any buttons, *ker* Chihin. I won't. I swear."

"By the gods better not. That board's got a link to fire controls. Why don't we shoot at the station for entertainment?"

From Tiar: "Just shut up, Chihin, godssakes, he said he was sorry."

"Everybody quiet!" Hilfy said. "We're almost on mark, I'm supposed to be off duty, can we have the crew paying attention for the next small while?"

"Sorry, captain."

"I'm sorry," Meras said, and Chihin:

"No gods-be place on the . . ."

"Shut it *up,* Chihin!"

("She's always like this," Fala whispered.)

"Gods-be zoo," Hilfy said, running her eye down the figures, watching the lines converge. "Shipped with two men and a kif that fought less." She hadn't been able to think about that in years. Certainly not to joke about it. There was something oddly comfortable about the kid sitting there, hulking over the controls that, one had to admit, he came aboard understanding better than *na* Khym had. Certainly better than Tully.

Numbers reached +14 and +14. Lines met, at 0 and 0.

Dead on. . . .

. . . Not bad, Tully said to her. Not bad. You could do worse than that young fellow.

Tully walked away then, down what might have been a dockside. She thought it was.

Wait, she said, Tully. Come back here. You can't leave like that . . .

. . . Stick to your own kind, Aunt Pyanfar said. And she: You're to talk. You work with the kif. You trade with them. In what? Small edible animals?

. . . They were home. Kohan was sitting on the veranda where he liked to sit, in the sunshine. His mane was gold, his eyes were gold. His hide shone like copper. The vines were blooming on the wall. It was the most perfect day of the most perfect year of her life. Papa talked about going hunting. . . .

But there was a shy, quiet kid sitting on the steps, whittling something. Dahan would sit in Kohan's presence and Kohan never cared, Kohan was not the sort that would drive a boy off, Kohan used to sit lazily in the sun and talk to Dahan about hunting, about boy-things. Sometimes Dahan would talk about his books and his notes and the stories he'd heard, and Kohan would talk about science and what he theorized, and about his herds and his breeding, that was a passion with Kohan, talk with him as seriously about house business as if Dahan were one of the daughters, and not a someday rival; while Dahan studied genetics not because he had any original interest in it, but because Kohan did. Dahan was the sort who should have benefited from Aunt Py's politics. . . . Pyanfar should have asked him up to station, taken *him* aboard *The Pride,* if only for a tour or two . . .

. . . but Dahan was dead. She'd seen his skull break. She'd seen the blood on the wall.

Things went darker. She didn't like this dream. She knew it too well. It tended to replay. But it was back to the porch again, and the sunlight. "What should we do?" Hallan asked. And her father said, "He's not a fighter, the gods look on him, he's not a fighter, he never will be, I've no reluctance to have him about. But I've got to talk to Pyanfar the next time she's here."

Before then, Kohan had been dead. Before then, Pyanfar's gods-cursed son moved in. Her Mahn half-brother. *Churrau hanim,* the old women called it. *Betterment of the race.* And she hadn't shot cousin Kara in the back. She'd played the game the age-old way. She'd married a challenger, Rhean had found another when *he* proved a disaster. On a civilized world, women didn't shoot fools, no, they let the Haruns and their ilk knock the likes of Dahan into a wall, spatter the brains that had theirs beaten tenfold. Women made up the deficit. Women had the genes that mattered, they passed down the intelligence and the quickness of wits, they passed down the cleverness they had gotten over generations. A girl got footloose, called her brother and set out for a place she thought suited her: her brother or her husband knocked heads to get it for her, and that was brains? That was the way civilization worked?

Tully, she said, refusing those images, Tully, come back here.

She could control the dreams. She could see him walking away from her thé way he had—walking away into this gray distance of gantries and lines, the same as Meetpoint docks where they'd met him. . . .

"Tully," she called after him, spooked by that; and to her relief he heard her and turned and waited to talk with her, alone for once.

"What are you doing?" he asked.

"Following you," she said.

"You shouldn't," Tully said. "You really shouldn't."

That made her mad. It wasn't the truth anyway. Tully never spoke the Trade that well. His mouth couldn't form the sounds. "You don't object to Chur. Or Geran or . . ."

"It's different. It's just different with them."

"It's not different! Don't listen to my aunt! She's trying to run my life. She doesn't know what's good for me. . . ."

"Have you asked what's good for me?" he said, and turned and walked away, leaving her with one of Aunt Pyanfar's favorite pieces of wisdom. From him, she didn't for a moment believe it, and she wouldn't *let* the dream be this way. She insisted not. She went walking along the dockside, in that jungle of then and now, and places that were real and weren't. . . .

The kid was there, of course the Meras kid was there, when your mind attacked you with images it didn't go by halves. Tully was acting like a fool and agreeing with Aunt Py, and of course here was the kid—

Couldn't be, couldn't be that Aunt Py had set it up. No. Py hadn't even known she was on her track. And the kid stood there staring at her, in his bewildered way, and blinked, saying . . .

. . . But she couldn't hear what he said. The alarm was going off. Illusions walked off arm in arm. Cousin Chur could see reality in jump. Or something beyond it. She'd tried to. Her mind just went off into hyperspace and lived in the past; and argued with itself; and with Aunt Py and with Things As They Were. And it did no one any creative good. . . .

... "Welcome to Kita Point. Armpit of this end of space. Kifish cultural center. Mahen religious objects, three the credit. . . . Stsho ambassadors, bargain prices. . . ."

. . . Chihin's sense of humor. Gods save them.

She reached after the nutrients pack, found it strayed and stretched after it, with muscles that protested. Couldn't go on at this pace. The mind was playing tricks. The body was arguing back. She left a smudge of fur on the chair arm.

And the stomach definitely wanted to heave, when the soup hit it unprepared.

"Is *gtst* honor still alive?" Tarras asked.

"Think so," Fala said. "I hear moaning."

"Not to their liking, stringing the jumps like this."

"Hope the ambassador thinks so. Hope *gtst* heaved up *gtst* insides, maybe *gtst* won't have shipped out of here."

"Bets on it," Chihin said. "The Preciousness for our chances."

"Gods," Fala said. "The com could've been open!"

"It wasn't."

"Cut it, cut it," Tiar said, "small mass-point here, we're ready for a double-dump, check your numbers. This isn't a nice one."

Gods-be right, Hilfy thought. She hated this . . .

. . . Bottom fell out of the universe and knit itself back.

"Gods." Male voice. What was that doing here?

Then she remembered.

"Here we go again," Tiar said, and the *Legacy* pulsed its field and broke the bubble a third time. Energy bled off into the interface. Hilfy gazed at a haze of instruments that informed her the ship was on course, proceeding in toward the brown mass that was Kita Point, at a sedate, manageable velocity.

It wasn't much of a place. The brown dwarf lent energy enough for the collectors that spread like vast wings . . . grandiose scheme. But it worked. The station had grown, within the span of her years in space, from nothing more than a repair and emergency services depot to a utilitarian nondescript can of a supply and manufacturing center.

It blipped at them, they automatically bleeped their identity. "Is that *it?*" she heard Hallan Meras murmur, doubtless confused by the small scale of things. "That's Kita?"

"Guaranteed," Fala said, "or Chihin's aimed us at Kefk."

"I'm never wrong," Chihin said. "When was I ever wrong? Tell me when I was wrong."

"Twice last year," Hilfy muttered, and punched in intraship com: "Your honor, how are you riding down there? Are you all right?"

A stsho muttering came back to her. *"Oh, the unwieldiness, oh, the heaviness . . ."* or some such. It was some planetary language.

"Your honor? We're at Kita. Is everything well with you?"

"With me? With us? With what creature? Oh, the misery. Oh, the discomfort and untidiness. We shall not be fit for viewing."

Gtst sounded normal enough. For a stsho. *Gtst* was alive. The Preciousness was on its perch and unbroken. And she hoped to all the gods respectable and otherwise that *gtst* excellency Atli-lyen-tlas of Urtur was here.

Ha'domaren was here, already at dock. *That* showed on the station schema the buoy had handed them on arrival. *Ha'domaren* had started well behind them again, gods blast them, and gotten in first, figuring Ana-kehnandian had no mundane problems, like cargo or other such inconveniences.

The first over-jump, at Urtur, might have been one mother of a powerful merchant ship.

Might have been just a courier, beating them in.

Not twice, it wasn't a simple courier.

"The devil," she said. "Berth 10. You notice?"

Chapter 10

There were communications you could make in transit and business you could do in transit, even blind tired and frazzled; even collapsing facedown on the galley table between calls and drinking gfi to stay copacetic enough to do routine business.

Chanur's Legacy *inbound to Kita Point Station, to Kita Point Customs Authority . . . we have items under seal at Urtur customs, therefore internal to mahen space, we don't anticipate a need for prolonged procedure as we are not crossing international borders. Our trading license is in order and we are prepared to present papers. Note also this crew will be resting after dock, due to repairs necessary at Urtur.*

Chanur's Legacy, *inbound to Kita Station, from captain Hilfy Chanur, her hand, to Ko'juit, at dock at berth 14: we have an urgent personal message for one Atli-lyen-tlas, passenger on your ship according to records at Urtur. Please place us in vocal contact. Translation is available on board.*

Chanur's Legacy, *inbound to Kita, from captain Hilfy Chanur, her hand, to Ha'domaren, attention Ana-kehnandian, chief scoundrel. We don't take kindly to being passed in jump. We have your position on record before and after. Be advised."*

. . . "Captain. Captain?"

Facedown on the galley table, fingers in the handle of the cup, and no memory of falling asleep.

"Sorry to wake you," Tarras said, "but we're heading in."

She grunted, disentangled her fingers from the cup and ran her claws through her mane, eyes shut.

"Couple of meaningful messages came in," Tarras said. "Nothing cheerful. The stsho we're looking for . . . disappeared."

"What, disappeared?"

Tarras laid a paper on the table. She blinked her eyes into focus.

Ko'juit, *at dock at Kita Station, Me-sheirtajikun captain, to captain Hilfy Chanur,* Chanur's Legacy, *inbound. Regret inform you not know passenger whereabouts.*

Ha'domaren, *at dock at Kita Station, Tahaisimandi Ana-kehnandian his hand, to captain Hilfy Chanur, why you so slow? You want know whereabout Atli-lyen-tlas, we find, you no worry.*

"I'll kill him."

"Nobody's told our passenger," Tarras said. "Figured you'd want to do that. It's not official, though. We can ask station authorities, see if there are any stsho on station at all. . . ."

"Do that," she murmured, resisted the urge to fall flat on her nose, and got up and wandered back to her quarters.

Should have taken the off-watch in her bed. Meras was asleep and harmless. Kita was going to be a disaster. They'd run as far as they could without rest. The crew had gotten half a watch of sleep before jump, but right now the draw-string waist of her trousers was loose, she'd dropped weight in jump, a pass of her hand across her chest turned up a palmful of loose fur, and if she were sane or fully conscious she would have a bath before she hit the mattress.

Wasn't near habitual that she slept through dock. But she was no use as she was. She fell into bed, dragged the safety net back over and locked it, and was unconscious for the next while.

Kita Point Customs Authority to captain Hilfy Chanur, in dock at Kita Point. We recognize Urtur customs seal, same good trade in mahen space. We clear all fine, only need stamp manifest which same you give at dock. All coopera-tion this office much appreciate.

Ha'domaren, *at dock at Kita Station, Tahaisimandi Ana-kehnandian his hand, to* Chanur's Legacy *captain Hilfy Chanur: You want talk? I got information you want. Make you good deal.*

A nap, a shower, and clean clothes didn't make the mes-sage more cheerful. "I'm going to talk to the mahe," she said to the assembled crew, Meras excepted. "I'm going to find out what he knows. I'm not going to shoot him no matter what the provocation. We can off-load as soon as we get the customs stamp. Tiar, you see to that."

"The stsho's calling up to the bridge," Fala said. "We keep telling *gtst* you're asleep and nobody can decide. And *ker* Pyanfar's mail . . . is piling up again. Do you want to see it?"

"I'm not available. Tell *gtst* honor we're already aware of *gtst* request and we're out seeing to it, it's our top priority. *Don't* let *gtst* out of *gtst* quarters. Jam the lock if you have to. Drown *gtst* in tea. Tarras, Chihin, I want the cargo out of here. I want the customs stamps clear. I want a list of what's available for transship to any port whatsoever, don't make any deals, we don't know *where* we're going. . . ."

Troubled faces stared back at her. Not a one said to her: This contract is a disaster. Not a one said to her: We may end up in debt because of this. Not a one said: You're a damned fool, captain.

"Take care of it," she said, on her way to leaving.

"What about the kid?" Chihin asked.

Extraneous subject. It was *not* what she wanted to think about. She cast a glance about familiar surroundings and familiar jobs and the thousand and one things that regularly wanted doing. And thought about a young man who had worked through pre-jump, stayed through jump, and was now, given a rest break, shut away again solo in the crew lounge. He wasn't a can of soup that you could stack on a shelf and forget about. He was an earnest stupid kid trying too hard—that was what she had read in their time together; and that enthusiasm was the biggest danger he posed. "He can have the run of the galley, he can do anything on this level he thinks he can do, but check it behind him and don't let him do anything stupid. He *doesn't* go off this level, he doesn't go near the lift, if the stsho gets loose . . . don't insult anybody, but get Meras under cover if you have to hide him in a locker. All right?"

"No problem," Tiar said.

"Gods-rotted mess," Chihin said. "There's got to be a hani ship headed off to Kirdu or somewhere."

"Not likely. And I'm not sure he's safe at Kirdu." That came from the gut. From the knowledge of *Ha'domaren* out there wanting a conference.

From things that weren't by the gods right. And she couldn't believe she was taking that position, but in coldest terms, she thought as she headed for the lift, neither Narn nor Padur could have told the Personage of Urtur they weren't giving up a crewman, *most* hani ships didn't have the Personage of Personages for a relative. . . .

Gods forbid they had to turn a hani kid over to mahen authorities, whose system of justice was nothing a hani boy was brought up to understand. He made mistakes? He was pampered by his sisters. He assumed and didn't ask? He hadn't been brought up to responsibility. He didn't think? He hadn't been encouraged to think. Thinking was what his sisters did. Consequences were what his sisters took.

Jumpspace did things to your mind. And the business with Tully walking off from her, that was a nightmare that didn't quite go away. You could get superstitious, you could start to think it was something external to yourself or that you were communicating with somebody across stellar distances, when an educated being knew that there was no such thing, that it was one's own subconscious and one's own inner thoughts.

So what was it with the kid, that she came out the other side of jumpspace with a gut-deep feeling they couldn't desert him?

She punched the call button. The lift door opened and she got in, faced the perspective of the galley-dodging corridor that led to the bridge as the door shut and the lift started down.

They couldn't desert him, because, by the gods, they weren't the scoundrels *Sun Ascendant* crew were, they weren't the sort to take advantage of the kid, they weren't the sort to have run and left him like abandoned garbage, and she wasn't the sort that could have left him locked away in a featureless room. . . .

Lift door opened. She got a breath, set out down the main lower corridor for the airlock.

Another gods-be small space. Which she didn't like to think about closing around her when she was in this kind of funk. She punched cycle and watched the lights run their

course, met the different-smelling air of another port and
walked the ribbed, lighted tube to the ramp and the dockside.

Where customs was waiting . . . "Welcome Kita Point,
hani captain! Sign all form. . . ."

And past that obstacle, just beyond the rampway access,
by the control console for the gantries and the lines that
were feeding the *Legacy* water and taking off her waste . . .

"H'lo, pretty hani." Haisi waved at her approach like an
old friend. "How you do?"

"Hello, you rag-eared scoundrel. What do you know,
how do you know it, and why shouldn't I file charges for
endangerment?"

The kid *wanted* to do whatever routine maintenance
wanted doing, and faced with such self-sacrifice, a body
thought of all the things nobody wanted to do . . . like the
cursed filter changes, that weren't exactly due, but almost,
and if they had somebody that wanted to lie on his back
and crawl halfway into the ventilation system, that was fine,
let him.

Meanwhile there were the customs people, and, left in
charge, with the stsho making calls from belowdecks and
the customs papers looking like a mere formality, a sensible
person in want of rest might draw an easier breath. Which
Tiar drew. And headed downside to talk with customs in
the captain's wake.

"Everything in order," the customs chief said. "All clear
with Urtur, all clear here. You captain sign, all fine." There
were benefits to dealing with the small stations, the newly
built. Luxuries were scarce. Necessities were short. If you
weren't armed and dangerous you could get through customs with most anything; and you didn't expect dispute.

But you did have to take the aforesaid customs report
and trek to the station office in person to file for various
services, and schedule for off-loading.

Which in the case of Kita Point and their berth was a
distance off, far enough to be inconvenient on a station too
small and too rough to afford a full time shuttle service.

So one walked. And walked, stood in line at the office
because Kita Point had no separate line for ships' lading
credentials or spacers wanting to certify a live pet for trans-

port, which made a very strangely assorted, unruly, and uncomfortable line to be in—a line that snarled and snapped in two instances, and struggled in wild panic in another.

"The hani trader *Chanur's Legacy,*" she was finally able to say, with the waft of kifish presence in her nostrils—two of them were in line behind her, but the mahendo'sat with the wildlife had gone through. She slid the physical papers across, left the mahen agent in peace to survey the requisite stamps, and made out the request for cargo receipt.

"Station load," she said, meaning it was for the station's own use. And that usually got priority. She stood waiting.

And felt something in the back waist of her trousers.

She reached back, suspecting wildlife or an off-target pickpocket.

And found a piece of paper.

She looked around, found nothing but a blank-faced shrug from the mahe immediately behind her in line, and saw a whisk of a white scuttling figure in a gray cloak vanishing around the corner.

Stsho. But no way was she going to leave her place in line to give chase.

"Sign," the agent was saying, and she took the stylus and the tablet and signed, in the several places marked.

"You when want off-load?"

"Ready now. Soon as possible." She tried to sneak a look at the paper, but the agent was saying,

"You got volatiles? You need sign form."

"Right. No problem." She got a look. It said, in bad block print, *Help. 2980-89.*

A phone number? An address?

"You sign here," the agent said.

She looked distractedly at the form. She read the variables and signed, collected the requisite form and took the paper with the message with her, on her way to a public phone.

Better *not* involve the captain.

Haisi Ana-kehnandian took a puff on the abominable smokestick, blew the contaminated air into the neon-lit ambient, and smiled lazily. "I tell you, pretty hani, you got one bastard lot luck. Just so, Atli-lyen-tlas come here like we know. Then . . . not good news. Atli-lyen-tlas gone kif ship."

"Kif!"

"And four stsho dead like day old fish. Big damn mess."

She didn't want to owe Haisi a thing. She didn't want to have to ask. But the mahe sat there smiling smugly and knowing she had no choice.

"So? Why?"

"Kif big suspect. Or maybe scare to death."

"Residents here or come in with the ambassador. Don't string it out, out with it."

"You so impatient. Got pretty eyes."

"Who were the stsho?"

"Three resident. One secretary Atli-lyen-tlas." Another cloud of smoke in the pollution zone. "I got photo, you want see?"

He reached into his pouch and pulled them out. She leaned over gingerly and took the offering, fanned them in her fingers. Not a pretty sight, no, especially the close-ups. "What did they die of?"

"Poison, maybe. Maybe scare to death. Stsho delicate."

"Where'd you get these?"

"Got cousin in station office."

"You got cousins everywhere."

"Big—"

"Big family. You said."

"Same like Chanur. Big fam'ly. Influ-ential fam'ly."

"I'm a merchant captain trying to make a living! I've got no influence with my aunt, I don't know her business, she doesn't know mine, we don't speak!"

"Hear same. Sad, fam'ly quarrel."

"None of your business."

The waiter set the drinks down. Iced fruit for Ana-kehnandian and iced tea for her. Intoxicating tea. She sipped hers carefully.

"What's the truth?" she asked. "Who's your Personage aligned with? Who does she do business with? What's her connection to my aunt or does she have one?"

"A. You want I say my Personage business."

"Might increase my trust of you."

Another puff on the smokestick. "You long time on *The Pride,* now you not speak? What story?"

"Not your business either."

"You clan head."

"I am. In name. *Ker* Pyanfar appointed me."

"You not forgive her for that, a?"

"Maybe not. What's it to do with anything?"

"Just lot people know you pret' damn good."

"Good for them. I'm so pleased."

A laugh and a puff of smoke. A lot of smoke. Hilfy wrinkled her nose.

"You a lot like the Personage. You same bastard like her."

"Family resemblance. Family temper. You want a demonstration?"

Another grin. Mahendo'sat and humans did that. Bad habit. Could get you killed, on Anuurn.

"You nice. No bad temper. Just hani."

"You're a prejudiced son, aren't you? You want a deal? You tell me what difference it makes what we're carrying. You tell me what difference it makes to the stsho and what's at stake."

"You not know."

"We haul cargo. We're being paid. The stsho didn't hire mahendo'sat to do what we're doing. Don't you think if they'd trusted you very much they'd have let *Ha'domaren* carry it?"

"Maybe they look for damn fool."

Point. "So you know so much: what is it? What significance does it have? Convince me you're our friend."

"Lot status. Lot status with stsho." Puff and puff. Sip of fruit drink. "No'shto-shti-stlen number one bastard, want run whole Compact. Stsho all same lot disturb by give this thing."

"So what does it matter what it is?"

"Same make difference what kind *oji*. Some got big presence. Some got histor-icity. Some got art. Some make suicide."

"Make suicide."

"You get *oji*, you got respond or you lose big. Number one dirty trick."

"You mean they have to equal the item."

"Or lose status big."

"And Atli-lyen-tlas doesn't want to receive it?"

"Maybe." Another sip. "What kind *oji?*"

"Sorry. Not enough information. Why should I help your Personage? She might not be my friend."

"We *good* friend! We number one good friend! Whereby you get idea? Long time mahendo'sat been friend hani. Who get you into space? Who bring ships to you world? Who give you number one help make ships and trade? You damn hani fight each other with sharp sticks two hundred year gone. Now so smart you tell mahendo'sat goodbye, no need help."

"Well, that's not a question you ask a merchant captain. Go tell my aunt what she owes you. Tell my aunt tell me tell you what I know, no trouble."

"You say you don't speak."

"Haven't had a reason. If we had a reason we'd speak."

"How much you want tell me what is?"

"You can't buy me."

"You want know where gone Atli-lyen-tlas?"

She was really tempted. Not to trust this Haisi person. But to trust him more than the stsho. Historically, the mahendo'sat had been more allied with hani than not. But not *all* mahendo'sat were on the same side. "Not many choices out of here. If it's Urtur I'll have your ears. Suppose I said it was a piece of art."

"Need know more than that, hani."

She took a sip of tea. Her last. And got up. "I give you something, you give me nothing. Wrong game, mahe. I'm not playing anymore."

"Kshshti."

"With the kif."

"They *hire* kif. Sit, sit, talk."

She sank back into the chair, leaned her elbows on the scarred table and gazed at the mahe's eyes. Green neon didn't improve his complexion. Green shone on his dark fur, on his uncommunicative, flat-nosed face—on the smoke he puffed out of his nostrils.

"So talk. What kif ship?"

"Maybe . . . *Nogkokktik.*"

"Why?"

"No'shto-shti-stlen got lot enemy. Plenty old, plenty smart. Enemy want *gtst* come home, give up be governor. That enough?"

"No'shto-shti-stlen is an old friend of my aunt. Why should I betray *gtst* interests?"

"No'shto-shti-stlen nobody friend. You know how long live stsho?"

It wasn't a known fact. There were guesses . . . in what she'd read.

"How long?"

"Maybe two hundred year. Hard make figure. Stsho change sex, change person, change everything, not remember. How you know when born, when change? Nobody sure. But what make stsho care? You Phase, same you dead. You don't got memory who you were. Same like dead."

"Who knows whether they remember who they were?"

"They say don't remember. You don't believe stsho?"

"I believe I got paid. And I get real nervous when people start asking questions about my business or about passengers on my ship."

Another puff of smoke, green in the neon. "You want make contact local stsho?"

"Maybe I will. Maybe I'll use the station com, like any civilized individual."

Haisi grinned. "Maybe you don't get answer. Damn scare' this stsho."

"Who is this?"

"Name not matter. Same aide to Atli-lyen-tlas, got real scare', not go with kif. I got contact. You got *oji*. And No'shto-shti-stlen messenger."

"So?"

"So you stsho make this stsho talk damn fast."

Tempting. "I'm under contract. I can't say what I can agree to. Interesting idea. I'll say that. But I have to go back and take a look at the document I've signed."

"Not safe place, Kita. Mahendo'sat upset, stsho upset . . . kif upset. You want talk new governor at Meetpoint, lot change. Change make money, change lose money. Lot people got lot stress. Bad for health."

It didn't make one feel confident, sitting in a mahen bar, with a mahe with unknown interests bankrolling his ship and making deals through him with unknown parties with unknown intentions.

"I'll get back to you," she said, and got up and left him
the bill.

2980-89 *was* a phone number. And an address, that being
the system on Kita Point Station. Which made it just about
as easy to take a walk to the lift and a ride up to the
residential levels, up to Deck 2, Section 80.

Not a bad neighborhood, Tiar said to herself, seeing the
immaculate paneling and the neat plastic address plates,
and the plastic signs that said, in the universal alphabet,
Silimaji nan nil Ja'hai-wa.

Meaning, for a mahen maintenance worker who might
not speak the pidgin, *Through traffic prohibited.*

No clutter, no smudges, none of the graffiti endemic on
the dockside. Pri-cey.

She rang at number 89, and waited, while optics in the
wall doubtless advised the occupants of a hani in spacer
blues in the spotless corridor.

"Who? Identify!"

"*Ker* Tiar Chanur, of the merchant freighter *Chanur's
Legacy.* I had a notice to call."

Electronic and manual locks clicked. The door shot wide.
A stsho was standing there, taller than most, painted in
curlicues of palest lime and mauve, about *gtst* plumy crest
and moonstone eyes. "Chanur, honorable Chanur. Protect
us! You must protect us!"

It was hardly a conversation for a hallway. But she had
no desire to let a door close her in some stranger's apart-
ment, either. "In what way? From what?"

Hands waved, trying to beckon her inside. "In, in, the
danger, the danger, honorable hani."

"Danger of *what?*" She backed up, evading the white,
beseeching fingers. "I don't know you. If you want help . . .
come to the ship."

"Most excellent hani! I have little baggage, very little,
please, please, you will bring me safely aboard your
ship . . ."

"I didn't say that! The captain has to clear any
passengers!"

"But if the distinguished captain admits this honest person, where will my baggage be? How shall I live? What

should I do? I must have certain things necessary for my existence! All is ready, all is gathered, I need only gather it up, oh, please, *please,* estimable hani, most honorable . . ."

"Get the gods-be bags! Hurry, if there's danger!"

Gtst wailed, *gtst* dashed back as fast as a stsho could move, and, indeed, *gtst* dragged out bags and bundles in feverish haste, from lockers, from cabinets, from various quarters of the pastel room, until it made a sizable pile.

"You can't carry all that."

"This honest person had hoped, had most earnestly hoped that a strong, a most excellent and trustworthy hani would be kindly disposed to . . ."

"Gods rot it." She went in, not without a wary glance about, grabbed up the heaviest bundles by their strings and handles and left the stsho to manage the rest, on her way out the door while *gtst* was still filling *gtst* arms.

"I'll take this lot," Tiar said over her shoulder, "you take the rest and don't look like you're with me, if you don't want publicity. And if the captain doesn't like the look of you, you and this whole pile are out on the dock, hear me?"

"Oh, most clever, most wise hani, most excellent . . ."

"Stow it! Close the gods-be door!" The creature had no concept of intrigue. *Gtst* shoved a note in an alien stranger's trousers and never thought an open door might raise questions.

So might a lift full of baggage, a hani, and a panicked, muttering stsho. A mahe with a child in tow got on at Deck One, and rode down with them. The child bounced around the walls, grinning at its own cleverness, and managed to knock into both of them in the short time before the doors opened on the cold grayness of the docks. Perhaps the mahe meant to space its offspring. Perhaps the mahe hoped someone else would do it. Tiar clutched the bundles and dragged them past the overanxious doors, held them for the weak-limbed stsho, and snarled, "Move, kid!" in such a tone the mahe grabbed the brat out of their path.

The stsho was clearly impressed. *Gtst* pale eyes were very wide. *Gtst* murmured, "Kindly restrain the offspring. It is very annoying," and followed her out.

For a stsho toward a stranger, that was amazing. *She* was impressed. *Gtst* had more fortitude than seemed evident.

"Berth 10," she said, and led off at a moderate stride, a moving obstruction on the docks, in the abundant foot traffic.

She looked back, just to be sure the stsho was still following. And *gtst* was, slogging along with *gtst* swinging, pendant baggage of small bundles, limping on lime-slippered feet.

"Go on, go on," *gtst* panted, shaking *gtst* crest from *gtst* eyes. "We are in great danger. I shall seem not to know you. It will be a ruse. Please, keep walking!"

She walked. There were kif about. There were mahendo'-sat. Not another hani, not another stsho. Of a sudden their dissociation seemed exceedingly naive and dangerous.

"Come on," she said. "Hurry it! I don't like this."

She was ever so glad to see the *Legacy*'s number on the display board, and to see the first of the transports already arrived. The hold was open, the ramp gate was showing green for unlocked.

"We're all right," she panted, hoping for the sight of Tarras or Chihin. There was the stsho, valiantly (for a stsho) struggling after.

There were three kif, just standing, watching them.

She was never so glad to walk up the ramp and find the gate opening to her request. The stsho was gasping at the bottom of the incline, trying to gather up *gtst* baggage, the cords of which had tangled with *gtst* robes. One of the kif was headed toward them, with deliberation in its moves.

"Get up here!" she said, regretting the laws that meant the nearest gun they owned was in the locker in the airlock. "Now!"

Gtst stumbled and limped *gtst* way up. The kif stopped, and for a moment looked straight at her, a stare that made the hair stand up on her nape as she shepherded the struggling stsho into the chill of the ramp.

"Oh, the cold!" it breathed.

"Kif," she said. "Move!" She dropped the baggage in the rampway, on the *Legacy*'s side of the doors, and ran for the airlock and the locker. The stsho shrilled a protest at the desertion. She heard it attempting to run, wailing and gasping.

She hit the airlock controls, waited through the cycle and, inside, used her first and third claws in the sockets that opened the locker. She seized the gun inside, clicked the safety off, and scared ten years of life out of the stsho that came gasping and struggling through the airlock.

"I'm going back after the baggage," she said. "*You* stay in the airlock."

Gtst wailed, *gtst* gasped, *gtst* sobbed. "Let us through! Let us through! Oh, murder, oh, vilest murder on us . . ."

Gtst was still wailing as Tiar walked back to get the baggage. The fragile tube was no place to start shooting; but her eye was toward the gates down there, that anyone with a key could open. And if a kif did, he was in dire trouble, by the gods, he was.

. . . *it shall be the obligation of the ship's captain to secure the item and to maintain its safety and its confidentiality from all unauthorized persons . . .*

. . . *the representative of the person issuing the contract shall be the final arbiter of the disposition of the object unless the person who has been the representative of the person issuing the contract shall be determined to be no longer in substance or in fact the same individual entrusted and declared by the contract to be the individual representing the person issuing the contract.*

Gods.

Hilfy raked a hand through her mane, stared at the screen. *Final arbiter of the disposition of the object. The representative of the person issuing the contract.*

Meaning Tlisi-tlas-tin representing No'shto-shti-stlen. Meaning ask Tlisi-tlas-tin, as the final arbiter.

She keyed out, got up from the desk in lower deck ops, and went to see the representative of *gtst* excellency . . . who, one hoped, was capable of assuming responsibility, or at least of discussing the matter in a sane and reasonable fashion.

She should tell *gtst* about Ana-kehnandian. She had never contemplated working in any close way with a stsho. *No one* contemplated working closely with a stsho. They were only preferable to the methane-breathers, in reason.

But if she had an ally now who could explain any-thing it was Tlisi-tlas-tin.

She went to the door and signaled her presence. "Your honor? *Ker* Hilfy Chanur. A word with you."

It took a little for a stsho to respond—a little longer to

rise and arrange *gtst*self and walk to the door. In unusually short order the door slid back and *gtst* honor Tlisi-tlas-tin gave a languorous ripple of *gtst* fingers in respect.

"Most honorable captain."

She didn't even have time to break the news. The lock cycled, and a shrill warbling entered the main corridor. *Gtst* honor's eyes went wide and *gtst* ducked back within the doorframe.

"Who is that?" *gtst* cried. "Oh, murder, oh, mischief! What distress is that?"

She had not a thing in her hands. It sounded like murder, and something was in the ship that did not belong there.

Something turned out stsho, and disheveled and woefully frightened, a figure hung about incongruously with parcels and strings and tangled pastel garments.

And behind that apparition, cousin Tiar, gun in hand.

"Refuge!" the stsho cried. Tlisi-tlas-tin's door shut, quickly, and Tiar got between, motioning the panicked stsho to stay still, casting a disturbed and hasty look in Hilfy's direction.

"What's going on?" she demanded of Tiar. Guns, for the god's sake, and a stranger on their deck.

"Kif," Tiar breathed. "Captain, I'm *sorry*. I was out on the docks—this . . . person . . . wanted help. . . ."

Her heart was thumping doubletime. But *seeing* a stsho, finally, proved they did exist here, stsho seemed on the receiving end of the trouble in mahen space, and this one was no threat . . . terrified, rather, distraught, exhausted, at the visible limit of *gtst* resources.

"Help for what?" *Kif* was still echoing in her ears, but if the inner hatch had opened, the outer hatch had shut; and no kif was getting in here.

"Oh, great hani, *kindly* hani person . . . please, refuge from this terrible place, please, violence, terrible violence . . ."

Four stsho dead, Haisi had said.

And beside her the door opened and Tlisi-tlas-tin put *gtst* head out. "Oh, woe! Oh, distress! Is this the person? Is this the one?"

"Captain," Tiar tried to say, but there was too much stsho wailing from both sides, and Tiar gestured helplessly with the gun in hand. "Kif, watching the ship!"

And Tarras and Chihin about to open up the hold for the dockers.

"Have we got a docking crew out there? Have we got any station security on the cargo lock?"

"Just the dockers. . . ."

The intruder had edged forward, toward Tlisi-tlas-tin, babbling and bowing . . . was all but at the door, and that set off old, war-honed instincts. Hilfy put out a warning hand and laid her ears back, by no means eager to let *gtst* near the *oji*.

But the intruder-stsho bowed and bobbed and babbled in manic frenzy, *gtst* moonstone eyes wide and bright, paint streaked on *gtst* face and arms and onto *gtst* pastel robes . . . *gtst* reached Tlisi-tlas-tin, *gtst* honor nothing protesting, with the parcels dangling about *gtst* limbs, but Tlisi-tlas-tin had retreated inside *gtst* cabin, and the intruder seemed overcome, hanging on the doorway and wailing.

Tlisi-tlas-tin hissed and straightened *gtst* robes, a hand on the pedestal of the *oji*. "This is by no means Atli-lyen-tlas!" *gtst* declared. "This is a juvenile! What unseemliness has turned an unformed individual loose without face-saving escort?" . . . or something to that effect. It was a barrage of high stshoshi, indignant and outraged, and the intruder covered *gtst* face and cowered.

"Aide to *gtst* excellency!" *gtst* protested. "I am no juvenile! I am an honorable person, gainfully employed and competent!"

"What," demanded Tlisi-tlas-tin, "what is your wretched and undistinguished name?"

What had *gtst* done? Hilfy wondered, stunned by the viciousness of Tlisi-tlas-tin's attack. Stsho weren't violent. Stsho avoided conflict, and unpleasantness, and *gtst* attacked a stsho *gtst* called a juvenile . . . who hovered in the doorway murmuring,

"Oh, the beauty, oh, the elegance, oh, oh!"

Tlisi-tlas-tin's crest lowered and lifted. *Gtst* blinked rapidly, and the young stsho bowed repeatedly, and turned and patted Hilfy's arm.

"Tell *gtst* excellency, tell *gtst* excellency I am overwhelmed, I cannot remember the unworthiness in the face of this magnificence, I admire *gtst* excellency, please say this!"

"*Gtst* says . . ."

"*Gtstisi,* oh, *gtstisi!*"

Gtstisi. The Indeterminate. The Transitory.

They had a gods-be Phasing stsho on their hands, a personality overwhelmed and disintegrating.

"*Gtstisi* says . . . *gtstisi* is overwhelmed." It was all of it she could construct. It was all that made sense.

But Tlisi-tlas-tin turned *gtst* back and walked a few steps before *gtst* deigned to answer.

And *gtstisi*—assuming it was Phasing—crouched on the floor at the doorway.

"Your honor," Hilfy said, trying to attract *gtst* attention. "*Is* this—" One could not directly refer to the former identity of a stsho in fragmentation—it was abominable manners. "Is this someone with whom your honor might have business?"

Gtst was clearly agitated, pacing and wringing *gtst* long, white fingers. "Excellency," *gtst* had the presence of mind to declare, promoting *gtst*self a notch, for the visitor's benefit, one could think. "I do not notice this distasteful event. If *gtstisi* remains, *gtstisi* remains. Where is Atli-lyen-tlas, what am I to think?"

"Excellency, I have had a report *gtst* moved on, likely to Kshshti. This could not possibly . . . *possibly* . . . be the identical person, please forgive my forwardness."

"A servant," *gtst* said, at which the intruder wailed and covered *gtstisi* head with locked arms. "Take this juvenile from my sight. It is insane."

One hesitated to make any disposition of the wretched creature. One hesitated to lay hands on it: stsho were fragile, and bones might break. But she took it by a fold of cloth and tugged, wondering what she might do with it, thinking of the accommodation they might improvise out of the remaining passenger cabin next door, and recalling that cabin was dark gray and a definite blue.

It might drive the creature over the edge, or pry its last grip loose from reality. *Final arbiter,* the contract said, of the disposition of the Preciousness. And that was the loader clanking into motion, those hydraulics were the cargo hatch unsealing the *Legacy* to the dockside and the dockers and kifish bandits, by Tiar's report.

"White paint," she said, and cast about desperately after

resources of personnel or energy. "White paint. Panels. There have to be some pieces in storage."

"I think there were," Tiar said.

"Get on the com. Advise Tarras and Chihin there's kif out there. Get—" She had the stsho in hand, Meras topside, *gtst* honor in the passenger quarters . . . and *gtstisi* was wilting in her grip, wiping at its body paint and its crest indiscriminately. "Lost, lost," *gtstisi* wailed. "I was someone and I forget, I forget, oh, the misery I have had, and I forget!"

"Get on it!" Hilfy said, and dragged the fainting stsho to the neighboring cabin. "This is temporary," she said. "It has no taste, no distinction. It will change."

"Oh, the despair!" *gistisi* cried, and slumped inside. "I die, I perish, oh, woe and obliteration . . . where is my name to be? What shall I become?"

"An honest stsho!" she said irritably, and shut the door and locked it.

And leaned against the wall, surveying over her left shoulder a scattered trail of small abandoned parcels. Tiar was not in sight. Probably Tiar would gladly be several lights away at the moment, and the hold was not far enough.

But she could not blame Tiar entirely. Nor blame Hallan Meras for this disaster. This one came of being here, came of kif stalking them, came of dealing with a scoundrel of a mahe who wouldn't tell her what she needed to know.

She had the most sinking feeling that *this* was the stsho Haisi had claimed was still available and knowledgeable, *this* was the source of knowledge still available to them, and *gtst* had just lost touch with *gtst* own mind—was, in effect, dying to the stsho *gtst* had been, and becoming another entity, if *gtst* could pull the bits and pieces of a personality together.

But *gtst* might not remember once *gtst* had made that transition. *Gtst—gtstisi*. Indeterminate, desperately trying to sort out its reality, and locked, within that storage compartment, in an environment that could lend it no cues.

She shoved herself away from the wall, opened Tlisi-tlastin's door without *gtst* permission and met shocked, offended eyes. "A mahe named Tahaisimandi Ana-kehnandian has been following us since Meetpoint. He said that some of Atli-lyen-tlas' staff remained . . .''

Gtst honor . . . *gtst* excellency, as *gtst* lately styled *gtst*self . . . flinched. "This is extremely distasteful."

"Because that unformed person *is* Atli-lyen-tlas?"

"No! A thousand, thousand nos. This is a person beneath our tasteful notice. We would not undertake a mission to such an individual. Do not distress us further. This is a juvenile. Atli-lyen-tlas has abandoned *gtst* post and fled in our face. The treachery, the abysmal treachery! I perform heinous insults upon this gift of *gtst* shapeless servant! It will not dissuade me!"

"You mean *gtstisi*—"

"Is surely a servile leaving of *gtst* excellency. Can you look at the magnificence of my surroundings and affront me with that disheveled and untidy person? *Gtstisi* may serve here. The lack of servants offends my dignity, which surely your honor knows. I will accept this individual as resident in my quarters, but *gtstisi* must be clean and respectful!"

"I will inform *gtstisi* of your—ah, excellency's offer."

"My order!"

"Exactly." She kept her expression sweet and her ears up, and bowed politely and went to the neighboring cabin to run *gtst* new excellency's errand. "*Gtst* excellency wants you," she said to the huddled figure inside. "But I suggest you make yourself presentable. There is a thoroughly tasteless place where you may find water and organize your baggage. Follow me."

"Oh, oh," was all *gtstisi* managed to say. "Despair and disaster."

But *gtstisi* followed, through the litter of the abandoned baggage, while thumps and bangs and the action of the loader heralded the exit of cargo from the hold, and, one could hope, not the entry of kifish pirates off the unregulated docks.

She saw the nameless stsho to the washroom, let *gtstisi* gather up *gtstisi* trail of baggage that was strewn from Tlisi-tlas-tin's door to the airlock, and meanwhile used the com at the intersection of the corridors to call the cargo lock.

"Tiar? Are you alive out there?"

"Things look quiet," Tiar said. *"They're gone."*

"Are you armed?"

"Gun's right here in the lock. We're legal."

Thank the gods for favors. She called the bridge:

"Fala. Where's Meras?"

"Doing the filters."

"Remind him keep off lower decks. We've got a problem."

"What kind of problem, captain?"

"Two stsho. One's Phasing. Ours, thank the gods, is still sane. There are kif on the docks, Tiar's working outside, they know she brought the stsho here . . . where's Tarras?"

"Right here, captain. You need some help down there?"

"Just be my eyes and ears on dockside. And investigate cargo for Kshshti. Don't agree to anything yet."

"Kshshti!"

"I know, I know, best I can do. I'll be on com. I've got a scoundrel to call."

"Aye, captain."

"So can you still deliver what you asked about?" Hilfy asked, and the scoundrel in question said, via station com:

"You number one bastard thief! How you find?"

It was the only pleasant moment in a disgusting day.

"Guess."

"What you propose now, hani bastard?"

"Manners, manners, Haisi. We all lose a few."

"Repeat: what you propose?"

"We might have something to talk about. But now we have the information and you're buying."

There was a moment of silence on the com. Hilfy leaned her arms on the ops station counter, and flicked her ears to listen to the rings jangle.

"What you offer?"

"I don't know. Let me think about it."

"You head for trouble. I number one good friend. Who else you trust?"

"Dear friend. Good friend. You don't want to rush my decision, do you? You want to give me time. We have to maintain good relations."

Now and again there were mahen words she hadn't

heard. There followed some. Then: *"Of course. Number one fine. Talk to you later, pretty captain."*

Tarras was looking up cargo for Kshshti. And if they didn't want to be charged with abducting the Preciousness, if they didn't want to pay back a million credit deal . . . Kshshti looked to be where they were going.

And out of Kshshti . . .

Out of Kshshti, Maing Tol, or back to Kita . . . or worse choices. Kshshti lay in the Disputed Territories. It was still a mahen station.

But it was too close to the kif . . . far too close for comfort.

And *gtst* excellency had taken a kifish ship at Kita Point?

Or the kif had taken *gtst* excellency. Certainly the young stsho Tiar had rounded up on station might have told them what the facts were, if the young stsho had not been driven straight out of *gtst* mind, either by the harrowing run to the ship, *gtst* conditions on the station, or the sight of Tlisi-tlas-tin. The fact was, they didn't know and might never know what had been the triggering event, or whether it bore on what had already happened.

So they had to go on. But she would feel ever so much better if she knew how far they were going to have to chase this Atli-lyen-tlas, or into what.

Hallan really, truly did not want to make another mistake. He knew how to clean the filters and maintain equipment, but he had read the manual and the instructions just the same, to be absolutely, unmistakably certain what he was doing. He didn't think speed was going to impress anyone . . . since he was sure they had given him the job to keep him out of the crew's way; and because it *would* save the crew a little time. He wished he could find a disaster in the making that he could fix, and by that, impress the captain and make up for what he had done at Urtur.

He had nightmares about that. He had nightmares about the tc'a showing up and demanding he come methane-side and parent its offspring. And of strangling in the atmosphere. But there were probably laws to protect him from that.

There were none to protect the ship from the fines it had

suffered because of him, because of having to close the section doors, and scaring all those people. . . .

He didn't think he could ever live that down. Sometimes he thought he would be better off to go home and live in the outback and do things the way they had always been done and not be a problem to anyone. He was not really a fighter, he never had been, he was just clumsy, which he daily proved, and his elbows continually found something to bash, or his head to knock into, but there was just no use for being his size on board a ship.

He heard someone come up near him. He did everything as precisely and efficiently as he could. Whoever it was stood there watching. And he finished the job before he looked to see.

"*Ker* Fala?"

"I was just watching."

That made him nervous. He put the tools away and got up, intending to take them to the storage. He supposed he should go to the crew lounge then, because he hadn't any other instructions.

She was still staring at him when he walked away. It made him feel—highly uncomfortable.

The crew aboard the *Sun* had behaved like that too. And he didn't feel the same as he did with Sahern clan, he felt confused, but it wasn't a confusion he wanted to think about. It scared him. He was afraid she was going to be waiting in the lounge when he got back, but she wasn't, she was in the galley making lunch. And maybe he should go help her, and not sit in the lounge as if there were nothing on the ship his intelligence could discover to do, but he didn't want to be alone with her, so he started aft.

But Fala said, to his back, "Want to help?"

And there went his available excuse. "All right," he said, not cheerfully, and came back to the very small galley.

"I think the captain's getting softer," Fala said, with a wink. "If she let you sit on the bridge, she's giving some. You want to get the *cghos* out of the refrigerator?"

He looked. He found it and put it on the counter, and she said, "You can turn on the steamer, it's the red button." She was busy and in a hurry, whacking slices off the lunchmeat with a knife, and piling them onto a plate with the cheese. "You can roll those if you want to, it's just sandwiches. I figure everybody's going to be eating with one hand and working with the other."

"Have we found the stsho we're looking for?" he asked, and Fala gave him a glance.

"Somebody who finds out less than I do," she said with a flick of her ears and a frown. "No. *Gtst* skipped out ahead of us. We don't know why."

He wondered if she expected him to know. For that moment she sounded friendly and not threatening, and he suffered a moment of panic, reminding himself he shouldn't slip into that kind of thinking, he shouldn't be here.

"Probably Kshshti," she said. "That's what I hear."

Kshshti was a border port. A dangerous place.

"Are we going there?"

A nod. A flick and settling of her couple of experience-rings, that said *she* was a real spacer. "I think so," she said soberly. "You ever seen it?"

"No. No, I never was at the far stations. Except Meetpoint. And Maing Tol."

"I've been there," she said. "You really feel foreign there."

He had slid into a personal conversation. He didn't *do* that with spacers. He tried to stay businesslike. He lowered his ears, looked away and found occupation rolling up the sandwiches and skewering them together.

"Something bothering you?" Fala Anify asked. "You *worried* about something?"

"No," he said.

"Scared of Kshshti?" she asked.

That was next to insulting. He wasn't scared of Kshshti, he hadn't been brought up to run in panic. But he supposed it looked that way to her, and he wasn't willing to explain, he just didn't want to look her in the face and talk to her, because she could really mess things up for him. He had wondered if there was a way he could possibly mess up in this port, and he had found one, that was certain. Because he didn't think Hilfy Chanur was going to tolerate him getting involved with the crew, especially the youngest of the crew. Chihin was safer. At least she was less complicated.

"We'll be all right," Fala said, as if Kshshti were the center of his problems. "The captain knows what she's doing. On *The Pride,* she was in and out of all kinds of situations. And we're armed, the *Legacy* is, if we ever run into anything that needs it, we've got it. The captain knew when she set out that a lot of people could think of getting at *ker* Pyanfar through us . . . so we're outfitted for most anything. We're not a ship anybody should mess with."

"That's good to know," he said, and flinched when Tarras put her head in and asked,

"What have we got here, a romance or a lunch?"

He could have died. On the spot.

Fala's ears went down, flat, in complete embarrassment.

Chapter 11

There was tea, while the loaders clanked away. The galley annex that had somehow gotten established in the lower-deck laundry had found another use, now that *gtst* excellency Tlisi-tlas-tin had acquired a . . . staff . . . fit for *gtst* station in life.

Meaning the nameless servant had acquired an interim name: *gtstisi* was *Dlima*, which meant something like Scant Necessity: not a flattering designation, in Hilfy's estimation, but one could have settled any indignity on Dlima in the present state of affairs, and *gtstisi* could not on the one hand protest it, or, on the other (by all she had read on the matter, written of course by non-stsho) could not integrate it into a meaningful reality. In *gtstisi* condition, experiences fell randomly, and had no order. *Gtstisi* would follow orders, to be sure—mahen scientists suggested (and stsho were tastefully silent on the matter) that *gtstisi* actually required orders, so that *gtstisi* had a hope of discovering structure in the events that tumbled in apparent chaos.

So, distressful as it might be to outsiders, outsiders were advised to ignore their personal scruples and to be as arbitrary, as harsh, as demanding as a stsho of rank might be, because, contrary to mahen expectation, and, as it happened, contrary to hani attitudes, the stsho in question would not hold a grudge, would scarcely remember, and would probably benefit by the experience.

So they said.

So she settled into the cushions, accepted the tea, ceremoniously served, at the foot of the pedestal on which the Preciousness rested, while the loaders worked and the cargo left their hold.

While Haisi was doubtless scouring the station for answers he might suspect she had. And while Tlisi-tlas-tin was discussing the poor but essentially necessary service *gtst* had acquired, "by the good offices of the esteemed hani captain."

"Has this individual discussed . . . hem, . . . any smallest detail of *gtstisi* former life?"

A distressed waggle of fingers. "I should never accuse the esteemed hani captain of a lapse in taste, but I really cannot discuss these distressing matters. Obviously this life contained affairs which *gtstisi* could not organize in any tasteful or useful fashion. These are . . . iiii . . . *biological* matters. Is enough understood?"

Hilfy thought; and thought; and thought in widening circles . . . with the confusions that came of studying alien language and custom much of her life, and not least among them the stsho. When everything else failed, the maxim ran . . . ask the alien how to ask the question.

"Then," she said carefully, and paused while Dlima poured; and paused further while Dlima served Tlisi-tlas-tin. "Then how shall I ask what information you might have gained in this port?"

"Nothing is easier."

"How shall I ask? I wish to benefit from your unquestionable good taste and elegant gracefulness. You have shown most extraordinary virtues . . ." *Never* attribute exact words like frankness to a species which might not value it. ". . . in dealing with the stresses of this voyage. And I am moved to wonder if your resourcefulness and intelligence might have gained information which would make your person far safer if the captain of this ship should learn it."

Moonstone eyes blinked several times, and the tiny mouth sipped at the delicate cup. "You have discovered a graciousness uncommon in your species."

And other species could be, by other species' standards, great boors. But she smiled and kept hani opinions behind her teeth, as invalid in this venue, even on her ship. "I thank your honor."

"As to the answer to your question, I think it very clear that the nameless person of no distinction was at one time a close associate of a person who has behaved tastelessly. Whether this abandonment was intentional or not, it is equally clear that this movement is not coincidence. The designated recipient of the Preciousness has gone to Kshshti."

"Could your excellency possibly enlighten me further as to the doubtless impeccable reasoning that has led your excellency to that conclusion?"

"Kif are involved. They would not readily convey this person closer to mahen centers of power. They had rather seek areas where circumstances are more favorable to them."

Meaning the border, the Disputed Territories that were still, despite Aunt Pyanfar's good offices, a matter of disagreement between kif and mahendo'sat. She had no quarrel with that reasoning. She was only glad to hear it confirmed.

"But, enlighten me again, excellency: how has this individual known we were coming? How has *gtst* managed to evade us not once but consecutively? Or is this *gtst* doing?"

Tlisi-tlas-tin carefully set down *gtst* cup, with that twist of the wrist that signaled an end of tea, and a seriousness approaching severe.

"I cannot say."

"I have trespassed. But may I ask: do you advise us to continue as we are, and pursue this individual to Kshshti? And is there reasonable likelihood that there we may discharge our responsibilities and increase our respectability?"

"We must continue. We must go to Kshshti. There is no question."

"I thank your excellency for your most extreme good will. I am always enlightened and invigorated by your discourse. As your excellency knows, there is a mahe pressing us closely, who has offered us bribes and threats in his insistence to view the Preciousness. . . ."

"Unthinkable!"

"I take it our refusals of this individual are wise."

"Villainy, utter villainy. Avoid this person!"

"He thought he could lay hands on your excellency's servant and extract information. The foresight of my crewwoman prevented him doing this. I therefore suspect he does not have the full cooperation of the directors of this station, or he could have laid hands on *gtstisi*. I think that he knew of *gtstisi* existence here, but not the exact whereabouts, nor could he discover it before we did . . . quite unexpectedly and by the forwardness of this juvenile person, and thanks in no part to the mahe in question."

"Most impressive." Tlisi-tlas-tin gave a slight glance aside to the servant. "Most desperate."

"I understand from this mahe that stsho were murdered here, most recently. He implied this was connected to the disappearance of Atli-lyen-tlas."

"Distressing. Most distressing. Is there other information which may be tastefully asked?"

"He implied that the sight or even information about the nature of the Preciousness might enable him to make a critical judgment of its meaning."

Gtst crest fluttered, lifted and lowered. "Unmitigated and unjustified arrogance!"

"I take it your excellency does not approve of his proposal."

"I perform indignities upon his graceless proposal."

"Is he possibly telling a falsehood?"

"In a most shameless fashion. This is a trading style well-known among mahendo'sat, this obtaining piece after piece of what one wants."

"A mahe could not possibly understand the meaning in the sending of the Preciousness."

"You are far more tasteful than he and you do not comprehend."

"Most certainly so, excellency."

White fingers reached for the cup again, and turned it. The conversation was ended. "A symmetry of information has been reached," *gtst* said. "Do you agree?"

There were a handful of questions she would ask that would not get answers—questions like: what part are the kif playing? Are they working for anyone but themselves?

The stsho might think they were. That was the trouble. Everything was the stsho's estimate of what was going on . . . and the stsho had had their fingers burned before. The stsho might be the last to know what was going on. The stsho might be the last to know that they were understood by the mahen scientists who wrote treatises on their psyche.

Gtst excellency said that no mahe could comprehend the

nature of the Preciousness—but Haisi chased them from star to star trying to learn what it was?

One *could* conclude that a mahen Personage might not be the only player in this contest . . . that the information Haisi wanted might be going to someone who *could* interpret it.

"I have a thought, excellency."

One did not break the symmetry of a conversation. Tlisi-tlas-tin's brow knit and *gtst* mouth drew thin in displeasure.

"Would a stsho *hire* a mahe to ask us about the Preciousness?"

The frown deepened and lifted.

"Or enter into collusion with some mahe for that purpose?"

Another frown settled on Tlisi-tlas-tin's brow.

"These are disturbing questions," *gtst* said.

"Are they wise questions, excellency?"

There was no immediate answer.

She cleared her throat. "Graceless as it might be, I might purvey him false information, and I would for your excellency's protection do so, if it would not offend you. But I would not know what falsehood might be believed by whoever hired him."

Tlisi-tlas-tin's respiration increased markedly. "These are most distressing ideas. I must consider them."

That the stsho would deceive . . . was well-established. But lying was not a word one tossed about carelessly, dealing with other species. Some species did. Some didn't. Some would, individually. Some would, collectively. And what some called lying others called an answer for indecent curiosity. Meddling with reality *or* its perception was, at least among oxy-breathers thus far studied, what intercultural scientists called a potential flashpoint—a ticking bomb in any interspecies dealings: the more alien, the worse in potential.

"I take my leave of your excellency. I entrust matters to your wisdom and discretion. Should I fail in elegance, I trust that your grace and most excellent sense will advise me to a more proper course."

"Most gracious."

"Most excellent and enlightening."

She *hated* bowing and backing. It wasn't hani. And she didn't do it all the way to the door, not quite. Being hani.

No question then where they were going—and since they had missed that wretch Atli-lyen-tlas twice due to *gtst* damnable haste in going wherever *gtst* was going (one suspected now, away from them) speed might be of the essence. Which meant no delay in loading cargo, no great mass to what they could take, and no time to fuss about the niceties of what they took.

"Got a few possibilities, captain," Tarras said. "Kshshti not being an unusual destination out of here." Meaning that they couldn't be too picky on that account either.

Hilfy read the list. It was a matter of figuring what they could load quickly, and one of the best answers was something light and valuable and easily disposed of in a port that bordered kif territory (she shuddered to think, and refused to carry small edible animals) and likewise lay on the receiving end of two lanes coming out of mahen territory, and one port away from stsho space and tc'a.

Methane load, maybe, which she hated almost as much as the small edible animals.

Or pharmaceuticals. She read the latest market reports from a ship inbound from Kshshti, ran it through the computer program that could spot the relative bad deals and bargains compared to markets elsewhere, factored with points of origin for the goods in question, plus a set of keywords like shortage and various diseases and rise and fall of prices in the business news. It advised, at least, it read news faster than a mortal eye could scan it, and it liked the pharmaceuticals possibility, the radioactives (another load she was not fond of, since one was at the mercy of the company in question's packaging practices, inspection was not easy, and some of them were appallingly naive about what a loader did to cans). But Kita was an importer of such materials, while Kefk, one step farther on from Kshshti, was a moderate exporter of said materials and reasonably would be shipping them to Kshshti . . . figuring trade possibilities was a headache on a border, because you *couldn't* get thoroughly accurate information across said border: traders lied, governments lied, and the black market flourished, but a well-known ship was ill-advised to play that game.

You wanted something . . . something that *you* knew about that the rest of the universe didn't. And the only thing they knew about that the rest of the universe didn't was the exact nature of the Preciousness, and (at least as regarded the average trader) that they carried some sort of stsho psychological . . .

. . . event.

She punched in data with sudden energy and factored in *political uncertainty* and *instability: stsho* . . . and even, thinking about Tahaisimandi Ana-kehnandian and his meddling personage . . . *instability: mahendo'sat.*

The computer silently worked and worked, and came up with a whole new set of projections. Under those conditions, a person wanted essentials in store and a government or a station wanted information and strategic necessities in greater abundance than ordinary. And it projected price rises and scarcities in different patterns.

The only difficulty with that scenario, the glaringly clear difficulty, was that inside information didn't do you a bit of good if the people making the decisions to buy weren't *also* privy to it. It was good for playing the futures game. But perfectly smart investments could bankrupt you if the secret stayed secret. As, contractually, it was supposed to.

Strategic metals, strategic materials, and out of a place like Kita, which was a quasi-star of so new a generation it hadn't heavy elements and wouldn't exist except that it provided services and repairs, and that those services and repairs had employed people who wanted first food and then luxuries to ameliorate their barren lives, and then employees who served up the luxuries, and then food to feed the purveyors of the unnecessary, an ecosystem of elegant simplicity beginning to run to the baroqueries common to civilization.

All of which told you, as every trader knew, that Kita was a place that imported as much for its own use as it could afford to have, and exported surplus luxuries, which it might well have; surplus necessities, which it was more reluctant to release; surplus people, who wanted out of Kita Point; and finally the final layers on the developing economy of a new station, Kita served penultimately as a cheap warehouse for speculators to store what could be imported from its neighbors and unloaded at a more advantageous time, at a higher price; and most baroque of all, it *manufactured* things out of the pieces, parts, and materials which the speculators warehoused; and employed workers who in turn began to want luxuries, and so on, and so on . . .

Dreadfully crazed, a developing economy. But Kita did produce some of the damndest things, geegaws, items in incredibly bad taste, the product of idle minds and fertile imaginations, and occasionally, just occasionally, some product that actually had unanticipated popularity in some other port.

She scanned the lists for materials in future necessity, for materials all species tended to hoard in time of trouble, and idly, finally, for odd items that might prove an inspiration to some local merchant . . . least reliable: *never,* as a through-passing trader, gamble heavily on fads.

But you never knew what might lurk there, and along with the life and comfort necessities . . . a methane-side curiosity, a compression-jewel that, exposed to oxygen and water . . . blossomed and ablated unpredictably.

Perhaps she'd been dealing with stsho too long. Perhaps she'd been *speaking* stshoshi too long.

But there was a word: *niylji,* art-by-irreproducible-chance.

The image of the exploded object was . . . white with pale mineral stains.

And the legend said you didn't know what you'd get until you uncased it. Or detonated it, as the case might be. An electronic fuse. Pull the tab to admit oxygen, and run for your life.

Art by explosion.

How *big* were the things? Palm-sized. The finished—pieces—were unpredictable. Some went to fragments. Some just puffed up to about the size of one's head.

Done on methane-side, under pressurized oxygen, they mostly eroded to a fist-sized mess. Done on oxygen-side, they absolutely . . . flowered. Somebody on Kita must have found it out the hard way, because it was certainly the first time she had seen the offering. The picture and explanation of the exotic was intriguing, although you could expect the entrepreneur who had actually *dealt* with methane-side (an accomplishment) to get the globes manufactured there, had picked the biggest of the lot.

Certainly worth a try . . . *they* had the franchise. It was a mahen company, trying to market them as geological curiosities, cross-listed under collector's market. They were willing to enter a partnership agreement with a company that could deal in a can lot . . . gods, that was no small number.

Inexperienced entrepreneur. They *hadn't* found any takers. Kita got mostly kif, tc'a, and, mahendo'sat in the trades associated with industrial companies, and traders, a lot of traders.

Call the fellow. See if he'd deal.

The merchant ship Chanur's Legacy, *captain Hilfy Chanur, to Ehoshenai Karpygijenon. In exchange for exclusive trading franchise under your patent of creation we meet your price and will contract with you for future shipments based on sales and returns, patent holder to assume legal liabilities relating to manufacture and compliance with Compact safety codes. We are at dock for the next twelve hours.*

That was a short time frame. But either the seller had the merchandise or he didn't. Either the seller had been waiting long enough with his funds tied up . . . or he hadn't. If it was inexpertly packed, they were making very low-*G* passage, for reasons other than that cargo, which most merchant carriers would worry about.

The merchant ship Chanur's Legacy, *captain Hilfy Chanur, to Tabi Shipping. Order for purchase: item #2090-986, 4 cans. Item #9879-856, 10 cans. Please confirm availability. Order valid for delivery within twelve hours or cancel.*

That would hurry them. But it was a fair-sized order.

The merchant ship Chanur's Legacy, *captain Hilfy Chanur, to Aisihgoshim Shipping. Order for purchase . . .*

And so on, with three more companies.

Then she called Haisi.

"Haisi?"

"I hear, pretty hani." It was not a cheerful mahe. *"What fine doublecross deal you got?"*

"By what I can figure," she said, "you're right."

"What you mean 'right'? What mean, 'right'?"

Agitated, he was. "You know and I know you know. So let's not play games, Haisi. We're headed out, you know we are, and I've got a list of futures I'd recommend to you if you want to play the market."

"Want talk."

"I'll bet you do. Safe voyage, Haisi. See you."

Drive him crazy, that would. She had not an inkling *what* Haisi knew. But Aunt Pyanfar always said, If you're up against a smart opponent, make him *think* himself to death. . . .

Com came live, an excited, effusively grateful Ehoshenai Karpygijenon, who spoke very little Trade interspersed with an obscure mahen dialect.

"Find same one time go bang I unload geo-logics. I say why not sell, lot people want like collect, like make go bang, like real lot many. . . ."

And more like that. The entrepreneur in question was a dock worker who'd sunk his whole savings into buying this can of rocks from a tc'a trader and hiring tc'a to assemble them into tolerably high-pressure methane/nitrogen globes. Detonators came separate. Put them on with double-sided tape. That was very nice to hear. The mahe was not an utter fool.

And, yes, oh, yes, the mahe was ever so excited to learn that a relative of the great, the esteemed Pyanfar Chanur was indeed in port and had expressed an interest, and of *course* the mahe would be delighted to franchise his product via Chanur's well-reputed trading company. . . .

Well-reputed at least where hard bankers weren't taking a close look at the amount of debt Chanur was carrying.

But for a dock worker who'd had a geological grenade blow up in his face, gambled his life savings and had sudden interest from a Chanur ship, after months of advertising in the list at ruinous rates, gods, the fellow offered her everything but a pledge of marriage, and called on mahen divinities to look on Chanur with outstanding prosperity and confusion upon Chanur's enemies unto a thousand thousand generations . . .

One would do, she thought. But the franchise offer was absolutely to the mahe's liking, he was completely thrilled, he was sure the Chanur name would lend respectability to his enterprise . . . she could have *had* the marriage proposal if she'd written it in. Her proposal to put him in for a percentage of sales thereafter was, he professed, full of such real business terms he knew he was in honest hands. . . .

Gods protect the fellow, Hilfy thought. Real business words, indeed.

For the rest she was sure Haisi was investigating every deal she'd just made, and drawing conclusions about the degree of her understanding based on what she was buying.

Which meant Haisi's Personage was going to learn in short order, plans might well be laid in accordance with Haisi's best guess about what she had learned from the stsho, and so much the better.

Aunt had used to din into her juvenile and unwilling ear: Trade isn't about goods. Trade is about information. Goods sit in the warehouse until information moves them.

Gods, she hadn't felt so alive since she was a teenager. She was in a situation up to her ring-bedecked ears, and by the gods she felt . . .

She felt something she hadn't felt in years. She felt . . . as if she had suddenly understood what her aunt had been trying to make her feel, talking about responsibility to the ship and the responsibility of the merchant trade and things that had just gone into an over-hormoned young brain and out the other ear . . . she outright *shared* something with Pyanfar Chanur, over the absent years and across light-years of space.

A feeling Aunt Pyanfar had given up, for . . .

For what Aunt Pyanfar had sworn she despised—politics. Gods-rotted politics, Pyanfar had used to say, cursing the practitioners thereof.

And then she went and joined the forces.

Led them—was the truth. And why?

Hilfy began to see a certain sadness in that. Even to have *sympathy* for Aunt Py, and to think that maybe having *na* Khym with her was a necessary consolation. . . .

And what was she doing wandering down tracks like that? What in the nine or so mahen hells was into her? And *why* had she called Haisi back to rattle him and make him do desperate things, when Haisi going away was what she wanted most?

Pyanfar-nerves, that was what she was experiencing. She'd learned from a past master at chicanery and if she weren't convinced she was half-crazy, she'd say she'd waked up, come alive . . . that she'd challenged Haisi Ana-kehnandian because she was Pyanfar's niece, not Kohan's well-behaved daughter.

Gods, she'd just contracted for a can of exploding rocks. And a franchise on them.

She'd just sent a very dangerous mahen agent wandering through station computer records to ask himself *why* she'd bought what she'd bought, and why station life-support chemicals, basic foodstuffs, and exploding rocks nobody in Compact space had wanted to buy . . . all interested her in the light of what she'd learned from a stsho Haisi didn't know had Phased out of *gtst* former identity and out of *gtst* sanity.

Did hani Phase?

She wondered. She wondered about mahendo'sat.

And listened to the sounds of the *Legacy* giving up cargo to create space for the deals she'd just made.

"I was terribly embarrassed," Fala said. "I'm terribly sorry," and Hallan, cornered in the crew lounge, with no excuse to leave, murmured what he hoped was a polite agreement and tried to think of somewhere else to look but Fala Anify's face and something, anything, that could look like an assigned job.

"Tarras just jokes," Fala said.

"I know," he said.

"You're awfully nice," Fala said.

He tried desperately to find occupation in sorting through the tapes in the rack.

"Tarras and Chihin both joke a lot. It's just their way of being friendly. They really like you."

That didn't exactly help.

"Where is Meras, exactly?"

"Ruun. Near the mountains. It's a real small clan."

"I ought to know. But I wasn't at all good in geography. I can astrogate. That's fine. But I just wasn't interested in planetary stuff. My aunts went with *The Pride*. They used to send me things when they were in port." She bounced down to sit on the end of the couch, which made it harder not to look at her. He must have sorted the tapes beyond twice. He looked stupid, he knew he did, and his ears twitched like a fool's if he tried to keep them up. So he had to look like he was sulking, and that might make her mad.

She asked, in his silence: "Meras isn't a spacing clan, is it?"

"No. No, it isn't."

"How come—?"

"I just wanted to." Gods, they were around to that.

"Anify's up in the mountains. My uncle's a lump and my aunts walked out on him and I think they sort of drifted into *ker* Pyanfar's business. But I'd get presents from space and Anuurn just didn't matter to me. I wanted it so bad, to go to space, my mother used to box my ears about my lessons, and finally she just told me spacers had to know this and spacers had to know that and if I didn't do my divisions and my tables and my geometry and my biology and my Compact history no ship was ever going to want me. But she couldn't make me believe it about agronomy and geography and classical poetry."

He liked classical poetry. But he could understand what she was saying.

"I just nattered my sisters into helping me," he said. "They got me a ride to station. They said I wouldn't last the first winter in the woods. They were right. I was a scrawny kid. And I don't have any aptitude for politics or farming. So if somebody *handed* me a niche in the clans I'd foul it up."

"I think you could do anything you wanted to."

"You could learn geography. If you wanted to."

He hadn't thought that was particularly clever. But she started to laugh, until the all-ship blared out:

"Fala? Where's that systems check? We're in count, gods rot it!"

"I've got to go," she said, and scrambled for the door. But she stopped there and looked back. "Can I bring you anything? Gfi? A sandwich?"

"No. No, I'm fine."

"Fala!"

She ran for it—*not* using the com unit by the crew lounge door. The door shut. He found himself exhaling a pent-up breath and feeling as if he should adjust the cabin temperature.

So they were in count for leaving this port. That was fast. That was very fast. And he was anxious to get out in space where there was something maybe the captain would let him do, so he had an excuse not to be cornered.

They were in count and the clanks and thumps of off-loading cargo kept going. That was a first too, so far as his experience went.

But usually crews wanted to take a few days' rest and liberty on the docks. And the *Legacy* had urgent business, very urgent business, with *two* stsho aboard, now, one of them crazy and the other apt to go that way if *gtst* met him again.

He was absolutely, resolutely, positively resolved he was not going to make one single more mistake on this voyage and he was not going to do anything the captain would disapprove of. . . .

Which meant not getting caught with Fala Anify in the crew lounge. The door opened. Fala put her head in. "You have the *prettiest* eyes," she said. And ducked out.

He dropped his head into his hands. His career in space hung by a thread, he had nothing to think about but stupid tape dramas and the aux boards manuals he was *trying* to din into his reflexes so he wouldn't foul up the next chance the captain gave him, and he had a junior and Chanur relative trying to get his attention.

Gods, *please* let the captain keep her busy.

Chapter 12

"Well, there's *Ha'domaren*."

That from Chihin, at scan. Four hours out from Kita docks and they were approaching jump.

"I don't think I'm surprised," Hilfy said, pursing her mouth. "I *wonder* what he made of the rocks."

"One real happy mahe," Tarras said. "Karpygijenon, I mean. Not our Haisi-lad."

Laughter on the bridge. It was a good sound. Except it was a slightly off-color joke, involving Haisi's morals, and *na* Hallan was probably mortified.

Well, let him be. He could adjust. He would have to.

"You know," Tiar said, "whoever's backing him has got to wish he'd carry cargo."

"I wouldn't bet *where* his mass is. He's shorting his jumps. He probably could do Urtur-Kshshti direct."

"Unless he's carrying a mortal lot of armament," Tarras said—their own gunner . . . if, the gods forbid, they ever had to use what they carried.

Propulsion stuff, Tarras was implying. And that jogged a very bad thought. "Heavy stuff is all government issue."

"So they've got a permit?" Fala asked.

"If they're running with a heavy missile load."

"I wish," Hilfy said, "that we had a source for this Paehisna-ma-to that son claims he's with. I'd like to know if she's in the government."

"If she is," said Chihin, "she's a whole different kind of bad news."

"Probably he's just shorting the jumps," Hilfy said. "Doesn't want to show off to the locals."

"They've got to ask," Tiar said, "the local officials, that is . . . why this ship doesn't offload or onload."

"Gods, no, they're not going to ask," Chihin said. "That

son reeks of influence. That ship's probably real well known here and there."

"Suppose *ker* Pyanfar knows him?" Fala asked.

"Wish *ker* Pyanfar would come get him," Tarras said.

"I *don't* like the idea he's got government ties," Chihin said. "If the mahendo'sat go unstable . . . and the stsho already are . . . that's not good."

"We're out and away," Hilfy said, "and I'll tell you how I'm betting. We're bought into staples and strategics, and as soon as sell it, I'd rather warehouse it on Kshshti for a sale when the stsho do go crazed . . . *or* find some reseller I can talk into taking the whole lot at enough profit."

"Rocks and all?"

"Are we serious about the rocks?" Fala asked plaintively. People put jokes over on Fala. Long, elaborate, and sober-faced ones. And Fala wasn't willing to fall for another one.

"They're tc'a eggs," Chihin said. "That's what they really are."

Wicked dig at *na* Hallan, that was. Hilfy looked in the reflection on a dark screen, and saw Hallan Meras trying to look as if he were utterly absorbed in the boards.

"No tc'a jokes!" Fala said.

"Was that a tc'a joke?" Chihin asked.

"*Ker* Chihin," Fala said sternly.

Getting serious, it was. And Fala hadn't the rank. "Chihin," Hilfy said.

"Aye, captain. No tc'a."

"*Na* Hallan?"

"Aye, captain?"

Kept his temper, he had. She saw his reflection looking at her, ears at half mast, then pricked up respectfully as she delayed answering.

"You may hear about tc'a from time to time. Do you take jokes, *na* Hallan?"

"Yes, captain."

"Can you make them?"

"I—don't think of one, off-hand, captain, I'm sorry."

"Tc'a," Chihin said.

"Chihin!" Fala said.

"I was just suggesting."

"Chihin," Hilfy said, and saw Chihin dip her ears and

lift them again. No gods-be way to stop her but an AP at point blank range. Or losing her temper, which didn't work with Chihin Anify, no more than it had with her cousins.

"Tc'a," Hallan said gravely, and Tarras sneezed, or laughed. Chihin scowled, and Fala grinned at her boards.

"I think that was a joke," Tiar said.

"You've got to tell me," Chihin said.

"That was a joke," Tarras said dryly.

Chihin's ears twitched. Chihin's mouth pursed into what might have been a smile. You could want to kill her. But Chihin was as ready to take it as give. Not from strange men, be it noted. Not from men in general, that *she* knew. Or most wouldn't try: definitely old school, Chihin was, and radiated her willingness to notch ears. Not unlike her cousins.

Fact was, Hilfy thought suddenly, and for no particular reason but many bits and tags, *Chihin* was pushing in a very odd way, for Chihin. Gods-be patient, she was.

And she *knew* the looks young Fala threw in *na* Hallan's direction.

It could get down to a sticky situation trying to get *na* Hallan's highly attractive self off the ship. Which by the gods she was twice determined to do. They had a smoothly functioning crew. They got along. The ship didn't need the scandal, Chanur didn't need the gossip, Meras didn't need it, and if she had her hands on *ker* Holy Righteousness Sahern at this moment she'd give her a lasting remembrance of Hilfy Chanur.

The crew was nattering at each other again. Quibbling over the jump, which was all right—exactitude saved fuel and saved money.

But they were coming up on the mark.

"Stow it. We're away, on the count. Are our passengers set, Fala?"

"*Gtst* excellency says they are."

"On the mark. How's our shadow?"

"Just blazing right along. I *wish* that son'd give us more room. We don't need to bump him in the drop."

"That son or his pilot is probably just too gods-be good. He could jump that ship onto a dinner-plate, you want to lay odds? They don't give just any captain a hunter-ship. And that's by the gods what it is."

"I'd lay odds our stsho passenger might know more about that son than *gtst* is saying."

"I'd lay odds our other stsho passenger did know more than *gtst* is sane enough to say. But we've no guarantee *gtstisi* is going to sort out anything like the stsho that was."

"Spooky," Tarras said. "Spooky lot. *I* wouldn't want to go through jump with a crazy person."

"I wouldn't want to be a crazy person in jump," Tiar said. "Can you imagine?"

"I'd rather not," Hilfy said. "Are we watching where we're going, please? We're coming up . . ."

The coordinates blinked.

She punched the button. The *Legacy* . . .

. . . dropped out of Kita Point space . . .

. . . "Well, well," Pyanfar said.

"Go away," Hilfy said. She didn't *want* her aunt. It frightened her that it *was* her aunt who kept disturbing her dreams—and it was beyond any doubt a dream, it was that comfortable thing the mind did when it didn't want to handle space that wasn't space. Except her gods-rotted aunt wouldn't stay out of them lately. Maybe it was the political stench about the *Legacy* on this voyage. Maybe it was her good sense trying to tell her she'd made a mistake. She wasn't superstitious about the illusions.

Not much, anyway.

"You're indulging yourself," Pyanfar said, sitting on something or another—furniture and rocks materialized when you wanted to sit. And Pyanfar usually sat down when she was going to meddle, parked herself like a gravity sink and insisted on affecting things around her. "Woolgathering's a bad habit, slows your reflexes, fogs your thinking. . . ."

She tried to imagine Pyanfar into the encompassing gray haze.

Pyanfar said, obstinately present: "You *live* in jump, don't you? Just your own little place where you can have your way with Tully and nobody can object. Not even Tully."

Her subconscious was getting vicious.

"Try living in realspace," Pyanfar said. "Try living where you are, Hilfy-girl. Try your own species, for starters."

"Gods rot your interference!" She was as mad as she'd been in years. "If you'd stayed out of my business I wouldn't have married that gods-cursed fool—"

"You're not listening. This isn't a life, niece. Life's not this. Your cousin Chur doesn't time out. Your cousin Chur *sees* the stars in a way I almost can. And you spend your time wishing for what wasn't. *Wasn't*, niece, wasn't ever, and wouldn't be, and couldn't be in a thousand years, and if you want me to say more, I will."

She didn't. That rarely stopped Pyanfar Chanur. But her aunt tilted her chin up in that lock-jawed way she had when she knew she'd won a point, and changed subjects.

"That's a hunter-ship out there. And it wants what you've got. It could blame things on the kif. It could be rid of you, get hold of your passengers and the *oji*, pin the raid on kif pirates, and *still* show up in civilized ports smelling like a spring morning. Think about that. They could be lying silent when you show up at Kshshti. They could clip a vane and strand you, for a least thing they could do. Kshshti's not going to investigate. You *know* what Kshshti is. . . ."

She was on Kshshti docks—red lights flashing, black-robed shadows closing in on them in some trading company's dingy freight access, fighting for their lives, and Tully going down—

She didn't want the rest of that memory. She tried to come out of it. She hadn't flinched at going to Kshshti when she'd known she had to, she hadn't let what had been affect what would be . . . she wasn't a coward, she hadn't been and wouldn't run scared. She'd *go* there, she hadn't given herself time to think and none to recall the jump out of there, the absolute black despair of a kifish hold. . . .

Kshshti was where it had started. That was where she had made the worst mistake of her life, when the kif had been waiting for nothing so much as a chance at any of them.

Leave it to the kid.

She'd been younger then. Hormones in full spate. A fool.

A kif leaned close to the cage, and talked to her, its speech full of clicks from inner and outer rows of teeth.

A kif reached into a cage and devoured small live creatures that squealed and squeaked pathetically. Kif were delicate eaters. Their appetites failed, with other than living food. And nothing went down their gullets but liquids—of whatever viscosity.

She wanted out of this dream.

. . . But it was forever before she heard the beep of the alarm, telling her they were making the drop . . .

. . . here and now.

"That's first dump," she said. And remembered the hunter-ship. "Where's *Ha'domaren?* Look alive! Can you spot him?"

"Got the buoy," Fala murmured.

And from Chihin and a deeper voice almost simultaneously, a set of coordinates, as Tiar's switching sent the buoy system-image to her number one screen.

She was relieved to know where that son was, damned sure.

Meanwhile Fala was talking to *gtst* excellency, who seemed to be alive, and Tiar was handling a message to station.

"Rocks didn't blow," Tarras said.

"That's nice. Advise *gtst* excellency we're going down again."

Pulling the dumps close together. But they'd come in close. Showy precision. She pulled a nutrient pack from the clip and downed it in three gulps.

"Kshshti Station," Tiar was saying, talking to a station central that wasn't going to hear them for another hour. "This is *Chanur's Legacy,* inbound."

Not *The Pride.* Now wasn't then. Maybe on Kshshti docks a stsho was running for cover. Maybe they'd caught Atli-lyen-tlas this time, maybe *gtst* hadn't had time to get out of port. A stsho didn't have the constitution for consecutive spaceflights. *Gtst* had to be feeling the strain of the chase by now. *Gtst* had to be saying to *gtst*self that maybe running wasn't worth it.

Gods-for-sure certain no *kifish* captain had provided *gtst* the comforts they'd given Tlisi-tlas-tin. That kifish ship held the dark kifish eyes preferred, the sullen glow of sodium-lights, the perpetual stink of ammonia . . .

. . . on anyone who dealt with them. . . .

A stsho couldn't flourish in the dark. *Gtst* sanity would go.

On the other hand . . . considering Kita Point . . . maybe it already had. Maybe there *wasn't* an Atlilyen-tlas by now, just a body, and compliance to kifish orders, and no knowledge who *gtst* had been.

Disquieting thought.

One she refused to deal with until she had found their recipient.

They traveled at insystem *v* now, good, peaceful citizens of the Compact. They had the output of the buoy computer that, constantly updated by real events in its vicinity and events transmitted from Kshshti Station, maintained a timewarped relity of its own, shading from the truly real and contemporaneous, or at least minutes-ago truth to the many-minutes-ago truth of Kshshti station.

The station schema was, at the time they got it, some 52 minutes old. That was a benefit of the peace: stations were no longer so paranoid as to think that two enemies might go at each other in full view of a station—or with one linked to its fragile skin. Kshshti Station showed *Ha'domaren* ahead of them . . . where else? And a ship named *Nogkokktik*, captained by one Takekkt, at dock since yesterday.

Closing the gap, by the featherless gods.

Hani traders didn't even *go* to Kshshti. But there were sixty-seven messages for aunt Pyanfar here, one outstanding legal paper suing for information, and a stray package pickup (from a mahen religious foundation?) postage due.

Meanwhile the kifish ship *Kogkokktik* remained at dock—wasn't *talking* to anyone except station, and claimed, through station communications, not to know anything about any stsho passenger.

Likewise *Ha'domaren* received their salutations, welcomed them to Kshshti, and, no Ana-kehnandian was not available. Ana-kehnandian was in his sleep cycle and could not be disturbed. Amazing how the watch officer's command of the pidgin declined as soon as he'd said that.

And was there a stsho ambassador or anything of the sort on Kshshti?

No. The ambassador had taken ill and died last month.

"Gods *rot* it!" Hilfy cried.

"There's something," Tarras said, "going on."

Notable understatement. She gave Tarras the stare that deserved.

"I mean," Tarras amended that, "major."

A long breath, slowly exhaled; unwelcome reminiscence of ship stalking ship, the chill of hearing a safety go off behind one's back. Of seeing a ship die in a silent fireball, and hearing the voices over com . . .

She didn't want those days back again. She didn't want to be in this port playing tag with a kif.

But gods be. She hadn't the habit of giving in. Not even to her aunt. And never in a mahen hell to outsiders, notably not the kif.

She sat with her chin on her hand, thinking through their options, since no one was talking. Kshshti authorities were no reliable source of help—unless someone had come in here and swept out every official who had ever taken a bribe, and she had never heard that that had happened.

Of resources they had . . .

"Deal with customs," she said. "Offer the cans for sale . . . except the rocks. We're keeping the rocks."

"Keeping the rocks," Tarras echoed. "Right."

"If we get a decent offer, let me know. If we don't get a decent offer, look us up an honest warehouse . . ."

"At *Kshshti?*"

"Best we can do. I want everybody on Kshshti to know what we're carrying; and that we're willing to warehouse it if we don't get our offer."

Tarras gave her a curious, thoughtful look.

"Why would a Chanur ship come in carrying strategics and staples, and insist on warehousing . . . if we don't get a top price?"

A line developed between Tarras' brows. "You'll panic the market," Tarras protested. "Captain, . . . begging your pardon . . ."

"They know they're dealing with Chanur. The dockside bartenders probably know we're carrying an important stsho object. We're in this to make a living, cousin. So are they."

"You'll shove the market into a war scare. It'll proliferate. Captain, people can get hurt."

"There's nothing they'll buy they won't need. And that's the market, isn't it, cousin?"

"Not starting gods-be rumors!" Tarras cried, and immediately lowered her voice. "Captain. This isn't right."

She scowled at Tarras, at disloyalty, at a clear challenge to her methods, her character, and her ethics. They had had doubts under Aunt Py's command, too, there had been scary, sticky moments, a good many of them here at Kshshti, but, by the gods, the whole crew had stood by her.

Py had a few more gray hairs, be it known. Py and the four senior crew had been in tight spots before they had ever gotten into the mess at Kshshti, and they'd known Pyanfar was smart enough to think her way through it.

But Tarras didn't know that about her. Tarras knew she'd gotten the captaincy because she was Pyanfar's niece, that was what Tarras knew about her, the same thing all Chanur's rivals knew about her.

"If we let this loose," Tarras began.

"It's already loose, cousin, it's already part of the record, what we got at Kita, what we're doing, who we're carrying, where we're going . . . People *watch* us, people rake over everything we do . . . that message stack is in our files because every gods-be station *assumes* we're in thick with Pyanfar's doings, and all right, why don't we just call up station central and tell them who we've got aboard, what we're carrying, what we think Haisi's up to, why don't we just stand out there and see what happens then, cousin? So we lie to them, so we flash a few pieces of information and let whoever's out there wonder if they've got the picture. If we told the gods-be truth they'd go insane trying to figure out which part of it was a lie."

"I'm not for creating a war scare! I'm not for throwing the whole commodities market on its ear because we've got a problem!"

"So what if there *is* a war? What if, at least, the mahendo'sat and the stsho are maneuvering for position and somebody's going to double cross Aunt Py and the whole glass house is going to come down? How many people are going to get hurt then? How fast will some kifish *hakkikt* appoint himself to grab power? The market's a small casualty, cousin. A tick or two in the price of grain's something the smart traders will ride smart and the amateurs are going to get stung with, but I'm not responsible for that. I can't do anything about small investors' mistakes, I'm trying to keep Chanur afloat, I'm trying not to let this blow up in Aunt Py's face—which it could—or let Chanur's troubles with the *han* erode her influence to keep the peace, that's where my thoughts are running, because if you're right, Tarras Chanur, a good many more people can get hurt if the peace goes than if the market bobbles."

"We don't know what side the stsho is on!" Tarras protested. "We could be doing harm rather than help for all we know!"

"People who do something can always make a mistake. So can people who do nothing."

"That's all fine. Do we know what we're doing?"

"We rattle a few doors and see what puts its head out, cousin. And if you'll do what I ask and publish us on the list, I'll go rattle one in our own basement."

"The stsho?"

"They'd better find out their ambassador here's dead. And the other one's missing. People have already gotten hurt, if you want the morality of it. They're all stsho . . . but they still count. They're still dead. Somebody was willing to kill them. And we've got a piece of the puzzle on our deck."

"*Aye,* captain."

So maybe Tarras was easier in her mind. She wasn't. She walked out of the bridge and past *na* Hallan, who was doing a scrub-down and inventory of the galley cabinets, past Fala, who was doing a life-systems check, and got furtive stares from two eavesdroppers who'd probably rather be in the cold-hold.

Amazing the industry that appeared. She punched the lift button and rode down to lowerdecks, heard the clanks that meant Tiar and Chihin were busy in ops . . . their refueling and their readiness to move was the number one priority, ahead of cargo, ahead of customs, ahead of any other business.

Gods, she hated politics, she couldn't believe she'd said what she'd said up there . . . no wonder Tarras was confused.

She walked to the passenger corridor, signaled her inten-

tion to open the door, but while she was listening for a
response, the door opened, and Dlima, quite nicely painted,
gossamer-robed, quite gracious, bowed and let her in.

"Your excellency," Hilfy began, "how have you fared?"

Tlisi-tlas-tin reclined in the bowl-chair, a cup in hand,
and *gtst* beckoned her closer, quite at ease, quite pleased
with *gtst*self and life in general, as seemed. "Will you take
tea, captain?"

"Honored." It was the only appropriate answer. She
stepped in and settled herself as Dlima brought her a cup
and filled it with graceful attention. "Most elegant."

Dlima fluttered, and subsided, tea in hand, to snuggle up
to *gtst* excellency, no trace of the confused person abandoned at Kita Point.

So, so, and so, Hilfy thought. *Gtst* excellency was not
suffering. One wasn't so certain about Dlima's mind.

"Tell the captain," Tlisi-tlas-tin said, with a gentle nudge
of *gtst* elbow. "Or shall I?"

Feathery white lashes veiled moonstone eyes, and *gtstisi*
squirmed deeper into the nook against *gtst* excellency. "I
have the rare pleasure to make your honor's acquaintance."

"This is Dlimas-lyi," Tlisi-tlas-tin said, with *gtst* arm
about *gtsto* and a look of thoroughly foolish contentment
on *gtst* face.

Good, living gods, Hilfy thought in despair.

"*Gtsto* is a person of such inestimable quality, such wonderful refinement . . . beyond a consolation. I am beyond
fortunate."

So Dlima was something like male . . . as Tlisi-tlas-tin
*gtst*self was something no other sapient species on record
had.

"I am ineffably honored by the event." One didn't refer
to gender in polite conversation. What she was seeing was
intimacy verging on the indecent, by every book on stsho
etiquette she had read. How did one deal with stsho in
this condition?

Don't refer bluntly to the integration, the books said.

Don't use the *gtsto* pronoun without clear permission.
Use the universal *gtst*.

Don't refer to mating.

Don't act embarrassed.

"That *gtst* excellency has discovered such happiness as

my guest," she added desperately, "is a delight and an exquisitely unexpected honor to our hospitality."

Gods rot it. She had business to discuss. Urgent business.

But *gtst* was pleased. *Gtst* sipped *gtst* tea and *gtsto* was quick to refill the porcelain cups.

"Such excellent kindness," she said, and *gtsto* fluttered with pleasure. A spidery white hand reached out to stroke her probably frazzled mane, and she valiantly refused to flinch.

"What a curious and unexpected texture."

If *gtsto* proposed a threesome she was going to run for it.

"Dlimas-lyi," Tlisi-tlas-tin said gently. "Would you absent yourself? There is such tedious business at hand."

Dlimas-lyi bowed, and bowed, on the retreat from the bowl-chair. Tlisi-tlas-tin sipped *gtst* tea and Hilfy did the same.

Thank the gods . . . the third gender was the one that dealt with outsiders, business, and stress.

But outsiders didn't *meet* the sexed genders—or most rarely did.

"I am vastly moved by the trust *gtst* excellency has bestowed."

"Your tastefulness fulfills my extravagant expectations of a foreigner. If I had not come on this voyage I should never have met Dlimas-lyi. As a result of your hospitality I have . . . iiii . . . no, I shall be daring . . . affected a person of such exquisite worth as I could not dream of. *Gtsto* was the offspring of Atli-lyen-tlas, *gtsto*, ruthlessly abandoned, *gtsto*, hitherto *gtste* . . . who most valorously hid from *gtst* enemies until Chanur had come to port. Then, seeing my magnificence, and surely to afford me comfort, *gtstisi* became *gtsto*. . . ."

So Atli-lyen-tlas' daughter had hid from assassins, and, attracted to Tlisi-tlas-tin had become . . . call it male. It didn't bear offspring in this hormonal condition. If she presented what *gtst* had said to the universities at Anuurn or Maing Tol, she could justify a second certificate in Foreign Studies. Scholars would kill, to hear what *gtst* confided to her . . . but scholars were not going to hear it. That was the other thing you learned in Foreign Studies—not to sell out your source.

And in Protocols . . . never to let your source know you had.

"I am overwhelmed," she said honestly. "You are a most gracious guest. Admiration of your virtues has compelled me to personal efforts to fulfill our promises. And I must tell you—we are again frustrated in our attempts to reach Atli-lyen-tlas. The kif ship is here. It will not give us any information about passengers. But we have not abandoned effort."

"They are offensive individuals."

"I concur. Also the mahe about whom I spoke, Anakehnandian, aboard *Ha'domaren*, is notable by his presence at this station and his clear intention to meddle in your excellency's affairs."

"What does your honor propose to do about this annoying person?"

"This is Kshshti. We have no confidence in the authorities to do anything. We shall attempt creativity. Has your excellency any advisement? We would receive it with all attention. Or had your excellency rather wait on further information—" *Never* press a stsho for decision. "—we should certainly attempt to obtain it."

"As a hani, are you contemplating . . . iiii . . . violence of some sort?"

"By no means! But we *are* dealing with kif. Therefore it is a possibility, if instigated by them."

"The Preciousness must be safe!"

"At all costs."

"I am then willing to wait on your wisdom."

Gods *rot* the son.

"I have one other . . . em . . . distressing piece of information. Your ambassador here is dead."

"Wai! This is beyond all coincidence!"

"Is there possibly any advice your excellency could impart?"

"I will think on it."

"Perhaps . . . your excellency could step into that lately vacated place, and advise station authorities from that authority that you disapprove the silence of this kifish vessel?"

"Ambitious."

"But within your excellency's scope. Well within your abilities."

Gtst moon-pale eyes blinked, and blinked a second time, and *gtst* expression never changed.

Until *gtst* took a deep breath. "What would your honor do?"

"I admire the extraordinary graciousness of your excellency to consult a foreigner and understand your excellency is merely curious. I would deliver a message to the station of extreme displeasure, assuming the authority of the late ambassador, without leaving this ship, and demand that information on Atli-lyen-tlas be forthcoming at once."

"This is a very sudden step."

"It will startle them. But no more tasteful approach could gain notice from the authorities of Kshshti."

"A bold venture."

"You have been bold in defense of propriety before this."

Tlisi-tlas-tin's eyes were wide. *Gtst* nostrils flared in rapid breathing. "You instill in me a most curious excitement, distinguished captain."

Emotional imbalance, the book said, is to be avoided at all costs.

"I have never before perceived elegance in such reciprocity of hostility. I feel a poetry in it. Dare I take such advice?"

"Modified of course by your excellency's own wisdom."

"No, no, these are foreigners! And I have confidence in your honor's elegance. Convey such a message. I am most displeased with such behavior. I shall certainly relate their answer to the authorities at Llyene!"

"Your excellency most certainly has the right words. Shall I provide your excellency a communications link to station central?"

"Absolutely! I shall execrate their offspring and their dealings!"

For a stsho, Tlisi-tlas-tin was acquiring very hani sentiments.

For a hani, she was acquiring a very curious empathy for a flat-toothed, group-following stsho.

*   *   *

Gtst excellency certainly rattled the appropriate doors.

"I am outraged to learn of the demise of *gtst* excellency and *gtst* staff! This is villainy! I demand recompense! I demand the immediate cooperation of station authorities! I demand serious inquiry into the kidnapping of *gtst* excellency of Urtur! I demand serious action against the harassment perpetrated against us by the mahen ship *Ha'domaren!* Failure to comply instantly will jeopardize trade with all stsho!"

Strange to say, the Voice of the Personage of Kshshti immediately surrendered the mike to the Personage himself.

And strange to say, the Voice was quickly thereafter on the com, in person, to expedite customs for the *Legacy,* and to declare that officials were on the way to make serious inquiry into the issues raised by *gtst* excellency.

"*Most* efficacious!" Hilfy said, and restrained herself from slapping Tlisi-tlas-tin on the back, *gtst* was so pleased with *gtst*self . . . positively beaming as *gtst* leaned back from the ops room com console.

"Let them reflect upon the consequences I have named! Nothing is idle threat!"

The futures market, on the number two screen, showed an immediate five point rise in strategics and necessities. One could predict an active bidding for the *Legacy*'s cargo.

One could also predict a message from *Ha'domaren* . . .

"You damn lot ignorant hani! You don't listen, this *no* place to act like fool! I want talk! Now!"

"I'll bet you do," she said, stroking her mane into order.

Old nightmares, old sounds, remembered smells . . . now and then traded places in rapid succession. Kshshti docks hadn't changed that much. It was still a raffish, rough place of bare metal, cheap plastics, leaking pipes, and condensation that made rainy weather in the high cold chill of the towering overhead, obscured in the multiple suns of the lamps—hydrogen and sodium spectra that gave everything multiple shadows in bilious colors. It might have been years ago. It might be *The Pride* at dock behind her instead of the *Legacy,* and it might be those dark and dangerous times.

But it wasn't Tully walking beside her, it was Tiar, who hadn't said a word about old history, or anything of the sort, only pounced on her in the airlock with: "You're not going out there alone, captain. And you're not meeting that son by yourself."

So she hadn't gotten away. Orders be damned, Tiar would follow her. Two of them wandering around out there solo was asking for trouble. The dockside office, Haisi had finally agreed—which was line of sight. Haisi refused to come to the *Legacy,* she wouldn't come to *Ha'domaren,* not even close to it: the registry office, where one of them had to go anyway to get the loaders scheduled, was as close a compromise as they could arrive at, and she didn't have that much to say to Haisi anyway.

A couple of lines, like Stay off my tail, and Tell me who you're working for or we're through talking.

"More bars than restaurants," Tiar muttered.

"By actual count, probably." She was trying not to let her nerves get the better of her. It was her personal nightmare, this dockside: kif waiting in ambush, an alley that promised safety turning into a trap . . .

They'd fought, she and Tully had. But there'd been too many of them. And they'd ended up on a kifish ship, a prize Aunt Py had to buy back at cost—

—at a cost that might have changed the Compact forever; or might have had no bearing on the outcome: she could never reason it out. Her wits went down too many tracks when she even tried to figure it, and it was more than meeting a mahen agent that brought her out of the *Legacy* and onto this dockside: she had to go. She had to walk out here and see the place again, and, now that she was here, she could tell herself it was a place no different than other places, and that if things were equal, they would take a liberty here, disgrace their species in several of the bars, and leave Kshshti as they left any port in the Compact, maybe better, maybe worse.

Nothing mystical about this place, at least. And nothing that remarkable about the tall mahe who stood with arms folded outside the station office.

"Go on," she said to Tiar, "take care of our business. I'll talk to this son."

"Bad language," Haisi said. "Shame. Shame you lie."

"Got you, did they?"

"No, just make damn mess."

·"Listen, mahe bastard, you ride my tail one more time in jump I'll have your ears! I don't care how good your pilot thinks he is—"

A hand landed on Haisi's dark chest, fingers spread. "I. I pilot."

"Fine! I'm glad to know who I'm insulting! You're a damned fool, I've seen better, and I by the gods resent your taking chances with us! I don't care who your Personage is, you have no gods-be right to risk my ship!"

"No risk. I damn good."

She jabbed a claw at said chest. "I mean it! I'll sue you for endangerment. My passenger will sue you!"

"Where damage?"

"My nerves, mahen bastard! I'm carrying a stsho and you by the gods know it! You don't do it again!"

"Maybe same you use sense don't make trouble with stsho. Maybe now you talk deal what kind *oji.*"

"No deal!"

·"Oh, now we big confi-dent! Now we got make trouble honest mahe station—"

"*Gtst* isn't kidding, mahe! You want trade shut down, you want that on your Personage's doorstep, you push me."

"You damn fool! You listen me! You want make friend kif? I think you got same real dislike with kif!"

"Kif aren't giving me any trouble right now. You are!"

"Kif give you big lot trouble a'ready. Who got Atli-lyen-tlas?"

"You, for all I know."

"Not true. Kif got."

A blunt mahen claw jabbed *her* in the chest, and she batted at the offending hand. "You listen," Haisi said. "True No'shto-shti-stlen send Tlisi-tlas-tin go you ship?"

"So?"

"True you go visit No'shto-shti-stlen?"

"So?"

"True same got kif guard?"

"You got a point, mahe? Get to it!"

"You *like* kif guard?"

"I said get to it!"

"All same No'shto-shti-stlen got lot kif. Kif got No'shto-shti-stlen. Same in bed like old friend. No'shto-shti-stlen want be number one stsho and here come stupid hani—"

A wave of a dark, blunt-clawed hand. "Believe everything *gtst* excellency got say. Take *contract*. You hold damn *grenade*, Chanur! Thing go bang in you face."

"Same like be friend with damn mahe reckless no-regard-for-life!"

"Same like be smart mahen accent. Chanur *protocol* officer not damn polite."

"I'm always that way with navigational hazards. I have an allergy to fools!"

"You calm down. You listen. You want go bed with kif, you like fine No'shto-shti-stlen. You listen! You aunt be damn fool, all time 'ssociate with kif bandit. Oh, real polite, real nice. But same call you aunt *mekt-hakkikt*, great leader, like real fine . . . All same kif pirate. All same kif steal, kill, lie, I no got tell Hilfy Chanur about kif—"

"You can sit in your own *hell*, mahe, you're way past the limit with me. What I am and what I know, what I did and what I'll do . . . aren't your damn business, they haven't been your damn business, and I absolutely *resent* your trying to manipulate me! No luck, *no* luck, mahe, and you can tell that to the Personage that sent you to maneuver Chanur against itself."

"I try help, hani fool!"

"Stay out of my way!"

"You listen—"

"No."

"You *listen*, hani! You want kif be number one power in the Compact, you keep go what you do!"

"Fine. What's my choice? A smart-mouthed mahe?"

"Don't be fool!"

"I wasn't born one and I won't be made one. Good *afternoon*, Ana-kehnandian. And our regards to your Personage. Maybe she'll send someone polite next time she wants favors from a hani!"

"Fool!"

"Twice a fool!" Shouting was drawing an audience . . . mahendo'sat, a wall of brown and black, no sign of the stsho one might have expected here. "This isn't a place to discuss anything."

"Fine, we go my ship."

"I don't go near your ship. And it's no good you coming

to mine because you're not going to get what you want. We're drawing a crowd. Forget it!"

"Hani!—"

"Forget it, I said!" She walked away, shouldered a couple of mahendo'sat on her way to the registration office door, walked through into the brighter light—with some satisfaction in Haisi's discomfiture at being what no huntership captain ever wanted to be: public.

He didn't follow her in. There were stares all about them, mahendo'sat, mostly, and the inevitable (at Kshshti) clutch of black-robed, cowled kif, whispering in their own language of clicks and hisses.

Hani, was one word her ears caught. Chanur, was another.

Tiar was at the desk. She walked up to Tiar's elbow and waited while the mahen clerk processed the information.

"Not a real happy mahe," she muttered into Tiar's canted ear. "He claims he pilots that ship. Cocky son, says *he'll* miss us, we don't have to worry about collision."

"What did he want?"

"Oh, the usual, warn us about a plot to take over the universe, that sort of thing. What else is new?"

Tiar's ear flicked. "Captain, somebody might speak hani."

Dear, literal-minded Tiar. For the first time in a decade she felt alive, felt—

—by the gods, ahead of the situation instead of chasing after it.

Didn't know what she was going to do, precisely, but she knew what she was doing—and whoever was against them, didn't: that was the name of the game; and quite comfortably she turned her back to the counter, leaned her elbows there, and simply stared back (smiling pleasantly, of course) at the mahendo'sat and kif staring at her.

Crazy as the rest of the family, she thought. It probably onset with age. Aunt Py had been relatively stable until she became captain of *The Pride*.

The business at the desk concluded, Tiar putting in her bid for loaders to their dockside, no, they hadn't *sold* the cargo yet, but they'd put in a destination when they agreed with the loaders, so much per section the load had to go

around the rim of Kshshti, and no, they didn't need provi-
sioners soliciting them. Everything was fine.

Meanwhile she watched the room in the remote but not
impossible chance someone might turn up with a weapon
or some sort of trouble might come through the door.

Somebody like Haisi. Somebody like a few of his crew.
Probably Haisi was thinking hard what to do about trouble-
some hani. And if he was connected to anyone responsible,
gods rot him, he could have produced credentials from people she knew. She didn't need any, to prove to him who
she was.

"I think we're ready," Tiar said.

"Let's walk back," she said. "Sort of watch it."

The crowd at the door moved and let them out onto the
dingy, multiple-shadowed docks. "Haisi's left," Hilfy said
under her breath.

"Wasn't highly helpful?"

"You could say that." Another time-flash, on the smells
and the sights and the sounds of the dock, a bus passing,
on its magnetic guide strip, rattling the deck plates at a
service access. And not a hani in sight . . . just not a place
hani had gotten to, lately. Peace might have brought
prosperity . . . but merchant ships tended to establish quiet,
regular routes. There weren't the disruptions, the wild inci-
dents, the rumors, that tended to send the timid running
and the foolhardy kiting in on the smell of profit: and,
absent those motives, a merchant ship tended to carve out a
route it followed and stick to that route for fear of someone
moving in to compete . . . from a cooperative, rumor-
trading free trade, they'd become misers, close-mouthed on
information, jealously protective of their routes and resentful if somebody moved in on them or undercut their
prices—a mercantile age, it was, a greedy, tight-fisted age.

And what was a hani ship saying by *being* out of its
normal route these days, or what was a mahen hunter-ship
doing sniffing about? That there was something different
about them? That, being Chanur, there was something
other than trade on their minds?

That murdered stsho were significant?

Trust Kshshti to spread the rumors it got. That little business with Haisi was already spreading on a network more
efficient than the station news, bet on it.

"Ever been on Kshshti?"

"No," Tiar said shortly. Tiar had an anxious, distracted look. And she *knew* Tiar hadn't been here: Aunt Rhean hadn't favored this area of space. Aunt Pyanfar had been the one to run the edges, preferentially, using her experience of foreigners to make *The Pride* profitable.

But Aunt Pyanfar hadn't spoken the languages with any great fluency. And *she* could. She'd gone into that study to give herself an edge in getting into the crew, she'd had an aptitude for words, a mind quick to grasp foreign ideas, and a tongue that didn't trip on stshoshi . . . best bribe she could have offered Aunt Py, who couldn't say Llyene without dropping an essential l.

And where had it brought her?

A car swerved near them. "Gods-be *fool!*" Tiar exclaimed.

"*Na* Hallan would be right at home here," she said—nasty joke; but *na* Hallan wasn't here to hear it, and she was in a joking mood, crazy as it was. Maybe it was discovering Kshshti was a real place, and debunking it of the myth of nightmare . . . she hadn't flinched from coming here, hadn't let herself, but by the gods, maybe she should have come here years ago, walked the docks, had a look at the place and told herself . . .

"Kif," Tiar said suddenly, and her eyes spotted them at the same moment, a handful of them standing about in the shadows near the *Legacy's* berth.

Her heart was beating faster. She told herself there was no reason for panic, the station was civilized enough these days that an honest trader could get from the dock office to her ship's ramp without a gun; and that calling on the pocket com would be an overreaction.

One of them was walking toward them, strobed in the multiple shadows of the lights and the flash of a passing service truck. The matte black of his hooded robe was only marginally different from the skin of the long snout that was all of him that met the light. She couldn't see his hands, and while what had once been gunbelts were mere ornament these days . . . knives weren't outlawed.

"Captain, . . ." Tiar said.

"If something happens, break for cover behind the number two console, call station on com, I'll take the number

one, call the ship . . ." She monotoned it, under her breath:
her mind was on autopilot, her eyes were on the kif . . .
all the kif. They were predators, highly evolved, and *fast*
over short distances. And no weapons ban covered teeth.

"Good day, captain. What a rare sight . . . hani back at
Kshshti. How pleasant. Captain Hilfy Chanur, is it?"

"We might have met," she said flatly, ears back and with
no pretense at friendliness. "Have we?"

"That unfortunate incident. I assure you I was light-years
away and not involved. Let me introduce myself. My name
is Vikktakkht, *ambassador* Vikktakkht an Nikkatu, traveling aboard *Tiraskhti.* Perhaps the *mekt-hakkikt* has mentioned me."

"I doubt it. If she has, we haven't been in the same port
in years."

"Ah. And your companion, your chief officer, perhaps."

"Tiar Chanur."

"Another name to remember. How do you do, captain?
And I won't ask you such a meaningless question as why
you're here. I know why you're here. I know where
you're going."

The hair prickled at her nape. The last she'd seen there
were only mahendo'sat back there in front of the office,
but there'd been those inside. And she had no inclination
to wait here through kifish courtesies. "Nice to meet you,
give my regards to the *mekt-hakkikt,* and excuse us if we
don't stand about. We're running a tight schedule." She
took Tiar's arm and started around the obstacle, but there
were more of them beyond him, between them and the
consoles and the ramp.

"Captain," the kif called after her. "Tell Hallan Meras
I'd like to talk to him."

Dangerous to turn her back. It wasn't *Pride* crew she was
with. "Watch *them,*" she snapped, and turned to see what
Vikktakkht was up to.

"Just tell him," it said, with a lifting of empty, peaceful
hands. "We're old acquaintances."

Smug. Oh, so smug.

"Good day, then, Vikktakkht an Nikkatu."

"You have a very good accent."

"Practice," she said succinctly, and turned her back and

swept up Tiar on a walk for the ramp access, past the kif who attended Vikktakkht.

The bastard thought she'd panic. The bastard thought she'd still twitch to old wounds. Wrong, kif.

Dangerously wrong.

"What's he want with *na* Hallan?" Tiar asked, glancing over her shoulder. "What's he talking about? Do you know him?"

"Not yet."

"What's the kid possibly got to do with him?"

"That's what I want to ask *na* Hallan."

They were down on several spices, they'd run low on tissues, and they were out of shellfish, but they certainly had enough staples from here to Anuurn.

"*Ker* Chihin," Hallan said. "*Ker* Chihin. I've got the—"

Straight into the captain's presence.

"—inventory," he said. But by the captain's frowning, ears-down look, by Tarras and Tiar Chanur standing behind her likewise ears-down and frowning, he didn't somehow think they wanted the inventory. He didn't *think* anything he'd done in the galley could have fouled anything else up, unless maybe he'd messed up the computer somehow.

Maybe dumped their navigation records . . . something that bad. . . .

"Vikktakkht," the captain said, and his heart skipped a beat. Or two. He remembered the jail. He remembered the kif he'd talked to every day. He remembered the richly dressed one who'd said . . .

. . . said, "Remember my name. . . ."

"Meetpoint," he managed to say.

"Where on Meetpoint? Was he the one you hit?"

"I—don't know."

"But you know this name."

"He said . . . 'Someday you'll want to ask me a question.'"

"What question?"

"I don't know." He shook his head in utter confusion. "That was all he said. I was in the jail. And that was what he said."

"You know him from there."

"The day they . . . brought me to this ship." He didn't know whether what he'd answered was enough. He tried to think if there was anything else, any detail he could dredge up from memory, but nothing came clear to him, nothing had made sense then and nothing made sense now.

"That's all he said, captain. I didn't know what it meant. I still don't. I don't know what question he's talking about. I don't know what he wants."

"What *would* you ask him?"

"What he means. What he wants. I don't know!"

He was scared, really scared. He hadn't thought about the jail. He had put that place behind him. He trusted them, that there was no way he was going back to that place. But he'd found the way to foul up, it seemed. The captain just stood there looking at him, and finally said, "Are you willing to go out there, Meras?"

"Yes, captain," he said. But the prospect scared him of what else he could find to do wrong. "Whatever you want."

"It's what *he* wants that worries me. Go back to work. I've got some calling around to do. I'll let you know."

He was through with what they'd assigned him to do, but it didn't seem a good moment to bring that trivial matter up with her. He said quietly, "Aye, captain," and took his list and his pocket computer back to the galley to create something to do.

Chapter 13

"Captain?" Fala slid a cup of gfi under Hilfy's hand, and she murmured thanks without looking. Her eyes were on the screen, while the search program located the most recent of the letters for Pyanfar, the ones that had just missed her at Meetpoint, the ones that had been backed up at Hoas and Urtur and Kura and Touin. A lot from mahen religious nuts who wanted to tell the *mekt-hakkikt* about prophecies (one never understood why they were never good news) and a handful who had an invention they wanted to promote, which they were sure the great Personage of Personages would find useful (no few hani were guilty of this sin). There were a few vitriolic communications from people clearly unbalanced. The prize of that lot was from a mahe who had "written four times this week and you not answer letter. I tell you how solve border dispute by friendly rays of stars which make illuminate our peace. You make power color rainbow green and make green like so . . . when Iji orientate in harmony with rainbow color red with orange. Please take action immediate." (With illustrations, and important words underlined.)

But nothing, so far, no hint of Aunt Pyanfar's business in this stack.

A question Hallan Meras would like to ask Vikktakkht.

There *was* no question that she knew of . . . except the whereabouts of Atli-lyen-tlas.

And had the kif known that would be a question, back on Meetpoint, before a kifish guard handed Meras over to the *Legacy*?

Or was it some other thing, something Meras didn't remember or was afraid to say? Pyanfar had passed through Meetpoint not so long before: No'shto-shti-stlen had said

so, and the huge stack of messages assumed she would
come back through that port.

Hilfy sat, and sat, sipped gfi and stared at the blinking
lights that meant incoming messages. The computer was
set for the keywords Atli-lyen-tlas, stsho, ambassador, Ana-
kehnandian, *Ha'domaren,* Pyanfar, hani, and Vikktakkht.
She figured that should cover it.

But a quick scan of what arrived in the priority stack
were mostly inquiries from various mahen companies asking about conditions at Kita. Not a word from the kif. If
kif were talking to each other out there, they were not
talking to her. Possibly they were occupied with the local
investigation. Possibly they were couriering their messages
to each other around the rim, not using com at all.

"Fueling's complete," Tarras reported from downside
ops. *"I've got a good bid on the goods. The market could go
a point higher, could sink a little. My instinct says take it."*

"Do it. Very good. —Tarras, when the loaders get here,
go ahead and open the hold, but keep someone monitoring
the cameras. Whoever's going out, wear a coat, stuff the
pistol in your pocket, never mind the regulations."

She still wasn't panicked about the threat, and she kept
asking herself whether she were really this calm, or whether
she was operating in a state of flashback. Kshshti was the
site of her nightmares, and things were going wrong, but
she found herself quite cold, quite logical. She could wish
Aunt Py were here, she could wish her crew had had some
experience beyond the years-ago skirmish at Anuurn. Out
there on the docks—her one split second of panic was realizing she had to tell Tiar which way to look: *The Pride*'s
crew had known, at gut level, which side to step to, who
would do what, who was likeliest to cover whom. They'd
done it before. They'd worked out the missteps. Paid for a
few of them.

But Aunt Py wasn't here. Sorting the mail stacks, even
with computer search, for some answer to what was going
on . . . could take weeks: the people with the real information were less likely to dump their critical messages in
among the lunatic communications the stations collected in
general mail, unless there was some code to tell *The Pride*'s
computers to pay attention; and she didn't know what keywords to search. Meanwhile it was her ship, her crew. It

was her responsibility to get them through alive, and that
included telling them when to break the law, violate the
peace, the treaties, and the laws of civilized behavior.

It was up to her to decide a course of action on a kif
who had gotten his claws into someone on her ship—before
they signed the contract. Surmise that the stsho contract
was the kif's interest: if it was, surmise that it had known
about that contract, it had expected them to get it, and that
it was up to its skinny elbows in the disappearance of Atli-
lyen-tlas.

They had guns enough aboard—only prudent, never
mind where they had bought them, or how, but it had involved a mahen trader; while weapons were such a cultural
necessity among the kif, such a part of life-sustaining self-
esteem, that the Compact peace treaty had had to except
knives and blades from the weapons ban, figuring that kifish
teeth were no less dangerous, and that it was far better to
have the kif signatory to the peace than not. . . .

Of course, it had taken considerable efforts in translations and cross-cultural studies to explain the word *peace*
to all the several species. Granted, *war* did not translate
with complete accuracy, but kif had understood neither
idea. Kif weren't wired to understand war since they were
at constant odds with each other, cooperated when hani
least would, betrayed when hani would be most loyal, and
hit the ground at birth competitive, aggressive, and (some
scholars surmised) having first to escape their nest before
they were eaten.

As to the last . . . that was speculation. But she did
understand their minds better than most hani. It wasn't to
say she was forgiving. The kif weren't either. Circumstances
either changed or they did not. They had that in common.

She got up from the console, she walked back to where
na Hallan was puttering about in the galley, and said, with
a queasy feeling,

"*Na* Hallan,—how do you feel about talking to the kif?"

"If you want me to," he said.

"You take orders?"

"Aye, captain." Dubiously.

"You foul this up, Meras, and I'll shoot you myself. Lives
are at risk, yours, mine, more than that, do you understand? You go out on the docks. And I'll suggest a question

you can ask this Vikktakkht—that is, if you can't think of
one of your own. Nothing comes to you yet, what he might
have meant?"

"I've been trying to understand what he meant, captain.
I don't. I can't imagine what he's talking about. It doesn't
make sense. It didn't then."

"What would be important to ask him?"

"I don't know . . ."

"Like in the myths, Meras. You get one wish. What
would help us?"

His ears went down and lifted again, tentatively. "Knowing where the stsho is. Getting hold of him. . . ."

"*Gtst*. Not him. They're quite touchy on that score. But,
yes, that's the question—unless you think of a better one."

"I'm sure I wouldn't—"

"I'm sure if you think of one, you'll tell me. I'll find this
Vikktakkht. And if we meet him, if knives or guns come
out, you take orders, and you don't act the fool. Do you
hear me? Do you absolutely, beyond any question,
understand?"

"Aye, captain," he said faintly. But if she had said the
local star is green, she had the uneasy feeling that *na* Hallan
would have agreed.

Give him credit, he would have tried to see the star that
way. But it didn't make Yes the best answer. And it didn't
tell you what he'd do when the shots started flying.

She stared at him long enough to let him think about it.
"I'll see if this Vikktakkht is by any chance in touch with
his ship."

"You," Hilfy said to Fala, in the lower deck main corridor, "work the hold. Can you handle that?"

"No trouble," Fala said, "but . . ."

"No 'but.' I *need* you handling the loader."

Ears went down. "Because I'm the—"

"Because I have things on my mind, Fala! Gods!" She
headed down the corridor toward the airlock, where, if
Chihin and Tiar had gotten Hallan downside, their expedi-
tion was organizing.

The dockers had lost no time: the *Legacy*'s cargo lock
was open, and Tarras, in the requisite coat, was out there
going over the final customs forms.

There was no graceful way for a hani to wear a cold-hold coat on dockside: Tarras could justify it by going back and forth inside, and perspiring by turns. But they couldn't. So that meant the lightest arms, lousy for accuracy, but they fit in a formal-belted waist with no more than a slight bulge . . . and it was their office-meeting, formal reception best they wore.

Except *na* Hallan, who went in ordinary spacer blues. But when they walked down the ramp to the dock, there was no question where the stares went—straight to the hani a head taller than any of them, the one with the shoulders and the mane that matched.

Work stopped. A transport bumped the one in front with a considerable jolt. Hallan watched his feet on the way down. She watched their surroundings and said, under her breath, "I don't expect it, but watch left and right and say if you see anything untoward. *Na* Hallan, if there should be trouble, you do understand that getting your head down doesn't necessarily cover your rear. There's a lot of you. Wherever we go, I want you to have somewhere in mind that you could get to that would be a solid barrier; and where you'd duck to if you had to fall back. I want this whole dock to be a map like that in your head, do you follow me?"

"Yes, captain. I do, thank you."

He might. Boys learned hunting, bare-handed; boys learned tracking and hiding and all such games as fitted them for defending their lives. It was heroics she worried about. Boys learned to show out, and bluff, and trust the other side most often to follow the rules, although *na* Kohan had said once, reflectively, that men learned to cheat in the outback, because some did, and once that was true—you couldn't assume.

So with Chihin and Tiar. The rings in their ears meant a lot of ports and each one of those rings a risky situation, in space or on the docks. But they weren't *Pride* crew, and they hadn't studied this together. She just trusted they were thinking now, better than Tiar had been when she had felt that cross-up of signals.

They walked through the traffic of transports and past the towering gantry that held the power umbilicals, took that route for the next three berths, before they tended around the off-loading of another ship, mahen, as happened.

There were stares. Hallan cast an anxious look back at them and stumbled on a power cable.

"Feet," Chihin said.

"Sorry," he said.

There was the kifish trade office, number 15, opposite berth 28, as listed—an unambitious and functional looking place, conspicuous by the orange light behind the pressure windows; but beyond the section doors was a district where that lighting was the norm, where kifish bars, restaurants, and accommodations mingled with gambling parlors where kif played games no outsider would care to bet on, and where bloodletting was not an uncommon result, at least . . . it had been that way. Maybe they had cleaned it up. One reminded oneself these were civilized times.

But that might be fatal thinking.

"This is the place. If there's trouble, have your spots picked and don't look after anyone but yourself—at least you know what you're thinking and where you're going."

"Too gods-be close to the kif section," Chihin said.

"We're dealing with kif," Tiar said.

Now she was nervous. Now the hair down her backbone must be ridged, and her claws kept twitching in their sheaths.

But not notably scared. It was like sleepwalking, saying to herself, I've done this before, this is the life I chose for myself, this is the way the Compact is, not—

—not the safe, law-hedged half-truths the treaty made. Safe, as long as you're within twenty lights of Anuurn, civilized, as long as it's only hani you deal with, altruistic, as long as you're not dealing with species who have to have that word explained to them.

A methane-breather wove past, in its sealed vehicle; a bus followed, humming along its mag strip. Never *could* convince the tc'a to rely on the magnetics. Something about their sensitivities. You couldn't get that clear in translation either.

That was the truth out here. It wasn't law that got you by. It was good manners. It was giving in on a point that wasn't fatal to you, and might be to them.

There were kif about the door—not unnaturally. And it said something strange, that these kif showed less surprise at them than the mahendo'sat had done . . . these kif simply made soft clicking sounds of attention and backed away to allow them the door. There had been a time when kif didn't share information, when one kif knowing a fact didn't guarantee that other kif did.

Was that a change Pyanfar had wrought, the *mekt-hakkikt,* the leader of leaders, the power over powers, that had unified the kif for the first time in their existence?

Maybe they were all Vikktakkht's. Those were the kind of kif to watch out for, the ones that came in large, strongly-led groups.

The doors opened. They walked into dim sodium-light, into ammonia stink that stung the nose, and Hallan did sneeze, loudly in the silence. Black-robed kif kept nothing like a mahen office. It might have been a bar, a restaurant. There were tables, and one was in among them, and at the end of the room a kif with a silver-bordered robe beckoned to them.

That was Vikktakkht. She would lay money on it. As she would lay money there were guns beneath no few of these black robes.

They walked that far. "Good day," the kif prince said. "So pleased you could come."

"Admirable fluency on your side too."

"I even have a little hani. Not much. But enough to resolve differences."

It was disturbing to hear her own native tongue slurred over with kifish clicks and hisses. And one who learned your language might not be doing so for peaceful reasons.

"This is—" she said, "Chihin Anify. And Hallan Meras you know."

"Delighted. Kkkkt. *Na* Hallan."

"Sir."

"You've done as I hoped—served as my introduction. My character witness, I believe your term is. I behaved well toward you, did I not? You've no cause to complain of me?"

"Not of any kif, sir."

"Not of any kif." A soft snuffling that set Hilfy's nape-hairs up. Kifish laughter. Kifish mockery. They knew no other humor, that she had found. "You're such a soft-spoken hani. Yet they do insist you're quite aggressive."

"No, sir, not by choice."

"Don't try him," Hilfy said sharply. "You don't understand us that well. Between species, one can make fatal assumptions. What do you want?"

There was a soft clicking, a stir of cloth, all about them. The orange light glistened wetly on an analytical kifish eye, black as space and as deep in secrets.

"I said that you would want to ask me a question," Vikktakkht said quietly. "Kkkt. Do you have one, *na* Hallan?"

"Yes, sir," Hallan said. "What are kif doing, transporting the stsho ambassador?"

Hallan's question. Her wording. Don't give the bastard a question he could answer with yes or no. And Vikktakkht made a soft hiss and wrinkles chained up the leathery snout.

"Following *gtst* request," the kif said. "And I will be more informative. I will answer a second question. —From *na* Hallan."

Gods rot the creature. It was his territory, his terms. And if he spoke hani he likely knew what he was doing, insulting Meras, insulting Chanur.

Hallan stayed silent two, maybe three breaths, and she opened her mouth to say they were leaving; but Hallan said,

"What do you gain by doing that?"

Gods, good question, Meras.

"The good will of the stsho ambassador. Next question?"

Another small pause on Hallan's part. Hallan might have exhausted the permutations of the question she had suggested. And *she* was curious what he would ask.

"Is that—all you want?"

"Kkkt. It would be very valuable."

"But," Hallan repeated quietly, respectfully, "is that *all* you want?"

"No," the kif said. What else could a kif say?

But then Vikktakkht added: "The ambassador is at Kefk. Next question."

It was beyond bizarre. In honor, she ought to object and pull *na* Hallan out of this game. But Hallan did not seem to need rescue.

"Are you a friend of the *mekt-hakkikt?*"

Gods, that was a mistake. Kif had no word for friend.

"My alignment, you mean? *With* the *mekt-hakkikt.* Next question."

"What are you asking my captain to do?"

"To go to Kefk, where *I* have allies. There, I will have custody of the ambassador. There, you may ask me one more question."

Hallan flicked an ear in her direction. It was not a time to dispute the matter. There was silence all around them. This is a dangerous kif, she thought.

"Yes, sir," Hallan said.

"Chanur."

"Hakkikt?" Hilfy asked, sure that was what she was dealing with.

"You flatter me."

"I doubt it."

"Kkkt. You're free to go. At Kefk, Chanur."

There were arguments possible with mahendo'sat. None with this. A quality called *sfik* was life and death. And *sfik* in this case meant swaggering out of here on equal terms.

"At Kefk," she said, that being the only choice. She turned abruptly and walked out, praying to the gods her crew did the same, and that *na* Hallan, good heart that he was, didn't linger to push a point.

All the way the kif were estimating them, testing them with soft clicking sounds, the threat of their presence, and cleared their path only at the last moment. They lived as far as the door, and as far as outside, and no one had said anything and no weapons were out. They crossed the traffic pattern of the docks quickly now, toward the cover of the gantries and the shadows beneath the structural shapes.

"Was it all right?" Hallan asked. Now she could hear the nervousness in his voice.

"Good job," she said. "Good job, Meras." Because it had been. It still was. They were out of there.

But in the shadows, in those places where the girders and the double lights overhead made eye-tricking shadows, it was too easy to imagine black, robed figures.

"Kefk," Tiar panted distressedly.

Kefk was across the border, kifish territory. If they were anxious here, doubly so there. Hani were theoretically free to use that port, theoretically safe there, the way kif were theoretically safe at Anuurn, but neither hani nor kif had tested the treaty in regular trade.

Ally of Pyanfar's, was he? Kif could lie. Kif were quite good at it.

"I tell you what," Chihin said. "We sell *our* stsho to the kif."

"I could be tempted," Hilfy muttered. Chihin didn't say the contract had been the stupidest deal they had ever gotten into. Chihin was being polite.

But it was true. And there was no way out of it, at this point. To cut and run wasn't even a remote option, that she could see, not if they hoped to have a reputation left, not if they hoped to have their trading license, not if they hoped the whole gods-be Compact would hang together. Threads were unraveling. Two, now three, mahen stations had lost their whole stsho population to violence.

And they were in it up to their—

Something popped, with that nasty sound of exploding tissue. Chihin stumbled against her, and she yelled, "Cover!" on a half a breath, trying to hold on to Chihin and drag her out of fire if she could figure where it had come from. She saw the red dot on a girder, knew it was from across the dockside, and flung herself behind a pump housing, Chihin actively trying to tuck her legs into shadow and to get up on an elbow.

"How bad?" Hilfy panted.

"Don't know," Chihin said. "Arm. Feels like I was punched; but it works. Sort of." The shock was setting in, and Chihin's supporting arm began shaking, her breathing to shorten. Hilfy had her pocket com out, made a breathless call to the *Legacy:*

"Tarras! Sniper fire! Get to cover."

She was shaking now, light tremors, which was no good. She put a hand on Chihin, and risked a look out where they had been, where none of her party still was, which was good news. Everyone had made cover of some kind.

"Tarras!"

"Aye! I hear," the welcome voice came back. *"I'm calling the police!"*

Police, for the gods' sake! "Tiar, Tiar, do you read?"

"I'm here," a breathless voice said, thin and distorted by interference.

"Don't give position!" she said, and caught a breath of her own. "How are you doing?" she asked Chihin.

"All right," Chihin said thinly. "Give me a minute. We can run for it."

"That's a sniper. Laser targeted. Light arms, but they can cut us up piecemeal. —Tarras, I think the p.o. is the business frontage. Hang on . . ."

She leaned to get her gun from her belt, plain projectile weapon, with a vid display, and she drew a bead on the suspicious alley . . . couldn't get vid resolution. Couldn't go firing blindly down there: she could hit some poor mahen shopkeeper. But she sighted the structural supports where the laser spot had showed, and calculated the angle of fire across the dock. It had to be coming from that alley, that narrow nook between two freight company offices.

"Can we get an ambulance out here? Chihin's hit—don't know how bad. . . ."

A flurry of footsteps arrived out of the shadows. She rolled on her hip and saw red-brown hide, not black robes—a scared, almost too large for cover Hallan Meras.

"What do we do, captain?"

"We keep our heads down."

He was making as small a target as he could, arms locked about legs.

"Ker Tiar's over there," Hallan said, nodding toward the other console.

"Good." A movement and a crash from the *Legacy*'s area. A truck had started up and hit a can. It kept coming. "Tarras! Is that you in the truck?"

Fire hit it and blistered paint. The sniper didn't think it was on his side. She let off a few shots at neutral real estate to keep the sniper pinned. A neon sign. That blew with satisfactory fireworks.

"You see the son?" Chihin asked, squirming for vantage.

"No. Stay down!"

The truck bashed the gantry console and clipped the girder, crash-clang! It reversed and hooked a bumper.

"Gods," Hilfy groaned. Hooked solid. And it wasn't Tarras driving, it was Fala Anify. Fire pasted the vehicle. It rammed forward and jerked the bumper half off, then it hit the gantry console where Tiar was.

"Tiar!" she yelled into com. "*You* drive!"

There were sirens somewhere distant, under the electric whine of the truck as it backed. Hilfy sent a few more shots into the sputtering neon display, figuring only fools hadn't found cover by now.

And the smoke picked out the source of the opposing shots as they pierced the cloud. Chihin had her gun out, firing at the same area. The truck whined away and backward.

Bang!

Hit another truck.

"Gods in feathers!" Chihin moaned. "What are they doing?"

"They're stuck," Hallan said.

"Most gods-be embarrassing mess I ever . . ." Hilfy began, and a shot blistered paint on the girder just past their position. She leaned an elbow on the decking and put another round after her last, then fished in her waist after the spare clip. The truck was still backing and maneuvering, and she shot a distracted look at the situation as it clipped a control console and shot free, leaving the bumper clanging on the deck plates.

She sent a covering fire across the traffic lanes, and saw an open-sided pedestrian transport lumbering along the dockside, oblivious. "Gods!" she breathed. And to the com: "Hold fire, hold fire, there's bystanders out there!"

It wasn't the only vehicle coming. It rolled through. So did a couple of transport trucks thank the gods not carrying volatiles, and a cab. Then fire set up again, with a smell of blistered paint from the other side of the console that provided them cover.

"They made it," Chihin breathed. Hilfy looked; and ducked her eyes behind her hand.

Bang.

Into a loader arm.

"Fifty thousand," Chihin muttered under her breath.

"Where are the gods-be police?"

Another volley hit the console.

Cars passed, wheels thumping on the deck plates, traffic oblivious to the invisible barrage of laser fire and the pop of small caliber weapons.

She leaned painfully on her elbow, a new clip in her gun, with no desire to hit a passer-by.

And saw a bus coming from the other direction.

She pointed to the dark. "Hallan! *Carry* Chihin! Run for those shadows!"

"I don't need—" Chihin began, and yelled as Hallan obeyed orders, grabbed her and darted, brave lad. Hilfy ran behind them, cast a look back as their bus outran their diagonal, and fire popped after them.

Good for the smoke. She pasted rounds back, four of them, and dived for the cover of a girder.

"Keep going!" she panted. "Ramp shadow!"

"Gods be feathered!" Chihin gasped, but Hallan's shoulder cut off her wind, and he ran.

Hilfy fired another shot, darted back one way from cover and ran the other, after *na* Hallan.

A shot burned her arm. That was how close it was as she skidded over the deck plates in a slide for the shadow of a truck.

The far-side tire deflated with a hiss. The mahen dock workers stared back at them out of the shadow with dismay writ large on their features.

Then the police transport pulled up, with yellow-flashing emergency vehicles, ambulances, civil vehicles . . . repair trucks. She put the gun away, out of sight, and looked at Chihin, who had gotten a knee on the decking, *na* Hallan still holding on to her with both arms. Chihin shoved her gun into her belt, out of sight of the police, she had that much presence of mind, as they began swarming around the vehicles. Hilfy started to get to her feet to deal with them, safely behind the cover of the slightly tilted truck.

A shadow turned up next to her, around the truck's back end: Haisi reached for her arm to help her up. She snatched the arm back and got up herself, glaring.

"I try warn you," Haisi said. "I say, watch you back, I say don't deal kif. You got be damn big hurry. . . ."

"Big damn *help,* mahe!"

"You want help? Easy deal. I help carry . . ."

"No!" She barred his path to Chihin, who was bleeding on Hallan. "We got enough help."

"You number one stubborn hani."

"Get away from my ship!"

"Also crazy."

"I said leave! This is *our* business!"

"Maybe better you ask stsho, ask, You want die, you want take ride with kif? Maybe you listen somebody know who friend and not friend."

"Police!"

Haisi cast a look over his shoulder. Police *were* moving in.

"You got answer their question. You got answer, Hilfy Chanur? I got."

"Like you gave me an honest warning! —Officer, this mahe is a gods-be nuisance! I want him off my dockside! Now!"

Haisi said something in dialect, the police officer said something back, put a hand on his shoulder, and the two of them stood in close conference for a moment.

Maddening. But it was what you got, in another species' port. The medics were looking confused, and she motioned them toward Chihin. "There's a surgery on my ship. She goes *there!* Fala, Hallan, stay with her."

"We got regu-lation."

"I got a surgery. There. Go, gods rot it! No argument!"

"Captain?" The com had been nattering at her for the last few seconds. *"Captain? Are you all right?"*

"All right," she said, glumly watching the medics confer with the police and Haisi Ana-kehnandian. "We're coming in. Just keep monitoring."

The Personage of Kshshti to the hani ship Chanur's Legacy, *attention captain Hilfy Chanur.*

We not responsible this fool incident. We do investigation high priority. Hope you not take us do this. Hope well soon your crewmember. We do no charge medical service.

Bill for truck and loader arm attached. Also store sign and panels. You sue party responsible recover damage.

The hani ship Chanur's Legacy, *captain Hilfy Chanur, her hand, to his honor the Personage of Kshshti.*

We thank the police and emergency services for their response. We assure the Personage we took all precautions against endangerment of bystanders, and urge that the party responsible when discovered be prosecuted to the full extent of the law.

We accept the bill for damages and request that, when

responsibility is fixed, the suit be lodged by proxy by your office and monies forwarded to us.

Like your honor we are very glad that no bystanders were injured and ask your honor to extend our personal apologies to affected residents. We did not seek or provoke this assault.

The hakkikt *Vikktakkht an Nikkatu to captain Hilfy Chanur, the hani merchant* Chanur's Legacy, *at dock: Our congratulations for the damage inflicted on your enemies and may you eat their hearts.*

Tahaisimandi Ana-kehnandian, mahen ship Ha'domaren, *at dock, to captain Hilfy Chanur, the hani ship* Chanur's Legacy.

You one damn stubborn hani. See what kif do if you not got respect. They try make you scare. I make guess. They tell you go Kefk, yes? Damn stupid. You go Meetpoint. You can do Meetpoint if you carry no cargo. I escort you Meetpoint.

You friend try look out for you, you all same got arrogant mouth.

You deal with kif you got kif problem. How good now? Repeat same offer. You want ally, you ask. Number one good friend. You call say help, I do.

Chihin called it a patch job. The mahen surgeon, operating in the *Legacy*'s small medical station, called it a close call and wished Chihin would check into hospital.

Hilfy called it a lucky thing it had hit the arm and missed anything irreplaceable. And she was mortally glad to get the dockers furloughed over the next watch, the station medical team off her deck, the airlocks sealed, and the situation down to manageable.

Thank the gods the station had turned a blind eye to the gun law violations.

Thank the gods no sharp station lawyer had yet suggested they'd foreknown there was a risk . . . or they wouldn't have gone out on the docks armed.

To their credit they'd at least advised station that they'd been harassed. To their credit they were Pyanfar Chanur's relatives, and they had special and real reason to worry. As they need not argue with the Personage of Kshshti, *if* the Personage wasn't friendly to Ana-kehnandian's Personage, which was yet to be proved. She *hadn't* liked Anakehnandian's friendliness with the police.

And she didn't like the feeling in the pit of her stomach.

It was all right on the bridge. There was too much potentially to do to let the mind settle in old tracks. There was just trained response and a bucket of water on every fire that popped up . . . in fact, there were gratefully few of them; but that left an old *Pride* hand wondering where the rest were smouldering.

And when she walked back to her quarters to wash the blood and the sweat and the ammonia smell out of her memory . . . when the steam of the shower was around her and sound was down to the hiss of water from the jets, then the thoughts came back, then the mind went time-wandering and couldn't remember then from now—except the shower was fancier and the responsibility was hers. All hers.

With a crew who'd, admittedly, made only one less mistake than the sniper had made, in opting for a silent and invisible weapon on a moving target. *Not* an outstandingly well-informed or accurate attempt, all told.

And that was worrisome . . . that was just naggingly worrisome, because it didn't add up, except to a random lunatic.

Which almost excluded the kif. Kif slept with their weapons. Kif lived and died, among themselves, by their weapons. And a mistake like that wasn't the style of a Vikktakkht an Nikkatu, unless he gave orders to miss.

It wasn't the style of a mahen hunter captain, in a mahen port, with all sorts of resources, either.

Certainly wasn't the stsho, unless a stsho hired some other species to do the deed. *Could* be stsho: they weren't connoisseurs of violence. They couldn't judge the competency or the honesty of the guards they hired. They only paid them well enough that most wouldn't risk their job.

The same as a stupid hani taking a cargo full of stsho trouble, for a price too good to turn down.

They were in it. That was the fact. They were in it and on the dock out there, with shots flying, they'd made mistakes that weren't going to let her sleep tonight, that threatened to replay behind her eyelids and that stacked up ready and awaiting the idle moment, the dark, the unfilled silence. They'd deserved to lose their lives out there. Every time she thought back through it she found a new mistake— theirs, hers trying to cover them, layer upon layer of foul-ups, from the minor glitch to the decision to walk it and not take a taxi.

She scanted the dry cycle, went out damp and sat down on the side of the bed, staring at the locker, within which was a box, and within which was a ragged printout she wasn't supposed to have, and did. Pyanfar likely hadn't even thought about the ops file in her possession when she told her go downworld; or at least, the level of bitterness between them hadn't gotten that high, that Pyanfar had ever asked if she had more than the printout she had officially turned in.

She'd taken it to learn from it, to understand it, and maybe, in her mind at the time, as a slice of Pyanfar to analyze and figure, when no other clues had served. She still resorted to that printout now and again, when captain Hilfy Chanur had wanted to figure out what Pyanfar had done on some point and what Pyanfar's rules and policy had been on some obscure matter of dealing with certain ports—a compendium of experience that Pyanfar had gathered over a long number of years—some were procedures she'd laid down after certain close calls. Some were just universal good sense; and she had borrowed some inoffensive bits of it to cover the gaps in the *Legacy*'s own freer, easier-going rules, rules that didn't have a lot to say about firearms or being shot at. A lot of that manual her own procedures contradicted, because a lot of it was Pyanfar's own perfection-driven convictions, and some of it just didn't apply in the peace Pyanfar had built.

But a lot of it the *Legacy*'s written rules didn't cover, or didn't mention for one important other reason, because somewhere at the bottom of her resentment she was still Chanur clan-head, and *The Pride*'s operations, secretive as they were, and likely dangerous as they were, still relied on those procedures. Things she knew about *The Pride*'s standing orders, *The Pride*'s policies and tendencies and biases and likely choices in an emergency . . . were in that book; and one of them was that you didn't talk about that book existing, you didn't take that printout off *The Pride* and you didn't discuss those policies anywhere but on *The Pride*'s deck, because there were agencies and individuals that would kill to know what was in there.

But she didn't have time to reinvent everything. She didn't have time to modify a system that wasn't working. She'd nearly lost lives out there because she hadn't breached *The Pride*'s security to tell them. They were peacetime traders. The crew hadn't come in with the close-mouthed wariness *The Pride*'s crew had. Tiar wasn't a Haral Araun, she was a good-humored spacer with a pilot's hair-triggered instincts about survival and a common sense about the information flow. Tarras was a canny trader and she scored highest on the simulations with the weapons systems—Tarras had been hours on the simulators, but that didn't say the *Legacy* had ever launched one of its missiles or fired a gun, or done more than drills. The captain had. Gods-rotted right the captain had. And Rhean's crew had handled sidearms and done the drills and given a fair account of themselves in the battle before the peace, so it wasn't that Tarras had never fired a missile in her life; and it wasn't that Tiar and Chihin hadn't run coordinations or been back-up pilots under heavy fire . . . but too many ships had died at Anuurn and Gaohn, of mistakes *The Pride* hadn't made.

Because of The Rules. The by the gods Pyanfar Chanur way of doing things, which *wasn't* the exact way every hani ship ran its business and which she dared not have her peace-time crew talking about when they were home, or complaining about in a station bar.

And maybe in some remote part of her brain she didn't want to think in those terms any longer. The Compact having changed, peace having broken out—hani wanted to get back to their own business, and take their own time, and not worry about wars, and not hurry more than they had to. The crew was all right, they got along, they were still after their few years together, making adjustments to working together: they had their operating glitches and they yelled at each other, but no serious glitches, absent hostile action. It was a different age, and instincts dimmed, and fools could steer a ship or a planetary government: precision just didn't matter any more.

Medium was just all right.

Till you rusted or some amateur assassin nailed you for a reason you wouldn't ever find out.

Mad, she was. That son had shot at her and hit Chihin.

That in itself was a sloppy presumption. Aunt Py would say.

If Aunt Py were here to lecture . . . or to haul a young captain out of the mess she'd contracted herself and her crew into.

Not *experienced* enough for a captaincy, they said in the *han*, and behind her back.

More by the gods experienced than some—especially in the *han*. And a crew that was getting smoother as time went on.

But there wasn't time to let Hilfy Chanur figure out her way. There hadn't been time for Hilfy Chanur to figure things out, all her life.

She got up, took the printout from the locker to her office, and scanned it in.

She edited off all the references to *The Pride*. She searched the crew's names, and subbed in her own . . .

And she came to a dead stop on the matter of Hallan Meras, on the auxiliary post.

Lock him back in the laundry?

Forbid the crew to discuss ops with him, whatsoever?

Why had Vikktakkht wanted him? Why had Vikktakkht insisted to speak to him, except to get a less wary answer, and because Vikktakkht understood hani well enough to know they'd protect him. Meras was a vulnerability in their midst that her own curiosity had made available to the kif, and she couldn't deny that. She had a certain ruthlessness, a certain deficiency of pity, a certain willingness to run risks with other people's lives . . . she had discovered that in herself. Or maybe it was just that nobody planetside understood the things she'd seen, and the experiences she'd had . . . nobody who'd only been a merchant spacer could ever understand . . . and she grew angry, *impatient* with people who were naive, and people who were safe, and protected, and innocent. . . .

But that she'd taken Meras with her . . .

There'd been a good reason. There'd been a kif offering information they had to have. There'd been a kif who could have gone off with what he knew and refused to tell

them . . . (in a mahen hell: Vikktakkht wanted them to
know what he'd said) . . . but at the time, she hadn't known
what Meras' possible connection to Vikktakkht was, when
she'd taken a young man into that place—she had, who
above all knew what could happen to him. And it wasn't
all the good reasons for doing it that upset her stomach. It
was the *angry* reason for doing it. That he wasn't Tully.
That he was hani, and male, and blindly naive as every
charge-ahead brat of a mother's son was brought up to be,
worse, he was a feckless fool of an innocent like Dahan
had been, and the world wasn't kind to them, the old ways
Aunt Pyanfar had sent her back to didn't by the gods work,
and she didn't care what her biology nagged at her to do.
That didn't work either.

And she hated . . .

. . . hated a wide-eyed, good-natured, handsome kid looking at her with worship in his eyes, reminding her what
she'd lost, what she'd compromised, and what she'd let Pyanfar Chanur . . .

. . . strand her planetside to do.

She was by the gods mad. She was still . . . that . . .
mad. . . .

It still hurt. She could look at Hallan Meras and see
her junior over-eager self, and be perfectly forgiving and
understanding; but when she looked at him and *felt*
anything . . .

She got mad, just cruelly . . . mad . . . at things
unspecified.

That was a problem, wasn't it?

Py had cut her off from Tully, cut her off from her
dearest friends in the entire universe, and sent her
home . . . where Py couldn't go again. Ever.

That also . . . was a problem, wasn't it? It was Chanur's
problem. And Py sent her to solve it, and washed off Chanur, and Chanur's politics, and everything to do with the
clan—forever, at that point.

Direly sad thought . . . for Aunt Py.

Py had gotten hot when she'd said no. Py had said
things . . . maybe because Pyanfar Chanur was feeling pain,
who knew? Pyanfar wasn't ever one to say so.

So bad business had happened at Kshshti, so she'd had

a rough few years and she hated her unlamented husband with a passion.

But *why* was she so shaking mad? *Why* in all reason was she sitting here at her reasonably well-ordered desk upset and wanting to do harm to a young man who'd had no connection with Py except a conversation on a dockside years ago. She was a self-analytical person. She had sore spots and she knew where they were: she might have nightmares that made her throw up, but she didn't let them dominate her waking life, and she didn't let them sway her from what made business sense . . . gods-be right she'd deal with a kif if he had a deal she needed. She'd felt no panic at going to Kshshti. She could contemplate going to Kefk, clear over the border into kifish territory, and as it seemed now, they *were* going.

So she didn't have a problem, outside the occasional flashes on the past. She was free, she went where she chose, she had no problems that a financial windfall and peace in the family wouldn't cure.

So why did she feel that way about Hallan Meras?

Instinct? Something that deserved distrust? Something that threatened them? She hadn't read that between him and the kif. And she generally understood her own behavior better than that.

Attraction? She'd noticed he was male. So? She was also exhausted, distracted, and too harried by petulant stsho, pushy mahendo'sat, and a ship with potential legal problems, to think about any side issues.

She just didn't figure it—being at one moment perfectly at ease face-to-face with the lad and then, in the abstract, when he wasn't even at hand—

Enough to make you wonder about yourself, it was, what sore spots did go undiscovered, and what that one was about. But it wasn't about Hallan Meras personally. No. He was just a problem—

A security problem where it concerned the manual. Tell *na* Hallan to keep a piece of information to himself forever, and she honestly had every confidence he'd try. But this was the lad who'd fathered a tc'a by backing a lift-cart.

And, no, she wasn't going to accept him in the crew. Maybe that was what made her mad: that they weren't *The*

Pride, but that given time to work together, their way, her way, they might have become their own unique entity, nothing complicating their lives, no family divisions and feuds, no favoritisms. No mate problems. No jealousies.

And now there wasn't a chance for that to happen. Now she had to do something different, in the incorporation of Aunt Py's ideas, Aunt Py's personal notions, that there wasn't time to take part of.

Maybe that was why the Hallan matter touched her off. Maybe it was watching things go to blazes and knowing that Hallan's slips weren't harmless, that while they were trying to keep his skin whole and interrupting their life and death business to do it, he had become first a vulnerability, and now an obstacle to shaping her crew into what *she* wanted.

That might be it. That might be why she wanted to kill him, because a part of her had been seeing all along that he was that kind of danger.

And with the ship utterly still, the loaders silent, and the only sound the air whispering out of the ducts in the medical station . . . she called in all of them *but* Hallan Meras.

"Come in," she said to Tarras, who hovered at the door. "Sit down. —Chihin, *don't* sit up. Don't push it."

Chihin muttered and stuffed a pillow under her head, one-handed. "Nothing said about not sitting up."

"Orders," she said. "Mine. Nice if someone obeyed them. Just a wistful thought, understand."

There was general quiet. A respectful moment of general quiet. But it wasn't blame she wanted to start with. "First," she said, "the assassin made more mistakes. None of us are dead. The truck—"

"I'm sorry," Fala said faintly.

"It did work," Hilfy said. "It wasn't a stupid thought. Nothing we did was a stupid thought. But the unhappy fact is that we didn't win because we were good. He lost because he fouled up—*if* he lost. We don't know that he didn't accomplish what he wanted. He certainly made a lot of noise. And he's made us have to assume from now on that we're somebody's enemy." She had the thin manual printouts in her possession. She handed them out. "This is procedure from now on. Eat and drink it and sleep with it, but don't talk about it, don't joke about it. *Na* Hallan's not to get this. He's not to know about it. No copies go off this ship, in any form."

Fala was frowning. Chihin was trying to leaf through hers, one-handed, the booklet propped on her knee. Tiar and Tarras gave theirs a dubious look.

"A general change?"

She didn't intend to tell them, she hadn't intended to admit it. But she didn't intend to claim it for a daughter either, and you didn't just rip away everything an experienced crew knew and tell them do differently without saying why. "It's *The Pride*'s ops manual. I'm not supposed to have it. You're not supposed to know it exists. Read it. Follow it. We can talk about it. And maybe we can think of better ways. But we've got to live long enough. This fixes responsibilities, it talks about how many decimal places in the reports, it mandates when we do certain maintenance, it talks about some technical details that are just Py's idea, but let's don't quibble about that for now. She's a gods-be stickler for some details you're going to call stupid and you're going to find some procedures in there that were illegal even before the peace. But my word is, memorize this, understand it, don't mention it in front of outsiders, and I pointedly include *na* Hallan: he's not staying on this ship and he can't take this to another crew. Questions?"

"Are we *going* to Kefk?" Tarras asked.

"Very possibly," Hilfy said. "I don't see anything else to do."

There weren't questions beyond that. Maybe there was just too much reading to do.

"Dockers are on paid rest until 0600. I'd suggest you catch some sleep."

"I'm going to be fit tomorrow," Chihin said.

"You're going to be sore and impossible," Hilfy said. "You can sit watch in the morning. Run com."

"The kid, you know," Chihin said, not quite looking at her, "didn't do too badly out there."

"I noticed that." Of crew, she began to understand Chihin was angry too, in the same way she was, only more so. But Chihin, owing *na* Hallan, was being fair. Chihin set great personal store on being fair, even when it curdled in her stomach—for exactly the same reasons that were bothering her, she could surmise as much and not be far off the mark.

"No reason he can't sit station," Hilfy said. "No reason I don't trust him. He just doesn't know everything. Doesn't need to know. That's all." And Chihin looked somewhat relieved.

So they were going to Kefk. And the captain declared a six hour rest, come lawsuit or armed attack, which made the ship eerily quiet after the clangor and thumping of the loader and the irregular cycling of locks.

Hallan gazed at the ceiling of the crew lounge, faintly lit from the guide-strips that defined the walls and the bulkhead, and listened to that silence.

Fala had said, "It was terribly brave what you did."

Chihin had said, "You drive worse than *na* Hallan." But he couldn't take offense at that, because Chihin, the one who didn't like him, had also said, to him, "Thanks, kid."

She was honest, and she did mean it, even if it choked her; and he *liked* Chihin—he liked her in a special, difficult way, because Chihin was one of the old guard who was willing to change her perspective on things. You could find people sitting on either side of opinions who were there just because things had landed that way and they went along with it; but Chihin didn't just land, Chihin probed and picked at a situation or a person until she could figure it, and she didn't let up. And she made jokes to let you know what was going on with her. And she made them when you deserved it.

Fala—she was younger than he was, in experience. She'd done what none of her seniors had been in a position to do. And backward across the docks was faster and it didn't expose any different surface to fire; which wasn't stupid . . . even if she didn't go a very straight line.

She'd said to him, "Oh, gods, I'm glad you're all right. . . ." in a way that made him go warm and chill and warm again, all the way down to his feet. He'd stood there like a fool, not knowing what to say, except, "You too."

Because a feeling like that was what you got in families, and what a boy always had to give up, and couldn't count on finding again anywhere: you couldn't count on it in the exile you had to go to and you couldn't count on it from whatever clan you fought your way into. If you were stupid and your feelings for some girl led you to fight some clan lord you couldn't beat, it mostly got you in trouble.

That was what was wrong with this going to space, that *na* Chanur wasn't here, *na* Chanur who was also overlord of Anify hadn't the least idea he existed. It was like in the old ballads, like in that book, the young fools meeting in the woods, and things getting out of hand and the clan lord not knowing about it. Only when he found out, *na* Chanur was going to want to kill him, and *na* Chanur and in particular *na* Anify was going to be upset with Fala, which was going to make her sisters and her mother mad at her, which was going to set the family on its ear, at the least, and get *na* Chanur after *na* Meras, who wouldn't be happy with him at all, or with his sisters, for helping him get to space, and creating a problem with Chanur that *he* might have to fight over. Not to mention *na* Sahern, who wouldn't like the publicity of a truly famous incident.

Love was all very well in ballads. It was nice to think that it was possible, and maybe it happened in legitimate relationships, like Pyanfar Chanur and *na* Khym, who had to love each other, besides being married. But in real life it got you killed and messed up families, and he and Fala both had been shaky-kneed from rescuing Chihin, and he'd been wide open. The rush of action, that kind of thing. A moment, an incident, that wouldn't be the same tomorrow, if *he* kept his wits about him. . . .

But the feeling just wasn't going away tonight. He really wanted to go off with Fala somewhere and if he did that, and the captain had *na* Chanur to think about, it just wasn't going to help his case. If he did that, it could make it absolutely certain Hilfy Chanur would get rid of him, and that—

—that, in itself, began to have an emotional context it hadn't had, because he couldn't deal with the idea of not being on this ship. He couldn't lose that. He couldn't risk losing this ship or these people, and he didn't know when he'd begun to feel that way.

Oh, gods, he was in a lot of trouble.

I'm saying get out of here, get out, I won't live with a gods-be fool!

But it wasn't Korin Sfaura, it was a pillow Hilfy found

herself murdering, and she rolled onto her back in a tangle of bedclothes, sorry she hadn't killed him herself—and gotten him out of her repertoire of bad dreams and stupid mistakes.

She'd gone at him in a blind rage and at a vast disadvantage, that was all—though she hadn't been concussed, as Rhean said she had been, as Rhean was in a damned hurry to say, bringing in cousin Harun for what amounted to a power-grab, and a takeover of Chanur's onworld business.

Which Rhean did all right at. And she was rid of Korin without offending Sfaura, which it would have done if she'd done what she wanted to do. Politics. Korin Sfaura was dead. And that business was forever unfinished, and she carried that anger, too, but she wasn't sure all of it was at Korin, who'd been a pretty, vain, brute-selfish fool. And she wasn't sure why she waked dreaming about a man she wouldn't waste a waking moment thinking about.

Fact was, she'd picked him. Her judgment had been that bad. She still tried, on bad nights, to figure out why it had been that dismally bad, or what failing was in herself. And "pretty" about covered his assets. Maybe "stupid" had been another one—because deep down she had wanted a piece of furniture, something decorative, something you didn't have to justify anything to or argue with, because when her father had died she hadn't wanted anybody in his place, no *real* lord in Chanur, just something that would get heirs and not interfere in the politics between her and her aunts.

Only Rhean, who'd been furious at Aunt Py going off from the clan, had had her own ideas how Chanur should face the new age, and what was important, and maybe— no, probably—Rhean had been right: Rhean cared, and Rhean had given up her command and come home and done what needed doing. Mauled her in the doing, granted. She'd been mad as hell about that, and about *na* Harun, and stung by Rhean's reaction to her. But truth to tell, Rhean hadn't been happy to go downworld either. No more than she had been.

The power . . . Rhean liked that. It was a warmer blanket than the husband Rhean couldn't bring home to Chanur and couldn't likely get to that often. A continent away was a good political alliance, and what was a continent but a half an orbit when Rhean had come in from space, but things were different now.

A lot was.

And she wasn't coming home often, herself. Could marry again, but had no enthusiasm for the institution.

There was Meras. Who was on one level like Korin: pretty face, no source of opinions. Amazing how attractive that still was to her. But not fair to a kid with brains; and he'd shown with the kif that he did think, thought right well for a young man, and clearly enough Fala was taken with him, Tarras and Tiar were. . . .

But, but, and but. It was the middle of her sleep cycle, thoughts like that were a credit a hundredweight, and gods rot it, she didn't want to go through the husband business again. He was bright, he would get ideas, and the politics involved at home were already difficult.

Besides, he'd made irrevocable changes in their operations, he was a liability the kif had used to get her into a face-to-face meeting with unforeseeable consequences. She'd been mad enough to kill him a handful of hours ago, she and Chihin both.

She grabbed the pillow and buried her head under it, looking for some place void of images.

Chihin understood what was happening, Chihin had seen it coming before she did, Tiar and Tarras were too good-hearted to space him and Fala was suffering a late puberty. She didn't know what to do with him, she didn't know where she was going to unload him—Kefk, maybe. Let him bankrupt the kif.

At which thought she saw that room, smelled the air, felt the ambient tension kif generated with each other, and remembered there were creatures in the universe to whom the highest virtue was the fastest strike and who didn't lose a wink of sleep over blowing a shipful of living beings to radioactive dust. There wasn't evil. She'd studied cultures too thoroughly and learned too many languages to believe in evil. She just knew that she'd tried to arrange her life so she didn't have to deal with the kif at all . . . and here she was again; and there it was, the kifish offer . . . deal with us, learn to strike faster and first, learn to think our way, because we aren't wired to think yours, we can't understand hani thoughts . . .

You always hoped they could. You were always tempted to believe they might cross that uncrossable gulf and deny their own hardwiring, turn off the triggers that led from impulse to action, the way a hani could turn them on, the way a hani could use instincts that *were* there, if you wanted to tear up the stones civilization laid over them, worse, you could get into the game, dealing with the kif—the very primal-level game, that had its very primal rewards, that competed with civilization.

Hilfy Chanur had delved a bit too deeply into kifish minds. Hilfy Chanur had become expert in the language, to understand what she hadn't understood when it was her alone and Tully, and kif had talked outside the cage. She'd learned words she couldn't pronounce, lacking a double set of razor teeth, and words she couldn't translate, without resorting to words of psychotic connotation in every other language she knew.

But you didn't say crazy, you didn't say evil. They weren't. No more than outsiders were what kif would say, *naikktak*, randomly behaving, behaving without regard to survival.

Which said something about how kif thought of hani . . . and about the frame of mind in which Vikktakkht had asked *na* Hallan to ask him questions.

Asked a hani male, who was notorious for unpredictable and aggressive behavior.

Respect for the aggression? Possibly.

Curiosity? Possibly. Kif had a very active curiosity. Kif could be artistic, imaginative, and curious. All these dimensions. They valued such attributes.

But Hallan Meras . . .

Using him as bait to get her closer, that made sense. That was very kif.

But refusing to talk to her, insisting *na* Hallan do the business they'd clearly come for . . .

It snapped into focus. Gamesmanship. Provocation aimed at her.

Why?

She was Pyanfar's relative, but kif didn't understand kinship, not at gut level. They weren't wired for it. They'd understand it as potential rivalry, but the ones that knew outsiders were too sophisticated to make that mistake. That wasn't what Vikktakkht was doing. It felt too gods-be *personal*.

She rolled onto her back and mangled the pillow to prop her head, staring at the profitless dark. *This* was what she did instead of sleeping, too many hours of free association. Why couldn't the mind come to straight conclusions? Why did she have to think about Hallan Meras, her unwarranted temper, and *kif*, all rolled into one package with Vikktakkht's odd gods-rotted motives? Her mind was trying to put something together out of spare parts. And it wouldn't fit together.

What was the kif—

—*after*, by the gods?

Hunt. Prey. Run or fight and you got their attention. Stand still and you got eaten.

She'd escaped the kif. That story was probably famous among kif. But this kif had been right there at Meetpoint, set up with a prisoner guaranteed to get a hani's attention . . .

In jail for hitting a kif. One wondered how far *that* was a set-up.

Any hani might have done. But he'd just missed Pyanfar, who'd just gone through there. Pyanfar went through, the Preciousness suddenly became an urgent matter that No'shto-shti-stlen *had* to get to Atli-lyen-tlas, and Atli-lyen-tlas ran off with the kif while the mahendo'sat ran in panicked desperation to find out what No'shto-shti-stlen had sent.

No'shto-shti-stlen was guarded by kif. So Vikktakkht had either had access to information or had been pointedly excluded from information.

Atli-lyen-tlas had either run to the kif for transport or fallen into their hands as a prisoner. And who even knew *which* kif? Allies of Vikktakkht? Allies of Pyanfar Chanur?

It was No'shto-shti-stlen who'd rather urgently wanted Hallan Meras in her hands. That urgency might have been stsho anxiety about having a hani male on their hands— stsho didn't understand hani touchiness about their menfolk (stsho were no more constitutionally certain what "male" meant than hani were about the stsho's third gender) but àn old diplomat like No'shto-shti-stlen certainly understood that they were touchy, and that it was an issue that could come back and cause trouble of unforeseen dimensions.

So had Vikktakkht given Meras that odd promise at No'shto-shti-stlen's urging . . . or had he outmaneuvered the stsho to get into the jail and set a trap for her?

And had he set it up for *any* hani ship they could get, or had the fact that a second Chanur ship had shown up . . . either suggested to Vikktakkht a connection between events that wasn't connected, or had it offered him a second chance to involve Chanur in this mess?

He certainly would know who she was. He certainly would know she'd had an experience with kif. That she'd survived and come back to Meetpoint with a ship meant, in kifish eyes, she'd increased in rank, not diminished. In kifish eyes, Aunt Py hadn't thrown her out, she'd promoted her or been unable to prevent her rise. She was Chanur clan head, and one could bet the average kif knew what she was.

So Vikktakkht had ignored her in that interview and let himself be interrogated only by *na* Hallan. If she were kif, she might have casually shot *na* Hallan and insisted he talk to her. That would have gotten his respect. But he was too sophisticated a kif to expect a hani to do that, or to consider it in purely kifish terms that she didn't. He was sophisticated enough, like the Meetpoint stsho, to know that hani didn't tolerate affront to their menfolk, and probably to know that it was indecent for hani males to deal with outsiders, except when sex was directly at issue.

So was it some bizarre kifish joke? Or the careful playing of a Chanur's desire for specific information against her awareness that if she interrupted the game or refused his rules she might not get everything he would give if she didn't?

Interesting question.

She punched the pillow, battered it with her fist and tried for a comfortable spot in the tangled bedclothes, on a mental hunt through tangles of information. Too many weeds and not enough substance. The merest shadow of what she was looking for. Clearly enough, the kif wanted her to cross the kifish border.

Another punch at the pillow, which refused to take a

convenient shape. She wanted to sleep. Please the gods, she could dump it now and not think through what just didn't have an answer.

But what in a mahen hell made all these various pieces add up?

Chapter 14

You could manage to read printout and work cargo. The cold-suit mittens had a spike on the thumb next to the first finger that you could use to turn pages, and Tiar read on, with the loader banging and booming overhead, the giant cannisters fuming from their passage out of the cold-hold into the pressurized so-called heated hold, on their way to the docks.

Chihin had the dockside post, with her arm in a sling and a button-fuse on her temper. ("Gods-rotted nitpicking doesn't gods-be make a *difference,* half this stuff! She says she's going to enforce this? She's serious?")

That was somewhat Tiar's own opinion, but: "Whatever we're doing we better all do it," was her second one. And Chihin, who had read the whole thing, had muttered a surly, pain-infected obscenity and declared *The Pride*'s crew obviously had to bolt everything down and double-check the readouts because *The Pride*'s captain was crazy.

But that was the ship's-manual ops section, and every spacer in the clan knew Pyanfar Chanur was a stickler for neatness, double and triple checks, and logging every sneeze. The part about arms maintenance, about who went armed and where and when and when not to fire, who in a group was to watch what and who was to break for help, what the ship would stand good for and what the captain would not tolerate . . . all that, in Tiar's estimation, was a piece of good sense. The instructions might violate five separate Compact laws and two Trade office regulations Tiar could immediately think of, not mentioning local ordinances, but it was comforting to think that there was a standing order for a rescue, that station police no matter with what warrant were not going to take a crew member from the dockside for any reason whatsoever, and that the ship would seal up and leave dock at any moment to protect its crew, disregarding cargo and disregarding station central control. That was against the law. That would get them barred from trade unless they had a good story for the tribunal.

But Hilfy Chanur said that the new rules were the rules and she was going to follow them. It was a major lot of trouble if they ever had to do what was set down here: lawsuits, blacklisting, the various fines and penalties and loss of license Compact law threatened them with evidently didn't matter, if they had another incident like the one yesterday—because *ker* Hilfy said that was the way it was, and in Tiar's experience, Hilfy meant it, come fire come thunder. *Ker* Chanur had no few faults, but if she promised something this drastic, she wouldn't back down if it went operational.

No wonder they didn't want a copy leaving the ship. They weren't trade rules. They were a manual for . . .

A manual for, it occurred to Tiar Chanur as she thought about it, a *hunter* ship, an outright privateer . . . as, at least in the speculation of some in Chanur clan, that was what cousin Pyanfar had been for certain forces in the *han,* for years before it became official and war broke out and the *han* tried to bring her under control.

If we ever do any of these things, Tiar thought, we'll go over that same edge. At that point we'll no longer be a trading ship: ports won't treat us as one. We might get into port—but no knowing who'd trade with us.

And if the *Legacy* goes over the edge, if Chanur has two ships operating like this . . . how can we claim we're still just another clan? The *han* won't stand for it.

She wasn't sure how she felt about that. The captain was upset, she'd picked that up clearly enough. She'd seen it in Chihin, who was in pain, and had a right to be, but she could read Chihin, and it was more than the pain in the wounded arm, Chihin was rattled, ambivalent about this business, and mad as she'd seen her in years.

Because the kid had saved her neck? Maybe. Chihin really, honestly, didn't approve of the boy being here, particularly on this voyage . . . even if Chihin had grudgingly

called him a nice, cooperative kid— ("Too gods-be nice,"
Chihin had put it. "Mincemeat in a month, at home, at
his age.")

So it probably wasn't the kid, probably not even the
stsho. Chihin was walking around this morning with a head
of steam built up and a set to her jaw that said the pain
was only an aggravation, she was holding it in, and the wise
wouldn't cross her opinions.

Cargo was getting moved—Hallan Meras was back working on the dockside, where Hilfy had sworn he wouldn't
be, but Chihin was out there, unstoppable as a star in its
course, and Fala was working the pre-launch checks and
Tarras was making calls after cargo, running comp and
turning a page now and again, a frown on her face.

That was all right, Hilfy thought. She didn't expect expressions of delight when crew found out they were getting
less sleep and more work. And that the standing orders
amounted to outlawry. She went back to her office to fill out
forms for the station legal office, not something she had
rather do, but if they had a hope of recovering what they'd
just paid out, those forms had to get in before any undock.

Which might come sooner than later.

And there was the matter of the contract, which now, in
printout, could fill three of those cabinets. She'd given up
on printout. She asked the computer to search *borders/
international* and *flight/unwillingness/refusal.*

Search borders/international *negative,* it said with idiot
cheerfulness.

And reported . . . *In the event of the refusal of the party
accepting the contract to deliver the cargo to the designated
recipient . . .*

She knew that part. Double indemnity.

It came up with three similars and a couple of other
irrelevancies. Then: *End of search.*

Tarras put her head in the door, with the same worried
expression. "Captain. I have a question."

Crew was touchy, crew was upset, crew had a right to
be. It wasn't convenient, she was trying to logic her way
through subclauses and obligations and Vikktakkht an Nikkatu's behavior, but crew was a priority above priorities. It
had to be.

"About what?" she asked, and Tarras eased her way through the door, the Book a rolled-up and well-thumbed set of pages in her hands.

"First off, I was calling the police yesterday. I was trying to get them in there . . . that's why I didn't answer you right off. . . ."

"This thing isn't to assign fault. You weren't at fault. The police got there. That's not what this is aiming at. Absolutely not. If you think I'd better have a word about that . . ."

"I understand what I should have done, by this. But if I'd done that, if I'd threatened station . . ."

"You're *authorized* to threaten station. That's in there. It doesn't mean you open with that bid, cousin. You use your well-known sense. I don't fault you that you were talking to the police. I hoped you were talking to the police. I'd rather you were talking with them, I was a little gods-be busy at the time."

"If we did this, we'd be outlawed. It breaks the law, captain. We'd be blacklisted in every port. . . ."

"We'd be alive."

There was silence in the office. A shadow in the corridor. So Tarras hadn't quite come alone. Fala was listening, too, juniormost and without Tarras' disposition to ask the dangerous questions.

Tarras was thinking about the last one, and maybe thinking alive and outlawed wasn't the career she'd planned for herself.

"I'm not qualified," Tarras said, "to make a decision like that. I'm not a lawyer, I'm the super-cargo."

"You're also the weapons master. Don't tell them you're a lawyer. Tell them you're the gunner and you're left in charge and if somebody doesn't do something you will . . . if I were stationmaster, I'd listen."

Another silence. "You mean bring the weapons up."

"If you have to. Yes. And there's no stationmaster going to enforce a warrant on you. That's not a thing we'll accept."

"There's treaty law! There's the treaty Chanur helped make, Chanur can't break it—"

"You're right," she said, "you're *not* a lawyer. You respect a treaty. They won't."

"I didn't sign on for this!" Tarras said, which she supposed might mean Tarras was resigning, which she would regret to the utmost, but Kshshti was the wrong place to do that. Then Tarras said, in a quiet voice, "Are you under Pyanfar's orders? Is that what we're doing?"

Far leap of logic. But Tarras wasn't a shallow thinker. And couldn't be led off.

"Honestly, no. I don't say Pyanfar's not crossed the path of this deal, but there aren't any orders, I don't know where she is—No'shto-shti-stlen, may he rot, said she was off in deep dark nowhere, and *would* we take this boy and *would* we take this marvelous deal he had? It was my judgment to take it. It looked reasonable at the time. It isn't. But that gods-cursed thing has a double indemnity clause, for value *and* shipping fee. We're stuck. We are quite thoroughly stuck, Tarras, it's my fault, my bad decision to deal with that son, *knowing* he's a canny old stsho and a politician, and here we are. If we get out of this alive and unbanished, I'm taking no contracts but steel plate and frozen foodstuffs, I'm through with exotics, and you can write that one down to the captain's youthful foolishness. I don't want to lose you. I for gods-rotted certain don't want you to walk off the ship here: it's not a safe place."

Tarras stood there looking troubled, ears sinking to a backward slant. "I'm not walking out," she said, as if she'd been misunderstood all along. "I'm not complaining about the deal, I just wanted to know if there was something we didn't know."

"I'm not Pyanfar's. I never was Pyanfar's. Does the crew think that?"

"It was my question. I don't say you'd want to lie to us. But, yes, there's been a little question. In some quarters."

"How I got the command, you mean."

"I didn't say that."

"Py's guilty conscience."

"Huh?"

"How I got this ship." Things came clear to her even while she was talking, absolute clear insight. "She trained me. She knew how I'd react. She wanted me as clan head, at least enough to counter Rhean, who's good where she is." She was perfectly aware she was talking to one of Rhean's former crew. And maligning a closer kin to Tarras than she or Pyanfar was. "I'm a radical lunatic. Rhean's solid conservative. She hates the *han* but she'd back it against the universe. And I've peculiar foreign tastes, Anuurn knows that. As long as I'm clan head, the *han* knows Chanur's led by a depraved young radical. They cooperate with Rhean. Anything, so long as Hilfy Chanur doesn't come home." She shrugged. "Rhean and I get along fairly well, actually. We agree on finances. We agree I should be out here. That's quite a lot."

Tarras might have taken umbrage at that. Tarras merely tightened her lip in irony, acceptance of a situation neither of them could mend: that was the way Hilfy read it, and she generally could read Tarras.

"Aye, captain," Tarras said. "That's all right."

"I want you," she said, lest there be any mistaken doubt whatsoever. "I *need* you, Tarras. But I respect your other obligations."

"I'm all right," Tarras said. "The rest of us are. It's just—we needed to know we know."

Ker Chihin was hurting, Hallan could tell that. But she wouldn't stay out of action on the dockside. She kept walking back and forth, overseeing everything, talking to the mahendo'sat in the pidgin, which Hallan couldn't speak, beyond a few words.

He only tried to anticipate what she was going to want, and what was right and what was wrong. He personally, with gestures and his lame command of the Trade, insisted the loaders park on the mark, and the loader kept going without jamming. That was the best help he knew how to be, and *ker* Chihin didn't disapprove it. She finally sat down on the rampway railing and watched, and he took over watching the mahen foreman's check-off on the manifest—brought it back for her approval when they had completed the number two cold hold, and Chihin looked it over minutely and cast looks at the cans last on the truck.

"All right," she said grudgingly, signed it, and he took it back to the docker chief and the customs representative, full of the excitement that came of *doing* something real and useful, and actually dealing with the mahendo'sat himself, talking and being talked to by outsiders—a very queasy, scary situation, if he believed what he'd been taught at home; but it was what he had to do if he ever hoped to find his place among spacers, and the *Legacy* gave him his first real chance.

"You not damn bad," the docker chief admitted. "Not crazy."

"No, sir," he said. "I'm a licensed spacer."

They said something among themselves. Not all of them spoke the pidgin. But they didn't laugh at him, so far as he could detect. And he felt it a delicious wickedness, to be actually making sense to them, and answering a point of debate, which ordinarily a sister would step forward to do in his stead.

He took the completed form back to Chihin and then went back and told them to signal the next load, which was the number three cold hold, and listed for . . . he could make it out . . . Ebadi Transshippers. "All fine, do," the foreman said without quibble, and shouted at his workers. He trekked back to Chihin to say that was what he had just done—she growled at him, but not angry at what he had done, he felt that, only at being asked a needless neo question.

"You're going to wear a track in the deck," she said. "Sit down. They're doing all right. They understood you about parking on the line."

"You speak it?"

"I understand it," she said, and indicated the spot beside her. "Sit. Stay out of their way."

He sat. Chihin didn't sound annoyed, only tired. She said, "We've got cargo coming in. It's Kefk we're going to. You know about Kefk?"

"I know it's on the kifish side."

"It's not a good place. I've never been there. But it's not a place I ever wanted to go."

"I'd go anywhere," he said, consciously pleading his case with her. "If there's a chance I won't come back . . . that's better than home."

"Is it?" Clearly Chihin didn't think so.

"I'm not a fighter. I'm really not. Not for—for what I'd have to fight for if I stayed on Anuurn."

"Is this better?" Chihin asked. He was surprised at Chihin talking seriously with him at all. But it wasn't asking if Chihin was going to reason long with him. He said only the short answer.

"I want to be here."

Chihin was quiet after that. He thought he had exhausted her patience and his welcome, and he should get up and go be useful, somehow. But Chihin reached out and caught his wrist with the hand that worked.

He didn't know what she wanted. He stared at Chihin for what felt like a long, uncomfortable time, and Chihin said,

"You kept your head. You did all right under fire."

"Thank you, *ker* Chihin."

"I don't like your being here," she said bluntly.

"I know that."

She let go his hand. She didn't say anything for a while. Then: "What do you want? What do you really want?"

"I don't understand."

"You want to be out here? You want to spend your whole life running from port to port, with debt at your tail? Or did you think you were going to get rich and be lord of the spaceways?"

"If I knew I could be lord Meras, it wouldn't matter. I don't want what's down there. I want to be here."

"You're a fool."

"They've told me that. But I want it. I don't mind being junior. I am. I just want to be here."

"You tell me that the other side of Kefk."

"I will. I promise you I will, *ker* Chihin. There's nothing ever going to change my mind."

"Kid. The captain wants you out of here."

It hurt. He'd almost hoped. He kept a polite expression all the same.

"Most ships," she said, "are going to want you out of here."

"I'll find someone," he said.

"You can't work dockside. Stations aren't going to want you."

He shrugged, said, with a leaden feeling, "I'll find a way."

"It's sense to go home."

"No, it isn't. I don't want to go back there. It's not sense to do what you don't want."

"Ships have their ways of getting along. Hard enough for any outsider to come in. *The Pride* was . . . under duress. You've got to understand. We get called to station, sometimes in the middle of the night, you haven't got time to dress . . . I mean, it's a thousand things like that. . . ."

"I don't mind."

"Yeah. Well, others do. People talk. And heads have to be cracked for it, I mean, you get no respect if you let somebody make a remark, you know what I mean."

"Yes."

"Yeah. *Yeah,* that's the problem. Shit. —Look at you, your ears are flat."

He brought them up with a mindful effort, started to get up to excuse himself and get back to work, but Chihin took hold of his arm.

"You understand what I'm saying?"

"Yes, *ker* Chihin."

Chihin's ears went down and then to half. She was looking him in the face and he stared right back.

" '*Yeah,* Chihin,' " she said.

"Yeah."

She had let him go, having made her point. He started a second time to get up, and a second time she stopped him.

"Kid. I don't know it will do a bit of good, but I'm going to talk to the captain, say maybe we should do a wait-see. Mind, she might not go with it. But in my book you earned a chance at it. Not because you hauled me out. But because if you hadn't, a couple more of us might have been fools."

With Chihin you often had to replay things to figure out if they added up to favorable. And it seemed that way. He didn't know what to think: she was canny and she was sharp and he was afraid of her jokes.

"You probably could be lord Meras," she said. "If you wanted to."

He shook his head. "Not me. No."

"Your papa approve what you're doing?"

Another shake of his head.

She patted his leg, which he wouldn't have liked, but it was more like a dismissal: Go away, kid. Behave yourself.

He liked Chihin more for that. He got up and went back to work, feeling her watching him, weighing what he did, approving or disapproving. And, gods, he wanted to do just competently well—flashiness didn't impress Chihin. She'd made that clear, about the rescue. Just common sense. Just doing what you were supposed to do, consistently right. And it made sense to him, the way no one else in the universe had, not *ker* Hilfy, not Tiar, not Fala nor Tarras nor his mother or his sisters. Just do your job and be right.

He thought he could do that. He had a real hope of that, if that was the mark he had to reach.

. . . If the party receiving the goods be not the person stipulated to in Subsection 3 Section 1, and have valid claim as demonstrated in Subsection 36 of Section 25, then it shall be the reasonable obligation of the party accepting the contract to ascertain whether the person stipulated to in Subsection 3 Section 1 shall exist in Subsequent or in Consequent or in Postconsequent; however, this clause shall in no wise be deemed to invalidate the claim of the person stipulated to in Subsection 3 Section 1 or 2, or in any clause thereunto appended, except if it shall be determined by the party accepting the contract to pertain to a person or Subsequent or Consequent identified and stipulated to by the provisions of Section 5 . . .

It didn't read any better now than then. And subsection 3 section 1 and 2 and clauses thereunto appended made it abundantly clear: the Preciousness went to Kefk.

And the captain went down to the lower deck, to *gtst* excellency's quarters.

She made her presence known at the door. She received no word from inside. She stood waiting.

There were enough disasters. She opened the door, stsho willing or stsho not, and stared in momentary bewilderment at the drapery spread above the bowl-chair.

It was decidedly occupied. It was decidedly not the moment to call a conference. Stsho were notoriously touchy in personal matters.

That *gtst* excellency and *gtst* companion Dlimas-lyi were bound for Kefk was a matter *gtst* excellency might care to know about. But the captain decided *gtst* excellency could find out about it later.

The captain prudently closed the door, mission not accomplished, question not asked.

Is there a plausible lie I can tell Haisi Ana-kehnandian?

So let Ana-kehnandian wait to be told anything. He was loading up the message board, demanding to speak to her directly.

But the captain had things to occupy her. The captain had to get them out of port before the lawsuits started, as they could, the mahendo'sat being a litigious lot.

That they'd used firearms surely had circulated in the rumor market; and a lie was an unreliable weapon—*gtst* excellency's weapon, if *gtst* chose to use it; and a very dangerous thing in the hands of a hani with no notion what it meant.

She had never thought she might look on Kefk as a refuge.

Everything was ahead of schedule. The loader hadn't jammed, *ker* Tiar was insisting she could keep at it, she was getting used to the ice, and she could go into the heated observation room, seeing that the loader was running without a glitch. The cans just kept locking through the rotary platform and the arm kept picking them up and putting them on the chain and the chain kept rolling, delivering them to the arm that delivered them to the waiting trucks.

"I think you fixed this gods-be loader," Tiar said.

Hallan was very proud of that. *Ker* Chihin was going to talk to the captain, Tiar said he'd actually solved something instead of destroying something, and he *knew* Fala would vote for him. And Tarras had tended to. He had real hope, *real* hope. He just prayed the gods of every persuasion not to let anything happen, just let him finish one job that didn't blow up in his face.

Then a one-can truck showed up, with its load, coming back to the *Legacy's* dockside. The mahen driver got out and talked with the foreman, talked with customs, mahendo'sat (it was always the species name when you were talking about more than one) were waving their arms and saying not a word he understood. *Ker* Chihin was on her feet, but he was closer, and he had the tablet which might tell the story. He didn't think a proper spacer would hang back and wait for his supervisor, it wasn't a male/female business, it was a can trying to come back as damaged or wrongly addressed or not cleared or something, and he didn't want Chihin to have to solve a problem he'd created.

He walked up to the shouting mahendo'sat with his tablet and his manifest list.

"Excuse," he said. "Got list. All right, not all right, why?"

He was reasonably proud of that sentence.

But they waved arms and shouted at him. He looked at the frost-coated can, number 96, lot 3, and he looked at his list, about the time Chihin walked up, asked, "What's the matter? —What matter, here?"

More shouting. Something, when the mahendo'sat recovered their command of pidgin, about the can being a mistake, that the contents didn't somehow match the manifest, that the contents were listed as grain, the buyer had stipulated dried fish, and there was a complete foul-up.

"Load wrong at Kita!" the customs agent said. And the truck driver shouted, "Off my truck! Not my fault what got!"

"*Na* Hallan," Chihin said wearily.

"*Ker* Chihin," he began, with reference to the checklist, but the mahendo'sat thrust an arm past him and began pointing to numbers and trying to clarify what they meant, he supposed, loudly, in his ear.

"Quiet!" he said, louder than he intended to. But they got quiet, all at once.

"Dangerous," the customs agent said, retreating.

"He's not gods-be dangerous!" Chihin shouted, and Hallan folded his tablet against his chest, calling out, "I'm sorry, *na* mahe, for the gods' sake!"

More shouting, then. And the mahen truck driver saying he was going to offload it, now, here, and they could handle it.

"Now wait," Chihin said, but everything was getting confused. He said, "*Ker* Chihin, . . ."

Chihin paid him no attention. The trucker was getting up on the truck bed, threatening, evidently, to roll the can off and let them handle it; which wasn't a good way to treat a heavy canister, and the dockers were yelling.

"*Ker* Chihin," he said, and nobody at all was paying attention.

He shouted, *"It's not our can!"*

And everything was breathlessly quiet after.

"Not our can?" Chihin said.

And everybody started shouting again, but Chihin was looking, while he was trying to point at the manifest entry, which showed a different local weight.

"Make mistake at pickup!" the foreman said. "Got no pilfer here."

"Open can," the customs agent said.

"No," Chihin said. "You take it, you open it. It's not our can. You get it off our dock!"

"The can is list dry fish," the customs agent said. "We open. Find out."

"We've had one gods-be incident!" Chihin said. "Hallan, get off the dock. Now."

"But—"

"Get!" Chihin said, and waved her good arm at the docker crew. "Bomb," she said. "Blow up. Explosive. *Boom!*"

He was horrified. So were the mahendo'sat, who looked dubious, then in one mass, took out across the dock. The truck driver left his truck and ran for the far side of the dock, while the customs agents hesitated beside the suspect canister, big enough to hold a lift-car full of people or a godsawful lot of explosive.

He knew better than to disobey orders. But Chihin was still there, talking on the com to the ship, and he ran back toward her and met her as she started toward the ship, running and trying to cushion her wounded arm.

He didn't ask. He just grabbed her around the waist on the good side and hauled her up the ramp, as the *Legacy*'s outermost gate and cargo lock began to seal.

"Gods rot!" Chihin gasped.

Up the curving yellow tube, and he was dragging her, now. He stopped to snatch her up and ran as hard as he could, for the airlock still open for them.

He set her down there. Chihin had the presence of mind to slam her hand onto the Close plate, and it sealed in a rush. Then she leaned against the wall, and he did, panting from the run, trying to be sure she didn't fall.

That meant an arm around her, and hers around him, and as she caught her balance, all the way around him. He held on, she did, and since the universe failed to end, it ended up with Chihin patting him on the shoulder, and him feeling—very short of breath, very, very short of breath, and her likewise, and then both of them with their arms about each other.

Then it wasn't a thought-out thing at all, they were just holding on to each other, and the bomb still hadn't blown up. Tarras was asking, via com,

"Are you all right? Chihin? Na Hallan?"

But holding on seemed more important than making sense, and breathing more important than answering, and Chihin was all right, that was what he kept thinking, Chihin was the senior officer, she ought to answer if she wanted to.

"Chihin? Na Hallan?"

He hadn't any breath at all to answer.

"They look all right," he heard Tarras say, almost off mike.

And someone else, a younger, outraged voice: *"Gods rot her!"*

He knew he was in trouble then, he didn't want to make Fala mad, but he didn't know how to extricate himself, he didn't even try—he wasn't thinking quite clearly, and knew it.

"Is it a bomb?" the captain's voice said, off mike.

"I think they're calling in the bomb disposal people. The customs agent left."

"I think we're going for Kefk."

"Now?"

"We're off-loaded all but two cans. We call the dealer, say we're unable to deliver those two, we deduct the price, we get our tails out of this hellhole, right now. Advise gtst excellency and gtst—whatever. —Can you get those two fools out of the airlock?"

The captain was up there. Fala was. Tarras. Everybody. There was a bomb on the dock as large as a country haystack and the ship was going to leave. And all he could think of was the face, the very mature face of someone he couldn't believe was attracted to him.

"Got to get inside," Chihin said. And he was scared of the ship going or the can blowing up outside, but more vivid was the thought that Chihin was too different and too common-sense and too steeped in spacer morals to realize he cared for her, he truly, really cared for Chihin—who, with every prejudice she had, honestly made the effort to understand him.

"You gods-rotted idiots, get topside, report in immediately, do you hear me?"

That was the captain. Chihin said a word his sisters never said, then with the rake of a claw through his mane, breathed, "We better do it, kid. Or she'll make us hike to Kefk."

Chapter 15

It was one way to get out of station—station traffic control couldn't rightly refuse an emergency undock, a fire squad had their last two lines shut down, and they were on their way.

With empty holds and running light; with *Ha'domaren* and the kif still at dock and trying to get clearance, Hilfy was sure: one could imagine the messages flying back and forth. If they hadn't a stsho aboard, if they weren't for other reasons reluctant to demonstrate to the universe at large what the *Legacy* could do unladed, they could kite out of here.

As it was they put as much push on it as they dared use and listened to Kshshti try to solve its problem.

With nervous ships trying to bolt, the doors of that section of dock shut, and the whole population of Kshshti under seal-failure warning . . . station police were looking for the driver, who had disappeared, the truck was registered to a warehouse two sections away, no one they'd dealt with, it was stolen, so far as the manager claimed, and the can, which could match almost any ship's ink-written sequence-number for the manifest, didn't match anyone's serial numbers in the embedded ID that a laser reader would pick up: the manufacturer was Ma'naoshi on Ijir. Mahendo'sat. But cans scattered from their point of manufacture by the very nature of carrying freight. It could be anybody's; and being a cold-can, and being handled only by robot and by gloved personnel, any exterior biological contact could go all the way back to the day of manufacture, or to some truck driver on Gaohn station three years ago.

"Probably some load of frozen vegetables," Tarras said.

"Funny thing they haven't cleared anybody to leave the station," Tiar said. "I'm surprised they cleared us."

Station hadn't been at all happy when they declared themselves outbound. Station had threatened them with legal action. But station was silent on that point now that they'd entered the all but vacant traffic pattern and declared course for Kefk.

"We're getting the traffic advisories," Tiar said.

"Guess they've decided not to sue," Chihin said.

There was a markedly subdued atmosphere on the bridge—*na* Hallan hadn't said a thing, Chihin had been remarkably quiet, and Fala maintained a business-only report on the comflow.

One could say one had foreseen this situation, one could toss *na* Hallan off the bridge and lock him in the laundry, except if anyone deserved to be locked in the laundry the senior scantech ought to be first for that accommodation.

"They're saying," Fala said with a sudden edge of alarm in her voice, "they're saying there's something electronic in the can. They're taking it real seriously. Wondering if they should jettison it out the nearest lock."

"Could be a pressure trigger," Tarras said. "That's a cold-hold can. Could be vacuum sets it off, could be thermal. . . ."

"Thermal's the better bet," Tiar said, "rig it through the environmental sensors. Think they want advice?"

"They've probably thought of it," Hilfy muttered, "but gods know . . . relay that, Fala. If they're going to kick it out, better they maneuver it out sun-side. . . ."

"Thing could be thermonuclear for all we know," Chihin said. "Somebody's out of their godloving *mind*. They didn't think we were going to let that thing aboard."

"Enough if it's sitting on our dock when it . . ."

". . . goes off. Plain gods-be timer fuse. They should quit messing around and kick it out of there."

Fala was relaying that, too, she could hear the gist of it. It was useless. Kshshti had to know its possibilities, a few more, maybe, than they could think of.

But the perpetrators had to be on the station or on one of those ships still at dock.

"Methane ship's hit system."

"Gods, that's the brick too many on this load."

Add the confusion of an inbound methane-breather to a stationside catastrophe and there was no telling what could happen.

"They are going to jettison the can," Fala reported. Station wasn't answering its traffic inquiries, wasn't acknowledging calls, evidently . . . station's internal calls were probably reaching crisis proportions. What was coming back to them was the ops channel station made available to nervous ships at dock.

"*Tiraskhti* is breaking dock. The kif have given station five minutes to shut down their lines. Station isn't happy."

"One gets you ten *Ha'domaren* is next."

"Won't take that bet," Tarras said.

"Oh, good . . . *gods* . . ."

Number two screen. A white light flashed on Kshshti's side, flashed and died.

Like a lot of innocent station workers.

There was quiet on the bridge. Station ops com was dead. Then some other channel came through, reporting a major explosion, the decompression of sector 8, ordering Kshshti citizens to remain calm and stay put, ordering ships not to complicate matters by launching.

"Those sons are going anyway," Chihin said. "Gods rot it, there's—"

"Methane-breathers are going out," Fala said. "They're talking to the one inbound, I'm not getting any sense on the translator—all that comes clear is *destruction* and *hani* and *stsho,* and *kif* and *mahendo'sat.*"

Chilling message. You could read a methane-breather's many-brained matrix output in any direction at all. And it all said the same thing.

Chihin said, "Got more than you bargained for, *na* Hallan. Nice quiet trading voyage . . ."

"Let him alone," Fala snapped.

"Touchy. Touchy."

"Cut it out," Hilfy said. "You want to end up as a dust cloud, let's just have an argument in ops."

"She—" Fala began.

"I don't care!" Hilfy said. "I don't care who did what. Shut down! People are dead back there. Let's have attention to what's *important,* shall we? The ones that did that don't by the gods care who else they kill. Does that fact reach you?"

"*Tiraskhti*'s away," Chihin reported. "Going slow. No real hurry. Tc'a are away. Two of them. I'm looking for ID on our station chart. Station's not giving good output, I think they're confused. Hallan, double me, I've got my hands full."

"I want those gods-be ID's," Hilfy said. "Hallan! Acknowledge, rot you!"

"I'm watching, captain."

"*Ha'domaren*'s delivered an ultimatum to station. They get the lines shut down or they let them fall. . . ." Fala was back on the job. With her whole brain, hope to the gods.

Vectors were shaping up. *Tiraskhti* for Kefk, no question. *Ha'domaren . . . Ha'domaren* was going askew from that.

Meetpoint, Hilfy thought, about the time Tiar said it and Tarras swore.

"What's he up to?"

"I don't know." They could *do* it, unladed as they were. They could burn off *V* and go the other direction, as *Ha'domaren* was headed. They could arrive at Meetpoint with their contract unfilled, in debt for money part of which they'd spent, and have No'shto-shti-stlen suing them, along with Kshshti and Urtur. Or they could go to Kefk, alone with the kif.

"Fala. I want to talk to that son Haisi."

"Aye," Fala said. And made the try. It took a while. They were not cooperative.

Then Fala said, "They say he's not available. He's asleep."

"And I'm the Personage of Iji. Tell his crew I had a message for him, but it's not available either."

Fala did that. Of course they offered to take it.

"They—" Fala said.

"No. I'll talk to *him*."

There was a delay. And they were still headed for Kefk.

Then Haisi came through, loud and clear. "*You damn fool, hani. What message?*"

"What's the matter? Tired of our company?"

"*You not learn lesson? Go kif? Good luck. Have nice funeral. What message?*"

"What message? Regards from *gtst* excellency. What was it you wanted to know?"

"*You chief number one bastard, you know!*"

"By the gods right I know, mahe! I know you didn't level
with me. So I know and you don't. Good luck yourself."

What followed was mahen dialect, and the gist of it was
not polite. It was Haisi who broke off the contact, with: *"I
don't tell you go hell, Chanur. You already got course set."*

"Not happy," Tiar said.

Out of Vikktakkht's ship, *Tiraskhti,* not a word.

"Tc'a!" Fala said, and matrix-com shaped up on the
number 4 screen.

Tc'a	tc'a	tc'a	chi	hani	hani
birth	chi	rescue	birth	go	go
danger	danger	danger	danger	danger	danger
see	join	make	divide	danger	danger

"What's this 'birth' business?" Tarras muttered. "I don't
like that."

Neither did she, all considered. "Urtur," she said, of the
inbound tc'a. "That son's from Urtur."

"Mama," Tiar said. "Not son. That's *mama.*"

The hours ran on, and the tc'a sent the same message,
over and over, an accusing presence on the number four
screen persistent as the presence on the scan display. No
one said any more about it, but they didn't have to. It was
in the tail of Hallan's vision, and the scan display showed
the tc'a moving on their heading, not accelerating, but
definitely tending toward a meeting of the incomer and the
two local ships, and all three tc'a vessels transmitting that
same message again and again.

It's my fault, he thought. They blame us.

He had heard how the methane-breathers would attach
themselves to a ship, and how they could change vector in
jump, which physicists couldn't explain, but tc'a and knnn
could do; and chi, who always traveled with the tc'a, aboard
their ships, but no one knew whether they were allies or
pets. . . .

The captain had warned him. The captain had said he
was a fool and the ship could be in danger. Now it was in
danger, from the methane-breathers, in addition to everything else, and the tc'a might follow them into hyperspace,

where the gods only knew what might happen—if they
could change directions, they could *do* things in hyperspace,
and having them attack the ship there, he didn't want to
think about. . . .

Besides which there was the station back there with a
hole in it; and Fala was upset with him, he could see it in
every move she made . . . not that he'd done anything or
promised anything. But *she* thought he'd insulted her—
which he hadn't meant to do. And the crew was feuding
with each other, just the way they said would happen with
men on ships.

Besides which—gods, he only had to think about Chihin
to think how he'd felt down in the airlock, and that was
just *stupid,* he didn't want to do what he'd done, he didn't
want to feel what he felt, he wanted to use his common
sense and straighten things out . . . probably nothing was
even wrong in Chihin's eyes, except for Fala: Chihin probably didn't think it meant anything more than the crewwomen on the *Sun* had thought it did. But Chihin was like
them and unlike, so unlike and so different in the way she
dealt with things that he knew the spacefarers he'd
thought existed, both tough and kind, did exist . . .

And she might not care. That wasn't as important as
her existing.

"Stand by for jump," *ker* Tiar said.

They were going. This part always scared him. And the
tc'a were still there. The kifish ship *Tiraskhti* was pacing
them. People were still dead back there.

". . . here we go."

Fala said, "Why was I so unimportant? Is there something wrong with me?"

He didn't know how to answer that. But Chihin did.

"Nothing but youth," Chihin said, "and time cures that
if you don't make fatal mistakes."

"Let me alone!" Fala said.

He was dreaming. He knew he was, and he could make
it stop. He wanted Chihin and Fala not to quarrel. He
looked away.

But he could see the ship around him as if it were made
of glass. And a shadow of a ship rode close beyond the hull.
Serpent bodies moved and twined within that ship, trans-

parent as their own. He heard sound too low for sound. It quivered through deckplates and through bone, and shrieked until it passed above hearing.

Another ship came dangerously near them, within the proscribed limit, wailing. He leaped up, passed behind Chihin's frozen shape and reached past her shoulder. There was a warning button on that console and he pushed it.

Lights flared red. A siren wailed.

"Go away!" he shouted in this dream, as the shadow loomed larger. It was coming at them. Foolishly he waved his arms to warn it off.

But it swept right through them, with a dimming of the lights, a rumbling of sound, a feeling unlike any heat or cold he remembered.

Then all the ships were beyond them and retreating, the rumbling gone fainter as they became a triple shadow against the stars, smaller and smaller and fainter.

He dropped into his cushion, breathless and numb— raked his fingers through his mane and caught a frantic breath.

People had dreams in jump. That was surely all it was.

". . . Welcome to sunny Kefk," Chihin was saying. "A friendly sodium burner, no planet, but then, we can't have every convenience. . . ."

"Look alive," the captain snapped. "Where's the tc'a?"

"There's *Tiraskhti*," Chihin said, and Hallan saw that, and murmured so, but, searching the scan for the tc'a ships . . . nothing showed. An alarm had gone off in hyperspace. One of those anomalies, Chihin called it. Sometimes things happened.

There were things she'd rather lose track of than a clutch of methane-breathers bearing on their tail at three quarters light. "Gods-be snakes could drop out right on top of us," Hilfy muttered, when scan persistently showed nothing but their kif escort.

"With real luck," Tarras said, "they'll drop on *Tiraskhti*."

"Don't count on it," Tiar said, and toggled a screen change, view of the mass itself: Kefk, sullen apricot orange.

Then it was real to her. The wan sun evoked that reflection on steel bars, that spectrum cast triple shadows on the decking of a kifish prison, lit distant objects in a deathly

imitation of sunlight, recalled the clangs and clash of doors
and the working of machinery. And over all the smell of
it . . .

Sunny Kefk, Chihin said—leading edge of kifish territory,
first of a nest of same-generation suns they favored. Pirate
territory, before the treaty, space no other species ever
wanted to see.

Well, so, this is an experience, Hilfy thought to herself.
The young kid that had come to space with Pyanfar had
longed after the strange and the dangerous. And found it
once. And now again.

You fool, she said to herself—you utter fool, Hilfy
Chanur.

It must be all right, Hallan decided. Everything was normal on the boards. He felt after the nutrients pack. His
hands were shaking. He'd never come out of jump so dehydrated or so wobbly. He could scarcely handle the pack
without sticking holes in it, he couldn't make his fingers
work.

Truth was, he was scared—because there was nothing he
could do for himself, because there was, beneath the ordinary and necessary chatter the crew made, a grimness that
hadn't been there on the jump before this. And it might
very reasonably be because it was a kifish port and their
lives were in imminent danger, and they'd lost track of the
tc'a ships, all of which was very good reason to be upset.

But there was just this subtle turning of the shoulder
Fala did toward him, and somehow she avoided looking at
him or at Chihin at all. Everybody was upset with Chihin,
the captain had been angry on the starting side of jump,
and tempers might be a little cooler on this side—time
passed, in hyperspace, a lot of time; and you didn't come
out of it as intense about most things as you'd gone in,
even if it felt like only an hour later. It was a lot more
than that, the body had had a chance to cool down, and the
angers and the fears had a chance to settle and evaporate if
they had no reason to start up again on this side of jump.

But he'd made a public scene; and as soon as people
weren't busy they were going to remember it, the same as
Fala already did, as his fault.

He wanted to say something to Fala, he wanted to do

something to set it right, but Chihin was sitting between them out there, and his brain was still caught in that sugar-short haze that deprivation created in jump. He was doing well to get himself to his feet when the captain told him: Go fix breakfast, be useful; and his trousers started a slide he only just stopped with a grab at his waistband.

Thank the gods Fala was busy on the bridge and the captain didn't send her too. He couldn't deal with it now. He could scarcely walk. He felt his way into the galley, which was next to the bridge for very good reasons, and giddily, wobbly, started locating the frozen dinners, keeping a hand sort of near safety holds, because a ship coming in from above a sun could find some other ship dropping in too close to them, even yet, and the ship could have to maneuver without warning.

But you didn't plan for it. And probably you couldn't really hold on if it did. Most times the off-duty crew began to stir about just now, only the *Legacy* didn't have that many hands, and they took their breaks close to the bridge, where they could answer a sudden recall. People took breaks as they could, did necessary maintenance on the bridge and thereabouts . . .

And snacked, if they could keep it down. He popped another nutrient pack and shed fur over everything. He *wanted* a bath, but that wasn't possible till they'd reached the inner system boundary: he'd asked for duty and he had it.

Crew was up and moving. Chihin went through, and gave him some kind of a look he didn't dare meet; and came back through again, with her face wet and her mustaches dripping.

He was scared to death she was going to speak. But she didn't. He had some chips, galley's privilege, to keep his stomach from heaving, and it didn't help much. He followed it with cold tea, from the fridge. And he thought he was going to be sick right there, he was cold from the drink and shaking and his stomach was trying to turn itself inside out. He leaned on the counter trying just to breathe, wondering if he should go for the facilities, or if jostling wasn't the right thing to do just now . . .

A hand landed on his shoulder. "You need some help?" Tarras asked, and when he stood against the counter: "You all right?"

"Fine," he managed to say. And prayed to keep his stomach still, while Tarras wandered around and looked in the oven and put a pot of gfi on to brew . . . the smell was almost more than he could take.

"Looks like you've about got it," Tarras said, and came and leaned against the counter beside him. "Hits you hard sometimes."

"Yes," he said.

"You want to go back to the bridge and sit down?"

"No," he said, monosyllabic, desperate. No, he did not.

Silence for a moment. Then: "Prickly situation," Tarras said, and he felt his stomach knot a little tighter, *hoping* she was going to talk about the kif and the ship out there or anything else but—

"You and Fala have something going?"

"No!" He kept his voice low, hoping to the gods they didn't carry over the noise of the fans. "She's just nice, is all."

"She's a good kid," Tarras said. "You're the most attractive thing she's seen in a year. The only. But that's beside the point."

"I didn't—" He didn't want to talk about this. But he was cornered. And Tarras might be on Fala's side, but Tarras was easier to talk to than Fala. "I didn't want to upset her."

"Chihin's a full-time pain. It's her aim in life. You're not obligated to put up with—"

He didn't like Tarras saying that. He didn't want to hear it. He shoved off on his way to the crew lounge, as the only refuge he could think of, and Tarras caught his arm, caught it with a claw, and it hurt, but he kept going.

She caught him again. Most wouldn't. Nobody ever had, on this ship. But he'd learned on the *Sun,* that defying orders meant getting dumped. So he did stop. He didn't have to look at her.

"*Oh,* gods," Tarras muttered. *"Chihin?"*

So Chihin joked. He knew that. It didn't change the fact he felt it in the gut when she walked past him. It didn't change the fact he liked her, and it didn't change the way he'd felt, and the way he still felt.

Tarras let out a breath and leaned against the wall. "Kid, Chihin isn't the most serious-minded soul in the crew."

"That's all right," he said without looking at her.

"Ow," Tarras said, and after a moment of silence. "Look, *na* Hallan. She's *not* a bad sort. —Gods, I've landed in it, haven't I?"

He didn't know what to say. He wasn't mad at Tarras. He wasn't mad at anybody. Mostly his stomach was upset and he wished Fala wasn't mad. The oven timer went off, to his vast relief, and he said, "It's ready."

"I'll call them," she said, and ducked out while he took the dinners out.

And burned his fingers.

Something about *na* Hallan and Chihin . . . Tiar didn't wholly pick it up on the first hearing, with Tarras leaning and whispering into her ear.

And then she didn't believe it. But Tarras said, "It's serious."

She unbelted and got up; and went over to the captain and whispered, "The kid and Chihin? We got a problem."

Hilfy turned her head, looked at her nose to nose and said, ominously: "Problem?"

Tiar made a glance back toward the galley, another to Chihin and Fala, working side by side. An unnaturally quiet Chihin.

"She hasn't said a word."

The captain evidently added the same chain of figures. *Chihin* was deathly quiet. Not a joke. Not an ill-timed jibe about the situation. A lot of efficiency out of her, this last hour, but seldom a word, since the first.

And Fala—Fala was talking to the kif, but not to Chihin.

"I want this straightened out," Hilfy said under her breath. "Good *gods,* we aren't in a place we can afford this! Grow by the gods *up,* can't we?"

"I don't think it's Fala," Tiar said as faintly as she could, and got a second furious look from Hilfy.

"I don't *care* what's going on," Hilfy hissed. "This is deadly serious, cousin. The kif aren't playing lovers' games out there. Breakfast at stations, nobody's getting a break."

Good idea, Tiar thought to herself, and went and relayed the order out loud: "Stay at your posts. We've got a situation shaping up. We're in an ongoing caution, here, we can get the food out, but we're not taking any breaks, got it?"

Let them *think* she and the captain had been consulting

on the kif. Give them something outside the ship to worry about. She went back to the galley. "General alert. Get the trays out here, keep them clipped down, no open hot liquids. Tarras, arms board shakedown."

Tarras' ears went back, and sobriety happened fast, in a hesitation between the oven and getting back to her post.

"Get the trays out," Tiar repeated, to the young gentleman at the center of the storm, and he wiped the scowl off his face and started snatching, ignoring singed fingers.

"That's the way," she said. "Let's move! Get in those seats and get belted. This isn't Anuurn system."

She took her own tray back, grabbed a drink, and settled in while Tarras and Hallan were passing out trays off the stack and drinks out of a box.

The captain started giving system check orders. The captain ordered a condition three on the armament. And that was the first time the *Legacy* had ever brought the weapons board up full. There was a different kind of quiet on the bridge when that order came down, and various stations had to crosscheck with targeting.

Hope to the gods it was a test. The fact of the weapons got to her nerves too, even knowing it was a calculated distraction. The war memories came up along with that long-silent board. Her reflexes wound themselves tight as a spring, and her heart beat a little faster.

Because now that she thought of it, kif being kif, the arms computer on *Tiraskhti* was probably completely live. And probably had been, from the moment the kif went for jump toward his own border.

There were mining craft. There were construction pushers. They looked, except the major kifish ships at dock, like ordinary miners and pushers in any system in hani or mahen space.

Well they might, Hilfy thought. They were probably stolen.

But the ships at dock at Kefk had no look of honest traders. Huge engine packs. Cold-haulers that could release their cargo or blow off their mass with the flip of a toggle: hunter-ships, clutching cargo cans in their clamps, like many-legged insects; purported tankers, whose tanks probably were false mass.

"Captain," Fala said, "Vikktakkht."

"I'll take it," she said, and a clicking, soft voice said,

"Chanur captain. You'll go first and we'll dock beside you. For convenience' sake."

"Understood. And do we understand this trip is worth our time?"

"Put Meras on. I find him amusing."

I won't talk to you, that meant. "Later," she said shortly, and punched out. "—Tiar, I want one course laid out for Meetpoint, and courses for Kshshti, Mkks, Harak, Lukkur, and Tt'a'va'o. . . ."

"Tt'a'va'o!"

"If we go out of here with kif on our tail, *better* the methane-folk than Lukkur. But we take any vector open and deal with it when we get there."

"Aye, captain."

"Their prices aren't bad," Tarras said.

Tiar said: "Gods, load their cans aboard, after Kshshti?"

"I was kidding," Tarras said. "Kidding, cousin."

The *Legacy* still had the option to run, Hilfy thought. She could do a sudden break and sight on Meetpoint and get the *Legacy* out of here.

But you didn't run from kif. If you ran, they were wired to chase—sometimes literally; sometimes, more dangerously, they merely wrote you down for weak and apt for more abstract predation.

A Chanur—if she ran—would weaken Chanur clan in the eyes of all kif. It would prompt ambitions. It would encourage seditions. Assassinations, to which Aunt Pyanfar was all too vulnerable.

But rational as everything had seemed the other side of jump—they weren't just the only hani ship in system, they were the only foreign ship anywhere: not a mahendo'sat, not a stsho, not a methane-breather showed in the revolutions of the station. Not even a ship that was clearly a merchant ship.

"Those are hunters," Tiar said. "Every one of those are hunters. What's building here?"

"I don't like this," Fala said. "I really don't like this."

"Don't panic," Hilfy said quietly. "Never panic with them. It's a guarantee of problems."

"Chanur," came the kifish voice over her earpiece, *"you're clear to dock now."*

"Thank you, *hakkikt.*"

The schematic flashed up, glowing lines channeling their approach and their mandated velocity.

Scary enough on a small station. But the numbers, the indicators, were kifish characters, base 8.

"They're offering automated approach," Fala said, in a voice a little higher than her wont. "They say they have translation programs."

"So do we and No. No input from them to our computers. Absolutely not. Just calc it."

" 'Just calc it,' " Chihin muttered in a tone of desperation. "Calc it" was herself and Tiar and their computers, in rapid cross-check calculation. While they were aimed at Kefk Station like a missile.

But numbers started popping into the display of their own instrumentation, distance to dock, rate of spin, moment of contact.

"Fine it down," Hilfy said. "That's a stand-down on the weapons board, Tarras."

"Confirm, captain. Standing down and locked."

The kifish station was protesting their irregular approach. The Kefk control center wanted, they *demanded* computer to computer contact. They ordered them to brake and abort. The emergency flasher was on the station output. And if there was a time *Tiraskhti* could be absolutely certain weapons were at stand-down, it was now, preparing for dock. If there was a time *Tiraskhti* could get a shot that might miss their own station, it was in the next few minutes.

"By the book," Hilfy said calmly, and kept her claws out of the upholstery of her seat. "Extra decimals. Let's not have a repair bill at this place."

Station was still objecting. From *Tiraskhti,* moving in just behind them, there was silence that meant, one hoped, observant respect, waiting to see whether they could justify the defiance of station control, respect that grew or died a dangerous death on the skill with which they touched that docking cone.

And bet that the station wouldn't be quick to warn them of an impending mismatch.

"Rotation shutdown," Tiar announced, and the next queasy part started, as the *Legacy* gave up its own internal *G* and the ring coasted into null. They were coming very slowly, at a tangent to the station's scarily rapid spin. This was the point where panic could set in, and a point where, as an insystemer, you were either licensed to do this or you linked to tenders who were, and got cabled in.

Or you docked, like the ore carriers, in null at the mast.

A long hauler didn't have either option. Just the mobile cone that gave you a little guide and a tangential approach, and took you up at a distance that wouldn't let you crack the bulkheads, before the grapple snagged you and the docking assembly took you into sudden 1.2 *G* sync with the station's rotation.

Tiar made a lightning reach: the *Legacy*'s portside thrusters shoved her one way and then braked that motion null. A quick flurry of small adjustments truing up with the calculated appearance of the cone. You didn't track the cone until the last moment, didn't see it until it was too late to brake: and station computers weren't talking to theirs: theirs was just talking to their engines, now that it had the intercept plotted.

There was the cone. The last correction to put the probe right down its throat and a brisk shove from the mains that put the *Legacy* into the guide zone at intercept with the station's rate. The jolt of capture rang through the bow; the contact moved the whole passenger ring for a stomach-wrenching second and pressed them down in their seats. Grapples banged, the braces touched and boomed against the hull . . .

"And we are *in*," Tarras declared.

In. At a kifish station. Solo. Wonderful. "Good job," Hilfy said in the collective breath that followed. "Good job. The crew earns one for that."

By the Book, Fala was already sending her fueling request, arguing in the Trade with the Kefk dock authority.

And by the Book, by Aunt Py's lately sacred and mandated Book, there would be no bending on that point: fueling and offloading of wastes before the *Legacy* ever opened an airlock, Aunt Py's procedures, in places Pyanfar didn't trust; and a very good idea, in Hilfy's present estimation— but meanwhile a kifish *hakkikt* would, publicly, be compelled to wait on his hearing until that fuel was in, and that was a dangerous slight, in a game of volatile egos: *sfik*, kifish elegance, was life: offend it, and expect attack, as they expected a move of you under like circumstances. Kif were much on etiquette . . . their own etiquette, to be sure, a pricklish protocol of arms.

An air of competency, of hauteur, of willingness to take extreme action . . . with the firepower to back it up: those were assets; while generosity was the gesture of a superior to a servant; kindness fell in the same category; and loyalty lasted as long as a leader had *sfik* intact.

Courage? Fierceness in a fight was a plus. But so was deviousness. Self-preservation was the highest virtue, and risking one's neck could be self-preservation—if it demonstrated an arrogant competency to potential rivals.

A whole other universe, Hilfy thought to herself, a very solitary, dark, and aggressive universe. You could do anything you could carry off with style—or at least with sufficient firepower on your side. That counted.

Come to Kefk, Vikktakkht had insisted, certainly aware that she had been a prisoner among his kind, and perhaps, as many kif were surprisingly educated, aware that hani minds, prone to emotional might-have-beens and what-ifs entirely alien to his species, might come adrift from what was, and wander into delusion . . .

Vikktakkht might hope for that.

But there was a benefit to fluency in other languages. She could *think* in kifish: see things from kifish perspective—and, so doing, feel the shift in her heartbeat, the change from twice a month hunter to hair-triggered, hard-wired round the clock predator.

If they expected her to have balked at coming here— not likely.

To panic at being here—she had yet to reach that state.

Here I am, *na* kif. What am I thinking? What will I do? Do you know me that well?

You made me half crazy. If I'm here alone, I must be one tough bastard of a hani.

And you know I don't like you much. So *you're* taking the chance, *na* kif. You'd better pay off. Because by your rules—if you cross me, I can only start a war by *not* blowing you to hell.

"They're going to fuel us," Fala said. "They say they want payment transferred at the same moment they start pumping."

"That's fine. We'll transfer it bit by bit. They reach an eighth of our load, they get an eighth of the payment. In international trading certificates, and *they* can run courier and check the authenticity. *No* computer links to their bank. And we're not talking to Vikktakkht or anybody of his ilk until those tanks are full." Gods, did she know this routine! In her sleep, along with the nightmares. "—Tarras, get a bid on the datadump. We're still traders, that's what we're here for, let's not give them any other ideas. And everything in cash."

Hallan, quietly: "There's some sort of light keeps blinking on com."

"That's the incoming mail," Chihin said. "It's autoed. Com incoming isn't feeding to any computer that's connected to anything; it's deloused before it's available to read and it won't store. Don't worry."

Hilfy keyed up the file list, wondering what in all reason messages could be waiting for the *Legacy* at Kefk.

Pyanfar's mail.

Of course it was.

Chapter 16

The hoses coupled on, the pumps started their heartbeat thumping. Are we safe to do that? Hallan wondered nervously, as he'd begun to worry about every contact with this station. But the crew was busy, there were probably safeguards engaged he didn't know about, and if the ship had to refuel, it had to, for them ever to get out of this port; and there was no use asking stupid questions in that department.

Na Vikktakkht had invoked his name again, and meant to talk to the captain through *him*, and he didn't know why. Maybe it was something to do with the incident on Meetpoint. Maybe they just wanted to get him off the ship where they could arrest him, after which . . . after which he had heard very gruesome stories about kifish habits.

But maybe he wasn't as scared of that as he ought to be. And maybe he shouldn't be upset about what Tarras had said about Chihin. Chihin wasn't upset. She explained things to him where he was ignorant. She acted as if everything was all right. Fala was still ignoring him, but Fala was too busy to pursue a feud, and he didn't know whether she was madder at him or at Chihin. Fala was somebody who wanted anybody; that was the way he read her, fair or not. While Chihin didn't *need* anybody, Chihin didn't expect favors, either, she just did what came into her head and she was honest, it didn't matter that he wasn't the most important thing that had ever happened to her, he was just—

—out of his gods-cursed head when he thought about her being beside him; and he didn't know why, or what the logic was. It was certain enough she could live without him, he never doubted that. It was—

It was that Chihin just didn't expect to have anything,

and people didn't get close to her, because of her jokes, and if somebody told her back off now, she probably would.

And *if* she backed away, he couldn't stand seeing her every day, and putting up with Fala, who'd have been . . . nice, if there wasn't Chihin just out of reach.

It was going to take hours to do the fueling and all the coming and going, and he didn't want to confront anybody about anything, and he didn't want to be around Chihin, in case she *was* making a joke, and was going to make a bigger fool of him before she was done—she didn't always know when to stop.

He wished they'd hurry and go talk to the kif, and he could go with them, and maybe—maybe just have a whole new set of worries besides this one. The kif *might* want him. If Chihin didn't, maybe that was better than living here.

Maybe the captain would just say Fine, all right, good luck. Hoping he'd foul up with *them,* and cost them money.

"*Na* Hallan," the captain said, "filter check, life-systems check, don't drag your feet. We don't know how much time we've got. We could have to go out of here at any minute. With no undock procedures."

"No undock" got his attention. "Aye, captain," he said, galvanized into movement; he went to do that, obscurely relieved that the captain found something useful for him to do besides slit his wrists.

He could be mad, if he really wanted to think about it. He could really be mad, and he didn't even know who to aim it at, not Tarras, not Chihin, not Fala. Not the captain, who might be rough with him, but who'd given him chance after chance after he'd fouled up beyond all reasonable limits.

Certainly not Tiar, who had done nothing to him but good.

Maybe he was just mad at himself, for not being better, or smarter, or more able to handle things. He hoped to redeem himself. He did. He tried to think of the best question he could ask the kif, since the kifish lord had said he would have at least one more chance.

But he had no inspiration, no understanding that would help him. And maybe after all, it wasn't the real issue. Maybe it never had been. The kif had drawn the captain in by curiosity and used him, and maybe it was nothing but

that same ploy again. The kif had the stsho, or the stsho
was dead, and they were in a place surrounded by a very
dangerous species.

He just hadn't been much help to anyone.

"Your excellency?"
Silence.
"Your excellency?" They were alive inside. Hilfy signaled intent to enter the cabin, waited a moment for decency, and opened the door.

The sleeping-drape was still over the bowl-chair. Completely over the bowl-chair. There were two lumps under
it, and they moved.

They weren't sick. The tea service beside the pit that had
not spattered itself into bits and pieces during dock proved
someone had been up and about, undoubtedly Dlimas-
lyi . . . was *gtst* excellency going to bestir *gtst*self to work?
Not in her experience.

She cleared her throat. "Your excellency, I have the
honor to report our safe arrival at Kefk. Does your excellency require anything? We will negotiate with the persons
who may have the person of Atli-lyen-tlas as soon as fueling is complete."

A muted squeal from beneath the cover. A white head
popped above it, crest tousled, wide-eyed. "Your honor is
very kind. *Gtst* excellency will wait."

"Has—" Gods *rot* the creature. "Has *gtst* excellency any
influence at this port? Any contacts to pursue? Any knowledge of stsho personnel in this area? We are in a port
foreign to us in which we have neither introduction nor
credentials, and a kif named Vikktakkht an Nikkatu who
has led us here with dubious promises now wishes to speak
with a young male crewmember regarding *gtst* excellency
Atli-lyen-tlas."

A second head popped up, as disheveled. "With a *male*
person? A juvenile male person? Could this possibly be the
juvenile male person who assaulted our sensibilities in the
corridor, the carrier of refuse, the unstable and aggressive
individual? The same?"

"This Vikktakkht wishes to talk to this same individual.
I disapprove. I am insulted. However I will not permit this
strategem to distract me from the fulfillment of the con-

tract. I shall go. I shall prompt this young male person in his answers to this outrageous provocation. I shall learn by that means and determine my course of action."

"Most resolute! Most deserved on his part! Let him speak to the juvenile carrier of refuse!"

Not exactly the impression she'd wanted to convey of *na* Hallan; but argument with two sheet-wrapped stsho seemed precarious. "The object, however, is the presence of Atli-lyen-tlas, safely on this deck, which I shall attempt, against all obfuscation and misdirection. I should, however, caution your excellency that every other ship in this port is kif, they are not honest trading vessels who are here, and there is the remote but not disregardable possibility of a precipitous and scarcely warned undocking and high velocity departure which would render, for instance, that most exquisite tea set a cluster of projectiles of great hazard. An alarm will sound in the event of emergency. It will be a very loud and unmistakable siren. In that eventuality, abandon all decorum, cast any loose objects into the nearest locker, preferring your own safety above all. I shall provide an abundance of unfortunately inelegant cushions, which you may pack within your bowl-chair while fastening safety belts."

"These are frightening precautions!"

"Far less so than a departure inadequately protected. If there is time, a member of my crew will assist you. But if your excellency will excuse my forwardness, which is motivated only by our deepest regard for your safety, I wish to have conveyed these cushions into this cabin immediately. I wish to take no chances."

Tlisi-tlas-tin waved an urgent hand. "At once, at once! Dlimas-lyi, assist the honorable crewmember!"

"*Most* gracious!"

"How like your thoughtful and hospitable self to take extravagant precaution!"

Interesting sight. She had never seen a stsho without a stitch of clothing. Dlimas-lyi scrambled out and hurried, bowing often. One tried not to show startlement, except to return the bow.

Every pillow on the ship, as happened. Hers. The crew's. Every pillow out of storage, including those from the dismantled passenger cabins, and mahendo'sat slept in nests

of pillows, so there were no few in reserve. Plus a couple
of inflatable airbags for emergency use.

"In the lift," she said, and did not say, Would your honor
care to dress, we are not in that great a hurry. But she
was unsure of the proprieties, and only put the door at
Open-Hold.

"I remind your excellency that a face-upward reclination
on any safety cushion is safest during any sustained engine
use, to keep breathing passages unobstructed."

"This is a dire contemplation!"

"Think of it as a hopeful one, as in the worst and most
violent eventuality your excellency and *gtst* companion will
rest in a serene and safe nest."

"Your concern and foresight on behalf of your passengers is most greatly appreciated! You are white to my
eyes!"

"I am deeply touched." Actually, she was. It was a far
step for Tlisi-tlas-tin. "I have profound regard for your excellency's opinion."

As pillows and airbags arrived in great abundance, hasty
waddling bundles of them, on two different-hued sets of
legs.

The filters were all right, except one: Hallan pulled that
one to wash it in the galley, which had to serve, since the
downside was proscribed stsho territory. He rinsed it clean
and looked around in startlement as someone strolled into
the galley.

Oh, gods. Chihin. He didn't want to be here. He even
considered flight. Locking himself in the crew quarters. But
dignity kept him set on his job, and he only hoped she'd
come after a sandwich or something and wouldn't say anything.

He kept working at the sink, drying things off. Chihin
leaned past him after a bag of chips from the cabinet over
his head, bodily leaning on him, resting her hand on his
shoulder. And he didn't believe then it was chips she was
after—but he didn't know whether it was affection, a joke
at his expense, or whether she was asking him to recipro-
cate or what. She got the chips. She opened them and she
left, and he didn't yet know what to do or what he should
have done. His stomach was upset. He wanted to make

sense of things and not to make matters worse, and now he didn't know at all what was going on, except just having her near him was enough to send his temperature up a point and make him short of breath, forget any clear sense, and she might have wanted him, and she might have thought he was trying to ignore her.

And if *that* was the case Chihin wasn't going to come back for another rejection, if she felt rebuffed. He could have hurt her feelings . . . if he even had a hope of understanding somebody like her. He was lost. He was just lost.

The sensors read what was going in as untainted and completely proper. And to Hilfy's small surprise, the station paid for the datadump like a civilized port, a relatively fair price, fifty-fifty with *Tiraskhti*'s competing arrival; and deducted it from the fuel bill, which likewise wasn't exorbitant for a place like Kefk, which didn't have overmuch surplus.

No trouble on the bank certificates: the kif sent a representative to the airlock to accept the certificates; and sent again at each major fraction of the load—which was more cooperation than you might get at Urtur. Tarras, delivering the certificates, was armed; the kif was clearly armed: Hilfy watched the entire exchange from the lower deck ops station on vid, with a pistol beside her hand, quite ready to shut the lock from there and trap a kif bent on mischief of any kind.

Not a hint of trouble.

And of Pyanfar's purified mail, *here,* among kif, the religious cases were completely absent, the entrepreneurs were nonexistent—there were numerous individuals offering the assassination of whatever enemies she might designate, some on speculation. There were numerous individuals listing their credentials, which might read like a police report in another society; but murder was not a prosecutable offense under kifish law. There *were* no prosecutable offenses between individuals under kifish law, only offenses against necessary collective institutions. It was, for instance, against the law for a kif or a group of kif to attack the bank and rob it; or to take independent action against a foreign government or against the kifish government, or to attack a space station in contravention of the dignity of the *mekt-*

hakkikt. Pyanfar had probably dictated that one herself—since there *was* no kifish legislature, as such, merely a general consent to follow a given *hakkikt* so far as it looked advantageous, and what the *hakkikt* said *was* law so far as the *hakkikt*'s influence went. Violate it and find oneself delivered to the offended *hakkikt,* who might demonstrate his or her *sfik* above that of the offender by having the offender for dinner. Literally.

And of all the ranks Aunt Pyanfar held, that she leaned the most heavily on her authority among the kif—might simply be that she had to exert it, constantly, to stay *mekt-hakkikt,* without which—all her laws were null and void; and that without her in that post, there would be no peace.

But it occasioned no few shakes of the head among hani on Anuurn, who were only disturbed that kif were constantly *about* Pyanfar Chanur. Of the realities inside kifish space, no one came here to learn.

Except Pyanfar Chanur.

Did she ever *take* any of these offers, Hilfy found herself wondering uneasily. If you were offered universal peace, and someone was in the way of that peace, grievously in the way of it, and you had this many offers, from a species that truly, earnestly didn't mind murder, either of its own kind or someone else—would one begin to weigh relative evils?

Oh, *gods,* aunt, what a daily set of choices, what a difficult No, to say time after time—or is it always No, with the peace at stake . . . when the potential violator might be kif?

What a narrow ledge to walk, aunt. Why ever did you take it?

Except no one else could have, in that day, at that time. . . .

Pyanfar, one message said, *got talk you. Got wife no sense. A.J.*

A.J? Who went by A.J? Why no header? No date. She didn't know any—

A.J? Aja Jin?

Jik?

That was a Personage among the mahendo'sat. And *Aja Jin* was a hunter-ship. Wife no sense? Woman no sense? I was ambiguous in mahendi.

Jik wasn't married, last she knew. Jik . . . with more turns than a tc'a . . . was still, if he had held loyal, one of Aunt Py's number one agents, and *Aja Jin* was one of those ships that didn't file its course with any trade office, or carry cargo. *Aja Jin*, like *The Pride*, just showed up here, and showed up there, and how far it could go at a jump and where it refueled was something Aunt Py probably knew, but probably nobody else did.

Not even the bother to code it. And left *here*, at Kefk, across a border only fools crossed?

What in a mahen hell was this she'd let herself be maneuvered into? Aunt Py's private mailbox? A place . . . if one thought about it . . . where a ship like *Aja Jin* could kite in on the sudden, drop a message in plain mahen Trade, not even troubling to code it, beyond the necessity to know who A.J. was . . . because kif had no motive to go to anybody but another kif with the news: kif high up enough to use it were either loyal to Aunt Py or outright plotting against her, but in no case would they deliver what they knew to empower any random outsider. It was just not in their interest to do so.

And make a move against the *mekt-hakkikt*, where she picked up her mail? Consider all those messages of hopeful underlings, desperate for some credit with the highest authority in kifish space.

But Vikktakkht wanted Hilfy Chanur *here?*

Necessary to tread very, very carefully. You flatter me, Vikktakkht had said when she addressed him as *hakkikt* at Kshshti—but here his message before docking had used the title: The *hakkikt* Vikktakkht an Nikkatu, no quibble about it.

The *hakkikt* said here they would find Atli-lyen-tlas, and here he would assist them, and here was where everything had to be, in what if an absolutely wild guess was right, was a place Pyanfar came, and a place presently *full* of hunter-ships, and nothing else; and a place it was going to be very difficult for the *Legacy* to leave against this *hakkikt*'s will.

On the one hand, it was possible a mahen lunatic with domestic problems had left Pyanfar an inane appeal for assistance.

But there were 248 messages already in Pyanfar's message stack, and more were backed up waiting for the computer's version of bomb detection. This was not a place that had low expectations of seeing Pyanfar Chanur. No few of said messages had points of origin like Mkks, and Akkti, and distant Mimakkt, all in kifish space—messages sent to Kefk.

On the one hand this could be Pyanfar's kifish base of operations.

On the other hand—it might not be. And that "might not be" held the most dire possibilities.

The screen flashed blue: the computer spat up a message with a keyword.

The hakkikt *Vikktakkht to captain Hilfy Chanur, at dock at Kefk: Contact me.*

The message before dock was halfway cordial. This, after dock, was terse, guarded against insult, a simple and moderate demand which a mere captain would be extremely ambitious to refuse.

On kifish terms, a very clear and entirely reasonable warning: fueling was *nearly* complete. The *hakkikt* gave her a way to both comply and save her own *sfik*, having held off a superior force this long.

Definitely time to comply, if one didn't wish to challenge him outright.

Step by step down the kif agenda. And no question but that the kif wanted her, in person.

She didn't let her mind dwell on that scenario. It would come. It wasn't on her to-do list at the moment.

She swung the chair around and keyed in the com function.

The hani ship Chanur's Legacy, *at dock at Kefk, captain Hilfy Chanur, head of Chanur clan, her hand, to the* hakkikt *Vikktakkht an Nikkatu, the kif hunter* Tiraskhti, *at dock at Kefk: We are pleased to open communication.*

A moment, then:

The hakkikt *Vikktakkht to captain Hilfy Chanur, at dock at Kefk: I have the person you seek. Bring Meras.*

She did *not* like that juxtaposition. And every second of delay was a possibility of a blow-up, a loss of *sfik*, an unwanted challenge of the kif's intentions . . . the ramifications were wide and rapid.

The hani ship Chanur's Legacy, *at dock at Kefk, captain*

Hilfy Chanur, head of Chanur clan, her hand, to the hakkikt *Vikktakkht an Nikkatu, the kif hunter* Tiraskhti, *at dock at Kefk: When?*

Her hand was shaking as she keyed it out. Thank the gods the kif couldn't see that. She couldn't flinch aboard *Tiraskhti.* Not if she wanted to get out alive.

The hakkikt *Vikktakkht to captain Hilfy Chanur, at dock at Kefk: An escort is on the way to your lock now.*

Gods rot the bastard! They weren't prepared for this. It was an ultimatum. They could refuse it. But you measured every such action and bet everything you had on it. She had made a play, coming in here. The hakkikt was making his throw, now, and it was a test or it was an outright kidnapping.

The hani ship Chanur's Legacy, *at dock at Kefk, captain Hilfy Chanur, head of Chanur clan, her hand, to the* hakkikt *Vikktakkht an Nikkatu, the kif hunter* Tiraskhti, *at dock at Kefk: I look forward to the meeting.*

Let *him* wonder if she was going to shoot him on sight— because *he* would have to raise the level of threat to tell her she wasn't going in there armed.

She was in formal dress now. There was the mini-pistol in her belt. There was the gun on the counter, its holster in the wall-clip, and she punched in all-ship while she was getting out of the chair. "Hallan Meras, Fala Anify, report to lower main *now,* formal dress, code red, Fala. Hallan, just wash off, clean clothes, and get yourself down here."

"I'm going," Fala said from somewhere.

"Hallan, answer the gods-be com!"

"Yes, captain! I'm on my way!"

Tarras arrived, full of protests. "The kif? You're going out there? With those two kids?"

"The Rules, Tarras. The Rules. I want the gunner, the pilot, the scan officer on the bridge. You don't deal with the kif solo, I've got to have somebody, he wants to talk through Meras: Fala's the only expendable, that's the way it is, Tarras. I'm *sorry,* cousin. It's the way it adds."

Tarras stood there in silence, hard-breathing. Then: "Tell them the gunner's unstable and gods-be upset about this."

"I'm telling them we want Atli-lyen-tlas. Or a good excuse. Keep *Chihin* on the ship. Read the Rules at her till she hears you."

"Aye," Tarras said. Thank the gods for Tarras' basic intelligence. Tarras left, grim and upset; and collided with Tiar inbound.

"Captain,—"

"Won't work this time, Tiar. Crew to stations, by the Book. *Trust* me I know what I'm doing."

"Risking your gods-be neck, captain!"

"That's fine. Neither Fala nor I navigate. Your course is Meetpoint by Lukkur or Tt'a'va'ao, if that's the only route open—if I get into trouble, run for it and let somebody know besides the kif, does this make sense to you?"

Tiar didn't like it. Not in the least, but she went with Tarras, and both of them were going to have their hands full with Chihin, bet on it. For the first time this crew was going to make the hard choice and do what they were told, by the ever-living gods. And she was deeply sorry to be taking two kids into this mess, but it was exactly as she'd told them: no choice.

She heard the lift descending. That was either Tarras and Tiar on their way up—or . . .

She heard the shouting. That was Chihin. Protesting, she could figure, that she'd calc'ed all the possible courses already, and she was going. Hilfy couldn't hear the words, but she could pick the argument out of the rhythm. The voices went quiet then—muted by the doors, perhaps; the lift ascended. But someone was coming down the corridor, she heard the hurrying approach.

"Captain," Fala panted, still damp from the shower. Scared, no question of it.

"This is where we see if you can keep your head, *ker* Anify. Sorry I can't take senior crew, you're it. Remember everything—*everything* you read in the manual, and if you're scared out of your wits you don't let *them* know it. There's another gun in the locker there. Put it on."

"Aye, captain." Fala got into the locker, got the gun and holster out, and put it on. Her hands were shaking: neo nerves, the unknown, the never-experienced. That was all right. She had a few flutters herself.

"They're going to try to spook you. You put your hands on your gun, they'll do the same, just don't for godssake escalate a gesture into a firefight, do you follow that?"

The lift had come down again. Another runner came

down the corridor, heavier—out of breath when he got to the door.

"Sorry I'm—"

"You two," Hilfy said, "listen to me very soberly. I don't know what you've got going on personally, I don't care. Either you shake the stupidity out of your heads or you and I are going to blow the peace to bits, do you understand me? It's not just two young fools who're going to die if somebody doesn't get their wits together. We could be at war again, and several billion people could get killed. Is this more important than your personal business?"

"Yes, captain," Hallan said faintly.

"Yes," Fala said, ears up, scared, and not looking at *na* Hallan. "*Yes,* captain."

"That's good. That's just adequate. Can we ascend to flawless competency?" There was a beep from the board, the motion sensor on the airlock's closed hatch. The vid monitor showed two black-robed shadows coming down the access link toward the door, two doubtless armed kif. "Our escort's here. *Na* Hallan, the question, should you get the chance . . ."

"Yes, captain."

"Flatter the son. *Don't* embarrass him in front of his people. And find out what he knows about Atli-lyen-tlas."

"Is that the question, captain?"

"That's the question. What *he* knows, not where the stsho is. The second question, if we get one—there isn't one. There's nothing that isn't dangerous. Watch out for the words 'want' or 'need': a kifish *hakkikt* doesn't *need* anything; and don't push him: the odds are completely in his favor. Don't make him demonstrate it." She shepherded them out the door and settled the gun tight in its holster— no feeling in the universe like making a fast dive for cover and seeing your gun go spinning off across the floor. "Fala, you don't draw unless they do, and then don't waste shots on the hired help: shoot the highest rank target you can hit and run for the door. You *go for the door,* don't sightsee, that's all the instruction I can give you. Threat for threat, let them make the first move."

"Aye, captain."

"Gods-be right, 'Aye, captain.' *Follow orders.*"

Chapter 17

The docks at Kefk had only sodium glare in the overheads, were all gray paint—kif didn't see color, at least not the way hani did; didn't see the yellow of warning signs, just the dark-light pattern; and on Kefk, it was only pattern that identified the conduits, and pattern that said walk here and not there. In all this gray and black universe, oddly tinted by the glare of apricot light, there arrived the color of hani, bronzed: Hilfy's trousers went a peculiar muted red; the spacer blues went a grayed blue; and rifle barrels and gun-belt metal on their five-man escort acquired apricot high-lights, while the matte graphite gray of kifish hands and kifish snouts, all that showed from beneath the robes, actually took on a livelier shade.

Do the kids credit, Hilfy thought, they didn't balk at their escort, they didn't sightsee or wrinkle their noses in disgust at the ammonia tang in the breath-frosting air; they paid attention to their surroundings, and Hilfy watched every-thing that passed in front of her and in the periphery of her vision, where neon signs lit a spacer's row no different than any services zone on any station trying to attract cus-tomers, except the words were kifish, and never ask what delicacies those establishments offered, and what entertain-ments they advertised. The neon signs were white, or the sickly color of kifish daylight: or they were neon red: *ask* what kifish vision responded to.

While all down the dockside, black-robed, weapons-bristling bystanders clustered in small groups and watched, talking behind their hands, talking with the turn of a shoulder.

Look at the fools, they might be saying.

They passed two berths where not a thing was going on; the ships might be in count, or, Hilfy thought, might be primed and ready to pull out on a second's notice; passed a third berth, where canisters were going in, but they were all the ship's-supply sort, with accesses for hoses and dispenser attachments; and just pulling up on a transport truck, cages of live animals that squealed a thousand irate protests when a loader jolted them, and swarmed like a flow of ink up the sides of the fine mesh cage.

Akkhtish life, a kif had once said: as voracious and fast-breeding and nasty as a species had to be to have stayed alive on the kifish homeworld—the only species in the universe, in her opinion, that *deserved* the kif for predators.

"This way," the kif officer said, with a flourish of a hand from within the sleeve, and directed them to an access gate beside which a board burned with the kifish letters *Tiraskhti.*

Here we go, Hilfy thought, and climbed up the ramp in the lead, taking two kids into what could be a very, very bad situation. The kids would be the pressure point, if something went wrong. The kif understood the use of hostages, in some convoluted way that had nothing to do with sentiment and maybe a lot to do with taking a valuable item and diminishing the *sfik* of the opposition by withholding it.

The airlock opened ahead, dimly lit. The ammonia stink inside was far stronger. But not improbably kif smelled hani presence just as strongly: as for the lighting, they hated the light of yellow suns, and disliked the noon even of their own. So the theorists held.

They occupied the lock, a tight, uneasy company, less the two that took up guard at the outside of the airlock; the lock cycled them through to a corridor, and more crew and personnel than a hani ship needed—met them there.

"Kkkkt," they said, that odd sound that betokened interest. Or a preface to attack—calm, she wished herself, thinking if she could get the youngsters through this corridor without incident they would be safer in wider spaces, out of the convenient, curious reach of a kifish claw. "Kkkt," ran like a wave beside their presence, as their escort shoved a way through the crowd, ahead of and beside them on their way through to the hall where a kifish dignitary entertained, and held court, and whatever other business the *hakkikt* had in mind.

That was where they came, through a door into a wide space ringed about with armed kif—she *knew* this place, or its exact likeness; and suffered a confusion of time, as if no years had intervened. There was the kifish prince, in silver-edged black; there was the same low table, with two chairs, there was the inevitable ring of witnesses about them, in light so dim a hani eye could not pick out the edges of shapes.

"You don't sit," she muttered to Fala and *na* Hallan, and walked as far as the table, seeing *here*, not the flashbacks on another ship, another place: no place to act spooked, she told herself, no place to get spooked: she had two kids to get out of here alive. The *hakkikt* had to score points, *had* to, now that she'd called his bluff all the way to this table, but he couldn't get everything without her cooperation, or he wouldn't have called her here.

She pulled a chair back, sat down across the round table from Vikktakkht, with Fala and Hallan behind her, and settled back in deliberate casualness.

Vikktakkht sat with one thin arm over the low back of his chair, his face shadowed within the silver-edged hood, except the snout—except the fine modeling of vein and muscle in what one could imagine was a very handsome, very fearsome type of his species.

"Kkkt. Captain. And Meras. Meras may sit with us."

"*Na* Hallan," she said without looking, and the boy carefully lowered his huge frame into the remaining empty chair.

"Meras," Vikktakkht said. "Ask your next question."

"Sir," Hallan said, in a quiet, respectful voice, and hesitated.

For the gods' sake, boy, Hilfy thought, *remember the question.*

"What do you know," Hallan asked, "about Atli-lyen-tlas?"

Kkkt, the murmur ran around the room. And Hallan, to his credit, didn't flinch.

"A broad question." The *hakkikt's* arm lifted. A silver bracelet showed on a bare dark wrist, as he made a gesture about him. "I defer that answer for a moment—and offer another question."

Don't improvise, Hilfy thought. Boy. Don't try.

"May I ask a favor of you, sir?"

She hadn't expected that turn. She translated it frantically into kif, looked for ambiguities. The room murmured with startlement, seemed to hold its breath, and a few muttered, "K-k-k-kkkt," in a surly tone: *they* would not have dared that; and her heart was beating doubletime, her brain trying to figure what she could say.

But Vikktakkht made a casual motion of his hand. "Audacious. Make a request of me. If you amuse me, I may do it."

Hilfy stopped breathing, thinking, *Careful, na* Hallan. *Think,* boy.

Kif edged closer to them, listening, hissing at each other for room and silence. She felt Fala's presence closer at the back of her chair—dared not caution her, *hoped* the kid didn't shove back.

"I'd like you to understand, sir, I don't belong to Chanur. They weren't even at Meetpoint when I was arrested. They tried to get me back to my crew, that's all. So nothing I've done is their fault."

"Kkkt," broke out from a hundred throats, and died in hisses. Hilfy translated that one into kifish, running it down path after path of logic. "Offended" had too many ramifications to track.

"Kkkt," Vikktakkht said softly. "So, Meras? Is that your request? My understanding?"

While Hilfy thought: "Understand" doesn't mean "forgive." Boy, give it up. Stop there.

"If you're Pyanfar Chanur's friend, they need—they . . . ."

Gods, boy, don't assign him a job in front of his followers. . . . *"Hakkikt,"* she said, but Vikktakkht made a preemptive move of his hand.

"Meras?"

A silence. Then: "They think you can find the stsho," Hallan said.

"Is that your request?"

Yes! Hilfy thought. Gods, bail out, boy!

"Yes, sir."

"Isn't that two requests?"

"Then the second, sir. But I just wanted to clear that first up, in case that wasn't in your record."

"Kkkt." A motion of the hand. A servant hastened to

put a cup in it. Vikktakkht didn't drink. Instead, a motion of the cup ending in their direction. "What motives, this hunger for responsibility? Is this a challenge? Is that the word?"

"No, sir. It is the word, but I'm not challenging you. At all, sir. It's my obligation to Chanur, to make clear—"

"He's saying—" Hilfy began desperately, and the preemptive hand moved sharply, then made a second gesture.

"Translate, Chanur. I recall you have some fluency."

"Nakkot ahigekk. Sh'sstikakkt Chanur."

"Now he follows Chanur, you mean."

"Yes."

"And what does Chanur want?"

"Nakkot shatik nik'ka Atli-lyen-tlas."

"Ah. And what opposes you? What do you suppose opposes you?"

"Paehisna-ma-to."

The long jaw lifted. The *hakkikt* stared at her down a long, dangerous nose.

"Kkkt. But the mahendo'sat *support* the *mekt-hakkikt.*"

She couldn't be wrong. She could *not* be wrong, and have followed the wrong ship. "Do they?"

"What does Hilfy Chanur think?"

"I didn't come here because I believed Ana-kehnandian."

"Kkkt. You came here because we have Atli-lyen-tlas."

"Do you?"

"Kkkt. Kkkt. The flat-toothed stsho face every breeze. They attempt to please Chanur. They launch an initiative in this direction, in that direction. *Gakkak.*"

"Herd creatures."

"Herd tactics. Exactly. They launch an initiative at Chanur's presence. They launch initiatives to mahendo'sat of rank. But the mahendo'sat are not *gakkak.* They go all directions. If you chase one, others escape, and another may join you. Thus, Paehisna-ma-to."

"Not a friend of Chanur."

"Not well-disposed to kif. Some say Hilfy Chanur is not well-disposed to kif. Some say—Hilfy Chanur would be the logical ally of Paehisna-ma-to. The logical successor to Pyanfar Chanur."

She drew in a slow, ammonia-tainted breath. "Where *is* the *mekt-hakkikt?*"

A vague move of the hand. "Where the *mekt-hakkikt* chooses. Recently at Meetpoint. As you know."

Assassins, after Aunt Py? *Mahen* assassins?

"Who blew up Kshshti docks? Who fired shots at us?"

"What do you think?"

"There aren't any kifish dockworkers at Kshshti."

"As happens there are not."

"Difficult for you to get into a warehouse and steal a can."

"Not impossible."

"But why would you need to stop me? I'd agreed to go to Kefk."

"Hani have not always done as promised."

"The bomb would have heavily damaged us, without destroying the ship. And the sniper wasn't of your quality. While Kshshti wouldn't let a mahen hunter-ship undock. Those ships have priority in any situation. Wouldn't you think they'd let them leave, if they let us leave?"

"But we are historic enemies."

"Kshshti put bureaucratic delays in a hunter-ship's path. It more than suspected Ana-kehnandian. I haven't heard of this Paehisna-ma-to. So she's new. A rising power. Urtur—was cautious with Ana-kehnandian. Kshshti was *bravely* cautious . . . *nakkti skskiti.*"

"Kkkt." This time it was laughter, laughter that shook Vikktakkht's stillness, and rippled around the room. "*Nakkti skskiti.* That *is* Kshshti. A banner for all winds."

"I'm not. And I'm not such a fool I think kif think like hani. Or that a *hakkikt* of your stature, who wished to contact us, would make two attempts designed to scare us without killing us."

"Kkkt." A motion of Vikktakkht's hand. "You think we have no subtlety?"

"Blowing out a docking port on Kshshti?"

More laughter, that clicked and hissed all around the room.

"Salutation," Vikktakkht said, "from the *mekt-hakkikt.* Who assured me you would not be diverted by her rival."

By Paehisna-ma-to, he meant; and meant that Pyanfar leaned to the kif, to *kifish* support, which would always be loyal, while they feared the subordinates that feared her. . . .

She felt queasy at the stomach, having reasoned her way to that truth, having looked at it from all sides, and having decided that this *was* a place Pyanfar expected her mail delivered—however dark the paths Pyanfar traveled these days.

Maybe Paehisna-ma-to had reason, the thought came fluttering to the surface.

And drowned. Whoever had shot Chihin was not her friend. Whoever had killed innocent stsho and mahen security personnel was not her friend.

"And No'shto-shti-stlen?" she asked.

"An ally with enemies in Llyene. Hence *gtst* moved to form an alliance with the ambassador to Urtur, of a nature which you doubtless know and Ana-kehnandian does not."

"I don't know."

"You've not seen the object."

Caution held her tongue. Even with this so-named ally of Pyanfar's. "What would that tell me if I could?"

"The nature of the alliance. No'shto-shti-stlen's position within it, which of three."

"You mean sex?"

"An emblem of proposed gender."

She hoped she kept her mouth closed. Kif, fortunately, had no embarrassment in such matters.

"You have come here to present this to Atli-lyen-tlas. Is this not so?"

"Yes, *hakkikt.*"

"We have provided the ambassador such comforts as we found possible. But I think the ambassador would be far more comfortable on your ship."

"Possibly so, *hakkikt.*"

"Sagikki aku gtst!"

Bring the stsho! the *hakkikt* said, and with no delay whatsoever a door opened, admitting the blinding spectrum of a paler sun. There was a moderate commotion in that quarter. Hilfy turned her head cautiously and saw, past Hallan's shoulder, kif moving within that light. A waft of perfume came out, and kif made soft sounds of disgust.

Then came the spindly outline of a stsho body, *gtst* gossamer robes backlit against the glare in her watering eyes. She was blind, as the stsho seemed to be, hesitatingly as *gtst* moved; so likewise the kif. Perhaps, she thought, it was eloquent of the condition within the Compact itself.

But the creature did not seem to get *gtst* equilibrium in the dark, and had to be guided by *gtst* kifish attendants. Something's wrong, Hilfy thought, rising from her chair. Something's vastly wrong with this stsho.

"Perhaps," Vikktakkht said, "your care will restore *gtst*. The practice of medicine is not a priority among our species. One argues for it. But medicine is still a secretive matter, practiced upon oneself. There is not, on this entire station, a medical facility, only a few supplies."

"I would first suggest," she said, she thought politely, "that *gtst* not be required to walk."

Not in time. *Gtst* collapsed. Fala made an instinctive move to assist and safeties went off guns all around the room. Fala froze. Hallan lurched for his feet.

"*Hakkt!*" Vikktakkht said sharply, that untranslatable word that meant something like Off guard, and safeties went back on, a more random clicking.

"And if you would tell your crew to go back on station power," Vikktakkht said, "station central control would be far more easy in its dealings."

"They're coming back," Tiar breathed, and only then realized the degree to which her nerves were wound, when she heard the advisement from *Tiraskhti* com, on aural-only.

"*I'll trust it when they get into the airlock,*" Chihin said in her ear, on ops com; and Tarras: "*They're saying they've got gtst excellency!*"

"I'll believe *that* when I see it," Tiar said. And made up her mind she would start believing it when she heard from the captain's own pocket com, and when there didn't come any of the codewords for coercion that were in the Manual. She sat gnawing her mustaches to ragged ruin, and then got that thin, static-fractured advisement:

"*This is Legacy One. You're going to see a transport truck pull up. Only bus this station runs. We're all right, we're coming home, we got our addressee, put on a pot of gfi, we could use it.*"

"*That means it's really all right,*" Tarras said, the edge of

excitement beginning to grow in her voice. And the Manual
was on the bridge: they'd fed into com voice analysis every
codeword that might come through. If Tarras said it was
clear it was clear, and there was a next step.

"Chihin, get down to the lock, arm, don't open till
they're on it, we don't trust it."

"I'm gone," Chihin said, and cleared her board to Tarras.

Everybody was all right. There was a little tremor in
Tiar's hand as she reached to key aux monitoring over to
her two low-level screens.

Everybody was all right. They'd gotten the stsho, *ker*
Hilfy had pulled it off somehow and they could go to Meetpoint with Chanur honor intact.

Please the gods it didn't blow up in their faces.

But she didn't think she should advise *gtst* excellency yet,
stsho being the easily worried creatures they were. She
didn't think they should provide any good news until they
knew there were no catches.

And even after the captain and the rest of them were
secure in the airlock *she* wasn't going to be able to leave
station. According to the Book, which had gotten them
through it this far, the senior officer parked herself in the
number one station, kept systems up, kept a close monitor
on transmissions around them, whether or not they could
decode them, the number of coded transmissions versus
non-coded: and if anything surged out of recent
parameters—

Then the senior officer was permitted to panic.

Gtst excellency Atli-lyen-tlas was not at all in good
shape—half-dead, to Hilfy's eyes; and when the driver
pulled up in front of the *Legacy*'s berth (most adamantly,
she had insisted neither Hallan *nor* Fala drive) she called
on *na* Hallan to vault down to the deck and stand ready
to receive *gtst* excellency into his arms.

"She is a very large hani," *gtst* excellency was heard to
mutter. "She will not drop us."

"She won't," Hilfy said, and *na* Hallan shut his mouth
and reached up his hands. "She's a very competent person." At which *na* Hallan gave her a startled look, as if to
ask did she possibly mean that.

But she had her hands full of fragile stsho at the moment,

and together she and Fala lowered Atli-lyen-tlas into Hallan's arms.

"I have your honor," Hallan assured *gtst*.

Hilfy clapped Fala on the shoulder, and the two of them jumped down. A whole squad of kif had turned up, with rifles evident, and that was worrisome, but their driver got out and waved a black-sleeved arm toward the ramp and the waiting kif.

"Essscort," the driver said. "The *hakkikt*'s. Sssafe."

It wasn't how she defined safe, but they walked and the kif didn't threaten them and didn't move, so she supposed there were no orders on the part of the *hakkikt* to try to rush the airlock. "Watch their hands," she said to Fala. "Rule of measured threat. You did just fine in there. Let's get home."

Fala didn't say anything but "Aye, captain." The kids were trying to be right. They walked past the kif, with the half-fainting stsho, and up the rampway. The access gate opened for them, which argued somebody was observing from where they'd been ordered to be, and possibly someone was waiting for them downside, which they were supposed to be. That gate shut, meaning, however fragile the tube that connected them to their ship, they were alone behind seal, and there was, one hoped, no kifish guard at their lock.

"Nobody behind us," Fala said, having actually cast a look back to see.

"Bravo, kid, you're learning." She punched in the pocket com. "Tiar, Chihin, Tarras?"

"We're on it, captain, lock's about to open."

Upon which, it did, pale and inviting light.

Things happened, things happened on schedule and with checks, if the crew had had to do it with the manual in one hand and thumbing from page to page. She found her own anxiety like a spring slowly let go—as if somehow she didn't have to check up, she didn't have to *wonder* was anything unseen-to: things were getting checked, and when the airlock shut behind them, and the air was cycling, she could feel a queasy confidence someone was monitoring the situation outside, without her—to her giddy relief—having to think of everything at once and give the orders.

She by the gods resented it. Py scored a point, and she

was absolutely scowling when the airlock door opened and it was Chihin facing Fala and Hallan with a double armload of stsho.

"We need the gurney," she said shortly. "We need *gtst* excellency to the sickbay and we need the medical supplies, probably vitamin and mineral supplements—"

"A bath," *gtst* breathed, "oh, estimables, a bath, among first things, cleanly light, *wai*, the distress and the suffering I have endured—"

"*Gtst* shows improvement," Hilfy said dryly. "*Na* Hallan, never mind the gurney, just carry *gtst.*"

"Aye, captain," he said, and walked on.

"Tarras," Hilfy said, "to the dispensary."

"She's down there," Chihin said. "She's already setting up."

Good gods, initiative. Right decisions.

The *crew* knew what was going on, the *crew* all of a sudden knew it was their responsibility to move in advance of orders: it wasn't—it never had been that they didn't know what they were doing. Three of them had come in with experience.

The captain hadn't. And the old women had been right: Rhean had been right: she *hadn't* had the experience.

Mark another one for Aunt Pyanfar. The crew wasn't unhappy, the *crew* suddenly had the latitude to do what it reasonably thought it ought to, the crew might be a little gods-be scared at the moment, but it was by the ever-living gods functioning ahead of the game for the first time in recent memory.

"I want a—"—thorough check against stsho parameters, she was about to say when she faced Tarras in the lab, but Tarras said to Hallan: "Put *gtst* excellency there, I've got the tests set up."

She could on the one hand feel superfluous. On the other she had enough on her hands—like getting the entire conversation down as she recalled it, like running it through the kifish translation program, looking for significances and omissions.

The captain wasn't strictly speaking a flight officer on this ship, but the captain with her head clear could make judgment calls that a protocol officer could make—and if there was a time to make them it was now.

Tell *gtst* excellency Tlisi-tlas-tin that *gtst* excellency Atli-lyen-tlas was lying disreputable in sickbay? Not yet. Not until they knew whether *gtst* excellency was going to live or die—or whether *gtst* excellency *was* still Atli-lyen-tlas.

Chapter 18

There was a time one was superfluous, and Hallan had learned to know it. He hovered near the doorway while Tarras gave orders to Fala, and Fala gave him looks while she was carrying this and carrying that.

"I *do* like you," he contrived to say, when Fala's fetching and carrying paused her near him. "I really do, Fala, I just—"

Fala retrieved the kit she was after and went across the small surgery to where Tarras was ministering to *gtst* excellency with small and delicate needles, murmuring words of encouragement, assuring *gtst* that it was exactly what the computer had said to do.

Fala didn't want to talk to him. He didn't entirely blame her. He didn't feel welcome here, where people who knew what they were doing were trying to save the stsho gentleman's—or lady's—life. . . .

He found it more convenient to edge toward the door, and when no one seemed to notice that fact, to edge out it, and into the main lower corridor.

But ops was down there, and Chihin was working lower-deck ops, and he didn't want to go down there; and did, desperately. . . .

Except it was too desperate and dangerous a situation to cause anybody more trouble than he had.

He wanted to apologize to Fala; and, really, truly, he wanted to patch it up: yes, he was attracted to Fala, at least she was pretty and she was clever and she was somebody he wanted very much to have like him, except it wasn't anything like the feeling he got when he even thought about Chihin.

Which told him it was the last place in the universe he needed to be when things were at a crisis and Chihin was supposed to be doing her job and there was a problem between them.

No business on a ship, the captain had said; and he didn't want to prove that by creating another problem for the captain. The crew lounge was where the captain had appointed him to go when she wanted him out of trouble and out of sight, and he went down the corridor as carefully as under fire, avoiding Chihin and avoiding any chance of running into the stsho, and got as far as the lift and rode it topside.

Then he could draw an easier breath. Then he could feel as if he wasn't in the way. And he soft-footed it as far as the corridor that led to the lounge.

But it equally well led to the galley and the bridge, too; and he wasn't forbidden to be there: he actually could do something useful; and Tiar was there, she'd been talking back and forth with them from some ops station and he didn't think it was downside.

Tiar was on his side, she'd always been friendly to him, she *hadn't* made his life difficult—Tiar understood what was going on.

He tended cautiously up the corridor in the direction of the bridge. The captain was in her office. The door was shut and the light was on the lock panel that meant she was there and the door wasn't locked, if you wanted to risk your neck. He didn't. He walked softly past and through the galley and onto the bridge where, sure enough, Tiar was sitting guard over the boards, with most of hers live and the screens showing the docks outside, and the station's scan-feed, and the station's docking-schema, and inputs he didn't recognize, but they were analytical, he thought, probably running system checks on the engines or something he wasn't familiar with.

He went and sat down very quietly in Fala's usual place, next on Tiar's right, the other side being the captain's place, where to save his life he wouldn't dare trespass.

She glanced at him, and looked back at the boards. So there was silence for some few moments.

"Can I help?" he asked softly, so as not to break her concentration.

"We're getting a little warm-up in a circuit. Not ops-critical, but we've put a load on us this trip. It's just symptomatic of a long run with very little sitting time."

"Dangerous?" Getting lost in hyperspace wasn't a thought he wanted even to entertain.

"No."

He was anxious, all the same. He was just generally scared, of a sudden, or it was easier to worry about a remote chance of breakdown in subspace than to worry about things that were definitely wrong, and he recognized that mental diversion for what it was. He'd nerved himself to walk in here, Tiar wanted to talk machinery, and now he'd lost his opening, which went something like . . .

"How's the stsho doing?" she asked.

"Pretty weak. Excited about being here. Glad to get into clean air. I don't blame him."

Tiar wrinkled her nose, a grimace. "It does sort of cling to you."

He hadn't washed. Nobody had had time below. And he was embarrassed. "I'm sorry. I didn't realize it was that bad."

"Not. Stay. I want to talk to you anyway."

Oh, gods. Everything was out of control.

"What did I do?" he asked.

Tiar's ears flicked, an impressive flicker of rings. "Nothing you did."

"Oh.

"What's the score with you and Fala and Chihin?"

The blood drained to his feet. His brains went with it. He sat there a moment trying to think how not to offend anybody, or look like a thorough fool.

"Do you think Chihin likes me?"

Tiar tried very hard to keep a straight face. It wasn't quite, for a moment, and then she got it under control, quite deadpan. "I'd say it looked that way at Kshshti. Is she being a problem? Is that what's going on?"

"I—" Everybody wanted to blame Chihin. Everybody thought she was taking advantage. Which maybe ought to tell him that was the case.

Except he just didn't pick that up from her. He hadn't. He didn't, below, he had just made himself scarce, which he thought everybody appreciated, since they were busy and thinking about saving their lives, and following the captain's orders.

"You tell her back off," Tiar said. "There's no way she's going to vote for or against a berth on this ship for you or

that basis. She's a bastard, but she's an honorable bastard—
she just doesn't play the game like that. She's made Fala
mad. But that's happened before. Mostly Fala's mad at
Chihin playing games."

"You think so."

"Hey. You're not hard to look at, Fala's smitten, doesn't
mean she's got proprietary rights. Tell *her* back off, if that's
the way you feel. Then you can have her *and* Chihin annoyed at you for at least a week. They'll live."

It sounded like good advice. Except it sat on his heart
like lead where it came to Chihin; and he wasn't used to
talking back to people, not at home, not on the *Sun*. He
just hadn't mastered the art of saying no.

Hadn't grown up before he'd left home. And maybe
hadn't yet, he thought. In spite of banging his head on
shipboard doorways, and sitting in the chair he was in with
more of him than the chair was designed to hold.

He just felt awkward. At everything. And he didn't know
if he could say that to Chihin. Or even Fala. In which case
things could only get worse.

"You don't like that advice," Tiar said.

He didn't know what to say. He shrugged, knew he wasn't
going to follow her advice, which was stupid, and maybe could
lose him his place on board. But he couldn't do it.

"I'm not good at telling people no," he said.

"You want me to tell them?"

That was cowardly. And it would hurt Chihin's feelings,
in a major way, he kept thinking that, even when everybody
else told him Chihin was having a joke at his expense. And
it would last until about the next time the two of them
were in the same area of the ship.

"I like Chihin," he said. "And I don't think she's joking."

"She's *not* joking, if you mean is she serious," Tiar
warned him bluntly. But Tiar wasn't stupid, and she seemed
to catch on, then. "You *like* her."

He nodded.

Tiar raked a hand through her mane, sat back and stared
at the boards a second as if she were dumbfounded.

"I don't think," he said, in the chance she hadn't just
dismissed him, "I don't think she's acting the way everybody says she is. I just don't think that."

Tiar looked in his direction, and slowly swung her chair

around. "I've known her a long time. I know her in ways Tarras and Fala don't. And if that's what you're picking up—next serious question: do you want a rescue?"

He shook his head; and Tiar looked oddly, vaguely satisfied.

"You're sure."

He nodded; and Tiar frowned and seemed to have thoughts she wasn't saying.

Finally she did say: "You're gods-be young. You won't always understand her. But if you get to that side of her— good luck, you'll need it; and I'd like to see it happen. Just don't let her run over you. She needs a full stop now and again. Keeps her honest."

He sat there a moment, trying to sort through that, and deciding it meant he wasn't crazy and things were the way he thought, and things could *be* the way he hoped for—

"But Fala," he said.

"But Fala," Tiar said. "I'll talk to her."

"No!"

"She'll live. You don't dislike her."

"No. I *like* her fine, just not—"

"People have to respect that, in clans, on ships, doesn't matter: there's serious and there's not-serious, and Fala will forgive me saying she'd run the other way from a real commitment. That's what I think. I've been wrong before, but I don't think I am. If you want my further advice, I'd say Fala's more interested in feeling she's not unattractive to young men."

"Fala? She's *beautiful.*"

"Beautiful doesn't matter. She wants to be attractive. Doesn't everyone?"

"I understand."

"So you pretty well know how to handle it, don't you?"

He was just not used to things going right. Something in him was still knotted up expecting disaster, like maybe the ship would fall apart in hyperspace just when things were about to sort themselves out. The gods didn't intend he should get absolutely everything he wanted. The captain was going to throw him off the ship. Chihin was going to decide she didn't like him.

The kif were going to turn on them after all and all the ships around them were going to join in.

"I hope you're right," he said.

"Kid, you go follow your instincts—but don't present too much temptation to anybody till we get this ship out of this godsforsaken port in one piece."

"Yes, *ker* Tiar."

Besides, the stsho were down there. So he couldn't get to downside ops. He decided he should go clean up, and when he had showered, he was hungry. All of a sudden he had a ravenous appetite, when nothing had much appealed to him since before he was arrested on Meetpoint.

Even Kefk seemed wonderful to him of a sudden. He was grateful to Vikktakkht. He liked the stsho gentleman. He hoped the stsho would be all right and all of them would be happy. He liked everything and everyone around him, and he scrubbed the galley down and set up the meals for undocking, and did everything he could think of to do, the way everyone else aboard was seeing to every detail they could find. . . .

He was absolutely happy. In this port, with kif all around them, and with the ship feeling the strain of a lot of quick turnarounds. Because when Chihin came topside and off duty he could talk to her.

And beyond that prospect he couldn't get his thoughts straight at all.

Gtst was clean, at least. *Gtst* looked very feeble.

Wants to talk to you, Tarras had said, although in Hilfy's opinion Atli-lyen-tlas could do with a few hours of sleep and a minimum of excitement before they even talked about business or arranged what could become a very stressful meeting.

"Your excellency," Hilfy said. "I have the honor to introduce myself: Hilfy Chanur, captain of *Chanur's Legacy*. How may I make your excellency welcome aboard? I apologize for the utilitarian nature of this present accommodation. . . ."

"Most, most gracious." The voice was very faint. "You're more fluent than any hani I ever met."

"I was protocol officer and communications on *The Pride*. Please make requests of us for your comfort or information. I shall answer everything to your satisfaction, and not ask but one question myself, in order not to exhaust your excellency's strength at this moment. Please feel that

you may be very direct and brief in your answer as we
know your energy is limited. Were you fleeing us, with the
kif? Please be assured we mean your excellency only help."

"Do you know of Paehisna-ma-to?"

"I have met one of her agents."

"This vile person . . ." A pause for breath. "This tasteless
individual has committed violence against my staff at
Urtur."

"Some of your staff left aboard a mahen ship."

"They dared not . . . dared not the darksomeness of a
kifish vessel. I am greatly apprehensive for their lives and
persons. The mahendo'sat are in fear of the Momentum."

Numa'sho: it was in the mahen psyche that a new force
that suffered no setbacks had something—mystic about it;
they were loath to fight against what had never been
beaten.

"Paehisna-ma-to has met reverses. Her agents have resorted to extreme measures which may cause fear in some
governments, but which have met brave resistance from the
Personages of Urtur and Kshshti. And we have eluded their
efforts to divert us."

"This is excellent news," *gtst* whispered. "Most excellent
news, as my staff relied on these individuals regarding the
selection of transportation. Please accept my profound gratitude that you followed where few hani venture. The kif
made small efforts at hospitality, and they would have conveyed me on to Meetpoint, but I should have perished by
then. The long, long flight . . . the food . . . I cannot
describe . . ."

"We will place your excellency in tasteful surrounding
and delay in this port until your excellency is able to
travel."

"Has No'shto-shti-stlen sent you? Is your ship the bearer
of the *oji*?"

"Yes. I hope that this is a felicitous event for your excellency. Please advise me if otherwise."

A weak hand fluttered and fell. "I am otherwise. I shall
make all effort to accept. But I fear that I have fled too
far and lost too much."

"Your excellency will recover!"

"It is indelicate to say. Forgive me. Persons of my stage
in life have lost all energies in such regard. I am *gtsta*."

Neuter?

Perhaps she let the dismay show. No'shto-shti-stlen sent a . . . whatever it was . . . and the object of *gtst* proposal was—

"*Gtsta,*" Atli-lyen-tlas said faintly. "I am incapable of accepting the inestimable distinction which *gtst* excellency of Meetpoint wished to convey. This—iiii—rarely changes."

"I should not wish to distress your excellency further. Please advise me where a hani might be ignorant, but be aware I view this as a personal matter of most extreme delicacy, and ask only for your excellency's welfare: Is there medical treatment which might avail?"

"Most excellent hani, it is age. To attempt to sustain the energies will take years from my life, yet I am motivated to do so. Paehisna-ma-to has conspired within stsho space itself to create disaffections and hesitations, which have threatened *gtst* excellency of Meetpoint, whom I most ardently have admired. I overestimated my endurance. I underestimated the persistence of the agents of Paehisna-ma-to. I can only hope to find the strength."

"Your excellency, *gtst* excellency of Meetpoint has sent a representative, one Tlisi-tlas-tin, as custodian of the Preciousness and arbiter of propriety. The Preciousness rests within *gtst* cabin and in such tasteful surroundings as we could best create."

"Take me there! I must see the Preciousness. Please assist me!"

She was apprehensive. She had visions of fragile bones breaking in the mere attempt to walk, of a stsho circulatory system failing in the effort.

But the will to live was important too. She looked at Tarras, who hovered in the neighboring surgery, ostensibly taking inventory, but watching. Tarras walked to the small screened area and Fala turned up with her.

"*Gtst* excellency wants to go to Tlisi-tlas-tin," she said. "I think it's important. Can *gtst* do it?"

"I don't know," Tarras said. "I don't know what I'm doing, but following the book. I . . . just don't know. We can see."

"Try," she said, and Tarras and Fala came in and helped *tst* to *gtst* feet, very gently, very carefully. There was no other transport but a gurney, which would undoubtedly offend *gtst* dignity. And calling down *na* Hallan . . . *gtst* excellency Tlisi-tlas-tin would surely advise Atli-lyen-tlas that *na* Hallan was not an unusually tall crewwoman.

Which might be too much for *gtst* heart, or the system that passed for one.

The lift engaged, upward bound. And it might be the captain coming back topside, or it might be Tarras or Fala; but Hallan, polishing the chromalic of the galley to a fine gloss, paid attention, paid heart and mind and hope of finding it was Chihin.

And maybe it was the way the whole day had been going—it was. *Ker* Chihin came wandering onto the bridge by the outside corridor saying to Tiar something about a rest break, could she monitor downside ops; and Tiar saying—he eavesdropped shamelessly—that that was all right, everything was quiet, there wasn't a need for her down there, and why didn't she get a sandwich or something and take a break and then relieve her?

Ker Tiar knew he was topside, *ker* Tiar knew he was here, oh, gods, he wasn't quite ready to think and talk . . .

But Chihin walked in, did this little flick of the ears as a hello and looked into the fridge.

"Can I make you something?" Hallan asked in a small voice.

"I thought you weren't speaking."

"I don't—I didn't—I never meant you should think that."

"Oh?" Chihin said.

He was totally desperate. He said, "*Ker* Chihin, were you joking or not?"

"No," she said plainly. "Not really."

"I wasn't," he said.

Chihin's ears did a back and forth and finally didn't know where to settle.

His didn't.

"I really like you," he said desperately. "I really do."

He'd rather have faced his father with that intimacy. And that was the most dangerous hani he personally knew.

Hilfy pressed the button, signaled her presence, said, to the intercom: "*Your* excellency, I have the honor to presen *gtst* excellency Atli-lyen-tlas of Urtur, would you kindly cause the door to be opened?''

There was silence.

"*Your* excellency?"

Gods *rot* the son.

She pressed the button.

On a nestful of pillows and cushions, covered with a sheet, which showed—

One preferred not to think.

"What is *this?*" asked Atli-lyen-tlas.

There was movement beneath the sheet. She had given, she was sure, adequate time for whatever was going on decently to cease.

But Dlimas-lyi's head popped up. *Gtsto* went wide-eyed; and *gtst* head popped up beside, in a blossoming eruption of pillows.

While Atli-lyen-tlas fell back into Tarras' arms, murmuring, "Oh, the beauty, wai, the elegance of this appearance. . . ."

She found no elegance. But *gtsta* breathed, "This is my offspring. This is my offspring. I have no further to see, I have no further to know. Wai, what ambition have you? Wai, the magnificence of this nest you have made!"

While Dlimas-lyi and Tlisi-tlas-tin scrambled up clutching the sheet about *gtst*selves and floundering among the pillows.

"Atli-lyen-tlas!" *gtst* said, and *gtsto* bowed profoundly, again and again. Hilfy stood ready to catch Atli-lyen-tlas should *gtsta* fall. But *gtst* excellency of Urtur seemed to draw strength from the encounter:

"Do not take distress of my presence," Atli-lyen-tlas said. "How is my offspring now known?"

"Dlimas-lyi," *gtsto* whispered, "may it add distinction to your excellency."

"I have resigned Urtur," Atli-lyen-tlas said. "And I have no more attachment to this time."

"You are *gtsta!*"

"Just so. Nor need distress my serenity with what is beyond my reach. The *oji* is not for me now. This person Dlimas-lyi is not for me. I am free."

"Your holiness," Tlisi-tlas-tin whispered. "Please utter assurances of your good favor in our condition."

"I do so. Please," Atli-lyen-tlas said, reaching a trembling hand toward Hilfy. "Please convey me to a place where I may rest. My course is clear now. I am without obligation of any tasteful sort and would not struggle to achieve more. I am completed."

Try *that* one through the translation program, Hilfy thought in dismay. There were things which one did not ask a stsho. Sex was right in the same class as Phasing. *Gtst* excellency and Dlimas-lyi stood naked as they were born and she now had a holiness of some kind on her hands, an aged stsho, resigned, retired, unmarriageable, and sexless; and *therefore* not eligible to receive the Preciousness.

Gods save them.

"We will find your holiness suitable and tasteful quarters immediately adjacent. It will take a time to prepare. Is this acceptable?"

"We should be very honored," said Tlisi-tlas-tin.

"Most profoundly," said Dlimas-lyi, "we beg your holiness to do so."

A flutter of fingers. "I am beyond needs. But yes, this would be pleasant. I have no cares. Free. All free."

Whereupon *gtsta* indicated *gtsta* would walk back in the direction from which *gtsta* had come. Tarras and Fala offered tentative support; but *gtsta* said,

"I am free of needs."

Fall on his holy rump, Hilfy thought distressedly. But whatever reserve of strength Atli-lyen-tlas had found, still held. *Gtsta* fingers had been burning hot when they had touched hers. *Something* metabolic was going on, whether healthy or not—the stsho medical diagnosis program would have to tell them that one.

Gtsta walked ahead of them, wandering a little in *gtsta* steps, taking time to examine the texture of the walls of the corridor, the wall-com at the corner, *gtsta* fingered dials and button sockets *gtsta* had no claws to access, or there would have been loud-hail all over the ship, providing a most unwelcome and tasteless startlement to *gtsta*self.

Holiness seemed to have a direct and negative effect on the brain, Hilfy decided. And on the tendency to push buttons and take walks, and the holiness' door was going to be *locked*, the minute they had *gtsta* inside.

"Guard *gtsta*," she muttered to Tarras and Fala. "Keep *gtsta* away from buttons and sharp objects."

"What do we do if *gtsta* wants something?" Tarras asked.
"What's wrong with *gtsta?* What's going on?"

Tarras and Fala hadn't followed a word of it. One forgot.

"That's a holiness," she said. "Don't ask me whether
gtsta is Phasing or what. I don't know. And I've read every
gods-be book on the species."

"Nobody knows?" Fala asked.

"Nobody but the stsho," she said. "And they've refused
to talk."

"I . . . you know." Hallan didn't feel he was doing well.
Chihin just kept watching him, the two of them standing in
the galley, Chihin leaning back against the counter, himself
with nowhere reasonable to put his hands. "I just . . . well,
I didn't know what you thought." He didn't want to say
that Chihin's own best friends had warned him: that wasn't
kind. "I just wasn't sure you were really meaning what I
thought you meant, so I didn't want to talk to you until I
could sort of figure out . . ."

"Same," Chihin said. "You want to go back to the quarters? Sort it out where we don't have to be proper?"

"I—" He was going to hyperventilate. He wanted to take
the invitation and he was unaccountably scared to, because
it would change things, and change them all of a sudden
and too fast. "I—"

"Don't trust me?"

He thought about what Tiar had said. That he wouldn't
always understand her. But, Do you want a rescue? Tiar
had asked; and he'd said no.

"All—" he began.

*"Chihin. Report downside. Pull the white paneling out of
storage—move it, we're on short schedule."*

Chihin scowled and said a word.

"I was going to say all right," he said desperately.

But the captain said hurry and Chihin left.

*"Hallan. Report downside. We need some equipment
moved. Be extremely quiet. Remember the passengers."*

If he ran he might make the lift.

The hakkikt *Vikktakkht an Nikkatu to captain Hilfy Chanur, the hani merchant* Chanur's Legacy, *at dock at Kefk, by
courier: Has the stsho survived in any useful way? Ships arriv-*

ing from Meetpoint say that the stsho of Llyene are creating sedition and division. We must soon deal blood upon the leaders of this movement. ·Give us an estimated time of departure.

The hani ship Chanur's Legacy, *to the* hakkikt Vikktakkht an Nikkatu, *of* Tiraskhti, *at dock at Kefk: We are making modifications necessary for the transport of this person. We are finding more rapid recovery than we had thought. What is a holiness? We lack reference.*

The hakkikt Vikktakkht an Nikkatu *by courier to captain Hilfy Chanur, the hani merchant* Chanur's Legacy, *at dock at Kefk: A stsho incapable of the reproductive act. A holiness has no ability to make the alliance on which our mutual ally has placed all gtst expectation. The agents of the rival Personage will immediately take advantage and by information lately come to us, have already moved against the mekt-hakkikt. Advise us of your departure and we will delight to accompany you. Peace is advantageous. We will eat the hearts and eyes of the enemy.*

. . . it shall be the reasonable obligation of the party accepting the contract to ascertain whether the person stipulated to in Subsection 3 Section 1 shall exist in Subsequent or in Consequent or in Postconsequent, however this clause shall in no wise be deemed to invalidate the claim of the person stipulated to in Subsection 3 Section 1 or 2, or in any clause thereunto appended, except if it shall be determined by the party accepting the contract to pertain to a person or Subsequent or Consequent identified and stipulated to by the provisions of Section 5 . . .

Hilfy tapped a claw on the desk, glared at the monitor, and asked the library: *Atli-lyen-tlas who is the recipient has become a holiness. What is the result ·to the terms of the contract?*

It took an entire cup of gfi for the computer to run that request through translations, permutations, legal definitions, Compact law, stsho custom references, and the cursed subclauses.

Then it said: *Answer to print? File? Both?*

File, she said, having learned.

The answer, when it came up, said briefly: *The person accepting the contract must designate a second recipient who exists as the nearest degree of consequence to the first named recipient; if, on the other hand, the party issuing this contract disapproves this recipient, the person accepting the contract is obligated to double indemnity and the return of the cargo.*

Hilfy stared at it and stared at it, then got up and blazed a direct path down to *gtst* excellency's white, expensive nest, signaled her presence and opened the door without waiting—there being little of Tlisi-tlas-tin or Dlimas-lyi she hadn't seen.

"Your excellency, forgive a most hasty but necessary declaration! You must become the recipient!"

A tousled crest and wide moonstone eyes appeared from beneath the sheet.

"Of course," said Tlisi-tlas-tin. "Of course. Was this not understood?"

It was white. It was clean. There was carpet over the deck tiles and they'd contrived a plastic frame and some bent struts to improvise a stsho bed; they'd *made* a mattress out of plastic sheeting Chihin said she hoped to the gods didn't give way, but it held air, and it held water, and when they'd covered it with white drapery it would at least protect the old stsho, Hallan was sure it would. He crawled backward out of the pit with utmost care not to put a claw out and create a disaster.

Chihin gave him a hand on the escape, and sprawled, sitting, with a swipe of stiffened paint on her sore arm and plaster bits in her mane. She leaned against him, he leaned, they were all over with spatters and the way she looked at him, brow to brow and a little out of focus, said she was as tired and sore as he was.

And they had one thought, both, in that moment, it didn't take that much reading—his went something like a dread and an anxiousness to find out, and a fear of getting into what took time to discover and being called up short.

She said, "There's the downside shower. We can clean up, catch a snack . . ."

She wasn't young and rushing at things. He had that figured now, it wasn't on again, off again signals, it was just a sane sense of how things worked; and he didn't know

where they could go to figure out the rest of it, but he tried
to slow down his breathless haste and use his wits the way
Chihin did and tell himself if they got involved in *this* room
and didn't report in, the captain was going to ship them to
the kif. . . .

"Wonder if the mattress works," Chihin said. But he
thought he could read her now, when she was serious, when
she was being outrageous.

"I don't want to walk from Kefk," he said; and he must
have guessed right, because she put her arms on his shoulders then and laughed and got up.

"Shower," she said, and left him with his burning haste
to be a fool, a sense things could always go wrong from
here, there might not be another chance . . . Chihin could
come to her senses and decide something else, or they
could die and chances might not come again.

"Tiar," she said, talking to the intercom. "Tiar, we're
about finished. Give us a chance to get our objectionable
selves out of the passenger corridor and you can ferry the
old fellow in. . . ."

*"Thank the gods. Captain says get up here, we're in count,
we're just about to clear the umbilicals."*

Chihin's ears went flat. "In *count!* Gods *rot,* what kind
of schedule does the captain think we're up to? We got a
dying stsho, we got us so tired we can't see straight . . .
what in a mahen hell *in gods-be count.* . . ."

The thump and clang was the umbilical bundle coming
clear. Chihin was upset, besides mad. She stopped arguing,
cut off the com, and looked at him, and he didn't know
what help to be, but that Chihin was worried, worried him
about this departure they were making, the haste they
were in.

"Are we running from the kif?" he asked.

"From dead stop at dock?" She put her arms around
him a moment. Stupid question, he thought. Totally stupid
question, but he'd thought the situation might be more
complicated than that. Maybe it was and she knew and
wouldn't tell him, they never told you anything . . . it's not
your business, boy, we'll take care of it, don't worry
yourself . . .

He was scared of jump this time. He was really scared.
"There were tc'a," he said. He could only be twice the

fool. "In jump. When the alarm went off. I saw them go right through the ship and nobody was moving and I hit the alarm. In my dream, I did. And it was going off when we came out. I know it's stupid," he said, when she stood back to look at him in a worried way; and it was more disturbing that she didn't laugh, didn't offer the immediately obvious: You were dreaming, stupid kid.

"Nobody was moving," she said.

"In my dream."

"Chur dreams like that."

Chur Anify. On *The Pride*. Chur the map-maker. Chur, that they said could walk through hyperspace and see what kif saw and maybe knnn and tc'a . . .

He didn't believe that. People exaggerated, especially the world-bound ones who didn't know the limitations. You didn't expect it out of Chihin, who was Chur's cousin, if you reckoned it.

"What did you do?"

"I just got up and reached over and hit the alarm. But maybe it went off itself and I just dreamed—"

Chihin was looking at him in all seriousness, maybe thinking she didn't want to be associated with somebody that crazy.

"It's my fault, about the tc'a," he said. "Maybe that was why I dreamed it."

"Kid. If you punch any more buttons on my board you by the gods be sure what you're touching."

"Most adequate," *gtsta* pronounced, walking on strange bare feet onto the carpet they hadn't used in the decoration next door. Gods-be *right*, adequate, Hilfy thought, while the seconds ticked down in the count, and bare stsho toes curled into the white pile. "Most curious, the sensation."

"We assure you *gtst* excellency and *gtst* companion are next door," Hilfy said, while Fala and Tarras hovered near to prevent falls. "I must caution your holiness to watch your st—"

—on the rim, she had been about to say, but *gtsta* put a bare foot on the edge of the improvised bowl-chair, and Tarras made a futile grab as *gtsta* slid down the plastic footpad, plump! to what was surely multiple fractures.

Gtsta sprawled and bounced, a tangle of legs and gossamer. *Gtsta* trilled some note that did not seem of pain and, flailing *gtsta* arms, made another bounce that made the whole mattress quiver.

And a third, while three very time-pressed hani hovered at the edge and tried to assess the damage.

Another bounce, and a quivering like jelly. Is *gtsta* able to get up? Hilfy wondered. But *gtsta* seemed not to be distressed. Crackpot idea, she thought, a bagful of water. But if it didn't pop and drown the old son during acceleration, *gtsta* had a chance. A water-filled bowl-chair . . . and all the essential nutrients they'd been able to pump into *gtsta* fragile veins.

"Pull the nets over," she said. *Gtsta* had already had the medication, Tarras had seen to that, and it seemed to be taking effect. *Gtsta* lay flat on the ripples and rebounds, waving a languid arm, *gtsta* mouth pursed and *gtsta* eyes half-open, while Tarras and Fala hauled the safety netting over the pit and made it fast with cord.

"Blessing," *gtsta* holiness said. "Well wishes. I see the tides of the many suns. I see the oneness of them. I shall tell you their names. . . ."

The tranquilizer definitely was taking hold. And she for one had rather rely on the navigational computer.

Chihin was saying Meras might be a sleepwalker, that the kid was spooked and seeing tc'a, and that *that* had been the alarm during system drop. They had a clearance from the kif for undock and a schedule they'd agreed to in a star system the kif were clearly touchy about protecting; and, gods save them, they had a Preciousness and a handful of stsho to get to Meetpoint alive to back up No'shto-shti-stlen against the allies of Paehisna-ma-to,—*if* the old son could live through the experience.

They had a contract to declare filled; and get out of there alive and solvent—because they'd been out nearly a year as stationers counted time, and Tahaisimandi Ana-kehnandian had routed himself straight to Meetpoint out of Kshshti, three months ago—as Meetpoint counted time.

"*Gtsta* has *gtsta* nutrient packs, *gtsta* is comfortable . . ." Hilfy began; and *gtsta* murmured, "The oneness of it all. The ineffable contentment, after the darkness of my voyage. The light, go to the friendly light, for the sake of the peace. . . ."

Pretty gods-be out, Hilfy thought, and squatted down and looked through the net to be certain *gtsta* nutrients pack was still wrapped about *gtsta* frail arm. For the sick and the frail one didn't depend on the strength to hunt for it: it would feed continually, or as continually as anything happened in hyperspace.

Ask the kid, Chihin said, and was spooked, herself. They had one in the family. And she'd watched Chur go thin and otherly and sometimes as sensible as *gtsta*, when she was tracking something. What do you see? was the logical question.

And gods save them, she recalled with a chill down her back, Chur had talked about the light and the tides. . . .

They were underway, launched, outbound, so fast there was no time to wipe the dust off; and Chihin sat by him at her post, grinned at him, with a twitch of a white-smudged ear.

"I probably ought to tell the captain," Hallan said, not happily.

"I did," Chihin said. "It's all right. It's all right. . . ."

"That's *Tiraskhti*," Fala said. "They're away."

"Salutations to the *hakkikt*," the captain said. "Send it."

Fala did that. He heard the lisped kifish. "The *hakkikt* says," Fala reported back, " *'hold your exact course.' 'Ssak-kukkta sa khutturkht.'* —Is that right?"

"That son's going to jump with us, I knew it. Tell him we copy. Gods-rotted payback for our dock at Kefk."

Surely not for that, Hallan thought. It was dangerous. Even kif cared about their own lives.

"Tarras, Tarras, do you copy?" That was Tiar talking to Tarras, who was down below doing something the captain had sent her after. "You're clear to move."

"Aye," the answer came back, and in a moment more the lift worked and opened; and Tarras came stringing hand-line, clipping it into recessed rings along the way. So they could move if they had to, Hallan thought, without *G* or against acceleration. It wasn't something the *Sun* had ever done. It was a scary contemplation. And when Tarras got into her station, the captain ordered the arms board brought up to ready.

"Na Hallan?" the captain said, startling him, and he was

ready for the usual Be careful and keep your hands off things. "*Na* Hallan, config to scan, Chihin, take a stand-down and trank out, I want you on-line when we come out."

"Aye, captain," Chihin said, and Hallan punched the requisite buttons to bring the aux board over to scan, his hands wanting to shake quite embarrassingly.

"Good night," Chihin said to him. "Good luck."

Panic quickened his breathing. No, not panic, healthy respect for his responsibility. Just a monitor-the-dots problem. But Chihin wasn't going to be there if anything went wrong this side.

"I'm here," Tarras said at his other elbow. "Take it easy, do your job, kid. You shouldn't get any input the computer doesn't recognize."

But in another minute or so a dot leaped on to his screen, at Kefk Station rim. His heart jumped. Chihin swore—but she'd just taken the drug. "That's number 10 berth," he read off his screen, trying to stay calm. "*Mu—Muk-jukt,* captain."

"Friendly to the *hakkikt* or what?" Fala wondered aloud.

"Ask the *hakkikt,*" the captain said; and Fala did; and said, "He says, quote, he knows. . . ."

Meanwhile another kif left the station. He reported it and he didn't push buttons.

"Gods-be kif show-outs," the captain muttered at one point. "They've got to see, they've got to be there, they'll cut Vikktakkht's throat if this goes wrong. His and ours."

You mean they're not taking orders? Hallan wondered to himself. It wasn't any hani way of doing things.

"Up *V,*" the captain said. "Let's just put a little more push on it. They've got the pillows, below." They hadn't taken on cargo. They hadn't had the time. Or they hadn't trusted it.

They were just going, and Chihin murmured, drowsily, "Wake me if you see any pretty lights, kid. Otherwise, see you otherside."

Another one and another one. Fala said, "*Na* Hallan, I forgive you."

"What did I do?" he asked, surprised out of his concentration, and between reports. Lines were converging. They were going, gods, they were going . . .

"Stand by," Tiar said sharply. "This isn't the standard drop, cousins. Let's not miss a stitch. . . ."

. . . "Well, well," Aunt Pyanfar said, arms folded, feet set, the very image of herself, "you've committed yourself to the kif, have you?"

Hilfy was not surprised at the appearance. She was surprised at herself, that questions leaped into her head, Have I done the right thing? Am I a total fool, Aunt Py? . . . not angry, not resentful, not any of those things, just wishing she *could* ask across space and warped time . . . ask the real Pyanfar, not the one that came and went in her mind . . .

Like what was going on at Kefk, that kif kept Pyanfar's doings behind a screen, a whole unguessed power that wasn't just *The Pride,* wasn't just one ship and a well-reputed hani who mediated the Compact's trade and treaty disputes . . .

Like: Aunt Pyanfar, what have you gotten yourself into? Who *are* you, since you threw me out, downworld?

The *mekt-hakkikt,* indeed, the leader the kif could never find to unite them; the Personage of the mahendo'sat, with whatever religious mandate that conveyed—until some rival like Paehisna-ma-to came along; the President of the Amphictiony of Anuurn, no gray-nosed, doddering grandmother to quibble about two thousand year old privilege or ceremonial inheritance; that was not what was based at Kefk.

They were committed. They were beyond recall but not beyond disaster.

"Good luck," Tully said, remote from her. And she had too much on her mind, too much on her hands, to play those games of make-believe. He'd been right to walk away. He wasn't the property of some teen-aged child: it wasn't Tully's obligation to set her life in order, or to provide her some strange halfway creature to be, instead of hani: Take care of Chanur, Pyanfar had said, shoving her out of their midst, and wrapping time and black space about herself.

Who *are* you, Aunt Pyanfar?

And what are you doing, in deep space, where the methane-breathers go?

Humans live in that direction. They don't come to trade. They might have; but they insisted we take sides in their war—thank you, we have enough trouble, Aunt Pyanfar had said, and drawn a firm line, verbally at least.

But perhaps it was more substantial than one guessed; and vaster and more needful—

—of force? Of hunter-ships at Kefk? Of spies and assassinations of hapless stsho and bombs on Kshshti dock?

. . . "Coming down," she heard Tiar say.

So they were there. Over the edge. In it up to their ears.

The song wavered, there and not there and there again. It seemed he'd heard it for a very long time; and he'd been anxious entering jump, but it was only the dream of a guilty conscience . . .

He only heard them now. And it wasn't a threatening song, just very different.

He tried to watch the screens, but they were garble. The ship was riding the fabric of space-time, skittering along the interface, to fall into the next dimple, that only a stellar mass could make, and he could see that interface going on and on and skirling anti-mass along the disturbance they were.

Maybe it was only, after all, a dream. . . .

"Going down," he heard Tiar say . . .

He tried to capture it. The moment of dropping out of the interface. But a vast disturbance sheeted down around them, and he heard tc'a voices, or what passed for it . . .

. . . Heard a machine-voice saying: "Proximity alert, proximity alert."

"Around us!" he tried to say, his eyes full of vision and dark, but Chihin said calmly, "Got it, got it, aux; Tiar, the system buoy's gone nuts and we got a heavy surplus on hunter-ships out here. . . ."

"I saw ships," he said, "ten, twenty—off in the dark—"

"Dark of where?" the captain snapped. "This side, that side, where?"

"Otherside," he said, but he knew he was wrong, the ships were here, around them, arriving one after the other

Chapter 19

Twenty sleek kifish hunters, suddenly another one dropping in—and never, under these circumstances, believe all that the system buoy schema showed you, Hilfy thought, seeing what unfurled itself on her flanks. It wasn't a position she'd ever hoped or wanted to be in—center position in a fleet of kif, aimed at Meetpoint . . . a Meetpoint the station buoy showed busy with shipping: hani ships, stsho ships, mahen traders, kif, and tc'a and chi, as ordinary as she'd ever seen it, and deader emissions-wise than she'd ever heard it.

"Fala," she said, "all channels input. Stats. Percent. Who's who. It's too quiet for what they're showing."

"Aye," Fala said. Stats be feathered, the number of contacts flickering through com told her it was way down. And not due to the kifish presence: they were an hour out from station, light. The station had an hour yet to wait before Meetpoint learned they were here, and what was here with them and what maneuvers they were performing. An hour before station could react. But not before something might react that was lying silent and closer.

"Arms live," she said to Tarras, heard the acknowledgment, saw another set of lights come on her own board. They were now breaking the law. Several laws. Lane violations, safety violations, the disarmament treaty, the Station Immunity Act . . .

"Captain," *na* Hallan said faintly. "When you've a moment."

"Query, aux one?"

"I've got something. I recorded it—I think I did . . ."

Frightened neo. He didn't know how to give a report or switch images. Tiar had her hands full. "Fala," she said, "advise station we're inbound for dock and take the feed from Hallan."

It popped over from Fala's number one: matrix-com, raw transcript.

Chanur	advise	Paehisna-ma-to	mistake	No'shto-shti-stlen
Hilfy	you	kill	violent	right
all	wrong	not-law	bring	choice
stations	death	ambassador	now	change
listen	kif	stsho	on	Meetpoint
kif	now	is	all	governor
tc'a	know	guilty	party	. . .

Chanur advises Paehisna-ma-to ((she is) mistaken (about?)) (of the error of?) No'shto-shti-stlen. Hilfy, killing a violent (person) will be right. All unlawful wrong (deeds) bring choice/change. Stations (because of) death of the ambassador now are changing. Listen, kif, to the stsho on Meetpoint. Kif, now the governor is falling. The tc'a know the guilty party (incomplete statement).

Killing a violent person will be right? Aunt Pyanfar?

"What is it?" Tiar asked. "What's she talking about?"

"Gods-be thing's in kifish records too. They sleepwalk, most of them. —Give me the *hakkikt!*"

"Aye," Fala said, and the click and hiss of kifish communications came through strongly in her earpiece.

"Nakgoth na sti!" she said. "Hilfy Chanur nak, nakgoth na sti, hakkikt-tak skkhta."

"The tc'a are most difficult to persuade to lie," the voice came back, cultured and fluent. *"In fact, they can't."*

"*Hakkikt,* with profoundest regard to your wisdom, this isn't Pyanfar. This isn't right!"

"Right?" Vikktakkht asked. *"What is 'right?' Tell us 'right,' Chanur captain. We are Pyanfar's allies. Has there been cause for her to change sides in this?"*

Kif would. On a puff of contrary wind. Intellectually Vikktakkht knew that hani were otherwise. In his gut, in a chancy situation, he might not. "Give me a moment," she said, looked desperately at the screen, and made a reach and unbelted, dizzy as she was. She snagged the nutrient pack beside her chair, bit a hole in it, and got a swallow down as she was getting up.

"Captain?" Fala said. "We've got a station message."

"You can't have a station message. We're time-lagged."
Another swallow.

"It says—"

"It's a gods-be lie-in-wait. Transmitted to our call number from the buoy. They know who we are. They've prepped the buoy with a false system schema. What do they say?"

"It's—" Fala half turned, as she hand-over-handed her way to Fala's station, where the translator main keys were. "They're saying . . . in the name of the stsho government . . ."

. . . and the han *and the* hani *you are required to dock immediately and open to inspection. You are in violation of Compact Treaty and will be subject to severe criminal penalties if you do not obey instructions. We will accept a single ship in approach with weapons deactivated.*

The ship Chanur's Legacy *is cleared for lane 1280. Acknowledge.*

"We're getting the system detail," Tiar said. "What now, captain?"

"We're getting their word what's in this system, that's what we're getting. Chihin, look alive, Hallan, we're on live-scan only, don't believe a thing station images tell you. Fala, give me the raw data on the tc'a."

"It matches—"

"I don't care what it matches, I want to see it, now!"

The kid was rattled. She shouldn't have yelled. Fala made a false start on the order and a second one and got it.

Chanur	998	Paehisna-ma-to	86-786	No'shto-shti-stlen
586	8	798-897-22	46	567
6	57	868-897-22	1872	98
9-9	786	7	6-75	299-786t
96	76	10-69	7657	40y8
786	8=999	8/659	6-976	6-7/0
5/8	98	768-./768/865	6868/5	. . .

"It's not tc'a."

"How isn't it tc'a?" Fala protested, and Hilfy reached past her, punched up the rough again.

"It's not tc'a, I've just seen too many of them. You don't get that many unknowns in the transcript. It's driving the translator crazy. —Tiar, course change to that lane and transmit compliance."

"Captain," Tarras said, and Chihin nearly on top of that.

"I know. Did I say we were going? —Where did this gods-be thing come from? *Na* Hallan? Did you capture this transmission?"

"I—heard them. I think it's what I heard. They were with us . . . I could hear them. But I couldn't see them, captain."

"Couldn't see them. 'Couldn't *see* them' doesn't explain this output. Something odd's going on with it. You can't get a capture this clear out of hyperspace."

"Mechanical?" Fala asked. "Could it be a patch-together? Something the buoy's sending us?"

The kid was using her head again. Somebody using some complicated equipment might have assembled it out of other tc'a transmissions, and rigged the buoy to send it to their specific ship ID when they dropped in. But she wasn't that sure it was an answer. The *Legacy* made a gentle burn and she caught at the chair back and the hand-line. "Look sharp, all stations. Don't gawk. They've given us a lane down which they'll be lying in wait, friends, let's not get caught by it. Tarras, missile up."

"Aye," came the flat acknowledgment.

"Fala, vertical sort. Read it down."

Chanur	Hilfy	all	stations	listen	kif	tc'a
Advise	you	wrong	death	kif	now	know
Paehisna-ma-to	kill	not-law	ambassador	stsho	is	guilty
mistake	violent	bring	now	on	all	party
No'shto-shti-stlen	right	choice	change	Meet-point	governor.	

Chanur to all stations; listen to the kif and the tc'a. (I?) advise you of the wrongful death (because) kif now know Paehisna-ma-to is guilty of murder of the stsho ambassador. Mistake now will bring violence on all parties. No'shto-shti-stlen makes the right choice to change the governor (on) Meetpoint . . .

"Third sort. Diagonal on the left."

Gods-rotted matrix brains.

"Aye, captain."

* * *

*No'shto-shti-stlen: mistake right. Paehisna-ma-to violent
choice. Advise killing brings change. Chanur you not-law
now Meetpoint. All death ambassador on governor. Stations
kif stsho all ? listen now is party. . . .*

"Garbage. It's not tc'a. *Hani* translator, idiomatic, vertical pass."

"Captain." That from Hallan, quietly.

"Chain of command. Chain of command, Meras."

*Chanur to all stations: listen to the kif and the tc'a. They
will advise you the death was murder. The kif now have
proof that Paehisna-ma-to is guilty of the murder of the
stsho ambassadorial personnel. A false move now will loose
violent behaviors on all fronts. No'shto-shti-stlen made the
right choice when he decided to bring in a new governor.*

"It *is* Aunt Py. Gods rot her, why in a mahen hell did
she set up a hash like that? Broadcast *that* translation to
the kif. Broadcast it system-wide. And watch it! That's not
going to make certain individuals happy—" Meanwhile
they were inbound on 1280 with an ambush of some kind
set for them, no question. And *na* Hallan was sitting there
with something bursting to say, for which she had no present time. "Fala, get me the *hakkikt* again. And find out if
our passengers are in one piece."

She oozed back to her chair, fell into it as the earpiece
sputtered kifish.

"Nak."

"Chanur nak. Pakkaktu hastakkht. 1280 lakau."

A soft kifish laughter. *"Tc'a? Mau lkkto mekt-hakkikta."*
Put nothing past her.

She broke off transmission for a second. "Fala, are the
stsho alive down there?"

"Not happy," Fala said. "Alive. Scared. The two in cabin
2. I'm trying to raise the holiness. I'm getting sounds, I
can't swear to else."

She switched *Tiraskhti*-com in. "We're going in there,"
she said in the Trade. "I'm calling station, advising them
we're going in alone. They don't frighten us." They did,
but you didn't explain that to a kifish ally. You didn't stand

back here and trade ultimatums with hair-triggered kif and mahendo'sat and hope to avoid escalations.

Though wherever the trap was, their scan hadn't bounced off anything out there. And the kif hadn't seen anything they were telling about.

"Captain," Chihin said, "*na* Hallan thinks there're more ships out there."

"Where? Vector, Hallan."

"Up," came the faint answer. "They were *there,* captain."

"Tc'a?"

"I heard them. I could hear them over the com. I heard *something.*"

Gods-be spookiness. Chur was spook enough. When you had a neo wandering around in jump, the gods knew what you got. More ships? Messages at the buoy?

The buoy was the intersection, the place where ships dropped toward the local sun. The buoy recorded presences, and hadn't recorded anything but them and the kif.

Nothing, at least, that that buoy was programmed to confess to the *Legacy* and its kifish companions.

But would Aunt Py set up a message that ambiguous?

"More of her gods-be mail," she muttered. "Filtered through a tc'a brain. They've dived down like a fish breaching. They're *up* there."

"*Hovering* in hyperspace?" Tiar said.

"You can't do that," Hilfy said. "You can't change vector in hyperspace, either."

But knnn did it.

"I'd hate to pay their fuel load," Tarras said.

Tc'a did take on fuel, in realspace. Tc'a did pay bills, like the rest of them. There were surely constraints of physics on what they did in hyperspace. But one had to remember that ships didn't entirely *enter* hyperspace, didn't leave the interface, please the gods they didn't . . .

"Message to station," Hilfy said, "we have tc'a ships in the vicinity. A navigational caution is in order."

Let the mahendo'sat hunter-ships lurking out there worry about that one. Tc'a didn't obey lane restrictions. Not on Kshshti docks. Not in the regulated space around a station

And the gods knew, you didn't shoot at one. Never shoot at anything, Aunt Py had used to say, that you can't talk to

"Let's get us a little more *V,* Tiar, full 1 *G* sustained."

Sustained 1 *G* push, and one hoped the stsho aboard had taken advice and remained in their beds. Things tended to go rapidly to the aft bulkhead under these circumstances.

"*Kkkt,*" came over her earpiece. "*This amuses. We are going with you, Chanur.*"

You didn't tell a kifish *hakkikt* mind his own business, either. Thank the gods it was only *Tiraskhti* that moved. And she'd never thought she'd live to say it, but that sleek hunter moving with them was a welcome sight.

And all those kif out there . . . if anything happened to the *hakkikt,* there would be a twenty-way sort-out after the leadership of that fleet. Station surely knew that. Station surely knew that it would be very dangerous to deprive the kif of a leader, if it didn't want a firefight in its territory.

But one had to ask oneself why station was staying silent—besides the fact it didn't yet know, and wouldn't, for some few minutes, that they had a kif inbound.

She punched the intercom. "How are you both faring, excellency?"

"*Wai,*" came the breathless answer. "*Wai, the dreadfulness of ships! We are most uncomfortable! I fear for the holiness! I fear for the Preciousness! I fear for our lives!*"

"We're going to cease acceleration, your excellency, in just a few moments. —Tiar, establish with *Tiraskhti* helm, we don't want to surprise them, just stay in link with their pilot. —Fala, I'll take your board, get downside, see if *gtsta* needs attention. —Go inertial, Tiar, at your discretion."

"Standby."

The weight that had been pushing them slantwise into their cushions became ordinary, regular orientation revised up and down. "I'm going," Fala said; and Hilfy keyed over to basic com functions on her own board. "Station, this is *Chanur's Legacy,* inbound on your instructions. Inform *gtst* excellency No'shto-shti-stlen that we return delighted with our success in *gtst* instructions."

That was stshoshi. *That* for the representatives of the *han,* who would not bother to learn the language of their trading partners.

But after the due round-trip time-lapse, mahendi came back: "*You stay lane, Chanur ship. Same ask kif ship Tiraskhti. Stay lane. Legal matter here. No gun.*"

A crackle of kifish followed, with no time-lag: *Tiraskhti.*

"In the name of the mekt-hakkikt, *we will follow the treaty and we will enforce the treaty.* Parau'a mekt-hakkikta ras-surrn na uunfaura, uunfaura sassurrn ma . . ."

Hani, by the gods.

And from belowdecks: *"Captain,* gtsta *is saying some-thing about tc'a and the sun and* ker *Pyanfar. Something like the stars speaking with one voice . . ."* She could hear the babble from elsewhere, something about star-drives and resonances and talking with the fields . . . *"Otherwise* gtsta *looks all right. Should I release the netting?"*

"No!" She amended that more quietly. "Tell *gtsta* where we are, tell *gtsta* the situation, tell *gtsta* it's a safety mea-sure, and get your agile young bones up here as fast as you can."

There still wasn't a guarantee there wouldn't be shooting; but the opposition would have to be crazier than the holi-ness. The opposition had Meetpoint. The opposition had the Treaty and the Compact itself to hold hostage—because if the opposition didn't start shooting, the opposition held Meetpoint, and Momentum continued on the side of Paehisna-ma-to; while if *they* started shooting, the *mekt-hakkikt*'s own side would have broken the Treaty. And it all came unraveled from there—even if they had the force to take Meetpoint without damage, which, with a mahen fleet hidden out there—they didn't have.

Not a nice situation, she said to herself. Not at all a nice situation, Hilfy Chanur. *Why* did you take the gods-be contract?

"*Berth 22,* Legacy," station deigned to say.

"Are we going to take their computer input?" Tiar asked.

"No," Hilfy said. "What's one more law? You and Chihin, just figure us in. We'll take their 22. They'll proba-bly have guards. Lots of guards."

"Kif?" Tarras wondered.

"I'll bet you they aren't. I'll bet there was a reason old No'shto-shti-stlen had gtstself nose-deep in kif. And I'll bet there were casualties. On the other hand—"

"On the other hand."

"On the other hand, stsho aren't prone to commit them selves until it's absolutely safe. So cancel the last bet. There may not have been. There may not have been a shot fired here. It's not the *han*'s style. Or Llyene's. Leave that to Paehisna-ma-to. Well, well—"

She was playing with the optics. Scan wasn't showing the ambush, which in Meetpoint's sparse system didn't leave many points of cover—like keeping the station between them and the opposition, hence the lane assignment; like keeping some of them lying off in the system fringes, like between their ships and system exit, to nadir of the star.

But ships in dock caught the wan sunlight quite nicely, besides all those working-lamps and warning-lights that kept outside tenders and pushers from going splat! into a station structural part or a ship at dock. Optics was a major function on her board; and she had already been watching and capturing images.

"Ah. There's *Ha'domaren.* . . . Not out there where he could get hurt, not our Haisi."

"Gods rot him," said Tiar.

"Couple of kif we don't know. Tc'a ship shows up as a seen-before, at Urtur."

"My heart won't take the surprise," Tiar said.

"Oh, here's one. *Ehrran's Honor.*"

"Ehrran!"

"We do have a *han* presence here, friends. Can we assume it's that faction which hates us with a passion? We have Paehisna-ma-to's pet hunter captain. We have assorted mahendo'sat, we have—*Padur's Victory.*"

"Blast them if they're in on this!"

"Could be coincidence. They were coming this way, for probably honest reasons. But I'd *sure* like to know who was at Hoas while we were at Urtur."

"What about the *Sun?*" Hallan asked.

"I wish I could tell you not." But there it was, in evidence between two other hani ships, *Nai's Splendor,* and *Doran's Golden Hope. Sahern's Sun Ascendant,* plain to see. "*Lslillyest,* a good clutch of stsho ships, none of which I know, none of which library knows, which indicates they're not traders, they're from deep inside stsho space . . . do I guess, the capital at Llyene, if they've set No'shto-shti-stlen aside?"

"Politics," Tiar said. "Gods, there's something three days dead here."

"We could get out of here," Chihin said. "We could tell the kif we've had our closer look, goodbye, good luck."

"They'll outlaw us. They'll have their evidence, a cargo not delivered, right on the books. Chanur will lose this ship, Chanur will lose Momentum with the mahendo'sat."

"Better free-running than clipped at dock."

"It's one thing to say, cousin."

"We're not giving up!"

"Oh, no, no, no, Chihin."

"What are we going to do?" Tiar asked.

"I don't exactly know. Neither do they. They can try their writs and their papers. Those don't make many holes in the hull. And they'll talk to us. Talk is what they're here for. They're here to prove a case against us."

"It's a trap," Hallan said. "If the *Sun*'s with them, it's a trap—they're going to file some complaint, captain."

"Good lad, good thinking. Gods-be right they are."

"I don't want to get you in trouble."

She had to laugh. Probably to Hallan Meras it wasn't funny.

"They're not getting him back," Chihin said.

"Just run the calc," she said. "First thing is not to hit the station. Then we'll worry about Sahern clan. They're a minor problem."

"It's not a minor problem," Chihin said.

"Say he's not going to Sahern. It's one thing for *me* to throw him off. No gods-be Sahern is taking him. Two plus two, cousin, let me handle the legal work, you have your hands full and I don't want to make a mistake here. Fala, you want to make another run belowdecks?"

"Aye, captain, I will."

"I'd say we have another half hour. Get down there, there's some shifting about I want done. You *may* have to do take-hold down there. Have something in mind."

"Aye, captain."

Nervy kid. It was a dangerous thing, moving about in approach. Things could happen. But the stray cargo pusher that happened into the *Legacy*'s path was going to be out of luck.

"Captain," Tarras said, "I'm still holding that missile live."

"That's where you're to hold it."

"Just confirming," Tarras said. "Thank you."

Calc was shaping up. Fala called up for instructions. Station called to protest they were out of calibration, check their computers.

"Oh, we're not using your feed," Hilfy delighted to say. "Since you can't prove you're authorized. We'll just guess our way in."

"You damn fool!" Meetpoint Control screamed.

"How are we doing, Tiar?"

"Oh, maybe five, ten percent one way or the other. Who knows?"

"You lose your license!"

"Hope we're good, Meetpoint. Or give us No'shto-shti-stlen."

"Not can do! Not can do! Brake!"

"Have Paehisna-ma-to's adherents so little nerve?" Vikk-takkht cut in over com. *"We, on the other hand, are braking. And our weapons remain live."*

Credit to the *hakkikt,* not one word about the missile they had armed, which with his systems he most probably knew about.

"Thank you, *hakkikt.*"

"You stop, you stop, I call superior!"

"Like give us access to No'shto-shti-stlen?"

"You stop, I try!"

"Are we calc'ed, Tiar?"

"We're steady on."

"Sorry, Meetpoint. Not in the mood now. Maybe we'll take that missile off-line. Maybe not."

"You bluff!"

"Oh, yes, sometimes. Not all the time." She shut off that com-link. "Shut it down, Tarras."

"Gray hairs," Chihin muttered, "forty of 'em."

"Just put us in soft," she said.

Hallan's mouth was moving. Reading numbers or committing himself to the gods, Hilfy thought. And punched in the take-hold.

"You damn fool break five hundred law!"

"He's hysterical," Hilfy said, accidentally into a live mike. "Take care of that, Tiar." And cut the contact. "Your excellency, I report a safe dock. You may move about now. Felicitations on your excellency's return to

Meetpoint. We are now attempting to make contact with
gtst excellency the governor, but mahendo'sat have occupied station offices. . . ."

"*Wai!*"

"We believe by the number of stsho ships here at dock
who are not traders that some treachery is contemplated.
There are han officials who have historical antipathy
toward Chanur; there are mahendo'sat including Ana-
kehnandian; but the ship of his excellency the *hakkikt* Vikktakkht is holding position off the station with the threat
of weapons and of the Treaty and of the displeasure of the
mekt-hakkikt. As to *gtst* excellency No'shto-shti-stlen, these
outrageous persons are withholding contact with *gtst* excellency. We are in fear for *gtst* safety at this moment, or
wonder if your excellency might have a word with these
individuals."

"*I shall execrate them.*"

"Please prepare to do so. I am putting your intercom in
direct radio contact with Meetpoint communications. For
obvious reasons we are not accepting the umbilicals, most
particularly the com lines."

"*We are prepared.*"

"You are in contact," she said, and pushed the button
and eavesdropped, chin on fist.

"*Outrageous and shameless behavior,*" was the opener,
at a pitch that made the indicators spike. While on a wave-
length belonging to hani official business: "Chanur's Legacy, *put me in contact with Hilfy Chanur.*"

"You are there," Hilfy answered. "Good day. Is this Ehrran clan?"

"*Insolence will not improve your case with the* han! *You
are personally and as a crew charged with piracy, kidnapping, rape, and murder; you are as a head of clan charged
with treason, sedition, violation of Treaty law, . . .*"

"Speeding. You forgot speeding and irregular docking
procedure, Ehrran. This is a political show and we both
know it. Gods, is there a dirty business this side of Aji
you don't have your hand in?"

"*I demand to speak to Hallan Meras. On behalf of Meras
clan and Sahern.*"

That was bound to come. Hallan threw her a desperate
look, Chihin looked like thunder.

Hilfy punched the transmit again. "Demand what you like, Ehrran. Chanur doesn't permit it."

Captain, Hallan was saying soundlessly. She shook her head.

"Do I have that for the record, Chanur?"

"Absolutely you do, Errhan."

"Captain," Hallan said distressedly.

"You're married. Shut up."

"I'm—"—married, the jaw said.

"As of about half an hour ago. Signed by a stsho official, a stsho holiness, an impartial witness and me as captain of this ship. Congratulations and don't disgrace us."

"Who—?" Hallan shut up again. The Eyes of the *han* was reading more charges on com.

"Better be me," Chihin said darkly.

"First listed," Hilfy said. "Excuse us we didn't ask preferences. You were calculating approach and I thought they'd pull this."

"But," Hallan said. Before Chihin shut him up. Ehrran was repeating some question. She just transmitted the document in facsimile. And the one charging Sahern with desertion, abandonment, public insult, public indecency, malicious suit, and nine infractions of the common law of Compact space.

"And I'm adding conspiracy and defamation under the law of the Amphictiony; and conspiracy to commit breach of the Peace under Treaty law, Ehrran, against the captain and crew of *Sahern's Star Ascendant.* If she wants to go to court, by the gods, I have names and dates logged."

Strange the silence that followed that. The contact broke off. Somebody was consulting somebody.

She punched in on the conversation on the other channel. Indicators were still hitting high levels.

Let it run, she thought, and shoved back to give her legs a stretch. "I think we'll stand down a while. Put us on alarm, Chihin. Put the recording on. Go clean up . . . do whatever takes your fancy. Good luck, *na* Hallan, congratulations, welcome to the clan, we'll give you the formal party when we get out of this."

There was a general clearing out. She didn't ask to where. She sat down again, and started reviewing the messages that they weren't admitting receiving.

Not everyone had left. She saw the shadow in a dead
monitor, looked back at Tiar over her shoulder.

"Need any help?"

"Might."

"The *han*'s not through yet."

"The *han*'s not through yet and Paehisna-ma-to hasn't
even started."

"The bribes have to be flying. Paehisna-ma-to to the
stsho, to the kif off-station, the kif on-station . . ."

"The *hakkikt* has been loyal to Aunt Py for a long time."

"Some of them could be getting restive. Including the
hakkikt."

"I have thought of that."

"They say you can buy anything at Meetpoint."

"Except certain things. I'd say maybe the Preciousness
isn't on the open market. Maybe a holiness isn't. The stsho
are fragile people. They'd never take a chance that wasn't
forced on them. They're hanging back now, I'm betting on
it, trying to see where advantage lies."

"Politicians."

"Not all bad, politicians. The stsho are good at it. They'd
have been a mouthful for somebody long since if they
weren't. And if they weren't a prime source of goods; and
if they hadn't ties with the methane-folk."

"The tc'a business? That was extremely odd."

"It was very extremely odd. Py sent that in symbol-set.
The tc'a that received it didn't read it in the ordinary way.
It thought the sentences were separate-brain paths. It inter-
preted them that way and just nearly got us all in trouble."

"You think she's near here?"

She considered that answer a long moment. Then: "No.
I don't. I think she knows what's going on but she can't
get here in time."

"You can't transmit in hyperspace!"

"You can't change vector and you can't transmit. Correction. *We* can't."

Tiar made a rumbling in her throat and shook her head.
"If you could do that—"

"—to blazes with the futures market, the whole way we
trade? Yes to that, too. Aunt took a big chance getting
that message here. Possibly Vikktakkht knows. Possibly it

surprised him. Possibly he won't rush to the nearest gathering of kif and tell what he just heard. I have the feeling it scared hell out of him."

"Keep the fear in him?"

"Certainly it shook him. Certainly it made him think. Certainly we've got one ally out there that's got something new to think about. That's why I'm inclined to make a bet that we've got a little leeway with Vikktakkht. And I may do something I wouldn't dare, if *gtst* excellency can't find *gtst* excellency very soon now."

"What's that?"

"Surrender our stsho passengers."

"They are reprehensible individuals!" *gtst* excellency cried, waving *gtst* arms. "They are covered in shame and perfidy!"

"Your excellence could not then discover the whereabouts of No'shto-shti-stlen? Or is it tasteful for me to ask—"

"Your honor has every attribute of taste! Your honor is the only whiteness in a thousand worlds, wai! the treachery, wai! the reckless and shameless behavior of individuals who were born with better advantage!"

"What is the condition of No'shto-shti-stlen?"

"Dire. *Gtst* bravely holds *gtst* post. But *gtst* confides to me that *gtst* despairs. The influence of Paehisna-ma-to has reached even to Llyene, and the capital has lost confidence in *gtst* excellency, the capital has sent out other persons to displace *gtst* that may be more pleasing to Paehisna-ma-to."

"And not pleasing to the *mekt-hakkikt?*"

"One can hardly please both, as *gtst* excellency foresaw. I must take the Preciousness, I must advance onto the station, I must show these emissaries that I am disdainful of them and their gross displays of foreign force, these—"

Gtst ran out of breath and subsided onto the pillows, while Dlimas-lyi tried with gentle touches to calm *gtst*.

"I shall go with *gtst*," Dlimas-lyi looked up to say. "I shall not permit *gtst* alone to venture among strangers."

"*Your* excellency," Hilfy said in all honesty, "your tastefulness and good qualities make me admire you exceedingly. You are the most excellent of stsho."

"You are likewise the most excellent of hani," Tlisi-tlas-tin declared, reaching up a thin, white hand. "I value your estimation."

Was it possible a hani could grow fond of *gtst* excellency? She thought so, quite profoundly fond of the fellow and *gtst* nestmate.

She knelt down, to bring herself eye to eye with *gtst* excellency, who gazed at her with no lowering of lashes or nodding away.

"Your excellency, may I ask the most extreme trust? The most reckless trust? And perhaps something of great delicacy?"

"Ask."

"May I—em—transport the Preciousness elsewhere for perhaps an hour or two? May I do things in your name which I may try to perform tastefully, but which, if I fail, will attach only to me and my ignorance? In no wise would I risk your excellencies' honor or your reputations."

Eyes lowered, hands fluttered. "You ask a most dire favor!"

"I am—aware of the nature of the Preciousness, and I will treat the Preciousness as if it were my own honor in question."

It seemed *gtst* excellency might faint or Phase, so great was *gtst* agitation. Then *gtst* seized her hand with all *gtst* slight strength.

"*Gtsta* might handle the Preciousness! In this fashion would our honor be kept!"

"Most resourceful of stsho!" she said, and leaped up in a thoroughly tasteless haste, on her way to the door before she remembered a courteous bow.

"Wai, go!" *gtst* excellency cried, waving *gtst* gossamer sleeve. "Go, at all necessary speed, dear hani, and work necessary disarrangements upon our enemies!"

Chapter 20

For a while there was just no thinking, even about hazards around them. It helped that Chihin was crazy; or as crazy as he was, with everything that had happened, and it helped that the other four of his wives *didn't* insist on conjugal privileges. . . .

But for a while one's brain just shorted out, and then wouldn't work, and when common sense finally came back, the two of them seemed to find it together.

"I think—" Hallan tried to say.

"Yeah," Chihin breathed.

"I think maybe we better get back. . . ."

"I think so too," Chihin said, and started getting up, so he did. He thought, We could be killed. We could all be arrested. What kind of fools are we, acting like this?

But Chihin looked at him and he straightway lost his good sense again, until she made a face and swore and shoved him out the door, where the air was colder and clearer and the ship-sounds in the corridor reminded anybody with a brain at all that there were urgent operations going on.

They went to the bridge but only Tiar was there. Tiar twitched an ear back to take in their presence, Chihin flung herself into station and punched buttons—he settled into his chair more carefully, and didn't.

"What's up?" Chihin asked.

"Captain's downside, talking to the mahendo'sat."

"What, talking to the mahendo'sat? What have we got to say to the mahendo'sat? Blow their—"

"That's what they're doing," Tiar said. "Fala's got ops lowerdeck, Tarras is with the captain, and, well, we know where you two were."

"Don't give me that! What in a mahen hell's going on?"

"Main ops channel," Tiar said.

"Well, well, now we got make deal." Haisi stood, arms folded, on the dockside, at the bottom of the *Legacy*'s ramp, and blew smoke into the frosty air. "You give *oji*, we give you clear undock, go home, safe, no trouble . . . small difficulty with kif, same we fix."

"Fix like you fixed things at Kshshti."

"Not us, hani, you got bad information. You got real close experience with kif. You forget?"

"No. But it doesn't matter to the bottom line."

"What matter?" Another puff of smoke, green and blue against the neon of some shop along the Rows. "What make matter? You in one damn bad mess, hani. You look bad, Pyanfar Chanur look bad. You got find way out . . . because if that kif out there attack this station, who bring same here? If you start shoot, who got trouble? You got."

"You say. Looks to me like we're both here."

"Wrong." With hand on large expanse of dark-furred chest. "We here with invi-tation stsho government. We got word maybe kif problem, stsho from Llyene ask us come in here, toss out kif guard on account of no good deal No'shto-shti-stlen make with marry Atli-lyen-tlas. Atli-lyen-tlas got too many 'so-ciations with kif. Llyene government have got embarrass' by No'shto-shti-stlen, official come here, examine record, got prepare replace *gtst,* maybe severe reprimand. Meanwhile here come kif. Damn right here come kif. Want old job back. Want commit little piracy, a? You been number one suckered, hani."

She laid her ears back. "If you're so friendly with the stsho, how come you had to come ask *me* about the *oji?* How come that? A?"

"You know stsho. Three sex. *Gtst* do politic, *gtste* and *gtsto* very private, do sex, no public. No'shto-shti-stlen and Atli-lyen-tlas both *gtst.* So somebody got to step down from politic. Stsho at Llyene don't like Atli-lyen-tlas, long time want *gtst* come back stsho space, long time No'shto-shti-stlen protect same, now want marry *gtst.* So what sex No'shto-shti-stlen be? *Gtst* propose same in the *oji.* Maybe if No'shto-shti-stlen stay *gtst,* stsho at Llyene not upset enough come here make new government. But stupid han won't answer question, so they come. They say you give them the *oji,* all fine."

"So where are they?"

"They watch. I promise same. Not worry."

"Where's No'shto-shti-stlen?"

"With stsho. We not touch. I tell you, you give *oji,* everybody go away happy. 'Cept maybe kif. You no worry. We fix kif."

"Vikktakkht's a friend of my aunt."

A laugh. A long draw at the smokestick and a slow exhale. "Vikktakkht kif. Nobody friend. Don't got word, 'friend.' Just 'advantage.' Just stab in you back when you no more scare him. Why he not come in station, a? He wait. Let stupid hani fight the mahe. Tell you what. You give *oji,* stsho at Llyene happy, we happy, no problem."

"I don't *give* anything, mahe. I'm not a charity. I got it, I keep it. Maybe I take it to my aunt."

"Make big mess. Meanwhile you got go out there tell kif sorry you make mistake. You look real bad, hani. You look like dessert. Maybe like hos-tage, a? Kif go make deal Pyanfar, hey, you want? You pay. You got experience that game."

Trying to shake her nerve, he was. She wrinkled her nose, not a friendly gesture. Or a patient one. "Maybe I get along with them just fine."

"Then you two time fool. You got chance win big here. Pyanfar got lot commitment No'shto-shti-stlen. *You* make new deal, be friend new gov'ment, all fine, easy new gov'ment be friend Pyanfar. You big important. Lot good deal for you."

She stared at him, thought about the directions power would run in the Compact, asked herself what was in it for Paehisna-ma-to, and came up with: "doublecross." Not quite a coup for Paehisna-ma-to, but no prosecution for the explosion at Kshshti, they'd blame that one on the kif; no absolute gain of power but no stop to the Momentum of Paehisna-ma-to either. Net gain, no loss, No'shto-shti-stlen out of the way, net gain there, too, putting Meetpoint in the hands of someone more attuned to other voices.

Gods, she did hate politics. And hated worse being suckered.

But if Haisi tossed off a kifish strike force of twenty hunter ships as a "we fix," Haisi had a lot of firepower out there hidden in the system—

"So?" Haisi asked her. "You want be logical? No good, the *oji*, got no value 'cept to stsho. Chanur don't want lose face. We don't want lose face. 'Specially Vikktakkht don't want lose face: what you got do is make him look good, make him go 'way."

So maybe there *wasn't* such a large mahen force. And Haisi was one good negotiator.

"You want me to tell him to go away, huh? You worried?"

A quick frown. Haisi snatched the smokestick from his mouth to jab it in her direction. "You want peace? You not want? That are whole question. You not just stupid hani captain, you *Chanur*. You got youself in politic, all right, you play smart. You only damn one can get that kif go 'way now. You only one can save Vikktakkht *sfik* so he don't get throat cut by own follower. Kif damn fragile, all time damn fragile. You got save him, or we got fight. I *rather* not fight. I rather not have this kif sit point gun at Meetpoint. Lot nervous people here."

Maybe Haisi was saying the same about himself—he was in a bind, a serious one. He wanted a way out.

So she'd done him damage. She had that.

"I have to give him something," she said. "I have to bring him in on the negotiations. I have to be there. This has to save face for everybody. You understand me?"

Haisi looked relieved. "Number one fine. You got million credit deal. You walk away clear. What more want?"

"No, no, no, it doesn't work that way. We've got to talk to the stsho. We've got to have a slice of this, so does Vikktakkht."

"What you want? You dumb hani captain, no make gov'ment."

"I'm Chanur, mahe. You've been using that, that's the game you've been playing, and I demand to have something out of this that's going to satisfy that kif out there, that's going to satisfy our honor, and not have any trouble with our papers, our cargoes, or the Personage's affairs. I have an obligation to her friends. I have a contractual obligation to No'shto-shti-stlen. That's *gtst* property. I can't just hand it over. I've got, for that matter, an obligation to that kif out there, who's played tolerably fair with me. So you've got what you want here, you haven't got what I have, you're not secure until you've got it, and you'd better damn well settle with our honor, and our claims, and our—pardon me—finance, because anything else is going to be expensive to the stsho and to this station, which *isn't* going to make the stsho damn happy with you, a?"

"So what you got have?"

"In trade? First off, not to have that stsho contract hanging over my head. I've got to have trade agreements with the new government, including trade agreements for Vikk-takkht's interests. I've got to have Chanur's friends out of here: we're not leaving any hostages in anybody's hands."

"What friend you talk about?"

"No'shto-shti-stlen."

"No, no, no good deal."

"What no good deal? What threat is *gtst* to anybody if he's not the governor?"

A few rapid puffs of smoke. The whole dockside was unnaturally silent. "You give *oji,* I present deal to stsho."

"No. You give me No'shto-shti-stlen, or no *oji.*"

"You no damn position to bluff, hani. You want see Chanur take bad damage, you go ahead. Meetpoint dock get blow to hell, all you fault, you bring kif in. Look damn bad. We throw out kif guard for stsho, you bring back, blow up dock. . . ."

"I could *destroy* the *oji.* So nobody gets it."

Brows went up. "Not good. Holy antiquity. Belong big stsho fam'ly."

"So somebody gets badly upset if anything happens to this *oji,* huh?"

"Stop play game! We talk about you trade agreement. We get damn kif leave this system!"

"Agreements with the kif too."

"We talk."

"You want him out of here, right you talk. You talk damn serious. No doublecross."

"First give *oji.*"

"First give No'shto-shti-stlen."

"Simul-taneous."

"All right. You bring No'shto-shti-stlen, I bring the *oji.*"

"Maybe so you got Atli-lyen-tlas. Maybe you think pull trick. I tell you, we see stsho, that stsho dead before foot touch this deck. Same hani."

Now the masks were off. *Now* they knew the players. She stared at the mahe as eye to eye a hani could, at a species head and shoulders taller. "I've said what we have to have. Simultaneous transfer. Then we start talking—and talking seriously, mahe, no damn tricks on your side either."

"You got pocket com? You crew follow all this?"

What's he up to? she wondered; and said aloud: "They're listening, damned right."

"Same mine. Same stsho. We stand here, you crew bring *oji,* stsho bring No'shto-shti-stlen. All fine."

"Fine." She folded her arms. "Tiar?"

"Aye, captain," the answer came back.

"When I see No'shto-shti-stlen on the dock, I'll advise you. Nothing leaves the ship before then."

"Aye, captain."

"Advise the *hakkikt* we're in negotiation and we'll keep him posted."

"I'll do that, captain."

She gave a wave of the hand. "Your turn."

A casual puff of smoke. Haisi rattled off a string of mahendi language she didn't follow that well. But it contained words like No'shto-shti-stlen, *gtst,* and stsho.

There was argument.

Haisi said, "Stsho want know no guns."

"No guns." She switched to stshoshi, figuring on Haisi's bug to pick it up. "I wish to establish friendly relations with the most distinguished representatives from Llyene. I should in no wise wish to perform a tasteless act of violence or to endanger them in any way."

Haisi didn't understand all of that, either. It was not altogether Trade-tongue.

Haisi looked just a little uneasy. So the stsho weren't prisoners. And, being stsho, they were probably treating No'shto-shti-stlen tolerably well, so long as events were uncertain, so long as there was the remotest chance of anything going contrary to their plans.

Probably too, No'shto-shti-stlen, the canny old fellow,

had held out hope, so long as he had a throw of the dice left. Haisi had said *gtst,* and maybe it was the standard, safe term, and maybe it was something else. Some stsho might have Phased under such stress. But she fully expected to see *gtst* in possession of *gtst* name, *gtst* dignity, and *gtst* claim to the *oji.*

And the stsho would not be safe from *gtst* until they had the *oji,* that seemed likely from the persistence with which Haisi wanted to lay hands on it.

When *that* went into hostile hands, this emblem of whatever gender it was, evidently No'shto-shti-stlen posed no threat. And she *wished* she knew she was doing the right thing.

But time passed, and passed, here in the dockside cold with, she was sure, a good many eyes on every breath they took. Haisi smoked one smokestick down to a stub, extinguished it with a pinch and put it in the pouch of his kilt, from which he took out another and lit it with a good deal of fuss.

"That *can't* be good for you," she said, and Haisi let out the breath he had been drawing in while lighting it, put the lighter away and laughed.

"Not good," he said. "Keep want quit. How you? Got no bad habit?"

"Husbands," she said. "Just got my second."

Another laugh. "You marry! Heard same. Maybe you cheat on husband, we get together next port. Big party."

"With *you?* No thanks. I have *some* taste."

Haisi grinned wide. "I bet you good."

"Number one right I'm good. Ask me again sometime, oh, three, four years. I might be in the mood for a pirate."

"Honest citizen. I tell you, Hilfy Chanur, you got learn tell difference, quit lie down with kif."

She'd heard about every nasty comment on that topic there was. She put on a perfect smile. "What *is* the difference? Hah?"

"Cute hani. Pretty nose. Pretty eyes."

"You are a bastard, Haisi. A charming bastard. But you are a bastard." There had been movement just then, across the dock, on the merchant strip, a pale-robed shadow, and another, now. "Looks like stsho."

Haisi didn't turn his head to look. He angled his whole body, to watch her and Tarras up by the gate; and to see what was happening.

"They bring No'shto-shti-stlen. Where *oji?*"

"So how do we do this? Meet halfway?"

Haisi stretched out his arm to the left. "Halfway there, you bring *oji.*" And to the right: "Same halfway there, No'shto-shti-stlen. We take, you take, all fine."

"Fair," she decided, and touched the pocket com. "Tiar, they're coming. Did you follow that? We're to bring the *oji* out and put it down on the dock at about the same pace they bring No'shto-shti-stlen to a similar place some little removed. You can bring it as far as the gate, now."

Haisi was talking to his own crew, and then, apparently to the stsho, saying much the same thing.

There was the chance of a switch. But it was not a time to argue. It was highly unlikely one stsho would place *gtst*self in jeopardy by posing as another and it was unlikely the stsho with *gtst* would risk their lives by bringing a substitute. And if she slowed down the proceedings Haisi would do exactly the same, at which point everything could come unraveled. People could get shot. Including No'shto-shti-stlen.

Which was still a possibility, once Haisi had the *oji,* which was one reason Tarras was up there, in a high position relative to the dockside.

One thing she would bet on: no one in the *han* could read stsho signatures. *She* couldn't, with any certainty. It was within the realm of possibility they would have shown the marriage document to stsho, to *Haisi*'s stsho, for verification . . . so it was within possibility that the Llyene stsho knew that Atli-lyen-tlas was a holiness: signatures did indicate Mode, Phase, and Gender, among other Life Events of significance. It was within possibility that the Llyene stsho recognized the identities of Tlisi-tlas-tin and Dlimas-lyi, *and* their relationship. And the negotiations had still gone as they had gone, which didn't prove one way or the other that the stsho had told everything they knew to Ana-kehnandian . . . but by all she knew of stsho, Tahaisi-mandi Ana-kehnandian was in their estimation not to be confided in. Nor wholly in power over the situation: there-fore not to be confided in. Perfectly logical stsho reasoning, who held self-preservation and tasteful behavior paramount.

She knew just enough to know how much she didn't know. But there was no choice, absolutely no choice. She'd done the best trading she could with the goods she had. She thought she'd come away as best she could—but she never thought that Ana-kehnandian was going to play fair.

Not by the gods likely, Haisi.

Haisi gave her a nod and walked off to stand at the appointed spot to receive the *oji*, where others of his crew showed up, armed . . . of course: *they* replaced the kif as station police.

She walked off toward the stsho, to receive No'shto-shti-stlen. And she said, into com, which doubtless was being monitored on *Ha'domaren*, by electronics the mahendo'sat had had time to install around the dock, "Is it in position?"

"Aye, captain," Tiar said.

"Everything's on schedule. Bring it on out, down to the dock. They start walking, we start walking, that's the way it works. I'm going out onto the dock to wait for No'shto-shti-stlen. When you carry it out, go toward Ana-kehnandian and his crew at the same rate you see No'shto-shti-stlen going toward me. When *gtst* reaches me, you set down the case and go back to the lock."

"Got that," Tiar said. The instructions were for Fala. But Tiar understood. *"She's coming out now. You'd better see them moving, captain."*

She didn't turn to see. She had her attention divided between the stsho, who did begin tentatively to move, and Haisi and his lot, and the possibility of snipers somewhere about the dock—which was a fearful lot of real estate to monitor. At a certain point one just hoped to the gods.

"They're moving," she said.

Stsho were not going to dash into possible danger. It was a nervous, sometimes halting advance. She could see Fala now, doing almost pace for pace the same thing as the stsho, with the black case within her arms. And she could pick out the one she thought must be No'shto-shti-stlen, among the gleaming gossamer of the others, a figure no less richly dressed, no less adorned and painted, but less interested in the surroundings than looking toward her, only toward her, as if she were the destination of hope.

Closer and closer.

"Your excellency?" she asked. "No'shto-shti-stlen?"

There were bows, a deep one from the one stsho, nervous ones from the others.

"Wai, most gracious hani," said the one, in stshoshi, which the others might not know she understood. It was the only proof she could look to have . . . *gtst* looked right. *Gtst* sounded right.

"Please accompany me with all tasteful speed," she said, and added, for the others, "Please abandon this exposed place. There is danger."

No'shto-shti-stlen was willing. She struck out for the *Legacy*'s dock at a fair pace, the others were dithering, and of a sudden *all* the stsho were bolting with her.

Herd-mind, Vikktakkht had said, My gods! She didn't know what to do but run, all the stsho were running, and Fala sprinted for the ramp, but no shots came. Hilfy stopped there, a momentary pause, in the middle of a lot of stsho who were probably wishing they had bolted the completely opposite direction. "Get *gtst* into the ship!" she ordered Fala. "Your excellency, go with her!"

As she saw Haisi with the box on the decking, yonder, saw the stsho with her begin to go uncertainly in that direction. But Haisi was bound to check out the goods—to be sure of them.

Haisi opened the box. A silver spheroid rolled out—a small one. And if their wiring worked right—

Haisi dived for the cover of a station girder, right behind his men. The stsho shrieked with one voice and retreated the only direction they could, toward the *Legacy*. A moment later the silver ball exploded with a fearsome shock, a ball of upward-wafting fire, and a huge cloud of smoke.

Stsho yelped into silence, Haisi was sprawled flat not quite into cover, and just then apparently realizing the explosion behind him had not done major damage.

Thank the gods of space.

Haisi was getting up, beginning to figure it, and glared at her. She laughed and laughed harder, in spite of the fact snipers were possible. The smoke was beginning to clear and a shape to appear out of it, a pale, twisted structure tall as he was, twice as wide, lacy, white, with subtle ochers

"Exploding rocks," she said, and shouted it, she couldn't resist it. *"Exploding rocks, Haisi, you son of an earless mother!"*

She herded the stsho for the *Legacy*'s rampway, just a little out of the way of snipers, or a direct shot from Haisi, who was just standing there, probably with his brain rattled from the shockwave, and maybe adding up the fact that that *hadn't* been the *oji*, which was still on the *Legacy*, and that she had, presumably, No'shto-shti-stlen, and that, thanks to stsho instincts, she had the Llyene officials uncertainly sheltering in the shadow of the *Legacy*'s access.

And she had a lot of kif allies out there.

"Pray go inside," she said to the stsho, "where your excellencies will find more safety. This mahe is of uncertain mood and possibly tastelessly violent behavior."

"What *is* this object?" a stsho asked.

She hadn't exactly decided what to call it. But she threw it another look, standing there wreathed in the smoke of its birth, and said, considerately, "An . . . artwork, actually, most excellent, and never of any hazard to the station."

"An artwork," one said, and something she couldn't catch. "An artwork," another said, or a variant on that. There was a sound among them she'd never heard the species make, with waving of hands and bobbing of heads, and a general milling about.

Then a mass "Iiiii," of uncertainty, but not a thing more, as she and Fala together urged them into the rampway chill, away from snipers, please the gods, away from imminent attack.

"Advance to the airlock," she advised them above their murmuring and hesitations. "All will be well." She certainly hoped so.

Tarras had the gun discreetly out of view behind the gate: "Tiar," she said to the pocket com, once they were through, with Tarras still keeping a careful eye on the docks, "Tiar, shut that gate and open the airlock, we're in, we're all in, we're clear."

She was breathlessly glad when that gate slid shut: no way to lock it against somebody stationside with a key or a master control, but she heard the lock open, out of sight around the curve of the tube—safety and their own deck was that close, and if nobody started an interstellar war while they were traversing this very fragile tube she vowed she would turn religious.

Then just as the foremost of the flock of stsho rounded the curve of the tube toward the airlock, they stopped dead in their tracks and exclaimed in startlement, refusing to budge as the back ranks crowded up against them.

A totally naked stsho was walking down the tube, bearing the Preciousness in *gtsta* hands, as inane and as happy an expression on *gtsta* face as she had ever seen on a stsho.

"No'shto-shti-stlen!" *gtsta* exclaimed delightedly. "Blessed be the receiver of the gift, blessed be the bearer of young, blessed be you, O most excellent of excellences!"

No'shto-shti-stlen—it was *gtst*—came and took the Preciousness in *gtst* arms, and bowed and bowed—there being nothing the captain, walled away from the proceedings by a phalanx of murmuring and bobbing stsho, could do to object to the situation.

Gtsta then walked, naked as the day *gtsta* was born, through the yielding wall of stsho, and past them . . . since the stsho did not stop *gtsta,* it hardly seemed safe for a hani captain to do so: she held Fala with a press of her hand, as *gtsta* walked blithely past them and on down the yellow-ribbed shadow of the rampway.

"Better open the outer gate again," Hilfy said to Tiar. "*Gtsta* wants to go out there, and we've got no right to argue."

"But—" cried No'shto-shti-stlen, standing the other side of the parted stsho, "but, Holiness, who have I married?"

Gtsta swung about, walking backwards, and waved *gtsta* spindly arms. "Tlisi-tlas-tin and Dlimas-lyi, my Dlima-lyen-lyi, my egg, my loveliest, most favored, most blessed—"

Gtsta was out of sight, then, warbling something to *gtsta* self, and the stsho around them were apparently congratulating No'shto-shti-stlen, No'shto-shti-stlen bowing and bowing, and holding the Preciousness.

It was time to get the whole party out of this tube, Hilfy said to herself, to get them somewhere safe, like the passenger quarters, if that was tasteful . . . at this point a hani was definitely out of her social depth and proceeding on guess and luck.

She worked her way through the crowd with a great dea

of bowing and apologies for tasteless dutiful necessities, . . .
"Including your excellencies' personal safety. Please urge
everyone toward the ship, please make some decorous
haste. There are infelicitous persons outside and the gate
is open." Tarras and Fala, thank the gods, had taken up
guard at the rear and one of them had disappeared, probably to see if *gtsta* was clear of the gate.

Evidently *gtsta* was. She heard it shut.

"We're sealed," Tiar said, breathing a sigh, and looked
around to her crewmates. Who were congratulating each
other, and probably not listening.

She gave her attention back to the dockside camera
hook-up, which *was* operating, of a sudden, stsho officials
having seemingly decided that it should. There was not a
notable lot going on, except a completely naked stsho who
was walking around and around the object that, reacting
with the station's oxygen, had expanded into a pillar of
lace.

Gtsta seemed delighted with it. *Gtsta* ran fingers over it,
gtsta examined it high and low and from every angle. Eventually another couple of stsho showed up, fully dressed,
bowing repeatedly, and likewise admiring the accident.

Not a sign of Haisi and his crew. Not a transmission out
of *Ha'domaren*, which was at dock, tightly sealed.

Of a sudden, though, they were getting real station information, real system information. She contacted her opposite number aboard *Tiraskhti*, and found herself in direct
communication with Vikktakkht.

"Things are quiet right now," she said, "*hakkikt*. We
have the *oji*, we have No'shto-shti-stlen, the Llyene stsho
are apparently aboard, and I haven't heard from my captain
yet, but I think they're making some sort of contact with
the stsho we have aboard."

"We have station output. Is this truthful?"

"I think it is, *hakkikt*. I've no way to be sure that's the
case, we're not in direct communication with station
authorities."

"Most probably you have them aboard."

"Yes, *hakkikt*."

*"Kkkt. Amusing. I wonder if Ana-kehnandian has a no-
tion of calling in his forces . . . or what those ships out there*

*will do as soon as the wavefront reaches them. I will offer
him safe passage—for the next several hours. Advise your
captain to abide by this."*

"Yes, *hakkikt,* I will tell her." Arrogant son. But thank
the gods they were talking about safe retreats now. In her
guess, *Ha'domaren* was trying to figure out what to do, and
what it had left, and whether a fight to the death right now
was in Paehisna-ma-to's interest.

Or if there was a way to recover the initiative.

Not that this hani could see. Not from the moment that
son had realized he'd let No'shto-shti-stlen and the Preciousness get together.

She eavesdropped on the passenger cabin. There was a
great deal of stsho ooohing and warbling going on. There
were numerous people in there.

"What are they up to?" Chihin asked.

"Weddings breaking out all over," Tiar said, not without
a thought that, by the gods, the *han* had not a word to
say: and Meras clan, remote and rural, and probably old-
fashioned, was going to find itself in alliance with powerful,
now solvent Chanur—

Counting a can full of what was beginning to draw a
curious crowd out there; and a franchise.

Sahern was not going to say a word else on the Meras
affair, by the gods not, unless they wanted an active feud
with Chanur, which didn't look like a smart bet for anyone
at the moment.

So a few more years for the enemies to regroup. But it
didn't mean Chanur would be sitting still.

She didn't let her guard down, didn't stop paying attention to the screens. Chihin and Hallan took over watching
station scan, and eventually reported outward movement
out of the mahen ships that were now clearly identified
on scan.

"Leaving him, they are." That was worth a call belowdecks. "Captain."

"Problem?"

"Mahendo'sat appear to be leaving system, not real organized. *Gtsta* holiness has drawn a crowd out there around
the rock. No apparent trouble on the docks. I think the
hakkikt's going to stay where he is until he's sure what

Ha'domaren's doing, but he's offered Haisi a safe passage, I'm supposed to tell you that."

"Haisi take it?"

"He hasn't budged. Hasn't made a move. —No, wait." There was a change on the station schema. "Son's just appeared as in count for departure. He's going."

"Ha!" the captain said. *"We got him."*

Chapter 21

It surfaced like a diver in an upside-down ocean, breached near the system buoy, and dived again—up—into the interface and perhaps deeper. It was there long enough to have gathered a system map: the buoy output one; and to sing a message of its own, in its harmonic voices. This one was simple.

tc'a	stsho	kif	mahendo'sat	hani
hani	hani	hani	hani	hani
peace	peace	peace	peace	peace
Chanur	Chanur	Chanur	Chanur	Chanur
Meras	Meras	Meras	Meras	Chanur
peace	peace	peace	peace	peace

"Well, look at that," Tiar said.

"How did it know my name?" Hallan asked.

"Famous, I suppose," Chihin muttered. "The kif certainly know you. They set you up. And I'm beginning to wonder about the tc'a."

"I wonder where that son's headed."

"Same place *The Pride* is," Chihin said.

"Or maybe they don't have to," Tiar said. "I'd about bet you cousin Pyanfar *knows* what's just happened. I'll bet you that son just transmitted."

Chihin shook her head. "If we start talking through the tc'a, gods save us. It's no way to run a trading business."

"Back to trade and thank the gods," Tiar said. "Enough of politics. We got the wedding party off our deck, the Preciousness and all, we got Tlisi-tlas-tin for governor, No'shto-shti-stlen's a happy bride, and we've got a can of exploding rocks to sell."

"Another Kita run, to nail down that franchise," Chihin

muttered. "The stsho love the idea. I've a notion we can sell it to the mahendo'sat—"

"Kif might have an interest. To each their own uses."

Tiraskhti was in. The rest of the kif still hovered, firmly under the *hakkikt*'s command, one could trust, since the effort was a success. High-level stsho turned out to welcome the *hakkikt,* to bid him to the intimate offices, along with Chanur. This was, perhaps, an unusual reception, kif and hani at once. Possibly it was unprecedented.

Or perhaps not.

"Honor to you," Hilfy said, with her escort, Tarras and Fala; and Vikktakkht with his dark-robed crew, meeting at the lift.

"Death to our enemies," Vikktakkht said courteously, and as the car arrived: "We will *share.*"

Faktkht. Share-prey, it meant: but Vikktakkht put *sotk* with it, meaning territory. Unprecedented idea in kifish, so far as she knew.

And it solved the question of precedences, with a kif who outranked a mere captain. Polite.

"You first," Hilfy said. Which required trust, of a species that didn't like to be followed.

"Kkkkt," the guards said, uneasy. So they sorted it out, with a kifish thumb on the hold button: Vikktakkht, then her, then his guard, then hers.

They stood on opposite sides of the car. There were probably weapons under the kifish robes. There were, inside their own dress-uniform belts.

The car rose.

"Profitable," Vikktakkht said, "this *peace,* this *sharing.* We will eat the hearts of those that oppose it. Anakehnandian will not go to his Personage with this failure. He must find a new service. I am considering taking him up myself."

"He made mistakes," Hilfy said. Kif hardly tolerated such. She was amazed that Vikktakkht was secure enough to propose such a thing. Most would not. Most would not dare.

"He was badly instructed," Vikktakkht said. "And he knows Paehisna-ma-to and her agents. Not a bad acquisition. Perhaps he will take instruction. Perhaps not. If not, his loss. I will have the information, honor to the *mekt-hakkikt.* He has not many ports of refuge. I will make him an offer."

"Generous of you."

"Extremely. And he will know it. Our guards return to duty here—our agreements are bettered. Paehisna-ma-to is now an uncertain influence at best. The Momentum is reversed. He would have no future in her service."

The car stopped, and opened its doors onto the white, nacre curtained formal hall of the governor's offices. And kifish guards were in evidence, bowing and showing all respect—to the *hakkikt,* if not to a hani captain.

Vikktakkht brushed them aside with a sweep of his sleeve. "Our escort will stay *here,*" he said in the Trade. "The guards will stay *here.*"

A bow from the guards, profound and quick. So much for the stsho's hired security. "Wait here," Hilfy said, wondering what the kif was up to, and somewhat glad of the pistol in her belt—wondering if there might be some kifish purpose against the governor, and if they might not, after all, have a piece of treachery on their hands.

But she played the game. She walked beside him, innocent as a stroll in the country, past the arches, the freeform white statues, the blowing drapery.

"We know each other," Vikktakkht remarked as they walked side by side; and, before she could leap to the unpleasant and hostile conclusion, of her own captivity, and her kifish guards: "We were crew on the same ship."

My *gods,* Hilfy thought. The kifish slave. Skkukuk. From aboard *The Pride.*

But this wasn't at all the place to recall that name.

"Why didn't you simply say—" She started to ask. "No. Of course not. Stupid question."

"Indeed," Vikktakkht said. "It would have given Paehisna-ma-to her best opening. Had I claimed that, you would have doubted me instantly. You would have rushed to ally with Ana-kehnandian."

A member of *The Pride*'s crew. Amazing.

"Not rushed," she said, and still wondered if this kif was loyal to Pyanfar. He *seemed* to have acted in Pyanfar's interest. "But I would have doubted your intentions."

"Kkkkt. As you do now?"

Never mince words with a *hakkikt*. "I respect your evident power."

"Admirable discretion. But if I aspired to be *mekthakkikt* the peace would end. And I find it, as I say, profitable. I am *hakkikt hakkiktun*. In the name of the *mekthakkikt* I stand first among kif. There is nothing more a kif can gain."

"Indeed," she said conservatively. "As in Chanur. I prefer where I am."

They strolled through the last arch, into the presence of bowing stsho.

"Kkkt. Profitable. Profitable to both, Chanur."

CJ Cherryh
PRETENDER

"Serious space opera at its very best by one of the leading SF writers in the field today." —*Publishers Weekly*

The *Foreigner* novels introduced readers to the epic story of a lost human colony struggling to survive on the hostile world of the alien atevi. Now diplomat Bren Cameron has returned to the atevi star system, only to find that civil war has and that his very life depends on only two allies: Illisidi, grandmother of the deposed atevi ruler Tabini, and Cajeiri, Tabini's eight-year-old son. Can one eldery ateva and a young boy protect Bren in a civil war most atevi believe he caused?

0-7564-0374-X

To Order Call: 1-800-788-6262

www.dawbooks.com

DAW 8